The Artifacts of Power Trilogy

BRIAN RATHBONE

ISBN-10: 1-945465-10-7
ISBN-13: 978-1-945465-10-9

DEDICATION

For my readers.

THE WORLD OF GODSLAND
FANTASY SERIES

THE DAWNING OF POWER TRILOGY
CALL OF THE HERALD
INHERITED DANGER
DRAGON ORE

THE BALANCE OF POWER TRILOGY
REGENT
FERAL
REGAL

THE ARTIFACTS OF POWER TRILOGY
THE FIFTH MAGIC
DRAGONHOLD
THE SEVENTH MAGIC

ACKNOWLEDGMENTS

Special thanks to Andrea Howe for her editing and Lawrence Mann for his artwork.

THE FIFTH MAGIC

Chapter 1

Honor feeds no children.
--Sevellon the thief

* * *

Lies.

Like the patina of a thousand years, deceptions, half-truths, and full-on lies coated everything in Sinjin Volker's life. He had things he'd never have dreamed of: a beautiful wife, a dragon, and the Dragon Clan at his command, but it was tainted.

As he gazed out along the horizon, across the Endless Sea, wind gusts resonated within Windhold, casting Sinjin's long hair back. Kendra said she was responsible for cutting his hair, but he was afraid to ask, partly because he wasn't sure he trusted her with a knife near his neck at the moment and partly because she'd made it clear, to him and others, she hated it when his hair got long. To ask for a haircut would mean admitting defeat. Though he knew it was childish, he refused to give her the victory. He justified it by telling himself he needed the Dragon Clan and the Drakon to respect him. Giving in to Kendra was unlikely to better their opinion of him. Using a strip of leather, he pulled his hair back and tied it up, which kept most of it out of his mouth and eyes.

The air smelled of a coming storm. Wind gusts grew more frequent and powerful. Windhold was aptly named, and riding out storms in the hold was unpleasant at best. Better to saddle the dragons and fly. The Dragon Clan could retreat to the lower hold and stay warm and dry. He turned back to those in the hold to give the command, but no one was looking at him. Even Durin was already saddling Valterius, and Sinjin's dragon watched his friend with a mildly suspicious eye. Durin had saddled Valterius many times, but Al'Drak liked to keep everyone sharp; his status among the dragons was unchallenged. Sinjin tried not to be upset no one had looked to him for command or even guidance. It was a sign of his poor leadership skills and it stung. Valterius moved suddenly to one side, and all Sinjin could do was watch. The words of warning had barely formed on his tongue when the dragon's tail flicked, catching Durin in the back of his knees and sending him flying. The Drakon pretended not to see, though a few smirked, knowing Valterius had a sense of humor.

Durin pulled himself from the stone floor. "Your dragon."

"Yeah. I know," Sinjin said. Valterius managed to look innocent, and he couldn't help but laugh.

"Thanks," Durin said. "You never seem to find it funny when he does it to you."

"Not for a while at least," Sinjin said, and he helped Durin finish saddling Valterius. The dragon was happier with two of them working on him. As long as he was the center of attention, he was well behaved. Sinjin had been working with him on obedience. Convincing the dragon he was the leader and that his commands were to be followed was proving to be something of a challenge. Still, there was something new in their relationship. Perhaps grudging respect, Sinjin thought, but he flinched when the dragon twitched his tail, which made him reconsider. He mounted without incident, but Valterius stared at him, and he could rarely venture a guess at what the creature was thinking. "Let's make for the shallows," he said after strapping himself in. Using the reins, he guided Valterius into the main wind hall.

Rather than walk toward the opening as they normally would, Valterius chose to show off his skill. Spreading his wings, he hovered in place for a short time, and with nothing more than minute, barely perceptible muscle movements, he moved with the wind and soared from the hold without ever flapping his wings. The Drakon followed. Like leaves from a mighty tree, shaken and thrown into the wind, they glided away. Inescapable wind gusts more violent than Sinjin was comfortable flying in were inescapable. The storm rushed in and surrounded them faster than thought. Strong fliers, the Drakon not so easily overcome. Pushing along the storm's outer edge, Valterius used the winds to their advantage and sent them racing to the south and west, toward the shallows.

For once he'd chosen to allow Sinjin to set their course with nothing but his knees. A squeeze to one side or the other was all it took to express his intentions. Kendra flew Gerhonda close; Valterius didn't object.

"We should just fly straight to the Terhilian Keys for the council," she shouted. "We could sweep the area and make sure there are no surprises."

"This is a council designed to keep the peace. We cannot show up with our entire strength. That would be an act of aggression."

"I see nothing wrong with a little aggression," Kendra said. "From what I've been hearing, Trinda and the Dark Queen have some of their own."

"We've no proof of that," Sinjin said.

"Have you any proof otherwise?" she asked.

He didn't answer.

"Then how can we discount either possibility? We cannot."

"Valterius and I are going, and you may ride with me if you wish, but we will not bring a show of strength to the Council of the Known Lands."

The air between Valterius and Gerhonda grew turbulent, and some distance soon separated them. Valterius continued to fly toward the shallows, and Sinjin realized he might have finally won an argument. He'd always wondered what that might feel like.

* * *

The *Serpent* was a ship like no other, despite the masthead being an imitation of the legendary *Dragon's Wing*. The *Serpent*, too, bore a Kyrien's likeness, but it was much more hastily created and was best seen from a distance. Both ships could fly but in entirely different manners. Where the *Dragon's Wing* flew by the power of a flightmaster and thrustmaster, the *Serpent* flew under her own power and the wind in her sails, as her captain said a proper ship should.

"Perhaps the best way to keep a ship from sinking is to never put it in the water," Kenward Trell reminded Brother Vaughn as they moved through the mostly clear skies with almost graceful ease. The smell of burning wood and coal, along with the black smoke pouring from the chimstack and a constant low-pitched whistle proved brute force was required to keep them aloft.

Brother Vaughn asked himself once again what he'd been thinking when boarding this ship. Kenward was world renowned for his recklessness, and the *Serpent* appeared to have been built under the premise it might soon be scattered across a mountainside. The lure of knowledge held by those within the Heights had been enough to blind Brother Vaughn, but he'd regretted it ever since they departed the Firstland. The chance to see verdant dragons under peaceful circumstances also drew him on, but it was less and less likely they would get there alive.

"Airships once ruled the winds," Kenward said. "And so they will again. The *Serpent* proves any man can sail the skies, whether they are touched by the gods or not."

Brother Vaughn caught himself about to run his hands along the railing, but he'd already gotten two splinters that way, and a third one would be his own fault. In truth, much of what was shoddy about the *Serpent* was a result of the materials from which she'd been built. Though rare and difficult to find, flakewood was by far the lightest building material strong enough to support a ship this size. The archives revealed much, and Kenward had proven determined to use the ancients' knowledge to his advantage.

Aside from being light, the flakewood splintered easily, possessing none of greatoak's malleability. Gaps between the planks made Brother Vaughn shiver, knowing the ship was in no way water tight. "You could've at least made the planks fit together," he said.

"No point in making her seaworthy if you're never going to put her in the water," Kenward said. "Besides, flakewood floats better than lightwood, so the *Serpent* should still float."

"Should . . ."

Kenward shrugged. Brother Vaughn had already heard his argument.

"We've only tested the *Serpent* in the air. If she ever ends up in the sea, we'll find out if she floats."

Even Kenward had shown his concern a number of times during their flight over what was called the Endless Sea. But they'd stayed aloft, and Brother Vaughn had long since tired of seeing water beneath them through the cracks in the deck and the hold below.

"Never have I worried so much over weight, Vaughn," Kenward said. "Maybe you could catch a ride to the council with Onin. Based on my calculations, I'll have plenty of room in the hold but too much weight aboard to fill it. A partially filled hold offends my sensibilities."

"If Onin will have me," Brother Vaughn said. He'd have said more, but he didn't want to give Kenward any more reason to toss him overboard.

"Sevon!" Kenward shouted, and a short, skinny man with thin, straggly hair answered the call. "Go tell Farsy to redo our estimates assuming all passengers find their own ways home."

The man nodded and did not meet Brother Vaughn's eyes when he turned. Brother Vaughn kept his hands in the pockets of his robes to keep them warm, and he fondled the ornately carved cube he always kept with him. Kenward had been the one to reveal its true purpose, and it had kept him up at night ever since. A key. It was an elaborate and ancient key meant to open a ship's secondhold--the place where a captain might hide his or her greatest treasure. Brother Vaughn knew the location of the ship this key went to. It taunted him, making him wonder, over and over, what might be within the secondhold of a ship resting at the bottom of the God's Eye for thousands of years. But the God's Eye was denied to him, as was all of Dragonhold, making it a puzzle with no solution.

This trip, in a way, had been about escaping knowledge he could not pursue. The cube was a reminder he sometimes wished he'd left behind, but he could entrust it to no one else, and there was no place he considered safe enough to leave it. Thus, its constant presence continued to make him wonder.

"Land below!" came a shout from the crow's nest, and Brother Vaughn gripped the rail. It took a moment for the clouds below them to clear, but when they did, the view was magnificent. Beneath them was an emerald marsh, teeming with life. Rising from a still-distant plain, waited the Heights. There, Brother Vaughn knew, wrapped in low-lying clouds, was the forest in which Thundegar and Allette had lived. Seeing this place so alive gave him greater context for the tale reshaping his world.

Knowledge spread following the first Council of the Known Lands. Even the design of this ship would have been unknown to them if not for that communication. Revelations from the scrolls Catrin had found within Ohmahold and other discoveries within Dragonhold had profound impacts on those within the Heights, the Mids, and across all of Godsland. Most agreed a new age was upon them; Brother Vaughn hoped it was an age of enlightenment and not an age of conflict.

Thus far, the Council of the Known Lands succeeded in maintaining peace, but rumors of tension reminded nothing was certain. Diplomacy was the reason most believed Brother Vaughn was on this trip, and he did hope to foster good will, but he wondered just how much he could do. In many ways, Kenward was a far better ambassador. Trade was a language everyone understood, and Kenward brought with him as many valuable items as he hoped to leave with.

A cold wind descended on them with sudden force and ferocity. The ship dropped through the air like a stone, and Brother Vaughn's guts raced toward his chin. There had been no warning, and crewmen were tossed about. When the ship just as suddenly slowed its descent, people slammed into the *Serpent's* unforgiving deck.

"Boiling downbursts!" Kenward cursed. "Anyone injured?"

Moans broke the silence, and Kenward moved toward the closest source. Just before he reached Bryn, another body collided with him, and he reached out to steady the man. It was the one they called Sevon. Brother Vaughn hadn't known him prior to this flight, but Kenward had been forced to find some new crewmen to man the *Serpent*. It was not a change all sailors could make; Sevon, though, was at home on the airship and generally moved about with lithe dexterity.

Brother Vaughn steadied him.

"Sorry," Sevon said.

Attended to Bryn, who was now coming around, though he was bleeding from his forehead, Brother Vaughn paid Sevon no more mind.

"Pelivor warned me about these blasted downdrafts," Kenward said, "but I'll be boiled if I can see 'em coming."

Luckily, no one was seriously injured, and Kenward moved back to the rails. The marsh was a great deal closer now, and Brother Vaughn could see the swamp pigs Thundegar had described. Glistening, the creatures moved through the channels they created, cutting the otherwise complete carpet of vegetation into pieces like a woodsmith's puzzle only with sunlight reflecting through the gaps.

Beneath them flashed darkness embodied, and the ship's hull issued an echoing thrum. With terror in his heart, Brother Vaughn watched the feral dragon slip just as quickly away from them and out of view. Looking around, frantic, he could not locate the dragon, and he once again knew true fear. He had faced these creatures before and barely survived, and now he was exposed and vulnerable once again. The feeling grew more intense as the *Serpent* lost altitude.

Black smoke poured from the chimstack, and steam billowed around it.

"We got a leak!" someone cried from belowdecks and the crew worked to stem the flow. The ship's shadow danced along the vegetation and grew closer. It was just a matter of time before they crashed into it. Not far in the distance, the greenery ended and desert began. Brother Vaughn wasn't certain what to wish for, so he simply prayed the crew could fix the steam leak in time. The billowing air bags rippled above them in danger of collapsing. Brother Vaughn braced himself. He'd thought flying on a dragon or on a ship with a flightmaster was terrifying. This took fear to a new level.

The ship's shadow raced along the desert, a sand cloud swirling in their wake. The cries from below changed in pitch, and after a fevered moment of shouted orders, the steam rising from belowdecks decreased. The wind socks--or bladders, as Kenward called them--firmed and snapped taut. The ship began to rise, and Brother Vaughn prayed they were not too late. A stiff wind now pushed them toward the heights faster than any of them would have liked. Kenward called out more orders, and the *Serpent* responded--somewhat. As if waking from a long sleep, the ship lumbered upward; cast like a leaf in the wind, it twisted. The ropes holding the air bags popped and whined but continued to hold. By some luck, the wind straightened the ship, line, and sail.

Pointed in the right direction, Kenward took advantage. "More flame!"

Black smoke grew thick. The ship ascended into it then leaped higher, supported by thermals rising above the sands. With the increase in smoke came more steam, and Farsy shouted from belowdecks, his words distorted but his intention clear. The black was choked to a fraction of what it had been, and the steam lessened. The *Serpent* could climb only so high so fast. Fortunately the thermals did most of the work, leaving them drifting higher and higher in a lazy circle. Tilted sails caught uprising air, the angle of one side less than the other, allowing them to spiral upward.

The people of the Heights had been notified the *Serpent* was coming, but Brother Vaughn still wasn't certain what to expect. At that point, just about anything would be better than being on Kenward's airship. What had he been thinking?

The captain appeared to be feeling quite good about himself. Brother Vaughn could imagine his words, "First person to ever fly a steam-powered ship across the Endless Sea and do trade with the Heights."

A crowd appeared along the edges of the gaping openings in the mountains. With the sun setting behind them, Kenward guided the *Serpent* away from the thermals and toward the tallest spire. There waited an official delegation, and he guided the airship closer.

Erratic wind gusts and vortices tossed the ship during the final approach, and those waiting within the cavernous chamber scattered. With the lines creaking and groaning from the strain, the *Serpent* cleared the expansive opening with excessive speed. Again the wind gusted, catching the air bags in the gale. Into the stone floor the hull slammed, jolting all those aboard, before changing direction and being dragged back toward open air.

"Cut the lines!" Kenward shouted, his voice high. "Quickly!"

Moving with all the speed they could muster, the crew worked to cut the ropes. They would not be quick enough. Brother Vaughn would have jumped, but he was not strong enough. Others made the leap and landed on solid stone, but he remained rooted and would go where the ship went. The world stopped moving suddenly and completely. A deep boom rattled his being, and Brother Vaughn's eyes felt as if they might be torn from his head. When he opened them, his vision was blurred, and it took a moment to see the largest eye he'd ever seen gazing down upon him. The mighty verdant dragon, his head nearly as big as the ship, snorted and rattled the chamber, then roared. Brother Vaughn would always remember it as if the dragon had roared at him personally.

Grateful for the leviathan's help, Brother Vaughn tried to be thankful while he pulled himself over the rail to drop onto the cavern floor. The dragon had stopped the *Serpent* from being dashed against the rocks, but he had also nearly deafened Brother Vaughn and risked giving him a heart attack. Men in white linen robes with shoes that shone even in the failing light approached.

"I am Brother Vaughn."

"Your people certainly know how to make an entrance," said a fat man with a lopsided grin.

Sensi, Brother Vaughn presumed as he picked himself up from the cold stone.

Chapter 2

Change threatens all that is and shall be met with fire.
--Sensi, chamberlain to the lord chancellor

* * *

Diplomacy was made difficult by the lord chancellor's refusal to meet with Brother Vaughn. The best he could do was talk with the people at the market while trying to keep Kenward out of trouble, the latter of which was like trying to keep the wind from blowing.

"For all of these," Kenward said to a gem merchant, "I will give you one of these." He produced a dried and preserved yet still lustrous saltbark leaf.

"Do you think me a halfwit?" the man asked, his voice high and accent thick. The interaction did not go unnoticed, and guards moved closer to where they stood. Brother Vaughn had the distinct feeling he was being watched from above, and he gave Kenward a nudge.

"I mean no offense," Kenward said. "This saltbark leaf will cure almost any ill and is considered as valuable as a life."

The merchant made a show of being unconvinced but soon reconsidered. "Half," he said. "Because I cannot know it is real until it's needed."

"It's real," Brother Vaughn said. "I was there when it was harvested, and I have seen the healing it can bring. It's real."

"Half," Kenward said, "but I pick which half."

The merchant cast Kenward a sideways glance then smiled, "Deal."

With every stone selected, the merchant acted as if he were being robbed. This was apparently not all that unusual since the guards and other merchants ignored it.

"How will Umair feed his children?" he cried.

"Hold this, Sevon," Kenward said, but Sevon did not answer. Brother Vaughn turned, but the little man was nowhere to be seen.

When Kenward had only one selection left to make, he was torn between a pretty, red stone growing out of a darker stone and a much smaller translucent stone with but a hint of green giving it color. His hand hovering near one then the other, Kenward read Umair's eyes. He grabbed the smaller greenish stone, feeling apprehensive, but Umair cried out as if he'd been assaulted. This the guards could not ignore, and they closed in on the merchant's shop.

"What's the problem, Umair? Are you being robbed again in the broad light of day?"

"This man tricked me into thinking he was an idiot, and instead he's a thief!"

"I may look dumb," Kenward said, "but it's just a disguise."

"You see? He tricked me."

"Move along," the guard said to Kenward, and Brother Vaughn sighed in relief.

"Can we go back now to see if the men are done repairing the *Serpent?*"

"I need some more rope," Kenward said. "The crew can't fix the ship without materials, but everything here is expensive."

"It's all imported," Brother Vaughn said.

"That's crazy," Kenward said. "Give anyone control over your food and goods, and they'll eventually use it against you."

Secretly Brother Vaughn was dreading getting back on the *Serpent*, but it didn't appear he was going to make any progress here on his own. The *Serpent* might be his only way home, which was a less-than-comforting feeling.

"For rope?" Brother Vaughn heard Kenward say and he turned. "Did you spin it out of rainbows and dragon tears?"

The merchant did not respond.

"We'll have to use what we've got," Kenward said, finally convinced to go back to the ship. It was a long and uncomfortable walk. He spent his time grumbling over the prices merchants dared ask for their goods, imported or not. Brother Vaughn knew returning to the vacuous hall where the *Serpent* lay on her side like a grounded whale might also mean getting another chance to see a verdant dragon up close. He hoped any he encountered would refrain from roaring at him. His hearing was just starting to return to normal.

His dreams of seeing another verdant dragon were fulfilled when they entered the hall, except this dragon was different from the rest. Jehregard stared down at Brother Vaughn, one eye more like a gemstone than eye. His mottled black and gray skin was like rock with moss and lichen growing between his mighty plates and giving him a greenish hue. There was no malice in the dragon's stance, eyes, or the energy he exuded, but he was intimidating nonetheless. One false step could kill a person, and having been stepped on by multiple horses, Brother Vaughn wasn't certain how close he wanted to get. Atop the dragon's back was a smaller version of the tierre, which could still hold ten people comfortably.

"I wonder how the old boy might feel about giving us a nudge," Kenward said.

Brother Vaughn shivered at the thought. It hadn't been Onin's verdant dragon that saved them from being dragged over the ledge, but he was certainly powerful enough to push the *Serpent* back into open air. What happened afterward being the true cause for concern.

Onin appeared a moment later, along with Sensi. The rotund man had been nothing but rude and seeing him was not a hopeful sign.

"Onin, my friend," Kenward said.

The older man cast him a flat glare. "What?"

"My men should soon complete the repairs needed, but my ship is now much heavier, and I was hoping I could beg a favor of you."

"What?"

"A push," Kenward said. "More of a nudge, really. Just enough to send us on our way."

"Not soon enough," Sensi said in a voice just loud enough for everyone to hear.

"Fine," Onin said.

"Are you going to the council?" Brother Vaughn asked.

The looks returned to him were cold.

"Yes," Onin said.

"May I go with you?" Brother Vaughn asked before he lost his nerve.

"That would be most appreciated," Kenward said. "I can use the extra weight."

Brother Vaughn didn't appreciate being judged by nothing but his weight, but he saw Kenward's point. Onin turned to Sensi, saying nothing.

The fat man groaned. "If you must."

Knowing his welcome was tenuous at best, Brother Vaughn did his best to fall in behind Onin, remaining silent and invisible. Jehregard continued to watch them approach.

Bryn ran out to meet Kenward. "Almost ready, sir," he said, "just need that rope and we'll be airworthy in no time."

Lying on her side and belching black smoke, the *Serpent* was an ominous sight. The wind socks started to reinflate, and Kenward bade them a brief farewell. "Got to go," he said. "I'll shout when I need that nudge. Be gentle, will you?"

Onin grunted.

Not a moment before Kenward reached the *Serpent*, Sevon appeared from within the crowds gathering to watch them depart--or perhaps just burn to cinders. There was shouting coming from aboard the ship, and flames leaped up from between the decking. Kenward, Sevon, and the rest of those not onboard raced back to the ship. Wind gusts, powerful and insistent, threatened to pull the *Serpent* into the open air as well as fanning the flames.

Brother Vaughn wasn't certain how pleasant his trip to the council would be, but he knew he'd made the right decision. Kenward's orders echoed through the chamber, and Jehregard added his deep baritone roar. As the *Serpent* moved closer to the edge, so did Kenward's voice go up in pitch. Steam poured out and black smoke engulfed the ship, leaving the crowds to gasp and wonder her fate. Jehregard moved closer before Onin could reach the agitated dragon. Every step made the stone tremble, tierre and harness rattled and popped, and the mighty beast was lowering his head when the smoke suddenly cleared. Kenward and his crew scrambled over the airship, checking lines and shouting. The same wind that cleared the smoke also dragged the *Serpent* from the hold.

"I think we're good," Kenward shouted just before the ship dropped from sight. The crew's screams grew distant. Brother Vaughn ran toward Jehregard, his fear outweighed by the need to know what happened to his friends. Though he was glad not to share their fate, he would never have wished them harm. Snaps, cracks, and screams echoed as he ran, and his heart pounded. Jehregard gave a great trumpeting call, but Brother Vaughn didn't know what it meant. It only added to his anxiety and confusion. When he did finally reach the edge, he managed to keep a goodly distance between himself and the agitated dragon. Peering down, the *Serpent* resembled a falling toy--how far it had dropped was terrifying. With full and taut wind socks, though, the ship righted herself. Trees in their wake reeled from recent impact, but Kenward's laughter could be heard even from the heights.

"That man is quite insane," Brother Vaughn said. No one argued.

"Come," Onin said, pushing him from behind. Sensi approached more slowly, but even he appeared to be moved by a sense of urgency. Jehregard extended his leg, providing an easy climb to the tierre. Onin went first and Brother Vaughn followed. Sensi offered a few choice words to the wind before doing his best to climb in a dignified fashion. When he reached the tierre, the big man was breathing hard and had to wipe the sweat from his forehead. "Tie yourselves in," Onin said.

Brother Vaughn didn't hesitate for an instant. Nothing he'd seen of flying thus far gave him any reason to believe he had the ability to stay where he was on his own. Sensi halfheartedly pulled at the too-short ropes and managed to secure himself, if just barely. Brother Vaughn couldn't help but check and recheck the knot he'd tied. He was considering untying it and retying it to make it more secure when Jehregard issued another deafening call, one Brother Vaughn could feel in the seat of his pants even when he held his hands over his ears.

A cold feeling unsettled his stomach, but Jehregard proved his skill. Extending his wings, the dragon left the cold stone without any noticeable sensation to those aboard. Seemingly without moving a muscle, the verdant dragon sailed into the open air as smoothly as could be. Brother Vaughn breathed a deep sigh of relief and wiped sweat from his own forehead. Sensi gave him a disgusted look.

No sooner had Jehregard executed a turn than shouting from within the mountain hold began. One word rang through the air, "Thief!"

Sensi cast an accusing glare at Brother Vaughn, who shrugged and turned his hands palm up.

"Go back," Sensi said.

"Why?" Onin asked, surprising Brother Vaughn.

"Because something has been stolen, and it's possible the thief is aboard," Sensi said without looking at Brother Vaughn.

"Did you steal anything?" Onin asked Brother Vaughn, turning to look over his shoulder.

"No."

"He didn't do it," Onin said.

"You're just going to believe him?" Sensi asked, incensed.

"My tierre, my rules," Onin said, and their course did not change.

"This is why the lord chancellor doesn't trust you," Sensi said.

Brother Vaughn shrank into the padded chair and checked his knot once again. Roars echoed from the heights. A pair of full-sized verdant dragons gained the skies, their huge tierres bristling with activity. Like war on wings, they instilled fear.

As if guessing his thoughts, Sensi said, "There'll be more."

"It will take them time," Onin said. "The great oafs are too big to be nimble. That is, after all, why you are aboard, is it not? Do you wish to try to have one of those beasts land amid the keys? I think you would never come back. I am no thief, you are no thief, and the monk is no thief. We fly. Let them chase the airship; there they will find fools and thieves alike."

It was the most Brother Vaughn had ever heard Onin speak, and he turned to Sensi, who appeared annoyed but otherwise calm. Something about that bothered him, but he didn't get the chance to reason it out.

"Hold on," Onin said. "The ride may get a little bumpy."

In the next instant, clouds engulfed them, and Jehregard's smooth flight was anything but. Sensi was holding the ropes with white knuckles. Brother Vaughn did the same. Ropes were small comfort when the bottom dropped out.

* * *

Convincing Kendra to leave Gerhonda wasn't something within Sinjin's power, which left him going to the council alone. There would be advantages, but he had to admit he would be vulnerable. It wasn't something he liked to admit, but there was a time and place for foolishness, as his mother had always said. Sometimes he thought of her in the past tense, which made it easier to cope--easier to avoid slipping around Kendra or anyone else. She had never accepted his reasons for not searching for his mother's saddle. Perhaps the greatest reason to think about his mother in the past tense was to keep his anger at bay. He'd been deprived of a mother, though she still lived. He'd been deprived of an honest relationship with his wife. The guilt wore on him, and he blamed his mother for swearing him to silence, especially with regard to Kendra. What was he supposed to do? It was a question threatening his sanity.

Seeing the shallows in the distance added to the sense of urgency. He needed to have his words sorted out before he and Kendra next spoke. He loved her and didn't want to hurt her, but he could not give in this time. Valterius snorted and dipped low over the water, knowing their destination was near. Pillars loomed above saltbark trees, and soon the channel through which the *Slippery Eel* once sailed would come into view. Sinjin had never seen the place, and it was like having something from a fairy tale materialize before you. He knew the stories his mother had told him were all true, but they had never felt like the real truth. He'd been unable to visualize such things as exploding mountains. Yet before them was the remains of a towering peak, as if a god had cleaved it with a mighty ax.

Valterius soared lower and Sinjin was thrown forward as they slowed. With a triumphant cry, Valterius thrust skyward, a glittering silver and green fish in his claws. More splashes followed as the Drakon fished, and Sinjin was glad for it. They all needed rest. While the dragons fed, the Drakon could prepare a more palatable meal than raw fish. When his mother told him about this place, he had dreamed of swimming in such magical waters. Tales of giant sharks gave him pause. By the size of the fish the dragons pulled from the waters, ample food existed to support predators.

When they reached the pillars carved with visages of madness and faded over eons, the winds were still, so Valterius could not do what Kyrien had done and hover within the pillars. Instead, the dragon had to land on a saltbark tree. As soon as he landed, a stiff wind blew, nearly knocking Valterius from the tree. It was the only way the dragons could stay dry in the place without landing on the mountain itself. He felt bad for treating the trees poorly, but he could not bring himself to camp in a place where a mountain had once exploded. The pillars were close enough, and he didn't expect to stay long. The Drakon could feed their dragons and return to Windhold when they were rested. He would leave for the Keys of Terhilian with or without Kendra.

She and Gerhonda perched nearby. "Do we really have to sit here like so many blackbirds? Why not camp on the land surrounding the mountain?"

"The mountain gives me the crawls," Sinjin said.

"It already blew up. What are you afraid of?"

"It feels like it wants to explode again."

Kendra made no response to those words and remained quiet while climbing down from Gerhonda's back. The dragon remained saddled but could eat more comfortably without Kendra's weight on her back. Sinjin slid down as well and settled on a low branch, careful not to crush the leaves. Valterius had already destroyed sections of the tree's precious foliage, but there was nothing to be done except try to do no more harm.

"So you're going alone?" Kendra said from her own branch.

"I didn't say that," Sinjin snapped in response.

"You didn't have to. I won't fight you, but I'll never forgive you if you don't come back."

"It'd be better if you went with me," Sinjin said.

"You said only one dragon."

"I did."

"Then we will ride Gerhonda?"

"No."

Silence.

Sinjin expected a number of things, but he had not expected to hear his wife crying. It was not something he could abide, not at his word or his action. Slipping into the cold water, despite knowing the danger, he faced his fears to reach her.

"I'm sorry," Sinjin said. "I didn't want to make you cry."

"I can't leave her," Kendra said, a catch in her voice.

"Then I'll go alone."

"No," Kendra said. "That's not an option."

Pulling himself from the water and onto the branch where he could put his wet but, he hoped, comforting arm around her.

She leaned against him. "I know you're right about only one dragon," she said. "But going alone is too risky. You need a good sword at your back. But I cannot send Gerhonda back to the Firstland."

Sinjin sighed and thought for a while before saying anything else. His wife wasn't being unreasonable, yet she still managed to be impossible. At times such as these, a man must think fast. "Then we'll achieve both. You and I will fly to the council on Valterius, and Gerhonda will remain nearby but concealed."

Kendra said nothing and instead kissed him on the cheek. Sliding one hand up the back of her neck, he turned and kissed her in a manner she could not ignore. Gerhonda snorted.

* * *

Despite knowing where Onin and Jehregard were going, no verdants awaited them when at the Keys of Terhilian. Brother Vaughn breathed a tentative sigh of relief; at least he would not have to live the nightmare of facing angry verdant dragons. These beasts could tear down mountains if they so chose. He had no interest in seeing them fight one of their own. He'd seen what they and those in their tierres could do in times of war. It was something that still haunted his dreams, though he'd admit it to no one.

Jehregard landed not far from where the oversized table would be placed. The table would come by ship from the Greatland, and Jehregard would most likely be asked to hoist the heavy table from the barge onto shore. It was a service Onin said the dragon was happy to provide. Brother Vaughn was glad for Onin. Though he was gruff and opinionated, he was a great deal more pleasant to talk to than Sensi. Brother Vaughn got the distinct impression his very presence offended the fat man, and he couldn't wait to be away from him. It was something he had done nothing to deserve, which raised his ire.

"Mids," Onin said pointing. A tall ship moved under full sail. It was indeed a Midlands ship.

Not long after the ship was spotted, Brother Vaughn scanned the horizon and saw a dragon approaching. Shielding his eyes from the blinding sunlight, he saw a single dragon with two riders. Storm clouds still gathered along the horizon, and the shifting clouds played tricks on his eyes.

"Dragon riders," he said, pointing.

"And Greatlanders," Onin added.

The atmosphere grew heavier and thicker with the new arrivals. Tension fouled the air. Longboats had been dropped from the Midlands ship, and the barge was being assembled alongside the Greatlanders' ship. Sinjin and Kendra were visible as the dragon grew closer, and Brother Vaughn had the nagging feeling more dragons were near. Valterius landed not far from Jehregard, and the two dragons greeted each other. It was difficult to tell if it was an amicable greeting since all dragon greetings sounded alike to Brother Vaughn, which was odd given how many bird songs he could identify and imitate. It was something to which he decided he would someday devote more time.

"Hello, Brother Vaughn," Sinjin said as he approached. "Hello, Onin and Sensi."

Onin grunted in response, and Sensi gave Sinjin a brief nod but made no other attempt to communicate. Brother Vaughn offered a brief hug and whispered, "Good luck."

In keeping with the treaty, two people came to shore from the Midlands, though more longboats waited nearby. It was a clear sign of doubt and fear. Brother Vaughn didn't like how this was starting. If only the rest would arrive and they could get this over with. The whole thing made his guts churn.

The barge's arrival was a good distraction, and it gave the gathered people a common sense of purpose. Though the Midlands delegation offered no help, they did watch the proceedings with an approving eye. Jehregard performed his customary service as a living crane and took the ropes in his monstrous jaws and moved the oversized table to the beach. Only two people from any delegation were permitted on the shore at one time. Other delegations pitched in by carrying chairs from the barge to the table. Participating lowered walls the Midlands delegation had built up around themselves.

Light conversation was just beginning between Sinjin and the man Brother Vaughn thought was Lord Bercheron. Some cast Brother Vaughn curious glances, most likely since the Cathurans had negotiated their own seat on this council, and he wasn't certain if more of his order would be in attendance. His standing with the order was questionable, and he didn't want to cause a fuss at such an important meeting. He just couldn't keep himself away. If it was a problem, he would allow himself to be taken to Jharmin Kyte's ship. Lord Kyte had just arrived now that his men were no longer needed to transport the table and chairs. With him came not his wife but Madra of Far Rossing. Madra was a good woman, but she was prone to bickering, and that was not what this council needed, though Jharmin's wife was no wilting flower either.

Nat Dersinger's ship dropped anchor not long after. Only Trinda and Allette were missing. No one expected Allette to come, but Trinda had historically come and managed to confuse everyone one way or another. Given the rumors of the two queens' colluding, the anticipation grew even more palpable.

With most of the council members seated, conversation grew more organized and intense.

"I'm not certain how long we should wait," Jharmin said. "Neither Trinda nor Allette has responded to the invitations sent. I don't hold much hope of them coming, myself."

"Perhaps that is for the best," Lord Bercheron said. "This will give us a chance to discuss what to do about them."

"As long as they keep to themselves," Jharmin said, "I say we do nothing."

"That's because you don't share a border with either of them," Lord Bercheron said. "Every day those ferals reproduce and grow is another day closer to war, and what if they are better prepared this time? Better to stomp them out of existence while they're still weak."

Sensi and Onin nodded in agreement, and Brother Vaughn did not like the direction the conversation was taking.

"I understand your concerns," Jharmin said, "but I can commit no resources to attacking Allette without leaving us open to attack from the Godfist."

"And we would be caught in the middle . . . again," Nat Dersinger said.

Ahem.

Brother Vaughn wasn't certain he had heard something at first, but then he heard it again.

Ahem.

This time everyone heard, and all those seated at the council table craned their necks. Nestled high in the rocks, sat Trinda Hollis, the child queen. She'd been there the entire time. Trinda waited for silence. "Any act of aggression against my ally, Allette, the one the people call the Black Queen of the Jaga, will be considered an act of war against the Godfist and against me, personally. My friend thought perhaps we should solve all of our problems today. She said if all the snakes put their heads in one place, draw your blade."

Outrage shone on faces around the table, and Kendra Volker stood ready for a fight.

"I told her snakes could be beautiful and have their purposes. Good snakes keep the rats away. Only those who dare enter the master's house need lose their heads. So be good snakes and keep your heads. Make a move toward myself or Allette, and feel our sting."

Jharmin Kyte stood with clenched fists on the table. Gold-tipped, green flames crept over his hands.

"Mind your manners, Greatlander," Trinda said. "Your people couldn't take the Godfist when you had the ferals on your side. How do you think you'll fare with them at your backs?"

"This is a violation of the council charter!" Lord Bercheron said.

"Actually it isn't," Trinda said. "I've read the charter. And while the fact that you did not previously note my presence is not a violation of the charter, those are." She said, pointing out to sea.

An angry roar built among those gathered as they saw the fleet of warships gathered on the horizon. Blades left sheaths and Kendra stood ready to defend Sinjin. Lord Bercheron's eyes narrowed as he regarded Trinda. Jharmin Kyte appeared ready to blast them all, and yet Trinda exuded cold calm.

Distant cries reached out across the water, and Brother Vaughn could soon make out the familiar curses. Bursting from the clouds, the *Serpent* left them roiling in her wake. Moments later, the clouds burst apart; three massive verdant dragons emerging in pursuit.

"Ambush!" Jharmin Kyte shouted.

Those on the shoreline moved away from the council table. Trinda alone remained where she was, smiling like the cat that caught the bird.

Chapter 3

Within the deepest darkness, the light shines most brightly.
--Gemino, sorcerer and artist

* * *

Sinjin took two steps backward, running into Kendra, who held her ground. It felt good knowing she was there, protecting him and allowing him to protect her. He wished he had violated the charter and brought the Staff of Life or Koe with him, but he was not defenseless. The staff and Koe had helped him gain access to his power, but he did not need them to glean at least a small amount from the air around him. Comets in abundance helped in that regard, though they made his powerful enemies even more powerful. This was among the best arguments he'd heard and had even repeated with regard to attacking Allette while she and the ferals were still weak. Now that would mean war with the Godfist, and he could think of nothing he'd like less.

When Jharmin turned to him, flames still dancing along his aging but still muscular form, Sinjin offered up his open palms. "Prepare to defend yourself, Nephew," Jharmin said. "My boat will be here soon. You should be away from here."

"Yes," Trinda said from above them. "You should be away. Fly back to your rock. You don't want to be here when my ships arrive."

With a glance over his shoulder, Sinjin saw Onin and Sensi climbing aboard Jehregard. Brother Vaughn was left standing with his arms extended, his plea ignored. Sand and debris soon filled the air and caused Brother Vaughn to retreat into his robes. Valterius cried out and Sinjin pushed Kendra in his direction. All the while, the *Serpent* drew closer. Black smoke billowed from the chimstack accompanied by a high-pitched whine. The ship moved with more speed than he would have guessed. It was amazing it flew at all, let alone over great distances. There were things about the *Serpent* he didn't understand, but he doubted Kenward would give up his secrets.

"Get them off my tail!" Kenward screamed as they passed. Free of the clouds, it wouldn't take long for the verdants to chase down the *Serpent*, no matter how nimble she was. Kenward executed a daring move, circling back. Sinjin was mounted before the ship passed the beach a second time. Kendra was climbing up behind him when another dragon appeared atop the cliffs. Gerhonda issued a challenging call and swooped toward Kendra. Before she reached the beach, though, she passed the child queen. With a single sweep of her tail, Gerhonda sent Trinda tumbling to the sand.

Though she landed on her feet, Trinda had fire in her eyes. The air stank of power; it washed over those who remained in waves.

"Any harm to her will come twice to you," Kendra growled the ancient warning, standing her ground before Trinda.

The child queen smiled. "You're a pretty little snake. Fly away."

Verdants circled overhead. Trinda's warships drew ever closer. Without taking her gaze off Trinda, Kendra mounted. The child queen rewarded her with a goading smile.

"Brother Vaughn!" Sinjin shouted.

The man ran toward Valterius.

"Grab my hand!" came a shout from behind. Brother Vaughn turned to see the *Serpent* approaching and Kenward reaching out for him.

Brother Vaughn continued to run to Valterius and did not look back.

Nat Dersinger's shouts were the last thing Sinjin heard before leaving the keys behind.

"There will be blood and fire!"

* * *

The *Serpent* flew toward clouds gathering in the east, and there was nothing Sinjin and Valterius along with Kendra and Gerhonda could do about the verdant dragons still flying in pursuit. All he could do was wish his friends speed and luck. Brother Vaughn clung to him. The prayers he uttered were not for his own safety but that of the madman and his crew. Sinjin had sailed with Kenward but not aboard the *Serpent*; doing so took a special kind of madman.

"Do these two dragons seem like too much of a show of strength now?" Kendra asked the wind, not looking at him.

"Say you were wrong," Brother Vaughn whispered.

Biting his lip, Sinjin had to think about it for a minute. "I was wrong."

Kendra just harrumphed and continued to look anywhere but at him.

"You took too long," Brother Vaughn whispered.

"Way too long," Kendra said, and she wheeled Gerhonda to one side, ending the conversation.

"Thanks," Sinjin said.

"I was just trying to help," Brother Vaughn said.

"I know," Sinjin said. Kendra was right. All his optimism and seeing the good in people couldn't make it so. People given the opportunities for quarrel will eventually find a reason to do so. He had never wanted to believe it, but fate was proving it true. "I'm not certain the Council of the Known Lands will meet again."

Brother Vaughn offered no argument. Kendra assumed the lead position, which annoyed Sinjin, but he let it go. At some point in the future, he would have to nicely remind her he was Al'Drakon. It wasn't purely his ego that required this; it was responsibility to the Drakon and the Dragon Clan as a whole. They needed him to be strong and in charge. Anything otherwise confused and agitated them. Kendra knew this but when she wanted to be spiteful, dominating him was her preferred revenge.

Fortunately for Sinjin, he was not alone, and Valterius would tolerate only so much. Before they came within view of the hold, Sinjin's dragon swung to one side and gained altitude. Without warning, he dived, gaining speed and bringing his bulk directly over top of Kendra and Gerhonda. Kendra's dragon issued a petulant call and gave way, allowing Valterius to lead. Sinjin couldn't help smiling for what Valterius had done, but he also knew he'd bear the blame for his dragon's actions.

Behind him, Brother Vaughn fidgeted.

"What are you doing?" he asked, made uncomfortable by Brother Vaughn's twisting and turning in his seat.

"I'm sorry," Brother Vaughn said. "I think I've lost something important to me."

"Your cube?" Sinjin asked.

Brother Vaughn hesitated before answering. "Yes," he said after a long moment. "I must've lost it during the flight with Onin. I love dragons--don't misunderstand me--but I might be happier observing them from the ground."

Sinjin understood his sentiment, but he'd begun to overcome his fears and feel more at home in the saddle. Nowhere else did he have the freedom he did flying with Valterius, and nowhere else was he more powerful. Comet light bathed him in power, and though he might never achieve Trinda's or Allette's abilities, he was no longer powerless. It was something he was still getting accustomed to. For much of his life, he'd been passive, trying to stay in the background and avoid a fight. He still didn't like conflict and prevented violence whenever possible, but he was no longer afraid. He was no longer powerless. These things he reiterated and reminded himself as Windhold came into view.

Behind him, Brother Vaughn said a prayer as wind gusts tossed them about. Valterius wasn't bothered by such things, and Sinjin was growing accustomed. Brother Vaughn was pale and trembling. Sinjin patted Valterius on the neck and did his best to ask his mighty steed for a smooth landing. Though his dragon couldn't possibly read his thoughts, he was surprised when Valterius landed as gently as he ever remembered, and he had to wonder just how much the dragon did understand.

Durin rushed out to meet them, and the dragon was all too happy to be returned to Durin's care. It took Brother Vaughn a moment to dismount and Sinjin empathized; his own thighs hurt, and his stiff muscles resisted his commands. Time in the saddle took its toll, and Sinjin walked slowly as he went to where Kendra stood. Brother Vaughn wisely stayed with Durin.

"You could've gotten us both killed," Kendra said.

"You're right," Sinjin admitted.

"Well, it took you long enough to figure that out. And if I hadn't insisted on bringing Gerhonda, where would Brother Vaughn be?"

Sinjin had no answer.

"No more illusions and wishes. Just real truth," Kendra continued with conviction. The Drakon watched her in a way that made Sinjin think she should be Al'Drakon. He flushed. "War is coming and we must prepare. We need to firm our allegiances and monitor our enemy's activities. There can be no other way."

"I agree," Sinjin said, soft but firm.

"And how are you going to do that? What, exactly, are you going to do?"

"I don't know," he said.

"Yes, you do," Kendra said, coiled like a snake ready to strike him. Sinjin steeled himself and prepared for the onslaught. "You've known all along. You just won't tell me what it is. You don't trust me enough to share your secret. How can any of us trust you when you don't trust us?"

It wasn't fair, he thought, knowing it was childish, but that failed to banish his anger. "Durin!" he shouted. The hold went silent.

"What?" Durin called, peering out from underneath a wing.

"Saddle Valterius!"

"But I just got it off of him!"

"Do it!" Sinjin commanded. Others moved to assist Durin. He didn't need the help, but neither did he turn it away. Valterius flicked his tail, but he tended to behave a little better when other people were around him. Sinjin generally found this amusing, but anger kept the smile from forming. His anger was mostly with someone who wasn't present, and he did what he could to control it. From Durin he accepted his staff and Koe. Kendra stood watching him with her hands on her hips. She'd said nothing since his outburst, which was probably for the best.

With Valterius saddled, Sinjin climbed aboard. Now Kendra raised an eyebrow. After inserting the ancient staff in its holder, he reached down and offered Kendra a hand up. She made a rude noise and walked back to Gerhonda. The minutes spent in the saddle waiting for Kendra were uncomfortable. There was little doubt Kendra kept him waiting longer than necessary just out of spite. At least she was preparing to go with him. It was enough.

"What happened?" Durin asked.

"The council meeting did not go well," Sinjin said.

"I figured as much."

"Trinda and Allette are aligned, and Trinda's warships ambushed the council."

Durin's eyes bulged.

"And then the *Serpent* arrived."

"At the council?" Durin asked. "I thought he wasn't supposed to get anywhere near there."

"He wasn't," Sinjin said, "but you know Kenward; tell him he can't do something, and that's just what he'll do."

"In his defense," Brother Vaughn said, "three verdant dragons were chasing him."

"There was that," Sinjin conceded.

"Maybe I should have left it at 'the council meeting did not go well,'" Durin said.

Kendra brought Gerhonda to stand behind Valterius, a clear rebuke for the flight in. Sinjin did his best not to prolong the display. Valterius moved back toward the skies. He cast one unhappy glance back at Sinjin before leaping into the air. Gerhonda followed an instant later, and they soon flew side by side.

"Are you going to tell me what this is about?" Kendra asked after a long silence.

"You want to know everything, so I'm going to show you everything."

"It's about time."

"This isn't a matter to be taken lightly," Sinjin said. Kendra made a show of acting apologetic. Sinjin refused to look at her. No matter how he wished the flight to be over, they had enormous distances to cover. There was nothing to be done but fly with all the speed the dragons could muster.

* * *

Deep within Dragonhold, time was nearly meaningless. Sleep threatened two men unaccustomed to sentry duties. Most who guarded the child queen had been selected for their strengths, for their ability to protect Trinda should the need arise. For others, however, it was sometimes their weaknesses that served her best. Neither guard standing watch over Trinda would be much use in a fight. Keen eyesight they did not possess, nor the sharpest hearing. What they did have were voices loud enough to summon more capable men stationed not far away.

No matter how bright the room, given the many herald globes resting in various holders, these men should not be able to see the object holding Trinda's attention. It had been Trinda who discovered the herald globes' more deadly properties, yet she felt most safe when surrounded by them and bathed in their light. The holders bore Strom's mark, and no one could deny Catrin and Osbourne's artistry in creating the globes, but those barely mattered.

Before her rested an ancient scroll, rotted and discolored with age. The words were largely illegible and their forms archaic, so much so that Trinda had to squint at them. The one with illuminated illustrations, however, made clear Dragonhold's true nature and power. A smile spread across Trinda's face, but she started like a guilty child at the sound of approaching boots. Some secrets must be kept even from those closest to her, and Trinda scrambled to conceal the disintegrating scroll without further damaging it.

Finally, her life had true purpose. Finally, she understood why she had been made to suffer so, why the dark men had come. Surviving what they'd done to her had made her stronger, the things they'd asked of her had prepared her well for the challenges she'd already faced, and her greatest struggles lay ahead. Trinda Hollis would not be a martyr; she was too smart for that. The child queen would instead change the world.

She heard not a word uttered by those who'd come to brief her, and they clearly did not understand when her inner smile refused to remain hidden.

* * *

"Are you sure you don't want to just tell me?" Kendra asked. "Maybe you could save us the rest of this flight to nowhere. You could've mentioned we were going to the other end of the world."

Sinjin remained silent, unable to find the words. His mother had made him promise not to tell; she hadn't made him promise never to bring Kendra to her. He wasn't breaking his promise to her, but still he felt guilty. Valterius and Gerhonda sometimes slept while they flew, which made Sinjin too nervous to sleep. He and Kendra drank from the clouds and ate from the stores in their saddles. Their flight back from Terhilian had taxed their supplies, but the Drakon practice of storing extra food, herbs, and fluids within the saddle had proven wise. It had already served the Drakon well. Kendra had been the first to have been blown far off course by storms when on patrol. Sand bars and islands could sometimes be found, but the Drakon had learned it was best to be over prepared and to be as self-sufficient as possible when in the air.

"Really?" Kendra would ask every now and then as they continued to fly over near endless waters. Valterius flew based on Sinjin's general sense of direction, which he communicated through his knees. The dragon was extraordinarily well behaved, and Sinjin wasn't certain why, but he wasn't going to argue.

"Really?"

Even knowing she was incensed, Sinjin kept his head down and mouth shut. He wasn't certain of the Black Spike's location, but he knew they were getting closer. Kendra would just have to wait a little longer for the answers she sought. Then it appeared, little more than a dark spot on the horizon. The instant it came into view, Sinjin could feel it, tingling and pulling at him, at the same time making his instincts scream for flight.

"You're not taking us there, are you?" Kendra asked, seeing the lone structure rising from deep seas, the only solid thing visible in any direction.

Not trusting his voice, Sinjin remained silent. Their path pointed unerringly toward the Black Spike. Waves assaulted the fortress on one side, deep blue mountains capped in white slammed into stacked basalt stone. Somehow the unlikely fortress withstood the force, leaving huge troughs on the opposite side. Kendra kept silent as they drew closer.

Sinjin guided Valterius to hover before the Black Spike, despite feeling a nearly irresistible urge to leave. "Let us in!" he yelled despite his better judgment. "Let us in!"

Nothing happened except wind gusts pushing Valterius away from the fortress.

"What is it, Sinjin?" Kendra pleaded, emotion coloring her voice. "Who is it? What have you been hiding from me?"

Anger burned within Sinjin. He hadn't asked for this. He could see no more reason to withhold this from his wife. It had been vastly unfair for his mother to ask this of him. It was a burden he could no longer bear. Using his pent-up emotion, he attacked the waters around the Black Spike. His attack was unimpressive, resulting in no visible effect.

Somehow, Kendra must have perceived it. "Sinjin, no!" she said.

He'd come too far. He'd let his anger grow to a conflagration, and he needed to release it before it consumed him. Using what his mother had taught him, he looked at the problem from a different angle. Was there a way to use nature to his advantage? It took a moment before he realized there was.

With each towering wave crashing into the fortress, driven by the growing wind, deep depressions were created. These alone came close to revealing the entrance. If he were to add his energy to the wind and push even larger waves into the stronghold, it might be easier than trying to pull the water out of the way. Dragging in a deep breath, he drew energy from the Staff of Life, Koe, and the now frigid air around them.

"Stop, Sinjin! Please, stop. I don't need to know. We can go home now!"

Her words were lost to him. Comets whispered of their power, enticing him. The energy flowed through him as he had always wished it would; only it didn't feel at all like he'd imagined it. Drawing the air toward them, he fed the waves and made them taller, stronger, and more devastating when they struck the fortress. The mighty monolith swayed in concert with the waves.

Then he saw the entrance and pointed. Kendra looked back as if he were crazy; then she shrugged and urged Gerhonda downward.

"No!" Sinjin screamed, knowing the entrance was not yet clear enough to safely traverse. Much more had been visible when he and Valterius had last been there; right after his mother had made him swear to never tell anyone she still lived. Gerhonda showed her courage by swooping into the blackness only slightly darker than the obsidian stone surrounding it. Sinjin waited. Valterius was poised to follow, and he dived before Sinjin was ready. A monstrous wave crashed on the Black Spike just before Valterius thrust himself toward the still emerging portal. Cold overwhelmed all other sensations. Valterius swam deeper at the same time the water receded. The dragon swam as quickly as he could, knowing the water would return with deadly force. It roared up behind them, slamming cold air against Sinjin's back. They were thrust upward toward jagged stone formations, which supported the dock and stairs above.

Narrowly avoiding lethal and unforgiving stone, Valterius and Sinjin broke the surface a moment later. He sputtered and gasped for breath. Kendra sat on the dock next to Gerhonda; neither appeared pleased.

"Were you trying to kill yourself?" Sinjin asked before he could think better of it.

"You pointed at the entrance," Kendra said. "Far be it from me to disobey your orders."

"That certainly wasn't an order," Sinjin said, but he was cut off by a deep and guttural growl that made Sinjin's bones vibrate.

"You are not welcome here," a voice deeper than his mother's usual voice said. It was louder and more powerful than any human voice alone. "You have come uninvited."

"I cannot keep this boiling secret any longer!" Sinjin cried. "I have kept my word, and I've told no one. But I can put my wife off no longer. She deserves to know, and I deserve a life without secrets. It's tearing us apart."

The silence was heavy with anxiety. Kendra showed signs of shock, realizations, perhaps even regret. "I don't need to know," Kendra said. "I'm sorry. I didn't understand."

Again the deep growling made Sinjin's teeth hurt, even in the following silence. It was a trial of the soul. He wanted to give his wife the respect she deserved and still be a good son; that last thought hurt physically. No one wanted to be a bad son or daughter, but all felt that shame at some point or another. For Sinjin, it was intensified. He knew there would be consequences. He didn't know yet what they would be, but the world was falling apart anyway. How could this make things any worse?

"Kendra must know," he said. "She must know what it took to make me keep secrets from her. Too much has happened, to many feelings hurt because I made a promise I shouldn't have made."

"No, Sinjin. Stop. Please don't," Kendra said. "I'm so sorry. I could not see your pain."

"This ends now," he said, more determined about this than anything he'd ever done in his life. Though he hated to stand up to his mother, she needed to respect his marriage.

"He's right," came his mother's voice, and the sound of it made him cry. So many emotions washed over him as she spoke, he could only weep. "I asked you to keep my most precious secret. It was too much to ask; I knew it when I asked it of you. There is a kind heart in you, and I do not fault you, but I had hoped you would last a while longer.

"How did you survive?" Kendra asked Catrin, her face gone pale.

"Kyrien and the feral queen mated. It was a violent affair. It took quick thinking and ingenuity to keep me from drowning but we survived."

"I'm sorry," Kendra whispered, not looking at Sinjin.

"Is it enough?" Catrin asked, looking pointedly at Kendra, who shrank under the Herald's glare. "The less you know, the less dangerous you are to me. By coming here, you've already risked much."

"War is coming," Sinjin said. "Trinda and Allette have allied themselves and threatened the Council of the Known Lands."

"I know," Catrin said. "All the more reason you shouldn't be here. You risk everything I've done."

"I'm sorry," Sinjin said, guilt replacing his rage. "Come with us," he finally said. His heart would never forgive him if he didn't ask.

Pain flashed in Catrin's eyes. "I can't."

"What do you mean, you can't?" Sinjin asked, his voice involuntarily taking on a whining quality even he hated.

"Don't make me tell you why. It's bad enough I've had to reveal this much. You will both just have to trust me. Can you do that?"

"Yes," Kendra said with a sniff.

Sinjin took longer to respond. "I want my mom back."

"I would come with you if I could but I cannot. Forgive me, my son," Catrin said, her voice wavering.

Sinjin turned back to Valterius with unshed tears in his eyes, the strength of his soul all that held them back.

"I've always been there with you, my son, even if you could not see me."

The look Sinjin gave her made it clear he didn't want to hear her words.

"Think back and you'll know my actions, for I am the wind."

There were no more words spoken before Catrin raised her hands and with the full power of the true Herald of Istra, she held back the raging seas and provided an opening large enough to fly through. Valterius wasted no time, and Gerhonda touched the tip of his tail, she followed so closely. Both clearly remembered their entrance into the Black Spike. Once clear, the waters rushed back in to fill the void, and his mother was once more lost to him. He was no closer to understanding why. "I'm sorry," were the only words he could find.

"So am I," Kendra said. "So am I."

Chapter 4

Suffer the young. They know not yet their ignorance and frailty.
--Madra of Far Rossing

* * *

Within Dragonhold, it was easy to forget the outside world existed. News barely penetrated the mountain fortress and Trinda's security. Even if it did get inside, most news traveled slowly and to only those the source trusted. Some talkative folks disappeared. Strom didn't believe the stories offered. Certainly people could fall into the river and be swept out, but it stretched the imagination, especially since those missing did not work near the river. Dragonhold was the largest single hold on all of Godsland, and people did not just end up somewhere they didn't belong for no reason.

Sitting across from him, Osbourne grimaced. "I had hoped things would one day get better. If I listened just to what Trinda told us, I'd think they had, but the word from the Vestrana continues to be nothing but grim. I almost feel bad staying in here."

"I know," Strom said, checking over his shoulder, wanting to be certain they were alone. Those words in the wrong ears could get people killed.

"I miss Cat," Osbourne continued. "She might not have always known what to do, but she always managed to decide on something and set the course. Now I spend half my time trying to figure out if I'm doing the wrong things."

Strom just grunted and picked at a metal splinter lodged under his skin. He barely felt it, his hands desensitized by his profession. Swinging a hammer and beating metal into shape had its benefits, his powerful muscles among them, but there were also drawbacks. He'd been told his hands were as smooth as a cat's tongue, which was not something all ladies could overlook. Working with glass had left Osbourne with hands not much better though less rough.

Finally Martik arrived, slipping into Strom's chambers. There was plenty of room, but the engineer pulled a stool close. "Had to circle back twice," he said. "Kept running into people. It's unlikely Chase will make it."

Strom and Osbourne both nodded, knowing it was better not to give anyone reason to watch them more closely than they already were. Trinda knew they were loyal to Catrin, and they, along with many others in the hold, were surreptitiously watched.

"Things outside are happening fast," Strom said. "I'm betting Sinjin needs a smith, a glassmaker, and an engineer."

"You always were one to get straight to the point," Martik said.

"I don't think I'll be all that much help in either case," Osbourne said.

"Not much glass can do to help."

"You undervalue your skills," Martik countered.

Osbourne didn't respond.

"The only thing keeping me here are the wonders of this keep," Strom said. "There's more here than meets the eye, and she's up to something. Not sure what yet, but she's downplaying this. I can tell by the way she watches."

"What are you working on, anyway, Martik?" Osbourne asked.

"No one is allowed to speak of it, so don't say anything of this to anyone," Martik said.

Osbourne gave him a look indicating that was obvious.

"There's a stone wheel as tall as fifty horses standing on top of one another, and perhaps just as wide, though we can only see one side of it; the rest is embedded in the mountain itself."

"And?" Strom asked.

"Beyond the fact that I can't figure out how it was made, I cannot imagine what purpose such a gigantic mechanism could serve. I know this wheel is not part of what made the keep move and hasn't budged for perhaps thousands of years. That's what she wants me to fix."

"So you're fixing a machine you don't understand so it can fulfill its purpose, which you also don't understand. Sounds like a great idea. What could go wrong?"

"I know it sounds crazy, but I'm pretty sure Trinda knows exactly what this thing does, and I'm betting she's counting on it for something. I just don't know what."

"Can you sabotage it?" Strom asked.

"Not easily," Martik said. "This thing can take anything I can throw at it. The best way to keep it nonfunctional would be to never try to fix it. She's watching, though, and I don't think it would take long for her to catch on."

"It's not worth the risk," Strom said. "Maybe the best way to keep it from being fixed would be to remove you from the equation."

"It would buy you some time," Martik said. "But I've already had to explain to my best men how to get the job done. They're down there working on it as we speak."

"Still," Strom said. "You're the real brains behind it. Without you, they are bound to be delayed at the very least." It was clear Martik was reluctant to leave, and Strom was intrigued by what possible purpose this mechanism could serve. Knowing Trinda was trying to hide her interest made him think fixing it would be a huge mistake. The child queen had proven a capable leader, and her edicts were mostly palatable, but they were edicts nonetheless. The fact that the news from the outside world was so different from what the people of the Godfist were being told by Trinda and those loyal to her was reason enough to have doubts. "How long until you can be ready to go, Osbo?"

"Glass doesn't travel well," Osbourne said. "I can be ready within an hour."

Strom nodded, his friend was nothing if not practical.

"How long until you can be ready, Martik?"

"I could leave straight from this meeting with a clear conscience," Martik said.

"Good," Strom said. "I think the time has--" The rest of the sentence never left his lips. A mighty banging at the door made all three jump from their chairs. After taking a moment to breathe and gather his wits, Strom moved to the door. Osbourne and Martik did what they could to appear normal, but that somehow made their guilt and anxiety even more obvious. There was nothing to be done about it, as the determined banging rang out once again. "What is it?" Strom asked when he opened the door, trying to act angry rather than afraid.

"We've come for the engineer," said a deep voice, and the plumed helm of Trinda's elite guards preceded a face Martik recognized. Keenan was a good man but entirely devoted to Trinda and entirely too proficient with his weapons. There would be no leaving now--at least not yet.

"We'll have to finish our game another time," Martik said to Strom and Osbourne before following Keenan and another guard away from Strom's quarters.

"That went well," Osbourne said.

* * *

Dragonhold had been in the dark for eons until Trinda Hollis arrived. Benjin and Wendel may have rediscovered the fortress, and Catrin began cleaning her up, but Martik knew it was Trinda Hollis who breathed life back into this magnificent hold. For that reason, he could not fully dislike the girl. She had done some positive and amazing things, and had recently taken mercy on Master Edling by allowing him to leave his cell. Any threat he posed was long gone, and Martik wasn't certain how much of a kindness she had granted the man, but at least he was free from his cell. It had to be an improvement, except that many would be given their chance to seek vengeance.

Behind him stood a slope made from an uncountable number of hewn stones. High above, the mound stretched from valley wall to valley wall, forming a sort of bridge, which Sinjin, Brother Vaughn, and Trinda had used to escape the demons years before. A giant's bones had been found not far from where Martik stood. They had been picked clean. The light had chased many things away or left them to die without their favored darkness. Much of the hold was still dark, and Martik suspected there were things hiding in the shadows. It gave him the crawls.

Amber crystals, far larger than any natural specimen he'd ever seen, shed a jaundiced light on the immense stone wheel he faced. Around the wheel was a city created in a way no one could guess. There were no straight lines--anywhere. The place was all curves, imitating nature's gracefulness and including symmetry and patterns Martik had seen in the world around him. Men had been exploring the city for weeks. It appeared no people had ever actually lived there. There was only the detritus left by whatever had lived in the darkness.

All that was just a distraction to Martik. The wheel beckoned him. It was a puzzle waiting to be solved, and he was the perfect person to solve it, yet he had to question his motivation when Trinda was the beneficiary. Whatever mighty tool or weapon the ancients had left them, he would be delivering it into the hands of one plotting for war. That did not sit lightly on his gut. He didn't have much choice but to guide his crew closer toward freeing the giant wheel. When the crew retired for the day, he would make good his escape along with Strom and Osbourne. Together they would find their way to the Firstland. It all felt like a crazy dream, far from what his childhood on the family farm had prepared him for. In other ways, that life had prepared him for everything. It had taught him to be a problem solver, and that was what he did best.

His men struggled with mining tools to clear the debris from the wheel, and progress was painfully slow. They had originally thought the job would be easy since everything had been laid out for them. The wall leading up to the stone wheel was taller than three men, but it had circular holes alternating from side to side, providing toeholds for easy climbing. They soon found the rock cylinders strewn across the valley floor. Each one appeared to have been cut to fit within the holes along the base of the wheel, but his men had been able only to get them to slide part of the way into the holes. This had created a convenient ladder and platform once a few planks were added. From that point, they had all been grateful for the holes and cylinders but paid them little more mind.

Martik took Wendel Volker's advice and looked at the entire construction from a different perspective. Where else were there cylindrical holes within Dragonhold? he asked himself. It didn't take long to think of the water channels. Nowhere else, though, did they find these stone plugs. He wondered if perhaps these were the by-product of cutting the holes, but that still didn't explain why they were found only there. Near the bottom, one rung looked out of place. It was too low to be useful as a step, which made Martik further question its purpose. The stone cylinder wiggled free without much effort. The first thing Martik realized was the cylinder was made of a darker stone than the stone in which the shafts had been bored. These stone plugs had been made for a purpose, and Martik was feeling more and more confident that purpose was not to act as a ladder or platform.

Using his knife, he checked inside the circular depression and found it quite thoroughly clogged. After working at it for a while, he managed to clear the channel, and as he lay there breathing, a breeze cooled his skin. It wasn't emanating from the channel but rushing into it. It had to be!

Grabbing the stone cylinder, he wiped it as clean as he could and slid it into the channel. It was a nearly perfect fit; there was just enough play to allow the cylinder to slide in. When only a couple hand widths protruded from the hole, the shaft moved on its own. There was a sucking sound followed by a thud. Just enough shaft remained exposed to allow Martik to pull it back out. It resisted at first, but then came free with a sucking whoosh. Nothing else happened. He inserted it once again, and the suction pulled the shaft back, firmly locking it into place. This was it.

One of Trinda's guards was watching him a little too closely, and Martik realized his thoughts must have been written on his face. He had to make the decision in that moment whether or not to reveal what he'd found. Though part of him worried over the consequences, Martik could not resist.

"You men come down from there! And bring the planks!" he shouted to the crew, and the guard gave him a look that said he knew Martik was a traitor. It took much of the fun from what Martik was about to do. "You might want to get Trinda," he said to the guard.

"Queen Trinda," the man said. "And you don't want to test it first? You want me to drag the lady down here on your hunch?"

"Are you saying I should start the wheel turning without her here?"

The man glared at him for some time. Martik's crew was reaching the bottom of the stair. Finally he sent another guard with word for Trinda. He specifically did not look at Martik after that, which was not such a terrible result. It would take some time for Trinda to get there, but there was still work to be done.

"Remove the ladder stones, starting at the top. Hand the stones down and carefully stack them with the others," he said. "Do you understand?"

"Yes," Bradley said.

He was a good man whom Martik and Chase trusted. Though he normally served as a part of Trinda's guard, he'd been assigned to assist Martik in his efforts. Their friendship was no secret.

Martik stepped away from what he no longer considered a ladder; it was a lever, a gate, or maybe switch was the better word. The work proceeded more slowly than Martik would have liked, and he wondered why he had even opened his mouth. Sometimes his temper and ego got the better of him, and he reminded himself to keep his emotions under control. "Emotion destroys what logic builds," his father had always said. "Martik knew there was a place for emotion in his life, but he took his father's point: it could rule or ruin your life if not kept in check.

When Trinda arrived, she was carried by a well-muscled guard. She sat in his arms as if he were a throne, and the man did his best to descend loose stone slope with grace. There was a dangerous look on her face, and Martik hoped he was right. If not, his ego could have gotten him into serious trouble.

"I am not to be summoned," Trinda said before the man carrying her came to a stop before Martik.

"You asked for word should I have any progress, and I believe we've made significant progress today."

"I'm told you haven't actually done anything yet, as evidenced by this," she said, gesturing toward Martik's men, who were still working."

"I did not want to deprive you of the chance to see the wheel turn for the first time," Martik said, suddenly wishing he had no tongue. Now either the wheel turned, or he'd be a failure who had summoned the child queen to witness his disgrace.

"Yet you had no trouble depriving my guard of any of the details."

"I--"

"You deprived me of the information I needed. Don't do that again."

The words were said in a pleasant enough tone, but a chill enveloped Martik; he didn't want to "fall into the river."

The men proved why he considered them his best crew. The stone shafts were neatly lined up on the stone at the wheel's base. Feeling like a fool, Martik flushed and moved to the long, cylindrical stones. "These shafts are cut from a different type of stone; and they fit almost perfectly."

Trinda looked unimpressed.

Sliding the lowest shaft halfway in, Martik began re-creating the ladder, and even his men looked at him strangely, but then one sucked in a deep breath, the realization finally hitting him. With his crew handing him black stone cylinders, Martik reached the last hole, and this was the first shaft he pushed past the halfway point. He put his hands in the air and let everyone see the shaft get sucked in the rest of the way. There was an audible thunk when the stone was seated. Now those in attendance watched with a bit more anticipation. Martik's spirit soared but he did not want to get overconfident. Stepping back down a rung, he pushed in the shaft he'd just been standing on, and so he backed down the ladder, collapsing it as he went. With each shaft drawn into place, as if by magic, Martik's crew and perhaps even the guards came to believe. Every shaft brought them closer to solving a great mystery, and Martik couldn't help but smile. Then, though, he came to the last shaft, one he'd already tested. He knew it would work. It just had to work. When he tried sliding the stone into place, it resisted for an instant, and Martik swallowed, but after adjusting the angle, it slid in without resistance until being pulled from his grasp with a firm, almost greedy thunk. It was quiet and no one moved.

Nothing happened.

Someone coughed and Martik stood from where he'd been kneeling, his prayer unanswered.

Trinda glared down at him. "Do not summon me again."

* * *

"What were you thinking?" Strom asked Martik, his voice louder than he may have intended.

"I can't help it when something suddenly makes sense to me," Martik said.

"Quit pouting," Osbourne said.

"Trinda's guard has been watching me," Martik said. "Closer than I thought. He's not just watching me; he's reading me. And he knew the moment I figured it out; only I guess I really didn't figure it out."

"Stop whining," Osbourne said.

"I think they're going to try to stop us when we leave. I think they know," Martik said in a rush.

"They do," Strom said. "But they don't know when, and I'm betting they won't expect tonight."

"That's insane," Osbourne said.

"You're really not being helpful, you know," Martik said.

"Moving the conversation along . . ." Osbourne said. "You really think tonight, right after Martik's utter disgrace and humiliation in front of all those people, is the best time to make our escape?"

Martik stuck his tongue out at Osbourne.

"Our man is working the barges tonight," Strom said. "We just have to time it right. We still have time before the change of guard, and we know the day guard has had quite a day. I say we go."

Martik swallowed. It hadn't been real to him before, but now they were talking about actually trying to escape Dragonhold. Given how his day had gone, his confidence wasn't high, and he thought he might be sick. Osbourne didn't look a great deal better, no matter how much sarcasm he poured on it. Strom appeared determined but there was the slightest hint at the corner of his eyes: fear.

"How long do you need?" Strom asked, his voice low.

"I'm ready," Martik breathed. Nothing he owned was worth the risk.

"I'm ready too," Osbourne said.

Supplies already waited in the Upper Chinawpa valley. Beyond what they were wearing, they would be leaving their entire lives behind. In a way, their lives had been taken from them long before, and perhaps they would now take them back.

"I'll go first," Strom said. "Wait half a turn of the sand clock, and one of you follow. Then the other another half turn after that. Get to the docks, and we should be free. Deep breaths. Relax."

With that, Strom strode out as if nothing were amiss. Martik wasn't certain he could match the feat, and he had serious doubts about Osbourne.

"You go next," Osbourne said. "I'll be right behind you."

"You're not giving up already, are you?" Martik asked.

Osbourne laughed. "No. But I know I might give myself away. I'm not very good at hiding things. Strom has gotten better at it over the years."

"It helps to have arms like dragon jaws," Martik said, and Osbourne couldn't argue. Strom wasn't a man to be tangled with.

Half the sand had passed through the sand clock, and Martik let it run. With a nod, he walked into the hall, still unsure if Osbourne would follow. Shadows cast by the torchlight danced and taunted Martik as he walked. Gone were the days of herald globes lighting the halls. Those had been hoarded and stashed somewhere perhaps only Trinda herself knew. It was another puzzle. Did the girl hoard them to keep others from using them or so she could use them herself? Her alliance with Allette indicated she might be amassing a deadly arsenal for her own military purposes.

Martik realized he was mumbling to himself as he passed people in the halls, and he wondered what he might have been saying when people passed by. He would have to pay more attention. It was his nature to fixate on problems and ignore everything else, especially, as in this case, when his subconscious was handling the walking. Passing through the great hall made him feel as if everyone were watching him. They could easily see he was on his way to escape from Dragonhold, and surely he would be intercepted at any time. Every step caused his heart to beat faster, and sweat was running down his cheek by the time he reached the archway leading to the God's Eye. This would be the easiest place to stop him, and a man was moving in his direction. With every step, he wanted to go faster, to run, but he could not. That would ruin everything. He had to remain calm. The man was not someone he recognized, but when their eyes met, Martik quickly looked away, something he instantly regretted.

The man passed by the archway and moved back toward the kitchens. With a deep breath, Martik entered the hall, unable to appreciate the architecture as he usually did. He prayed with every step. When Strom saw him, he let out an audible sigh then looked embarrassed for having done so.

"Sound carries over water," Martik said softly.

Strom flushed and nodded.

Waiting for Osbourne was torture. Strom had turned over a sand clock when Martik arrived, and he frequently checked it. When half the sand had run out, Osbourne was not there, and a barge appeared. They would get but one chance at this, and Martik looked at Strom.

"I can't leave him."

Martik nodded. Either all of them went or none of them went. A moment after having that thought, Martik let out an audible sigh of relief. Strom gave him a look that said, Really?

The barge landed as Osbourne walked up, and they boarded without his ever stopping.

"Go," Strom said to the bargeman, whom Martik didn't recognize.

The man responded by pushing them into deep water. Every instant of the journey was etched in Martik's mind; he'd never been so frightened and exhilarated at the same time. They were so close to their goal, he could barely contain himself.

Strom grabbed his arm and leaned in. "Easy."

Martik hadn't even realized he'd been stepping forward and back as if about to make a running jump. Taking deep breaths, he did what he could to release them slowly. After what felt like ages, they reached the pocked stone shoreline. The bargeman said nothing as the three men disembarked. He simply poled back into deep water.

A single pair of guards was all that stood between them and the Chinawpa Valley and their freedom. Strom led the way, and it was clear he intended to fight if necessary. Martik followed with a bit less conviction, and Osbourne nearly outpaced him. They were at the checkered hall, which was what they now called the hall where Kyrien had entered and exited the hold with his dragon ore saddle on. The stones had left crisscrossing gouges in the otherwise smooth stone. It was a poignant reminder.

The guards' silhouettes came into view, and Martik could hear nothing over the pounding in his ears. Strom approached the man on the left and nodded in greeting. The man nodded back, and Strom walked into the valley beyond. Osbourne took another tentative step on his way outside, and nothing barred his path. Martik nearly sighed with relief again, but instead a hand closed over his mouth.

"You disappoint me, Martik Tillerman," Trinda said from within the cavern; the light of many herald globes her guards held hurting his eyes. It was an exaggerated show of force. A single overcharged herald globe would have been plenty. "First you failed to impress after you summoned me and now this. What am I going to do with you?"

Strong hands marshaled Martik back to where Trinda stood, and she spoke over his shoulder. "As for the two of you," she said. "You may never return."

Chapter 5

Words can cut as deep as a blade.
--Morif, soldier

* * *

The mighty wheel mocked Martik. He'd been so certain only days ago the shafts were the keys, and he was starting to realize they were perhaps one of the keys. The presence of a vacuum, that inrushing breeze, made him envision moving water. A river ran through this mountain, and it could be the suction's source. Those thoughts would have continued if not for heavy debris being cleared from atop the wheel. This irregularly shaped rock had not been created by the keep's crumbling. All the stone around it was smooth once the debris was cleared. This debris had been placed there to intentionally jam the mechanism, Martik knew. Someone had worked hard to make certain this wheel would stay as it was.

"Clear below!" Bradley shouted from above.

Martik moved to a safer place. The debris had to be thrown, or in this case pushed, from high above, and there was no guarantee it would fall where they intended. The wrong bounce on the way down could send it toward those gathered at the mighty wheel's base.

"Clear," Martik called back once he was satisfied his people were as safe as they could be.

Jagged rock appeared, only the tip at first, and it moved slowly before toppling over all at once and racing down the wheel's face, never touching the smooth stone. Hitting bottom with terrible force, it sent stone shards flying in every direction, some screaming as they went.

"Help!" someone shouted. "Man down!"

Martik cursed himself for not moving people farther back and pushed through the crowd.

"Stung me good," a man named Adger said. "But I'm all right. I think we should use that rock to make a wall we can take shelter behind."

Martik laughed. Leave it to someone from the Godfist to use the very problem itself as the solution. "Adger's right," he said. "Do as he says."

The man gave Martik a grateful nod but said nothing. Instead he just started moving rock. The others followed suit and placed their loads where he pointed. It proved something Martik's father had once told him. "Men of few words speak through their work."

With the shelter erected, Martik sent more men to the wheel's top to work the jam free. These men climbed on wooden rungs inserted in the boreholes. Martik had insisted the rock shafts be kept safe behind the new shelter. Leaving Adger in charge at the base, Martik climbed to join the workers above. Clearing the debris had not revealed much about the mechanism. Martik knew the wheel could possibly come free with devastating effect, and he wanted to keep his eyes on the situation. Though he thought the stone shafts were a key to starting this monumental machine, he couldn't be certain, and he did not want to risk lives unnecessarily.

Clearing the debris caused the rest to crack, move, and be generally unstable, making the process even more difficult. If only the loose sediment packed around the larger rocks hadn't set up like liquid stone. Not for the first time, he cursed whomever had done this. No matter what their reasons, they had now endangered his workers. Shouts rang out as debris suddenly broke free. The sound was like dragons fighting, and Martik truly wished he didn't know what that sounded like. It still haunted his dreams. It was among a small number of reasons he'd been happy to have been caught. Dragons could not fly through stone, so at least he was safe from the ferals. Curiosity about this wheel and the opportunity to redeem himself helped make the incarceration and humiliation bearable. He leaned heavily on those things whenever his thoughts turned to Strom and Osbourne. The two should be past the plateau where Catrin had released the floodwaters onto the Zjhon army. It had always struck him as an excellent demonstration water's power.

Water.

The debris was fused together, and doing that would take water, lots of water. Walking along the top of the wheel, Martik ignored everything, searching for what he knew must be there.

"Careful, sir," Bradley said, despite the fact that Martik had been telling him to stop calling him "sir" every day for more than a year. "Don't go too far in that direction; it gets steep and slippery."

"Walk with me," Martik said. "Where would you say the halfway point is between the sides of the wheel?" It was a point of contention, since the debris prevented them from seeing just how far back the wheel continued. Most of the wheel was enclosed in the mountain itself, leaving only the strip along the edge where the debris had been cleared visible.

"I think it's as wide as it is tall," Bradley said.

"What makes you say that?"

"Well, sir, when you cut a tree, you cut it down into manageable pieces, and those tend to be about as tall as they are big around. I know that must sound silly, but it just makes sense to me."

"It actually doesn't sound silly at all," Martik said. "You have an intuitive sense, and I think you are correct. No matter how skilled the people who made this, they would have had to move it, and the size you suggest would be less likely to crack in transport. And the ancients loved symmetry, which means if they wanted to place another key shaft up here, then it would be right about there." He pointed to a place above them lost in shadow.

Bradley turned back to the crew he managed. "We need some help over here," he said. "We need to get Martik up there so he can see."

Martik smiled at Bradley's crew's competence. They had worked under him for some time and had grown into the most capable crew he'd ever worked with. They were among the things keeping him from despair. Quickly they used the materials they had at hand to erect a structure Martik could easily scale. A torch was passed to Bradley, and he handed it to Martik.

"I hope I'm right about this," Martik said under his breath.

"Even if you're wrong," Bradley said, "you'll be the most brilliant fool I've ever known."

Martik had to smile. The climb was awkward but not unsafe, and the scaffolding was surprisingly stable given its haphazard construction. His heart jumped a bit when he saw a familiar-looking circular opening a short distance from where he and Bradley had estimated.

"There's an opening there," Martik said, and though happy for him, no one expressed surprise; that alone soothed Martik's bruised ego. "We need to move this scaffold to here." He was about to apologize, but the men didn't hesitate for an instant. Bradley jumped in and helped. Martik grabbed a young man among the most muscular on the crew. "Bring me one of those shafts, but be careful with it. We don't have the tools or knowledge to make a replacement. Understood?"

"Yes, sir," the young man said.

Watching him go, his step a little too anxious, Martik hoped the boy calmed himself before coming back up with the shaft, but then his attention was drawn back to the orifice itself. His crew had reassembled the structure, and he second-guessed himself, hoping he'd not had them rebuild it in the wrong place. Despite all his accomplishments, Martik still worried he would make another mistake. It was just part of who he was, he supposed.

After climbing atop the structure, though, Martik was rewarded with excellent access to the perfectly round shaft. This one was still clean and smooth inside, and all he needed was the stone key. It was soon handed up to him.

He hesitated. There was no way to be certain this orifice would do what he thought it would. He couldn't risk anyone but himself in the event he was wrong. If he evacuated the entire work site, as his gut told him to do, he would look like a dolt and might lose what faith he had remaining in his abilities.

Either way there was risk, but only by evacuating could he take all the risk on himself. "I thank you all for getting us to this point. What I'm about to do might be dangerous, or it might have no effect at all." People laughed.

"I can't risk any of you based on my feelings and hunches, so I am going to ask you all to move back to the top of the ramp." This was less enthusiastically received. It meant shutting down the entire operation for the day.

"I know," Martik said. "I'm sorry. If this does what I expect, I'll be able to get down safely. More than one of us coming down at once could mean big trouble. If I'm wrong, I'm wrong."

The crew didn't debate or grumble, they just cleaned up their work areas, gathered their tools, and made an orderly retreat.

Bradley stood beside Martik after everyone else had gone over the edge and down the ladder. "What do you think it's going to do?"

"Go on down, and I'll show you," Martik said with a grin.

"The crew and I agreed. I'm staying and protecting your back," Bradley said. When Martik opened his mouth to respond, he said, "They wouldn't take no for an answer. Surely two of us can escape whatever doom you face as easily as one?"

Knowing no discussion had taken place after his evacuation order, Martik shook his head and handed Bradley the torch. "Don't burn me this time," he said.

Bradley smiled. He hadn't burned Martik with a torch in a long time, but Martik would never let him forget it.

Once everyone else gained the safety of the upper slope, they climbed together. Martik could feel the crew's eyes upon him as he and Bradley climbed. The thought of sending for Trinda was quickly banished, though he thought he saw guards running from the chamber. That was fine with him. If they summoned Trinda, then she couldn't possibly blame him. Thinking back through their history, Martik knew she might still find a way, but at least he would make it more difficult.

At the top, Bradley held the torch overhead and to one side. Martik wasted no time and lifted the heavy stone over his head and tried to get it into the orifice. Bradley offered his other hand to steady the shaft and Martik smiled. It really was a two-man job. He'd have been hard pressed to do this alone, and he had to admit his ego was at times his worst enemy. The shaft slid upward as they guided it. Afraid to take his hands away, Martik glanced at Bradley, who was also ready to keep the shaft from sliding out and shattering atop the mighty stone wheel. Both were proven wrong when the shaft was sucked rapidly upward and seated itself with a resounding thump. The two men looked at each other, unsure how to react.

Nothing happened at first, and Martik was prepared for another humiliation. Then the stone around them began to thrum.

Thump . . . thump . . . thump . . . thud.

The last felt like a dragon had shoulder blocked the mountain.

"Run!" Martik said and Bradley was already leaping down their temporary structure.

"Come on!" Bradley said when he beat Martik to the bottom. "We've got to go now."

The two men had just made it to the ladder when the water began rushing over the wheel, soaking the debris and sending waterfalls down the wheel where the mechanism was still blocked.

As they climbed the slope to where a crowd of people cheered, Bradley turned to Martik, "Was that what you thought was going to happen?"

"I'll never tell," Martik said with a grin.

* * *

"Now how are we going to turn the water off?" Bradley asked.

It was a good question and one Martik hadn't quite puzzled out yet. The water rushing over the mighty wheel was less forceful than a flash flood, and strong climbers made it to the top despite concerns about the wood being slippery and the rungs themselves coming loose.

"I'm not certain yet," Martik said. "The water will surely have helped loosen up the debris blocking the mechanism, though."

Bradley nodded his agreement. "What about two ladders tied together at the top, so they lean on each other and can stand on their own. We can have someone holding each corner of the ladders in place against the current."

"There's a chance the debris will shift once we get up there, and that could put all of us at risk," Martik said.

"Yes, sir. We're going to have to be careful."

"Pick your best team. No more than we need but no less. I want to inspect the ladders before we do anything."

"Yes, sir," Bradley said, a twinkle in his eye. Martik knew he would do everything in his power to make him proud. It was a good feeling, but worry for Strom and Osbourne overshadowed it.

Even Chase had asked him if there was any news, despite Catrin's cousin being far better connected. Martik had trouble understanding why Chase was still within Dragonhold, but he admitted having his own reasons to stay. It certainly wasn't all bad. Trinda's leadership was mostly unobtrusive, and the people had flourished under her rule. Food was plentiful, people were productive, and they lived and loved much as they had always done. However, the guards watching him colored the illusion.

In less time than Martik would've thought possible, Bradley returned with his team: four men and two ladders. As promised, the ladders had been lashed together at one end to his satisfaction. It was good they hadn't been longer, since the water spilling over giant wheel's edge was filling the valley. The water was getting deeper, and the crew worked hard to lift the ladders up the slippery stair. With the rushing water fighting them the entire way, it proved more difficult than Martik had initially expected, and he hadn't thought it to be easy.

When they finally reached the top, the last man over the edge lost his footing and nearly fell, but he kept his grip on the ladder, which was held firmly at the other end. Martik and Bradley followed, helping each other manage the slippery climb. Twice Martik wobbled and both times Bradley was there.

"Sorry I'm having so much trouble," Martik said, breathing hard.

"To be honest," Bradley said, "it's kind of nice to see you have trouble with something. I know you've been having a bad run of luck, but you have a way of making a man think less of himself because of all the things you do."

Martik didn't know what to say and concentrated on making the climb. When he reached the top, the water's rush was nearly overwhelming. He could see why the crew had such difficulty keeping their footing. Bradley put an arm around him, and they moved one step at a time to where the crew worked on erecting the ladders. None of them was having an easy time of it. Martik's pride would normally have prevented him from accepting Bradley's help, but this was life or death. If someone fell and was swept away by the current, there wasn't much hope for survival.

Grateful instead for the support, he felt a little better when Bradley slipped. He shouldn't have smiled at that, but he did anyway. The entire scene was surreal, and the dim amber light danced across the water, making the stone move like a living thing, writhing beneath their feet. Those holding the makeshift structure looked less than confident, but Martik committed himself to climbing spindly ladders atop a giant rock wheel to pull a stone plug and turn off the waterfall. It was the kind of thing no one outside the hold would ever believe.

Though reaching high enough for Martik to grasp the stone shaft, the ladders flexed and moved in alarming ways.

"Let me do it?" Bradley begged, but Martik was determined.

The higher he climbed, the more it flexed and swayed. He decided to move more quickly, which worsened the problem. Finally, though, he was able to steady his weight using the shaft itself.

The force of his weight overwhelmed the vacuum. The shaft moved downward gradually at first but then fell without resistance. Martik did his best to hold on to it and had to grasp it with both hands, his legs trembling from the exertion of staying upright on an unstable structure. The lives of those below him were at stake, and he gave his all to hold on to the heavy shaft.

Though he secured it, his weight was on his heels, and he started to fall backward. Trying to shift his weight to his toes and failing, he had to reach out with one hand and grab the ladders. The shaft nearly slipped from his grasp, but the water flow had already begun to abate.

Once steadied, he shifted to a comfortable position, and Bradley met him halfway. It was an awkward exchange, but the stone was handed down, and Martik was able to use both hands to climb back to relative safety. The water was receding, which was good except for glistening silt now covering the entire surface in a thin layer. It moved and shifted under their boots and sent Martik to his knees.

He hoped it would be manageable when it dried and was pleased to see the source of this material had been the cement like sediment holding the debris together. What remained were big chunks of stone, which should be relatively easy to relocate.

After a slippery climb down, Martik was somewhat vindicated. He was now several steps closer to solving the mystery, and he could hardly wait.

Chapter 6

Passion razes kingdoms.
--King Venes

* * *

Martik sat with his legs crossed, watching the ancient wheel turn. It made no sense. After clearing the debris, the giant stone wheel began to move, the water filling the pool around it giving it buoyancy. It didn't spin; it bobbed. Bradley and Martik inserted the remaining shafts, which were sucked into place, and the mighty wheel shifted. A loud grinding noise followed by a thump made Martik's teeth hurt.

Nothing at all changed at first, but then it was clear the wheel was turning, albeit slowly. Little by little, the speed increased, and Martik wondered how fast it could go and to what purpose it moved. The wheel's movement had no perceptible effect. He had to be missing something. Bradley stood nearby and Martik knew the young man was worried about him, but he just needed to think it through. This was a complex machine, and there was no shame in not understanding it. The ancients surely knew things he did not. They had left him a puzzle, especially since he could find no way to gain access to the mechanism. The only possibility he could envision was to move the great slope behind him and fill the entire city with water, which stretched the imagination.

"There has to be another key," Bradley said.

Though he'd considered that before, Bradley's words made him stop and look at things from another perspective. "Bradley," he said, "when we decided to pile all the debris over there, why did we do that?"

The younger man thought for a second, and his eyes went wide. "Because there was already debris piled there!"

Martik didn't have to say anything more. Bradley organized his team and began the process of moving all the debris they had carelessly tossed down from above. Martik worried anything under all the shattered rock had also been destroyed. Part of him wanted to get in there and move the rock with the crew, but that was no longer his role. He had to trust his crew and Bradley to do what he asked of them. His role was to figure out this machine, and he was just guessing. If there was nothing under the debris, he'd be back in familiar territory.

Trinda had come twice to see his progress. She hadn't said a word to him since his attempted escape. He didn't care. He wasn't doing it for her; he was doing it for himself. Trinda's guards watched everything he did, and there was no need for him to report to her. His only job was to figure out this mechanism, and it was the one thing he was incapable of doing.

Even as those thoughts crossed his mind, Bradley shouted, "We found something!"

Martik didn't even remember standing up, but his legs were under him and he was moving at a reckless pace. Workers converged on the place where Bradley stood, and things went more quickly now that they were clearing a much smaller area.

"Bring water, rags, and an empty bucket," Bradley said, and he had water and rags by the time Martik arrived. Some debris remained, and he had to climb over jagged stone to see what Bradley had found.

There waited a new puzzle. Istra's likeness was set into the floor, only with holes carved into the stone where her eyes, ears, and mouth would be. Bradley wiped the area down and cleared what he could. Small bits disappeared into the holes, making not a sound; even when they used a stone on a string to check the depth of the mouth hole, which was the largest, they could find no bottom.

"And it gets even stranger," Martik said.

The crew continued to work at moving the debris while Bradley and Martik stared. The area was soon clean and swept. He walked the entire carving, looking for any other clues or hints as to its true purpose, or at the very least how to unlock it.

All the while, the giant cylindrical wheel turned just a little faster.

* * *

Strom walked with his shoulders hunched, and Osbourne followed, feeling about the same. Leaving Martik behind went against their values, but they really had little choice. If Trinda did not want them back in the hold, then there was little chance of getting back in. Instead, they were forced to carry on without him . . . and their supplies. It was bad enough that Trinda had intercepted Martik, but she could at least have left their supplies. Now they were being forced to forage in the same woods they'd had to forage all those years ago. It was reminiscent and altogether humiliating and demoralizing. "Maybe we'll find some black walnuts," Osbourne said, aiming low.

The truth was that these woods were no longer what they had once been. Now they supported the mouths of Dragonhold, and they had been picked nearly bare. Once there had been black walnuts by the hundreds arranged in circles beneath the trees, but now one or two might remain high among the branches, the grounds clear.

"The farther away we get the better and worse it will get," Strom said, and he knew the truth of those words. The lands were less forgiving to the east, but they shouldn't have been picked clean. The snakes alone were usually enough to keep people away. "Try not to step on any rotting logs."

"That's not even a little funny," Osbourne said, but both had a brief laugh. "While we're talking of memories, I seem to remember a hill with a big tree and some apple trees not far away. You think we could find that place again?"

"We can do that," Strom said, and Osbourne noticed he stood a little taller as he walked. An achievable goal had perhaps given them both a little hope. Perhaps the land was more welcoming now, or maybe they had learned with age to be more careful where they put their feet, but the journey across the swamps was not as unpleasant as it could have been. Rolling hills waited beyond, and the smell of apples was on the wind.

"I think we're getting closer," Osbourne said. He sighed. "I miss them all."

"I know," Strom said. "I'm glad you're here. A pretty lady would be better, but we can't have everything."

"I'd trade you for a sack full of sausages, cheese, and springwine. Or any one of the three in a pinch."

Over the next hill stood a place they both recognized; the mighty tree still presided over the sloping hills, and not far away, another tree cradled a stone as if gripping a mystical orb. The memories were overwhelming. Some made Osbourne want to laugh; others made him want to cry.

"Gather wood," Strom said. "I'm going fishing." In his hand the smith held fishing wire and a hook. They were the only tools they had, and Osbourne was grateful Strom had managed to sneak them out of Dragonhold. He hoped they would not have to live off the land for long, but he knew they could if they were forced to. Strom had sent a message through the Vestrana, seeking a ship, but there was no way to know if that message had ever gotten through to anyone willing or able to pick them up.

The realization they had no home was inescapable. All Osbourne could do was hope.

* * *

Even his memories of the Arghast Desert could not prepare Osbourne for the oppressive heat and searing sunlight. The sand reflected the heat, gradually cooking them. Strom had taken off his shirt, and his skin tanned like leather. Osbourne remained trapped within his long shirt, knowing the sun would boil the skin from his body; his fair skin would never tan like Strom's, and he envied the man.

Much as Wendel and Benjin had done all those years ago, Strom and Osbourne walked the coastline. Bordered on one side by nothing but blue salt water and the Arghast Desert on the other, they suffered from thirst. Here the heat from the sands burned off any moisture in the air, and everything was parched. The sea water was salty and would make a person sick, and they had nothing to help them distill it into potable water.

"We shouldn't go too much further," Osbourne said. "If we don't find water soon, we're going to need to go back to that last stream we found, and it was a long way back."

"Just a ways further," Strom said, just as he had three times before.

Osbourne knew they would eventually go too far and turning back would do no good. The only source of hope was the gathering darkness along the horizon. Rain would give them what they needed so badly. Lightning illuminated the growing clouds, and Osbourne decided he should take care in what he wished for. There was no cover along the shoreline, and he and Strom were the tallest things for some distance.

"What do you think we should do?" Osbourne asked.

"About what?" Strom replied, sounding irritable.

"About that," Osbourne said, pointing to the storm, knowing his friend had been in deep thought. Neither was at their best.

"We should look along the water for shells or anything we can use to hold rainwater," Strom suggested.

"What about shelter from the storm?" Osbourne asked.

Strom just shrugged. "Not much we can do about that."

Together they scoured the beach, searching for shells, but most were small, broken, and not much use. Strom had just found a conical shell the size of his fist when Osbourne saw something he would never have expected. Some kind of cross between a balloon and a ship emerged from the storm clouds, rocking and bucking like a prize bull, and the thing managed to lurch its way toward where Strom and Osbourne stood. The shell slid from Strom's hand as he stood agape.

"Is that who I think it is?" Strom asked.

"Who else could it be?" Osbourne asked in return.

Only Kenward Trell could be responsible for something as audacious as the airship. As she drew closer, they began to see the rough likeness of Kyrien. It was rough but not without charm.

For a moment, Osbourne felt lucky, albeit nervous. The nervous part grew as the ship approached, and Kenward's orders continued to rise in pitch. The winds driving the ship forward whipped across the beach and drove sand before it, stinging skin and eyes. Osbourne did his best to keep his eyes on the approaching ship.

"Be ready to jump aboard," Kenward shouted as the ship descended until she skimmed across the water without ever touching the waves.

When lightning flashed behind the ship, Osbourne could see it through the slats making up the vessel, and he swallowed hard, uncertain he wanted to board this madman's airship. This feeling grew stronger when the ship crashed into the sands behind him and Strom. It was a violent impact, but the ship held together. The wind socks rested on the sand for an instant before the wind filled them. They stretched the ropes tight and dragged the ship sideways across the sand, rapidly approaching where Strom and Osbourne now ran, trying to escape.

"Be ready!" Kenward shouted. "We'll pull you aboard! Just don't get run over by the *Serpent*. That wouldn't end well for you."

Osbourne looked over his shoulder, wondering if he could outrun the ship, but it was clear he could not. Strom had come to the same conclusion, and both turned at the same time. The ship rushed toward them, and Kenward's crew reached out while holding on for dear life.

"Now! Jump!" Kenward called.

It was too soon, Osbourne thought, but he was glad he jumped when he did. Clipping the rail, he spun in the air and landed firmly atop Kenward, which was only fair. Strom made it aboard much more gracefully, but they were far from safe. Sand built up before the ship, and she was threatening to dig in. Given their speed, it could tear the ship apart. "Get us back in the air," Kenward ordered.

Crewmen moved and shouted, but not much otherwise changed except for the gouts of black smoke filling the air and a whirring sound that grew louder and higher in pitch. The wind bags quite suddenly righted themselves and inflated, and the ship left the sand. It rejoined the sand several times before finally leaving the ground behind.

Kenward ordered a structural check and offered Strom and Osbourne a winning smile. "Welcome aboard the *Serpent*! If you see any giant dragons chasing us, be sure to let me know."

* * *

Flying aboard the *Serpent* was an experience Strom would never forget. As a craftsman, almost everything about the ship offended his sensibilities, but it was the only thing between life and death. It was not a good feeling. There were things about the ship he had to admire as well, which helped a little. Though the lashings appeared sloppy, for example, they also flexed, making the ship supple. Given the wood's brittle nature, this design made more and more sense. He still didn't like the deck shifting under his feet or the way the ship flexed and moved, but she flew. He had to give Kenward that point. Without using Istra's power, the *Serpent* flew.

When he probed deeper into how the ship managed flight, Kenward was guarded. "It's an ancient technology," he admitted. "I'm sworn to secrecy on its exact nature and source, I'm afraid."

"Coal fired," Strom said, sniffing the air. "Steam power and hot air as a by-product. How do you regulate the pressure?"

"Show off," Kenward said, grinning. "Come on. I'll show you."

Strom followed against his better judgment, although to the delight of his curiosity. The deckhouse was as flimsy and haphazard as the rest of the ship. Within waited unbearable heat, a coal pile on one side, and a huge boiler on the other. Men tended the fires, and Strom kept looking for the valves, the pressure releases. He found only one, and there was no gauge or any other way to measure the pressure. It was a nearly sealed system. They were flying on a giant bomb. If it didn't explode, it would likely burst into flames. The mounts holding the boiler in place were surrounded by smoking black wood. An impeller drove a shaft with a leather belt running between it and another. If the belt broke, as belts were wont to do, it could take out the less-than-sturdy boiler mounts.

"Isn't she a beauty?" Kenward asked.

Strom was impressed Kenward had lived as long as he had with such a terrible mental illness. "Your brilliance is only surpassed by your sheer lack of concern for safety."

"Thank you!" Kenward said with his irrepressible grin. "I knew you would see the beauty in her."

In truth, Strom could think of nothing but getting off this flying disaster before it came unglued. "How long until we reach the Firstland?" he asked.

"Not much longer," Kenward said, either blissfully unaware of Strom's misgivings or in complete disregard of them.

Strom suspected the latter. "Perhaps we should land at the beach. Landing within the hold is risky."

"Oh, but it's so much easier," Kenward said. "You'll be able to step right off the ship and into Windhold. That's how we do things here on the *Serpent*. No long journey's just to board and disembark, no, sir. We come to you and take you directly to where you are going. It's the way of the future, my friend. You just have to see my vision."

Strom was having visions of his own, most of which involved fire and a twisted pile of burning flakewood. Osbourne thought even less of the ship and refused to even walk around the deck. He had remained glued to the deckhouse in spite of the heat, and Strom thought he might have splinters from gripping the planks so tightly.

When the Firstland finally came into view, Strom found himself at a loss for words, despite having seen the Firstland before. No descriptions from fireside tales or books could convey the majesty of the place said to be the cradle of mankind. Osbourne even stood to get a better view, though he remained stuck to the deckhouse. Mountains reached for the sky and pierced the clouds, a natural harbor at their feet.

Strom decided seeing the Eternal Guardians from above was the most awesome way to see them. The entire Valley of Victors was amazing in how real the carvings of men were. Catrin had always said how it had bothered her that there were no women depicted at all, as if they hadn't existed.

Unpredictable surrounded the mountains, especially Windhold, which boggled the mind and the eye. The mountain had been carved out to leave only her bones, twisting sweeping shafts of hard rock shaped by forces long forgotten.

The Arghast, who Strom knew he must now think of as Drakon and Dragon Clan, gathered near the largest opening into Windhold. Strom questioned the wisdom of their decision. Gusts blew the ship sideways without notice, and there was little Kenward or anyone else could do about it. Perhaps one could fly without Istra's power, Strom thought, but should one? The answer was clear when the Drakon fled.

"We're coming in too fast," Osbourne shouted, but everyone else had already realized it.

"Vent the steam!" Kenward shouted. "Lower the sails. Brace yourselves!"

The *Serpent* struck Windhold a resounding blow. The mountain didn't budge, and thus the ship and her occupants absorbed the energy. Though the ship was still in one piece, Strom was fairly certain something important was damaged if not completely broken. Black smoke poured from the chimstack, and he just hoped the thing held together long enough for him to get off of it and never get back on again. He would swim wherever else he may need to go if that was what it took. No more flying with Kenward, he promised himself.

The wind bags pressed against the hold by the prevailing wind held the ship in place. Though Strom would have liked to have been the first one off the ship, he couldn't leave without Osbourne. He turned back to the deckhouse, but to the man's credit, he was already walking toward Strom.

"Get me off this ship," Osbourne said.

"Why do people always say that?" Kenward asked. No one responded.

Strom helped Osbourne over the rail, and his friend offered him an arm to grasp as he made his way down. His arms and legs tingled, and he had to take a couple of minutes just to bask in the glory of having survived flying to the Firstland aboard the *Serpent*. Osbourne hugged him in celebration. Kenward shook his head as if they were daft.

"I wish Martik was here," Osbourne said and Strom agreed. He deeply regretted leaving Martik behind but would have to live with his regret. Kenward and his men worked with rope and winches to secure the *Serpent*. The wind bags and the sails were stowed and the fires quenched, though the steam nearly filled the entire hold. The dragons, at least, seemed to like it.

Sinjin and Kendra approached, and Strom couldn't help but grin. "Look at you," was all he could think of to say. At least he didn't say, "Look how big you've gotten."

"Welcome," Sinjin said, smiling. Then he turned more serious. "Martik?"

"Captured but most likely well cared for," Strom said. "There are things Trinda wants him to fix."

"Fix?" Sinjin asked.

"Remember how well things went when the water got turned on?" Osbourne asked while poking Strom in the ribs. "Those kinds of things."

"What are those things supposed to do?" Sinjin asked.

"Sinjin," Kendra said, "you're interrogating the poor man. It's clear they've had a harrowing journey."

"Yes," Kenward said as he came to join them. "I'm certain the time they spent in the wilderness must have been quite harrowing. How lucky they were the *Serpent* arrived to pick them up."

"And how lucky they were verdant dragons have to eat and sleep," someone behind Kenward said, but he ignored it.

"Kenward," Sinjin said, "I must ask. Why were verdant dragons chasing you?"

"Oh. That," Kenward said. "Clearly a misunderstanding. They think we stole something from them. The crew and I have discussed it, and we have decided we did not steal anything. And yes, thank god and goddess verdant dragons have to eat and sleep." His crew roared in response.

"Please, all of you come in and have some tea," Kendra said. This was the most Sinjin had ever seen her attempt to entertain anyone, and he rather liked it, though he wouldn't tell her that. She might take it the wrong way. What he liked was that she was warm and welcoming, and she wasn't yelling at anyone. The last thought came with a chuckle. His wife was a spirited woman.

"They ambushed us as we were leaving the hold, grabbed Martik, and forced us the rest of the way out. Trinda told us we were never to return, but I'm not leaving it up to her. She even had the guards dispose of our packs and supplies.

"Had to rough it, eh?" Sinjin asked with a smile.

Seeing what the Drakon had done with almost nothing, Strom was ashamed to admit they struggled.

"It took months to get set up well enough I didn't have to worry over our day-to-day survival," Sinjin said.

"You worry too much," Kendra said while adjusting his shirt collar.

Strom looked to the dragon watching him from nearby.

"That's Valterius," Sinjin said. "He likes to know who's in the hold."

"He doesn't talk in people's minds, does he?" Strom asked, unable to hide the worry in his voice.

"No," Sinjin said with a smile. "Sometimes I wish he did."

"Don't wish for that," Strom said. "Trust me."

"What is this thing Martik is working on for Trinda?"

"It's a towering wheel of stone," Osbourne said. "No idea what its purpose is, but Martik is supposed to make it turn."

"Really?" Sinjin asked. "And then what happens?"

"I wish I knew," Strom said. "Martik is still trying to figure it all out."

"I don't like the sound of it," Kendra said. No one disagreed.

"I'm going to see if she'll trade with me," Kenward said. "She's got the perfect airship landing pad--something you need here, by the way, seriously."

"Good luck with that," Strom said.

"She'll do it," Kenward said. "She's cut off from the world, and there'll be things she wants. I might know how to get those things. And perhaps I can get you things."

"We'll talk about that later," Sinjin said. "I could use your advice. The Heights are claiming the ferals are very active, though not in as great a number as before."

"Give them a couple years," Durin said as he walked up. "The place will be crawling with them." He served tea and embraced each in turn, threatening to spill their hot drink.

"Anyway, the Greatlanders want to remain neutral, and the rest want us to fly in support of the verdants, so they can continue vital trade across the Jaga. We're not really fully settled here yet, and that would drain us of resources. What do you think?"

"I think you violated my first rule," Osbourne said. "Never be in charge. Failing that, my second rule is to care for yourself and your family first. If you can help more when those are cared for, then do so."

Sinjin smiled. "I thought so too. Thanks."

"You shouldn't second-guess yourself," Kendra said.

"People's lives are at risk, and these decisions could place a lot more in danger. I won't apologize for seeking good counsel."

"Nor should you," Kenward said. "And I shall give you my advice. Start by having some of your friends help your other friends fix their ship."

Chapter 7

Success lies in the ability to inspire others to action.
--Mother Gwendolin, Cathuran monk

* * *

Strom shook his head, and Osbourne mirrored his concern.

"You're defenseless in here," Strom said, and Osbourne nodded emphatically. "I bet a good storm would chase you out of here."

Sinjin flushed but didn't say anything.

"This place is great as a flight deck, but it's no place to live."

"The Dragon Clan occupies the lower levels of the mountain, and they are a little better protected from the weather."

"But not by much," Kendra said, and Sinjin flushed again.

"The problem with this mountain is it's full of holes," Osbourne said, and all eyes turned to him. "In order to secure it, you'd need to fill far too many openings."

"He's right," Strom said.

"They're right," Kendra said.

"I hear you," Sinjin said. "We cannot defend others until we can defend ourselves."

"Thank you!" Kendra said. "Was that so difficult?"

Strom gave her a disapproving look, and she closed her mouth forcefully.

"We've looked over the island," Sinjin said, "though not as thoroughly as I would like. We've found ruins but nothing more attractive than this."

"Perhaps we should look some more?" Kendra said with a twinkle in her eye.

Sinjin smiled. He loved his wife. "That's a splendid idea. I don't know about you, but I could use a second set of eyes."

Kendra just grabbed Strom by the arm and propelled him to where Gerhonda waited. Sinjin guided Osbourne toward Valterius. Durin was already saddling the dragon, and several people assisted Kendra and Strom saddle Gerhonda and get strapped in. Strom paled. "Perhaps you could just draw me a map," he said to Kendra and Sinjin laughed.

"It's not funny," Osbourne said. "I could make do with a map."

"It'll be fine and there is nothing like seeing for yourself. Am I right?"

Osbourne appeared dubious and looked Valterius up and down. "Do these things have a weight limit? I'm not made of flakewood, you know."

"I think Valterius can handle it," Sinjin said, and his dragon snorted, forcing Osbourne back a step. After climbing up, Sinjin offered Osbourne a hand, and his mother's old friend took it reluctantly. "I won't kill you.

Promise," Sinjin said.

With that, Osbourne grabbed tight and pulled himself up. Durin climbed up and got Osbourne strapped in; he also double-checked Sinjin's straps, something Sinjin had grown accustomed to but still appreciated. Once Durin jumped down, Valterius started for the wind channel.

"Are we really ready? Are my straps tight enough?" Osbourne asked.

"You've been cleared," Sinjin said, and Gerhonda fell in alongside Valterius. Before anyone could say anything more, both dragons surged forward and thrust themselves into the warm, blue skies. Lush greenery was already reclaiming the scarred landscape around Windhold. Evidence of the mighty battle was largely obscured, but skeletal remains along with circular impressions left in stone and sandy areas were difficult to miss.

Strom held his breath as the world fell away from underneath him. This was worse than flying with Kenward, as now rock and trees hurtled toward him at incredible speed. When Gerhonda extended her wings, Strom was pressed down into his seat by the force, and he couldn't prevent the scream issuing from his lips. Osbourne, apparently, couldn't either. But then an amazing thing happened, Gerhonda and Valterius found thermals and started riding them in lazy circles. The land below grew farther away and the view even more impressive. They had seen some of this scenery on their approach aboard the *Serpent*, but that had been a very different experience.

Once the dragons had gained sufficient altitude, Sinjin and Valterius turned first and dived toward the twisting valleys. Gerhonda followed and Strom had never felt such a rush of excitement in his life. It was terrifying and thrilling and beautiful all at the same time. Kendra pointed out the second hollow mountain they had mentioned, where the openings were too small for the dragons. He also pointed out the clearly man-made ruins giving evidence of the Firstland's distant past. Beyond that, they had to squeeze through a narrow and twisting valley, and it didn't appear wide enough to accommodate them. With wings trimmed, the dragons narrowly avoided the rocky peaks. As a passenger, it was difficult to do anything but ride along and watch the rapidly approaching trees and rock. Despite that, Strom turned his head and looked about as they flew. Just before they burst forth from the narrow valley, he saw a bright flash of green light.

Before them waited an amazing sight. The Valley of Victors was far more imposing when seen up close than from afar. The dragons flew along the twisting river, the Eternal Guardians rising up before them, only the giant statues were facing the other direction. Even from behind, though, they demanded respect. Strom could barely keep his breath for all the wondrous sights, though his eye was drawn by dark shapes moving through the trees and causing the canopy to shake. When the harbor came into view, shrouded by black beaches lined with glistening bodies, Strom forgot everything else. Corpulent seal-like creatures sunned themselves along the shores and on glistening rock formations.

Valterius winged toward a section of beach free of wildlife. As his shadow approached, many of the distended beasts thrust themselves into the water. With a few flaps of his wings, Valterius slowed and landed on the obsidian beach. Gerhonda landed not far away.

"I thought you might like a chance to catch your breath," Sinjin said.

"Is it safe to be here?" Osbourne asked.

"The dragons will keep most of the wildlife at a distance," Kendra said. "But if you see a big, black fin coming, get away from the water."

"Maybe I'll just stay up here," Osbourne said.

Strom unstrapped himself and climbed down. The flight hadn't been a long one, but it felt good to stretch nonetheless. Eventually Osbourne joined them.

"We considered moving closer to the beaches, where it is easy to land, but there are too many predators at forest level. The hollow mountains are the only inhabitable structures at a sufficient height above the tree line. We can look some more, but I'm not sure how much we'll find."

"It could be nothing," Strom said, and all eyes rested on him. "Have you ever seen green light flash in that gorge?" He pointed to the place through which they had flown.

"No," Sinjin said after turning his eyes to where Strom pointed. "That's a pretty tricky stretch. I've never noticed much of anything going through there. Too busy trying to stay alive."

"What did you see?" Kendra asked.

"It lasted only for an instant," Strom said. "But I saw a flash of green light come from up there, by where that flat spot is, next to the dip. See where I mean?"

No one did.

"If you'll fly us back up there," Strom said, "I'll show you."

"We'll have to get some serious altitude over the sands," Kendra said. "You know how dangerous the air above those peaks can be. One downdraft, and you'll be smeared across the mountainside."

"Maybe we should wait here while you look," Osbourne said. "I'm sure the extra weight just makes it more dangerous."

"Come on, Osbourne," Strom said. "I see a big, black fin coming. Don't get eaten."

"Very funny," Osbourne said until he, too, saw the giant fin racing toward shore. He managed to get back in his place atop Valterius before anyone else. The fin continued toward them, pushing a wall of water with it, and one of the oversized seals was thrown into the air by the wave. The shark's head and gleaming white teeth gnashed the air as the seal writhed, trying to escape its fate. The shark was ready and struck as soon as the creature hit the water. It was over in an instant, and Osbourne paled even further.

Strom wasted no time in regaining the saddle, and the dragons kept close watch on the shoreline. Strom didn't want to think about who would win in a battle between shark and dragon, and he triple-checked the straps holding him in. Kendra checked them herself once, and they were on their way. With a powerful leg thrust and a few wing flaps, the dragons gained the air. Soaring low over the water, they could see oversized shadows moving beneath the surface. Strom didn't want to know what those creatures were. Knowing such massive beasts now ruled the seas and the skies, he felt a great deal smaller than he once had. It was an adjustment all of them had to make. On the Godfist or even the Greatland, humans had been at the top of the food chain. Here the same could not be said. These days, no place was safe.

Soon black beach rushed beneath them again, and warmer air pushed them upward. Higher and higher they went, and it still wasn't high enough to suit Kendra or Sinjin. Strom's head felt as if it would explode, and he wasn't certain how much more he could take. Kendra showed him how to relieve some of the pressure by holding his nose, closing his mouth, and blowing. Though he felt much better afterward, he still wasn't certain how much more altitude he could withstand. Thin air left him struggling to breathe. Kendra noticed his discomfort and signaled to Sinjin.

"Be careful," he shouted.

Flying through the valley had been a frightening experience. Knowing it was a good bit safer than what they were about to do made Strom's stomach hurt. Clouds obscured much of the landscape below them. The air moved in ripping torrents, sheared by the peaks themselves. Tenacious trees clung to the heights, reaching out to them and coming perilously close. Valterius pulled away from the rocky peak, but Kendra would not be so easily dissuaded. Strom held on with a white-knuckled grip. If she or Gerhonda miscalculated, they could slam into the side of a mountain. Clouds obscured his vision, and he waited for death to come. Instead, they burst into an area almost completely surrounded by peaks. Misshapen spires surrounded a grove, and by their very shape, they directed the persistent wind into the hidden valley, creating a persistent updraft.

Gerhonda floated on the updraft, small movements of her wings allowing her to turn them in a slow circle. Moments later, Valterius burst from the mists, his roar echoing within the sheltered vale. No one spoke as they took in the beauty of the place. At the center stood a clearing of weathered stone with twenty-four towering green crystals on the perimeter. And in the surrounding valley walls were openings large enough to admit dragons. Each one was shaded by overhanging rock that made them difficult to see from above.

Valterius landed first and Gerhonda floated down beside him. The landing was remarkably soft. This time no one hesitated in climbing down and exploring what they had found. It was impossible not to be drawn to the crystals. With flat, glossy faces, they formed geometric shapes with no names. White striations broke up the green. They were beautiful beyond description. Each stone was unique, and the deeper you stared into them, the more texture you found. Strom backed up when he realized all of them were staring directly into the crystals.

"Do not get lost," Strom said. His words echoed.

It took a moment before the others responded, as if they had to cover a great distance to return.

"Wow," was all Osbourne managed to say.

"Beautiful," Kendra said, running her hand along a sheer face.

Strom walked to the center of the vale, to the very heart of the bare stone. Never had he known power like Catrin's, save maybe when her dragon had spoken in his mind or when he was at the forge and swinging a hammer. The world shimmered around him, the updraft warm, almost gentle in its caress. Perhaps it was just his mind playing tricks, but Strom would swear he felt something. This place had such power even he could feel it. For once, he was glad Catrin was not by his side; what might happen if she tapped into this power? He tried not to think about it.

Sinjin stared into the crystals until Kendra went to pull him away. Osbourne joined them. "It's creepy," he said.

Strom knew exactly what he meant. This was so much like the event in the Grove of the Elders all those years ago, yet it was so very different. It smelled the same, as if the air were charged, like right before a storm.

Kendra led Sinjin away from the crystals, but rather than coming to where Strom and Osbourne stood, she took him toward a shaded entrance. Strom moved in that direction, and Osbourne followed, still in an apparent haze. The air was cooler there, and there was less of an updraft. The openings themselves, five of them, were large enough to admit regent dragons, which meant no problems admitting the smaller regal dragons-- except all of the orifices were blocked.

Strom whistled when he saw the stones used to block the entryways. The blocks were well cut and would weigh as much as a warship. "They really didn't want anyone getting in there," he said.

Kendra had her arms crossed over her chest, her thoughts clearly intense.

"What would it take to move these stone blocks?" Sinjin asked.

"Dragons--" Osbourne said.

"And Martik," Strom finished for him.

* * *

Martik had never been more frustrated. Trinda had forbidden him to work any more on the great wheel, which continued to turn a little faster every day. He suspected there was a limit to how fast such a colossal stone could turn and not have disastrous consequences. Yet he was denied access to the vast new stores of ancient knowledge found within the hold. Surely there had to be clues if not the answers themselves, and they were just out of reach.

The only thing he was allowed to concentrate on now was the viewing chamber. He knew what had happened to Catrin and Prios when they had used the chamber without the metal-streaked stone throne, like the one present within Ohmahold's viewing chamber.

A stack of books with descriptions of the stone chairs and their composition were brought to him, but he was no miner or prospector. He was trained to build things made of stone, not figure out where to dig for rare and specific types of stone. He didn't know how much metal there had to be within the rock for the chairs to serve their purpose, or even exactly what types of metal were needed. All he had were dimensions and a vague idea of the required material.

He could deduce from what he knew of Catrin's work that she had commissioned stone thrones from the Greatland. This led him to believe the required stone was not known to exist here on the Godfist and that it was known to exist somewhere in the Greatland. It occurred to him that the thrones Catrin commissioned were probably still resting within Catrin's Vale upon the Firstland. That thought stuck and Martik struggled to find words capable of convincing Trinda to allow Sinjin to bring the throne.

There was nothing else for him to do regarding the viewing chamber. It was fully functional, had no moving parts, and essentially consisted of two holes cut in a stone wall. It was exasperating.

He could no longer avoid the inevitable. He needed to face Trinda. They had not spoken in person since his "betrayal," as she referred to it in her missives. She was clearly still not pleased with him, but he could stand his current assignment no longer. Perhaps if he was able to negotiate a trade with Sinjin, he would be allowed to go back to work on the wheel until Sinjin arrived.

Walking into the hall, he found Bernerd, Trinda's trusted guard.

"I need to speak with the queen," he said.

"Why?" Bernerd asked, disinterested.

"Because I need to speak with her about the viewing chamber."

"What, exactly, about the viewing chamber do you need to speak with the lady about? You see, the thing you must understand is that anything you wish to say to the queen must be said to me first."

"The thrones we need are on the Firstland."

"See now? That wasn't so difficult. And how do you propose to retrieve them? Do you require a boat?" Bernerd asked with a smile.

"I suggest we trade with Sinjin Volker for it."

It took a moment for Bernerd to stop laughing, but he finally wiped a tear and drew a deep breath. "This should be fun to watch. I'm going to allow it just to see her react when you say the name Sinjin Volker. Trade, he says . . ." Bernerd continued to laugh as he led Martik to Trinda's day apartments. It was rare for him to be allowed into her personal space. Bernerd wanted it as uncomfortable for him as possible.

"And why is he here?" she said by way of greeting.

Bernerd smiled. "He insisted on seeing you." Trinda turned to Martik with a raised eyebrow. Insisted wasn't the word Martik would have used. "He has a question he simply must ask you. Go ahead, traitor, ask her."

Could there be a worse setup for a question? Martik wondered. He thought not.

"You have asked me to understand the viewing chamber and bring it to full utility, as you put it," Martik said, pausing to take a breath under Trinda's cold stare. "It is my opinion the correct composition of stone is not known on the Godfist, and commissioning new thrones will be expensive, laborious, and take a long time. This all seems avoidable since the very thrones Catrin commissioned are resting on the Firstland."

Trinda's soured.

"Surely if we offered them something, they would be willing to trade. I'm betting they would bring the thrones to us."

"Only if the thrones are delivered by Brother Vaughn," Trinda said, shocking both Martik and Bernerd.

He knew the man had been close to Trinda, but it was an odd thing for her to request, especially when he had expected a real fight. "What may I offer them in trade?" he asked, wondering if this was where it would begin.

Trinda tapped her chin for a moment then gave him a wicked smile. "Perhaps I should offer them you."

Martik didn't know what to say.

"Or perhaps I'll keep you just a little bit longer," she continued.

The girl did have a cruel streak.

"Offer them food and goods of equal weight. They may select what they wish from the market when they arrive. I believe they are aware of the quality of our produce, herbs, spices, and other goods. You have way to get word to the Volker boy?"

"Uh . . . yeah," he admitted.

"At least you were honest about that bit," she said. "Go. Send your missive."

* * *

Sinjin sat across the table from Strom, Osbourne, and Durin and had Kendra by his side, along with Arakhan and Mikala. Surely they would find some solution to their problems, he thought, yet they mostly came up with more questions. What was in the head of Trinda Hollis was a subject of much discussion, but no one could say for certain what the girl was up to. She was as easy to understand as dragons, Kendra had come to say.

Sinjin thought the same could be said for women in general.

Durin sighed. "I'm worried we might end up spending a lot of resources and energy with the very real chance there's nothing in those holes worth having," he said. And Sinjin recalled Durin had just been saying how nice it was to have finally settled in to his new home.

Sinjin could see his point, but he also saw what Strom and Osbourne meant about the sheer lack of physical security. If the ferals wanted to attack, they could fly right in, just as they had when the regent queen had been here, and knowing where her skull rested made clear the outcome.

"It's worth at least investigating," Kendra said. "If you don't believe me, then I'll take you up there and show you. No one who has been there would feel as you do."

Durin waved his hands in front of him, "No need. I just wanted to make my point. Do what you need to do, just try not to use all of our precious resources in the process, and try not to get anyone killed. You all aren't the folks I'd call if I needed help moving dragon-sized rocks, except maybe because you actually have dragons. But seriously, don't kill yourselves."

Sinjin turned to Arakhan. "Who among you are the builders?"

Arakhan shrugged. "No builders, only shaman. There are Drakon shamans. I am one."

"Do you know how to move heavy stone?"

Arakhan shook his head. "Not much stone in Arghast Desert."

"I guess it's up to us, then," Sinjin said, turning at Kendra.

"We'll find a way," Kendra said.

As if summoned by her words, a young member of the Dragon Clan ran up, holding a pigeon. It bore a message. Sinjin smiled. The birds were working out well, even if he had to send many birds to get a single message through; it was better than being cut off from Dragonhold and the Vestrana.

After removing the tiny, rolled parchment wrapped around the bird's leg, Sinjin saw a simple note. Send stone chairs and Brother Vaughn in exchange for equal weight in food and goods. No dragons. As soon as he saw the words, his mouth watered. There were things from the Godfist all of them longed for and could not have. If this was a chance to open up trade with the people of the Godfist, Trinda Hollis aside, then it could be a boon for him and his people.

"It sounds like a trap," Durin said. "I wouldn't put it past her. That girl has issues. And she's sneaky."

"And why ask for Brother Vaughn?" Kendra asked.

"I really don't know," Brother Vaughn said. "Though I'll admit I'm not certain I wish to go. It's a long voyage by boat, and I don't remember seeing any docked in the bay. And she said no dragons."

Sinjin's visions of sausage breads and cheese faded.

Chapter 8

Potential is often smothered by doubt.
--Brother Vaughn, Cathuran monk

* * *

Within the dry dock, ropes sang with tension, as four regal dragons lowered the stone chair directly into the *Serpent's* hold. Even as a group, the weight was almost too much for the mighty beasts. Valterius bellowed and Gerhonda responded, as did Atherian and Grekka, ridden by Arakhan and Mikala. The four strained and struggled to work together against the wind and the weight; it was a perilous and risky venture, and it was just the beginning.

"I know they say I'm insane," Kenward said, "but this is beyond even my foolhardiness. Everything my mother has ever said to me tells me not to do this."

Those words made Sinjin consider his options once again. They could send for a traditional ship, but that would take months. The *Dragon's Wing* could do the job, but she wasn't due back from the Greatland for weeks either.

"The *Wing* is a faster ship, yes?" Brother Vaughn asked. "I mean no offense, of course."

"Under certain conditions," Kenward admitted grudgingly. "The journey between the Firstland and the Godfist is dangerous due to far more than just distance. A single storm can add weeks to the voyage. Those seas are among the stormiest I know, and it can be impossible to avoid them on the open seas. The *Serpent* can sometimes fly above storms that would relegate the *Dragon's Wing* back into the waves. The *Serpent* does not require someone with access to Istra's powers to stay aloft, which makes her the faster vessel under many circumstances."

Brother Vaughn nodded. "It's said that Catrin and Kyrien made the trip in under a week."

"If that is true," Kenward said with a shiver. "I suspect it was not an entirely natural occurrence."

Again, Brother Vaughn nodded.

"There is no way Valterius and I can travel that fast--at least not that I know of," Sinjin added. "We would be at the mercy of the winds as much or more than either ship."

Brother Vaughn sighed in frustration.

"I'm not even certain the *Serpent* can handle the weight," Kenward said.

Brother Vaughn stood next to Kenward, looking no more confident. When the throne had been lowered into place, the knots in his guts snatched tighter, making him fear he would be sick. It was the least of his troubles.

With but one stone chair in place, Sinjin and Kendra dismounted, knowing the ship could carry no more. Still, two trips with the *Serpent* should be faster than a single sea voyage.

"Trinda isn't going to be happy," Kendra said.

Sinjin shrugged.

The other Drakon went back to their usual business, some flying out to sea in search of fish bulky enough to feed growing dragons, others soaring low through the valleys or high above on patrol. Soon that rhythm would be disrupted, but Sinjin enjoyed the new familiarity while it lasted. The awkward ship reminded him change was inevitable and moving at a pace unrivaled in history.

"We've discussed this," Kendra said to Kenward. "Without most of your crew aboard, you'll need far fewer supplies, which will offset the additional weight."

"Myself, two crewmen, and him?" Kenward asked. "I mean no insult, Brother Vaughn, but you aren't trained in the workings of this airship, and your usefulness will be limited. That's about enough people to operate the boiler and man the tiller. What about the sails and rigging, and the lookout? Do you think the monk is going to climb to the crow's nest?"

Brother Vaughn said nothing, knowing that climb was truly beyond his abilities or desires.

"How much of your crew do you plan to leave behind?" Kendra asked.

"I don't want to leave any of them behind," Kenward sulked.

"And once you're in the air, you'll know if the *Serpent* can support more weight, correct?"

"I suppose so, yes," Kenward said.

"Then I'll bring Bryn on Gerhonda and we'll lower them onto your deck. Is that satisfactory?"

"That's a dangerous plan," Brother Vaughn said. "Gerhonda could easily get hung up in the rigging."

"That's why I didn't offer to have the Drakon ferry more of the crew onto the ship once she's in the air," Kendra said. "However, one or two I think we can handle. And if it truly is too dangerous, then we'll abort the mission."

"Don't mind my wife," Sinjin said. "She hasn't had sausage bread in too long, and the thought of Godfist food is perhaps more than she can bear." She elbowed him in the ribs. "You don't have to do anything you don't think you can handle. We could just wait until the *Dragon's Wing* arrives. I don't think she'll have any trouble."

"I may be pushy," Kendra whispered in his ear, "but you're evil."

Brother Vaughn remained silent. Part of him wanted to return to

Dragonhold and see all those he'd left behind. Leaving his wife, Mirta, in Windhold was not something he wanted, especially since he had just been gone to the Heights for so long. He'd also sworn never to board the *Serpent* again, let alone the *Serpent* with a skeleton crew and too much weight in the hold. Kenward had said he thought the ship would float, despite not being water tight, but the truth was that the *Serpent* had never touched the water and there was no way to know what would happen if she ever came down over the seas. This was particularly disconcerting knowing just how much water they'd have to cross to reach the Godfist.

"Where are the minstrels among you?" Kenward said. "Songs" will be sung of this."

Brother Vaughn swallowed hard. He'd secretly been hoping Kenward would refuse, for he could not. He'd long ago taken an oath to put the good of those around him before his own needs. It was an oath some of his order interpreted loosely, but Brother Vaughn had lived his life in accordance with his vows, and he wasn't about to stop now. His bravery had difficulty matching his nobility, though, and his knees trembled.

"I'll not ask anyone to board the *Serpent* unless they wish it," Kenward said. "I know she'll fly, but you must find your own belief."

Farsy stepped forward without hesitation. He'd been with Kenward the longest and trusted the man implicitly. Nimsy and Sevon stepped forward next, and neither said a word; they just took their places next to Farsy, having been integral in the design of the more experimental parts of the ship. Though new to the crew, Sevon's nimble fingers and uncanny understanding of mechanics had proven invaluable. All had known they were the captain's first choice, and they were unwilling to let him down; risking their lives for Kenward had long since lost its chill.

Next Bryn stepped forward, despite knowing he might not get aboard. He looked as if he were trying hard not to think about what he was getting himself into.

"Very well," Kenward said after a prolonged silence. "Farsy, Nimsy, and Sevon, pack the coal bins tight, stoke the fires, fill the barrels, and check the ropes. More weight requires more fuel, which means more weight. Anything more, and I'll have no crew at all. Bryn, you ride with the lady. May you find your way safely to my deck once again."

Bryn nodded solemnly. The *Serpent's* crew responded to these orders, and the ship was soon nearly ready to fly. Farsy and Nimsy manned the fires from belowdecks, and Sevon worked amid the rigging. Brother Vaughn wished the man well; all their lives depended on his work, which was something he tried not to think about.

Slowly the wind socks filled, the air pulling at them, and the *Serpent* sat lightly in the dry dock. Kenward rushed about the ship, checking and double-checking things usually the responsibility of others. His frantic movements did little to ease the knots in Brother Vaughn's gut. It was a terrifying feeling to know you were about to gain the air with no way of knowing if you would fly or come crashing back down. Trinda had requested him by name, and Kenward was unwilling to risk having Brother Vaughn flown in by dragon. The monk reconsidered the decision. Now that the time had come, flying in became more appealing.

"Maybe the dragons could escort the *Serpent* until we get near the Godfist," Brother Vaughn said as the wind picked up.

Black smoke belched from the chimstack, and the socks billowed one last time before snapping taut in the wind. The sound of flakewood grinding against stone gave the impression the ship was being torn apart. Those aboard had secured themselves and were as prepared for this as they could be, but there was nothing that could completely prepare a person for being taken by a sudden gust of wind with sail and wind socks fluttering around you.

A rocky shoreline rushed toward them, scrubby trees ready to provide a final embrace, Brother Vaughn screamed; he was not alone. The *Serpent* spun out of control, losing what little altitude they had. Shouting came from above as well, but he could not understand what was being said. The only thought his mind could comprehend was that he was about to die. Wings flashed by and Brother Vaughn saw Bryn leaning out with a gaff and trying to free a snagged rope. His valiant effort lacked the strength or leverage to free it. What the young man had done, though, was show Gerhonda exactly what needed doing, and she used her claws to untwist the lines securing the wind socks. The ropes snapped taut with a whip like sound, and the prow moved upward, righting the ship. Dragons latched on to the *Serpent* from all sides and helped to lift the otherwise doomed ship away from the jagged shoreline. Branches smashed into the hull even as the dragons strained, and black smoke filled the air.

Taking deep breaths, Brother Vaughn did his best to not hyperventilate. The ship gained the air, and the dragons peeled away, one by one. Kenward guided the ship out over the water, where the air was cooler. The *Serpent* did not fly as high as she had in the past, despite the fires radiating heat through the slats of the deck. Gerhonda and Kendra came closer, Bryn riding anxiously behind Kendra and still wielding a gaff.

"I'm sorry, m'boy," Kenward shouted over the sound of his hissing and whirring ship. "There's just too much weight. I can't get her higher than this without throwing the monk overboard."

Brother Vaughn swallowed, not entirely certain he was joking.

"May the winds be kind and bring you home," Kendra said. Gerhonda turned and wheeled away, back toward Windhold.

Bryn's expression made it clear he longed to be on the ship, and Brother Vaughn felt bad for having taken his place. Trinda had given him no choice.

What she could want with him, he had no idea, but he did not fear the girl. It was the waters separating them he dreaded most. Again, he wished the dragons would escort them, but he also understood the Drakon were still in survival mode and could scarcely afford to lose their most valuable resources for weeks or months on end. Still, a single dragon and rider could not have hurt, and they would soon burn enough fuel and consume enough rations to allow for additional weight. If Kendra and Bryn were not already beyond earshot, he would have called them back and begged.

Kenward approached with a smile on his face. That worried Brother Vaughn more than anything. "How are you with a shovel?" Kenward asked, his grin never fading.

* * *

Approaching Dragonhold was surreal. The Pinook Valley was wide, providing sufficient room to move, but Kenward still kept them as high as he could, which wasn't high enough to clear the peaks. It also wasn't high enough to reach what Kenward knew was an airship dock atop Dragonhold. It was from there Trinda had saved Brother Vaughn from the ferals. Kenward reminded himself of that act. She had been kind to him, and she had treated the people of the Godfist well. He had no quarrel with her, save the actual taking of Dragonhold. It was something he would need to bury deeply and quickly. The wrong words within the hold could get them all killed, no matter how kind she'd been in the past.

Denied the proper airship dock, Kenward reluctantly flew toward the main entrance to Dragonhold, which was far grander than when he'd last seen it. Rising from the valley floor was a bulwark to dwarf any other on Godsland. The stairways, once exposed to dragon attacks, were now concealed within white stone fascia. Near the top, construction continued, and the old gates remained in place. These gates had served Dragonhold well since their hasty construction and would still deny the *Serpent* entrance should the child queen wish it. The gates ponderously swung open. Kenward gripped the wheel, watching the approach with intense concentration. The *Serpent* had yet to land the same way twice.

The entrance to Dragonhold was large enough to admit them into the towering great hall, but there wasn't much extra height. Gusting crosswinds made this an even more perilous endeavor.

"We're going to have to come in fast," Kenward shouted. "We need all the air in the socks, and all the thrust we can muster. We can come in a little high, but we can't come in too low. The socks will likely catch, so be ready for a rough landing."

Brother Vaughn secured himself to the rail and stood with his knees bent. When Kenward warned of a rough landing, a wise man took it seriously. The valley felt much smaller, as Kenward guided the ship lower and lower. Towering stone walls rushed by in a blur, giving evidence to their speed. Too fast, thought Brother Vaughn. Kenward held his course. The mighty gates were now open as wide as they would go. Height wasn't the only issue; the opening was narrow as well.

"This is going to be close, people," Kenward shouted. "Brace yourselves!"

There were no dragons here to save them this time, and if Kenward misjudged, it could be the end of them. Brother Vaughn breathed fast and tried to be brave. It made him feel somewhat better when Kenward's screams matched his own.

The mountain consumed them. With little more than a whispered brush, the *Serpent* entered Dragonhold like an albatross--beautiful in flight yet awkward and dangerous when landing. Not everyone had been expecting an airship to enter the hold, and people scattered in all directions as the *Serpent* dropped to the cold stone and skidded. Slowly the *Serpent* rotated and slid, the wind socks cast forward by a gust even as the mighty gates swung shut. The jarring impact and subsequent bouncing threatened to shake the ship apart.

Brother Vaughn stood on trembling knees and couldn't help but feel anxious as the gates blotted out the sky. They were left in torchlight, which struck Brother Vaughn as ironic since Trinda had the largest stockpile of herald globes in existence. He knew there were a few in private collections that had escaped her grasp. It stung knowing the one Catrin had given him personally was among Trinda's hoard. It wasn't the kind of thing one forgot. He was also reminded of the cube he'd lost. Ever since he'd discovered its true purpose, he'd wanted to get back to Dragonhold and find out just what could be locked away with such an elaborate key.

The *Serpent* issued black smoke and steam for some time after entering the great hall, and Brother Vaughn wondered if it wouldn't be wise to open the gates enough to let the wind carry it away. As it was, most people were coughing and moving away from the main hall.

"I've allowed this ship within my hold," Trinda suddenly said, and Brother Vaughn looked up to the place from where her voice had come. Once again, she sat on the oversized throne left by the ancients. She gazed down on Brother Vaughn, and familiar feelings of confusion and distrust washed over him. He'd done what he could to help this girl--woman, Brother Vaughn corrected himself, no matter how she appeared--and she'd turned on those he cared for. And yet she'd cared for many of those he loved as well. Trinda Hollis was an unsolvable puzzle, and he put his feelings aside. He could do some good here, and that was what he intended to do. Foster relations, trading, and in general have a positive impact on the situation. At least that was what he thought he was going to do.

"I want to see the thrones," Trinda said, and Brother Vaughn's blood went cold. "Martik! Have your people unload my cargo."

"Begging your pardon, your highness," Kenward said. "We were only able to transport one of the thrones this trip."

Silence heavier than he'd ever known enveloped the hall.

"You insult me," Trinda said, her voice as cold as the stone surrounding her. "I asked for two thrones, and you have defied me!" As she said these words, Trinda slammed her fist on the throne upon which she sat, her arms nowhere near long enough to reach the actual armrests. She sat in the middle of the throne, like a child's toy. When her fist struck stone, however, it was clear neither was she a toy nor should she be trifled with. Cold air rushed away from her striking fist, chilling whatever it touched and leaving steaming frost in its wake.

Stinging from the cold, Brother Vaughn stepped forward, hoping to defuse the situation. "There was no other way, child," he said, realizing his error even as the words left his lips.

"Do not call me child!"

This time, when Trinda's fist met stone, there was fire. Blue flame radiated outward, singeing everything in its path. Feeling as if he'd been assaulted and smelling burned hair, Brother Vaughn braced himself for the worst.

"You will get whatever supplies you need to make the journey, and you will fetch the remaining throne," Trinda said, and there was no room for argument. At least she was providing supplies. It showed the girl had good sense and was not inclined to cruelty as a matter of course. Trinda Hollis was nothing if not intriguing.

"My lady," Kenward said, eyeing the *Serpent's* crumbling timbers. "My ship was damaged during our landing. I doubt the quantity of flakewood I need to repair her is within the hold. May I--?"

"Get him what he needs," Trinda said to a nearby guard. The man nodded and moved to face Kenward. A younger man with a wax tablet and stylus approached. "And do not let him rob me," she added. "This man is a scoundrel."

Kenward made no argument and instead bowed to Trinda. The woman in a girl's body was thoughtful, and Brother Vaughn knew there was far more intellect behind those eyes than most would admit. She was up to something, perhaps many things, and he wished he knew what she planned. Everyone within the hold said she had an uncanny ability to read Dragonhold, as if communicating with it. The underground fortress was expansive beyond reckoning, yet she continued to discover its secrets.

When Kenward finished listing the items he needed, the guard and his scribe turned to the throne. Trinda met the guard's eyes, and he nodded to her. She nodded in return. Kenward started breathing again. It was then he realized Martik's crew were about to unload the throne. "Wait!" he said. "She's gonna shift when you move that thing!"

Martik waved off Kenward's worry as he orchestrated his crew, who made him proud. Using a hastily constructed hoist with a thick, oiled rope, they lifted the hulking metallic stone chair and eased it away from the *Serpent*. Using braces and sandbags, the ship had stabilized and secured. The crew worked with speed and efficiency Brother Vaughn admired. Not many achieved such a high level of teamwork and competency.

Once it was freed from the ship's hold, the crew lowered the throne onto wooden braces then disassembled the hoist. Using the same materials, they built a platform around the throne. It would take many strong bodies to move the stone and metal chair; this platform with its raised supports would make it easy for them to do so. These people worked with smooth, quiet efficiency--impressive, indeed. Now if he could just figure out how to get Martik out of Dragonhold and to the Firstland, where he was really needed.

"I wish to see the throne in place," Trinda said. "All of you are to be present. Without you, the throne would not be here. All of you. My guards will care for your ship."

Kenward was hesitant but the size and number of guards nearby provided him ample motivation. They were in Trinda's hold and would need to do as they were told while they remained here. Brother Vaughn still had no idea why he'd been summoned. He thought perhaps it had been a mistake, or maybe she'd forgotten asking specifically for him. She hadn't so much as greeted him--another puzzle.

Martik and his crew were already halfway across the great hall when Trinda had her guards help her down. She followed the same path as Martik, and the *Serpent's* crew fell in behind, followed by more guards. This trip was not optional.

Being back amid the towering columns was reminiscent for Brother Vaughn, though it was in far better repair this time around. Under Trinda's rule, a great many things had been restored to their original luster or had been improved upon, as with the bulwark facade.

Even the throne had been commissioned by Catrin and Prios and fulfilled their desires. Both had nearly died in the viewing chamber because they lacked the anchor effect these very thrones provided. Catrin and Prios were gone. Emotion threatened to overcome him. Never would he get over the loss of them. Never.

The viewing chamber was much as Brother Vaughn remembered it: small, sparse, and with two holes in the chamber's outer wall, open sky beyond. This was among the very few places within the hold where one could see the sky. This alone made the room remarkable. The single throne cast the room out of symmetry. Two holes, one throne. The balance was gone, and it offended the eye.

"Do you see what you've done?" Trinda asked, her voice shrill.

"I apologize, m'lady," Kenward said.

"You should've brought the other chair and left him behind," she said, pointing to Brother Vaughn. It was the first she had acknowledged him. It was an ill auspice. He reconsidered the wisdom in coming here.

"But since you are here," Trinda said, "I'll be kind, as you once were to me."

A bit of hope bloomed in Brother Vaughn's chest. "Thank you," he said, trying to appear deferential.

"Come," Trinda said. "All of you." Brother Vaughn wasn't certain why she kept saying that, but she gave him little time to ponder. As they entered the hallway running between the great hall and the God's Eye, Trinda stopped. "Fetch the diver," she said, and a man sprinted back toward the great hall. Trinda, though, turned and walked toward the God's Eye. Brother Vaughn walked with a sense of anticipation and wonder. Did she know? he asked himself. What could she possibly want to show them in that expansive underground lake? He knew some of what lurked there, and he reached for the cube out of habit, lamenting the loss of it.

Logan, the diver, nodded to Brother Vaughn after catching up with them and making his way to the water's edge. He wore nothing but a loin wrap and looked out of place standing beside Trinda and her guards. From within her white robes, Trinda pulled a glowing orb. It cast warm light that bounced off the water: a herald globe. "Do you remember?" Trinda asked Brother Vaughn, who nodded. "I sang for you and summoned the fish. Do you remember?"

"I remember," he said.

"Good," Trinda continued. "You were kind to me, and I'll now return the favor."

Brother Vaughn didn't know how to tell her he'd lost the cube.

"Sevellon," Trinda said. "The time has come."

Sevellon, Brother Vaughn thought, how did he know that name?

From behind Kenward, Sevon stepped into the herald globe's light. Kenward hissed. Sevon turned with an apology in his eyes. "Mistress," he said.

"I do like it when you call me that, Sevellon," Trinda said with the closest thing to a smile Brother Vaughn had ever seen on her face. "What do you have for me?"

"Just the items requested, mistress."

Brother Vaughn watched in disbelief when Sevon--or Sevellon--produced a familiar cube from his pockets. He also handed Trinda an object Brother Vaughn recognized. At first glance, it appeared to be nothing more than a small figurine. He recognized it as the one the lord chancellor had asked him to hold during a welcoming ceremony. He'd not realized it at the time, but this was something of great value. But why have him steal the cube?

"It was only a precaution," Trinda said, as if reading his thoughts. "I always intended you to be here for this, though I wasn't certain you'd come. I needed . . . insurance.

"Do you know what this is and how it works?" Trinda asked the diver.

"No, m'lady. I dived for it and found it, but I don't know what it is."

"Tell him," Trinda said to Kenward.

Brother Vaughn was a little surprised when Kenward began to speak; he was not a man accustomed to taking orders.

"It's a key," Kenward said. "A unique and special key meant to open only one thing, a ship's secondhold." The diver looked confused. "The hold is where the captain keeps his cargo. The secondhold is where the captain keeps his most precious belongings. If there's a ship down there and that key opens the secondhold, there's no telling what you'll find.

These words once again ignited Brother Vaughn's imagination, and he could imagine a great many possibilities, but he'd done that for years. Now he wanted to know what was actually in the secondhold.

"How does Logan use the key?" Brother Vaughn asked, unable to keep the impatience from his voice.

Kenward raised an eyebrow but didn't argue with Brother Vaughn. Instead, he turned back to Logan. "Look for the captain's quarters; they'll be the biggest. Search for trap doors, false bottoms in shelves, that sort of thing. Look for a recessed area the right size to accept the cube."

"Then what?" the diver asked.

Kenward just shrugged. "That's all I really know. It should allow a trap door to open, but you might have to do something else, maybe push on it or pull a lever. If that doesn't work, try changing the orientation of the cube."

"He's going to be under water," Brother Vaughn said. "That all sounds pretty complicated."

"Your only other choice is to raise the ship. And even then you might have trouble," Kenward said. "There's no way you'll get a proper secondhold open without the key or a dragon."

"May I see if I can find the secondhold first," Logan said, and Trinda nodded her assent and handed him the herald globe. "Don't lose this."

He nodded and stepped onto the barge. After Bradley poled them into place, Logan took a few deep breaths, slipped beneath the surface, and swam downward. The light in his hand grew brighter the deeper he went. A sunken ship emerged from the darkness, its shadow form pristine with clean, sharp lines.

Chapter 9

The greatest threat our world faces is unyielding belief.
--Barabas the druid

* * *

Wonder and excitement emanated from the usually implacable Trinda. No one could say what Logan would find, but Brother Vaughn could feel the collective hope the diver would find something. Locating the secondhold would be a feat in and of itself; opening it and retrieving its contents a near impossible task.

When the man broke the surface and gasped for breath, Brother Vaughn knew he was pushing his abilities to their limits. Part of him feared the diver would swim into the ship and never find his way back out. It was a rational fear, and that was what troubled him most.

Glistening in the light of the herald globe he held in one hand, the diver had to breathe for a moment before he could speak. Trinda tapped her toe.

"I found the cabins," he said across the water. "Haven't figured out which is the captain's cabin yet. Some of the hatches are closed, so I'm going to check the open ones first."

Trinda sighed. "Do your best," she said.

After Logan took a few deep breaths, he dived and kicked his way back to the sunken ship.

Turning back at her guard, Trinda said. "Surely he's not the only person in the hold who can dive. Find the rest. Equip them and bring them here."

"Yes, m'lady," he said before leaving at nearly a full run, a wise move given Trinda's darkening mood.

Brother Vaughn watched the child queen and tried not to think about her that way. She'd hurt him, for certain, but that didn't seem to have been her intention. She never appeared to want to hurt anyone--except maybe Edling; she just wanted her way. Kenward was unusually quiet, and Brother Vaughn suspected it was because he was standing on solid ground, something the man quite openly detested. Even this marvelous body of water trapped within a mountain wasn't enough to overcome his discomfort. Trinda had almost complete control over him, his ship, and his crew, especially the thief who'd never been his to begin with; Brother Vaughn could understand his trepidation. Given the things that had come from Kenward's mouth in the past, he decided silence was the best he could hope for.

When the guard returned with three young men and two young women, each holding a herald globe as if it might explode at any instant, all of them were breathing hard.

"You bring me divers who are out of breath?" Trinda asked. "How good can they be?"

"I'm sorry, m'lady. I asked them to hurry, and these were the only people brave enough to answer the call."

Trinda nodded. "They are to be commended for their bravery," she said. "The water is cold and deep. Do not die. Your job is to help Logan and provide him light and not to die. Is that clear?" The divers all nodded, none bold enough to speak to the queen. They moved to the barge, but Trinda stepped in front of the smallest girl, who was younger than Trinda appeared. "Do your parents know you're here?"

The girl nodded.

"Do not die."

"I won't die, m'lady," the girl finally said, her voice quavering. "I used to clean the barnacles from our fishing boat before--"

Trinda nodded and stepped out of the girl's way. When she turned, her eyes were greeted by an incredible sight. Six herald globes cast overlapping pools of light onto the subterranean lake floor. Not far away, Brother Vaughn knew there were crystalline formations in a megalithic feral dragon's likeness. The divers had been urged to avoid the area, not because Trinda feared it, but she must have known the divers would. Brother Vaughn couldn't argue with the logic, since he, too, had been made to feel small, weak, and vulnerable upon seeing the mystical creature.

The ship itself was a design unlike anything Brother Vaughn had ever seen. It appeared there had been rowers in the middle decks, and she had no masts. There was no wind to speak of within this place. The ship must have been built within the cavern and would forever remain there. Trinda did not want the ship raised, even though it appeared perfectly preserved. Her only instruction had been to retrieve items of value, and specifically those items the ship's captain had considered most valuable.

"The ship has a name," Logan said when he next surfaced. "Drakon Ghar. Not sure what that means."

"I believe it means those of the dragon who protect," Brother Vaughn said.

"A guardian dragon," Trinda said, her visage unreadable. "I've never had one of those. I have wondered what it would be like. It's not all I expected it to be." No one made any response, and Brother Vaughn was trying to decide if it had been a joke. Unwilling to laugh at the wrong thing, he remained silent. Three more times Logan returned from the ship, though the rest surfaced twice as often. The young girl Trinda had questioned shivered so badly, her teeth knocked and her skin was a bluish color. "Out of the water," Trinda said, pointing to her. The girl might have protested but the glow in Trinda's eyes made her think better of it.

Smart girl, Brother Vaughn thought.

"Get her a blanket," Trinda said, and her guard went pale. Trinda just sighed and shook her head. "Someone had better go get some blankets, then, hadn't they?" He was already running.

Two boys got out of the water as well, and Trinda did not scold or chide them, nor did Bradley complain about conveying them to shore. When Trinda's guards returned with blankets, Trinda grabbed a blanket herself and wrapped it around the youngest girl's shoulders. She did, however, make sure the herald globes were returned to her guards. Logan broke the surface again and gasped for breath. "I think I found it," he said.

"The captain's quarters?" Trinda asked.

"The secondhold," he said. Subdued excitement rippled over those standing on the cold stone shore along the God's Eye. Trinda boarded the barge this time. When the barge reached the man who was treading water, Trinda knelt down and handed Logan the cube he himself had found and given to Brother Vaughn years ago. "Pardon me for saying this, m'lady, but if there's something in there that entitles a man to wine, women, and song, may I be first in line?"

Trinda laughed, her eyes twinkling. "You may."

"There's one other thing," Logan said, though he hesitated before continuing. "It looks to me like the captain of the Drakon Ghar sunk her intentionally. There's no battle damage, and all the hatches are open."

Brother Vaughn wasn't certain what to make of it, but his curiosity about the secondhold overwhelmed all else. Would Logan be able to open the secondhold? Would the ancient lock even function? Considering how well the ship was preserved, a part of him dared to hope. Another part knew the most dangerous dives were ahead. Twice more the diver came up for air, each time winded.

"Out of the water. All of you," Trinda said.

"I think I've just about got it open," Logan said. "Just one or two more dives, and we should know what's inside."

"Get out of the water, dry off, and warm up with some tea," Trinda said, and she turned her gaze on another of her guards. The man didn't know what to do at first, but then he must have realized there was no hot tea waiting for the divers, and he dashed away. "Fools," Trinda said under her breath; perhaps it was not meant for Brother Vaughn's ears, but he heard it nonetheless.

"Describe it to me," Trinda said to Logan once the barge reached shore. Kenward and Brother Vaughn stepped closer as the diver spoke quietly, still shivering. Trinda had been right. They needed to warm up. Had he misjudged her? Again?

"It's in what would have been the floor of the captain's cabin under a desk that's secured to the deck. I saw a square outline in the wood about the size of the cube. With a little prying, the wood plug came loose, and I saw the carvings within the recessed area. That's when I knew it was what you had asked me to find."

"You've done well," Trinda said. "Now tell me about the recess. What did it look like? Were the carvings the same as what's on the cube?"

Kenward listened intently but Brother Vaughn couldn't quite understand why she was pursuing this when he nearly had the secondhold open.

"It looked as if they had carved the cube out of that very piece of wood," Logan said. "The carvings on it fit perfectly into the ones in the recess once I had it turned the right way. That's what took me so long. I'm sorry."

"You have no reason to be sorry," Trinda said. "And here is your tea. I'm so glad you didn't have to wait any longer."

Trinda's guards had the good sense to look sheepish. "I've asked Miss Mariss to send hot food," Bernerd said.

"Thank you," Trinda said. "It's good to see you thinking for yourself."

"Yes, m'lady," he said, which annoyed Trinda. Everyone else wisely remained silent.

Runners arrived from the kitchens, and they brought thick stew in a kettle and loaves of bread. The stew was ladled into mugs and bread torn off in generous hunks. The divers eagerly accepted the food, except for Logan. "It's not good to dive with a full stomach," he said. "I want to get back in the water." The other divers hesitated, and he held up a hand to them. "I know where I'm going now, and I don't need any help this time. You all did a great job helping find it. Thank you. Eat."

Brother Vaughn thought Trinda might stand in his way, but she just nodded and stood aside. Logan handed his blanket to a guard and stepped onto the barge. Once back in the water, he dived without hesitation. Not for the first time, Brother Vaughn tried to understand why the herald globe shone more brightly the deeper it sank. Was it the cold or the pressure or the water itself? It should tell him something, but he couldn't figure out what it meant. No matter the mystery, the diver illuminated the floor of the God's Eye, and there appeared to be runes carved in the dark stone. Debris and artifacts from the sunken ship gave a tantalizing glimpse of the past, something Brother Vaughn had always longed for. History gave him context.

When Logan reentered the ship, he left those above with only shifting light beams as signs of his progress. Tension charged the air. Too many things could go wrong. Brother Vaughn was convinced that was why the diver had wanted the young people to stay on land; he was protecting them from what he knew might claim his life. Brother Vaughn admired the man's bravery and honorable intentions, but he cursed him under his breath at the same time. "And now we all just have to wait here and wonder if you're drowning or not," he said without meaning to.

"He's well," Trinda said, her eyes hooded, as if her thoughts were far away.

A moment later, Logan proved her correct and emerged from the Drakon Ghar, his legs pumping as he rushed back toward the surface. The diver swam to where Trinda waited. He was gasping for breath but held the herald globe steadily in one hand and a circular object in the other. "M'lady," he said. "I'm so sorry. I got the secondhold open, but this is all that was in there." He handed her a stone ring big enough to be worn like a bracelet. Brother Vaughn tried to get a better look at it, but Trinda turned away, leaning over as she examined it. He'd seen it for no more than an instant, yet he would have sworn it bore runes and maybe even a metallic glint.

He was about to ask Trinda what the ring was when Logan said, "Oh. And there was this." He reached down and pulled a rolled cloth from his loincloth, which was still submerged.

"Wait!" Brother Vaughn said as Logan moved to hand Trinda the rolled cloth. "Leave it under water. If you expose it to the air, it could disintegrate."

Trinda crossed her arms over her chest, met his eyes, and listened. Her expression was not entirely friendly.

He continued, speaking more quickly. "We need a vessel to move it out of the God's Eye without risking destroying it. And we'll need to move it to a colder part of the keep. There we can transcribe and preserve whatever knowledge it contains, even if we cannot save the item itself. May I enlist the help of your guards?"

Trinda stood silent for a moment, considering his words. "Do as he says."

People moved to obey her command and fill Brother Vaughn's requests. He wasn't certain it would work, but his studies on preserving knowledge told him it was his best chance. It also brought back painful memories of the order from which he was now estranged. He sought comfort in the fact that he lived his life by the Cathuran order's tenets, more so than many of his brothers and sisters, but those were prideful thoughts, and they shamed him. Only the knowledge of misdeeds at the hands of his brethren banished that shame. He was not innocent, but he was in the right.

"May we see the other . . . uh . . . thing?" Kenward asked seemingly against his better judgment.

"You'll get your chance," Trinda said with a smile that chilled Brother Vaughn. "But now's not the time. When you've secured the document, my guards will escort you to the great wheel. I think you'll find the conditions there favorable. By then, you should also have your supplies, and your repairs should be well under way." With a nod, she ended the conversation and walked away, most of her guards going with her.

Four guards remained. They would not meet his eyes. "You all know us, and you know we mean you no harm. Be at ease." The guards remained as they were, and Brother Vaughn sighed. So much in his world had changed, and little of it was for the better. He couldn't help but smile, though, when Martik arrived with a work crew and materials. Wood planks were assembled to make a small box, which they lined with oiled hide. The box was just wide enough to hold the rolled canvas. Martik instructed his men to build a larger container near the great wheel, one large enough to hold the unrolled scroll and still keep it submerged in elbow-deep water.

"I want water from the God's Eye to fill the container," Brother Vaughn said. "Don't use river water, please."

"Do as he says," Martik said. He leaned closer to Brother Vaughn and asked, "Strom and Osbourne?"

"They're fine," Brother Vaughn whispered. The guards pretended not to hear. "Though I'm not sure you'd get them aboard the *Serpent* again."

"Not sure you'd get me on her either," Martik said. Now it was Kenward pretending not to hear, though he was doing a poor job of it, his annoyance difficult to hide.

Once the transport vessel had been filled and checked for leaks, four of Trinda's guards lowered it into the water. The diver placed the rolled canvas in the vessel and climbed from the water.

"Move steadily and let everyone know if you are tiring," Martik said, "We'll get someone fresh to take over. The lady has made it clear she values this object and we are to treat it with care."

Brother Vaughn could barely contain his curiosity. Ever since they had found the cube, he'd wondered what purpose it could serve, and ever since Kenward had told him it was a key to the secondhold, he'd wanted to know what could possibly wait there. Part of him knew it might be illegible, its contents lost to the flow of time. Still he hoped.

Martik and his crew proved themselves as flexible as they were capable, and soon they were moving into parts of the keep Brother Vaughn had never seen before. The great wheel was a shock to see. He'd heard about it from Strom and Osbourne, but their descriptions failed to express the overwhelming presence and sense of unstoppable power the mighty apparatus conveyed. The water cascading over it kept it slick and glossy, and it reflected the amber light from enormous crystals overhead. The very scale of the place made Brother Vaughn wonder at how it had ever been constructed. Such mastery and power the ancients had! It made him feel small and ignorant.

A more permanent vessel waited there, ready to hold the document while he transcribed it, assuming there was something to transcribe. As soon as the scroll was moved into the more accommodating vessel, Martik turned to Brother Vaughn. "It's in your custody now," he said. "But if you don't mind, I'd like to stick around and watch what you do."

"I don't object at all," Brother Vaughn said, "though I can make no promises. It could be that the years have erased everything." As soon as he leaned down to examine the document further, he saw it wasn't so. Precise lines crossed what would be considered the outside of the rolled document. A single trip of cloth tied with a simple knot secured the scroll in spirit only and fell away at the slightest probing of Brother Vaughn's knife. It didn't bode well for the rest of the document. The parchment resisted being unrolled, cracking and splitting. Martik sucked in air over his teeth, and Brother Vaughn looked at him.

"Sorry," Martik said. "I hate it when people do that to me. Please, carry on."

Trying a different approach, Brother Vaughn used a straight edge to lift the seam all at once, and the document gradually revealed itself. The parchment had been used multiple times. There were messages then other messages between the lines of the first, and there were tallies and numbers jammed around the edges. Thick, dark lines emerged, revealing a more urgent message written over top everything else. It was only the beginning of a message, and Martik leaned in close, looking over Brother Vaughn's shoulder. The parchment resisted giving up the remainder, though. Again Martik sucked in air as the document tore and a chunk stayed where it had been for thousands of years. Brother Vaughn did what he could to recover the fragment, but it was completely fused. He continued, hoping the missing part could be reconstructed based on context, but he hated to lose anything. There could be many things to learn from all the messages on this document.

With trembling hands, Brother Vaughn continued his ministrations. The message emerged.

BEWARE THE FIFTH MAGIC.

He was fairly certain the third word was fifth, but much of it was missing. He could think of nothing else it might be, and he turned to Martik.

"I can't argue your translation," he said, "but I also can't be certain."

"You're right," Brother Vaughn said. "Fifth is my best guess, but it doesn't really tell us anything."

"That stone ring had writing on it too," Kenward said, but the guards' glares silenced him.

Brother Vaughn changed the subject. "I'd like to see if I can transcribe any of the older messages on this parchment."

"Those look like inventory tallies in the margins," Kenward said, "but if you want to translate an old love letter, be my guest."

Brother Vaughn wasn't certain the guards believed Kenward's last statement, but they did look at least a little less interested in what he was doing. Everything they said of any consequence was no doubt being relayed to Trinda, but maybe he could still learn something to give him an edge. Sadly, Kenward's prediction the other messages were love letters proved true.

"I don't think we're going to learn any more from this," Brother Vaughn finally said, and he stepped away from the vessel, his hands still dripping. To his surprise, the guards covered the vessel and stood watch over it. "I've completed my analysis," he said to one of the guards. "Can you please let her highness know--?"

"She knows," the man said, averting his gaze, making it clear Brother Vaughn would get nothing more from him. He was left with no idea what to do. Kenward fidgeted and Martik was already talking with men from his crew.

"I should be going," Kenward said into the awkward silence. "I'm sure her highness would like my ship out of her hall."

No one barred his path.

Chapter 10

Despite eons of disuse, weapons of the past threaten us all.
--Nat Dersinger, prophet

* * *

The *Serpent* was closer to being airworthy, but a few metal pieces needed to repair broken mounts had still not been sent from the smithy. Kenward wondered if Trinda had truly passed along his request since he hoped those working the smithy would not intentionally keep him waiting--certainly not under these circumstances. His attempts to visit the forge had proven he did not have free rein within the hold. He was left with two options: wait until Trinda decided to give him what he needed and let him go or risk coming apart in the air. People might say he was crazy, but he wasn't stupid.

The remaining crew checked rigging, joints, and lines, then double-checked. They grew restless, Kenward knew, and he could hardly blame them. Trinda was an enigma he was certain he'd never understand, and the best thing to do would be to get away from there. The child queen still wanted the second throne from the Firstland, and Kenward had already decided she'd have to find another way to get it there. He, his crew, and his ship were simply too precious to risk for someone who might turn around and have him killed or imprisoned.

What Kenward hadn't been expecting was to see Sevon coming from the direction of the kitchens and the forge, a place he himself had been denied.

"May I approach?" Sevellon the thief asked.

Kenward reminded himself to whom he spoke. "Don't come too close and keep your hands where I can see them."

There was pain in the thief's eyes. "I'm sorry. I know you're angry, but I hope you'll understand. I couldn't reveal myself, even to those I trust and care for."

Kenward was a pirate; he understood such things. "Did you ever steal from me or my crew?" he asked, not certain he'd believe any answer but yes.

"No, sir. There're few places in the world I've felt more at home than on the *Serpent*. You and the crew are like--"

"But you did steal something from the lord chancellor, which put the verdants on our tail and caused no end of trouble, did you not?"

"I did, sir," Sevellon said, his head hanging low.

"And how do I know you wouldn't do such a thing again?"

"I give you my word."

Kenward knew a thief's word was as good as a pirate's, which was to say it varied widely. Sevon had been a valuable crewman not easily replaced. Few were brave enough to board the *Serpent*, let alone work the rigging like Sevon. The man was physically as nimble and quick as his sharp mind. "How do I know you're not still working for Trinda? After all, you just came from places I've been barred from going."

"I'll not work for the child queen again, sir. She violated the contract by revealing my true name. This cannot be forgiven."

Kenward thought on this for a moment. It was a risk. Sevellon was a convincing liar; it was requisite for his profession. "I just don't know if I can trust you."

The thief nodded, sadness in his eyes. "I had hoped you would understand, but I hold no grudge. I endangered you and your crew. As a token of my appreciation, I bring you these, though I recommend you install them quickly and be on your way. I heard tell of orders to be ready to close the gates on a moment's notice."

He handed the metal pieces needed to repair the mounts to Kenward.

The value of the gifts and the information could not be overlooked, and Kenward extended his hand. "Come, Sevon. We've work to do."

Sevon smiled and did not hesitate. Soon they worked to quietly install the new mounts that would hold Kenward's prized experimental engine in place. Without it, they wouldn't get far. Most of the crew remained as they had been, obeying Kenward's silent command. No one could know just how close they were to being airworthy. Bringing the boiler to temperature would take time--time when it would be quite obvious they were preparing for departure.

"Light a test fire," Kenward ordered far more loudly than needed. "Not too much, now. We just need to test the pressures; we still haven't got all the parts we need." The guards nearby ignored him, and he hoped his luck would hold. When Brother Vaughn approached, Kenward thought that alone might give them away. He had no desire to leave the monk behind, but having him show up just when they were heating up the engines was more than inconvenient.

"Are you getting ready to leave?" Brother Vaughn asked softly.

The skin on Kenward's neck stood. He was stealing honey while the bees watched. "Still don't have the parts we need," Kenward said, again louder than needed before continuing more softly. "Be ready at a moment's notice, but do whatever you can to make it look as if we can't leave yet."

"I'll see if I can get some food for the crew while they wait," Brother Vaughn said so loudly Kenward cringed.

Brother Vaughn walked away and did his best to blend into the crowd. Kenward shook his head, knowing their plans must be all too obvious to anyone paying them the least bit of attention, which Kenward hoped would be their saving grace. His hopes were dashed, though, when Trinda emerged into the great hall flanked by rows of guards. She wore a long, white dress with a train rustling along the stone behind her. She came to stand before Kenward. Sweat ran into his eye.

"I would have had your parts brought to you, but you've apparently beaten me to it," Trinda said, her eyes landing on Sevon, who was high above. The rigging hung limply from the mast, which stood at an odd angle because the ship rested on her side.

Kenward remained silent.

"You were to deliver me two thrones," Trinda continued. "I will expect the other before the first snow. Is that clear?"

This was not an enemy Kenward wished to create. "I understand," he said, still unsure as to whether or not he would make good on the bargain.

"You should hurry," Trinda said, a knowing smile on her face. "The skies may not remain clear much longer."

Kenward turned back to the *Serpent*. "Stoke the fires and open the valves full stop!"

Steam and black smoke began to fill the air around the ship, and when Kenward turned back to Trinda, she was gone. He finally found her sitting on the humongous throne, her elbows on her knees and her chin in her hands. She watched Kenward intently, and his skin began to crawl. He returned to his work with full intensity. As much as he hated to admit it, that girl frightened him.

Moments later he knew the fear was warranted. Trinda Hollis, the child queen, began to sing.

* * *

Reunions were at hand and Sinjin smiled. It had been too long since he'd seen the *Dragon's Wing*'s crew. Kendra flew nearby and, though she might not be overjoyed to see Gwen again, seeing Benjin, Fasha, Wendel, and Jensen was enough to bring tears to her eyes. Sinjin pretended not to see them.

Gerhonda flew in close, and Kendra instructed them on where she wanted them to dock. It had been some time since they had been there last, and Kendra took pride in what she'd accomplished. Atop a rock shelf that protruded from Windhold, Kendra had orchestrated the construction of a landing field. It had dragon riders flying between the beaches and the plateau for weeks, but a black beach now formed a suitable dry dock. Wooden structures waited at the far end to secure the *Dragon's Wing*.

Benjin didn't appear sold on landing his ship in the dry dock, and he could see the disappointment on Kendra's face. Those eyes must be the same force that drove Sinjin to recklessness. Fasha could have countermanded Benjin's orders, but she did not. The way she stormed to the stern gave evidence as to her opinion, though.

"We'll guide you in," Kendra said, now beaming.

Valterius must have recognized the danger and followed even Sinjin's most subtle urgings. It was a magnificent feeling to have another creature acting as a willing extension of your own body, especially when that creature could fly. For most of his life, he hadn't known how freeing flight could be. Always before he'd been limited to moving on the ground or on the water, but now he could soar the skies and view the world from another perspective.

The *Dragon's Wing* slowed as she approached the shelf. Now that the ship was really here and moving in closer, the shelf appeared far too small, and the command to abort caught in his throat.

"Too fast!" Kendra shouted. "Slow down."

"I can do this," Pelivor shouted, and Sinjin saw Benjin and his grandfather brace themselves.

Black sand filled the air beneath the *Dragon's Wing*, but plenty remained on the shelf. Pelivor stood with power flowing around him, orchestrating the thrust and lift through his communication with Gwen. The two strained as the ship settled into black sand, but the crew barely moved on impact. It took a moment before a cheer rose up from the crew, allowing Pelivor and Gwen to release the energy they'd been channeling.

Sinjin squeezed Valterius with his left leg, indicating he wanted the dragon to execute a wide turn, which would allow him to share a moment's celebration with his wife, but Valterius did not respond. Being far less subtle, Sinjin tried again to get his dragon to turn. Valterius ignored him.

"Where are you going?" Sinjin heard Kendra shouting. "I said go back!"

At first Sinjin had thought she was yelling at him and Valterius, but then a cold feeling washed over him when he realized Gerhonda and the other dragons were also not responding to their riders. Shouts from the *Dragon's Wing* were lost in the distance as one of Sinjin Volker's greatest fears came to pass. He, his wife, and the Drakon were at their dragons' mercy as they flew off, away from the Firstland. He could only hope their wisdom was greater than his.

Kendra, on the other hand, decided to take a different approach. Screaming things that would make a sailor blush, Kendra berated Gerhonda until her voice failed. Not long after, the dragons showed the first sign of cognizance since leaving the Firstland. For hours they had flown as straight as arrows, as if drawn by a mighty lodestone to the north and west. Now, though, they flew lower, beneath the scattered clouds. A splash of land came into view. Twin mountain islands cradled a natural harbor, which shone bright blue. Towering needle trees dominated the islands and stood in contrast to the white sands and foaming waterfalls. It was to those falls the dragons went to drink.

Most Drakon had the good sense to stay in the saddle but not his wife. Kendra yanked back the straps as quickly as she could and practically leaped off of Gerhonda's back. The dragon nudged Kendra with her forehead, but Sinjin's wife was having none of it.

"How dare you drag us out here at such an important time?" Kendra shouted. "Those people needed us, and you just left them there as if they didn't exist. Explain yourself!" Sinjin shook his head but grew alarmed when Valterius finished his drink, trumpeted, and leaped back into the air. Gerhonda nudged Kendra back toward the saddle, but she crossed her arms over her chest and refused to move. "How do you like it?"

Gerhonda whined and pawed the soil, again nudging Kendra toward the saddle. This just infuriated Kendra further, and Sinjin thought she might actually hit her dragon, though he doubted Gerhonda would feel it if she did. Instead, Kendra just stood her ground. After one more whine, Gerhonda leaped into the air, leaving Kendra standing agape on the uninhabited island. Sinjin cried out, knowing just how terrible being stranded in such a place could be, and his faith was mostly restored in the dragons when Gerhonda turned back, swept across the beach, and scooped Kendra up in her claws.

Sinjin sucked in air; it hadn't been a smooth acquisition, and Kendra dangled in her dragon's grip. Gerhonda continued to whine and flew higher, which Sinjin wasn't certain was the best course of action. Soon, though, they were high above him and Valterius and the other dragons. Shading his eyes from the sun, he looked up and his blood went cold when Gerhonda dropped Kendra. Hearing his wife scream , Sinjin tried to direct Valterius to intercept her. Valterius continued on his path. It was his turn to berate his dragon. When he looked back up, though, he saw Gerhonda extend her claws and gently wrap them around the now repositioned Kendra. She made no sound and did not move, and he couldn't contain his alarm. Eventually she answered his calls and told him she was uninjured. The strain in her voice was clear, but at least he knew she was alive.

It was near dark the following day when finally Sinjin and the Drakon got some idea as to where they were headed. It came as quite a surprise when the *Serpent* materialized from within the clouds ahead. They traveled in opposite directions and there wasn't much time to speak. Kenward never slowed his ship, and Valterius stayed his course.

"Why are you going to the Godfist?" Kenward shouted.

"The dragons insist!" Sinjin shouted in response.

The last thing he heard from the *Serpent* were the words, "Trinda sang!"

* * *

When the Godfist finally came into view, it was no surprise. It felt inevitable now, as if an irresistible force drew them. Sinjin could almost feel Trinda's claws reaching out for him. He hadn't always been kind to her, but neither he nor the Drakon nor the crew of the *Dragon's Wing* deserved to be tormented. The place's harsh beauty and the new construction were lost on Sinjin. In his mind he tried to find the strength to deal with Trinda. He had no idea what it was he would say, but he knew he needed to keep things as civil as possible.

The gates to the great hall stood open, and people lined either side, as if waiting to greet them. It was a strange feeling. People Sinjin knew and cared for were among those gathered, but they were also loyal to Trinda now, or at the very least living under her rule. Sinjin no longer had a place within Dragonhold. His belongings had been delivered to him by Trinda and Pelivor what felt like ages ago. Now she had pulled him back in, and he wasn't certain how his former home and people would welcome him.

He realized his goal of keeping things civil was going to be exceedingly difficult when they flew into the hall's relative darkness and Gerhonda released Kendra several hand widths above the stone. Kendra made a loud "woof" when she struck the stone and lay still for a few moments--long enough for the remaining Drakon to land within the hall. Even with their numbers, the hall swallowed them easily and made them look tiny. Gerhonda whined and nudged Kendra with her snout.

Sitting atop her grossly oversized throne, Sinjin thought Trinda looked ridiculous, and yet she exuded undeniable power. Opening her mouth to speak, Trinda silenced the hall--even the dragons--with a gesture. Before she could utter a word, though, Kendra pulled herself from the cold stone. Sinjin and the others remained in their saddles. His grip on the staff tightened, and his fingers caressed Koe.

Kendra turned to Gerhonda, who did her best to look sheepish. "What in all of Godsland is wrong with you? Have you lost the use of your senses? How dare you carry me like nothing more than a plump tuna. What in the name of everything good and right in the world were you thinking? You dropped me in midair!"

The dragon just whined in response and nudged Kendra with her forehead. Sinjin's wife did not appear ready to release her anger.

"It's not her fault," Sinjin said, despite knowing it might make Kendra angrier. "Gerhonda was summoned like the rest of the dragons."

"I summoned the dragons. Yes," Trinda said to Sinjin. "But it is to you I wish to speak."

"And the rest of us?" Kendra asked, her face flushed, her posture aggressive.

"It is difficult to summon just one dragon," Trinda said, holding out her palms in feigned innocence.

Kendra fumed.

"I require your assistance."

It was clear she spoke to Sinjin, which infuriated Kendra even further.

"There are easier ways of contacting me," Sinjin said. "And I'm fairly certain you told me I was no longer welcome here."

Trinda took a long moment before responding. "I had hoped your love of your people would outweigh your hatred of me. The people of Dragonhold are in grave danger."

Sinjin wanted to say he didn't hate Trinda, but his wife came uncorked.

"People wouldn't hate you if you didn't just up and take over people's holds and throw them out and then summon their dragons without so much as a 'please'!"

Sinjin drew a breath to speak, and Kendra stared at him with eyes afire.

"Silence!" Trinda barked, slamming her fist down with emphasis, sending out icy air laced with cold blue fire. At this command, guards moved to close the mighty wooden gates. Even more guards emerged from all around, most carrying heavy crossbows. "Dismount and surrender your arms, and no one will be harmed." Kendra crossed her arms over her chest, daring anyone to disarm her. Trinda, though, wasn't watching Kendra; she was looking at Sinjin. "Surrender the staff and the cat, and they'll be returned to you when the time is right."

Sinjin doubted he and Trinda would agree on when the time was right so he resisted. Kendra gave him a firm nod. He looked for familiar faces among the guards, but Trinda knew better. Most of the men facing the Drakon had the look of the Greatland about them. None would have reason to be loyal to Sinjin. It would be a blood bath. Maybe he and the Drakon could defeat Trinda's forces, but at what cost? Perhaps they could fly in the darkness above them. The massive pillars disappeared in the heights, but Sinjin had no idea how deep that darkness was or if there were anything awaiting them there.

In the end, his temper cooled, and he began unstrapping his harness. The Drakon took that as their order to do the same.

"No!" Kendra shouted. "Don't you dare surrender!"

Sinjin stepped down from Valterius, knowing there was likely to be blood if ever he and his wife got the chance to discuss this day. Despite his own misgivings, Sinjin laid the staff and Koe at the feet of a guard who kept him at blade's end. The crossbowman next to him kept his bolt trained on Sinjin's chest. It was quite the welcome home.

The guard bent and retrieved the items with leather-gloved hands. When he handed them up to Trinda, blue light leaped between her outstretched hands and the staff. Pulsing light continued, wrapping around her grip. Koe gleamed in her other hand. The child queen drew a deep breath, and gusting winds filled the hold.

With a sick feeling in his stomach, Sinjin wondered what he'd done.

Chapter 11

If it makes your heart sing, do it.
--Barabas the druid

* * *

Standing before the huge stone cylinder, Sinjin didn't know what to think. The gargantuan wheel rotated at dizzying speed, lending credence to Trinda's claims, but he could not see what purpose this wheel might serve. Part of him wanted to scold Trinda for experimenting with things she didn't understand, but he and his were far from innocent, and the hypocrisy stayed his tongue.

"So you're saying you started this machine without having any idea what it does, and now you're worried it'll come apart and destroy Dragonhold?" Kendra asked.

"And a large piece of the Godfist. Yes," Trinda said, her eyes unfriendly, her patience with Kendra obvious.

Sinjin tried to convince Kendra to be silent using nothing more than a look, but that just made her angrier. It was another situation Sinjin found impossible to solve. Though he loved his wife's passion, he didn't want to see it get her killed.

Kendra snorted. "It's big, all right, and it's impressive, but I doubt much more than this immediate area would be affected in the event of a failure."

"You've not read what I've read," Trinda said. "You don't have access to the truth."

Before Kendra could speak another word, Sinjin jumped into the conversation. "I must ask," he said. "What, exactly, is it you think I can do to help?"

"It's . . . complicated. But you have already helped me," Trinda said, smiling in a way that gave no indication as to the thoughts in her head. "Soon I will return your staff and cat to you and I will ask you to help me stop the wheel."

"Then let's do what must be done," Kendra said, and Sinjin had to bite his tongue. "Give my husband back his belongings, and I'm certain he'll do what he can to help--just as I'm certain he'd have done if you simply asked him. He did, after all, facilitate the delivery of the stone thrones you so desired."

"Would you please let me do the talking?" Sinjin finally said to Kendra. It was not that he disagreed with her sentiments, but now was not the time to antagonize Trinda. The girl was unpredictable enough as it was, and Kendra's goading wasn't helping anyone. "My wife and I were engaged in important matters when we were . . . summoned," Sinjin said. "Please ask what you will of me and let us be on our way."

"Soon," Trinda said, and she turned and walked away. Her personal guards surrounded her as she walked, and the remaining guards closed ranks behind them, making it clear they were not to follow. A moment later, the guards moved to form an opening once again.

As was her way, even the child queen's gifts were unexpected. When Miss Mariss, his Uncle Chase, and Martik made their way past the guards, Sinjin couldn't help but smile and run to meet them. The three carried platters laden with food, and even Kendra smiled. The smell of sausage breads was unmistakable.

"It's good to see you, my boy," Chase said. "Have you word of my father and Benjin and your grandfather?"

"We saw Benjin, Fasha, Wendel, and Jensen very briefly, just before we were summoned here."

Chase's eyes went wide at the word summoned. "I knew she sang, but we had no idea what it was she was singing for."

"Apparently," Sinjin said, "she can sing and summon the regal dragons. She said she needed my help stopping that." He pointed at the stone wheel.

"It's good you came," Martik said. "I fear Trinda's concerns are not wholly unfounded. I've seen an ancient diagram she found, and it looks to me like that giant wheel is not the primary mechanism."

"What is it, then?" Kendra asked.

"A trigger," Martik said. "She wouldn't let me see the other diagrams, so I can't be certain. Even if I'm right, I have no idea what it's supposed to initiate. It could be entirely benign, just like the water system or the central forge, but . . ."

"Eat," Miss Mariss said, and no one argued. The Drakon waited in orderly fashion for the sausage breads and wine to be distributed. Each thanked Miss Mariss, and she appeared touched by their formality. Sinjin knew Miss Mariss's sausage breads were legendary even among the Arghast, and he wouldn't be surprised if they didn't attempt to take her with them when they left Dragonhold. Knowing they might never leave Dragonhold threatened to spoil his appetite. Deep down, he didn't think Trinda intended them harm.

"There are two things worrying me," Martik said. "First, the wheel moves ever faster, driven partly by the water and partly by the vacuum created by the underground river as it moves through a sealed chamber. However, there must be something else to account for the forces being applied here, and I don't know what it is.

"And though she often speaks in riddles, I don't doubt her words on one thing. If left alone, the wheel will continue to spin faster and faster, and some part of the mechanism will eventually fail."

"And you think this wheel is used to start some larger chain reaction?"

Kendra asked.

"From what Martik has described to me," Chase said, "this is not just some part of the hold waiting to be turned back on. It struck me as part of a defensive or even offensive feature of the keep. I doubt very much the application is civil; it has a far more military look about it."

"All of that is but speculation," Martik added, and Chase nodded sadly. "There's no way to know without those diagrams or access to the mechanisms."

Nearby guards monitored their conversation, and no one was foolish enough to ask if there was a way to get those diagrams, but Sinjin knew it was what they were all thinking. For a few moments, they ate in silence, and Sinjin actually tasted his food. It was just as glorious as he remembered, reminding him just how archaic life on the Firstland really was. When they returned, he silently vowed to talk with Kendra about ways to draw talented and experienced people to the Firstland.

"You cannot stop the wheel?" Arakhan asked.

"Not now," Martik said. "Early on, when it was moving slowly, we could probably have stopped it safely by jamming it with wooden timbers, but now there is simply too much energy. Anything we do will transfer that energy to the stone around the mechanism, and something would have to give. If we destabilize the mechanism, it may be worse than allowing the trigger to function normally and initiate whatever it's supposed to do. And if we stop the water, then it will no longer float freely. I believe it would bite into the stone and possibly bind up. I wouldn't want to be around if that happened. There must be a way to bring it to a gradual stop, but I haven't figured it out yet. If only we had more control over how much water flows."

"There's something I don't understand," Sinjin said. "If this thing is a trigger, then how is it initiated?"

Martik and Chase both shrugged.

"Wish I knew," Martik said.

* * *

Standing side by side at the prow, as they had done so many times before, Benjin and Fasha sailed the winds in silence. Neither wanted to voice the fears churning in their guts; there was no need. The Drakon had gone from the Firstland and hadn't returned. The crew of the *Dragon's Wing* had done the only thing they could, which was to offload the supplies and goods they carried. An empty ship was far easier to fly away from Windhold.

Kendra's idea for an airship dock had merit, but Benjin would stick with water landings and more traditional methods to transport goods inland. The dragons were supposed to be there to help guide them away from the dry dock and to keep the prevailing winds from smashing them against the hold itself. The memory of their departure from Windhold was something none would soon forget. The fact that the *Dragon's Wing* was in one piece was the result of good fortune as much as anything else, which wasn't the most comforting thought.

Few of his thoughts were pleasant. Not long ago, he'd believed they were making a new start. He'd hoped for a peaceful existence. He'd been wrong.

The path the Drakon followed had been unerring, and the *Dragon's Wing* now soared along the same path. No one knew what they would find, if anything. Their only information came from the general direction the Drakon flew: toward the Godfist.

This did not bode well, and Benjin was reminded of the events leading up to Trinda's taking Dragonhold. He did not like the conclusions he came to, and he was certain the rest on board felt the same way. Pelivor and Gwen kept the ship in the air with perhaps unhealthy dedication and commitment. Benjin didn't want them or any other crew member to burn out. Jessub Tillerman was now the backbone of his crew. The young man knew how to work hard and did his level best to keep up with Pelivor and Gwen.

"We must fish," Fasha said without preamble. "Set us down."

Gradually Gwen reduced the thrust, and the ship eased lower. His flightmaster and thrustmaster had more than earned their titles; they had gone beyond proficiency and now practiced flight like an art form. It required the two to work together, almost like a dance. Pelivor was leading, but without Gwen, the dance was incomplete. Either could act on their own to both fly and propel the ship, but when they worked together, the *Dragon's Wing* was the fastest and most nimble ship on all the seas and skies.

Benjin was reminded a moment later, though, they were not the only ship sailing the wind. Just moments before the *Dragon's Wing* would enter the seas, Jessub cried out from the crow's nest, "The *Serpent* to port!"

Though he'd seen Kenward's airship only once, the thing had managed to offend just about every one of Benjin's senses. Everything about it just felt wrong, yet he'd seen the thing fly. Now he had inescapable evidence the ship was still flying. It wasn't that he wished any ill on Kenward or his crew, but the *Serpent* had been designed to never touch water. The roughly carved masthead modeled after his own ship did not sit well with Benjin.

Though he flew the *Dragon's Wing* without reservation or fear, the thought of getting on the *Serpent* made him physically ill. He'd known those on Kenward's crew were less than sane from his days aboard the *Slippery Eel.* Many proved themselves fearless by boarding the *Serpent.* At least a few had shown good sense. They had been replaced.

Distant shouts drifted over the winds, fragmented and distorted.

"Bring us back up and make for the *Serpent*!" Fasha commanded.

Once again demonstrating their skill, Gwen and Pelivor aborted the water landing. The maneuver required a great deal of thrust, which sent Wendel to his knees, but he soon regained his feet.

"Sorry," Gwen said once they were gaining altitude. Wendel waved off the apology. No one could expect the two to have mastered things no one else had ever done.

The closer the *Serpent* got, the more detail was visible, and Benjin had to admit the roughly carved masthead was a suitable tribute from a distance. There was no way the flakewood airship could ever match the polished sheen of the greatoak.

Another problem arose as the two ships approached one another: speed. Though Kenward did his best to keep it a secret, the *Serpent* was propelled by more than just wind and sail. Still, the *Serpent* was far slower. The *Dragon's Wing*, which was heavier, needed to move faster than the *Serpent* to stay in the air.

"Bring us down," Fasha ordered after they had flown three circles around the *Serpent* without being able to communicate clearly. Gwen and Pelivor swiftly complied and brought them in for the softest landing one could expect when dropping into rough seas.

The ship's motion was like an old friend yet was foreign after so much time. The adjustment always took some time. Kenward proved his ship did have some advantages over the *Wing*; he could effectively hover as long as the winds cooperated. Though the seas were choppy, the winds were consistent and allowed Kenward to bring the *Serpent* in close.

"Not too close," Fasha shouted and frowned when Benjin chuckled. She shook her head, knowing the joke. Kenward had been making her think he would sink her for most of their lives. He hadn't actually done it yet.

He had managed to sink one ship, and another lay in the high reaches on the Firstland, which wasn't exactly comforting. Benjin admitted Catrin had a lot to do with the loss of the *Slippery Eel*. Thoughts of Catrin were painful, and he pushed them away.

"Hey, Sis!" Kenward shouted. Benjin couldn't help but smile.

"Have you seen the Drakon?" Fasha shouted back, never one to waste words.

"We saw them," Kenward said. "They're headed to Dragonhold."

"Why?" Benjin shouted before Fasha could take a breath.

"Trinda sang!" Brother Vaughn shouted from the place where he had quite thoroughly tied himself to the *Serpent*. "I think she must have summoned the regal dragons in the same way she once summoned the ferals."

These words made Benjin's blood run cold. He'd suspected Trinda was behind this, but having it confirmed made him feel even worse.

"I can't fly in circles all day," Kenward shouted into the silence following Brother Vaughn's words. "I've only got enough fuel and fresh water to get me back to the Firstland. Trinda really wants that second forsaken throne, and we can't pull it off without the dragons."

"Throne?" Benjin asked, a sick feeling in his stomach.

"The ones from the Eel," Brother Vaughn said, saving Kenward from having to say it.

Fasha turned to Benjin, her eyes pleading. Both knew how painful it must be for Kenward to go back there. How difficult it must be to once again transport the cargo that doomed the *Slippery Eel*. Benjin wasn't certain he wanted to go to Catrin's Vale, but he could not make his friend go there.

"Drop the fishing gear," Benjin ordered. "Once we have enough food to get us back to the Firstland, we sail."

Fasha nodded and though it was his and his wife's ship, Benjin turned to Wendel. Sinjin was Wendel's grandson, and the boy was flying into the child queen's hands.

"There is nothing we can do to help Sinjin if we can't even get into Dragonhold," Wendel said, his face grim and determined. "With the throne, she has at least a reason to hear us out."

"It's decided," Fasha said. "Kenward, fly on ahead. We'll be behind you."

"You'll catch up, Sis," Kenward said, and Fasha blew him a kiss. Benjin would never really understand those two. For much of their lives, they had been at each other's throats, yet as they grew older, they were almost nice to each other--almost; they were Trells, after all.

Benjin had made the decision, but he had a strange feeling in his gut. He watched the *Serpent* until she disappeared behind the cloud banks rolling in. Winds tossed the seas and the ship. Benjin would never admit it, but his sea legs weren't what they used to be.

"Fish aren't going to bite in these winds," Wendel said.

"We've enough stores for three more meals, sir," Jessub reported without being asked.

Benjin nodded and took in his surroundings. Everyone was waiting for him to decide. He was unsure, a sense of impending doom descending upon him, from where he did not know. For once he felt true empathy for Nat Dersinger. Now he knew what it felt like to have dark premonitions, and he liked it not at all.

Looking to his wife, he silently asked her. A weaker person would have deferred to him or had difficulty deciding what to do, but that was not Fasha. "Pull the lines! Get us back in the air, and point us back toward the Firstland. Jessub, prepare the next meal with one-third rations."

Jessub nodded and retreated into the deckhouse. No one protested, instead pulling in the fishing gear and preparing for flight. It was a mixed blessing when a pair of tuna came in with the trawls. While it bolstered their stores, it took time to clean and store the fish before they could prepare for flight. Benjin's impatience had rubbed off on Fasha, and she joined him in securing the rigging.

Dark skies harboring cold winds descended upon them by the time the *Dragon's Wing* was ready to take flight. The conditions made it easier in some ways since the winds provided lift, but these winds were gusty and unpredictable, which could unexpectedly drop them back into the water. Instead, the ship leaped upward and backward on a sudden, persistent gust. Turning the ship to use that wind to their advantage, Pelivor strained. It didn't take him long to bring the ship under control and gain altitude, but it felt like an hour to Benjin. He was just about to take a deep breath when a hulking form burst from the clouds and nearly collided with the rigging. With a deep, rumbling roar, the dragon swerved and missed them, but it was a close thing.

Shouting could be heard from the tierre, but Benjin couldn't make out the words. Onin of the old guard's voice was easily identified, and he recognized Jehregard.

The dragon continued toward the Godfist, his path unerring, and Benjin had a bad feeling in his gut. "Make all speed!"

* * *

Durin knew nothing. He was stranded on the Firstland with the Dragon Clan. Sinjin and Kendra would never have left them intentionally, and Benjin had told him about Trinda Hollis's singing before also leaving. He had no insight into her motives and nothing to ensure the future of his friends and his people. He wanted to scream, but the Dragon Clan watched. They saw him as some sort of measuring stick on Sinjin's and Kendra's motives and the intentions. The Dragon Clan were one people in name, but the clan consisted of three different cultures, and they had yet to come to fully understand each other. Harmony was difficult without understanding.

Normally Durin acted as a mediator between those with differences or ill feelings, but he didn't feel up to it on this day. For once, he wanted someone to try to calm his ragged nerves. Just one time, he would like it if someone solved his problems. This tirade was interrupted by the mental parade of problems that had been solved by others, and he drew a deep breath.

The storm had left parts of Windhold in disarray. Those parts of the hold were not anyone in particular's responsibility, and Durin knew he needed to organize work groups to get the windblown debris cleaned up and sorted from the still usable materials. They discarded almost nothing on the Firstland, and even windblown detritus could be what they needed to survive.

He was a few steps away from Valterius's stall when someone cried out. At first he couldn't make out the words, but the Dragon Clan gathered near Windhold's seaward openings.

Finally a clear voice rose above the din. "*Dragon's Wing!*" the man said.

Relief flooded over Durin; he'd begun to think no one would ever come back. He heard no cry of Drakon or Al'Drak, which quickly tempered the relief.

"The *Serpent!*" came another cry, and Durin slowed as he neared the opening, having reached a full run. There, on the horizon, were two flying ships in some ways similar to each other yet completely different. The *Dragon's Wing* outpaced the *Serpent* and reached the shallow waters off shore. There they glided into the smooth waters, barely disturbing the surface as they did. The process was so subtle, it was like an illusion to Durin.

The *Serpent*, in contrast, soared over the *Wing's* masts and continued toward Windhold. Caught up in the spectacle, Durin and the Dragon Clan failed to recognize the danger until Kenward's cries reached them. "Look out! We're coming in!"

At once, the Dragon Clan cleared the opening, and a few brave souls charged across the windblown open expanse, moving crates, bales of stick weed, and bundles of herbs. The *Serpent* continued an orderly approach. The winds directly surrounding the hold were anything but predictable. Sinjin had described entering Windhold on the wing as the most terrifying three breaths of his life. The *Serpent* exaggerated the effect and proved to Durin he belonged on solid ground. Twisting at the last instant, the *Serpent* tipped forward, slamming Kyrien's likeness into the stone. The ship stopped fast--too fast. Durin worried there would be injuries.

The wind socks deflated, but as they had in the past, they reinflated as they caught the wind within the cavern and began dragging the ship deeper into the hold. The Dragon Clan showed their tenacity and ingenuity by jumping on atop the wind socks, causing them to completely deflate. The first two or three were taken for a ride, but their efforts eventually paid off and brought the *Serpent* to a halt.

Kyrien's now badly scarred visage, struck Durin as a bad omen. Still, at least someone had returned to them. His heart was still sick with worry over the Drakon. He even missed Valterius trying to step on him or swat him with the sledge he had for a tail.

"Thank you for your help, Dragon Clan," Kenward said when he stepped from his airship and onto Windhold's solid stone. "Sorry for the abrupt entrance, but on a finer note, we could use some help unloading all these supplies. Trinda would have let us all starve, I'm sure, but a Trell is never without options."

Durin smiled. He'd long since lost hope in getting the requested supplies from the Godfist. For a time, there would be at least some comforts from home.

"Thank you, Kenward," Durin said. "We're in your debt."

"I'm glad to hear you say that," Kenward said, and Durin felt a little sick. What had he just gotten himself into? "You might want to get your fill of things from the Godfist before I tell you. I don't want to spoil your appetite."

"Tell me now," Durin said.

"As you wish," Kenward said. "Trinda sang and summoned the dragons to Dragonhold. And we need to get the other stone chair onto the *Dragon's Wing.*"

"Without the help of any dragons?" Durin asked without thinking. "Are you joking?"

"Still hungry?" Kenward asked in response.

Durin walked to where the supplies were being opened and inspected them, despite having far less appetite than he'd had a moment before.

Chapter 12
Marry the sword, sleep in a cold bed.
--Morif, soldier

* * *

Benjin found himself, once again, grateful for the Dragon Clan. Their strength came not from their dragons but from within. As ever in his life, when he needed help, they had been there for him. They had not always understood each other, and there had not always been love and respect between them, but that was long ago. Now Benjin considered himself an honorary part of the Dragon Clan, if not the Drakon. Sinjin had often said flying the *Dragon's Wing* made him and his crew Drakon, but Benjin knew his place.

Finding a way to sufficiently thank the Dragon Clan for the risks they took and the burden they bore this day would take years. Only a single mention that the throne might help keep Sinjin, Valterius, and the Drakon safe was needed to motivate the people. It gave Benjin great pride, not just in what Sinjin had accomplished, but for the Arghast themselves. They were, after all, his countrymen.

Flying any ship to the place where the *Slippery Eel* lay was risky and dangerous at best, and strong winds made it an even less viable option. Thus they found themselves carrying the bulky piece down the mountainside. Benjin had serious reservations about the plan's practicality as well, but his people never ceased to impress him. Once they had removed the throne from the *Slippery Eel*, it was apparent they had sufficient strength to bear the burden. Benjin prayed for their stamina as well.

Another reason Benjin was grateful for the Dragon Clan was that they had spared Kenward the need to revisit the *Slippery Eel's* resting place. The anguish had been clear in Kenward's eyes, and Benjin couldn't imagine how the man must feel. At least when he had sunk the Kraken's Claw, the wreckage had been lost to the depths. The *Slippery Eel* remained much as she'd been left, save the slow ravages of time. Encroaching mosses coated the wood, giving the appearance the ship was growing out of the mountain.

There were other restless spirits in that vale as well. It was a sacred place. The regent dragons had said the vale belonged to Catrin, but one couldn't visit the place and not be overcome by the fading presence of those majestic creatures, now gone from his world. Benjin shed more than one tear in their memory and that of Catrin and Kyrien. Not for the first time, nor the last, he sucked unsteady breaths past his quivering bottom lip.

Shouts brought Benjin from his mourning. Methodically he made his way around the narrow ledge to see the throne teetering on the precipice.

Those carrying one side had slipped on loose scree and were having a terrible time trying to get back under the timbers they were using the hoist the massive weight.

"Lower your corner!" Benjin shouted to the men opposite the low corner. As they did, daylight shone under the support braces, and the people wasted no time getting the timbers raised back up onto their shoulders. No one had been killed, and the throne hadn't been lost, which was a testament to just how strong these people were, physically, mentally, and spiritually. Somehow they knew they would not fail, which drove them to success. Benjin had always known the world worked this way, but never had he seen it quite so clearly demonstrated as with the Dragon Clan. Nothing would prevent these people from achieving what they believed they would do.

Their progress gave Benjin hope and belief of his own. They had made it past the worst of the descent. Here and there they would have to clear brush and take down a tree or two to clear a wide enough path, but they had essentially achieved their goal. Benjin worried less about potential loss of life.

It was nearing dark when they finally reached the lowlands, making their way onto the trail leading to the beach. As soon as Kenward's crew saw the Dragon Clan emerge on to the plain, they rushed to assist the now exhausted tribesmen. The windlass and ropes had already been prepped, and only Kenward and Sevon remained to mind the *Serpent*. Sevon was not known for his brute strength and would have been of little use. Still, knowing what he knew, Benjin wondered if Sevon had other reasons. Kenward said he trusted the man, but Benjin couldn't help but view him with suspicion. Anyone who'd been in the employ of Trinda was suspect. Knowing he could do nothing but guard his own coin purse, Benjin let his concerns about Sevellon the thief go and concentrated on the dangers they might face while lowering the throne into the *Serpent's* hold.

Kenward, though, proved he knew his business. Though it was full dark by the time they had secured and rigged the throne to Kenward's satisfaction, the actual act of loading the heavy chunk of stone went smoothly. Windlass, levers, and pulleys were all used with tremendous effect.

The captain of the *Serpent* came to Benjin and leaned close, "Don't tell anyone I said so, but I think this might be the most dangerous and stupid thing I've ever done in my life."

Considering what Benjin knew about Kenward's history and having been there for some outrageously reckless behavior, the thought made Benjin feel a little sick. "I still think it would be a lot safer and faster to take the throne on the *Dragon's Wing*. Pelivor and Gwen say they could handle the additional weight without much trouble."

"If all we wanted to do was deliver the throne to Trinda," Kenward said, "then the *Dragon's Wing* would indeed be better suited to this task, but there are other things that must be done. The *Wing* would have to dock in one of the harbors; the *Serpent* has the advantage of being able to fly directly into the hold. How do you think Pelivor and Gwen would feel about that?" Benjin didn't have to ask; he knew doing it safely was beyond the *Wing's* capabilities. "The best thing you can do for me is escort us back. You can fish and provide us with provisions so I don't have to carry the extra weight. That alone will make this journey safer than the last."

Benjin saw Kenward's point, but he couldn't help feeling they were playing directly into Trinda's hands.

* * *

Kenward Trell watched the Godfist growing larger with ever-increasing trepidation. He'd known this was a bad idea from the beginning, but something was telling him things were far worse than he'd thought. Soon they would leave their escort behind, and the *Serpent* would be on her own. Usually that was how Kenward liked it, but this time was different--far different.

"We'll wait for you in the harbor!" Benjin shouted from below.

Leaning over the rail, Kenward waved good-bye to his friends and his sister--he hoped not for the last time. Once they were over land, the feeling aboard the ship changed. Kenward's orders were often anticipated by the crew at this stage of the journey, and the severely shorthanded crew worked with alacrity. Kenward watched closely to make certain speed did not affect quality. These tasks were required not to suit his whim; they were matters of life and death; a single bad knot could send them crashing into the rock face or the valley floor. Despite his efforts, the *Serpent* moved with too much speed. One thing Kenward had never figured out was how to slow down his airship when pushed by prevailing winds. The crew's skill manipulating the sails gave him some control under good conditions, but stronger gusts sent the *Serpent* out of control. The lack of a solution was now Kenward's foremost concern.

When Dragonhold came into view, Kenward was glad to see the gates open. A part of him had been wishing for the gates to be closed, but Trinda awaited his cargo, and the trader in him knew a good captain always delivered. Darkness was all he could see within the hold, and he could only hope they were ready for his entrance. "Sound the horn! Secure yourselves!" Kenward shouted.

Farsy pulled down three times on a cord running into the boiler room, and three deep blasts issued from the ship's horns before Kenward's trusted friend looped a rope harness over his shoulders and grinned. Their speed was likely to send them deeper into the great hall than on their previous entrance into Dragonhold. Kenward did everything he could to scrub off speed. Nothing helped. The *Serpent* entered Dragonhold with her crew screaming in terror. Just barely clearing the gates, the ship turned sideways as the wind socks dragged against protruding edges. When the *Serpent* struck stone, she skidded and bounced on her starboard side, leaving everyone aboard bruised and scraped.

Kenward's vision slowly adjusted, and he cursed himself for not using the oldest pirate trick known. He should have worn a patch over one eye to preserve his night vision. Had he pulled off the patch upon entering the darkness, he would have been able to see with one eye, at least. A strange puff of warm wind buffeted Kenward for an instant, and his vision was slow to return. The air smelled of smoke and something else. He was worrying over the furnaces and boilers when his vision cleared. A dragon's head towered over them. The mighty beast's roar was more than Kenward's psyche could handle. He fainted, crumbling to the *Serpent's* angled deck.

* * *

A mature dragon's roar bellowed through Dragonhold like chained thunder. Sinjin wondered for a moment if the sound truly was thunder. It had been known to rain within these parts of the keep, but he'd heard that thunder, and this was different. This sounded alive and Kendra appeared to agree. Both turned to leave the inexplicable stone wheel they had been contemplating, and Sinjin feared someone would bar their path; it had happened before.

Mostly they had been honored as guests, but there was no question as to who was in charge and who determined their fate. Trinda was not unkind, but neither was she friendly. Not for the first time, Sinjin wished he'd been nicer to her in the past. They say the true measure of a person can be seen in the way he treats people less powerful than himself, and Sinjin was ashamed of things he'd said and done.

Regret was a part of growing up, but he'd been taught not to let past mistakes prevent great things in the future. Those mistakes taught him how to be a better person, his father had always said. Sometimes it was as if he could still hear his father's voice in his mind. He missed his father terribly.

"What do you think that was?" Kendra asked softly. Trinda's guards were never far away.

"I don't know," Sinjin said, not wanting to admit he hadn't been thinking about it.

"Not sure how much more excitement I can take," Kendra said.

Sinjin laughed. It felt good to release some of his tension, even if just a small amount. A crowd had gathered along the shoreline of the God's Eye, waiting for the barges to return from the far shore. These people wanted to know what was happening just as badly as he and Kendra did. Their arrival among the crowd did not go unnoticed, and though no one spoke to them, they did clear a way for Sinjin and Kendra, silently acknowledging Dragonhold's rightful masters. He wasn't certain what exactly the child queen had said to the people, but it was clear they feared communicating openly with him and Kendra. It saddened him.

The barges were larger and more substantial than the ones originally built under Catrin's leadership. These barges required four men to pole them and could hold many more people, though it appeared the original, smaller barges were also still in use. When they arrived, however, no one boarded. Instead, Sinjin and Kendra were left standing closest to the shoreline, and they boarded in uncomfortable silence. Even the young men manning the poles did not speak to them, despite Sinjin's knowing three of them fairly well. Bradley, at the very least, met his eyes and gave him a nod. The others were afraid to do even that. Such things made him dislike Trinda, and he remained conflicted with regard to the child queen. Only water lapping against the barge and moving poles accompanied their journey across the lake.

On the far side of the God's Eye, the passageway and the great hall beyond were eerily quiet and empty. Normally a steady flow of people moved through this hall, and now their boot steps echoed in the silence. A distant shuffling sound like leather on stone reached their ears but was too distorted to tell them much. A sinking feeling nauseated Sinjin.

A horn sounded three times, and he recognized its call. Screaming and shouting were followed by another deep roar, this one unmistakable.

Entering the great hall at a full run, Sinjin and Kendra slowed and stared at the spectacle unfolding. It took a moment before they truly understood what they saw. Clouds of black smoke mingled with steam rolling across the ancient mosaic floor of the hall. Rising out of smoke and steam stood a dragon that dwarfed the regals. Sinjin soon recognized Jehregard, still wearing his tierre, and Onin of the old guard glaring at anyone who dared approach.

Before the dragon, like a child's toy in disarray, the *Serpent* lay on her side. Nimsy and Farsy helped Kenward off the ship. Sinjin and Kendra were soon running again, seeing their friends in trouble. By the time they reached the others, much of the excitement was over. The fire on the *Serpent* appeared to have been quenched, and the wind socks, emptied. Kenward was unsteady on his feet, but he did stand, and that relieved much of Sinjin's worry.

As they approached, Jehregard lowered a wing, allowing Onin to dismount. Sinjin was surprised to see Thundegar Rheams as well.

"You gave me quite a start," Kenward said to Onin as Sinjin and Kendra approached.

"Are you all right?" Kendra asked.

"Onin's dragon nearly scared the wind out of me," Kenward said with an accusing glance at Jehregard.

"You have my apologies," Onin said. "If someone would lend me a sledgehammer, I'll make sure he's aware of my displeasure."

"A sledgehammer?" Kendra asked.

"The great brute won't feel anything less, and I want him to know just how much I appreciate him bringing me here against my will. And what, if I may ask, are all of you doing here?"

"We were summoned," Sinjin said. Onin noticed him for the first time, a confused look crossing his gnarled visage. "Trinda sang and summoned the regal dragons. It would appear Jehregard also answered the call."

"Regardless," Onin said, "I will greatly reward the person who brings me a sledgehammer."

Sinjin reminded himself not to cross Onin.

For a moment, silence fell over them, and Sinjin was momentarily overwhelmed by the strangeness of it all. He wondered if he were dreaming since none of this could really be happening to him. Moments later, the feeling grew.

Without warning, Trinda spoke, "Welcome, Onin of the old guard. Welcome, Jehregard."

Onin opened his mouth to say something, but Jehregard, whose head loomed just behind Onin, issued a deafening bellow directed at Trinda. Onin's hair--beard, braids, beads, and all--danced in the wind of his dragon's roar.

Holding his ears, Onin turned around and glared at his dragon.

When Onin did speak, he shouted far more loudly than needed. "Why have you summoned us?"

"I need your help," Trinda said.

"You've got a funny way of asking for favors," Onin shouted. "Can I expect to be compensated for this effort and the inconvenience?"

Sinjin was surprised by Onin's words, having expected him to take Trinda to task.

"What compensation do you require?" Trinda asked as if intrigued.

"For starters," Onin said, "I need a sledgehammer."

* * *

Sinjin was conflicted about the stone throne finally finding its way into its rightful place, the place his mother had intended to put it when she commissioned the stone chairs years before. Like many of the things taking place within Dragonhold, they were things his mother had strived for, yet they hadn't been completed until after Trinda took control. Sinjin heard speculation Dragonhold was better off under Trinda's leadership than under his mother's control. He couldn't help but resent it. His mother had worked for years to convince people to return Dragonhold to its former glory, and it was only after the accidental discovery of the hold's ability to reconfigure itself that Trinda was able to do what she had done, however remarkable it might be. Sinjin wondered what his mother would have accomplished given access to the entire hold.

He had to take a moment to shake his head. If not for his best friend's laziness, the hold might have remained forever divided. Again, Sinjin wondered if he were dreaming. When the second throne was finally resting in its permanent home, he had to admit the place was now. . . right. There was symmetry and balance. His mother had taught him how important each of those were.

Trinda cast him a coy smile, no doubt proud of once again fulfilling his mother's ambitions. Then, though, she gazed out the stone portal to the skies beyond. After sucking in a deep breath, she ran from the room. Her guards struggled to keep up.

Sinjin and Kendra ran behind, joined by Martik and Chase, who'd orchestrated the stone chair's placement.

"Stick with me if things go badly," Chase said.

"Or with me," Martik said. "Either of us should have a chance at getting you to a safe place."

"What's Trinda playing at?" Sinjin asked his uncle.

Chase just shook his head. "Wish I knew," he said. "I'm starting to wish I'd taken one of the opportunities I've had to leave this place. I've got a really bad feeling."

This made Sinjin feel even worse. No one asked any more questions.

When they neared the great hall, Chase signaled them to slow. He sneaked to the corner, peeking around. He just stood there, frozen, not giving any indication of what he saw. When Sinjin and Kendra walked up to join him, he jumped.

"I think we should try to get out of the hold. Now," he said, and he pushed them back.

"What is it?" Sinjin asked. "What's happening?"

Chase continued to push him back, but Sinjin was no longer a child. If he didn't want to go back, then he would not. The look on his uncle's face surprised him when he resisted. The older man just nodded and let him go. Where Sinjin went, so went Kendra.

Slowly he poked his head around the corner. Jehregard had moved deep into the great hall and was the first thing to grab Sinjin's attention. Toward the far end of the hall, Trinda, stood alone before the *Serpent*, her arms spread wide, holding two objects. Immediately he recognized the Staff of

Life. From the distance, he couldn't be certain it was Koe she held in her other hand, but he surmised it was so.

Perched atop the *Serpent* and crushing her under its weight was a nightmare made flesh. A maturing feral queen lashed the air with her tail in clear agitation. Sinjin knew animals, and this one was ready to shred anything that came close. He couldn't really blame it. Though ferals had been his enemy, this dragon had not come of its own volition, nor did those atop her. Dressed in black and wielding a staff of dark swamp root that glistened under a polished sheen, Allette Kilbor watched Trinda with deadly intent. Before her, the cloud cat dug its claws deeper into wooden panels built into the otherwise dragon-leather saddle.

The dragon hide offended Sinjin's sensibilities. Along with a host of other reasons, he was starting to think Chase was right. When he turned to leave, though, Kendra grabbed his arm.

"Wait," she said.

Torn, Sinjin decided to trust his wife's instincts. She'd been right before, and he also knew knocking her out would be the only other way to pull her away from something she'd decided she wanted to see.

"Why have you brought me here?" Allette demanded, her dragon's tail still twitching.

"I need your help," Trinda said.

"And why would I want to help you?" Allette asked.

"Because I am not your enemy," Trinda said.

"I recall differently," Allette said. Trinda's forces and herald globes had turned the tide of the Jaga War.

"You have not attacked us, and we have not attacked you," Trinda continued. "There has been peace."

"Until now," Allette said.

This was almost enough to convince Sinjin to drag Kendra from Dragonhold. Things were about to get ugly.

The feral queen shifted her weight, and the *Serpent* groaned beneath her. Timbers snapped and the sound was almost physically painful; Sinjin knew how much Kenward loved his ships, and though Sinjin had sworn never to board the *Serpent*, he felt a certain attachment to her.

"Whatever you two are going to do," Sinjin heard Kenward shout. "Leave my ship out of it!"

"Silence!" Trinda demanded, ringing the flagstone with Sinjin's staff, the same staff his mother had once guarded and Nat Dersinger's family before her. A frost ring radiated from the staff, stunning those around Trinda and striking the feral queen in the muzzle. The dark creature responded with a furious bellow.

The following events were instantly burned into Sinjin's memory. Kenward and his crew fled the *Serpent*. Timbers snapped when the feral queen launched herself. Hovering in the air above the child queen, who was dressed all in white, Allette and her dragon resembled death incarnate.

The feral queen snapped at Trinda. The girl hurled a fist of lightning to intercept the approaching dragon's muzzle. The two connected with a sizzling pop that left the air smoking. The feral queen reared, and Allette stood tall in the saddle. Leveling her inky black staff at Trinda, she sent forth black flames in a gushing font that stained whatever they touched. Trinda cast up a defensive shield, her power magnified by Koe and the Staff of Life. Dark flames washed over it on a raging torrent. Her energy shield still held around her, the child queen retreated, disappearing into the halls leading to the kitchens.

The feral queen settled herself on the overlarge throne. Now it was small and fragile under the weight of Allette's dragon. Sinjin stepped out and waved to Kenward and his crew. Once Kenward had spotted them and waved back, Sinjin turned to Kendra. He opened his mouth to speak, but the roar of the feral queen filled the hall. Jehregard responded with a deep bellow that vibrated the stone, and even the regal dragons trumpeted from the darkness above. Hearing Valterius made Sinjin want to cry. How in the world were they going to get their dragons out of here?

In the next instant, the question was irrelevant. Pointing her black staff at the gates, Allette issued a blast of darkness. The crossbar keeping the towering gates closed shattered. Slowly the massive timbers swung inward. Feral dragons flooded the hall. With them came twisted demons like those that had plagued the Godfist in the past, and Sinjin felt sick. The feeling grew worse when screams came from the God's Eye.

Chapter 13

To bend the wind is to hold hands with the gods.
--Pelivor, flightmaster

* * *

There was nowhere to run. Sinjin considered their options, none of them good. If Allette's forces were outside the hold, then fleeing would put them in greater danger. Allette stood between them and the tunnels leading to much of the hold. The God's Eye stood in the way of the only other route Sinjin knew of to gain the interior of Dragonhold. Staying near Valterius, the other regals, and Jehregard was a far safer thing to do.

Allette and the feral queen cleared most of the main hall, and demons made their way toward where Onin, Thundegar Rheams, and Jehregard stood. Thundegar had known the girl; he'd been a father figure to her at a critical time in her life, but when the man started walking toward her, Sinjin feared for his life.

"What in the world just happened?" Kendra asked in a low voice, still stunned over Trinda's retreat and Allette's sudden taking of the outer hold.

"We're in trouble," Sinjin replied.

There was no more time for talking. Thundegar had come face-to-face with one of Allette's demons, and the monstrous, twisted creature brought up a heavy maul with black metal studs, and a mere heartbeat before it brought down the weapon with the full force of its might, Allette spoke. "No." With her staff, she pointed at the demon, and it dropped its weapon before falling to its armored knees. There it remained. Those who had been approaching slowed then stopped.

"You have just come very close to death," Allette said. "Do not test me. I'm not the girl you knew. I am the Black Queen, ruler of the Jaga, and you will bow before me."

"I do not fear death . . . nor you," Thundegar said. "And I bow before no one. Nor should you or anyone else for that matter."

The feral queen lashed the air with her tail and coiled her serpentine neck all while moving closer to where Thundegar stood. Standing in her saddle, the Black Queen loomed over Thundegar. Perhaps she would have killed him then, but Rastas intervened. After struggling a moment to free his claws from the wood blocks he used to secure himself, the cloud cat took three long strides and leaped off the front of the feral queen's angular snout before the dragon had the chance to react. The dragon didn't appear to appreciate it and snapped at Rastas's tail. The cat Thundegar had raised charged toward him at a full run, never slowing. Just before he reached Thundegar, who braced himself on his cane, the cloud cat leaped, sending his considerable girth into Thundegar's chest, knocking him down.

The stone rushed up to meet Thundegar, air bursting from his lungs when he struck. Even as Thundegar struggled to regain his breath, the big cat rubbed his face along Thundegar's torso; then he was attacking the man's boots; after grabbing one boot and weaving his head back and forth like the great goofball he was, the cat actually coaxed a laugh from Thundegar. He rubbed his old friend between the ears, as he hadn't been able to do for so long. "Crazy cat," he said.

Those words softened Allette's expression, showing hints of the frightened and broken little girl who'd fled back into the Jaga after their last meeting.

"Why did you bring me here?" Allette asked him softly. "Why would you want to hurt me so?"

The feral queen growled, low and deep.

"I was summoned, same as you," Thundegar said. Allette looked dubious. "Trinda has the ability to summon dragons. I was riding the dragon you see behind me with my friend Onin when it happened to us too."

Suspicion showed on Allette's face and posture.

"There are other dragons here as well," Thundegar said. "They're hiding--first from Trinda and now from you."

Allette's eyes narrowed. "You lie," she said.

Sinjin stepped closer but Kendra grabbed his arm and held him fast.

"This is something I must do," he said. Kendra squeezed hard one last time before letting him go. He made a mental note to remind her how strong her grip was if he survived the next few minutes. "I, too, was summoned along with my dragon."

At the sight of Sinjin, Allette hissed and the feral queen's pupils narrowed. It was a disconcerting sight, and it stilled his breath for a long moment. "You know me," he said. "And I know I've brought you great pain in the past, but it was not out of malice."

Allette did not appear convinced.

"Sinjin is among those who voted to leave you in peace," Kendra said, stepping out behind him. "There're others who wished to attack you before you could regain your strength. I beg you not to prove those imbeciles correct."

"Where is your dragon?" Allette asked Sinjin, no warmth in her manner.

"Valterius!" he shouted. Nothing happened. Demons moved closer. Sinjin could feel the beasts' hot breath on his face. The smell alone was enough to make him want to flee, but he held his ground. To retreat would be to trigger instinct in the predatory dragon; this much Sinjin knew. He also knew standing his ground probably didn't increase the odds of his survival by all that much. "Valterius!" he shouted again, hoping his dragon would sense the urgency in his voice, but still nothing happened.

"Gerhonda!" Kendra shouted when Valterius did not materialize.

The feral queen hissed and turned on Kendra, ready to snap her up in her jaws. The creature's head was so big, it wouldn't even need to chew before swallowing her. The thought made Sinjin ill. Demons closed in on him now, perhaps only Rastas kept them from harming Thundegar. Sinjin and Kendra had no such protection.

Just as they found themselves back to back, the air pressure changed. Sinjin cried out as he was violently snatched from within the crowd of demons. In the next instant, he was flying, but not as he usually did. Valterius gripped him with both claws and flew through the halls of Dragonhold with incredible speed. Only when his wife cursed did he know Gerhonda followed. About the rest, Sinjin could not say. He was too busy being terrified.

Valterius wove through towering pillars, making himself a difficult target to hit. Jehregard's massive head appear before them, and Valterius flew just a little higher before turning on a wingtip and diving toward the hall leading to the God's Eye. There Kenward, Chase, and the others waited.

"Look out!" was all Sinjin had the time to shout before they flew through a too-small space. Valterius' scales made a frightening sound when scraping against the ceiling, and Sinjin's feet occasionally came into contact with the stone floor, causing him to nearly slip from his dragon's grip. The sound of Kendra's complaints gave him a little comfort--at least he knew she was alive. His breath and all other thought were taken from him when they entered the chamber containing the God's Eye.

Valterius flew higher, dodging the stalactites reaching down from the chamber ceiling. Sun- and comet light streamed in through a narrow opening in the ceiling of the chamber, and Sinjin had a sick feeling when he thought his dragon might try to escape through that too-narrow gap. Instead, Valterius continued toward the far side of the chamber. When Al'Drak was forced lower by a protruding formation, Sinjin saw the reflection in the still lake. It featured him and Valterius against the backdrop of daggers made of stone. That was until a demon burst forth from the water, breaking the illusion and nearly catching Sinjin's ankle as they passed.

Gerhonda swooped in, smacking the demon in the head with her bottom jaw. The demon quickly disappeared from sight, and Sinjin caught his first glimpse of Kendra, who hung upside down, Gerhonda gripping her by her ankles. Sinjin knew Kendra well, and if they survived this, he knew he might need to intervene on Gerhonda's behalf. Of course that would have to be after he and Valterius got a few things straight.

Those thoughts were washed away when Sinjin saw the barges under attack and the head of a feral dragon sticking in through the far entrance. Demons taunted those aboard the unarmed and overfull barges.

What had Trinda been thinking? Sinjin had to ask himself. Then he had to hold on as Valterius plunged him into the lake. The dragon's open jaws sent demons flying away from them. The feral dragon roared, trying to squeeze itself into the chamber without much luck. Though the feral dragon posed little danger as long as they did not approach it, Sinjin also knew they wouldn't be able to escape that way. Valterius fended off demons and placed Sinjin onto the barge. The dragon did not let go of him.

"Hold on to me," Sinjin shouted, and the people around him did as he asked, nearly crushing him with their desperate grasps. Valterius flapped his wings and moved the barge toward a nearby opening, one Sinjin knew led to the inner hold, perhaps their last chance at finding safety. Water splashed behind him followed by more of his wife's cursing, and he shouted, "Help her!"

Those nearest Kendra let go of Sinjin and reached out for his wife. The moment she was in their embrace, Gerhonda released her. The regal dragon used teeth, claws, and tail to fend off the encroaching demons. Gathered beneath the barge, the twisted, unnatural creatures rocked the unwieldy vessel, trying to tip it over. Those aboard were tossed about when a massive wave pitched the barge as Gerhonda dived beneath.

Moments later, Valterius's effort paid off, and the barge thumped into the wall of the chamber. As soon as they struck, the people let go of Sinjin, and Valterius flew on into an even smaller hall than the last. Sinjin had to keep his knees bent to not be dragged along the floor. Again, Kendra's shouts reached him. He turned long enough to catch a glance of her, now right side up and struggling the same as he.

Remembering this hall, Sinjin hoped Valterius could truly read his thoughts, for there were tight places ahead, places where he'd nearly died the last time, he recalled. The dragons proved their skill at flying even in tight spaces, executing swift turns that left their humans pale and queasy.

When at last they broke into the chamber with the mountain like bridge of loose, black stone, the true majesty of the city on one side of the bridge was revealed. Beside the titan wheel that spun ever faster, Trinda waited. Sinjin wondered what kind of reception they would get.

Valterius denied Sinjin a dignified entrance and sent him sprawling on the wet flagstone at Trinda's feet. Gerhonda, at least, tried to redeem herself by gently placing Kendra at Sinjin's side. His wife helped him stand and wiped blood from his lip.

When he looked at Trinda, he expected a sarcastic remark, but all she did was raise one eyebrow. This, he decided, was no better.

* * *

Occasional sounds of battle and the roars of dragons filtered down to where Sinjin and Kendra confronted Trinda. Or perhaps it was she who confronted them. The dragons had retreated to a pair of rock protrusions high above.

"None of this makes sense," Sinjin said. "Why have you done this? What purpose could it possibly serve?"

Trinda responded with nothing more than a smile. It crawled under his skin and made him want to scream, but when a growl escaped his wife's lips, he held her back. This was no time for tempers.

"Are you going to let them take over the hold?" Sinjin asked. "Or are we going to fight?" It was the most diplomatic approach he could take. Perhaps if Trinda could be persuaded to align her forces with his, then they would have a chance.

"Allette is not evil," Trinda said.

Sinjin blinked. "What?"

Trinda sighed with a pained look on her face, as if she spoke to a slow-witted child. "The sounds you hear are not the slaughter of people; it is the posturing of dragons trapped in a confined space and people being herded into areas where they can be controlled. I'm not saying no one will get hurt, but I can assure you the self-proclaimed Black Queen is not a mass murderer."

It took a bit of time for Sinjin to process the information.

"That still doesn't explain why you summoned the dragons here. What game are you playing?" Kendra asked, venom in her tone and flames in the corners of her eyes. By the gods, Sinjin loved that woman, and by the goddess, she did her best to drive him mad.

"Perhaps I don't want to tell you," Trinda said. "You haven't been very nice to me, so you shall have to wait and find out with all the rest." The words were said with cool power flowing through them. They escaped the child queen's lips like wisps of mist. Then her voice turned hard and icy. "But do not think for an instant I'm vapid or without cause. Perhaps someday you'll find understanding, but I doubt today will be the day."

Kendra audibly ground her teeth, and he could only hope she would maintain control of her rising temper. Kendra was no stranger to conflict. Clenching her teeth, she let Sinjin ask the next question.

"What are we going to do when they get down here?" Sinjin asked in as polite a tone as he could manage without sounding entirely insincere.

"Leave me to worry about that," Trinda said.

Sinjin couldn't help but feel betrayed and helpless. They'd never had any choice in the matter of coming here. He worried over these things to mask deeper worries. Trinda eyed him as if trying to read his anxiety, and he pushed those feelings deeper. Fortunately for him, he had an abundance of things about which to worry and let his thoughts remain a maelstrom of anxiety. The sounds drifting to them grew louder, and he wondered just how much time they had left.

"If we are to defend the hold," Sinjin said, "may I have my staff and Koe please?"

"That won't be necessary. Now is not the time," Trinda said.

He had known she wouldn't grant his request, and it further soured his mood. This trickster clothed in the body of a child was starting to push Sinjin's patience to its limits. Dealing with Trinda required Sinjin to constantly remind himself she was far more powerful and intelligent than her form would suggest. The girl was an expert at using this to her advantage. Even people who knew how dangerous she was still sometimes fell under her spell and underestimated her.

Considering some of her abilities, Trinda was perhaps the most powerful person on all of Godsland. Sinjin noticed Trinda staring at him, and he pushed that thought down as far as he could. Despite his efforts, blood rushed to his face. Sometimes he envied his mother's ability to speak with her subconscious. Maybe then he could convince his body to stop embarrassing him. Trinda's smile grew wider.

Given the chance, Sinjin would have said something, but his knees buckled when the keep shuddered. An instant later, a clap louder than thunder and a familiar roar filled Dragonhold.

"Well," Trinda said, her face a mask of innocence. "I think we have another visitor."

* * *

Kenward watched the events unfold in a state of increasing shock. Far too many demons and feral dragons flooded the hall, and the *Serpent* wasn't yet ready to fly. He eyed Jehregard and wondered if the huge dragon could push his way out of the hold. Visions of being in a wooden box atop that dragon forced Kenward to consider other options.

In the end, he turned to Chase and Martik to see what they would do. So far, they had remained near Onin and Jehregard for the semblance of safety the dragon provided. But it was clear Chase was looking for an opportunity to make their escape. Martik was eyeing the tierre atop the verdant dragon, but the longer he thought about it, the more color drained from his face.

Allette remained atop her dragon and appeared torn as to what to do with Thundegar. She'd been ready to cast him aside not long before, but Rastas stood defensively beside Thundegar, his tail wrapped around the man's leg.

"I'm not your enemy," Thundegar said.

"Nor are you my father," Allette responded with venom. "He's dead, along with all my friends and family."

"Not all of your friends are dead," Thundegar continued, his voice calm and level without a hint of fear. Kenward admired him; the gaze of the feral queen was enough to make his legs turn to jelly.

"I betrayed you!" Allette shouted at Thundegar as if he were deaf. "You've no reason to be my friend."

"You did not betray me," Thundegar said. "You were unable to help me, that is true, and you did what you had to do save yourself, but that doesn't make you a traitor; it makes you a survivor. If you had come back, it's possible none of us would've survived. Do you understand me?"

The hall was mostly silent. Kenward drew ragged breaths. The air reeked of power and left a metallic taste in his mouth that grew progressively worse.

"What do you expect me to do? Just leave? After I was drawn here against my will and threatened by that . . . that . . . child?"

"I only ask you to recognize that we are friends and that none of the people you see in this hall are responsible for bringing you here."

"I'm aware of that," Allette said with a heavy note of exasperation. "But it doesn't mean I don't want to at least pay my respects to our hostess and repay her for her kindness."

The venom pouring forth from Allette showed just how damaged this child was, and Kenward's soul wept for her innocence. He knew her story and could not help but relate to her. He'd lost a great deal in this life; some of it had been returned to him, but he knew the pain of loss, and he could see it all over the girl's face. Like Thundegar, he hoped she would come to see them as allies. The presence of the demons didn't help Allette's cause in anyone's mind, but Kenward also knew they existed before Allette had come to power among the ferals. The demons were the creations of the ferals, and Kenward wasn't certain just how much control over these dragons the girl really had. If it was anything like what he'd seen out of Valterius, Gerhonda, and Jehregard, then her control was little more than an illusion. From what Kenward had seen, the dragons were the ones in control; if not, they wouldn't be in this mess.

The taste was overwhelming, and a hum grew in his ears. Kenward opened his mouth to speak, but the humming shut out all other sound; even the feral queen's roar was drowned out. Chase had both his hands over his ears, but he pulled one away long enough to wave them toward the main entrance to Dragonhold, not far from the hall leading to the kitchens and deeper into the hold.

Kenward caught a flash of light through the open gates, and his mind could not fathom what it was he'd seen. At that moment, consumed with following Chase and the others, Kenward could give it no more thought. The feral queen loomed above him as they slipped beneath her tail. She and Allette were focused on the entrance to the keep, and those who fled were no longer of any concern. Kenward was glad to see Thundegar among those who made it to the hall, the cloud cat, Rastas, never leaving his side.

Something made Kenward stop and look back, despite his better judgment. When he did, he saw something he'd never have dared to hope for. Glowing like a new star and entering the hold at high speed came a dragon and rider. There was no mistaking Catrin Volker, the Herald of Istra and Kenward's dear friend, and her dragon, Kyrien. Never had Kenward seen either of them shine so, as if Catrin herself were on fire. The saddle upon which she rode spread rainbows of light. Ropes of multicolored lightning shimmered and leaped out at random.

"Flee!" boomed Catrin's forceful command. "I have to release the energy! No one will be safe."

She may have said something else, but Kenward couldn't hear over the thunder of his heart and his feet. Tears streamed down his face from the realization Catrin and Kyrien were alive, but he could not slow. When the Herald of Istra tells you to flee, anyone with the sense the gods gave them did just that. When the thunder began and the blast of air knocked them all from their feet, Kenward prayed they had gotten far enough away.

Chapter 14

Artifacts of true power are rarely hidden in the light.
--Ain Giest, sleepless one

* * *

The first thundering crash was the least of it. What Catrin was doing to release her energy, Kenward didn't know, but it added to his confliction. The joy of knowing Catrin was alive was unabated. She was among his most treasured friends, but she was also the Herald of Istra and was apparently in the process of grinding the great hall to bits. Those around him had the good sense to stay down, and none were injured by the blasts, but Kenward knew his ears would ring for days.

"It's Catrin," Kenward managed to say between blasts, and the looks he received in return ranged from fright to disbelief. Chase, though, stood with tears in his eyes and a determined smile on his face. The next blast knocked him back down, and he landed on Martik, who complimented his decision-making skills.

Eventually the blasts subsided enough that it was safe to stand again. Chase was already moving back toward the hall, and Kenward had to run to keep up with him, and even then, Chase pulled ahead. Others followed more slowly, and the two burst back into the hall, expecting to see the place littered with the bodies of ferals and demons alike. Instead, the demons huddled together against one wall. Jehregard was as still as stone, and Allette remained atop her dragon. They watched Catrin from a distance, the feral queen coiled around a stone column.

Catrin remained in her saddle as well. The air around her shimmered and sparkled. Kenward had seen her struggle to access her powers early in her journey, and now those very same powers might turn her to ash.

Though it was obvious Chase wanted to be reunited with his cousin, the danger was far from averted. From all appearances, Catrin might be a danger to herself. While they hadn't found the bodies they had been expecting, they did find scorch marks blistering the great hall. In places, the mosaic was now once again in disarray. The damage was confined to the general area around Catrin, and it was clear she exercised some control in venting the excess energy, or there might not be anyone left alive. Seeing scorch marks and a mighty split bisecting the oversized throne, it was clear where Catrin had concentrated her rage. Trinda would not be pleased, but Trinda had yet to face Catrin. The thought gave Kenward a chill. He'd said once that he'd happily give up adventure for a trader's life, yet here he was in greater danger than ever.

The feral queen slithered down the column and crept across the hall to face Kyrien. Kenward was trying to decide which was more intense, the looks exchanged between Catrin and Allette or between the dragons they rode. The four sized each other up.

Now it was Kyrien's tail lashing the air. Kenward couldn't imagine what the dragon was thinking. The ferals had been responsible for exterminating his race, making him the last of his kind, yet he'd mated with a feral queen, producing the regal dragons. Uncertainty hung in the air. Kenward knew the slightest thing could set these two to tearing the world apart. No one wanted to see how capable they truly were.

"I have no quarrel with you," Allette said. "I did not summon you. The child queen is responsible for that, and I would thank her for the kindness. Would you care to join me?"

"I have no quarrel with you," Catrin said, her face stony and cold, "but I take exception to the company you keep."

The feral queen extended her wings, made even more imposing. Kyrien remained as he was, which was perhaps even more intimidating.

"You and the dragon you ride were not part of the attack that killed the regent queen, but some of those here were; I can smell the blood of the regents on them, and I will make no peace with them. Their lives are forfeit--a small price for the loss of an entire species."

"You are correct," Allette said. "Vekkara and I were not a part of that heinous act."

Kenward wasn't quite certain the statement constituted an apology.

"For this day, I propose a truce," Catrin said. "If your forces do not attack anyone within this hold, with the noted exception of Trinda Hollis, then I will allow you all to live."

From any other person, those words might have been an idle threat, especially to one as powerful as Allette. But there was no doubt Catrin meant what she said. It looked as if Catrin could barely keep from killing them all. It unnerved him. Catrin would never intentionally hurt him, but a history of unintentional consequences made Kenward take a step backward.

"Accepted," Allette said.

"Where is Trinda Hollis?" Catrin asked in a frightening voice that carried throughout the hold.

"Cat!" Chase yelled, and Catrin turned to him. The expression on her face changed from a stoic mask to an emotional storm. A sad smile morphed into guilt. "I am so sorry you mourned me. I never meant it to be so."

"It's OK, Cat," Chase said, his voice cracking and tears streaming down his face. "You're here. That's all that matters."

Catrin released the saddle straps and climbed down. The truce was a shaky one, and Kenward was glad to see her not making any sudden moves. Though he loved her dearly, she did frighten him so. Of just about any other person, Kenward would chastise himself for the fear, but with Catrin, it was warranted. This was the only person in existence who might inadvertently destroy the world. Kenward wondered for one terrifying instant what would happen if Catrin had nightmares, but he pushed the thought from his mind lest it paralyze him. His world had become a dangerous place.

"The last I saw Trinda," Chase said, "she was near the great wheel with Sinjin."

Catrin's head snapped to the side, and she started toward Chase. "Take me there," she said in an unfriendly tone. "Now."

Allette dismounted a bit more quickly and walked to Catrin's side. "I will join you."

"My son--" Catrin said.

"Will come to no harm from me," Allette said. "You have my word."

Catrin said no more and pushed Chase into the lead. Kenward followed, knowing he was of no use at all. Despite that, he had to know what happened. The events of Catrin's life had permanently shaped his own, and he had to know what could possibly come next. He was especially curious to find out what it was Trinda wanted. Her story about the great wheel destroying the hold was almost certainly a ruse, but there was but one way to find out.

* * *

The arrival of the feral dragons had made it clear it was time to leave the Godfist, despite the fact that the *Serpent* had never returned. Benjin stood at the rail, watching the seas.

"Pelivor and Gwen will awake soon," Fasha said when she reached his side. The feel of her close to him was comforting; it was among the things he clung to. In many ways his world was dull and faded compared to what it had once been. His wife, his friends, their ship, and a daughter of which he could not be more proud were the things that kept him moving. Even with all that bounty, his losses had torn great holes in his heart. The pain of it was at times unbearable. Fasha sensed his mood and wiggled herself under his arm. He did nothing to stop her.

"Have I told you today, my wife, how much I love you?"

"No," she said. "You're late."

"Have I mentioned you're as beautiful as the sunrise? And I get to gaze on you even at night."

"Feeling poetic today?" Fasha asked.

"I'm feeling something today. I'm not quite certain what it is. I just needed to get a bit of air and clear my head. Did you finish the inventory?"

"I did," Fasha said. "We can make for the Firstland and not stop for food or water."

"We're going to need to keep our flightmaster and thrustmaster in check."

Fasha laughed. "They'll rest even if I have to knock them over the head."

Benjin knew it was so and let at least that one worry go. Gwen was his daughter, and he expected things from her he could expect from no one else in this world. But Pelivor was not his son, and he had no right to ask the man for so much. He knew just how twisted it was that he expected more from Gwen than he felt comfortable asking from Pelivor, but it was so. It was something Benjin had to accept about himself.

"I feel so helpless," Fasha said after a long silence. "There's nothing we can do on the Godfist and really nothing we can do on the Firstland. We're not even bringing trade goods. It goes against my heritage."

Benjin smiled. As he'd thought many times before: Once a sailor, always a sailor. Once a pirate, always a pirate. Once his, he'd never let go. He pulled Fasha a little closer. "I don't know what we'll do to help, but we'll find some way. We've managed not to be completely useless up until now."

"Speak for yourself," Wendel said from not far away.

"Eavesdropping?" Benjin asked.

"Normally I wouldn't interrupt your private conversation," Wendel said, "but I was drawn out here by a feeling. I tell you I'd've laughed at anyone who told me that years ago, but then Catrin came along." He sniffed. The rest of those aboard, most of whom had known Catrin personally, gathered with them and shared her memory. No one spoke. No words were required. Catrin's presence was overwhelming. Then the thunder started. Unlike natural thunder, this was continuous, though the intensity fluctuated.

Looking out at roiling clouds suddenly lit from within, Benjin held a hand up to shade his eyes. All those aboard were speechless when rainbows burst through gaps in the clouds backed by orange fire. Benjin's breathing quickened and he grabbed Wendel by the arm. In the next minute, he was the only thing holding his friend up. From the clouds burst a vision of the goddess reborn adragonback. Shining like a font of pure energy, both dragon and rider were engulfed in flame. Even from a distance, Benjin could see Catrin struggling'. His friend was alive, but she was far from saved.

Wendel's knees buckled and Benjin went to one knee with him, gazing back up to the skies with a mixture of fascination and disbelief. Had he gone mad? Then he thought he might be dreaming as Catrin and Kyrien dipped in close, just as Pelivor and Gwen arrived on deck. Like blowing a kiss, Catrin sent a twinkling ball of light speeding toward the *Dragon's Wing*. It raced over the ship, and as it reached the mainmast, it exploded into an umbrella of sparkling light shimmering and dancing in the air, closing in on the ship like a shrinking dome. Benjin extended his hands and let the sparkles gather there. They were warm to the touch and left a tingly feeling in their wake, long after they faded and disappeared.

Each burst of light brought with it a memory of Catrin, a laugh, a rare hug, more than a few giggles. Tears streamed down Benjin's cheeks. Wendel held his face in his hands, so powerful were his emotions. When the last of the glittering gifts had passed and Catrin and Kyrien had long since disappeared from sight, Benjin and Wendel lay down on the deck and slept better than they had in a long time.

* * *

"I am sorry about the regent dragons," Allette said as they made their way to Dragonhold's interior. It was dangerous territory, and Kenward dearly wished the girl would just remain silent and not push the issue.

Catrin nodded in acknowledgment. "Do you know the reason?" she asked.

Silence was broken only by their footsteps as Chase continued to lead the way.

"Bad blood," Allette finally said. "It goes back a very long way. The memories of dragons are far longer than ours. Has your dragon not told you this?"

Catrin's glare would stop a charging bull. "I asked what you are aware of. I already know what I'm aware of."

"There was war during the last age of power," Allette said. "During the long sleep, the dragons rest and keep themselves nourished until the goddess returns. Given the chance to avenge yourself the losses of the last age, what would you do?"

It was a rhetorical question, but Kenward half expected Catrin to answer nonetheless. "And now what do you and the ferals want?" she asked instead.

"To be left alone," Allette said. Kenward had to admit that for the time they had been left to themselves, they had caused no trouble. Many had insisted they would quietly rebuild their strength then attack again, but Kenward wasn't so sure. There was something in the Black Queen's eyes that made him second-guess himself. Such humanity existed there, though it was laced with dark, reptilian coldness. Kenward shivered when she caught him staring at her. Did she blush after turning away? Kenward wasn't certain since he couldn't look directly at her. Instead, he had to try to catch a glimpse from his peripheral vision. Whether she had or not, Kenward felt himself flush, and his knees were a little unsteady as unbidden thoughts flooded his mind. No matter how much he wished them away, they persisted. He hoped no one was looking at him.

Chase held up his hand, calling for them to stop. He moved to the end of the narrow, secondary hall they were walking through and peered around the corner. He came back shaking his head. "They're all there," he whispered. "It looks like they are waiting for us."

"Since we lack the element of surprise," Catrin said, "I'll be on my way. Thank you, my dear cousin. Now get out of my way."

Allette moved at Catrin's side. They were perhaps the oddest of alliances, and Kenward hoped the allegiance would last long enough for him to escape. It occurred to him, perhaps too late, that Catrin might best be loved and admired from afar. As she walked, the air shimmered around her, and as if it were contagious, a nimbus of power also grew outward from Allette. Hers was all violets and deep blues. Catrin's aura ran more reds, oranges, and yellows. Kenward had no idea what it meant, but a similar nimbus surrounded Trinda. She waited for them, arms outstretched and holding the Staff of Life and Koe. Fire and lightning danced around the serpent on the staff, showing Trinda was drawing deeply from the dragon ore stones in its eyes.

Catrin and Allette carried no dragon ore, and Kenward wondered if they could defeat Trinda within her very center of power. She had everything at her disposal, and they had been summoned. One did not, in general, summon someone she could not control or dominate. That fact had them all on edge. Trinda had proven unpredictable in the past, and no one knew quite what to expect. It was unnerving in the extreme.

Sinjin and Kendra watched with worry as Catrin and Allette approached. Something bothered Kenward about what he saw, but he couldn't quite place it. Sinjin's expression puzzled Kenward. Then he realized what was missing: surprise. Realization slammed into Kenward's psyche, and he couldn't decide if he wanted to punch Sinjin and Kendra or hug them. Keeping such a secret was a tremendous burden, he knew, but it was such a pointless secret. Pointless until he considered Trinda's ability to summon dragons and apparently their riders as well. He wondered about that last part, but then Trinda spoke.

"Welcome home, Catrin Volker," Trinda Hollis said.

Catrin and Allette continued forward. Neither spoke.

"And I thank the Black Queen for joining us. I know I've kept you waiting, but now that Catrin has joined us, we can begin."

"Begin what?" Allette asked, her tone miles from friendly.

Trinda lowered her hands, and it was only then Kenward noticed Trinda was straddling a hole in the black stone floor. The mighty wheel spun with dizzying speed now, and when Kenward looked closer at the hole, he saw runes around it glowing blue. A scream was forming on his lips as he realized the runes were actually on the stone ring found in the Drakon Ghar's secondhold. He remembered then the scroll.

"Beware the Fifth Magic!" he shouted.

Before anyone else could act, Trinda's hands were moving downward, inserting the Staff of Life into the now glowing orifice. The shaft sank in just deep enough to keep the serpent's glowing eyes visible. The child queen twisted the staff until there was a rocky click. Sound erupted from Kenward and everyone else at the same time. The cacophony prevented anyone from being heard, but there was no need for words or commands, only warning.

Trinda wheeled and retreated toward the giant stone wheel, reaching into her robes. Catrin lashed out, her attack followed a heartbeat later by Allette's. Both attacks struck the child queen's exposed back and she shuddered.

Falling forward, she did manage to free whatever it was she'd been trying to pull from her robes. In her hand, Kenward saw something he recognized--the figurine the lord chancellor had asked him and his men to hold when they had first met. He'd been told it was for ceremonial purposes and was merely tradition, but he now suspected it was something entirely different. Trinda rolled onto her back, stunned.

Guards moved to surround her, the window of opportunity closing. Catrin and Allette did not attack, though Kenward wasn't sure why they held back. Perhaps neither could stomach harming someone in a little girl's body, despite knowing she was older than Catrin. No matter the reason, there were consequences. They should have taken their chance while they could. Though placing the staff within the stone ring had no discernible effect, what Trinda did next would forever change the Godfist. With trembling hands, she placed the figurine Sevon had stolen from the Heights into a much smaller opening in the rock and gave it a turn.

Catrin's second attack raced toward her but too late. The delicate figurine of a woman in flowing robes went fully erect. With the hand gripping a lightning bolt held high, the figurine began to spin, the centrifugal force causing previously hidden blades to extend. For a moment, Kenward was struck by its beauty. He had no idea how such a thing could be made or why all these otherwise unrelated pieces interacted in such an amazing way. His infatuation was interrupted by a whirring sound from the spinning figurine, which was now rotating faster, causing the sound to grow higher and higher in pitch. Then the figurine suddenly and catastrophically stopped. The blades must not have been connected to the center of the figurine because the sudden stop allowed the blades to continue rotating until they crashed into one another. What had been beautiful a moment before was now in chaos. The trend would continue.

The stone ring holding the Staff of Life disappeared into the hole, and the staff dropped with it until only a single hand's width of ancient wood remained above the stone. Part of Kenward wanted to race to the staff and keep it from dropping any further. Never before had it been so clear that he was powerless.

For a few moments, the keep was silent. Trinda lay still. Bernerd knelt to check her for signs of life, but then the keep shuddered. A deep, painful vibration hurt Kenward's joints and gave the impression of giant gears being engaged. He had the distinct feeling his fate was already sealed. Whatever was going to happen was going to happen, and it was too late for him to change it. He'd been in dangerous situations before, but never had he been so utterly helpless. When the stone floor leaped up to meet him, he thought his luck might finally have run out.

* * *

The decision to return to the Godfist came down to Wendel Volker. It was, after all, his daughter who'd just effectively come back from the dead. And now she was flying back into danger. Benjin didn't know how to feel except worried. There were very few ways he could imagine this ending well. Almost all paths led to disaster. Again he tried to understand Trinda's motives but could make no sense of them. Why bring all the dragons to Dragonhold if not to get the most powerful people on Godsland in one place. It was possible the girl could not differentiate which types of dragons she summoned, but Benjin suspected she knew exactly what she was doing. He just didn't know why, which bothered him greatly.

Going back to the Godfist was an enormous risk, but the weather had worked to Benjin's advantage for once in his life. Though storms were something they normally sought to avoid, a storm fronted by strong winds and headed in the correct direction had made their already swift vessel even faster. Ferals had ignored the *Dragon's Wing* last time, but that didn't mean they would do so again. His wife and daughter were on this ship, and every crew member was a dear friend. All of them had agreed, which did nothing to reduce the responsibility weighing on Benjin. His family and friends were strong and craftier than most would give them credit for, and still Benjin felt he should turn back out to sea.

The Godfist loomed ahead like a beacon of inevitability. The problems there would neither go away nor fix themselves. People he loved were in danger there, and the *Wing* flew with single-minded determination. They weren't much of an army, but they would have to do.

"Bring us in fast and low," Benjin said to Pelivor. "The longer before they know we're coming, the better."

"Are you sure about this?" Fasha asked.

"You're the captain of this ship," Benjin said. "I know I've crossed that line on a number of occasions, but I'll not go back on my word."

Fasha stood for a long moment, silent. She glanced at Gwen and the others, as if committing them to memory. Perhaps she was, Benjin thought.

It nearly brought tears to his eyes. He couldn't bear to think about losing any of them, and yet if they landed on the Godfist, it was unlikely all of them would make it back out.

"Turn back," Wendel said. "I can't have any of your blood on my conscience. Let me off in the harbor. I'll go alone."

"I'm going with you," Jensen said, leaving no room for debate.

"No one will keep me away," Pelivor said, fire in his eyes. His posture dared anyone to defy him.

"I'm not staying here while my flightmaster saves the girl," Gwen said. Pelivor flushed.

It was, once again, unanimous.

"Low and fast," Benjin said again.

Shouts greeted them when they passed over the harbor and lift, but those who'd seen them couldn't send word in time. Flying low, as it turned out, had drawbacks. So many things jutted into the air. Trees and buildings jammed the valley, which had been uninhabited not so long ago. Benjin thanked the gods for Pelivor's skills. No one spoke for fear of breaking the man's concentration.

Deadly obstructions soared past with blinding speed. Pelivor masterfully avoided the dangers, but in doing so, he sent the ship leaning to one side or the other. The rest did what they could to predict the movements of the ship. Pelivor could offer little warning, able only to react when new dangers approached.

The valley widened a bit as they moved south, and the flight through Lowerton was much smoother. The place was abandoned and empty and lent to the spooky feeling. Seeing feral dragons circling high above didn't add to his confidence.

When Dragonhold came into view, the facade was still unfinished, the gates hanging open. Those gates were charred and splintered and wouldn't be closing any time soon. One door was perilously close to falling into the valley below, which would most likely take out the wooden stair on its way down. It didn't bode well for their climb. Few other options presented themselves.

Deep thunder rolled through the valley, far louder than anything Benjin had ever heard, yet there was not a cloud in the sky. This sounded different than Catrin's attacks, and he was still trying to figure it out when he saw dust clouds. Dragonhold moved. It didn't simply rotate internally this time; the entire mountain moved. Reaching from the ground like claws of stone, megalithic spires with smooth, elegant lines erupted. Dragonhold was in the grip of a stone god. Farther and farther the claws extended until nearly meeting in the air high above the tallest peak. How could anyone have created something grander than the mountains? Benjin asked himself. It was unfathomable, yet it was real.

Lightning danced between the stone spires. Then the stones themselves began to sing a wavering note.

"It's some kind of shield!" Wendel shouted. "We'll never get in there through that!" Desperation raised the pitch of voice.

"Whatever that thing is," Benjin shouted, "it looks like it's still warming up. Hold on!"

"What are you doing?" Fasha asked in a shrill voice.

"Bring us in hot," Benjin yelled to Pelivor.

"Are you mad?" Fasha shouted. The time for debate had passed. A spire stood between them and the front gates. Sliding past it would be the only way to gain the hold--that was, if they were not killed instantly by the shield. Mountain and spire rushed toward them at incredible speed. Benjin braced himself.

Dancing between the spires, lightning licked the rigging as they sped forward. Benjin hoped they weren't already too late and couldn't blame those screaming as they cleared the spire. No pain came but the gates were upon them in the next instant, even smaller than they appeared from far away. The opening was large enough to admit the *Wing*, but the speed and the angle of their approach was less than ideal, causing them to brush against one side of the entrance. A whole tree trunk protruded from the gate and sent them spinning. Pelivor showed skills he'd never used before as he straightened out the listing airship and brought her down. The landing was more abrupt than any before it, and Benjin thought hull might shatter, but it was as if they had struck something with a bit of give to it.

A moment later, Benjin made his way to the rail and looked down to see what had broken their fall. Kenward Trell was not going to be happy.

Chapter 15

Memory is short and civilization fragile; record precious knowledge in stone.
--Brother Vaughn, Cathuran monk

* * *

After the initial jolt knocked everyone down, Sinjin pushed himself up onto all fours. Kendra and others moved, and his wife did not appear to be hurt. Trinda was still, and her guards hovered over her. His mother's and even Allette's faces told him something was terribly wrong. All the color had drained from them, and Sinjin felt something unnerving. Though he possessed very little power, he could feel it . . . changing. It was a strange sensation and difficult to describe. He felt as if the power were being bent. What had always been a somewhat constant note had changed in pitch, and it buzzed in his mind. His mother clapped her hands over her ears, and Allette doubled over.

Accompanying all this was a grinding vibration, similar to what it had felt like when the keep moved, except this was far more intense and sustained. Darkness overcast the amber crystals allowing in the light, forming claw-shaped shadows. Like the hand of an awakened god tightening around them, colossal stone fingers enclosed Dragonhold in a tomblike grip.

"No!" Catrin screamed.

"Make it stop!" Allette added her shrill plea.

These massive stones warped the energy as they moved into place. Multicolored lightning danced along the rock, and waves of blue plasma washed over the spaces in between, as if some sort of barrier had been erected between them. The farther the fingers reached, the more defined the barrier grew. The energy vibrated at an ever-increasing pitch, making Sinjin's teeth feel as if they would explode.

His mother and Allette squirmed in obvious anguish. Never had Sinjin hated Trinda more. He'd been angry and hurt, but now it was different. Now he wanted to knock her teeth out. There was nothing he could tolerate less than someone hurting his mother, and it was clear those with power greater than his were in far more pain.

Trinda woke, her screams deflecting his anger. The certainty of their deaths was made clear when a second jolt rocked Dragonhold. The fingers of stone locked into place with sudden finality. It felt as if they had all just been sealed in a tomb. Though they had previously managed to stand, Allette and his mother both collapsed back onto the cold stone floor. What struck Sinjin first was the silence. The high-pitched note was gone, and its absence felt unnatural. It was like the feeling he got when flying and pressure built up in his ears; he could still hear but everything sounded wrong.

The silence didn't last long. It was soon filled with Allette's sobbing. Sinjin rushed to his mother and found her unresponsive. What had Trinda done? he asked himself with tears streaming down his face. She was breathing, which gave him hope.

Kendra reached his side. "What just happened?"

"I'm not certain," Sinjin said. "But I'm pretty sure it's not good. I don't know what it's done to her, and I don't know how to help." Despite his best effort, the anxiety and fear made his voice tremble.

Perhaps this sound triggered some maternal instinct in Catrin since her eyes opened and a sad smile formed on her lips. "It's OK, Sinjin," she said.

Sinjin could not hold back his tears. The wellspring of relief drove him back to his knees.

"What has Trinda done?" Kendra asked Catrin.

"The power is gone," Catrin said. Her words were followed by stunned silence, which felt as if it might last forever. "The Fifth Magic has been activated. The true nature of this place has come to light too late. Dragonhold is a prison."

* * *

Kicking at an empty oyster shell along a black shore, Durin walked alone. Holding out hope his friends and family were still alive was exhausting given what they knew, and Durin had long since grown weary of it. For the Drakon left behind by dragons summoned in their absence, the uncertainty was no less painful. It had been their inescapable worry and anguish that had driven him from the hold. Stopping, he picked up another empty shell and skimmed it across the still waters of his favorite tidal pool. It was this place he came to whenever he needed inspiration, and he was sorely in need.

A variety of fish swam within the pool, shocks of blue, yellow, and orange color danced beneath the now shimmering surface. Glossy black one-claw crabs skittered from the pool and up onto the rocks, concealing themselves away in crevices, making themselves nearly invisible. Durin knew where they were, though. The crabs were now considered a delicacy among the Dragon Clan, and though it took dozens to make a proper meal, Durin and the rest loved their succulent, smoky taste.

Thoughts of the Dragon Clan reminded Durin of his troubles. Morale was low. The Drakon were privileged just by virtue of having bonded with a dragon. None blamed them, but that didn't mean no one felt resentment, hurt, or disappointment. The Arghast had foreseen this day, long ago, and becoming Drakon was something they'd all aspired to. For those left to support the hold, "Dragon Clan" had taken on new meaning and was no longer something of the greatest pride; it was less than Drakon, and that would not do.

It was a puzzle Durin could not solve and was perhaps the least of his problems, but he wanted very much to avoid thinking about his most pressing concerns. He wasn't the one who'd been raised to hold great power as Sinjin had. Durin was in no way prepared for the role in which he found himself, yet the Dragon Clan respected him. They trusted him. He knew that trust was misplaced. It was given because of his relationship with Sinjin, not because he'd earned it. The idea of hand-me-down power did not sit well in his gut. His having power of any sort, least of all power he did not deserve, was unsettling. Sinjin, at least, had been raised for leadership. He'd been trained to handle situations just like this. Durin had been trained to carry water buckets. When he was honest with himself, he admitted that Sinjin had carried his share of water buckets and that some of what he'd learned had rubbed off. Still, the thought of these people relying on him made his stomach hurt.

He'd been an outsider not so long ago, a pasty-faced Pinook among Arghast, but all that had changed. They relied on one another now. They had saved each other's lives, which created a bond stronger than any but blood. Their trust and reliance weighed on Durin. He was going to fail them. It was among the few things Durin had done with any regularity in his life. The greater the possible payoff for his efforts had been, the more colossal the disaster. Sinjin had set him up for the ultimate failure, and Durin couldn't help but resent him for it.

Most of the time, Durin didn't feel this way, but Sinjin was gone along with the rest of the Drakon and those aboard the *Serpent* and the *Dragon's Wing*. The unknown was driving Durin to distraction, and there was absolutely nothing he could do about it. Again, Durin kicked at the loose shells around him. Seabirds filled the air with their calls, and more shellfish dropped from the skies around Durin. He had learned long ago to wear headgear when visiting this place. His hat of woven reeds was far from attractive, but it did protect him from errant projectiles. The rocks around the tidal pool appeared to be the preferred place for seabirds to drop the otherwise inaccessible morsels. The air was filled with their raucous calls, and Durin thought it might be time to go; shellfish wasn't the only thing to fall from the sky during these feeding frenzies.

Holding on to his hat, Durin jogged up the trail leading back to Windhold. Even with the noise of the seabirds, cries from the hold could be heard as soon as he cleared the black dunes. Panic set in almost immediately. Something must be wrong. Running up the difficult and, in places, treacherous trail, Durin knew he was being reckless. Sinjin would have counseled him to go more slowly rather than risk injury, but the uncertainty was going to consume Durin if he didn't get some indication of what was going on soon.

In record time, he reached the base of the mountain housing Windhold. Durin had to take a moment to catch his breath. It was then he saw a sight that made his heart leap: dragons on the horizon. It didn't take long, though, to realize something was wrong. His breath freezing in his chest, Durin came to a chilling realization. The dragons were saddled but riderless.

Durin couldn't get back to the hold proper soon enough, and when he finally burst into the main flight hall, everyone was talking at once. Durin walked to the giant opening and let the wind scour him with sand and occasional hints of salt spray. He had often marveled at the persistent wind giving the hold its name, but on this day, he ignored it. His tears mixed with the wind, and Valterius called out to him, a mournful wail. That alone was enough to make his knees buckle, but he steeled himself. This was no time for weakness or fear, Durin finally realized. His people needed him, and now there might be something he could actually do. Though he had no idea what fate had befallen the Drakon, he would not rest until he found out.

Valterius, Gerhonda, and the other dragons entered Windhold in silence. The entire scene was surreal. What happened next put a lump in his throat. Gerhonda approached Marra, the woman who usually helped Kendra care for her, but rather than letting the woman remove the bridle and saddle, Gerhonda used her forehead to nudge Marra. Her eyes went wider and wider as Gerhonda guided her to the saddle. The scene repeated throughout the hold, and even so, Durin jumped when Valterius nudged him.

Feeling as if he were in a dream, Durin mounted Valterius. His knees trembled. Though he'd secretly wondered what it would feel like to have his own dragon, this was not how he had ever hoped or imagined it might happen. The other Dragon Clan appeared to share this feeling--most of them at least.

Strom and Osbourne had been struggling to find their place in Windhold, and both were stunned when dragons approached, especially since they were not dragon grooms. No one protested, though, and Osbourne climbed atop Atherian. The man had no experience with dragon saddles, and Durin was proud of Chelene when she strapped Osbourne in. He sensed no anger or resentment from her. Ever-practical Chelene simply did what needed doing.

Strom, on the other hand, had a much more difficult time. Initially he refused Grekka, but the regal dragon insisted. After some words Durin would never repeat, Strom mounted. As with Chelene, Tressa helped Strom, who sat with his eyes closed. Durin wasn't sure if he was praying or just frightened. Strom had sworn to avoid dragons ever since Kyrien had invaded his thoughts and coerced him into making Catrin's sword. Tressa gave him a firm nod, indicating Strom was securely strapped in.

"Today, my friends," Durin shouted out, "we must be Drakon if even only for a time. If you'll follow me, we'll either find a way to save our people or avenge them!"

Valterius roared his agreement, and the Drakon answered. Before Durin was quite ready, Valterius leaped into the air, followed by Gerhonda and the other dragons. Solemn and determined, the Drakon flew. Durin knew not what he would find or even if they would survive, but for once he knew what he did was right.

* * *

"We've got to get her out of here," Kendra said.

"I'm not sure we should move her," Sinjin said. His mother had been drifting in and out of consciousness. Her fragile state worried him.

"She just needs rest and time to adjust," Kendra said. "I'm certain of it. They took Trinda away."

This was perhaps the sole reason Sinjin considered doing as Kendra asked. Most of the guards had left when they had carried Trinda somewhere more comfortable. His mother had said Dragonhold was a prison, and if they were going to escape it, this might be their only chance.

Looking around for something from which they could make a litter for his mother, Sinjin spotted the wooden basin constructed to preserve the parchment found on the Drakon Ghar. Without hesitation, he moved toward it, driven by single-minded purpose. He was rudely blocked by a spear point jabbed in his belly. Though it did not pierce his flesh, it was painful and Sinjin appreciated it not a bit. Taking the spear in hand, just below the tip, he pulled it away and did not release it.

"I've done what you've asked of me up until this point," Sinjin said, "but if you don't get out of my way, we'll find out just how good you are in a fight."

There was a moment of tense silence before the Greatlander stepped back. Another guard stood nearby and tried to pretend he hadn't been watching or listening to the exchange. Without a single thought for the document, Sinjin knocked the ends of the framed basin free, which left two longer rails with waxed leather between them. It wasn't quite as long as he would've liked, but it was better than nothing. Within moments, they had Catrin loaded onto the litter and carried her back toward the great hall. Through the tunnels and past the kitchens, no one barred their path. Though this was not the shortest route to the great hall, it didn't require use of the barges.

A commotion up ahead forced them to stop. Sinjin and Chase lowered Catrin gently to the ground. Only when Halmsa rushed down the hall, his face lighting up when he saw them, did Sinjin breathe again. The Drakon had come looking for them, and there were now ample hands to carry his mother. Though he wanted to care for her himself, it was more important he figure out a way to get them out of Dragonhold.

"What's happening in the great hall?" Sinjin asked.

"The Drak have gone," Halmsa said, and the air left Sinjin. "Feral and verdant are still in the hall. And the *Dragon's Wing*."

"What?" Sinjin asked, dumbfounded. "They shouldn't be here!"

"Here they be," Halmsa said.

The problems they faced felt insurmountable, but a glance at Kendra and his mother, who barely stirred, overcame his fears. "We need to get my mother on the *Dragon's Wing* and get her out of here."

"But there is . . . something surrounding the hold," Halmsa said.

"You said the Drak escaped."

"They did," Halmsa said. "Just before the . . . uh . . . thing closed."

While he was happy Valterius and the others had escaped, Sinjin wondered if the rest would be imprisoned within Dragonhold for the rest of their days. Though he had far less access to Istra's powers than others, he could still acutely feel its absence. He had never realized how strongly he'd felt Istra's energy until it was gone. It was as if something critical were missing from the air. He could only imagine what it must feel like for his mother or Allette. He thought for just an instant about how Trinda must feel, but she had brought this upon herself and them. He would never forgive her for it. In the past he'd felt guilty for the way he'd treated her, but that was no more.

Benjin, Wendel, and Jensen emerged from the kitchens laden with supplies, and Sinjin couldn't help but smile at the sight. Kendra briefed their friends since she reached them first.

"What in all of Godsland is going on around here?" Benjin demanded. "And what are those giant stone claws?"

"The best we can figure," Kendra said, "that thing is the Fifth Magic, and it appears to be a prison. It cuts us off from Istra's light."

"Can anything go through it?" Benjin asked, but no one answered. Instead, they started making their way back to the great hall. There they found Onin of the old guard and Jehregard making their way to the main entrance.

Kenward came to Sinjin's side and was about to ask him a question when Benjin interrupted. "Kenward," he began, "I'm more sorry than you can possibly imagine."

Without even asking what, Kenward pushed past Benjin and into the great hall. The *Dragon's Wing* resting atop the *Serpent's* shattered remains. "I know you never liked the carving on the masthead," Kenward said in a pained voice, "but you didn't have to do that to her!"

The *Serpent* had taken significant damage before breaking the *Wing's* fall, but now the ship was unsalvageable. In preserving the *Dragon's Wing*, the *Serpent* might have saved them all, but they would need to figure out a way around the energy field surrounding the hold. Now that he was in the main hall, Sinjin could see the field through the still open and damaged gates. It shone bluish green. The plasma rippled and churned like fast-moving clouds. He could feel wringing energy from the air. It felt as if it would suck the life from him, leaving nothing behind but a dried husk.

Escape was starting to feel like an unreachable goal. Chase was searching for something they could throw at the energy barrier, looking everywhere but at the wreckage of the *Serpent*. A wise move. Kenward was already volatile, and there was no sense in antagonizing him, no matter how handy the wreckage might be at that moment.

"Look out!" Sevon cried a moment later, and he ran back from the main entrance. Given everything that had happened, he acted on Sevon's warning without hesitation. Sinjin couldn't help but look back. When he caught a glimpse of what the thief had seen, his legs stopped cooperating. A mature feral dragon bore down on the keep at incredible speed. The barrier would be first tested from outside.

Striking the plasma barrier jaws first, the feral bull was all aggression. A loud crackling and a blinding pulse of light reported the impact. The thunderclap was almost immediate and made Sinjin's head ring. The feral continued forward, wings extended, but the life was gone from its eyes. Slamming into the timbers framing the main entrance, it reduced one wooden gate to rubble and flying splinters. Sinjin supposed there wasn't much need for the gates any longer since it was now clear nothing living could get in or out of Dragonhold.

* * *

Catrin Volker woke in her chambers. A herald globe rested in the stand as it always had, though the light it gave was soft and dull. It would soon need to be charged. Sleep played tricks with Catrin's memories. She almost expected to see Prios walk in with trays of food from the kitchens. Her chest tightened as she prayed that very thing would happen, hoped against hope for all the terrible things to be naught but a dream. It was not to be so.

Looking around with fresher eyes, Catrin's belongings were just as they had been. This surprised her since she knew Trinda had sent Sinjin's belongings with him when she banned him from Dragonhold. This one small thing Catrin was thankful to Trinda for. Here there were ties to her old life, to a happier time when she and Prios and Sinjin had been a family.

When the door did open, it was Chase who entered with food. The sight

131

almost made Catrin cry for a multitude of reasons, but mostly she was happy to see Chase.

"Stay there," Chase said. "You need the rest."

Catrin sat on the edge of the bed despite his protests. She hated trying to eat while lying down.

"How are they doing?" Catrin asked.

Chase knew whom she meant. "Sinjin, Kendra, and the rest are uneasy and still trying to figure out what to do with themselves. Trinda's guards don't quite know what to do either, and so far they've given us run of the keep except for the halls where Trinda's quarters are. We haven't seen a single sign of her. I assume she has the good sense to rest."

Catrin snorted.

"Kenward and Brother Vaughn have been looking after Allette," Chase continued, not acknowledging the outburst. "No one's been killed yet, so it's going reasonably well."

"I need a way to get word to someone outside of Dragonhold," Catrin said.

Chase considered this for a moment. "Who?"

"Anyone who'll listen," Catrin said with a hint of desperation in her voice.

"What about the stone forest?" Chase asked. "When you're better rested, we can try to get you there and see if you can contact Jharmin or Ohmahold."

"Perhaps," Catrin said. "The keystones fell into disuse once everyone knew Trinda could hear every word."

"You just never know," Chase said. "They may have people posted to eavesdrop just as Trinda has. I suppose there's the chance it won't even work without Istra's light." His mood soured as he talked himself out of his own idea.

"I understand why Sinjin is here, since Trinda summoned the dragons, but why are Benjin and Kenward here?"

"Kenward came after Trinda offered to open trade with Windhold in exchange for the stone thrones from the *Slippery Eel*," Chase answered, but Catrin's smile brought the realization to him as well. "No. You need to rest. Absolutely not!"

Chapter 16

Fortune favors the reckless but abhors the unlucky.
--Mundin Barr, speculator

* * *

It took hours for Strom to open his eyes, but the man eventually relaxed, if only just a little.

"Grekka won't let anything happen to you," Durin had told him. He wasn't certain it helped.

Osbourne had quickly grown accustomed to flight adragonback. "This is so much better than an airship! You're an extension of the dragon."

The Dragon Clan shared his enthusiasm. Durin didn't say anything, knowing he and Strom would probably be more at home on the *Serpent* or the *Dragon's Wing*. Durin had often chided Sinjin about his lack of control over Valterius. It had been more than just a little inconvenient on numerous occasions, but now he knew just how Sinjin had felt: helpless. He tried talking to Valterius but had no way to know if the dragon understood him. He wasn't certain how the dragon would communicate back even if he did understand. It was frustrating beyond belief.

The dragons knew what had happened to his friends, but they could not or would not tell him. Choosing to believe the former was easier than venting impotent rage on Valterius. He was fortunate to have worked with his mount from the time he was a hatchling. They already trusted each other.

Strom and Osbourne were at a disadvantage, but Osbourne and Atherian were bonding. Grekka checked on Strom often, as if worried her passenger might have died. Strom refused to move for fear of causing them both to fall from the skies. It was an unreasonable fear since dragons were designed to fly and could easily compensate for his shifting weight. Deep-set fears were rarely subject to reason.

Early in their flight, Durin had searched Sinjin's saddlebags for any sign of what had happened to him and the others. He'd found nothing beyond salted fish and mealcakes. Neither had appealed to him at the time, but now the coarsely ground grains in the mealcakes were just sweet enough to offset the fish's saltiness. The others had also found basic rations, but it would not be enough to get them . . . The uncertainty was maddening. How could he plan when he had no idea where they were going or what they would find there?

When the Keys of Terhilian came into view, the Terhilian Lovers at least confirmed they were, indeed, flying toward the Godfist. That was until Valterius led the other dragons lower and landed on the beaches beneath the statues. The mighty table brought here for the Council of the Known Lands rested at an angle, partially submerged in sand and making for an unnerving sight. Half a dozen ornate chairs surrounded the table in disarray. Other chairs had been carried far down the beach by tidal waters. Everything about the sight was creepy and spoke of the perils they faced.

Nipping at the straps securing him, Valterius made it clear Durin was to dismount. It was his way of saying, "Get off or I'll remove you."

Dragons landed along the beach, their riders looking to Durin. After he unstrapped himself, the Drakon did the same, equally reluctant but given no more choice in the matter. Valterius nudged Durin toward a chair that was mostly submerged in the sand, and he leaped back into the air. The other dragons followed, and Durin was left to wonder what it was he was supposed to do.

"Firewood," Strom said.

Grateful for the big, practical man, Durin cursed himself for being so dense. Soon the chairs had been reduced to kindling, and Strom set to work using flint Osbourne had found in his saddlebags and shavings from a chair leg. Fishing would be difficult without wire or hooks.

Valterius proved himself once again when he plunged his claws into the waters off shore and landed a fish half as long as a man was tall. He had thought Valterius might be hunting for his own meal until the dragon came soaring back toward them. Durin took two steps back as the dragon approached, aiming straight for him. Valterius was a few paces away when he released the still fighting fish from his claws. The fish caught Durin full in the chest and drove him back into the sand.

As unpleasant and uncalled for as it was, at least he knew what he was supposed to do. "Let's get the best impromptu smokehouse we can set up and preserve as much of Valterius's gift as we can," he said.

Strom said the table would be perfect if they could manage to cut a couple pieces off. They had no tools capable of cutting the thick table. Grekka proved no tools were required. After dropping the fish she'd caught nicely at Strom's feet, she looked up to Durin. He did his best to make gestures indicating what they needed. Stepping up, the dragon looked the table over and sniffed. Then she clamped down her powerful jaws and snapped off a section large enough to lean against what was sunken in the sand and form a workable smokehouse. Before the dragon completely disassembled the table, Durin stepped in.

"We need more wood to burn," Strom said.

Walking down the beach, searching for more chairs or driftwood, they gathered what he could find. The dragons had begun to eat their catches, and Durin watched them as he searched. None of this could be happening to him, and he walked as if in a dream. With few more answers than when they had left Windhold, he moved back to where skilled hands deftly cleaned the fish brought back by the dragons. It wasn't nearly enough wood. Osbourne joined him in the search, and they looked for a place where they might be able to climb up to wooded areas of the island, but the cliffs here were similar in height and steep grade.

"I have to admit I never saw this coming," Durin said as they walked.

Osbourne smiled and patted him on the shoulder. "The world once made sense," Osbourne said wistfully, "but that was before the return of Istra changed everything."

* * *

After weeks of anticipation, the Godfist came into view, and a sick feeling came over Durin. Did he really want to know the Drakon's fate? he asked himself. Though he and his fellow Dragon Clan flew with the Drak, none considered themselves true Drakon. No matter what he said, they were but passengers upon dragons belonging to others. Belonging was not the right word, but he knew no suitable way to describe the relationship between dragon and rider. Grekka flew in close; Strom looked almost comfortable in the saddle but not quite. The desire to get out of the saddle and stretch his legs was almost unbearable. Yet they were probably safest right where he was. There had been breaks in their flight that had allowed for time swimming when islands and sand bars weren't an option. Even accompanied by the dragons, Durin had feared swimming in such deep waters. More than once he'd regretted squandering the chance to loosen his sore muscles.

"There was a time when I longed for my homeland," Strom said, "but now I dread it."

His words reminded Durin of his own feelings. Trinda controlled Dragonhold, at least as far as he knew, and he'd never been very nice to her. Putting himself back under her control was something he wanted to avoid at almost all cost. The Drakon were not an acceptable bargain, though, and he had to steel himself to the possibilities. He'd have answers soon, whether he liked them or not.

The upper Pinook Valley appeared to be completely deserted, and Durin was saddened by how short a time the settlements had survived. He didn't blame the people for retreating into Dragonhold rather than being exposed to enemy dragons. Still, it bothered him and left his homeland scarred and dead. The feeling persisted and when they reached the plateau, they found it bathed in unnatural blue light. Instants later, Dragonhold came into view. Had he not been strapped in, Durin might have fallen from the saddle. Gasps of dismay burst from those around him despite the well-known need for stealth.

"By the gods," Strom said, though he kept his voice low.

Rising from within the land like giant dragon claws, symmetrical stone leviathans engulfed Dragonhold in their embrace. Power, embodied in sheets of blue flame, reached between the claws. The air sang with energy, and everyone could feel it. It was like a sunburn but more intense and coming from something on Godsland. Were Sinjin and the rest of the Drakon in there? Had Trinda summoned them just to imprison them?

Valterius was keeping his distance from this domelike structure until a sudden change in direction sent them straight for it. Durin cried out, thinking Valterius would send them plunging into the blue fire and to their certain deaths. A blast of hot air then warmed his back, and he turned to see a feral dragon closing in on them and more coming. There was no time to shout a warning to the others; Durin was too busy holding on and ducking beneath feral claws.

Picking up speed, Valterius narrowly evaded the closest feral and changed direction again only once they were almost upon the fiery barrier. Then he sent them climbing the almost vertical face. The feral's mass kept it moving forward, and it slammed into the barrier, passing through. For an instant, Durin dared to hope the barrier was but an illusion, but then lightning struck the feral from multiple directions, and the already dead dragon slammed into the cliff face before sliding down, taking out an expansive section of the wooden stair and the fortifications around it.

Breathing hard, Durin leaned forward in the stirrups and connected with Valterius. The dragon provided subtle cues as to which direction he would turn next, giving him just enough time to anticipate it. This made evasive flying far less abusive on his body, and Durin would've shared the tip if he'd been able to speak. Ferals closed in from multiple directions, and "flitting" was the best way to describe Valterius's evasive maneuvers. He'd seen birds do it, but being on the back of a flitting dragon was like being stuffed in a barrel and rolled down a hill.

The other regals were also hard pressed. Behind them a dragons screamed; a regal and feral dragon locked in a deadly dance. Though smaller, the regal dragon, Vartika, managed to bite down on a critical wing joint, sending both dragons and Jerrel into a fatal dive. Durin couldn't watch. Valterius bellowed and the regals responded. The number of dragons roaring gave him heart, and he crouched over Valterius's neck.

"We can do this," he said. "Together, we can do this."

* * *

The flight from the Godfist was far less harrowing than it could have been, though the anguish of leaving loved ones behind weighed heavily on them all. The feral dragons had chased them out to sea but had then returned to guard Dragonhold. If the ferals were there, Allette was likely there as well. Given the choice, Durin would have to pick Trinda. She was completely unhinged, but at least she didn't have dragons. He wondered about that a moment. If Trinda had summoned all the dragons, did she have control over them? Only a fool would draw such dangerous creatures otherwise. Trinda was insane but she was not stupid. He must assume she had some control over the dragons, which put her a step ahead of almost everyone else. The Drakon had formed an alliance with the regal dragons, but who was actually in control of that relationship was a matter of some debate. Given the current circumstances, he knew which side of the argument he fell on. He would have chosen to circle back to the Arghast Desert and regroup, but Valterius no longer responded to anything he did. It was as if Durin had ceased to exist in the dragon's world, and it infuriated him. Those who flew alongside him were no more at ease with the lack of control they had over their future. Not for the first time, he pondered the motivations of dragons.

Endless waves passed beneath them with almost nothing to break the monotony. Occasional aquatic life or patches of seaweed were welcome sights since they were something other than ubiquitous waves. Their supplies had long since dwindled, and no one had even the faintest idea of where they were going. Strom, Osbourne, and Durin speculated about their destination, but the midday heat was better suited to silence. Sweat ran into Durin's eyes, and he wondered how much longer they would last. No land had been spotted since the Falcon Isles, and Durin feared the dragons would arrive at the Greatland with corpses on their backs.

The only sources of fresh water were clouds and rainstorms, but those had been scarce. It was as if someone had driven all the clouds away. Another reason they had stopped talking about their destination was that there was nothing they could do about it. They had no control over where they were going, no way to help Sinjin and the Drakon--if even they were alive--and no way to return to Windhold to assist those who remained. Had something on the horizon not attracted his attention, he might have screamed. There was something, though, and it grew more distinct by the moment.

"What is that?" Durin asked out loud, his throat dry and sore.

It took a moment for anyone to respond. Finally Strom said, "That's perhaps the least inviting place I've ever seen."

Jutting from deep water was a black stone tower--no windows, no gates, nothing to indicate the structure was habitable. Waves as tall as greatoaks slammed into one side of the tower, leaving huge swirling depressions in the seawater on the far side. Seabirds flocked around it were the only life to be seen.

Durin muttered the same phrase over and over as he squeezed his eyes shut and prayed. Fly right by . . . fly right by . . . fly right by . . .

The closer they came to the tower, the more ominous it appeared. Fear clawed at Durin. Having no control made the feeling far worse. He trusted Valterius, to a certain extent at least, and he didn't think the dragon would do anything to intentionally hurt him. At the same time, dragons were proving unfathomable and unreliable allies. No matter how wonderful the ability to fly, he wasn't certain he'd ever get back on a dragon once he found his way home. Engulfed within the tower's shadow, getting home was less and less likely.

"Why would the dragons bring us here--wherever here is?" Osbourne said into the oppressive silence. "They could have left us to die any number of places along the way. Flying out here to do it seems like a lot of effort."

The dragons appeared irritated by the discussion, but Durin didn't care. He was pretty unhappy with the dragons at that point. "Whatever it is they plan to do, I hope they just get on with it and do it."

With that, Valterius climbed steeply. The other dragons followed. Though he was strapped in, Durin held on with everything he had. It was self-preservation. If a single strap failed, his grip might be the only thing holding him in place. Their ascent began to slow, and Valterius pumped his mighty wings before alighting atop the mighty stone tower, which stood as a grim monument to some long-lost civilization. No one in their time possessed the knowledge required to build such a massive structure in deep water so far from any shore. Well, that wasn't entirely true, but it frightened him to admit some people currently alive possessed sufficient power to do such things. Still, this place exuded a sense of ancient foreboding. Atherian landed not far from Valterius. Grekka soon followed. The other dragons circled overhead. Durin waited to see what Strom and Osbourne would do.

Valterius blocked his view and nudged him with his maw. Durin had absolutely no intention of removing his straps. He was comfortable right where he was. The dragon disagreed and nudged him again. Seeing Strom unbuckling, he said, "Don't!"

"They flew us all the way out here," Strom said. "What else are we supposed to do? They must have brought us here for some reason."

"I don't care what their reason is," Durin said. "I'm not going in there. I'm not even convinced it's possible to get in there."

Strom might have said something more, but Valterius had Durin's full attention. Now biting at his straps, Al'Drak might destroy the saddle completely if Durin did not dismount. Then he would never get home. Uttering words he'd thought he'd never use, he started undoing the straps. Valterius watched with an unreadable expression, and he couldn't help but stick his tongue out at the dragon, who snorted in response.

All three had dismounted, dangerously close to the tower's edge in Durin's opinion. There wasn't so much as a railing to prevent a person from plunging into the depths so far below. Valterius nudged him again, except this time pushing him toward the other side of the tower.

"If this isn't for a very good reason," Durin said to Valterius, "I'll find you and haunt you."

The dragon had the courtesy to look the slightest bit abashed before leaping back into the skies and flying away.

* * *

Much of Sinjin's childhood had been spent playing on the meeting chamber floor. It had been some time since the room had seen any use. On this day, Catrin had called a conference, and Sinjin felt more than a little strange sitting at the table as a participant. He felt like a pretender. His mother appeared fragile and weak without her power, and Sinjin wondered if the Fifth Magic weren't slowly killing her. Allette arrived a moment later, guided by Kenward. Few had been willing to tend to Allette's needs, but Kenward felt sorry for the girl. Sinjin could almost understand where Kenward was coming from, but seeing them together just felt wrong, and he couldn't shake it.

Chase and Martik were also in attendance, along with Brother Vaughn, Wendel, Jensen, and Miss Mariss.

"I've not had the opportunity to speak with all of you individually. I apologize," Catrin said. Even her voice sounded thin and weak. "I know my disappearance was terribly difficult for all of you. I'm sorry about that. I cannot tell you everything, but know that I did what I had to do."

"You shone like Vestra when you arrived here," Allette said, surprising everyone. "And then you vented the excess energy. Why draw so much?"

The question caught everyone except Catrin off guard. "I no longer draw energy. I cannot keep the energy out." Allette covered her mouth in shock. "You have a barrier or a doorway you must open to access the power, correct?"

"Yes," Allette said, her suspicion poorly masked.

"My barrier is gone," Catrin said, and more than one pair of eyes bulged. "I have access to all the energy around me all the time whether I wish it or not."

"That is why I invited you here," Trinda said from the doorway, once again proving her talent for stealth.

Again, Catrin did not appear surprised. "While I appreciate your invitation, I had the situation quite in hand."

Trinda smiled a knowing smile. How much did she know, Sinjin wondered, and how long had she known it? She had access to information within Dragonhold no one else did, but he suspected it went further than that--a lot further.

"This place is a sanctuary for those who need refuge from the burden of

Istra's power," Trinda said.

"I wasn't seeking refuge," Allette said, her eyes never leaving Trinda. "You violated the peace we declared. We are at war."

"And that is why I invited you," Trinda said. "The world is a safer place with the two of you within Dragonhold."

"I don't remember being invited," Allette said, her voice smoldering.

Trinda gave a slight bow of her head. "In the best way I knew how."

Allette maintained her aggressive posture. "And what of you? Why lock yourself within your own prison?"

"I have made this sacrifice for the good of my people," Trinda said, her face a mask of innocence. "I have done what needed doing. Tell me, how else would the world ever have been rid of you?"

The anger building within Sinjin knew no rival. Trinda had drawn his mother and Allette here, imprisoned them, and now she was taunting them. Before he knew it, he was out of his chair and moving toward the child queen.

"No!" his mother shouted, but his momentum carried him forward, and his anger drove his hand to her throat. Trinda's guards reacted just a moment too late, and he had the girl's delicate neck in his hands. He could crush the life out of her if he wished, but even after all she'd done, he didn't wish it.

Lowering his lips to her ear, he whispered something only she heard and that she alone would understand. Then he let go. Trinda's guards immediately pushed him back, and one drew a fully charged herald globe from his pockets. Sinjin's opportunity had passed, and Trinda once again had the advantage.

"We're going to have to find a way to get along," Trinda said. "We're going to have a lot of time to spend with each other."

"Thanks to you," Allette said.

"You're safe now," Trinda said.

Those words flummoxed Allette, and she said no more.

"I'm sorry to have interrupted your meeting," Trinda continued. "I thought I might save you a bit of time. The Fifth Magic is irreversible. There's no sense planning your escape. None of us are leaving this place. Ever. You might as well get used to the idea. And while the people here once were loyal to some of you, they are no longer. Try to subvert them, and you might find my patience at its end."

No one had to ask what power Trinda had over those within the hold. She held the herald globes, powerful weapons when over-charged, and she also had the staff and Koe. Those, Sinjin realized, were now the only sources of power within the hold. Somehow, he would have to find a way to get them back for his mother. The staff appeared to have been locked in stone during the activation of the Fifth Magic, and he wasn't even certain it could be removed. The dragon ore stones themselves pulsated with light, promising a fiery death to any who tried removing the serpent's eyes.

"You may go anywhere in the hold unless my guards say otherwise. Consider yourselves my guests," Trinda continued with a wicked smile. "I'll leave you to plot your escape."

Chapter 17

To soar above the land is to see it in a way the landbound can never understand.
--Onin, master of the old guard

* * *

Sevellon the thief moved through Dragonhold with casual detachment, as if only there to see the sights. Most ignored him; he was, after all, short in stature, and he'd spent a lifetime learning ways to keep people from looking at him. Being a good thief required far more than stealth and physical dexterity, though those were certainly important. A good thief knew planning was the key to success. Understanding the people and the culture and all the details of daily life could dramatically reduce the chances of being caught. Since most thieves are caught only once, it was a matter of utmost importance. Sevellon had kept his head on his neck for this long, and he hoped the trend would continue.

Those who did watch Sevellon pass had been trained to see everyone and everything and retain pertinent details: soldiers and guards. Even the off-duty guards and retired soldiers were easy to spot. There was a hardness about them that could come from only the difficult work they did, not to mention the way they held themselves and the way their eyes moved. Most people failed to see much of what was around them, but thieves, guards, and soldiers knew details saved lives.

For Sevellon, the life saved was generally his own or perhaps his patrons', but the master thief had never before known the pride of using his skills to help people he truly cared for, people who had given him a second chance. Few things had been given to Sevellon in his life. Almost everything he possessed had been taken from someone else, which made any sort of kindness or generosity stand out.

Kenward Trell had given him a second chance.

Part of Sevellon wanted to distrust; it was the thief in him. Why would anyone be kind to someone as undesirable as he? he asked himself. Surely anyone looking out for his best interest did so for reasons of his own. The thoughts made him hesitate, but he continued, doing something he'd almost never done: believing in someone else.

When he passed the guard hall, filled with observant men and women, he did not rush past, as his initial impulse urged him to do. Instead, Sevellon slowed and peered into the hall. Many eyes turned to him, and he gave them a nod of acknowledgment. It was all that was needed to put these people at ease. He moved onward with a smile on his face.

The entrance to the kitchens was flanked by sweating guards who didn't even look at Sevellon when he entered. The place was the heart of the hold and was never silent or dormant. Those who toiled there tolerated the intense heat for the sake of the people they fed, but it was known to keep tempers at the ready. Miss Mariss stood nearby, and Sevellon approached a young woman he'd never met. She wordlessly handed him a platter of potato and onion hash with a slab of whitefish over it. The smell made Sevellon's stomach grumble. Under the pretense of finding a place to eat his food, the thief moved deeper into the hold.

As he approached the forge, a discordant ring was audible. Even the rhythm of the hammer blows was wrong. In Strom's absence, someone had had to assume the smith's duties, and it appeared the available talent was limited.

Silence was all that emerged from the now dormant glass smithy, but beyond lay what had once been a storeroom and was now the secondary entrance to the inner keep. Sevellon half expected to be stopped there, but the guards posted simply made certain he stayed away from the supplies still stored there as well as the glowing runes recessed into the floor. Sevellon knew the purpose of some of those runes. Keeping them guarded was wise.

These guards looked at him differently than those flanking the kitchens. These men watched over something dangerous and powerful, and it showed on their faces and in their eyes, whereas the kitchen guards were posted more to maintain order and to prevent anyone from demanding more than their share of food.

Detecting these differences was the entire purpose of this stroll through the halls. Sevellon did not need to sneak through the hold to discover where the things of real value were being kept; all he had to do was walk past the places where guards were posted and read their faces.

His food was growing cold, and the thief soon found an open space where he could eat his meal and not be in anyone's way. Benches and other alcoves were spread throughout Dragonhold, and Sevellon seated himself at a nearby bench. Passersby paid him no mind. He listened to their conversations as they walked, trying as he always did to piece together many small clues to get a better overall picture of the situation in general.

The main thing Sevellon sensed from the people of Dragonhold was fear, followed closely by uncertainty. No one understood the exact nature of the barrier erected around the hold, and most of what Sevellon heard was speculation. Some conversations were far more telling than others. Despite all their training and experience, guards and soldiers were still people, and this day proved they didn't always know when to keep their mouths shut.

Eating slowly so as not to run out of food and be seen as eavesdropping, Sevellon blew on the already cold potatoes.

"Need to double up on the guard around the entrances to the queen's chambers, as well as those leading to the control room. Also, if you see anyone going to the stone forest, let them go but report back to me immediately. Is that clear?"

Keeping his eyes down and now playing with his food, which was almost gone, Sevellon did his best to become invisible. In this regard, he was ill prepared. When the captain of the guards finished speaking, he turned to leave, and that was when his eyes landed on Sevellon. Concern flashed across the man's visage, and the thief knew he was in trouble. Meeting the captain's eyes, he gave a respectful nod. For a brief moment, Sevellon thought the man might arrest or interrogate him, but then he returned Sevellon's nod and walked toward the kitchens. Knowing how men like the good captain tended to think, Sevellon did what he could to eliminate any remaining suspicion. Getting up, he followed the captain back to the kitchens to return his platter.

* * *

Kenward's snores filled the very hall where Catrin had once found Imeteri's fish. Not far from Catrin's quarters, these accommodations had been available and made sense on every level. Still, Sevellon hated them, no matter how much Kenward spoke about history. The place reminded him of a prison cell, something he'd spent his entire life trying to avoid. The time or two he'd spent in a cell had been brief and not for stealing. Sevellon did his best to shake off the feeling and decided not to count his many failings. On this night, he needed to focus on his strengths. A certain sense of invincibility was required to pull off something this dangerous.

Doubts threatened his confidence even as he removed painted clothes from beneath his cot. At least this room had given him a place to hide the things he'd been gathering to make this possible.

Memories also plagued him. Not so long ago, he'd been happy. With the wind in his face and nothing but clear skies around him. Flying aboard the *Serpent* had been the most enjoyable time of his entire life. Though he'd been under Trinda's employ, he belonged on Kenward's crew. They were a rare breed. Never before had Sevellon known others possessing bravery and audacity to match his own. They made him proud.

Up until this point in his life, finding a way out of the back alleys he'd grown up in had been among his greatest accomplishments. What he was about to attempt was perhaps the most daring act yet. If he did fail, he would know he'd never let fear stand in the way of helping those for whom he cared.

In a way, he also knew he'd be forcing their hands. Trinda had made it comfortable for them here, and the motivation to find a way out was far less urgent than Sevellon desired. Perhaps another man would have let others decide his fate or might even have enlisted help, but what Sevellon did best, he did alone. Still Kenward's snores echoed in the hall. Sevellon was thankful for them as they covered any sounds he made changing in to clothes he'd painted to match the mottled surface of the keep's inner walls. He wore no shoes and instead painted his feet and face and hands. A cloth covered his hair and the back of his neck, and he tied knots at the bottom of his pant legs to make them tight and to keep them from moving.

The halls were dark, but night vision was among Sevellon's strengths. The child queen had hidden the herald globes she horded, save on occasions when having them visible suited her needs. Sevellon had a good idea where they might be, but herald globes were not what he sought. Their absence from the halls aided him greatly. Since the keep was now reliant on torches and oil lamps for light, most were extinguished during the night, leaving occasional pools of light to expose him. It was not the initial part of this journey he feared, though even discovery by his allies would take some explaining.

Nearing the great hall, Sevellon slowed. A single shadow crossed the torchlight surrounding the entrance to the hall. The guard remained almost perfectly still, and Sevellon suspected he was sleeping, but patience was among his most trusty tools. He waited and watched. After a hundred breaths counted, Sevellon crept closer. He moved noiselessly, but it was probably unnecessary at that particular moment, since Jehregard's snoring drowned out all other sound. The dragons were on Sevellon's side. Each one taxed the hold's supplies. Feeding them had been among the greatest challenges. No one knew how long the creatures could survive without food, which created a great sense of urgency.

Kyrien had not helped his case when he disappeared into the God's Eye since he could presumably survive off the fish the mighty underground lake had been stocked with. There was some debate as to where Catrin's dragon had gone. His disappearance caused anxiety among his companions, but Catrin appeared unconcerned. And Sevellon, too, could tell exactly where the dragon had gone from scratches on the stone walls of the hall leading to the God's Eye.

Slipping past the sleeping guard, Sevellon looked over to where Onin slept. His tierre rested on the stone floor, and Onin's feet could be seen sticking out the sides. Somewhere in the hall was the feral queen, but Sevellon tried not to think about that. Moving perhaps more swiftly than was wise, the thief made his way toward the hall leading to the kitchens. This route was dangerous--well lit in some places and in use during all hours of the day. Sevellon had considered taking the longer, less-used route through the God's Eye, but there would be no hiding his passage on the barges, and the thought of swimming in that lake terrified him. Kyrien might mistake him for a fish. Few things in this world truly frightened

Sevellon, but dragons did the job. He'd have conquered his fear had it been practical, but getting wet would only have ruined his camouflage.

Using his mental image of the halls and all the places he'd seen where he might hide if the need arose, Sevellon moved with haste. Just before reaching the kitchens, his pulse quickened. Ducking into an alcove, the thief avoided a passing patrol. In the darkness behind the towering statue filling most of the alcove, Sevellon's bare feet were warmed and illuminated by the glowing rune beneath them. More than just a little disturbed, the master thief darted into the hall the instant the patrol moved beyond his immediate area. They could have looked back and seen him, but it was a risk worth taking. The sooner he moved, the less likely he'd encounter the next patrol. The smithies were silent, and Sevellon moved with ease. The supply room, however, boasted two guards.

These men were neither sleeping nor inattentive. Sevellon suspected this was a short-watch duty station, where the guards were rotated every few hours, keeping fresh eyes on the runes and the passersby at all times. No matter what Trinda would have them think, she was tracking their every movement. Sevellon smiled--almost every movement.

Retrieving a pebble from his robe, Sevellon threw it to the far side of the storeroom, not far from the runes. It made a small tick when it struck stone. Both guards looked in that direction. It was enough to get Sevellon into the room. This was the part of being a thief most couldn't stomach. Hiding in plain sight, he relied on the frailties of human perception. The brain sees what it wants to see, an illusionist once told him. Those words had changed his life.

A lesser thief would have lost his nerve and bolted, but Sevellon stood not two paces from an alert guard. He slowed his breathing and employed his practiced skill of remaining almost perfectly still. Time passed sluggishly. Sevellon started to wonder if he'd been wrong about the short watches, but it must have been his impatience skewing the flow of time. Everything, he reminded himself, was a matter of perception and perspective.

By the time a pair of young men came to relieve the current guards, Sevellon himself was having trouble keeping from falling asleep. The sight of the fresh guards brought him to immediate attention, and he did what he could to clear the fog from his mind. The man standing next to Sevellon saw the guards an instant after Sevellon did, and he stepped out to meet them.

"It's about time," he said.

"The queen has us working in that special project," one of the approaching men said. "Orders are to stand double watches."

"It would've been nice if someone told us," the guard still standing across from Sevellon said. He was staring directly at the thief, yet he did not see. Sevellon, not for the first or even the hundredth time, thanked The

Amazing Kells for teaching him. Even knowing, Sevellon nearly bolted. The guard held a spear as tall as he was and would have no problem skewering the thief were he to realize what he was looking at.

After a painfully long wait, the second guard, too, abandoned his post. For the briefest instant, the newcomer's view of the room was blocked by the guards leaving, which was all the time Sevellon needed. The lights had ruined his night vision, though, and he stubbed his toe on a protruding crate. Biting his lip, he moved to the next hiding place he'd previously scouted.

"Did you hear something?" one of the new guards asked, and Sevellon hurried, hoping no one noticed the trail of blood coming from his lacerated toe.

Human nature once again played to his advantage. "I didn't hear anything," the other guard said.

"Must've just been mice," the first said. "We need to bring a couple cats up from the meadow, so they can catch 'em."

Sevellon heard no more from the two and did his best to staunch the bleeding. He was in trouble, and he knew it. Already he was behind schedule and had almost been caught. The most dangerous part of this journey was yet to come. The ability to overcome such fears was what had made him such a good thief, and Sevellon moved down back halls and disused corridors. There were more of these than well-used corridors in this part of the keep. Dragonhold could hold many times more people than it currently did. They still hadn't figured out quite how to grow enough food within the keep to feed so many.

Using everything he could to his favor, Sevellon made up some time on his way to one of the most heavily guarded places in the hold, second only to the control room. When he reached the junction just before the hall leading to Trinda's chambers, Sevellon listened--silence.

Slowly he crept around the corner, and he could see the shadows of two guards dancing across the stone in the torchlight. A wispy drapery filled the doorway to the queen's chambers, and the torches burned low, casting small pools of light. These guards were nowhere near as alert as those who guarded the entrance to the inner hold. Again human nature. Those within the inner hold assumed the more closely guarded tunnels leading in meant they stood guard for appearances only. Guards who think they are in no danger tended to look more like these two young men.

Despite their inattentiveness, neither was fully asleep, which was less than convenient. But Sevellon had come up with a solution long before getting to this point. Keep it simple, he reminded himself, and take advantage of human nature. He drew a second pebble from his pants pocket, and he tossed it down the hall, past the guards. Both men heard it and looked. Sevellon moved as quickly as he could, the narrow halls now an advantage. With his hands pressed against one wall and his feet against the opposite wall, he suspended himself in the darkness above the guards. His arms and legs trembled by the time they had lapsed back into a collective stupor. Only one stirred when Sevellon grabbed the ledge above the doorway, swung himself down, and slipped inside the child queen's personal apartments. After landing silently, the curtain moving in his wake, Sevellon crouched down beside a footstool. The guard peered inside with no alarm on his face. Seeing nothing out of place, he looked back out at the empty hall.

Having been unable to get this far in his scouting mission, Sevellon was now in unfamiliar territory, and he hoped he knew what he was doing.

* * *

Nightfall atop the black spike was perhaps the most frightening thing Durin had ever experienced. He thanked the gods Strom and Osbourne were with him, or he might have gone insane. The place was creepy during the daytime, but at night it was terrifying. Heavy cloud cover left them in near complete darkness, and he was afraid to move for fear of falling over the edge, despite knowing they had moved to the center of the structure before the darkness enveloped them.

There was nothing here but black rock and salt water. Again, he asked himself why the dragons would leave them there if not for some purpose. Strom and Osbourne had walked the edges, searching for signs of an entrance but found none. When Osbourne had lain down on his belly and slid himself over each side, Strom holding his ankles, Durin had retreated farther from the edge. The mood worsened after the search came up empty.

Knowing it could be his stimulated imagination, Durin thought he could feel the presence of others around him. Strom and Osbourne had gone silent, and he presumed they were sleeping, yet the wind whispered to him. Even more disturbing were the conflicting messages he was getting. Some communications invited him inside, yet another presence just as emphatically wanted him to leave. At times the wind felt as if it were a hand pushing on his face and body, trying to push him over the edge and to his death.

Another more comforting presence joined him then, and visions of saltbark trees standing in calm, blue waters gave him solace. He could hear waves crashing in the distance, and the song of seabirds was like the music of nature. Somewhere in this idyllic setting, sleep found Durin, and his own imagination took over. Soon he was soaring above the trees, as light as air.

Chapter 18

Beware the vanquished, for they smolder like banked coals.
--Archmaster Belegra

* * *

Though he'd prepared most of his life for protecting Catrin, Chase had thought the need passed and it was, in fact, beyond his meager abilities. Now, though, Cat was here, in the hold, and without her power. Trinda had done a masterful job of taking Dragonhold and adding people loyal to her rather than to Catrin and Chase. There were many within the hold still loyal to them, but they were no longer the majority, and there were a great many armed guards supporting Trinda. The child queen was without her power also, but she retained the herald globes. How ironic, Chase thought, the very thing Catrin had worked so hard to create as a tool for peace was now being used as a weapon against her. Allette knew better than anyone the lethal impact of his cousin's invention. Though Catrin had created the globes as precious light sources in her underground fortress, it had been Trinda who discovered the ability to flood them with energy and use them as weapons. Most of Allette's forces had fallen to the herald globes during the Jaga War.

Remaining in the outer hold had been Chase's idea, and Catrin hadn't argued. Trinda's grip was firmer deeper in the hold, and there were tactical reasons as well. An awful feeling had been growing in his gut. Things were bad but he knew they could be much worse. People loyal to Catrin gathered in the outer halls. Chase did what he could to conceal what was happening, but he knew it must be painfully obvious to those loyal to Trinda. Whatever he planned, he must keep in mind what she might be planning as well.

What helped Chase the most at the moment, though, was having someone friendly in the God's Eye. Bradley had always been among better soldiers. He'd done any number of undesirable things in the name of service to his people. Chase trusted him. Being in charge of the barges in the God's Eye might not be the most glamorous position, but from a strategic standpoint, it was perfect. Though he'd had no particular destination, Chase found himself walking toward the God's Eye. When he arrived at the nearly still waters, he stayed back. There had been reports of demon attacks along the shoreline and on the barges. Fewer reports had come in the past few days, but Chase was given to caution. His home had become a very dangerous place. It had happened to him before. Old fears and anxieties rose within him, unbidden and unwilling to be suppressed, try as he might.

With only two people aboard, a barge approached. One was tall and the other was shorter. Traffic on the God's Eye was minimal, partly due to worries over the demons, but also because there were no goods or trade coming from outside the hold. Somehow Nat Dersinger and Catrin had foreseen this. It was something that pained Chase deeply to admit. Fundamentally he'd been proven wrong. It shook the foundation of his beliefs and left him feeling far less certain of himself than he'd once been.

The torches on the approaching barge cast wavering shadows, and the vessel was nearly to shore before Chase recognized the two men aboard. Simms poled the barge to shore with a sour look on his face. It was clear he didn't want to be there and resented anyone who asked him to venture out into the dark waters. In this case Chase couldn't blame him. With every trip, he risked his life, but that was the role of a soldier. Chase sighed. Not all people could share his philosophy. He reminded himself he could not expect the same level of commitment he had to this cause from anyone else. Doing so just about guaranteed disappointment. This was one of the things Trinda had done masterfully. She'd left much as it had been and gradually changed things that were insignificant in and of themselves. But when all the subtle changes to the power structure added up, the girl had effectively divided the hold, which would make revolution far more difficult to achieve and a much bloodier proposition. Chase didn't even want to think about civil war within Dragonhold.

The other person on the barge was Sevellon the thief. Chase felt the smallest bit bad for the fellow, whose identity Trinda had revealed. It must be difficult to be a thief when everyone knows your profession. Perhaps the man would take this as an opportunity to find some other way to apply his skills. The barge touched stone, and no one spoke. Sevellon stepped off the barge, and Chase noticed he was barefoot. His feet were filthy; they almost looked like . . . Chase swallowed hard and hoped his gut was wrong.

Meeting Simms's eyes, Chase was not surprised when he turned away and pushed back off without saying a word. Sevellon smiled at Chase and tried to appear unconcerned by his presence. Chase wasn't so easily fooled. The thief had it tough now, indeed. "What happened to you?" Chase asked, pointing to the crude bandage on his foot.

"I stubbed my toe," the thief said.

"And where are you going now?" Chase asked, his years as chief of the guards asserting itself.

"I need to speak with the Herald."

Chase hadn't been expecting that, and the statement raised his anxiety levels dramatically. "What have you done?"

"I did the only thing I could do to help," Sevellon said. "I need to see the Herald. Now."

Chase escorted the thief to the viewing chamber where he knew Allette and Catrin were talking. It was a meeting they were not supposed to disturb, but something told him this would not wait, which was also the reason he'd decided to let Catrin interrogate the man rather than doing it himself.

"Life has been unkind to you," Catrin was saying to Allette when Chase entered. She cast him a glance, conveying a sharp reprimand.

He nodded, accepted it, and remained as he was.

"What is it?" Catrin asked, her anger turning to exasperation. She knew Chase would not interrupt such a crucial meeting without a good reason.

"I need to speak with you a moment," Chase said.

"You may speak freely," Catrin said. "I have no secrets from my allies."

Allette appeared as uncomfortable with that term as Chase was, but he knew his cousin. There would be no changing her mind now. Casting a glance at Sevellon, he gestured with his head for the man to enter. No matter how he felt about thieves, he would not repeat what Trinda had done.

Sevellon entered the room and knelt before Catrin. "Lady Catrin, I bring you a gift. With this I also give my support to your cause." With those words, Sevellon handed Catrin a small bundle.

Chase was just starting to think the man had a good sense of self-preservation until he saw what it was he presented to Catrin. Her breath caught before she even opened it, and Allette could not take her eyes from the bundle. Coarse cloth fell away in folds and Koe was revealed, all glossy and slick as if he'd been thoroughly soaked in Istra's light. Now it was Chase who lost his breath. This was perhaps the most precious gift anyone could have given Catrin, but it might also hasten the onset of the very war Chase feared. He didn't know how much energy the dragon ore carving held. It would not be enough to destroy the Fifth Magic.

Allette was the first to speak. "It's so beautiful," she said. "May I touch it?"

The conflict on Catrin's face was brief, but then she said, "It contains a store of Istra's power. You may touch it, but I would ask you not to draw from it. I fear it will be precious little given what we're about to face. Sevellon has given us a powerful gift, but it comes at a great price." Sevellon looked as if he wanted to disappear. "What's done is done. The best we can do now is prepare for Trinda's response, which will likely be swift and lethal."

"There is one other thing, Lady Catrin," Sevellon said, pulling a torch from a nearby crevice. "Please come." Catrin did not appear entirely pleased, but she allowed Sevellon to lead her back into the hall. Allette followed closely, and Chase brought up the rear, on the alert for any signs of trouble. Already the hairs on his neck stood, and he knew it was coming. Dragonhold currently felt the same way the giant mountain in the shallows had felt right before it exploded. "A wise man once taught me to observe everything in my surroundings," Sevellon said after stopping at a nondescript section of hall. "That includes looking up."

The ceiling was high above them, but with the torch lofted, there was something there. It wasn't much, just a small hole in the otherwise ubiquitous stone. Sevellon handed the torch to Chase, and he held it higher. The additional light brought out previously hidden details. Chase knew what he saw: a tunnel-collapse mechanism. Sevellon had found part of the keep's ancient defenses. The only problem was they didn't have the specially designed release rods needed to safely trigger the cave-in. This shortcoming was apparent to everyone and the futility of the situation clear when rows of guards entered the hallway from the great hall. This was they had seen of such military movements within the hold. Trinda knew she'd been robbed.

Shouts from the God's Eye gave evidence of attacks from two sides, and Catrin stepped back from under the collapse mechanism. "Get back," she said in a dangerous voice. Sevellon obeyed her command, but Chase and Allette remained. "Go!" she demanded and even Chase feared her in that instant. Fire danced in her eyes.

Kenward had come up behind them, and he took Allette by the arm. To Chase's surprise, she let him lead her back to the viewing chamber. Walking sideways, Chase retreated. Worry for Catrin was foremost on his mind; his own safety and that of the rest, not far behind. The guards were nearing the cave-in mechanism, and Chase muttered under his breath, "If you're going to do something, you'd better go ahead and do it."

Catrin may or may not have heard, but it appeared she agreed. Holding up Koe, she pointed him at the release mechanism. Tinged with fire and lightning, a blackness leaped from the cat's open jaws like a bolt of night. Roaring like an angry dragon, the intentionally weakened stone shuddered and cracked upon impact. While it had appeared to be solid and permanent as the surrounding stone, the ancients had done their jobs well. Despite being triggered in far from the expected manner, the defense mechanism did what it had been designed to do. Before approaching guards' eyes, the ceiling collapsed, blocking the hall with granite chunks larger than yearling horses. Like the ancient barriers originally barring their entrance into the hold, this obstruction was considerable but could be removed in time. The sand clock had been turned, and Chase knew the last grain would eventually slip away.

Retreating from the dust and debris accompanying the cave-in, Catrin came with a grim expression. This was not at all how either of them had expected this day to go. When she shifted Koe in her hand, Chase saw chalky swirls left in the cat where Catrin's fingertips had been. That single burst of energy had already visibly drained the stone, and Chase's confidence waned. There would be no way to recharge the cat once it was drained, Chase knew, and if it could be drained so quickly, then it would soon cease to be useful. He would have to trust his cousin to be judicious in its use.

"Arm yourselves and gather 'round!" Chase shouted as they neared the halls where most of their people waited. Afterward, he looked back to Catrin. She had stopped walking, her eyes glazed and distant.

"The God's Eye is well defended," Catrin said. "Post guards but Kyrien says he'll keep any real danger from getting too close." Again she shifted Koe, and the cat's back was now cloudy.

"Now what do we do?" Chase asked no one in particular. Catrin shrugged. Both turned their eyes on Sevellon, who had the good sense to keep his eyes down.

Under the weight of their gazes, he said, "I just wanted to help."

* * *

Along the shoreline of the God's Eye, Catrin and Allette stood, unworried over demon attacks since Kyrien had briefly shown himself before disappearing in deep, dark water. The barge carrying Trinda approached slowly. Only the child queen and a single guard were aboard. Chase knew it was possible to conceal more soldiers under and around the barge since he'd trained his soldiers in the tactics, but Kyrien's presence made that less worrisome. The two overcharged herald globes Trinda carried, whose light was nearly blinding, were far more worrisome. Even as an effort of last hope, two herald globes could produce a devastating attack.

No one on shore spoke as the barge glided to a stop before them. Chase wasn't certain what he'd been expecting, but it certainly hadn't been seeing tears dripping from Trinda's chin. Never had he seen such a mournful look on her face, and his emotions churned.

"My sisters," Trinda began, her voice quavering. "I come in search of forgiveness. I have wronged us all in my ignorance, and I am sorry. I've also come because I need your help."

Her words were met with silence. Trinda possessed a knack for being unreadable and impossible to predict. Chase couldn't imagine a more terrifying thing than someone as flighty as Trinda with the powers she possessed. Perhaps from that aspect, what Trinda had done had been a good thing. If only she hadn't trapped the rest of them in Dragonhold with her. She claimed to have acted in Catrin's and Allette's best interests by protecting them from the ever-growing amounts of Istra's power flooding their world. What other escape could there be? Chase had wondered more than once. Catrin refused to talk about what had happened to her after her disappearance, and Chase was left to speculate. It was a cruel thing to do to a person, and he really didn't appreciate it, even if he knew she had her reasons. Sometimes being angry at Catrin was a never-ending effort. Add Trinda to the recipe, and Chase thought he might scream.

"What is it you've done this time, sister?" Allette asked.

Trinda bowed her head, accepting the reprimand. "I've made a terrible mistake." This admission was met with silence charged with resentment. "I learned long ago of the Fifth Magic. I was told it was a sanctuary shielded from Istra's power."

Thus far, Chase felt her argument was plausible, but he feared whatever this mistake was. To have reduced Trinda to what were to Chase convincing tears and emotion, his fears conjured terrible visions.

"You've said as much," Allette interjected.

Catrin remained silent and Chase marveled at her control. Somehow saying nothing delivered a more scathing reproach than any words could convey.

"After the Fifth Magic was triggered, I knew something was wrong. It felt as if I was being sapped of life."

"It's an unpleasant sensation, isn't it?" Allette remarked.

Catrin's gaze was unyielding and was starting to intimidate Chase as well. She projected the energy of an angry mother so strongly, everyone present was cowed, with the notable exception of Allette, who looked ready to pull Trinda's head from her neck.

"I retreated to the archives and scoured the oldest sections with my most trusted assistants. This is what I found." In her hand was little more than a roll of aged vellum. The image it bore was faded and stained but contained an unmistakable signature Chase had seen before on equally ancient documents. Most concerned abominations such as the Statues of Terhilian and dark tomes of compulsion and greed. This image was different than the others, though. It showed Dragonhold as it was now, the stone claws enclosing the keep, though the drawing looked far simpler and cleaner than the real thing. On the vellum, trees grew around the energy field, and Chase had seen the devastation around the keep, even if tinted by translucent blue flame.

What lay beneath was the last thing to draw Chase's eye. Seeing it first, Catrin drew a sharp breath, and Chase rushed to understand. There, at the bottom of the vellum, partly obscured by dark stains, were words Chase could mostly translate and understand, having studied alongside Catrin for years.

Here waits my final revenge on those who embrace Istra's abominable light.

Just below was the signature of Von of the Elsics, a madman if ever there was one. The name made Chase's blood run cold. Already thousands had died as a result of Von's weapons, and knowing he designed this keep to target those with Istra's power drove Chase to his knees. It occurred to him then that Koe might contain the only usable energy in the entire hold, save the explosive force of the herald globes. The energy Catrin had expended in collapsing the hall and communicating with Kyrien had essentially been wasted. When he considered how much work it was going to take to clear the obstructed hall, Chase wanted to slam his head against the cold stone.

"I bring these as gifts and tokens of my sincerity," Trinda said, handing Catrin and Allette each one of the herald globes. You now have the power to kill me if you so choose."

Allette appeared to be giving this option serious consideration. Chase was ready to run. He'd seen what overcharged globes did on impact, and he wanted to be well clear of the area if one was going to go off. He was no coward. A wise person knows when they are overmatched.

Again tense silence hung in the air, and no one knew what to do next. Chase feared Allette would kill Trinda out of frustration if nothing else, but all of them turned and looked as ripples of water moved toward them, growing larger by the instant. Glistening in the light of the herald globes, Kyrien raised his head and nudged Catrin. In doing so, he also nudged Allette, who laughed. It was the first sign of happiness Chase had ever seen from the girl.

Catrin, though, closed her eyes and laid her hands on Kyrien, communing with him. When she pulled her hands away, there were tears in her eyes. With a firm nod she said, "I know what must be done, and I like it not."

* * *

Chase didn't like any of what was happening. Events moved too fast, and so much was based on the word of the least reliable person he knew. If not for the communication from Kyrien, Chase would have demanded they stop. He didn't completely trust the regent dragon either, but Catrin did, and he would have to accept that. Looking forlorn, Trinda gave the strong impression of a child made to wait her turn to play with a toy. Allette refused to leave Catrin's side and occupied the other stone chair. Finally, the viewing chamber was ready for what they believed to be proper use. Brother Vaughn and Chase had trained groups on the chant, and there was melodious power in the vibrations, even just as a bystander. Watching from the corner of the room and feeling sick, Chase prayed to any god who'd listen to keep anything from going wrong. No one knew if astral travel was possible from within the hold, and none could say if Catrin would even survive. Allette was bound to the same fate since she insisted on doing as Catrin did.

There was no guarantee Koe contained enough energy for her to complete the journey, and Catrin had tried to dissuade her. If anything complicated her travels, as had happened in the past, she might not make it back at all. Allette was beyond reasoning, though, and only when it looked as if she might throw down her herald globe in frustration had Catrin relented. What had Trinda been thinking giving the Black Queen a herald globe? Then he had to admit knowing what Trinda thought about anything was among his life's greatest mysteries.

There was no sound or anything other than the distant look in Catrin's eyes to indicate she was gone, and Chase's guts twisted. Allette, on the other hand, was frantic. She, too, knew Catrin was gone, but it was clear she'd been unable to follow.

"Catrin once told me that hitting her head on the rock while staring out into the sky was how she first learned to astral travel," Chase said, unsure why he felt compelled to offer this advice. In the next instant, he wished he'd been a bit more specific.

With desperation on her face, Allette gazed out the portal and slammed her head back against the stone chair--hard. Chase wasn't certain if she'd successfully left her body or knocked herself unconscious.

Chapter 19

Few things match the power of imagination.
--Enly Mandone, bard

* * *

Twin beams of consciousness burst from the viewing chamber in tandem, almost immediately piercing the blue fire encasing Dragonhold. There was no perceivable effect. Catrin soared free, her spirit rejoicing. Behind her extended gossamer thread leading back to her physical vessel, and she suspected a smile was forming on her now distant body. Mother Gwendolin had introduced her to astral travel long ago, even if somewhat accidentally. Catrin took a moment to thank her. Brother Vaughn had been instrumental in determining what kind of stone the chairs needed to be made of and where they could be sourced. Kenward had sacrificed two ships to transport these very stone chairs, and she would make certain it counted for something.

Without her body, Catrin could not feel the sun or the wind, nor could she feel Istra's energy. Her only source was Koe, and she had to be mindful of the limited supply. She didn't know what would happen if they depleted the energy Koe held before they returned to their bodies, and she had no desire to find out. Another thing that worried her was the possibility of draining Koe to the point of destroying her precious carving, just as she had destroyed Imeteri's fish so long ago. She had no way to know how much energy she was drawing or how much remained, thus all she could do was attempt to achieve what she must as quickly as possible.

Had Allette remained in her body within Dragonhold, it would have been better, Catrin thought, but she sensed the Black Queen's presence gaining on her. Consciously Catrin slowed to allow the girl to catch up. Catrin had no inkling how much energy Allette was drawing from Koe, but the thread leading back to her body burned brightly.

We must conserve.

Communicating with Allette in the way Prios had once done for her, Catrin experienced physical pain at the thought of her beloved. That pain was foremost in her mind when the chanting within Dragonhold found a new level of synchronicity unlike anything Catrin had experienced before. Always before, the two disparate melodies had merged into one, but never before had Catrin realized her spirit was bound to one side of the melody; Allette's spirit was bound to the other. Even when Pelivor had once traveled at the same time as her, he'd been trying to save her and they had never achieved synchronicity. Now, with Allette, it was unavoidable. Even the energy beams trailing behind them were now intertwined, braided and

157

indistinguishable from each other.

Somehow the losses they had taken bonded them and brought them closer. Allette's pain was Catrin's pain. It suffocated her. Every moment that was seared into the Black Queen's psyche permeated Catrin's and overlayed her own experiences; she remembered being present and had memories of all the senses. Smells in particular triggered intense memory and emotion.

You were so afraid. Allette's disembodied words rang in Catrin's consciousness. You are so powerful, and yet you are so afraid.

Guilt washed over Catrin at hearing the words because they were true. Never would she have believed Trinda could trap her within Dragonhold. She'd been so foolish as to think she was going to scold the child queen for summoning Kyrien. If only she'd known, she would have done things differently. Now she had left the most dangerous things unguarded. She tried not to think about that since she knew Allette must be experiencing her memories as well. Both must have had the realization simultaneously, which wasn't by circumstance. Whatever one wanted to hide was foremost in the other's mind. The very act of trying to conceal something exposed it.

And now they knew they had to kill each other. They now knew the other's most closely guarded secrets, things far too dangerous for anyone else to know. Any sane person would want to distance her thoughts from someone now committed to killing her, but their energies were now inseparable. If only Catrin had known this would happen.

Both resigned themselves to killing the other later.

* * *

This wasn't the first time Catrin had left Chase, Brother Vaughn, and others waiting during her astral travels, but this time was different. Chase watched Koe in despair as streaks and milky swirls appeared within the dragon ore carving. The cloud cat, Rastas, was curled up in Allette's lap but watched everything taking place. Chase could almost see the energy streaming over their hands and out of the carving. He knew they both could die if they ran out of energy, and he also knew they might never hear his warnings. Brother Vaughn and the others continued chanting while Chase yelled at his cousin to come back, shouting that they were draining Koe far too quickly. Catrin had been gone for days during previous astral travels, and by the looks of Koe, they had hours at most. She'd told him she experienced time differently when traveling, and he worried his warnings would go unheard and unheeded. Resting in Allette's lap, the cloud cat continued to watch.

Only the energy flow told Chase that Allette also traveled, which made him uncomfortable. Seeing and feeling things others couldn't had always been Catrin's expertise. His anxiety increased ten-fold when a voice spoke in his mind.

We're coming.

Chase looked up to see Kenward watching him. The good captain was among the few people on standby to continue the chant. He and Chase had known each other for a long time, and the man must have read his face because he also went pale.

"Get everyone out of the main hallway and into the side halls," Chase said. "Get those replacements reserved for the chant divided up and squeezed into the chant rooms."

Under almost any other circumstances, Kenward would have balked at being given orders, or at least made a sarcastic comment, but he simply did as he was told. This unnerved Chase as much as anything else, at least until the roaring and rending of stone began.

From the great hall came the sounds of an angry feral dragon, muffled by the very barrier Catrin had released. Chase didn't know how long it would take a dragon to remove the stone obstruction, but he was betting it wouldn't be long enough. Trinda might not approve of this new alliance, and both Catrin and Allette were vulnerable.

When he turned back to the hall, a huge reptilian eye watched him from the doorway. Chase nearly fainted. When the eye moved away and a giant claw reached into the room, all Chase could do was back away from the opening. Never in his life had he felt so helpless and trapped. The claw landed gently on Catrin's chest, and Chase held his breath, having no idea what would happen next. In the hallway rang the echoes of a feral dragon trying to claw its way to them.

* * *

Finding consensus with someone who wants to kill you is a difficult thing, but it was something Catrin and Allette had to achieve if they were to survive. For some time, they had simply struggled against one another, neither willing to allow the other to have control, and thus they were no closer to Catrin's goal, no closer to achieving the mission Kyrien had sent them on. Catrin still had second thoughts about putting those she cared about in such danger, including her son's closest friend, but she had no other plan. At that moment, Allette was proving just how strong willed she was. Her father had raised a determined and capable soul. The thought came partly from Allette and partly from Catrin's shared memory of her upbringing. It was among the most bizarre experiences of Catrin's life.

Mired in stalemate, the two powerful entities struggled against one another to nullifying effect. They continued to go nowhere. Catrin tried everything she could to persuade Allette, but the girl knew as much about

Catrin as she did of Allette. The Black Queen knew what Catrin wanted and, at the moment, was diametrically opposed to it. If they continued as they were, they would burn each other out, and the world would be left to fend for itself. Simultaneously both committed themselves to that act. At least then neither would return to the world armed with the most dangerous knowledge possible. Catrin knew this wasn't the right answer. The people would not be able to protect themselves from what had already been set into motion. The Godfist itself could be destroyed. And what of Kyrien? His presence flooded into Catrin's consciousness. She drew strength from her closest friend and companion. He was there with her then, and the tide turned.

Allette was not cowed, but she could no longer hold them in stasis. Applying her will, Catrin's spirit merged with Kyrien's, his bright light adding to the texture and beauty of their interwoven souls. Allette's sense of wonder was palpable, and her resistance lessened. Across the waves, their spirits soared, and Kyrien helped Catrin find their way. Disoriented, only her dragon's ability to know his location no matter the circumstances kept them on the correct trajectory.

The Black Spike finally came into view. Engulfed in darkness, it was as if the storm clouds had gathered there to torture the ancient stone structure jutting from the deepest and most solitary waters on Godsland. The Black Spike should not exist, yet it did. Catrin had lived in this strange place, and she still had no idea how it had been constructed, although she had serious suspicions about exactly who had built this improbable structure.

No one could enter this mighty fortress in the way Catrin and Kyrien did since it required such a tremendous amount of power, along with the knowledge of where the entrance was. It didn't help Catrin's anxiety when she heard Allette's thoughts. Now there were two people powerful enough to enter the Black Spike.

Catrin also knew there was no hiding what she was about to do, and Allette would know even more secrets surrounding this most mysterious and dangerous place. Having slept within, Catrin knew dark powers waited in the depths, even if she didn't know the exact form they took. Still, she directed their energies to the top of the mighty fortress and did the very thing her spirit urged her not to do.

* * *

Sleep had come in fits, dreams melding with reality to create a waking nightmare. Darkness enshrouded the Black Spike, as if it were a magnet for storm clouds. It was unclear if the structure created the storms or attracted them, but it was unnatural and made Durin's skin crawl. Strom and Osbourne did their best to remain positive and optimistic but he despaired.

Here there was only darkness, and his spirit could no longer find the light. The blackness crept into him, seeping into his bones from the cold obsidian stone. It was as if the keep itself were drawing the life from him.

In many ways, it didn't matter. A quick death would be preferable to a slow one, and Durin once again considered throwing himself from the heights and ending it all. Something deep within him, though, knew these thoughts were not his own. It was as if the keep were defending itself by fostering these ideas. There wasn't much need to defend against them since they were stuck on top this boiling rock pile with no way to go anywhere else. Durin wasn't certain what he'd done to offend the gods, but it was clear he'd done so. To add insult, the wind cast sand into his eyes.

Holding up his arm, he was buffeted by powerful winds, which threatened to send him toppling over the edge even if he didn't go willingly. Burying his head in his arms, he hoped to wait out the winds, but they were insistent and pushed on him with relentless fury, somehow finding a way to blow sand into his shielded eyes. There was no shelter atop this abomination and he stood. Moving with the wind afforded him at least a small amount of relief. To his surprise, the buffeting air grew more gentle as he went, as if caressing rather than assaulting him. Not wanting to go any closer to the edge, he slowed and stopped. The gusts grew fierce, propelling him forward. Part of him feared the wind was trying to get him into a better position from which to hurl him to his death, but there was something else there, something familiar, and Durin allowed himself to be pushed.

Once again, as he moved in the direction the wind blew, it lessened but did not go away. When he was only a few paces from the structure's edge, Durin began to resist. The air grew still. The darkness drew closer as the storm clouds brooded above. Subtle at first but growing stronger and brighter, a faint orange glow outlined rocks not far from the edge.

Strom and Osbourne must have been watching, and they saw it as well, both coming to stand by his side. No one spoke; there was no need. As a team, they cleared away the rocks from atop the glow, finding a chamber within. Sitting within an alcove carved into a stone taller than a man, sat a wonder. An amber statuette in the shape of a woman emitted a ruddy glow. With a sudden wind gust, the glow brightened.

In the chamber floor was an ancient hatchway made of wood and metal, which somehow retained its luster after withstanding the elements. Strom spent a few moments examining the metal before shaking his head. Applying his muscles, the smith opened the hatch.

Durin, Strom, and Osbourne descended into darkness.

DRAGONHOLD

Chapter 1

There will never be another you. We must cherish the one we have.
--Brother Vaughn, Cathuran monk

* * *

There were no more secrets. Intertwined souls raced along woven gossamer threads leading back to their bodies. In synchronicity Catrin Volker and Allette Kilbor moved through combined will. Fear and exhilaration flooded the irrepressible bond between them. With time passed the duality. Merging into a single energetic force, threaded together like a glittering tapestry, they soared.

The journey back to the Godfist was not an easy one. The wavering cord of energy guiding them danced and grew difficult to follow. Panic and fear permeated the energy Brother Vaughn and those guarding their bodies sent. It was an experience Catrin found familiar; astral travel was by its very nature a dangerous endeavor. Part of her hoped never to leave her body again, but first she had to survive long enough to make it back. The world moved beneath them at a speed of its own choosing. Long before the Godfist came into view, fatigue whittled away at her resolve. Ripples of anxiety washed between the nearly ubiquitous souls of Allette and Catrin, threatening to overwhelm them both. Each drew strength from the other, and the bond grew.

Engulfed within towering plasma walls that shimmered before them, Dragonhold was visible from a great distance and promised a price for entry. Though they approached in a form other than physical, the luminous shield reached out with bluish green fire, burning and biting deep. Striking the shield was like being slapped then doused with frigid water. Once within, there was no relief. Perhaps they should have seen it coming, but neither was prepared for their intertwined souls to suddenly and violently separate. Just before the ropy light beam reached Dragonhold's stone walls, the woven tendrils were torn apart, each entering the hold through one of the two holes leading back to their bodies.

Slamming back into her physical form with percussive force, Catrin screamed. Numb fingers relaxed and Koe fell onto a pillow someone had placed there. Before anyone else could move, Brother Vaughn reached down and grabbed the cat figurine. It was chalky white and looked as if it might crumble within his grip. Catrin wanted to warn him of the danger Allette posed, to take her precious Koe back from him, but her body would not respond. At least the screaming had subsided. In its place came a cloud cat's warning growls and the sound of dragons in the hall--angry, determined dragons.

You are safe, Kyrien said in Catrin's mind, which made her head hurt. Looking to her right made it worse. Allette Kilbor sat, still recovering from her first experience with astral travel. It would take her longer to recover than Catrin would require. This might be her only chance to kill the Black Queen, and Catrin reached for the blade at her belt. Her fingers refused to grip the handle firmly, and the blade danced, breaking free, her hand trembling. Brother Vaughn gasped, and the cloud cat Rastas flattened his ears. Then Catrin's eyes met Allette's. Between them passed understanding. Catrin's will was shattered. This girl had a noble, if broken, heart. Allette could not be blamed for what had occurred. Other forces were at play, threats far more dangerous than Allette. Newfound knowledge, acquired while melding with the other woman, gave reason for fear.

The Black Queen stirred and Catrin flinched. Brother Vaughn snatched the knife from the pillow. Catrin barely noticed; her eyes were locked with Allette's.

"Can we kill each other later?" the Black Queen asked. "My head hurts."

Deep rumbles from the hall moved closer. The feral queen would tear down the hold to get to Allette. In the hall between the viewing chamber and the God's Eye waited Kyrien, equally determined. At either woman's command, the wrath of dragons could be unleashed. The thought made Catrin shiver. Kyrien's mind was his own, and he would do anything to protect her. She was all he had left.

Brother Vaughn brought them both cool water and steaming broth. Allette waved them off, but Catrin knew better. Sipping it, she refreshed herself. Though Catrin's memories and knowledge might not be foremost in Allette's mind, the Black Queen soon reconsidered and accepted what the monk offered.

Sinjin reached his mother's side. "Are you well?" he asked. At her nod, he continued. "What did you learn? Where have the regal dragons gone?"

After two more sips of water, Catrin cleared her throat. "Durin and the Drakon are well . . . for now." Part of her wanted to guard her words. Adapting to this new situation proved difficult. Allette knew everything she knew. Secrets would remain hidden at Allette's discretion. The lack of control twisted Catrin's guts. "I sent them into the Black Spike."

Sinjin gaped in return.

"We sent them," Allette said.

Catrin didn't argue the point. "Strom, Osbourne, and Durin are on a quest to . . ."

"To find a way to destroy me and Trinda and the Fifth Magic," Allette finished for Catrin, no humor in her words.

Catrin nodded the admission. Sinjin and Brother Vaughn exchanged confused glances.

"It would seem simultaneous astral travel from this viewing chamber creates an experience very different from traveling alone."

"In what way?" Brother Vaughn asked before Catrin could continue.

"Our souls became entwined," Allette said. "The Herald knows my every secret."

"And the Black Queen, mine," Catrin said.

After a dangerous silence, Allette smiled. "We'll eventually have to kill each other, but now is not the time. As I mentioned before, my head hurts. Do you have any humrus root?"

All the while, Rastas watched Catrin with distrust. Seeing the cloud cat through Allette's eyes and experiences, she smiled. Confused, the cat whined and backed away.

"Perhaps we should get you back to your quarters," Sinjin said, his eyes never leaving Allette, save once to glance at the doorway. The feral queen's roar, no longer dampened, echoed loudly. The time the defensive blockage had afforded them was alarmingly brief.

"Where's Trinda?" Catrin asked.

"We need to kill her too," Allette said.

Sinjin looked at Brother Vaughn before answering. "She left."

Catrin simply nodded. Allette made an unflattering sound.

"Allette can have the upper keep and the God's Eye," Catrin said. "I wish to move deeper into the hold."

The Black Queen's eyes narrowed.

"Will your dragon let us pass?" Sinjin asked Allette.

"No," Allette said, her face expressionless. "Go to the God's Eye, or surely you will die."

Catrin nodded. With Sinjin's aid, she stood more quickly than she should have, and her head swam. Allette wore a shrewd smile; the cloud cat tried to curl up in her lap but spilled over on all sides.

"Do you accept these terms?" Catrin asked before Sinjin could lead her away.

"I do," Allette said with a playful glint in her eye. "For now our goals are the same. When that ceases to be the case . . ." The Black Queen shrugged and showed a sad but knowing smile.

"There's always a way to find peace," Brother Vaughn said. The words sounded hollow and generated no response.

"Let's go," Sinjin said, pulling on Catrin's arm. This time she let him lead her back into the hall. Brother Vaughn preceded them, Koe in hand, and Catrin watched his every step, worried he would trip and let the carving fall to the stone while in its most fragile state. Trusting others with her fate was not something Catrin was comfortable with.

"May I have Koe," Catrin asked Brother Vaughn, though it did not come out as a question. The Cathuran monk nodded and handed the carving to Catrin with great care, making her feel guilty for doubting him.

Still, she felt better having Koe back in her hands. Once it was in her pocket, she caressed the stone, trying to give it back energy as it had done for her so many times.

She'd half expected Allette to make a grab for the dragon ore carving, but it would have been a hollow prize. With no more energy coming into the hold to charge the stone, it could forever remain fragile and inert. Catrin pushed that vision from her mind. The herald globe in Brother Vaughn's hand stood as a constant reminder. It, too, would soon cease to shine. Trinda had overcharged it, making it a viable weapon, but over time the light dimmed. When used as a weapon, the energy served to protect the glass. When the globe contained less of a charge, Catrin had her doubts regarding its durability. Having no way to tell just when delicate glass became a deadly weapon, she watched Brother Vaughn walk, hoping he wouldn't stumble and fall.

Deep growls changed the air pressure in the hall and made Catrin's ears hurt. The group moved toward the God's Eye at a brisk pace. Kyrien filled much of the hall ahead and walked toward the water. Having a feral dragon at her back raised Catrin's hackles. The realization of her own powerlessness set in. Koe had been drained. Still Catrin fingered the statuette, and she wondered if the surface wasn't just the slightest bit smoother than it had been.

Ahead, Kyrien slipped into the God's Eye as silently as a dragon of his size could, and only when Catrin had walked onto his back did she feel safe. She'd grown so accustomed to limitless power that its absence made her feel weak and vulnerable. Allette felt the same, and Trinda likely did as well. The child queen had no one to blame but herself, yet Catrin still managed to feel compassion. Her hands trembled.

No barges moved within the God's Eye; those who wanted to join Catrin would need to walk onto a dragon's back. It wasn't something a person did without considering alternatives. Even Sinjin hesitated.

"You've been invited," Catrin said. "Come."

With cautious steps, Brother Vaughn, Sinjin, Kendra, Kenward, Sevellon, and the others climbed atop Kyrien's back. Unlike the barges, the dragon's mass did not shift with their movements. And somehow he managed to swim while keeping the section of his back on which they stood perfectly still. To the observer, it must have appeared to have been magic. Eyes in the darkness watched, and Catrin wondered once again what game the child queen played. "Why did Trinda leave the viewing chambers?" she asked as they glided toward the enormous cavern's far wall.

"Don't know," Brother Vaughn said.

Kendra explained, "We were too busy chanting and taking turns screaming at you to tell you Koe was almost depleted."

"And that you were going to die." Sinjin nodded emphatically.

Catrin shook her head. "Astral travel is not for the delicate."

"Do you share Allette's memories?" Kenward asked after a long silence. "I mean, do you know what happened to her?"

Meeting her friend's eyes, Catrin nodded.

* * *

Durin took a tentative step. Each one was more difficult than the last. Every bit of his experience told him to get out of this unnatural place. Strom and Osbourne continuing onward kept him from fleeing. The steep entry stair ended at a landing that opened into the creepiest place Durin had ever seen. Outside light streamed in through myriad openings in the rock walls. The result was a crisscrossing pattern of light that left much of the chamber floor in darkness. Enough was visible to see writing carved into the stone.

Osbourne knelt with the amber figurine they had found atop the Black Spike and chased back the shadows with its light. The floor was a marvel consisting of perfectly flat tiles melded together along sometimes jagged, haphazard lines. Despite the irregular shapes, there was a distinct beauty to the formations. Even more remarkable was the writing covering every stone. It was as if someone had written a massive epic using a chisel. The runes were foreign, but their elegant form and embellishments made it clear it was as much art as writing. Nearby stones, adorned with sentences carved in a spiral pattern, further bore this out.

Near the center of the room waited a circular depression. Strom stepped closer, Osbourne and Durin moving with him, not wanting to be left in even partial darkness. As they approached a stairway, the writings on the tiles took more sinister forms. Durin had to credit the author for conveying threats even though Durin didn't understand the words themselves. Runes laid out in the form of fierce creatures grew more and more frequent until they reached the stair. There, runes formed images of dragons surrounding a portal into darkness, portraying more varieties of winged serpent than were known to exist.

"Not the most inviting place," Osbourne said.

Strom shook his head.

"I don't want to go in there," Durin admitted.

"Neither do we," Strom said. "But the dragons don't appear to be coming back for us. And short of climbing down the outside of this thing and swimming home, we don't have much choice. I know one thing, though: when I get back to my forge, I'm going to make a pair of steel-shod gloves."

"What for?" Osbourne asked.

"Because I don't want to punch a dragon with my bare fists." With that statement, Strom took a deep breath and the first step. Circular, steep, and tight, the stair was daunting. No railings provided safety, and there was nothing to indicate how deep the winding steps went. Given the Black Spike's height, no one expected a short climb. Not knowing the exact nature of the amber figurine, they had no idea how long it would continue to emit light, making the descent even more nerve wracking.

Never had Durin felt so helpless and doomed. "And I thought carrying buckets of dirty water was bad."

Shaking his head, Strom continued downward and almost immediately stumbled. Feeling guilty for distracting the smith, Durin cursed himself, but then a grinding sound made him look back. Cold stone closed over the entrance, blotting out the remaining natural light. They were trapped. Or perhaps entombed would be more accurate, Durin thought.

Drawing deep breaths, Strom and Osbourne looked at each other. Durin was afraid to speak. He hoped they would say something to make death less certain. No words came. Continuing into the darkness had been folly before, but now it appeared closer to inescapable madness. Under the shadow of fate and the weight of black stone, they continued.

The lower they climbed, the clearer the danger became. No landings emerged from the darkness. The narrow stair spiraled into the depths as if endless. Protruding from the outer wall, it was all that kept them from being swallowed. Vertigo threatened Durin's sanity, and he clung to the outside wall. Neatly mated stones didn't provide much grip, but it comforted Durin at least in some small measure.

"I need to rest my knee," Strom announced without warning. Durin empathized; his feet felt as if he'd been dropping rocks on them. Sitting next to Osbourne, they pressed themselves against the stone as far from the gaping chasm as possible.

"We don't even know what we've been sent after," Strom said. "How are we supposed to know what to do?"

"Look on the sunny side," Osbourne said. "So far the choices have been few, so chances are we're still on the right track."

The statement failed to make Durin feel any better.

"I wish we had more light," Strom said, an absent-minded note in his voice. Durin jumped when the figurine glowed more brightly in response to Strom's wish. Shielding his eyes against the blinding light, Durin caught a dizzying glimpse of what lay below. Morbid fascination drew him closer to the edge, they were but a fraction of the way down based on what he could see. The dread chasm continued into the darkness for no one knew how far. "Not that much," Strom whispered. Gradually the light dimmed. None of them spoke for some time. "I don't know what just happened there," he finally said.

"You've talents, my friend," Osbourne said. Strom made no response.

"You don't have to want gifts to receive them. If Catrin taught me anything, she taught me that."

"Thanks," Strom said. The light shone just a bit brighter.

Osbourne looked thoughtful. "Keeping the light only as bright as we need it is probably a good idea."

"I'll do my best to manage it." Strom half mumbled, seemingly embarrassed by Istra's touch.

"I'm glad you're here, Strom," Durin said, hoping to bolster the man's purpose, if not his confidence. Deeper they moved into the Black Spike.

* * *

"Why concede the upper hold to Allette?" Brother Vaughn asked Catrin as they walked deeper into the hold. Kyrien couldn't fit through some of the more narrow halls and stayed back to guard the entrance to the God's Eye. For a time, they wouldn't have to worry about attacks from behind. The truces were tenuous at best, and Sinjin did what he could to keep up with the rest.

Chase moved to the fore and forced Catrin to stop. "What is it we're after?" he asked. "I know you have reasons for keeping secrets, but it would be nice to at least understand our goal."

"I don't mean to hide things from you," Catrin said. "I want to find Trinda's library and read the passages that caused her to initiate this nightmare."

"And if we run into her and her guards?"

"We do our best to get what we want peacefully. If that fails . . ." Catrin shrugged.

Chase nodded. He and Morif were the only trained soldiers among the group. The rest were poorly armed and wouldn't be much help in a fight. Catrin, though deprived of her power, was still at least a capable fighter. Sinjin shared only some of her prowess. Though not all of them were handy in a fight, some within their group possessed other useful skills. When they reached the first junction, Catrin faltered. Sevellon stepped up to her side and met her eyes. Without saying a word, he looked to the left and nodded. Sinjin wasn't certain his mother would take directions from a known thief, but she surprised him by wordlessly turning left. At several more junctions, Catrin allowed Sevellon to guide the way. Sinjin was beginning to suspect they were hopelessly lost, but then they came upon a hall flanked by guards. Catrin stepped in front of the thief and approached those posted.

With or without her powers, the Herald of Istra knew how to intimidate with nothing more than a walk. She approached the guards with her head held high and steel in her eyes. Stopping before them, she let the silence hang until it became uncomfortable. Just as one of the guards was about to speak, Catrin cut him short. "I wish to see Trinda Hollis."

"She's not present," one of the men managed before Catrin silenced him with a stare.

Chase walked up beside her. "Brennan. Merk," he said, nodding to the men as he did. Both guards just stared at him. Chase pointed to each and silently counted. Then he counted those around him. He shrugged, smiled, and turned back to the younger men. Morif cast the guards a one-eyed grin. Sinjin knew just how disconcerting that could be.

"She ain't here, sir," Merk said.

"Then take us to her," Morif growled, looking as if his patience were nearly exhausted.

"Don't know where she is, sir."

"Then go find out," Morif said.

Merk looked at Brennan, an apology in his eyes. Brennan just shook his head. "She'll have your hide for leaving your post."

"I knew this time would come," Merk said, his head hung. Then he met Brennan's eyes. "I stand with Catrin."

Knowing there were still loyal folks within the hold renewed Sinjin's faith. Seeing Merk rush deeper into the hold made him question the truth of that loyalty, which made him feel ashamed. He did his best to trust Merk and the rest of his people. He dared to hope. It was always a risk since every time hopes were dashed, they were even more difficult to rebuild.

"What are you guarding there, Brennan?" Morif asked, taking a step forward. Chase matched his stride. To his credit, Brennan stepped in front of the men and used his spear to bar their path.

"Bend your knees," Morif told him. Brennan did as he was told, his face flushing. Sinjin guessed he'd heard it before during drills. "Keep your eyes on my hips, remember," Morif said, a gleam in his eye. "I might try to fake you out with my head and arm movements."

Brennan took a step back, a wild look in his eyes. He knew he was more than overmatched. Sinjin watched the debate unfold in Brennan's mind. He might be able to take down one or two of them with his spear. He seemed to be considering dropping the spear and drawing his sword. Morif and Chase both put their hands on hilts and Brennan swallowed. "It's a library," he said, laying his spear on the stone. He did clear his sword from the scabbard but only to place it next to the spear.

After collecting the weapons, Chase pushed Brennan into the library. What waited was beyond anything Sinjin had ever heard of. He'd seen extensive collections, but this place was like a city of books, scrolls, and stack after stack of parchments and tablets. The library consisted of multiple levels, with each getting larger the higher they went. Walkways lined each level, giving access to the multitude of racks and shelves. There were more words here than anyone could read in a lifetime. Overwhelmed,

Sinjin knew the answers they needed must lie within the pages found here, but he also knew it might take a lifetime to find them. Given the current circumstances, time was not a luxury they possessed. No one knew exactly how long it would take the Fifth Magic to fully charge and activate, and they had to assume it could happen at any time. Such realizations made solace impossible to find. The pressure was constant and relentless.

Chase seemed more interested in some of the other items within the room, whereas Catrin and Brother Vaughn were drawn to the books. Chase caressed the handle of a tall, edged weapon that gleamed when the layer of dust was cleared. Multiple metals had been used to fashion a weapon that was strong and functional but also a work of art.

Sinjin worried they would waste too much time sifting through all the information they didn't currently need to find what they so desperately sought. It would be so easy for all of them to become lost in the revelations such a place could provide, but his worries were cut short when a breathless Merk returned. "The lady would like to see you," he gasped.

Chapter 2

Determination is the fire within. Burn brightly.
--Barabas the druid

* * *

While trying to memorize the path they followed, so he could find his way back to the library, Sinjin allowed Kendra to pull him to the back of the group. "I don't like this," she whispered.

"I stopped liking this situation the moment we arrived," Sinjin responded.

"There's got to be a way out."

"I agree," Sinjin said. "That's what my mom's trying to find. We just need to help her. She's vulnerable in here."

"Seems like she's vulnerable everywhere now, but in here at least, she's not a threat to the whole world."

"What are you saying?" Sinjin asked, soon regretting the edge in his voice.

"I'm just saying your mom was clearly overwhelmed by the energy of Istra's direct light. You remember that part, right?"

Grudgingly, Sinjin nodded.

"We need someone on the outside. How did Brother Vaughn escape the hold? And what about the portal to the mountaintop? Surely there's some way to get out of here."

It took a while for Sinjin to respond. His wife was a practical woman, and she made a solid point, but Sinjin didn't want more blood on his hands. They'd seen what happened to a dragon when flying through the barrier, and he had no reason to expect a kinder fate for anyone else who tried. "There's no guarantee a person could escape the keep with their lives."

"Staying within Dragonhold is almost certainly a death sentence."

Sinjin made no response. He opened his mouth to speak but closed it again after more thought. Kendra glared at him, but neither got the chance to continue the conversation since they had reached their apparent destination: Trinda's apartments. Sinjin wasn't the only one uncomfortable about entering. Sevellon looked as if doing so might violate some kind of personal rule.

"M'lady," Merk said, preceding them into the child queen's presence and gesturing for them to follow.

Catrin strode into the room as if she owned it. Some would argue she still did, but Trinda paid her no mind. The diminutive child queen's form hunched on deep carpeting amid a storm of parchments, scrolls, tapestries, and even pottery. Each piece had a story to tell, but amid such disarray, Catrin couldn't imagine finding any useful information.

Finally Trinda looked up and said, "You're back."

Catrin stared in response.

"Yes. Right," Trinda said. "And the Black Queen holds the outer hold?"

"You don't need me to tell you that," Catrin snapped.

"No," Trinda admitted. "But it's nice to get a firsthand account of events. It helps me to make certain I haven't been lied to."

Merk flushed.

"Allette holds the Great Hall," Catrin said.

Trinda smirked. "Nice of you to confirm that."

"Enough of this!" Catrin said, stepping on ancient parchments to reach Trinda. The child queen gasped and squealed but could not scurry away from Catrin's wrath. The Herald of Istra might be without the powers the goddess granted her, but she was not without the internal fortitude her father and Benjin had helped her to build. "Tell me what you know. How do we stop this thing?"

"You're standing on part of the answer. Please do not turn your heel."

"Show me," Catrin said.

Sinjin wondered at the truth of Trinda's words. So much of what she had shown him in the past was false, he couldn't help but feel he was being told a series of well-crafted lies. His mother looked no more convinced.

"Von of the Elsics detested the use of Istra's power," Trinda reminded them, quite unnecessarily, which made Catrin grind her teeth. It was a warning sign Sinjin recognized but of which Trinda was oblivious. "He built the Fifth Magic as a way to create a place to isolate what he considered an abomination."

"We know that part," Catrin said.

"It was later, when he was stricken with madness, that Von redesigned the keep to serve as a prison, trap, and eventual extermination device. He planned to hold peace talks within the hold and then spring his trap. Von died before his work was completed, based on what I've recently learned, but someone carried on his work and completed the construction."

"Have you learned anything that might actually be useful, or are you just in it for the history lesson?"

Trinda sighed. "Patience has never been your strong point, Catrin Volker. My research has taught me the Fifth Magic includes no failsafe mechanisms or path of reversal. In order to stop it, we'll have to destroy it or circumvent it in some way. Is that information useful enough for you?"

It wasn't something any of them wanted to hear, but it was important. At least they knew not to search for a simple solution to the problem. Von and his successors had gone out of their way to make certain there were no easy ways out. Perhaps Kendra was right, he thought, and she cast him a knowing glance, though it was clear she took no joy in doing so. Sinjin, and he guessed everyone else, would be thrilled to be proven wrong. Instead, all the worst possible cases were being proven true.

"Brother Vaughn once escaped from the hold," Kendra said. All eyes turned to her, and she shrank under their scrutiny. Sinjin empathized. "It's possible the shield doesn't penetrate the water and that we could escape."

"Possible." Kenward spoke the word as if it were a snake.

"There's no way to know," Kendra admitted.

"I nearly died under normal conditions," Brother Vaughn said. "Getting out puts you under water for a long time. I don't know if I could do it again."

"What about Logan the diver?" Sinjin asked, surprising even himself. Those around him considered the possibility without immediately rejecting it. "I'd hate to ask it of him. He's already risked so much to help us."

"I'll do it." Everyone turned to the slight figure who'd been nearly invisible, so well did he blend in with stone walls. "I've violated the trust of just about everyone present," Sevellon said. "Perhaps this is my chance to regain what I've lost."

Kendra swallowed hard. Sinjin knew his wife. For all her bravado, she considered the consequences of her words. Sevellon's fate was now in her hands. If he died, it would be her fault. Sinjin did not stand in judgment; he simply read the emotions on her face. Sliding closer, he gave her arm a squeeze. When she didn't pull away, he knew he'd been right. It was also nice that experience finally told him when the wisest thing to say was nothing at all.

Trinda also appeared concerned about Sevellon's decision. If Sinjin was any judge of emotion, she wanted to object, but she remained silent.

"Perhaps it would be best to wait until we know more," Brother Vaughn suggested.

"We don't know how long we've got until the hold destroys itself," Kendra said, regaining her strength. She pulled away from Sinjin's grip. "If Sevellon makes it out, he'll need time to get word to any of the people who might be able to help us."

Sinjin doubted there was much anyone could do to help. In his mind, all Sevellon needed to do was prove it could be done, and all of them could escape in the same fashion. Learning the opposite would be devastating, no matter Sevellon's transgressions.

"How will we know?" Brother Vaughn asked.

The question left everyone in silence for some time as they contemplated.

"We can see into the Pinook Valley from the Great Hall," Kenward said.

"Which is held by the Black Queen, who may or may not be cooperative," Chase observed. "I vote we leave her out of this if possible." Morif stood behind him, nodding his agreement.

"The source of the river must be to the north of the hold, yes?" Sevellon asked, once again proving he possessed a sharp mind. Chase nodded. "There should be a lot of apples on the ground at this time of year."

"There's a chance whatever signal we choose will just float on past or get stuck," Morif said. "This underground river is only a small part of what continues on above ground. We also need a way to acknowledge receipt of the message. That way, if he doesn't receive our response, he can send another."

"Mushrooms," Kendra said.

Trinda looked incredulous. "Miss Mariss would lose her mind," she said. It was the closest thing Sinjin had seen to her being afraid of someone. The fact that it was Miss Mariss was a sign the enigmatic woman did have some sense.

"So if I live, I'm to go north, gather apples, and throw them all into the river at once. And then I'm to come back south to look for mushrooms. Is that right?" No one contradicted him. "And then what?"

Sinjin thought about the situation and finally overcame his distrust of Trinda. She wasn't in a position to do much with the information, and it might just save his mother's life. His mother's and Kendra's safety were his highest priorities. "Find a way to get to Lankland," Sinjin said. "Go to Jharmin Kyte, and tell him we urgently need the blanket he once lent me."

Catrin turned with surprise. It felt good to contribute, and Sinjin savored the moment. Jharmin Kyte had once hidden Sinjin from the ferals-- and his mother--and judging by her expression, she'd made the connection. That same blanket might be just what Catrin needed. If he was right, the blanket had concealed him by cutting him off from Istra's light, which would explain why he'd found it so hard to breathe when under it.

Kendra also understood the blanket's effects, but Trinda obviously did not. She stared at him as if trying to read the thoughts in his head. "I believe it might be able to lessen the effects of Istra's light on my mother." This was intended to give Trinda just enough information to satisfy her curiosity without telling her everything. It also didn't hurt to remind the child queen that Catrin was his mother; whether to instill fear or to evoke compassion, Sinjin didn't really care.

"If you don't see mushrooms downstream," Chase said, "try lighting a signal fire in the Chinawpa Valley within sight of Dragonhold's rear entrance, but I wouldn't stick around. Allette has forces outside the hold, and I wouldn't trust them, truce or not. For the same reason, I'd avoid the Pinook Valley no matter what."

"He'll need coin, preserved food in a waxed pack, and one herald globe," Trinda said. A look at Bernerd sent him scrambling to gather the items. Sinjin wanted to follow, to find out where Trinda had hidden the herald globes. He wondered if Merk knew where she'd stashed them and resolved to get the younger man alone soon. Sevellon looked to be having similar thoughts, but Brother Vaughn and Catrin were inspecting his clothes for anything they could do to increase his chances of survival. The best they were able to suggest was tying off a pair of breeches and using them to hold air. He could use them for flotation and a few precious extra breaths.

"You'll want all the air you can get," Brother Vaughn said with haunted eyes. "And take lots of deep breaths before you go under. This should also help."

Sevellon looked as if he had made the choice between a quick and slow death. There was no joy in it, only relief. When the guard returned with a full pack, the thief wore a sad smile. "I'm ready."

* * *

Descending into darkness for what seemed an eternity, Durin wondered if the infernal stairway might continue all the way to the center of Godsland. Memories of his lessons regarding the underworld conjured frightening images he did his best to banish. The three men climbed in near silence, any words echoing harshly within the well. Though living in such a place was unimaginable to Durin, Catrin had done so, and he imagined all kinds of creatures who might also live there. No matter how hard he tried to change the direction of his thoughts, each step took him closer to madness.

"I don't like this place one bit," Osbourne said. Strom cast him an accusing glare as his words echoed. "You don't really think we can sneak in here unnoticed, do you?"

Discarding stealth felt unnatural even if Osbourne was right.

"No sense announcing our arrival, either," Strom said in a whisper. "No matter how hopeless this may seem, I've no intention of dying today."

Osbourne quieted and they climbed once again enveloped in naught but silence and a small bubble of amber light. The statuette was warm, and Durin took comfort from its light. Each of them had held the figurine for a time, but Strom alone could control the light with his mind. The figurine had been left there for them; that much was certain. The wind had guided them to the softly glowing statuette; it hadn't been a chance wind. Dragons had brought them here for reasons all their own, but it added up to their being guided toward some greater purpose. He just hoped the hand guiding them was one he could trust.

Any comfort was welcome in the pervasive darkness, and for a brief time, Durin was unafraid. The monotonous climb also dulled his senses. When the stairway ended, his anxiety returned in full force, making his heart race and his knees tremble. Already his legs and calves ached from the climb, leaving him unsteady on his feet. Strom and Osbourne slowed and stopped on the final stair, as if about to step into another realm from which they might never return. The fact that this wasn't an unreasonable expectation set Durin's guts to churning.

Without a word, Strom caused the figurine to glow more brightly, illuminating a dragon's head, jaws agape. Light danced over carved black stone, making it look alive and momentarily startling them. To proceed, one must willingly walk into a dragon's jaws. Durin swallowed hard. Strom placed a hand on the younger man's shoulder. Together three men entered the underworld. None was completely surprised when the jaws closed behind them. Durin realized there was a limit to how much fear he could experience. This journey had only gotten worse over time, yet he hadn't been reduced to a quivering pile of mush. This, at least, gave him some measure of pride even if the slightest noise still made him jump.

Within the stairwell, all had been silent save the wind and echoes of sounds the three men made. Wherever they were now had noises of its own. Durin assumed they were below the waterline--a thought that threatened to smother him. Briefly he imagined the ocean rushing in to drown them all. Driving the image from his mind, he stepped lively to keep up with Strom and Osbourne.

"How much water do we have left?" Durin asked in a whisper, unable to drive water, salt or fresh, from his mind. Too much or too little, and they would die.

"Enough for two days, tops," Strom said. Osbourne nodded his agreement. "Nothing to be done about it." He must have taken Durin's question as thirst since he lowered his pack to the cold stone floor. The narrow hall continued on a meandering course from what they could see. Unlike the stair, this place lacked deliberate symmetry and clean lines as if haphazardly dug by enormous creatures. It was not a comforting thought.

Osbourne commented, "The problem with salted fish as survival food is that it makes you so darned thirs—" Before his sentence was complete, a long, vibrating moan interrupted him. Growing increasingly louder, it ended with a boom that sent tremors through the entire structure. Unable to find words, the group just ate and drank. Silence crept back over them, as if the booming had never been. A place like this could drive a person mad. What had Catrin done here? How had she survived?

As Strom stood and offered Durin a hand, he was no closer to having answers.

"For all those we love," Osbourne said as they moved deeper into the unknown.

Seeing the faces of those he cared about most, Durin held his head high. If he could be brave, it would be for them. They deserved this from him, and he did his best to move with renewed commitment; still, his knees trembled.

Whether intentionally or subconsciously Durin didn't know, but the figurine in Strom's hand grew brighter whenever something new came into view. The light ahead, though, came from something else. The glow was a similar hue, and it illuminated a junction. Still looking like a tunnel dug buy some enormous creature, this intersection showed no signs of being man-made. There was, however, a clear message left by someone. In the left-hand tunnel rested an animal skull. It was perfectly centered in the hall and pointed directly at them. A second glowing figurine of similar design was the light's source. It rested in the right-hand hall--a very clear message.

Osbourne reached down to grab the figurine, but Strom stayed his hand. He looked to be committing every detail to memory. After a moment, he let Osbourne go. When the glass smith closed his hand around the figurine, Strom visibly tensed, but nothing happened. So far it seemed they had a benefactor guiding them. Durin just wished he knew who it was. Part of him wanted to know what was down the other hall. "Can you make it brighter for a moment?"

Strom frowned. "No one disturbs the skull or goes past it. Agreed?"

Durin nodded. Osbourne moved to Strom's side, and all three got as close to the skull as they dared. While not an expert on animal bones, Durin knew a number of things it was not. His gut and experience told him it was a dragon skull. That fact alone made him want to give it a wide berth. Farther down that hall, another light source was visible. Faint shadows danced like leaves on a gentle breeze, and the air whispered of moving water nearby.

Extending himself as far forward as he could without taking another step, Durin leaned on Strom. Shadows gathered into a diaphanous form. Strom pulled him back. He'd seen it as well.

"There's water in there," Durin whispered directly into Strom's ear. The shadow hadn't seemed threatening to Durin. For some reason, he sensed it was shy and afraid.

The smith nodded but pulled them back. "And something else. If we can find no other source, we'll return here."

"If we're able," Osbourne said in a soft voice. "This place has a nasty habit of sealing us in."

Chapter 3

Madness is but a matter of perspective.
--Ain Giest, sleepless one

* * *

Sevellon the thief was not as brave as he appeared. While everyone else had been preoccupied, he'd taken numerous opportunities to observe the barrier surrounding the keep. At a glance it could be perceived as penetrating deep into the land itself, but Sevellon had borrowed Kenward's looking glass. Few things had survived the *Serpent's* destruction, but the leather-bound looking glass had been spared. Life as a thief had taught him to take advantage of opportunities when they presented themselves. It had also taught him a healthy amount of caution was required to stay alive. He prided himself on taking enough risk to gain the reward but not enough to end up dead. It was a fine line.

As he slipped the waxed leather pack's straps over his shoulders, he knew this might be his last risk. It was a familiar feeling. The faces around him wore equal concern, which was touching. So much of his life had been spent alone and afraid, it was difficult to understand why these people cared for him. The bond he'd shared with Kenward and crew was the closest thing to family he'd ever experienced, and those people he'd miss most.

"You have letters from Trinda, Catrin, and Chase," Kendra said again. "There's enough coin to buy a whole fleet of ships and sail them to the Greatland and back. And remember to take lots of deep breaths."

The woman's concern appeared genuine but made Sevellon uncomfortable. He was accustomed to blending in to the background; having anyone's undivided attention was disconcerting, and being fussed over gave him the shakes. After Kendra had straightened his collar and brushed his shoulders, he stepped into the water, as much to get away from her as anything else.

Now the terror was real. Deep breaths. Dark, frigid water tested Sevellon's confidence as it rushed inexorably into a narrow crevasse. Knowing the wisdom of the advice from his own training, he took more deep breaths. After one last look at those along the shore, the thief gulped air, held it, and disappeared.

Cold shock made him feel as if he already needed to take a breath, even though he'd only just passed into the darkness beneath the stone. The water twisted and turned him until direction became meaningless. Getting the breeches untied and to his lips was far more difficult than he would have imagined. After two desperate attempts, he discarded them and swam with all his strength. Darkness engulfed him, and he wasn't certain if it was because he was still beneath a mountain of rock or if he was about to pass out. His lungs burned and ached, and just before he drew in water, light filtered in from one side.

He would have screamed from the pain if he could, his body no longer obeying his will. Finally his lips parted. Water rushed in, choking him, but then he broke the surface, and air was mixed in as well. The coughing fit nearly cost Sevellon his consciousness, and he flailed in the rushing water, trying not to get pulled back under. Clothes, boots, and pack weighed him down, and he'd yet to gain control over his breathing.

Slowly and deliberately he calmed himself. Allowing his body to float with the current, he regained his composure and strength. Getting out of the water wouldn't be all that difficult once he got to land, but the river was swollen and turbulent. Though going with the current had allowed him to rest, it also sent him farther into deeper water, where the current was irresistible. Only a fallen tree obstructing the rushing flow gave Sevellon hope. Throwing his arms up, he latched on to the tree and was dragged underneath. Bark dug into his face and arms, but he was able to slow himself and lock his legs around a branch. Again, he took a moment to regain his strength. He lost no ground this time, but the cold water sapped the feeling from his limbs. There was no time to waste.

White-capped formations dragged at Sevellon as he clung to the tree, pulling himself closer to shore. Branches still bearing leaves made things more difficult, but Sevellon eventually reached dry land. Once there, he found a place to hide and watch, knowing there might still be demons and ferals about. While he was closer to his freedom, he was by no means safe.

Run. Hide. Become invisible. A familiar voice in the back of his mind warned. They aren't your friends. They don't care about you.

Pulling an apple from his pack, he ate with a sad smile. When he was done, he tossed the core into the raging waters, which carried it toward the ocean.

Go. Run. The nudge was less subtle now.

With regret and relief, Sevellon headed south--away from Dragonhold. Though these people had befriended him, they would eventually see his true nature and cast him out--or worse. Certainly Trinda had a score to settle with him. Given the chance to walk away, instinct and training demanded he take it. To go north, as Kendra has asked, carried far greater risk and got him no closer to safety. The Amazing Kells had also taught him the most difficult lesson of all: a noble thief was a dead thief.

* * *

Though the river water was more turbulent than usual, the cavern through which it passed had changed little in thousands of years. Stunted trees bore small but delicious fruit, and miniature deer grazed among them. Birds were far from plentiful, but some managed to eke out a meager existence within the mountain. Sinjin and Kendra sat, watching the waters and knowing it was too soon to see any apples or other indicators that Sevellon lived. Still, they kept vigil. Kendra would not rest if there was even the slightest chance of missing the signal. Sinjin couldn't blame her, but he wasn't spending much of his time watching the water.

For just a brief while, Sinjin allowed himself to enjoy spending time with his wife. She was rigid beside him, twisted up from the stress and anxiety, which came as much from what they knew as from what they didn't yet know. Leaning closer, Sinjin touched her hand. She pulled away at first, but he was undeterred. Lightly he brushed up against her, and she came out of her trancelike state of worry.

"I'm afraid to ask what's going on in that head of yours," Sinjin said.

"You should be," Kendra responded with half a laugh.

"I'm sorry, you know."

"For what?" Kendra asked, turning her full attention on him.

"For not telling you about my mom." They had never talked it out, and somehow the words just fell from Sinjin's lips. He hadn't really meant to say it.

"I don't want to talk about that right now," Kendra said, but she snuggled closer.

"How far do you think Sevellon has gotten?" Sinjin asked before he could think better of it. One day he'd have to learn to think first.

"I don't want to talk about that either." Her tone was colder.

"What are you thinking about?" Sinjin asked.

"Took you long enough," Kendra said. "What do you want to do when all this is over?"

That question caught Sinjin by complete surprise. "I want to spend my life with you . . . in our home, with Valterius and Gerhonda and the Drakon and the Dragon Clan. We have a big family now."

"Maybe," Kendra said. "But maybe our family isn't quite complete yet."

Sinjin flushed. "Maybe."

"Let me guess, you don't want to talk about that."

"I didn't say that."

"You didn't have to," Kendra said, putting a little distance between them.

Trying to figure out where he'd gone wrong, Sinjin sighed. That, of course, was a mistake. Kendra huffed at him and turned away. Silence hung between them for some time, and Sinjin tried to find the words that would make his wife less angry.

"Do you really think that awful blanket will help your mom?" she asked.

The question proved to Sinjin that no matter how hard he tried, he would never understand the inner workings of the female mind. "I think it might," he said. "When the Fifth Magic blocked out Istra's energy, I felt like I was suffocating, except I could still breathe. Do you know what I mean?"

"I know exactly what you mean," Kendra said. "Your mom described something similar, only more intense."

"It reminded me of the feeling I had under that blanket. I could even smell the stench when it happened. I don't know. I could be wrong."

"I remember it too," Kendra said. "It didn't strike me until you said it, but now I can't help but agree."

At least for a short time, they were of the same mind. Sinjin would take those moments when he could get them.

"There's something else," Kendra said.

A cold feeling gripped Sinjin.

"Did you see the way Kenward looked at Allette?"

The question made Sinjin stop and shake his head. He hadn't actually noticed, but the way Kendra said it told him all he needed to know. Kenward had never been known to resist going after something he wanted. How Kendra could twist Sinjin's guts into pretzels with a single question was beyond him, but he found himself unable to respond. Instead, he just shook his head.

"She and your mom are going to try to kill each other."

"I know."

"Sorry," Kendra said. "Sometimes the things I think just come out of my mouth."

"I know."

"And?" she asked, one eyebrow raised.

"It's one of the things I love about you."

"Thank you," she said.

No more words were spoken as dusk settled in, the amber crystals above growing dimmer yet still shedding faint, residual light. Sinjin wondered how his mother and the others fared. If Trinda had already found and hidden the answers, there was little hope they would find it on their own. The child queen would also be doomed unless she knew something they didn't. Sinjin's thoughts ran in circles. In the end, he baited a line and dropped it into the river. Maybe he could catch dinner.

No apples appeared in the water.

* * *

When days passed with no apples in the river waters and no signal fires reported, Sinjin despaired. Kendra was taking it far worse since she was responsible for the idea in the first place. It would appear Sevellon the thief had gone to his death on her suggestion. Sinjin wanted more than anything to fix this for his wife, but he could do little beyond being there for her. "My mother, grandfather and Uncle Chase are leaving in the morning to explore the rest of Dragonhold," he said, hoping she would show some interest.

"I'll stay here."

"We can post a rotating watch," Sinjin said not for the first time.

"I'd never be able to trust someone else to remain vigilant. I know Sevellon is probably dead. One sign of respect I will show him is that I'll not give up on him so easily. Just a couple more days, and I'll give up hope."

This wasn't something Sinjin wished for his wife, but in this case, it might be for the best.

"You can go, though," Kendra said. "Go. Be with your family. I'm sure they'll be better company than me."

"I always enjoy your company."

Kendra snorted. But then she leaned against him and held his hand. Chase approached with Bradley. They had a whispered conversation out of earshot, and Bradley stood off to the side while Chase continued toward where Kendra and Sinjin kept watch. He sat next to them but didn't say anything for a long while. Eventually he broke the silence. "I want you both to come with us tomorrow."

"No," Kendra said, her jaw set. It was a familiar warning sign.

"Every decision we make has consequences," Chase continued. Sinjin tried to gesture to his uncle to take another approach, but the older man ignored him. "Some are harsher than others, but we cannot let that paralyze us. I know how badly it must hurt."

"What do you know about how I feel?" Kendra shouted accusingly.

Every bird in the cavern took flight, fluffy white tails retreating into distant shadows to escape Kendra's wrath. Wise move, Sinjin thought.

"I've given orders that cost people their lives," Chase said. "You made a suggestion, and Sevellon volunteered to go."

"How dare you downplay what I'm feeling?" Kendra said, and she stood, hands clenched into fists. When his uncle stood, Sinjin wondered if he had any idea how close he was to getting punched in the nose. Sinjin's wife knew how to put her weight behind it as well. His jaw hurt just thinking about it.

"You may be angry at me," Chase said.

Kendra punched him in the chest. It was kinder than hitting him in the face, which showed a measure of restraint. Still, Chase took a step back and winced. Kendra struck him again and again, shifting from punches to pounding on his chest. Words poured from her, most incomprehensible, which was probably a blessing. Her words dissolved into a mourning wail, and her blows lost their force. Slowly she melted against the older man, who had withstood the assault as if made of stone. Sinjin flushed, knowing he never could have done the same.

His uncle must have known what he was thinking. "You're both still young, and like my cousin, fate has been particularly unkind to you. Do not blame yourselves for things beyond your control. You've acted admirably and should be proud of yourselves, though I know that may seem impossible while you are mourning. But understand what it is you're experiencing. Feel the pain. Allow yourself to let go of Sevellon and those you've lost, and someday the sun may shine on you again."

Kendra sniffed, wiped her nose, and elbowed Chase in the ribs. Sinjin smiled. His wife had a unique and often painful way of expressing her love. Somehow, Uncle Chase knew it as such.

"That's your last free shot," he said. "The next one will cost you some bruises."

Kendra actually laughed.

"Let me post Bradley here," Chase said. "He's a good man, and he'll make sure vigilance is maintained."

Kendra nodded and allowed him to draw her away. Sinjin shook his head. His uncle looked back over his shoulder with you're welcome written on his face. Sinjin had to smile. There really wasn't much they needed to do to prepare for the journey. The kitchens remained neutral territory at the moment, and so far everyone had followed an unspoken truce in that area. The kitchens continued to operate as they always had and managed to feed those within the hold. Miss Mariss insisted she would let no mouth go unfed if there was any way she could help it. Still, she did not skimp on the supplies she and her staff packed for the journey.

Dragonhold's true size was unknown. Trinda had given indication of some exploration beyond the stone forest but had not elaborated. Sinjin suspected they would need far less in the way of supplies but didn't mind the weight in his pack. He'd gone hungry before and knew too much food and water was far better than not enough. Despite others having packed food and bedrolls for them, Kendra's list of things needing doing was long. It kept her occupied and from dwelling on Sevellon's supposed death. For that reason, Sinjin was happy to play along and did his best to help.

He'd long since grown accustomed to living away from the sun and stars, relying solely on his internal clock to tell him when it was time to head for his bedroll. He and Kendra shared a cot not far from the kitchens. Sinjin found it strange since he had grown up in the hold and had his own chambers. Allette held that part of the hold. No matter the truces, it might not be the safest place to sleep. Here they would be guarded, which allowed Sinjin to fall asleep. Otherwise, he probably would have stayed awake, watching Kendra breathe, knowing she wasn't really sleeping either. She'd always told him his snoring somehow pulled her eyes closed. Letting his cares go, Sinjin drifted to sleep.

* * *

The Great Hall had probably never before seen such disarray. There had been chaos there before when refugees erected a tent city, but that paled in comparison to the *Serpent's* wreckage, crushed as it was beneath the *Dragon's Wing*. Onin and Jehregard huddled against the exterior wall, far from the main entrance, which had become a dangerous place. In an apparent fit of panic and rage, the feral queen attacked debris blocking the God's Eye tunnel. It was difficult to understand what was happening.

The more time passed, the less likely he and Jehregard would escape Dragonhold alive. His chances were better than the dragon's, given he needed far less food to survive than the mighty beast. He wasn't sure how long his valiant companion could go without food and water, but the verdant dragon was already showing signs of negative effects. If it came to it, he had decided the two of them would fly from the hold. They would either make it through or they wouldn't; far better to choose their own fate. Jehregard moaned and came as close to a sigh dragons could accomplish.

"I know, old friend. I know."

Onin was still stroking the dragon's eye ridge, which had purposefully been placed low enough for him to do so, when Miss Mariss arrived with a half dozen helpers. "I don't blame you for not wanting to leave your dragon, but you must eat."

Onin grunted in response.

"I'm told my brisket is unmatched in the world. Would you care to judge?"

By the aroma, the woman did not boast, and a fine woman she was. "How is it that you are unmarried?" he asked.

"Well . . . I . . . uh . . . I mean . . . I . . . uh . . ."

"You're a beautiful woman whose food is art," Onin said, despite the deep crimson Miss Mariss was turning. "Were I not married to this great oaf of a dragon, I do believe I'd chase you anywhere you chose to run."

Those who had accompanied Miss Mariss did their best to pretend they'd heard nothing and concentrated on filling Jehregard's water and food troughs. What they brought was not enough to sustain him, but Onin could ask no more. Those within Dragonhold took a great risk to feed his dragon. When the food was gone, it was gone. Dragonhold had never achieved the ability to feed its inhabitants without food from the outside, and that was no longer an option. Onin recognized this and wondered how much longer they should remain a burden on these people. He was an old man, and he'd lived a rich, full life. Then he laughed. He was too stubborn to die.

Miss Mariss watched him as if he were an unfathomable mystery.

"You're kind to an old man and his dragon," he said. "We both acknowledge and appreciate what you do for us. Do not worry over my words. I was never very good at giving compliments."

"You did just fine," she said with a kind smile that melted Onin's battered heart. When she squeezed his arm, he felt things long since lost. "If you need to get away from here, for some time to yourself or whatever you need, call for me. I can have someone sit with Jehregard while you're gone."

"Thank you," Onin said. Jehregard gave a mighty woof of gratitude that struck the retreating people like a wind gust. Miss Mariss looked over her shoulder one last time as she walked away.

"We're going to have to figure out a way to survive this," Onin said to his dragon. Jehregard shook the hold's foundations with a deep baritone roar.

Moments later, Allette Kilbor strode into the Great Hall unannounced, save the sound of the feral queen moving behind her. So much for staying out of trouble, Onin thought. The Black Queen moved directly toward him, leaving little doubt as to whom she sought. When standing before him, she stared flatly, no emotion on her face. Her dragon, however, made its intentions plain. Rising up to her full height, the feral queen extended her wings and poised her head, ready to strike. Though she was smaller than Jehregard, it was not by a large margin. Onin didn't want to find out which, if either, would survive such a fight. In all likelihood, both would die.

"You're a good man, but you are powerless," Allette said by way of greeting.

"You are beautiful but tactless," Onin replied.

Allette wasn't quite prepared for that response, and it took her a moment before she spoke again. "Onin of the Old Guard, do you believe there can be peace between the Jaga and the Heights?"

"Relative peace existed for thousands of years," Onin said.

"But the feral dragons were in hiding for most of that time. They cannot hide now. They will not hide."

"Still," Onin said. "Would you allow the verdants to fly high above the Jaga, as they once did?"

The feral queen had not relaxed much, but she either understood his words or read Allette's thoughts. Those massive eyes narrowed, and the dragon moved her face closer to Onin. Behind him, Jehregard shifted his weight, agitated.

"If your dragon strikes," Onin said, his voice going cold and hard, "there will be no peace."

The Black Queen turned and hissed, and to Onin's surprise, the dragon was cowed. After giving him a look that spoke of a painful death, the feral queen assumed a less aggressive posture. Jehregard gave a woof, as if to say that was how it should be.

"There must be trade. No sanctions," Allette said.

This caught Onin off guard; never before had there been relations between the Jaga and the Heights. The Jaga had always been a wild place inhabited by dangerous creatures and even more dangerous people. The lord chancellor's policy had always been to avoid contact with the Jaga's inhabitants at almost any cost. Verdant dragons were more comfortable than ferals at high altitudes, and flying high above had worked for many generations. Now a single individual represented the Jaga--a unifying force.

Onin had no real power over those in the Heights, but that didn't mean he couldn't try to talk sense to them. "Done."

"You can make them do this, Onin of the Old Guard?"

"What other choice will they have?"

At this, the Black Queen smiled. "You're a good man."

The burly man nodded, metal rings tinkling in his beard.

"Will you help me get out of this place, Onin?"

For a brief instant, the Allette Kilbor of old was visible. As Thundegar Rheams had once said, Allette was no evil dictator; she was a good girl who'd been damaged by a cruel streak of fate. Onin knew something about that, as did Jehregard.

"We wish to leave this place as well," he said. "But how?"

"Come with me. I'll show you."

Allette and Onin walked side by side. A good bit of noise accompanied them as their dragons did their best to keep up, sometimes knocking down anything in their path to not let the other gain an advantage. Onin noticed Thundegar Rheams watched from not far away, and he wondered if the man's presence might be a boon, but then Thundegar stepped back into the shadows. Onin decided to pretend he hadn't seen the other man. He hadn't seen Rastas the cloud cat make his way back to Allette's side, and he was caught by surprise when the cat swiped at him with needle-sharp claws. Onin's reflexes weren't completely gone, and he narrowly avoided a new scar. Allette hissed at the cat, who continued to stare at Onin, tail twitching with mischievous intent.

The remains of the main gate gave the cat other things to hold his attention. The shield enclosing them was wholly unnatural and blotted out everything else. Allette walked all the way to the edge and pointed to the megalithic stone spire jutting from the ruptured landscape. With their graceful curves and runic inscriptions, these stone fingers stood at the heart of their problems. Between them stretched a membrane of pure energy. How and why, Onin didn't know, but that much he could see.

"We can leave the hold," Allette said. "We just can't yet escape the barrier. But if you look closely, you'll see that the barrier does not envelope the stones, it only fills the air between them. There is weakness we can exploit."

"What would you have me do?" Onin asked.

"Help me figure out how two dragons and a handful of people can take down one of those spires."

Chapter 4

Dreams are fueled by belief.
--Enly Mandone, bard

* * *

Jessub Tillerman was torn. Part of him was loyal to Catrin. She'd done so much for his family and had changed their lives. Some would say he and his kin lived solely because of her actions; it was a difficult debt to overlook. The same, however, could be said of the crew of the *Dragon's Wing*. Benjin and Fasha had taken him in as their own, even if he'd had to be a little pushy about it. The deck of the *Dragon's Wing* was his home. There he'd grown into manhood. Though Pelivor taught Gwen to propel the sleek, graceful ship, Jessub thought he might have learned just as much. The thrust tubes themselves were of Pelivor's design, even if he still struggled to use them. Jessub helped fashion those Gwen now used and couldn't help but feel proud of being part of what seemed an important moment in history. Fasha, Benjin and later Wendel and Jensen had all mentored him at one time or another. He'd learned so much.

The time Pelivor spent teaching Gwen to fly the ship was his favorite, though; not that he would ever tell her that. She'd been so determined but found little success. Jessub would always remember memorizing Pelivor's words to help her practice. Helping her overcome the frustration and embarrassment made him feel good, even if she hadn't quite succeeded in the end. Then there were the things he couldn't admit to himself.

Still, the opportunity to explore Dragonhold with Catrin would be the adventure of a lifetime, though it had the potential to make that lifetime significantly shorter. Rarely had fear prevented Jessub from doing anything, but even brave men had limits. Travelling with the Herald of Istra carried risks, yet he was pulled so strongly to go with her. Something had been growing inside him, and he needed to understand it. The Fifth Magic changed everything, Istra's energy both blessing and curse; only those with power were affected by its absence. It was the need to understand himself that drove him.

The thought of facing Gwen was almost more than he could bear. But he could not live in her shadow forever. At some point, he would need to accept his own role in his fate and embrace them. He'd watched her and learned from her; perhaps more than he'd ever realized. What she and Pelivor did to fly the ship fascinated him; perhaps now he understood more of the reasons.

He was no coward, but his guts hurt. This was the most difficult decision he'd ever have to make. No safe choices remained. There was no sanctuary. Part of him wished for the simpler life he had back on the farm with his grandparents, but those times and those people were gone. With an aching heart, Jessub sighed. When Benjin approached, he tried to pretend he hadn't been sitting there thinking, and just as soon realized how silly that was.

"It's not often in life that the way forward is clear," Benjin said.

How Benjin knew such things was beyond Jessub's understanding. The older man's wisdom and wit proved Jessub had a long way yet to go. He did not live in the shadows of others because they placed him there, he realized; he lived in their shadows because he had a lot to learn from them.

"It's always the silent ones you have to look out for," Benjin said with a wicked smile. "I know the reason for that."

Jessub Tillerman looked up at Benjin, a question in his eyes. Somehow that reason meant a lot to Jessub. Waiting to know what it was left him in suspense.

"I think it's because they're too busy thinking to open their mouths."

Jessub smiled, for he knew it to be true. Always one to consider his words these days, he wondered at how much he himself had already changed. Somehow he managed to let the silence hang too long. Again.

"If I'm going to talk to myself," Benjin said, "then I get to choose the subject. You're a good man, Jessub Tillerman. You've done everything asked of you and more. You've come a long way. It has been an honor to serve with you on the crew of the *Dragon's Wing*. But I want you to know you're free to live your life in any way you choose. You will always have a home on the *Dragon's Wing*, but it is not a prison. No one will hold it against you."

The words did not sound true to Jessub. Perhaps this was a shortcoming on his part, but he could not simply walk away from his responsibilities to the *Dragon's Wing* without leaving a hole in its place. He did not have as critical a role as Benjin or Fasha or Farsy or Grubb or Nimsy or Bryn or Gwen . . . He stopped his mental tirade before he came to tears.

Patting the young man on the shoulder, Benjin sighed as well, as if he knew his words weren't helping.

"Thank you," was all Jessub could get out. His quivering chin made him feel weak. Shame flushing his cheeks, he looked down.

"I believe in you," Benjin Hawk said before walking away.

* * *

Kenward walked toward the Great Hall, knowing Catrin and the others would soon depart for their explorations. Following what his gut told him was chief among the things that had kept him alive. The moment he'd heard Allette and Onin had aligned around the purpose of destroying one of the spires, he knew a likely fatal decision point lay ahead. No one could say what would happen if one was brought down; by Kenward's estimation, it had an equal chance of saving or destroying them. The Black Queen would hear no solution that would not free the dragons along with humans, which meant either take down the entire barrier or bore a large enough tunnel through one of the spires. While the stone fingers had sufficient girth, Kenward had his doubts.

Onin stood near the main entrance to Dragonhold as the sun rose. It was among the few places in the hold a person could achieve a certain sense of connection with the outside world, even if the barrier cast a bluish green hue over everything. Kenward wasn't certain if the man was in meditation or prayer, and he stood alongside him in silence. Together they watched the first sunlight strike the peaks on the valley's far side. The morning sun was at their backs, and they would not have a clear view until late morning. Still, watching the light inexorably reveal the landscape, painting it in a parade of textures that shifted over time, was a magical thing. The color would have been spectacular if not tainted by the barrier, and Onin turned to Kenward. He said nothing.

"You'll help Allette?" Kenward asked.

Onin nodded.

"Why?"

"If the dragons do not escape, they die."

Kenward nodded, not given to frivolous words himself. "Do you trust her?" he asked after a long moment. Onin grunted. "Do you really think your dragons can take down the barrier?"

Onin of the Old Guard just glared at Kenward and held out his open palms. "Won't know until we try."

Pulling information out of Onin was starting to wear on Kenward. Thundegar Rheams joined them, and Onin was no happier with his company than with Kenward's. It didn't make him feel all that much better.

"What do you think?" Kenward asked Thundegar. "Can the dragons possibly bring it down?"

"I mean no offense to Jehregard when I say this, but he is of smaller stature than most of his kind," Thundegar said with a glance at Onin. The old warrior grunted in acknowledgment. "Had we a full-size verdant within the hold, perhaps. I'm not certain Jehregard and the feral queen are up to such a monumental task. Though the smallest of the three, Kyrien is powerful and his help could make a difference. Catrin's help couldn't hurt either. Perhaps you could talk to her?"

Kenward had no sway over Catrin. She was his friend--most of the time--and would listen to him, but he could make no promises. "You'd be better served to talk with her father, Wendel, or Benjin. They came in on that ship you might have seen resting on the remains of mine."

Thundegar sighed. "I already did. I've come to the conclusion what you or I think makes almost no difference at all." Kenward gave him an ungrateful look. "You asked."

The truth of the words was plain, but they did not help Kenward. He had to decide what to do, where to place his efforts and his loyalties. Journeying deeper into the hold was counter to what every one of Kenward's instincts told him to do. He would add no value to that expedition, and it would likely get him no closer to the open air and seas. He had other reasons for not wanting to go with Catrin and other reasons to stay here, but he wasn't ready to face those things yet.

"Rock is rock," Onin said into the silence.

Kenward waited a moment for him to continue, but he just stood, staring at the stone spire. "Um . . . what?"

Onin looked at him as if he were daft. "We know how to break rock."

"Fire and water," a female voice said from behind. All three men jumped. Realizing how close the feral queen had gotten without their noticing, they each jumped again. It was one thing for Allette to sneak up on a person; the feral queen was another thing altogether. Jehregard rested nearby, snoring. "We need all the wood and coal we can get. And water buckets."

A sick feeling gripped Kenward, and he started to reconsider going with Catrin.

"We all make sacrifices," Allette said, locking eyes with Kenward.

He was trapped. Like a moth in a spider's web, he could not escape. Those eyes drew him in and held him. She knew him. She possessed Catrin's memories of him. It was perhaps the strangest relationship Kenward had ever had, yet she pulled at his heart. Something about this woman captivated him. He wanted to reach out to her, to touch her, to save her. But like a beautiful rose, he must be wary of thorns. This was no innocent dockside maiden; Allette was a woman of a different kind, and she had enemies Kenward called friends. Not to mention that the girl's allies came from his nightmares. It wasn't her fault, he knew, but even Catrin would not tell him what had happened to her. He was angry about that and for a number of other things he'd yet to forgive.

"Will you hate me too?" Allette asked, gazing into his soul.

"I don't . . . I wouldn't hate . . . it's just . . . Why must the ones I love destroy the things I treasure most?"

"It is a test of your love, Kenward Trell," Allette said.

Kenward laughed. He never did anything the easy way. Why would falling in love be any different? His knees trembled at the thought. No matter how loudly warnings screamed in his mind, they were overwhelmed. There simply was no choice in the matter. "You may burn the remains of the *Serpent*," he said with his head hung. And though smitten, he could not keep the retort from his tongue, "But do be careful not to scratch the

Dragon's Wing."

After being angry for a moment more, Kenward looked back at his sister's ship, perched atop the wreckage of his own. The *Wing* was still seaworthy and airworthy. No matter how unfair it was or how much it hurt, the *Serpent* was gone. Part of him had always known she would be short lived, but she had done her job well. The *Serpent* had proven one could fly without the aid of Istra's power. Ways to improve the design continued to fill his dreams; someday he would build a new ship in the *Serpent's* honor. Kenward sighed. "If you'll work with Benjin to build a makeshift dry dock and move the *Dragon's Wing* safely, I should be able to get you coal and buckets."

Onin chuckled.

Thundegar, at least, showed some sympathy. "I will go with you."

The feral queen moved to one side, clearing a pathway toward the kitchens without a word from Allette. Kenward looked at her one last time, knowing he risked losing another piece of himself in doing so. She nodded in return, not meeting his eyes. He appreciated the confirmation and hoped it truly was safe to walk past the feral queen. Which of the two was truly in control remained a mystery. Allette cared for Thundegar as well, so it was less likely the glossy black dragon would attack. There had been nothing stopping the towering predator from striking at any time. It was an unnerving thought.

"You're a brave man," Thundegar said as they walked between the rock wall and the feral queen. Enormous eyes tracked them, and scales shifted as the feral queen moved to watch them pass.

Kenward wanted to run and hide and never come back out. He could feel the breath of his demise descending. It was not imagination alone tormenting him. The feral queen fostered his fear and backed it with deadly intent.

Entering the tunnel leading to the kitchens at a brisk walk, Kenward finally breathed again.

"The queen has a unique way of expressing herself, don't you think?" Thundegar asked while wiping the sweat from his forehead.

"I'm not sure I can go back out there," Kenward admitted. "Brave I might be, but suicidal I'm not. My place among the stars will have to wait."

"I think she likes you," Thundegar said.

Kenward wasn't certain if he was talking about Allette or the feral queen; he was afraid to ask. This was not a conversation he was prepared to have. The low murmur of many voices in another part of the keep caught their attention. A crowd blocked the corridor up ahead, and more people arrived from a side passage.

"What's going on?" Kenward asked, acutely aware of being an outsider.

"Lady Catrin's going to explore the hold," a young man said.

That wasn't news to Kenward and did little to explain why people jammed the halls. "Why the crowd?" Kenward asked, hoping not to offend by asking the wrong question.

"People loyal to Catrin began to talk, and we decided we want to help. Turns out, there are a lot of us."

"We have important news for Lady Catrin," Kenward said. Half expecting to be snubbed, he was surprised and a little embarrassed when the young man began shouting the Herald's friends needed to come through. The deeper they moved, the more necessary the shouts became. Bodies crowded the constricting halls, the din consuming all but the loudest cries. Trapped amid a mass of humanity, Kenward had never felt so confined and thought he might suffocate.

"Easy there, friend," Thundegar said. "Make some room! Give this man some space!"

Packed against those around them, people did what they could to give Kenward room. In a way, it almost made the feeling worse. Guards wearing uniforms with Trinda's insignia guided the two men to where Catrin stood atop a stack of crates, tears in her eyes. The sight left Kenward breathless. He truly loved her in spite of all the pain their relationship had caused him. She'd always done her best to save those around her and even those who opposed her. He knew she'd never felt like a true ruler within Dragonhold, but this gathering was a clear majority and showed the people chose her as their leader.

When Kenward and Thundegar made their way to where Catrin stood, bereft of words, she shook her head, and tears fell to the stone floor. Her father moved to her side and put his arm around her. "Thank you all," Catrin finally said in a voice thick with emotion. A great roar traveled through the halls, rivaling that of the dragons.

When the roar died down enough for Kenward to be heard, he shouted, "Catrin! The *Dragon's Wing* will surely be destroyed if you don't come quickly!" He had her full attention.

"I need to get to the Great Hall," Catrin said in a tone that set people instantly moving. Kenward had never seen anything to match the way the people responded to Catrin's words. Wendel Volker marched ahead of Catrin, barking at anyone who got in their way. The tunnels that had nearly cost him his sanity coming in cleared so fast, they strode through at a quick walk.

"We're going to need coal," Kenward said, "and buckets to satisfy Allette. They want the wood from the *Serpent*."

"For what?" Catrin asked, sounding offended on his behalf.

"Allette and Onin are going to attack one of the spires," Kenward said.

Looking shocked, Catrin grabbed his arm and dragged him forward at a half run. He would've said something about buckets and coal had she given him the chance. Within the Great Hall, the feral queen glared at the *Dragon's Wing* with impatient eyes. Her head snapped in their direction when Catrin entered. With Thundegar, Kenward had a chance of passing peacefully, approaching with Catrin he'd likely wind up dead, and he questioned the wisdom of going any farther.

"Stop," Catrin said, her voice echoing within the hall. "I wish to speak with Allette."

The feral queen coiled herself before Catrin, ready to strike, but the Herald showed no fear. Kenward admired her. Without Istra's light, she was less powerful than he, in many ways. Yet she stood before death itself and chastised it.

Allette appeared from behind her dragon. "Do not stand in my way, Catrin Volker."

"We've no idea what effect destroying one of the spires would have," Catrin said. "Give us some time to learn more of how the Fifth Magic works, and we may find a better way."

"Your dragon may be able to live on fish and mushrooms," Allette said, glancing up at the feral queen. "Unless you have a herd of cattle hidden away, we either escape soon or die."

Jehregard and the feral queen both reacted to the sound of another dragon entering the hall. Kyrien's movements spoke of agitation and aggression. Jehregard issued a whine that ended with a trumpeting roar.

"Has the time come so soon?" Allette asked Catrin. "Shall we kill each other now?"

Those words were a clear invitation to leave, Kenward thought, and he took a step backward. Before he could turn and run, the feral queen edged into the space between him and the kitchens. Rising up to her full height, she hissed and flapped her wings, buffeting him with wind. Kyrien issued a warning growl that pulled the feral queen's attention away from Kenward, though she still blocked his path. Shouts echoed from behind the dragon, and Kenward worried the people of Dragonhold might attack the feral queen in their fervor, which would surely end in a massacre.

"Stop this at once!" Onin demanded, and Jehregard trumpeted his displeasure. Though normally docile, verdant dragons could be fierce when circumstances called for it. Kenward had seen them fight in the Jaga War.

"I don't wish to kill you," Catrin said slowly. Allette held her ground and said nothing. "I just want you to wait before attacking the spire. Damaging the Fifth Magic could be worse than leaving it as is. I doubt it can be defeated through brute force. Give me three days . . . please."

"No," Allette said. "I'm sorry but I cannot do what you ask. You, of course, understand."

Kenward could not imagine what passed between the two women, having experienced each other's lives and knowing the other's secrets. He shivered at the thought. If either had access to Istra's power at that moment, Kenward suspected lightning would be flying. As it was, all three dragons appeared ready for a fight.

In the end, Catrin nodded. "Help us preserve the *Dragon's Wing*, and I won't stand in your way."

"If the ship can be moved quickly, then let it be done. If not, it'll fly one last time."

Once the feral queen stood down and moved well clear of the halls, people poured in. Word spread regarding what was needed. Catrin ordered buckets filled with coal and delivered to Allette despite her misgivings. The Black Queen accepted the gifts and waited impatiently for Martik, Benjin, Wendel and a handful of others while they figured out how to move and preserve the heavy vessel. The conversation was heated, and Kenward decided he didn't feel strongly enough about it to interject.

"We've a lot of straw," a young man said. The boy looked at the ground when no one responded. Men with louder voices talked right over him.

"Straw," Kenward said loudly, and the boy's eyes went wide. "This young man says you have a large supply of straw."

Martik turned and blinked at Kenward a moment, his thoughts almost visible on his face. "Get it up here as fast as you can. We need people to start clearing the debris from this side."

Kenward flinched at the word debris.

"We need the longest and strongest poles you can find to support this side," Martik continued, not even noticing the dirty look the captain of the *Serpent* gave him. Kenward tried a little harder.

"Don't forget you've got dragons at your disposal," Thundegar said.

Martik took a moment to consider. Kenward imagined many of the things Martik had done would have been made easier with a dragon's assistance. The man surprised him, though, when he said, "All the same, I think we'll do it ourselves. I don't know that I could communicate well enough with a dragon to keep anyone from getting hurt. It'll take us a half a day, but we'll get it done."

Allette grimaced at the prospect of waiting, but she was getting the coal and buckets she'd requested. For the moment, it had to be enough. The people of Dragonhold rallied around the common purpose, looking as if they might complete the task in far less time than Martik had predicted. A wise man always overestimated the difficulty of a task, and Martik Tillerman was a very wise man.

Chapter 5
Nothing belongs to anyone.
--Sevellon, thief

* * *

The Godfist had never been an easy place to live. The years following Istra's return had made it even more difficult. Anyone who saw Sevellon looked at him with distrust, not because they knew he was a thief, but because they trusted no one. Complacency was a thief's best friend. Here, though, the people had already lost much. This was why Sevellon chose not to go anywhere near the Masterhouse or Lowerton, but instead to the outskirts, where much of what had been destroyed had never been rebuilt. Many had died here. What most would see as modern ruins represented opportunity for the thief. Such places often held some small treasure if you knew where and how to look.

The cover of darkness was another tool he'd learned to use well, and preserving his night vision was a skill he'd finely tuned over many years. Still, avoiding frequent patrols sent out from the Masterhouse and remaining watchful for dragons, demons, gray soldiers, and giants proved difficult. Outsiders were not welcome here; that was something Sevellon understood, and he had no good way to explain his presence. Lying came naturally to him, though. In the event he was captured, he had a number of tales prepared. He hoped to play on their sympathies since trust was unlikely.

Guilt was not an emotion a thief could afford, and once again he suppressed it.

The metallic click of harness announced another patrol's imminent arrival. Sevellon crouched down behind an old chimney. Much of the place had burned, but charred floor slats remained. Part of being a good thief was knowing what things were valuable, what things you can manage to get away with, and where most people hide the things they cherish above all others. Remaining still, Sevellon relied on the fact that these patrols had found nothing lately, based on their idle conversation. These people were bored. Understanding human nature was another tool Sevellon relied on heavily. But one thing he had very little control over, much less understanding of, were animals.

Perhaps these beasts could sense him in ways humans could not, or perhaps it was simply the smell of him. It mattered little since the end result was the same. Two of the patrol's horses spooked. Sevellon could not see the whites of their eyes from where he hid, but the way their hooves pounded against cobbled stone spoke of fear. Next came the sound of boots. His muscles tensed and his heart raced.

"Probably nothing," one man said.

Sevellon was already moving, half walking, half running straight back from the chimney that had hidden him. Near the crumbling remains of a barn, he broke into a full run. If not for the torches the patrol carried ruining their night vision, they might have seen him. And if not for the horses' continued fussing, they might have heard him, but Sevellon had the thief's luck. Soon, having found nothing around the dilapidated house, the patrol moved on. Beneath the light cast by the moon and twinkling comets, Sevellon went back to pull the strongbox from its charred resting place. A strongbox was only as good as its lock, and Sevellon was confident. He'd not only opened better quality locks than those available on the Godfist, he'd made better during his time as a locksmith.

In the end, he was wrong. While this lock was poor quality in comparison to his own work, the softer metals used had melted and fused during the fire, making the lock far more secure. With the right tools and a bit of time, he could have opened the box, but it might as well have been sealed with magic in his current circumstances. After restoring the slats to order, Sevellon moved on. The closer to the harbor he went, the closer to inhabited structures he came. Old instincts and heightened senses rose from years of training. Here, at least, he might find what he needed.

Few dared to trade with the Godfist these days, and even the fishing ships rested, dormant, in the harbor. The thief needed a way off this forsaken rock, and that would require gold. At the moment, he had neither ship nor gold, and the odds of his surviving the winter continued to drop.

Moving into the shadows between two buildings, both of which appeared to be occupied, Sevellon froze. Patrols approached from two different directions, showing the Godfist remained in a state of alert. Times of tension, war, and distrust were among the least productive for thieves. An old friend had once taught him that war raised the stakes and provided even greater wealth for those willing to risk their lives. That same friend had gotten greedy. It was the type of lesson Sevellon wished he'd learned some other way.

The silhouette of a familiar ship crept through the harbor, close to the shoreline, its lighting kept low. In general, one did not question the thief's luck. In this case, however, Sevellon was uncertain whether he should be relieved or terrified. He knew from experience this ship would run under complete darkness if not for the rocks along the shoreline. The *Nightfist* was a mercenary ship and not one Sevellon had ever hoped to see again. His time aboard had been brief, which had been the best part about it. Kenward Trell had sometimes dealt with those perhaps best avoided, but the thief did not question the life of the pirate. Perhaps, if he was lucky, the *Nightfist*'s crew would remember him as a pirate and not the man who had lightened their purses.

Go. His instincts warned. Run.

* * *

Kenward oversaw the placement of the planks he and his crew had cut not so long ago. Then they had been building a ship that would be the first of its kind; now they were burning the remains of that same ship. There was the chance this would return to them their freedom and get Kenward out of this tomb, which would make it all worthwhile.

When the boiler and pressure tanks from the ship had been lowered, Kenward wasn't certain what to think. Those would be the most expensive and difficult parts to re-create but new designs would also provide better performance. From atop her dragon, Allette directed the placement of the tanks and boiler, and she dictated they be filled with water. When she ordered all the pipes sealed, he immediately remembered the warnings the ancient writings had about pressure release valves. He wasn't certain how long it would take, but he vowed to get well clear of the area once the fire was lit.

It had been Martik who suggested using some old, moldy barrels to store water atop the boiler and tanks. Kenward wasn't certain he understood the exact principles but suspected it would result in a spectacular display; all the more reason to get clear. There wasn't much room to maneuver within the domelike shield. The dragons had far more difficulty staying clear of the plasma barrier. Some places could hold multiple dragons, while others were barely wide enough to allow passage. Jehregard had settled into one of the larger cavities, which put him close enough to exert force on the spire with his enormous head. The feral queen moved more nimbly, which allowed Allette to survey the pyre's construction from multiple perspectives. For her sake and his own, Kenward hoped it worked.

Catrin had left, gone in search of another way out, and Kenward wished her luck as well. He didn't care who found a solution, as long as someone did. The *Dragon's Wing* was safely dry-docked, and thanks to the ingenuity, strength, and tenacity of the people of Dragonhold, the ship was even pointing in the right direction. Kenward wasn't certain such a takeoff would be possible for the heavier, more traditional and seaworthy ship. This was where his design had so many advantages. His mind whirled with possibilities.

Leftover straw mixed with coal was poured into every crack and crevice of the wood pile resting at the spire's base. Already the feral queen had attacked the spire with tooth and claw, showing just how devastating those weapons were, but the barrier pelted her with lightning. Every bit of rock she tore away came with a price, and even the feral queen could not endure such punishment for long.

Having done his best to oversee the placement of the timbers, Kenward hoped it was all worth it. If this didn't work, he might throw himself into the plasma barrier in frustration. His mother had warned him about such thoughts. Better to clear his head during the difficult and time-consuming climb back to the keep. Looking down on him, even Trinda watched the spectacle. Climbing the obliterated stair, his arms grew tired and sore. Ropes hung down over missing sections of stair, challenging his endurance. Somehow he found the strength, though his arms trembled.

The order to light the fire was given long before he reached Dragonhold. Smoke and heat grew worse as he climbed. By the time he gained the entrance, smoke filled the valley, obscuring all except an orange glow where the flames were highest. Swirling winds created wandering vortices of ash floating around them. Trinda coughed and looked over to Kenward, who was still catching his breath. She rolled her eyes as if believing there was no chance this would work. He wondered at the expressiveness of her face. The ability to communicate without words was a valuable skill, and he respected those who did it well. Still, her attitude annoyed him. Why would she hope for this to fail? Was it because it hadn't been her idea? Had Kenward wanted her support, he would have tried to make Trinda believe it was her idea, but it was not her support he needed. Trinda's power within Dragonhold continued to dwindle.

People filtered in and Kenward did what he could to help people make the last of the climb. He remembered how tired he'd been, and these folks had worked longer and harder. No one left afterward. They all stayed behind to witness events for themselves. They had been a part of this and were not ready to walk away. Kenward couldn't blame them.

Trinda, on the other hand, looked as if she were being punished. The ash stained her white dress and collected in her hair. A carpet of it danced across the stone, constantly shifting and moving in the wind, and it dirtied her shoes as well. "How much longer is this going to take?" she asked.

Kenward just shrugged in response. Trinda made a huffy noise. Not long after, though, a steady whistling grew in volume and rose in pitch. People came in faster now, and Kenward did what he could to help. Others joined in, the whistle's growing intensity increasing the urgency. Then, with unexpected suddenness, the whistling stopped. Now raging, the fire crackled and roared.

"What happened?" someone yelled.

No one got the chance to respond. A series of explosions sent shock waves up the barrier, which reflected into the hold. It started with a single, smaller explosion, immediately followed by two larger blasts. When the second shock wave hit, it knocked Kenward, Trinda, and most everyone gathered from their feet. Cries from the stair told of those who'd fallen as a result. Kenward scooted himself backward as the heat and glowing embers followed in a towering wave. Then the cinders got bigger--much bigger. A flaming chunk of pressure tank landed where Kenward had been sitting just a moment before. As fast as he could, he regained his feet and started pulling people away from the ledge.

Waves of steam and a thunderous crack followed the explosions in rapid succession. Cries echoed within the hold. A mighty dragon roar drowned out the flames, a thunderous boom shaking the Godfist's foundations a moment later. Jehregard had struck the spire, Kenward assumed, though he could see little through the smoke and steam. Allette's shouts also drifted up to where he sat, and Kenward admired the girl's courage. Even amid a firestorm, she maintained her composure. It was a skill few possessed.

The feral queen struck the spire next, which resulted in a much different, higher-pitched sound. Kenward felt each blow in his boots. Striking repeatedly, one right after the other, the dragons beat a rhythmic tune. Caged thunder filled the hold as stone gave way and the plasma wavered. Another cheer rose from those gathered. Lightning leaped out from the destabilized barrier, and from the sounds of their cries, it struck both the feral queen and Jehregard. Again and again lightning created a dancing spider web that almost continuously struck the dragons. Kenward felt helpless and useless, unable to do anything to ease their pain and knowing they wouldn't last much longer.

"Look out! Get down!"

Kenward had no idea who shouted the warning, but he was grateful nonetheless. Just as he hit the stone, ash swirling maddeningly around him, Kyrien flashed overhead at high speed. Smoke roiled in his wake, and no one had to wonder for long what he was doing. The dragon must have struck the spire at full speed. The impact caused the flagstone to jump up and smack Kenward in the face. He was still regaining consciousness when the snapping started. It grew louder and when Kenward looked up, the spire moved toward him. The goal had been to push the spire outward, and he would have thought Kyrien's momentum would have done just that, but no one had accounted for the energy field's grip. It flexed and pulled the mighty stone finger back toward the hold. It was then the spire's base failed. The stone megalith no longer lumbered toward them; it crashed down at full speed. Helping pull the last few people over and away from the ledge, Kenward went down for a third time.

The mighty pillar rushed toward him. Solid stone surrounding Dragonhold's main entrance was all that saved him from being crushed. Blocking most of the entrance, the spire now rested against the mountainside. What little open area remained was filled with a constant barrage of sparks and lightning. The plasma barrier remained in place, except now it bulged inward, closer to the hold and far angrier.

* * *

Kenward watched as the entrance to Dragonhold was effectively sealed, leaving Allette, Onin, and the dragons trapped outside with no access to food or water. Safety from the lightning was scarce. Kenward wasn't sure how long anyone would be able to survive trapped between the plasma barrier and the mountain. What had been only a matter of time for the dragons was now a matter of much less time. The few people who'd made it back were moved to an impromptu infirmary deeper within Dragonhold. No one ventured close to the front gates, afraid of being the lightning's next victim.

The keep resonated with a distorted note that warped the energy, making Kenward's teeth hurt. If he didn't get out of this place soon, he was going to go as crazy as most people thought he already was. Appearing to be a crazy fool had worked well for Kenward much of his life, but actually going insane was not a fate he relished. He'd seen powerful people, once vibrant and at the top of their mental games, reduced to shades of their former selves. Looking back at the gap between the stone spire and Dragonhold's gates, Kenward considered grabbing supplies and running through. Then he realized he could toss at least a few packs loaded with water, food, and other necessities through the narrow opening and remain unscathed.

Kenward raced for the kitchens, where Brother Vaughn was already explaining the situation to Miss Mariss, who looked more annoyed than ever.

"People just don't know when to leave well enough alone," she said.

Kenward would have defended their actions, but he knew better than to argue with Miss Mariss in her kitchen. It was the kind of thing you did only once. Despite her grumbling, Miss Mariss packed generous portions and included extra touches Kenward suspected were more for Onin's sake than Allette's. He was grateful when she handed him the packs and turned back to her work. He couldn't miss the worried look she gave him when he walked out.

"Don't go and do anything foolish!" she shouted after him.

He smiled. His aunt knew him well.

Though she'd given him water skins, he had to fill them himself. Not far from the kitchens was a small fountain perfect for the task. The things the ancients had built never failed to amaze him. Even as he filled the flasks, he imagined ways the wonders within Dragonhold might have been created. This led him to ponder how so much knowledge had been forgotten. Certainly things must have changed after Istra last departed, but that didn't explain how so much knowledge relevant to both Istran and Vestran phases had been lost. When he was honest with himself, he realized he was thinking about anything but Onin and Allette. Even if he could get supplies to them, what kind of existence would they have outside? Now more than ever, Kenward wished Catrin and her party success. Allette and Onin had both suffered enough in their lives, and Kenward wished no more hardships on them. His own memories proved just how painful such things could be, and he'd been lucky.

After capping the last water skin, Kenward walked back toward the Great Hall. Shouting and thunder quickened his step. When he turned the corner, two figures stood silhouetted against the fiery backdrop. Onin supported Allette, but even his strength was not enough to withstand the lightning. Dropping his burdens, Kenward ran toward them despite the fact that others were far closer than he. The lightning continued and the others slowed. Kenward did not.

It was a brave and foolish thing to do. Quicker than thought, a flash of light relieved him of control over his body. Through his pain, Kenward learned lightning's true nature and power. When finally the lightning relented, his body was slow to respond. Onin, the man he'd come to save, dragged both Kenward and Allette away from the entrance. One last time the lightning exacted its price for passage, sending all three to the stone. Other hands grabbed him then and pulled him to the infirmary.

He'd been fine moments before, but now his heart fluttered and his thoughts slowed. If this was how death felt, he liked it not at all. A woman he didn't recognize cut away his shirt to expose a charred wound, and Kenward cried out. His arms flailed at his sides against the shock of pain. His right hand met something warm and soft rather than the cold stone he'd expected. Calloused yet delicate fingers closed around his hand. Empathy and support flowed through the physical bond. Turning his head once he was able, he saw Allette staring back at him with pain-filled eyes. She'd given him strength when she was, herself, in great need. Kenward did what he could to communicate through touch, and he felt even worse when Allette gripped his hand hard, crying out in pain as someone tended her wounds. Her eyes rolled up into her head, and she passed out, her grip going limp in his hand.

Few things in this world impressed Kenward Trell, but reaching out to him in her greatest time of need and offering something of herself imprinted this woman on his very being. The rest had Allette Kilbor all wrong. This, Kenward was determined to change.

* * *

Walking beside Kendra, Sinjin could not believe what he heard. Even before they had split from the main party, the rumblings from deeper within the hold had begun. His mother had shown concern but said nothing. There had been speculation, but she had never confirmed or denied any of it. Now it was getting louder, and some was definitely not thunder, although Sinjin thought there had been legitimate thunder as well. This added to the confusion. High-pitched screams were a different matter altogether. The latest one sounded nearby, and Kendra grabbed Sinjin's arm, an instinctive defensive measure. She reached for what she treasured most.

With a lump in his throat, Sinjin cleared his sword from the scabbard. He made more noise than Kendra did performing the same motion, which made him blush. Next came a series of rumbling booms as if a god snored. It was impossible to know exactly what it was, but Sinjin's mind conjured gruesome images that made him sweat. He and Kendra were not untrained or unarmed but were no match for what Sinjin imagined waited in the darkness. There was something about exploring a place no human had seen in thousands of years. At every junction Catrin's party had come across, they had split up until broken down into pairs. No one was to go off alone. Despite the large number of people in the party, they got down to pairs surprisingly fast.

At first Kendra and Sinjin occasionally reencountered others who searched the halls, but there had been no signs of other humans in hours. Being in a constant state of alert took its toll on them, and Kendra motioned for him to sit and rest. She wrapped her herald globe more tightly in cloth to dim the light. Getting Trinda to provide the globes had been difficult, and the child queen continued to surprise. After sending one of her guards to retrieve the globes, she'd disappeared.

"Can you believe she just ran away?" Kendra asked, looking down at the glowing bundle in her lap.

"At least she gave us some of the herald globes before going wherever it is she went."

"You think he was telling the truth about not knowing where the rest are?" Kendra asked.

"I wouldn't put it past Trinda to hide them all over the keep and not tell anyone where they all are," Sinjin said as quietly as he could. Rumbling thunder obscured his words. Echoes danced within Dragonhold in strange ways. Sometimes the stone simply absorbed the sound, leaving people stranded where no one could hear them, and other sounds carried deep into the hold.

"What do you think we're going to find?" Kendra asked.

Sinjin shrugged, not wanting to reveal his fears. The question had come up before, and he hadn't answered then either. Knowing his wife as he did, Sinjin expected the question to come again. She wouldn't relent until he answered. She knew his weaknesses, yet he still wanted to be strong for her. Most of the time, she projected strength, but he knew her every weakness as well, and there were times she needed him. He'd let her down in the past and never wanted to feel that way again.

Reaching out, he squeezed her hand. After appearing confused at first, she looked up and smiled. Without warning, Dragonhold itself trembled and shook, tossing them helplessly about. When at last the tremors ceased, Sinjin jumped to his feet and helped Kendra up. Something was wrong. Sinjin's hair and teeth hurt, making him feel as if he'd been rung like a bell. When the feeling didn't abate, he looked to his wife, struggling as well, her eyes squinted from pain. Resonating within the halls and permeating the air around them, a discordant note threatened to debilitate them both. Like bees boring into Sinjin's ears, the feeling was inescapable. It nagged at him. High-pitched, panicked screams accompanied deep rumblings. If there were other creatures living within Dragonhold, surely now they were on full alert.

Moving as quickly as they could, they found the note more prevalent in some places than others and stopped to recuperate in a place where it was not overpowering.

"I can only imagine what your mom is going through," Kendra said.

Sinjin tried not to think about it. There was little he could do to help his mother, and thinking about her pain brought him physical and emotional anguish. It was a feeling no one should know, though many did.

So far Kendra and Sinjin had found little that was useful in their current circumstances. They found a beautiful fountain in full operation, though in need of a good cleaning, and they had discovered rooms filled with sealed clay jars as big as Sinjin. Halls cut in stone were indistinguishable from each other, the pebbles they dropped near each junction all they had to lead them back out. The deeper they went, the less likely they would ever make it back. The weight of the stone above pressed down upon them.

"You know Valterius is going to knock you down with his tail for months once you're reunited, right?"

Sinjin smiled and even laughed. It was the perfect thing to say at that moment. He loved his wife.

Chapter 6

Information from the past is changing our future.
--Brother Milo, Cathuran monk

* * *

Pelivor walked alongside Catrin in a state of disbelief. He'd mourned the loss of her, and she'd been returned to him. He'd lamented her previous marriage, and now his relief over Prios's absence in Catrin's life shamed him.

His old friend captured him with her eyes, just as she always had. She'd been his first kiss, and nothing could ever change that. He'd dreamed of her for years, which made him flush deeply. She spoke to him with softness in her eyes. Despite all the pain and danger, she still had a smile for him. Being so close to the very thing he desired was sweet torture, and he found himself staring too long.

"We somehow manage to find ourselves in the most dangerous situations," she said.

Smiling and nodding, Pelivor agreed. All along, he'd planned to stay by Catrin's side, and no one had challenged him. His pairing with her for this exploration had been at his desire, but she'd made no move to change it. That was the same as wanting it in his perception, and he tried to restrain his overeager heart. If Catrin hadn't been looking at him, he'd slap himself in the face. He should be thinking of ways to get them out of this colossal mess, yet he was acting like a foolish boy.

"I'm hoping all these dangerous situations will one day lead us to a peaceful existence," he said.

Catrin nodded. "Such a thing does exist."

Pelivor laughed. "What would you do?" he asked, knowing it was a silly question.

"Do you really want to know?" she asked, somehow managing to look innocent and fragile despite being the most powerful person on the planet, even if caught in a spider's web. "It's rather boring, actually."

Without realizing what he was doing until it was too late, Pelivor asked wordlessly, using only his facial expression. A flash of pain clouded Catrin's beautiful face. It was gone in an instant. Prios had always used a similar expression to coax words from people, and Pelivor had temporarily forgotten where he'd learned it. The result was that he'd made Catrin think of her dead husband. No matter how he tried, Pelivor always found a way to say the wrong thing around her.

The keep continued to rumble; the noise unidentifiable. Pelivor and Catrin exchanged a glance.

"Didn't Chase say Trinda had guards posted farther in than this?" Pelivor asked.

Catrin nodded. "He did. She's been monitoring the stone forest, and Chase said he thought she might have guards posted beyond there as well."

"I can't picture this forest," Pelivor said. "How much farther is it? It doesn't seem like a place this big should exist."

"Not that much farther," Catrin said. "The keep could go on for miles. I'm fairly certain the ancients exploited natural formations. The river that runs through this place is a big part of why the keep exists at all. It has worn away the soft rock over the millennia."

"You really are a know-it-all," Pelivor said, elbowing her in the ribs. The physical contact, no matter how minimal was thrilling.

"Sorry. I spent a lot of time studying, and I find these kinds of things interesting."

"Don't be sorry. That's one of the things I love about you."

The words were said before Pelivor could take them back, and the silence that hung after his statement was increasingly awkward. Searching for words, he drew a breath. Catrin gave him a sad smile, and he was about to apologize when someone knocked the world sideways. There were things in life that were part of the background, like the ringing in his ears, but when suddenly amplified and shifted to a frequency that set everything on edge, those things became unbearable. Reeling from the sudden change in the energy around them, Pelivor caught a glimpse of Catrin, her head cradled in her hands. He could not imagine how much worse it must be for her.

For years Pelivor had struggled to eke enough power from the air to fly the *Dragon's Wing*, and he couldn't even imagine how it must feel to have access to all the power all the time. The small amount he was able to draw was an elixir that left one wanting more. He knew the extent of Catrin's powers, and it frightened him if he thought too much about it.

"What is it?" Pelivor asked without realizing he was speaking.

"That fool Allette," Catrin said. "I think she damaged the Fifth Magic without actually disabling it. Why doesn't anyone listen to me?" She didn't give him a chance to answer. "We are powerless to do anything about the barrier. It's still there but now it's distorted; I can feel it. We must press on and hope we find some other way out soon."

Pelivor let the silence hang. The initial shock of the ringing was wearing off, and now it felt as if his teeth were going to crack. Catrin leaned on him for a moment; he put his arm around her. Why did it have to be so hard for them, he wondered, but he carried on nonetheless.

Only when they reached the stone forest did Pelivor really see the world around him again. His sole purpose was to take Catrin to the infernal ringing's source and make it stop. Thousands of trees, painstakingly carved with unmatched accuracy and detail, temporarily made the pain go away. For a moment the majesty erased all other thought. No guard could be seen, but evidence of their presence remained. Supplies and foodstuffs were stacked nearby, a cot tucked into a side hall not far from where the forest began.

Trinda might have recalled the guard, but Pelivor wasn't so sure. Perhaps it was the lifelike forest, or maybe it was the occasional carved inhabitants of those trees that unnerved Pelivor. Either way, he felt as if they were being watched. The hairs on his neck stood.

Neither wished to prolong this exploration, and they ate strips of dried beef while walking through the silent grove. Catrin unnecessarily motioned for silence. Others would be listening across the world in places just as improbable as this. Instantaneous global communications pushed the limits of imagination, yet it existed and Pelivor stood inside it.

While the high-pitched whine threatened to relieve Pelivor of his sanity, other noises indicated more immediate threats. No matter what anyone said, some of those deep booms were not thunder. Catrin had never said they were, and both knew the kind of danger they might face. It gave Pelivor great pride to walk beside Catrin into the unknown. They had fought overwhelming odds before, and though they hadn't always won, they had survived.

When Catrin drew a sudden breath and grabbed his arm, Pelivor wasn't certain they would again.

* * *

The maze beneath the Black Spike appeared to have been built by someone who was losing his sanity. Many tunnels went nowhere, some ending in vertical shafts. The construction was far rougher than what Durin had seen within Dragonhold or even Windhold.

"I knew a smith who made art by pouring molten silver into anthills," Strom said as if to chase away the ever-impinging darkness. "This place reminds me of the many tunnels and chambers the ants create."

Markers, presumably left by Catrin, saved them from exploring the entire place. Durin had to assume she was the one guiding them. Any other thought was just too frightening to bear.

"I'm convinced this place is the work of Ain Giest," Osbourne said. Strom glared at him as if mentioning the name might summon the immortal madman himself.

Durin wasn't certain he believed the old tales about Enoch and Ain Giest merging their consciousnesses and going mad, but someone built this impossible place. If Osbourne was correct, they were walking into the lair of the most notorious character in Godsland's history. Even the possibility gave Durin the crawls. They could do nothing to prepare and were essentially defenseless against whatever they encountered. Beyond the statuettes' light, darkness shifted and moved. Strom kept the figurines glowing low, afraid of discharging them too quickly, although there had been no perceptible lessening of the light they provided. Durin wished to see farther into the distance; not knowing if they were walking up on some ancient monster made his stomach hurt.

"If it was Ain," Osbourne continued, "I believe we are safe. He was never malicious as much as he perceived the world differently than others. No one can say what it must have been like always having his grandfather in the back of his mind, controlling his breathing, heart rate, and other functions. His frailty was the price of Enoch's folly. He was the one who'd taught so many of his people to heal themselves, not knowing how dire the consequences would be."

"No one should ever get into someone else's head," Strom said. "It's against nature and just wrong."

Durin could see his point, knowing Strom's experience with Kyrien was a driving factor behind his stance on the matter. There were others, though, who had benefitted from direct communication with the mind of another, sometimes across great distances. Had Prios not spoken in Sinjin's mind, assassins might well have succeeded in killing him. Some things were dangerous and needed to be used with care was what Durin took away from the conversation.

Ahead twisted carvings of trees materialized from the pervasive darkness. Winged gargoyles watched from glistening black branches as they moved deeper into a nightmare. Artfully carved, the trees may have once been accurate representations of nature. Now they looked as if they had been turned to wax, melted, then turned to stone. The creatures who occupied the upper branches were angular in comparison, lifelike images of things Durin prayed did not actually exist. And if they did, he hoped there were none within this place, which was horrible enough on its own.

Shuffling noises up ahead made Durin want to run and hide. Strom stopped them with a raised hand, and all three were on full alert. The light they bore would make them stand out to anything living in that darkness and might even drive some away. Durin didn't want to consider which of the creatures he'd seen in the trees might have been real, especially since far more terrifying monstrosities waited deeper within the twisted forest. Wings and tails emerged from human-looking torsos. Durin thought he might faint if one moved.

Nothing gave any indication of how large the forest was or if there were other tunnels leading out of the place.

Strom continued forward, as if drawn by magic, and Durin wondered if it might be true. He knew better than to ask the man. Strom was uncomfortable with his powers, and asking him would only make him defensive about it. Better to let the big man lead and follow his instincts. Durin smiled. He was finally starting to understand how to work with other people. He'd never known it could be so complicated or rewarding.

When Strom stopped without warning, holding up his hand again, Durin wasn't prepared and walked into Strom's back. He grunted loudly from the impact, and both Strom and Osbourne cast him scathing glances, demanding silence. When Durin recovered himself, he understood why. Voices came from not far ahead. Who in the world could possibly be at the bottom of this forsaken place, Durin asked himself, liking none of what his imagination conjured.

Strom quietly led them deeper into the nightmare forest, the pool of light giving them away to anything with eyes. Durin, too, felt compelled to move in silence. Someone or something else was there. The odds of its being friendly were decidedly slim.

No more voices came. Low rumblings and something akin to a growl were all that could be heard. Highly alert, all three jumped upon hearing a sudden intake of breath. Startled, terrified, and confused, Durin searched for a tree to hide behind but could find none that didn't bear some creature from his nightmares.

A mighty growl split the air, followed by a grunt, but Durin saw nothing. He exchanged confused glances with Strom and Osbourne but then remembered the tales of keystones. Sinjin had told him about them and had used them himself, so Durin knew such things really existed.

Grunts and cries filled the air but no words. Still, Durin felt some sort of connection. Even across the distance, he knew, even before Pelivor shouted, "Look out, Cat! Behind you!"

Though Durin was not there in physical form, Catrin's foes didn't know that. He made up his mind. "For Catrin!" he shouted with all the authority he could muster. Strom and Osbourne took a moment to understand his goal, but then they charged into the empty darkness, shouting battle cries that reverberated through the Black Spike.

* * *

Stopping cold when Catrin grabbed his arm, Pelivor held his breath. A hulking, shadowy form stepped into the light and did not shy away. Another approached from a different direction. Pelivor grabbed Catrin's collar and turned her back the way they had come. A third demon stepped into their path. There was a chance they could retreat through the stone forest, dashing between the trees to lose the enemy, but there were likely more where these had come from. Without their most potent weapons, they were in serious trouble.

His grip on Catrin loosened, and she darted away from him, dividing the monsters' focus. Charging toward the first one they'd seen, which wasn't far away, Catrin leaped into the air, executing a flying kick at the demon's knee. Too slow to react, the demon went down with a loud crack. The dark monster growled and thrashed in anguish but would pursue them no farther.

"Look out, Cat! Behind you!" Pelivor shouted. A mace made from a small tree trunk missed Catrin's head by a hair's width, but Pelivor had his own problems. The demon closing on him carried no weapons; instead, the foul beast wore twisted ironworks more like hammers than gloves. One soared past Pelivor's head, crashing into a stone tree, desecrating the eons-old masterpiece. Even as he sought to save his own life, Pelivor was aware of the beauty around him. What had seemed like a miss proved an effective attack, when a heavy branch came crashing down on Pelivor. Her eyes defiant, Catrin stood in the mace-wielding demon's path. Having no time to process what he saw, Pelivor rolled away. Two mighty hammers raced toward him, and there was little else he could do to defend himself.

"For Catrin!" came a sudden cry. Pelivor could hardly believe it. More cries split the air, and the course of the battle shifted. Pulling himself out from under the stone branch, he came away with cuts, scrapes, and bruises but little more.

The demon cast about, searching for this new threat. It was all the opportunity Pelivor needed. Following Catrin's example, he struck the enormous creature from behind, buckling the knee to take the beast down. It hit the stone floor with a resounding thud, its gruesome visage smacking the wall hard on its way down, knocking it out.

Limping away from a still form on the stone, the third demon fled. Running as fast as he could, Pelivor reached her side to find her still breathing.

"Can you hear me, Cat? Are you all right?"

She gave no answer for a time, and Pelivor sat, strangely alone.

"We were trying to help," came Durin's voice from the ether. "Is Catrin hurt?"

"I'll be fine," she said, stirring in Pelivor's grasp. "Thank you. You saved us."

"What do you need us to do, Cat?" Strom asked across the distance. He sounded as if he were standing right next to them. "We've done our best to follow your guidance."

"You're almost there," Catrin responded. "Keep going the same direction you've been traveling, and you'll find Ain's machine." A fit of coughing interrupted her words.

Pelivor helped her sit up. Demon calls rose in the distance. "We need to get out of here, Cat. Now."

"I've left you the very tool you'll need to activate the portals," Catrin said as Pelivor hoisted her back to her feet and hauled her away. Demons were coming.

* * *

Onin and Allette both walked under their own power, carrying their own packs despite Kenward's offered assistance. In the end he was glad for their stubbornness since his pack grew heavier over time. His aunt had been generous to him, and she'd been kind to Onin. Both were glad when she had agreed to show Allette similar courtesy. Miss Mariss was a woman of reason, and she'd nodded when Kenward reminded her that Allette hadn't come voluntarily.

"Catrin was correct," Allette said. It was as close as she'd come to an apology. "I can only hope she was right about going deeper into this tomb. At least here I can see the light, even if I can't feel it."

Onin shrugged. "Don't beat yourself up. Your idea had merit."

"I'm not angry with myself," Allette said. "I'm mad at her. How dare she be right?"

The comment took Kenward off his guard, and when he cast her a sideways glance, the Black Queen wore a rare grin. This young woman was a puzzle to match Trinda, Kenward thought. Most of the women in his life were mysteries to him, so he was undeterred by this fact.

"Catrin feels responsible for all of you," Allette blurted. "She feels terrible about the *Slippery Eel* and the *Serpent*. She'd take it back if she could."

Kenward gaped. He'd always known but somehow hearing it from Allette meant something more. Catrin and Allette had bonded in ways he could never understand and shared their deepest secrets. She had no reason to tell Kenward these things unless Catrin absolutely believed them. He supposed she told him to make him feel better, but it had the opposite effect. He'd cursed Catrin in some of the most creative and unusual language ever uttered on Godsland, and having her remorse verified removed much of his right to complaint.

"She really is your friend."

"Thank you," Kenward said. "You didn't have to tell me that, but I'm glad you did."

"Can she communicate directly with her dragon over great distances?" Onin asked.

His abrupt and specific question came as a surprise.

"Yes," Allette said after a moment. "But it's more difficult when she's deprived of Istra's light."

"Amazing," Onin said. "I can barely communicate with Jehregard when

I'm on his back and armed with a hammer."

Kenward had wondered just how brave Onin really was.

The man's next question proved he was the braver of the two. "Can you communicate with your dragons over great distance?"

All three continued walking, but Allette said nothing. Kenward wondered if she might scold the old warrior for his prying, but she proved capable of handling herself in other ways.

"I've no need of the hammer," she said.

Kenward smiled. She'd answered his question without really telling him what he wanted to know. Onin just grunted in response. Kenward had thought that might be the end of the conversation, but the old warrior wasn't quite done yet. Apparently he was determined to make the best of having the Black Queen's undivided attention.

"What do the ferals want?" he asked.

A bold question, Kenward thought. Allette did not respond right away. This was a sign of wisdom in Kenward's estimation. Those who speak with haste often fail to fully consider their words.

"To be left alone. If provoked, however, they'll seek revenge."

"Revenge?" Onin asked.

"The feral dragons did not fare well at the end of the last age," Allette said.

"That was thousands of years ago," Kenward said.

Allette's eyes were cold. "Dragons do not forget."

Onin grunted in acknowledgment. There was something she wasn't saying. After all, if the ferals wished only to be left alone, then why had they attacked the Greatland and the Godfist? Something wasn't adding up.

"And what do you want?" Kenward asked before he could think better of it.

Allette looked at him almost sheepishly. "I don't know."

It was perhaps the most honest thing anyone had ever said to him, and he recognized her vulnerability in that moment. She'd shown him something of herself, and he wanted nothing more than to comfort her. Life had been so unkind. She deserved some respite. She deserved to be loved.

"Not much chance you'll get it, then," Onin said.

Allette stuck her tongue out at him, and he actually smiled. It was something Kenward had never seen before. This day just kept getting stranger. Their journey had been relatively uneventful, and Trinda's guards surprisingly helpful in telling them where Catrin's group had gone.

"Heard Lady Catrin was going beyond the stone forest," one man said when he encountered the group. He just pointed in the general direction and told them to keep going.

It seemed odd to explore the hold by going directly down the main halls, but Kendra had most likely had this part of the hold thoroughly searched. If Catrin had good reason to believe she would find whatever it was they were searching for beyond the stone forest, then that would be the best place to start their search. That excited Kenward in one way: it was the chance to see this stone forest for himself. Some things simply are not real until experienced, and he could not imagine such a thing existing.

"What do you want, Onin of the Old Guard?" Allette asked the old warrior.

He grinned at her. "I'd like to live out my life with an eccentric dragon, a warm woman, and a full mug."

Allette laughed. "At least you've set achievable goals."

"You'd think. So far it's proven impossible."

"I just want to be free," Kenward said despite the fact that no one asked. "Give me a ship and open skies, and I'll be the happiest man alive."

"You actually want to fly one of those things again?" Onin asked.

"This from a man who navigates with a hammer," Kenward said, and they all laughed. It was an odd thing. All of them had reason to resent the others, reason enough to go to war in cases, yet they had found a common cause and were able to get along just fine. War was a prolonged and messy business Kenward wanted nothing to do with. Give him a good boarding and looting any day. No one gets hurt, and the pirates go on their way-- most of the time.

"Why did you not come to the council?" Onin asked Allette.

Her response was much faster this time. "I listened to what the child queen told me. It's a mistake I'll not make again."

"What did she tell you?" Kenward asked.

"She said none of you wanted peace and that the council was just a way to draw me out of hiding, so you could more easily dispose of me."

"And do you believe those words?" Onin asked.

"Not now," she said. "Many things have changed since then. I have changed since then."

Onin nodded his understanding, and Kenward could relate. Some of life's lessons leave us forever changed, and we cannot go back, no matter how hard we try. It was among the harshest lessons he'd learned: innocence lost could never be regained.

Kenward would have put those thoughts to words if not for battle cries echoing through the halls. The hair on Kenward's neck stood, and together they ran.

Chapter 7
Even the powerful have feelings. Tread lightly.
--Trinda Hollis, the child queen

* * *

The mysteries of Dragonhold grew in Sinjin's mind. He'd never been unable to imagine the scope of the place. Now that he'd journeyed so far and still not found an end, he tried to reconcile it. "The ancients must have been something to behold," he said without really meaning to.

"They frighten me," Kendra said. "Even long dead, they threaten us all. How do you fight dead foes?"

"You don't. You just do your best to clean up their messes."

"And not get caught up in them in doing so."

Sinjin laughed in spite of the truth.

"At least we're together," Kendra said. "It's not so bad."

She was right. Had they been separated, things would have been far worse for them both. They were stronger together. Her very presence made Sinjin a better person. He wasn't quite sure how she did it, but that didn't change it.

When they reached halls where the stone showed no sign of humans, Sinjin was disturbed to find evidence of clawed feet. They moved forward with even greater care. Something lay near the center of the hall and Sinjin slowed. Upon closer inspection, the shape turned out to be a skeleton, perfectly preserved bones resembling nothing Sinjin had ever seen. He was no expert, but the shape and elongated finger bones gave him the crawls.

More skeletons appeared as they moved deeper, each more mysterious and disturbing than the last. The keep had gone mostly quiet, which was even more unnerving than the noises had been. Now they had no way to know how far they were from the sources of those sounds.

"Look," Kendra said, pointing at the floor near an upcoming junction. The scratch marks in the dust almost all turned in the same direction.

If this was a test of courage, Sinjin was failing. Nothing anyone could say would make him believe turning the same direction as what were presumably demons was a good idea. Kendra appeared to be considering it. Sinjin pointed straight ahead rather than the more used tunnel to the right. Kendra frowned.

"Let's see if we can flank them," Sinjin said. "Look for the next hall to the right."

He hoped using tactical reasoning would resonate with his wife as it usually did. He'd married a fighter, and he'd eventually learned how to talk to one. Kendra nodded after a moment, and they crossed over the junction quickly, hoping nothing saw them pass. Kendra kept their herald globe tightly wrapped, but even a small amount of light was a beacon this deep underground. Not long after, they came upon another junction, the right-hand hall showing fewer signs of usage.

Kendra nodded in satisfaction and turned right. Looking over his shoulder, Sinjin had a bad feeling. Taking this hall had been his idea, which made it worse. Gently sloped halls curved in sweeping lines, much like the rest of the hold, which cut down on long-range visibility. This was an advantage in that it hid their light from others, but it also prevented them from seeing what lay ahead. Sinjin's knees trembled with anticipation. Part of it was fear, and part of it was being alert and prepared for anything.

Eventually the hall led to a flight of steps that descended into an oval-shaped chamber. Dust-covered forms filled most of the room but gave no indication of their true nature. Sinjin's imagination conjured frightening images that he sought to banish.

"You should go no farther this way," Trinda Hollis said in a low voice.

Kendra and Sinjin both jumped. It wasn't until Kendra lifted the herald globe over her head, still wrapped in cloth and glowing brightly nonetheless, that he saw her. On a rock shelf high above, Trinda sat. Had the girl not broken the illusion, the ledge would have been invisible.

"What game is this?" Kendra asked in a hiss.

"No game," Trinda said. "Just a final warning. If you go past this point, you are beyond any protection I can offer. My men do their best to keep the darker forces within the hold isolated, but I can make no promises. Dragonhold has more secrets than you may want to believe."

"And what of you?" Kendra asked. "What will you do?"

"I can take care of myself," Trinda said. "You should concentrate on what Catrin will do. She's a danger to us all, even if she does not wish it. I'm sorry. I know she's your mother, Sinjin, but please remember the rest of us when the time comes."

Sinjin nearly scoffed at her words. It was an old reaction and one that probably would not serve him well. It was a credit to his maturity that he gave what she said credence, even if he did not believe it to be true. His mother was one of the few things keeping darkness from claiming them all, and he could not imagine anything that would make her a threat.

"Thank you for your kind words of warning," Kendra said. "If you wanted to be of help, you'd provide us with the documents you used to make such wonderful decisions for all of us."

Trinda flushed at Kendra's scolding, but Sinjin could not deny the truth.

"You've never really wanted to help us," Kendra continued, and Sinjin doubted those words would improve the situation. "If you had, you would have given us the information we needed--the information we asked for. You couldn't even return all the herald globes to the person who created them. To tell the truth, Trinda Hollis, I've had about all I can stand of you."

Trinda just sniffed and looked offended. "Fine," she said. "If that is the reward I get for my kindness, then you're on your own."

The child queen then stood, huffed, and walked along the otherwise invisible ledge. When she disappeared around a corner and into a perfectly disguised rectangular orifice, Sinjin couldn't help but wonder if his wife had made a huge mistake.

* * *

There was no time to contemplate their route. All Pelivor could do was run away from demons and whatever else moved within the hold. Catrin kept pace but said nothing, the pain on her face clear. Coming here had been a terrible mistake. What had they been thinking? Exploring in pairs and lightly armed, they were no match for even a single demon, and by the sounds of it, there were many. Part of Catrin's pain came from not being able to help those she loved and now knowing she'd probably sent them to their deaths. Pelivor bore his own measure of responsibility.

A nearby growl caused them to scurry back the way they had come and around a corner. Catrin breathed heavily beside him. What a shock it must be for her, he thought. To go from having the power to rend the world to being helpless must be terrifying. Pelivor had considerably less access to the energy around them, but he knew how it felt to lose that power. It was something they might never get over if left in this wretched prison.

There was something that drew them both on, though: a persistent feeling. It wasn't that Pelivor knew which direction to turn or which chambers to explore; it was more the general sense he was getting closer to or farther from his goal. It was something he couldn't explain, and he did not even want to put the feeling to words for fear of breaking the spell.

When the demon patrols drove them in the wrong direction, Pelivor simply did what he could to find an alternate route toward their goal. Catrin must know, he thought. Why else would she follow his lead so blindly and without a word? She must feel it too.

At the next junction, he hesitated. Catrin drew him along, taking the lead and moving in the direction his spirit also told him to go. He'd been right. Both moved with increased confidence. They were getting close. He could feel it.

When Catrin reached out and squeezed his hand, a thrill ran along his arm, and he met her eyes. Whatever was going to happen was about to happen. Prepare yourself, her gaze said. There was something else there too, and Pelivor felt like a teenager all over again. Before the courage left him, he placed a hand on Catrin's hip, grabbed her face in his other hand, and kissed her like he meant it. When he released her from his grip, Catrin remained silent, her eyes unreadable.

Demons moving behind them drove them forward without time for further contemplation. Everything changed at once, and Pelivor's mind could barely keep pace with his senses. The first indication was Catrin's herald globe growing the slightest bit brighter. It could have been the result of the cloth it was wrapped in shifting, but then the ambient light level also increased. Amber in hue, natural light pooled in the hallway ahead, filled with texture and life. A familiar buzzing crept back into Pelivor's essence. It was something that had been undetectable until its sudden absence and now its equally sudden restoration.

Demons appeared in the hall behind them, and Pelivor dragged Catrin forward. She, too, appeared overwhelmed by the changes in the environment. The hair on Pelivor's arms and neck stood, and stepping into a hidden marvel stole his breath. Amber light illuminated a vast plain. Waterfalls and living trees within Dragonhold they had seen before, but this place was different. Raging from high above, the waterfall emerged from a stone god's open jaws.

The image represented no god Pelivor recognized, and its age was palpable. The water fell clear of the statue before plunging into a foaming pool below. The stone god sat, cross-legged and palms up, providing keys to life within Dragonhold. Clear, fresh water was not all the river brought into the hold. Pelivor didn't know through what mechanism it was accomplished, but a disproportionate number of large fish poured through the god's mouth and into the pool.

Sizable fins emerged from the depths and converged on newcomers, devouring them. Cradled in each of the god's palms were the largest carved gemstones Pelivor had ever seen. The stones themselves were a rich tapestry of light and texture behind smooth, clean facets. Whoever had cut these translucent green gems had been a master of the craft.

Above the god's head, roiling black clouds partially obscured amber crystals above. Steadily the waterfall provided additional moisture that gathered in thunderheads over the rolling plain. A bright flash brought Catrin and Pelivor from their revelry. Lightning leaped from the blackness and pulsed with blinding light, leaving purple streaks in Pelivor's vision. The resulting thunder rattled his soul.

The tree the lightning had struck sizzled and popped. It, like the other trees around it, was warped and twisted like a candle left in the sun. Some trees along the colossal cavern's edges were less warped, but those in open ground showed evidence of frequent strikes. Rich, green leaves harboring glossy, orange fruit proved they were a hardy lot.

If not for the demons behind them, Pelivor could have spent hours taking in the details. He and Catrin stepped farther into the open, exposing themselves in the process. Pelivor would have preferred having stone on at least one side. His back and flanks were poorly protected. The forest, with its short and widely spaced trees, would provide little cover. Given the size of the fins in the pool, Pelivor wanted nothing to do with those waters. He suspected anyone who ventured in would receive a reception similar to the fish falling from above. Pelivor could see how having a steady supply of stunned, fat, juicy fish could result in some enormous predators.

Bright violet birds with wings tipped in fiery orange swooped through the trees and danced along the mists' edges; flocks of stark white swallows soared higher, disappearing into the clouds. Given the place's majesty, overlooking critical details might have been forgivable, but Pelivor cursed himself when he saw demons watching from the hall. Standing at the edge of the natural light, they came no farther.

Catrin watched them as well, and Pelivor turned back to the seated god only to see him moving. He turned her around before his mouth could form any words. The upper portion of the stone god remained stationary, but behind the falls, the giant lap area shifted and moved. Scales appeared within the mists, and Pelivor's mind finally registered the horror awaiting them.

Perhaps the largest feral dragon to ever exist on Godsland overflowed from the god's lap. It was as if it had chosen its favorite sleeping spot when it was smaller and had outgrown it over time. Everything about this dragon spoke of age and power. It was nothing like those young and fresh dragons, so full of their newfound vigor. The feral dragons Catrin had fought until now had been but babies. Now they faced the elder statesman. At least that was how it felt to Pelivor.

Come closer.

The command was palpable, and Pelivor found himself drawn to the water's edge. Catrin walked beside him. The gems reached out to them, calling for him to embrace them and draw from the deep well they provided. He did not know what kind of stones these were, but Pelivor sensed the energy they stored, much like dragon ore. He could feel the energy the shield trapped being intensified and concentrated and forced into the stones with tremendous resistance, unlike the way dragon ore simply absorbed light. The frequency of their vibration made Pelivor's joints ache.

That's close enough.

Peering from behind the waterfall, the dragon's head, like a living mountain suddenly awake and hungry, moved. Pelivor looked to Catrin, who was entranced. The herald globe in her hand now glowing brightly, he wondered if he dared tap the power contained within this cavern. Already he could feel his innate abilities warming in the light, like feeling returned to a sleeping limb.

Your kind forfeited this place long ago.

Pelivor heard the statement but he was getting only one side of the conversation. With lidded eyes, as if in torpor, Catrin appeared asleep. He had to trust she was communicating with this ancient dragon and that he should keep his mouth--or mind--shut.

I am much pleased that you've given me back my power. You'll be rewarded for this act once you've completed the task.

Not knowing what the task was, a bad feeling festered in Pelivor's gut. The dragon looked down on them greedily. Catrin had said this place was a prison. She'd been correct, and it was occupied all along. No ordinary dragon, this beast had full and skilled access to Istra's power. Pelivor could feel the intricate control and subtle touch the magnificent beast possessed. Catrin had once marveled at his control and the complex structures he'd instinctively created, but both were clumsy hacks in comparison to this creature.

Mael.

The name thundered in Pelivor's mind; he was helpless to resist such power and control. The chance to run was past, and Catrin appeared to be faring no better. The fear keeping the demons from entering this hall was real and warranted, but Pelivor now realized even that was futile. Mael had long been manipulating the people of the Godfist, preparing to use them as the instruments of his release from this millennia-old prison.

Even the *Dragon's Wing* had not been immune. Mael sent Pelivor visions of the events that brought them into the hold. So many random and otherwise unexplainable things began making sense, which terrified Pelivor more than anything else could. If this creature escaped from Dragonhold, no one in the world would be safe, and Mael made it clear he would have no mercy on the descendants of those who'd imprisoned him. It may have been thousands of years ago, but dragon memories are longer than those of trees.

If Mael had been able to exert that much influence from within the most powerful prison ever built, then he would be unstoppable in the unfettered light. What had once been Pelivor's will collapsed under Mael's influence, staying his hand. Pelivor's fingertips itched with power, the attack ready to be unleashed with a flick of his will, but the dragon's desires preempted his own.

Pelivor was lost.

Chapter 8

Given a single chance, dragons will rule us all.
--Lord Bercheron

* * *

No matter what logic told him, Sinjin knew his wife would go the way Trinda had told her not to. Kendra was no fool. She knew the child queen was a trickster, and her presence likely meant they had found what they were looking for. The hallway beyond twisted and turned more than any they had encountered before. At times the tunnel would switch back to go in almost the opposite direction only to turn back again a few paces farther ahead.

Soon, though, sounds began to filter to them. A low, steady roar was accompanied by louder, more abrupt calls along with high-pitched noises. It was impossible to distinguish any of what they heard, which left them on edge. When the tunnel ended, they had to turn sideways to get through the intentionally narrow portal. Amber light poured through, and Sinjin thought he saw grass on the other side. Part of him dared to hope they'd found a way out of Dragonhold.

Kendra guarded the entrance while Sinjin squeezed through. What he saw when he emerged was beyond his ability to describe. A massive statue loomed over them, shrouded in mists. Twisted trees grew from rolling hills covered in lush grasses. A silver fox peered from behind a nearby tree and issued a high-pitched bark before scampering off, its glorious tail glistening with humidity. Sinjin wondered for a moment if the animals here had fallen into the river above and survived the plunge over the falls. It was unlikely given the feeding frenzy under way in the pool at the waterfall's base.

It was then Sinjin saw his mother and Pelivor standing, silent, staring at the stone god.

"I tried to spare you this," Trinda said after appearing nearby. "No matter what you think, I wish you no ill. If you turn back now, you might be spared his direct attention."

The presence of something in this place was undeniable, and Sinjin had no trouble believing a powerful being waited there. What were his mother and Pelivor doing? Every part of him was drawn there. He wanted to join her, to stand beside her no matter what she faced. He wasn't afraid of some ancient statue, even though history told him he should be. When something behind the falls moved, however, he adjusted his assumptions.

A huge dragon revealed himself, shifting his mass on a too-small resting place.

"Last chance," Trinda said. "Go back now or face him."

For once in his life, Sinjin believed Trinda, but that didn't mean he would take her advice. If his mother and Pelivor faced the dragon, then he and Kendra did so as well.

"Thank you, Trinda," Sinjin said.

"Consider my debt paid, Sinjin Volker. I wouldn't cross me again if I were you."

With those words, the child queen slipped between the trees, scaled a section of rough-cut rock with bare hands and feet, and disappeared into the rock wall itself. That girl was as mysterious as the wind.

She'd been right about one thing. This was his last chance to walk away, and he did one of the most foolish things he'd ever done. For his mother, he took a trembling step forward and drew a breath. Kendra did the same. Somehow she knew what he planned and stood beside him. Sinjin could not count the ways he loved his wife. Endangering her went against his every desire, but safety had long since fled. If they all died as a result of his actions, then he probably would have saved them some other imminent death.

When he spoke, his voice had Istra's strength, revealing to Sinjin he had some power in the stone god's presence. "If you wish my mother harm, then you'll have to deal with me!"

The words left him before he could fully consider the consequences. Water showered the plains as the dragon reacted. Echoing pops and creaks accompanied the sudden movement. More joints snapped and shifted as mighty wings spread for the first time in who knew how long. The dragon's wings were constructed of thin, frail-looking bones supporting membranes like overstretched leather. Light shone through tears in the membrane, and the claws on the ends of the bone structures gleamed under a patina of ages.

Water thrashed the plains when the dragon flapped his massive wings, sending the waterfall soaring across the cavern, fish included. Sinjin was distracted for the slightest instant when he saw the silver fox grab a fish from the lush grasses and run off looking like the cat that caught the bird.

With two more flaps of his wings and a single leap, the feral was upon them, seething with fury.

Who dares challenge me?

Anyone bent on living would have been digging a hole to hide in or running for his life, but Sinjin had already resigned himself to death. He could think of no better way to go than protecting those he loved. Opening his mouth to issue a taunting response, Sinjin froze, the words never leaving his lips. He'd been a fool to think he could resist the most powerful sorcerer ever to live. The thoughts were no longer his own. Mael's influence--for he knew the name as well as his own--blotted out his will, and that which was Sinjin was nearly lost as the dragon's eyes focused fully on him.

"Leave him alone!" Trinda Hollis shouted, and even in his stupor, Sinjin was surprised.

Taking advantage of the sudden shift in Mael's attention, Kendra grabbed Sinjin by the shoulder. "You're a brave fool," she said, pulling him back the way they had come. When it looked as if Mael would swallow Trinda in a single bite, though, Kendra stopped, picked up a fist-sized rock, and threw it with all her might. Her aim was uncanny, but Sinjin had to wonder who was the brave fool now.

When the rock struck Mael in the eye, the ancient dragon could not hide the pain. With an angry roar, the massive head swung back toward Sinjin and Kendra. His wife had done what she had to do, but it was too soon for their sake. Given the dragon's speed in spite of his age, they would never make it to shelter. Not to mention the fact that they would take time squeezing back into the hall.

Mael proved just how potent a foe he was. As his head lowered, blue-orange fire danced around the cavernous nostrils. Words of warning never left Sinjin's lips before Mael issued a stream of blue flame. Sinjin ran and pushed his wife ahead of him. She stumbled, but he propelled her forward with the full strength of his will and every measure of physical prowess he possessed.

In the next instant, Sinjin held his breath. A sheet of flame washed over them, but then it was gone. It left Sinjin stinging, smoking, and overwhelmed by the stench of burning hair. Thunder boomed as greenish lightning struck Mael from behind. Sinjin caught sight of Pelivor as he and Catrin, released from compulsion, came to his rescue. Mael swept his tail through the trees as Kendra and Sinjin ran, and the ancient dragon bore down, once again, on Catrin and Pelivor. Both retaliated, making their way closer to Kendra and Sinjin.

Not allowing Sinjin to watch, Kendra grabbed his jacket and dragged him away.

"Wait!" Sinjin said. "We have to help my mom!"

"We need to get out of here," Kendra responded. "Or your mother's and Pelivor's efforts will be for nothing. We aren't strong enough to face Mael."

"Sinjin? Kendra? Is that you?"

The voice reached out from empty air, and Sinjin spun in circles. "Durin! Where are you?"

"At the bottom of the Black Spike," Durin said. "Creepiest place ever. Your mom sent us here."

"Whatever you do," Kendra said, "don't do anything Catrin asked you to do!"

"What?" Strom's voice asked. "What do you mean?"

"There's a dragon sorcerer in Dragonhold manipulating us all!"

Those were the last words Kendra got to say before another wash of fire gushed toward them, despite the thunder of Pelivor's attacks. Kendra must be right, Sinjin realized. If Mael had been influencing them, his mother's instructions could well have been part of the dragon sorcerer's plan.

"What do we do?" Durin shouted across the massive distance, and his voice echoed throughout the cavern. Sinjin and Kendra were in no position to respond. Running as fast as they could, they barely outran the flames. Catrin and Pelivor redoubled their attacks to give Sinjin and Kendra time to escape. Trinda was nowhere to be seen.

Sinjin crouched in the darkness, presumably safe from dragon fire, and his mother's voice rang out. "Do as I've asked, Strom!" Her words were audible even from a distance. Sinjin had no doubt she was filled with Istra's power but also that her will was not her own. A more terrifying thought Sinjin could not imagine; that was until his wife gasped. She was closer to the opening than he was, and she could still see back into the chamber. Sinjin wanted her to come away from the threat of dragon fire, but she stood captivated and, by the look on her face, horrified.

"What is it?" Sinjin finally asked.

Benjin and Wendel walked into the open, moving toward the dragon, followed by Chase, Morif, and others.

"The rest of the exploration party has arrived."

* * *

Durin, Strom, and Osbourne moved deeper into the Black Spike. Greenish light split the darkness ahead, and resting in a pool of light waited something akin to a herald globe but different. Strom reached the stone first and picked it up. Durin wished he hadn't. The two had been at odds ever since leaving the twisted stone forest. Durin had a closer relationship with Sinjin, and Strom had always been loyal to Catrin. Given the conflicting information, it was impossible to know what to do. For Durin, it came down to his trust in Sinjin. He suspected the same was true for Strom with regard to Catrin.

It was an untenable situation that had placed a wall between them.

"Maybe we should just wait and see if we can get more information," Osbourne said, once again trying to bridge the gap. "We need a better understanding of what's happening. Too much is at stake to blindly act."

"Inaction is also a hasty decision," Strom said, his jaw set. Durin and Osbourne both knew that look, and neither tried to argue the point any further.

A sigh escaped Osbourne, and they stepped into the light. What they found there was unexpected. So much of what surrounded them was derived from madness, but this was a place of order, symmetry, and adherence to the natural world--at least to a greater extent than the rest of the Black Spike.

The cavern formed a perfect circle. At the center was a ring of carvings like those in the stone forests. This was another keystone by Durin's estimate; except this one was more elaborate and had an enormous lever in the middle. Standing at an angle, the lever was taller than Durin, as if made for a giant.

Motion was the next thing to catch the eye, and Durin turned to see what new threat waited. Instead, he found more orderly movement. A shaft as tall as fifty men oscillated in a way that gave Durin mental glimpses of what must lie out of sight. Its top and bottom encased within stone, the shaft moved up and left. Then at the top of its mighty stroke, the angle shifted to the right, and it moved just as swiftly downward only to repeat the cycle.

No matter who was right, there would be consequences--perhaps global. The keystones were intertwined in a way Durin didn't understand, but he knew they were connected. The fact that this keystone lay at the bottom of the blackest pit Durin had ever known should give evidence to its nature, but Strom was determined to satisfy Catrin's request. The man owed Catrin his life, just as Durin owed both Catrin and Sinjin his.

When Strom took another step toward the giant lever, Durin did the only thing he could think of. He ran out and faced the powerful smith. "I do not wish to fight you, but I cannot allow you to do this. Too much is at stake."

"Step aside," was all Strom said. He outmatched Durin in every way. He had physical prowess, strength of will, access to Istra's power, and the spider stone Catrin had left him. He could easily defeat Durin, but the smith had one other thing Durin was counting on: a conscience.

"Kendra and Sinjin are no fools, and they would not defy Catrin without good reason."

"Unless it was they who were coerced or tricked," Strom said. "I must place my faith in Catrin Volker, the Herald of Istra and my friend. And Sinjin's mother, I might add. I don't want to hurt you, but you will let me pass."

Sinjin had always told him to stand up for what he believed, and there was no one he believed in more. Sinjin Volker was his best friend, Al'Drakon, and son of the Herald. Durin held his ground.

"I cannot allow this," Osbourne said. "Catrin would not want this. There are three of us. We will put it to a vote."

Durin swallowed. His vote was already cast, as was Strom's.

"Do as Catrin asked." There was no joy in Osbourne's words.

Durin allowed Strom to pass despite yearning to stop him.

* * *

Keeping up with Allette proved almost impossible. The girl was in prime physical condition and an apparent rush. Fear built up in Kenward's belly when they encountered demons, and those creatures stepped out of Allette's path in deference. Kenward wanted even more to catch up just so he did not fall out of her sphere of influence. He had no idea how far her protection extended and no desire to find out.

Sprinting ahead would leave Onin behind. Kenward genuinely liked the man, and his honor simply would not allow it. He considered asking Allette to slow down, but her body language made it clear she would not be deterred. When they broke into a gigantic chamber filled with unusual sights, he felt as if they were late to the party. Most of those searching Dragonhold for a way to destroy the Fifth Magic gathered along the shores of a frothing pool. The waterfall above defied description.

What they had walked into, Kenward did not know, but he liked it not one bit. The dragon proved his instincts by breathing fire at the fleeing Sinjin and Kendra, which didn't make him feel much better.

Beside him, Onin cursed between ragged breaths.

Allette stepped into the cavern and walked toward the massive dragon. The girl feared nothing, Kenward thought, lacking the courage to follow her.

"What's she doing?" Onin asked.

"Whatever it is," Kenward said, "she's a better person than me for doing it."

Onin grunted. The Black Queen did something then that Kenward had not considered, and it chilled his blood. This girl was a dangerous flower. After stepping between the dragon and the stone god, Allette summoned the demons.

Glaring down at her, the dragon practically sneered. Who dares challenge Mael?

Giants and demons alike hesitated. With a single gesture, Allette obliterated that hesitation. A dangerous flower, indeed.

* * *

Reaching physically toward the gem wells, Allette gathered energy, creating a visible wash between them. A diaphanous river twisted and churned with captivating beauty. Demons converged from every direction, their numbers shocking. How had so many come to be in the hold? Knowing how many people had been living so close to such evil and corruption made Kenward shiver.

No matter what he felt for Allette, and he had no real understanding what that was, he could not abide the presence of demons. These creatures desecrated nature. For a moment, though, he had to ask himself what he would have done. Allette had not created these aberrations. Sometimes a tool is a tool no matter its nature or source. In this case she used her control over the demons to try to accomplish something for the good of them all, except perhaps Mael.

Despite his reasoning, fear gripped Kenward in the presence of so many agents of darkness.

Mael reared up to his full height before Allette and her approaching army. There was something akin to laughter in his ancient eyes. Catrin and Pelivor continued to make their way toward where the dragon stood, wings extended and flames coursing around his nostrils. Kenward knew not what they sought, but he wished them luck. This was like no foe any of them had ever faced.

Mael issued a torrent of fire directed at the approaching demons, which sent Allette, Catrin, and Pelivor scrambling. Even as they ran, Kenward saw the herald globes in both Allette's and Catrin's hands steadily growing brighter. With every attack, Mael charged the air in the cavern, and those nearby did everything they could to capitalize on it.

Taking the brunt of Mael's attack, the demons scattered.

We should have destroyed the Noonspire before it could corrupt the world so completely. Mael's thought echoed around him and thundered in Kenward's mind. He didn't know what the Noonspire was and didn't have time to consider further. A high-pitched tone, loud but not unpleasant, rang through the chamber.

I am well pleased. You've performed admirably, Herald of Istra.

Kenward could not see Catrin's face, but he'd have wagered everyone around him heard the words. Those who'd been a part of Catrin's exploration party now sought shelter from dragon fire, and they, too, reacted to Mael's thoughts.

Light poured from the circle of stone within the trees. Colors danced in streaks like misty wraiths, and Kenward could feel the energy. He knew how it felt to be in the presence of great power, and this dwarfed anything he'd ever experienced, as if the entire planet were being charged.

Like others in the chamber, Kenward was drawn to the keystone. Everyone and everything still alive and conscious within the chamber gravitated toward the shimmering and now singing artifact. There was a striking harmony, as if all the most talented singers in the world worked together. The beauty of this event was unmatched in Kenward's experience, and he prayed it would be for the good of the world. It was unlikely as Mael made his way to the stone. He did not rush, apparently relishing the experience. It had been a long time since he had been in power, and Kenward could see the conqueror for what he was. If unleashed on the world, Mael would subjugate them all.

That was when Kenward learned the keystones' true nature. Before him stood a gateway to anywhere, allowing him to see the other side. At first, he saw the mighty pillars amid the shallows, and as he shifted his perspective, the Grove of the Elders appeared, new greatoaks eagerly reaching toward the sky. The more he turned, the more he saw. Some places were familiar, but most were not. Some were dark and twisted, and in one such place, he saw his friends. There stood Durin, Strom, and Osbourne, looking as if they'd been struck dumb.

Mael's laughter was overwhelming as he crossed the final distance separating him from the portal.

"No!" Kenward screamed, hoping Strom and the others would hear him and undo whatever it was they had done. "Close the portal, Strom, or we'll all be doomed!"

Those were the last words Kenward uttered before Mael's tail blotted out the light. From one side came a flash. Allette was trying to distract the dragon. Just before the tip of Mael's tail smashed Kenward into the mossy soil, a blast of frigid air thrust him aside. The dragon turned his attention on Allette, the more dangerous foe, and Kenward prayed for her.

Running faster than he would have thought her capable, Allette darted through the trees, dodging dragon fire, claws, and the monster's tail, the demons remaining at her command too far away to be much use. The blinding glow of her herald globe, though, gave evidence she was anything but a frightened child. Recognizing the threat, Mael roared. Stones broke loose and dropped from above, the cacophony deafening. A flash of white within the trees caught Kenward's attention for an instant. He could just make out Trinda Hollis, and he prayed for her, no matter her evil deeds.

Some three strides from the keystone, Allette leaped into the air, her herald globe held before her, leaving a blue streak across Kenward's vision. Mael whipped around and lunged toward the flying girl, but he was too late. The herald globe never actually struck the stone. An instant before it would have, the object Catrin and Osbourne had crafted released its charge.

The shock wave caught Mael in the face and turned his head to one side. The initial blast triggered a far larger explosion that sent gouts of fire and lightning gushing from the keystone. For a brief instant, Kenward caught sight of devastation spread across the planet. Pillars amid the shallows fell and snapped in pieces. The black stone at the center of the Grove of Elders cracked open and spewed forth white-hot magma. The scene probably would have continued if not for the portal collapsing inward on itself, sending one last energy wave blasting through the cavern. Kenward could not see where Allette had ended up, but he doubted anyone could have survived such destruction.

Mael's rage was undeniable. The dragon looked as if he might tear the Godfist asunder. Turning his attention to Allette and the keystone had been a mistake, though, for he had underestimated Catrin's will. As the massive dragon swung his head around, preparing to incinerate them all with dragon fire, Catrin threw her blazing herald globe at Mael with all her might. The Herald of Istra proved her aim when the glowing orb disappeared into Mael's vacuous nostril. An instant later, the dragon's skull lit up from inside, and a different kind of flame shot from his jaws. His eyes rolling up until only white membranes were visible, Mael collapsed amid the trees.

Chapter 9

Sailing the skies is a lot like sailing the seas, except the people you throw overboard don't live as long.

--Kenward Trell, airship captain

* * *

Watching helplessly as Strom walked to the keystone's center, where the huge lever stood, Durin hoped he was wrong. He truly didn't want to be correct, but he'd come to trust his instincts. Unfortunately Strom and Osbourne had learned the same lesson, and their instincts had disagreed with his.

Osbourne stood beside him. "I'm sorry."

"Don't be," Durin said. "You did what you thought was right. Now all we can do is pray you were correct."

Durin's sudden pragmatism clearly unnerved Osbourne, but there was nothing to be done about it. They stood on the cusp of change the likes of which their planet had never seen. Durin wasn't certain he understood how or why; he just knew it was so. As he'd learned from his own past, opportunity for tremendous change was also opportunity for things to go terribly and irreversibly wrong.

Strom placed the amber figurine and the spider stone next to the lever and looked back one last time to Durin and Osbourne, an apology--and fear--in his eyes. This did nothing to calm Durin's nerves.

When the powerful smith turned back to the lever, Durin could see his muscles bulging from the effort, yet the lever did not budge. For several long minutes, he tried, and Strom could not make the lever move even a small amount. Durin dared to hope that he'd give up. He didn't know all that much about Strom in general, but he did know the man detested Kyrien's speaking in his mind and using Istra's power. Both things disturbed the man greatly. He said he wanted to be nothing more than a simple smith, but he was not. Durin found it ironic the big man refused to accept his own destiny when he'd been among those who'd driven Catrin to accept hers.

Given the way that had turned out, Durin couldn't blame the man. His hopes were crushed, though, when Strom bent down with obvious reluctance and picked up the spider stone. The smith would give up a small part of himself just to use the artifact, and Durin truly didn't wish it. Despite their disagreement, even considering the magnitude of the matter, Strom was his friend.

It hurt Durin's soul to see the mighty smith illuminated by the power he wielded against his own wishes. Strom did this for Catrin, they all knew. He owed her his life many times over and would not be deterred no matter what she asked of him. When Durin considered the situation, he realized he never had any chance of dissuading Strom. The man would die before betraying Catrin. Durin respected the smith for that but also recognized the dangers of such blind servitude.

With lightning pulsing around him, Strom applied his will along with his muscles and was rewarded with a deep grinding sound. Slowly the lever moved. Osbourne looked as if he wanted to help his friend, but the spider stone's power turned the smith into a frightening and imposing figure. Sweat dripping from his trembling muscles caught the light and flowed over the lines of his definition.

When the massive lever crossed over the halfway point, energy and anticipation thickened the air. The lever moved faster now, and Strom gave one final effort, which left him breathing hard. With a deep thunk, the lever seated itself.

Nothing happened.

Then a harmonious tune grew to fill the air. Luminous wisps danced over the keystone. Durin dared to hope he'd been wrong; there had been enough precedence. Strom stepped back, having the foresight to grab the amber figurine but ultimately appearing horrified by what he had done.

He returned to them, an apology still in his eyes. "When this happened to Catrin, I didn't understand," he said, his head hanging despite the spectacle happening behind him. "I should've been more kind to her."

It was an admission that shocked Durin. He'd always heard of Strom being among Catrin's most staunch defenders. He might have said more if not for Kenward's determined shouting. The blood drained from Durin's face and he went cold.

"Close the portal, Strom, or we'll all be doomed," Kenward's shout carried across the vast distance, sounding surreal.

Durin needed no more evidence. He'd been right all along. Strom and Osbourne hesitated, probably still coming to terms with the magnitude of their mistake. All Durin wanted was to undo that most grave of errors. Running forward, he grabbed the lever and tried to pull it back. Looking through the keystone almost made him release his grip in shock. A massive dragon loomed over Catrin, Pelivor, and Allette. Though he'd heard Kenward's voice, he did not see his friend there.

The lever held fast. Strom and Osbourne were just now moving to help. Knowing he needed to apply all his strength, Durin swung around to the other side of the lever. From there, he looked into an idyllic scene. Along a seacoast amid lush grasses, the world was at peace. The danger seemed so far away, and Durin considered stepping through, leaving all this behind. Instead, he pushed harder, hoping to save those he loved. No temptation could pull him away.

Sounds of fighting within Dragonhold drifted across the portal, the crescendo reaching a fever pitch. Allette's battle cry grew louder just before the keystone exploded.

* * *

Those within Mael's cavern moved to find the survivors, most of them wounded and, in some cases, the dead. The ancient dragon still breathed but was unconscious. Kenward ran straight for the now shattered keystone. He'd watched Allette dive onto the stone, and he'd witnessed the explosion, but after involuntarily looking away, he'd lost track of her. Now she was gone.

Catrin and Pelivor climbed the stone god, having left guards armed with overcharged herald globes near Mael's head. Kenward worried the dragon would find a way to manipulate and subvert them as he'd done in the past. He was among those who supported killing the ancient dragon. Such a threat should not be allowed to exist. It had been Catrin who talked most of them out of it. Kenward was a charitable soul as long as it didn't endanger his life. When he considered how dangerous Mael was, he couldn't help but reach the same conclusion as before. Had Catrin and Pelivor not both vowed to stay and watch over the dragon from a place of power and preparedness, Kenward might have tried to kill the beast himself. Even he laughed at that notion.

On his way to the broken keystone, which now bled fire and oozing rock, Kenward encountered Keenan. The man's face matched his own: concern, fear, confusion, and resignation. In spite of previously being on different sides, Kenward took pity on the man who was also trying to protect those he cared about.

"Looking for Trinda?" he asked.

Keenan looked at him with false hope. "You've seen her?"

"Not since the explosion," Kenward said. "I'm sorry." The disappointment in the man's eyes was difficult to bear. "Have you seen Allette?"

"The Black Queen?" Keenan asked then realized what he'd said. "No."

Kenward nodded. "If you see her . . ."

"Same," Keenan said, patting Kenward's shoulder on his way past.

"People of Dragonhold," Catrin spoke in a power-enhanced voice. "In order to contain the dragon, Pelivor and I will need to deplete his power source. We have discussed it, and we believe we can do so safely, but it will be best if all of you exit the cavern."

Moving toward the halls leading out of the cavern, Kenward did not leave. If he had to, he would duck behind solid stone. He'd come this far and refused to miss seeing how this ended. Someday he'd have to tell this tale over whiskey, and he hoped to do it justice.

A few others stayed behind: Benjin, Wendel, Chase, and Morif. They huddled together and watched, praying Catrin knew what she was doing and hoping she would be able to get them out of this mess.

Pelivor reached into the gem well he stood beside. The faceted gem towered over him, leaving him looking insignificant against the backdrop of the stone god and waterfall. Green light radiated when he tapped the stone's energy, a nimbus of power enveloping him.

Catrin connected with the stone she stood beside, the scale of her surroundings dwarfing her. When filled with power, though, she was impossible to ignore. Glowing like a new star, Catrin appeared strained yet determined.

After a glance at Pelivor and a firm nod from him, Catrin pulled Koe from her pocket. The dragon ore carving was glossy, translucent, and slick. The air itself changed when Catrin applied her will. Slowly she and Pelivor drained the energy from the stones and fed it to the surrounding soil and rock, which absorbed it easily. Everything seemed to be going as planned until Mael gave a single massive twitch.

There was a shift in the energy around them that was obvious even to those without any access to Istra's power. Without warning, power arced between the two stones with a thunderclap. Both Catrin and Pelivor went rigid, their faces masks of pain. The green light flickered and pulsed.

"Go!" Catrin shouted in a godlike voice. "Mael left a trap, but we are not defenseless. For a short time, the shield will be down. Go! Now! This may be your only chance to escape."

The words hadn't completely sunk in when Benjin grabbed Kenward and pulled him away.

"What's it going to take to get the *Wing* out of the hold?" Morif asked, moving at a brisk pace. There was far too much distance for them to run the whole way, leaving them at a fast walk no matter how great the urgency.

Benjin shook his head.

"Without Pelivor, I don't know if we can do it," Gwen said. "Even with his help, I'm not sure we could gain the skies."

"Worst case," Morif said. "We climb down from the main entrance."

Chase shook his head. "The stair is mostly gone."

Morif just shrugged.

The old soldier was right; they had few options.

When they finally reached the kitchens, they found Miss Mariss in frenzy, preparing packs for anyone who could escape the hold. Indeed, Catrin's words had been heard throughout Dragonhold.

Morif looked as if he would drag Millie and Miss Mariss from the kitchens, but Miss Mariss just placed her hands on her hips. "I'm not going anywhere. Catrin will need to eat. If she stays, I stay."

"And if they stay, I stay," Millie said in a tone that brooked no argument.

Turning to the others, Morif shrugged. "I'll help you carry your packs and see you off."

* * *

Kenward was torn. Getting the *Dragon's Wing* out of the hold was in many ways just his kind of crazy, but he wasn't certain it would work. If Pelivor had been there to provide the needed lift his wing structures afforded, then maybe, but even that was a stretch. Though Gwen was strong, she was the thrustmaster, and she had never successfully flown the ship. In the end, they had little choice. It was either risk being stranded outside the hold with no ship, or face the chance of being dashed to pieces when the *Dragon's Wing* dropped from the sky like a stone.

No matter what one wishes, his mother had always warned him, gravity will continue to function. Thus far her words had proven accurate. People rushed in all direction in preparation and the hopes the main entrance would soon be clear. The plasma shield was, indeed, lowered. Catrin had been good to her word and had perhaps saved his life once again. He'd not always been grateful to her, but he was very much so at that moment.

Kenward was unable to bear watching the preparations being made on the *Dragon's Wing* or the miles of coiled rope gathered. Fasha said Kenward was only happy when the crazy ideas were his, and perhaps she was right. The plan was almost guaranteed to fail, but neither Kenward nor anyone else had any better. What they also lacked was time. No one knew how long Catrin and Pelivor could disrupt the shield, and Catrin had made it clear this might be their last chance to escape.

Kenward was going to take her word on that. No matter what happened, he would be free of this infernal place before that shield was reestablished. Everyone assumed Catrin would be able to warn them before the plasma wall regenerated, but there was a chance she wouldn't. Itching to get out of the hold, Kenward walked closer to the main entrance.

In the back of his mind, he wondered what had happened to Allette. If not for a number of factors, he would have assumed her dead, but he wasn't so sure. Trinda Hollis's disappearance added to the feeling. That girl was no fool and had a healthy sense of self-preservation.

The keystones had been acting as portals at the time of Allette's attack, and she could have ended up just about anywhere. It was a thin hope, but Kenward clung to it. He'd grown attached to the mysterious woman and wished her well. Even Trinda, for all her quirks and misdeeds, bore no ill will from him.

The unfettered horizon was medicine for Kenward's soul. He could smell the salt on the air and feel Istra's light on his face. In every sense, he had not known what he loved until deprived of it. Viewed through a different lens, these things were newfound treasure. Despite everything else, Kenward couldn't stop grinning.

Seeing Onin atop Jehregard also made him smile. The two misfits were perfect for each other, and Kenward knew the value of that. When he realized the feral queen was watching him from the opposite side of the broken spire, he took a step back. The sight instilled fear.

Allette wasn't there, and Kenward had no way to know the dragon's loyalties or intentions. Roaring in disapproval, the feral queen backed away. A moment later, hot breath gusted like a spring breeze behind him. Kenward turned to see Kyrien regarding him with an unreadable expression.

Dragons would be a lot easier to deal with if you knew what they are thinking, Kenward told himself. Then he reconsidered, remembering how Strom had reacted to Kyrien's touching his mind without his permission. For that matter, Mael had apparently been doing it to all of them for decades. Perhaps not knowing what the dragons were thinking wasn't such a bad thing after all. Kenward just did what any wise person would have done; he slowly backed away.

Onin issued orders from outside the hold. Then something amazing happened. As one, the feral queen, Jehregard, and Kyrien latched on to the broken spire and pulled. Covering his ears against the overwhelming noise, Kenward watched a sliver of daylight appear between the stone floor and the mighty stone finger. Creaking and groaning, the spire did not go willingly, and Kenward feared they might lose their massive grips and send it crashing back down on them.

"Hurry!" Catrin's booming voice echoed through the hold.

The time for contemplation was past. Kenward did what he'd done for so much of his life: he followed his gut. Making a run for the *Dragon's Wing*, he helped Morif drag the huge length of braided rope toward the main entrance. As they approached, the spire reached the top of its arc then settled slightly askew, leaning outward in comparison to its original orientation. No one knew what would happen when the power was restored, and Kenward hoped to be far away before anyone found out.

"Thank you, my friend," Morif said. "Now go. Be free."

Kenward gave a quick, awkward bow. "Be well, Morif. If ever you need me, send word, and I'll come for you. We'll see each other again."

Morif gave him a one-eyed look that made it clear he didn't believe it but appreciated the thought nonetheless. Once again Kenward had to marvel at how men missing eyes and tongues somehow managed to be better communicators than he.

"Can't hold it any longer!" Catrin boomed, the strain in her voice evident to all.

"Go," Morif said.

Kenward ran.

The *Dragon's Wing* was perched, ready to slide onto a series of rollers made from rounded logs, many of which were too short for the job. Everything was in scarce supply, especially time, but they all hoped the lubricated logs would allow the ship to slide forward more easily than it would across bare stone. More people than Benjin and Fasha had wanted on their ship scaled the boarding nets. Those aboard would have to stay or make the jump back to unforgiving stone. There would be no time for climbing down.

Those who left Dragonhold would do so adragonback or aboard the *Dragon's Wing*, neither path certain. At the stern, Gwen looked terrified despite being secured in her usual spot. Kenward hadn't even considered the fact that the girl had been cut off from Istra's power and had access to only what little bit of light reached the ship from outside. His courage wavered.

Looking back at Dragonhold's main entrance, having dragons pull the *Wing* from the hold seemed an unlikely and audacious plan. Morif stood on one side of the entrance, swinging a rock over his head in a wide circle. The rock was secured to the rope using a series of knots--such a feeble thing. Bradley stood on the opposite side, trying to match Morif's feat and not quite succeeding. The weight of it was simply too much for the smaller man. Attached to mooring rings on the *Dragon's Wing*, these ropes might be the only thing to get them airborne, assuming the dragons succeeded in latching on to them in mid flight.

Onin's voice sounded again from outside, growing louder as he approached the hold. Kenward couldn't understand his words amid the furor and Gwen's straining to provide thrust. The air moved faster. The girl was succeeding to at least some extent. He was proud of her and hoped it would be enough.

"Make sure you are securely tied to something strong," Fasha commanded. "Be ready. This might get a little bumpy."

Kenward shook his head. His sister had a talent for understatement.

"Go now!" Catrin called out. "Can't hold it any longer!"

At the same time, Onin's cry reached them. Both Morif and Bradley released their ropes in near synchronicity. Morif's stone flew from the hold in a sweeping arc. Bradley's barely made it past the gate. The two men were nearly sucked into the air when Jehregard swept past at full speed. Catching Morif's rope in his massive jaws, the verdant dragon turned immediately and soared away. Dragonhold trembled when Kyrien struck the stone at high speed and latched on to the rope Bradley had thrown. The valiant guard stood, windmilling at the entrance until Morif caught the back of his coat and dragged him away.

The coils sang as the dragons flew away. Anyone caught in those ropes would suffer a quick death, and Kenward was glad to see the two safely away. Time passed slowly then as they waited for the last coils to run out. This would be no gentle ride. Gwen's thrust edged higher in pitch, her face glistening with sweat. What he hadn't expected to see was Jessub Tillerman run to where she was secured.

"No!" Gwen shouted.

Only a few coils of rope remained.

"Maybe I can help you this time," Jessub insisted. "Draw strength from me!"

"You're not sec--" Gwen's words were cut off when the shorter of the two ropes snapped taut, wrenching the *Dragon's Wing* sideways.

Had he not been tied to the rail, Kenward would have gone overboard, as would many of the others aboard. Jessub was the only one not secured, and he sprawled across the deck. Half a dozen people looked to be considering untying themselves to help the young man, but it was already too late. The *Dragon's Wing* lurched forward, and the second rope snapped taut, now jerking the ship back in the other direction, which righted her. They were now pointed toward the sky at least.

The logs beneath them creaked in protest but mostly did what the people had hoped they would. Saved only by slamming into the rigging, Jessub pulled himself from the deck and clawed his way to Gwen. All Kenward could see was open sky. It was a welcome sight; he just hoped it wouldn't be his last. He did notice another increase in the pitch of Gwen's thrust. It was not enough.

A slick, glistening log, not quite fully rounded and smooth, caught on something, twisting beneath the *Dragon's Wing*, and casting the ship sideways once again. The hull dragged along bare stone for a brief time. Sideways and with less speed than anyone had hoped, the *Dragon's Wing* burst into the Pinook Valley. The ship screamed as she came, or at least her passengers did.

The *Dragon's Wing* pitched downward and plummeted, leaving them staring at rocky, debris-strewn ground below. At that moment, lift was what they needed most, but Gwen specialized in thrust.

"You can do it," Jessub shouted. Repeating words still ingrained in his memory, he hoped to channel Pelivor's calm but soon failed.

The *Dragon's Wing* shot downward with incredible speed until the ropes went taut again and snapped the prow upward. Kenward prayed dragons were as powerful as they appeared since it seemed they were the only thing keeping the *Wing* aloft.

Now those aboard were treated to an unobstructed view of the horizon, a sight Kenward had dearly missed. Ahead Jehregard and Kyrien flapped hard, trying to pull the *Dragon's Wing* high enough to avoid the peaks on the valley's opposite side. It wasn't going to be enough. Kenward issued one last prayer as a rock wall raced toward them like the hammer of the gods.

Nothing could have prepared them for the sudden change in trajectory. The hull thrummed with impact. It was not the rocks they had hit but the feral queen. Wings extended on either side of the ship, and Kenward looked down in amazement. This was a sight he'd never thought to see. Silently Kenward thanked the feral queen and Allette, wherever she was. Somehow she'd managed to save them all. He hadn't misjudged her. That thought made Kenward Trell smile.

Clearing the highest peaks and soaring over open seas brought encouragement and a thrill. Their flight path leveled and stabilized, and Gwen provided sufficient thrust to keep them moving forward. Unfortunately no one had figured out what they would do next. There simply hadn't been enough time. No time remained, as the feral queen dropped from beneath them without warning and wheeled away, flying back toward the Godfist.

Kenward would have thanked her if he weren't so busy screaming.

Chapter 10

If you work with horses long enough, you're bound to get stepped on. If you work with dragons long enough, well, wear sturdy boots.

--Durin, dragon groom

* * *

A dispirited group gathered not far from where the kitchen tunnels opened into the main hall. Those assembled had various reasons for staying within Dragonhold as well as reasons, perhaps, that they might have wanted to go. For Miss Mariss, the *Dragon's Wing* carried with her bonds of blood and friendship. Watching the ship being hurled into the air tied her guts in knots. She'd had to see it firsthand, to know the fate of those she cared about. Strong hands steadied her all the while, knowing just what it was she watched.

Morif did his best to support both Millie and Miss Mariss, but she knew he, too, was probably struggling with his decision. Soon they would be trapped once again, with the chance none of them would ever escape Dragonhold alive, but Miss Mariss knew her place. If Catrin stayed, she stayed. Chase and Bradley stood nearby, pillars of strength and dedication. She was grateful for them as well. It was easier to be strong when those around you were strong.

Seeing the *Dragon's Wing* carried by dragons then lost from view was more than Millie could bear, and she walked toward the kitchens. "No sense worrying over the things I can't do anything about when there's work needing done."

Morif grunted in agreement.

* * *

None on the *Dragon's Wing* untied themselves. It was clear Kyrien and Jehregard would be able to keep them airborne for only so long. The ship would need to either fly on her own or end up in the water. Conventional sailing would have suited them all just fine if not for the distance between them and the waves. It didn't help that hastily tied knots were coming loose and weren't all that well placed to begin with. Setting the ropes farther apart would have lent stability to their flight, but there had been no time, and it was far too late to do anything about it. If the dragons had to lower them into the water, they would go in at a bad angle.

Gwen extricated herself from Jessub's overzealous embrace, leaving him secured with part of her harness she'd loosened enough to admit his torso. It wasn't perfect, but Kenward hoped it would keep him from going overboard. Jessub grabbed her hands and cast their arms out wide, emulating Pelivor.

"Create the leading edge first," Jessub said as calmly as he could. "Then pull back to create a completely flat surface that cuts the air." The air around them issued a steady low rumble. "And when you feel comfortable, shape the wing."

For the briefest instant, wing structures provided lift. Two dragons still supported them, but the ship swung between them like a crazed pendulum. The feral queen had held them high then dropped them. Not unlike a bird kicked from the nest, it was fly or fall. Jehregard and Kyrien flew with all their might, trying to account for the feral queen's absence.

Clouds obscured the light and Gwen faltered. Yanking her hands away, she placed them back on the thrust tubes and did what came natural to her.

"You can do it!" Jessub shouted. "You just about had it!"Gulping air, the young man leaned into the wind and applied his own will to support Gwen's efforts. Traces of light glittered alongside the ship but failed to take form. The wind tore at them, further destabilizing their attempted flight. Gwen reached out and put her hand on his shoulder. The pitch of her thrust went down dramatically, but the energy boost was enough to let the formations solidify. When the clouds parted, bathing Gwen and Jessub in full light, they achieved stability.

For the first time since they left Dragonhold, the *Dragon's Wing* flew on her crew's merit.

With the wing formations stabilized, Gwen withdrew her energy.

"I'm losing it," Jessub shouted as the wing structures wavered and faltered in turbulent air. Again the pitch of Gwen's thrust lowered as she bolstered his will. Simultaneously proud and embarrassed, Jessub did his best to concentrate.

"Can you keep us aloft?" Fasha asked.

Jessub remained silent, unable to do so by himself.

"We can do it," Gwen said. "Jessub and I can do it. We believe in each other."

At those words, Kyrien and Jehregard released the ropes. If the *Wing* was going to fly, she was going to have to do it on her own. The dragons parted and flew away. Onin and Jehregard flew toward the Firstland. Kyrien disappeared into the clouds.

Strapped in and with the physical, emotional, and energetic support of the crew, Jessub Tillerman did his best to take them lower--safely.

When the *Dragon's Wing* did grace the seas once again, she entered the water like a brick. Jessub managed to land the *Dragon's Wing* without sinking her, though he did soak the crew.

Gwen shook her head and unbuckled herself. "I thought you were going to kill us all."

"Sorry about that," Jessub said, his head hung so low, Kenward could barely see how red his face was. "It looked like you needed help."

Gwen smiled. "I did, and somehow being smothered by you did manage to improve the situation."

He grinned at that statement. "I told Gramma and Grampa I'd be a great adventurer one day," he said with a catch in his voice and a tear on his cheek.

"And that you are," Kenward said. "By the looks of it part flightmaster and part thrustmaster to boot. You're going to have to tell me how you learned so fast. You should have seen what it was like trying to get Pelivor to do it."

"I watched him and Gwen. Always thought I could see the wing structures but never believed I could do it myself."

"What changed your mind?" Kenward asked.

"I hated being in Dragonhold," Jessub admitted. "Once the barrier went up, I felt like I was suffocating. Most people seemed to be fine, but those with power suffered." he shrugged. "After that, I just acted on instinct. I thought we were all going to die."

"You did well," Fasha said. "Now we just need to figure out what to do next."

"Please," Sinjin said as he emerged from the crowd. Kenward hadn't even seen him board. It must have been terribly difficult to leave his mother behind. "Take us home."

This was the first time Kenward had heard Sinjin refer to the Firstland as home. It was progress, he supposed. Going there suited him just fine. Most of his crew was aboard and the Firstland was as easy a place as any to build a new airship. Having access to dragons tended to make a great many things easier.

After no one aboard offered any argument, Fasha set a course. Wind and sail propelled them, and Kenward could hardly believe it. Taking deep breaths and stretching out on the deck of his sister's ship, he enjoyed it while it lasted. A few moments later, a bird flew overhead and he grinned.

* * *

Reconciling figures and accounts was far from Nora Trell's favorite task, but it was among her most productive. A successful business did not thrive without a firm hand on the tiller. A firm hand was born of confidence. Her job was to make sure that confidence was warranted and their course true. Grimacing, she closed her long-term tallies. Costs were up and profits were down. The world changed and a successful trader had to change with it or become obsolete.

Beneath the ledgers rested a thick tome, weathered and aged but whole. A strip of white silk saved her page, and she resumed her search. She'd taught her children well, and they had discovered things beyond her wildest imaginings. Now that she knew what was possible, though, she could imagine a great many things. Knowledge was the key. Trade was always more profitable when you know things others do not. The Trell family had always thrived on innovation, their ship designs unmatched. But Nora knew the truth. The *Trader's Wind* would soon become at least partially obsolete. Each page of this faded text held the potential for discovery, though few did more than tantalize. So many things the ancients knew but did not write down. Their tales intrigued but failed to provide adequate detail. Even so, she'd already learned much.

The next page bore an illustration of a complex spherical object. Reading the description, Nora drew a sharp breath. When one of her runners entered without a knock; placed a small, rolled parchment on her desk; and silently left the room, Nora smiled. Having a well-trained staff was one of the keys to a successful business. She did not yet know the name of that young man, but soon she would.

The rolled parchment was difficult to open, mostly because it was so small, having come by bird. She also feared what it might contain. With her children, she never knew what to expect, and this message had without doubt come from Fasha. Some things a mother knew. "What trouble have my children gotten into this time?"

After reading the missive, all she could do was shake her head. Something would have to be done--something drastic.

* * *

Molten stone and sparks flowed from the keystone. The concussion from Allette's attack had knocked Strom and Osbourne clear of the major devastation. They had been pelted with hot rocks but bore mostly bruises and cuts that would heal given time.

"Durin." Osbourne said the name before Strom could get it out. No answer came.

The men moved with cautious haste to find the young man, and when they did, both drew sharp breaths. Durin did not move. Parts of his clothing and one boot were on fire. Moving as quickly as they could, they pulled Durin away from the molten rock spewing from deep fissures in the cavern floor. The damage to the Black Spike's foundation sent rocks crashing down from above. Delaying only long enough to put out the flames, they dragged Durin's unconscious form back to the tunnels.

"What are we going to do now?" Osbourne asked.

"You choose," Strom said, the consequences of his last decision still fresh.

Osbourne was silent for a moment after gently lowering Durin to the stone floor and checking his pulse. "He's alive."

Strom just grunted.

"We go back up the way we came in," Osbourne said.

Doing his best not to despair, Strom tried not to think about the stones that had closed in behind them during their descent. Having been so close to simply stepping into another place taunted him. Their chance had passed. They could have gone just about anywhere, and they had stayed within this black pit like fools. It was perhaps the stupidest thing he'd ever done, and he suspected they would pay with their lives. Durin may have already done so.

Strom was no fool. He'd seen people die from less grievous wounds, and Durin's comatose condition did not bode well for the young man. He needed the kind of medical attention they were neither trained nor equipped to provide.

Osbourne came up with the idea of making a litter from just their shirts and jackets. The result was more sling than litter, but it did make it easier to carry Durin's limp form. The thought of carrying the young man up the spiral stair made Strom quail, but he pushed the thought from his mind.

Getting back out of the tunnels didn't take as long as Strom had thought it would. Eventually they reached the place where they had found the dragon skull and the second figurine. Now, though, the skull was gone. Osbourne looked over his shoulder at Strom, who just shrugged. After a tense moment, Osbourne chose. He walked into the hall the skull had previously warned them against. Durin had said he thought there was water in this place, and Strom suspected that was what made the decision for Osbourne. It was the same call he would have made himself, and somehow that made him feel responsible anyway. Inescapable guilt tormented him.

"Stop there."

The voice came without warning, and the two men nearly dropped poor Durin. Strom shifted his grip on the makeshift litter and looked around.

"You are welcome here, but please come no farther for your own protection."

They eased Durin to the black stone. Before them a brightly illuminated chamber danced with ever-shifting light reflected off glistening rock. Glowing crystals jutted from what was, by the look of it, a naturally formed chamber. Beside a shimmering pool stood a saltbark tree; Strom would know the crystal-covered leaves anywhere.

Between them and the pool stood perhaps the most beautiful creature either had ever seen. Clothed in glittering emerald leaves, her long hair cascaded in intricate braids that sparkled in the light.

"The one you call Durin acted bravely. His wounds are grievous."

Strom nodded at this, a tear falling from his eye and his chin quivering. He faced judgment for his actions.

"You are loyal, faithful, and a man of integrity, Strom."

"You have us at a disadvantage, my lady," Osbourne said.

The beautiful woman laughed a tittering trill that set Strom's heart at ease. "Forgive me. I do not meet new people often and I forget my manners. I am a dryad. My full name is long, but you can call me Larissarelatarenfall."

Strom was grateful to his friend for knowing what to say.

"Forgive us, lady," Osbourne said. "Our tongues are clumsy. May we call you Larissa?"

The dryad laughed again but soon returned her attention to Durin. "He has suffered enough," she said and carefully removed a sparkling leaf from above her left breast. The leaf was bigger and had more crystals than any Strom remembered from the saltbark trees in the shallows.

Larissa bent down and gently took Durin's head in her hands. Her pale white flesh stood out in contrast to Durin's tanned and now burned, soot-covered skin. With motherly care, she tilted his head back until his mouth opened. Placing the leaf on his tongue like the greatest treasure, Larissa slid a hand under Durin's jaw and pressed his mouth closed.

The young man made no reaction.

"Will he live?" Strom asked, choked with emotion.

Larissa met his eyes. "There is nothing I can do that will heal all his wounds, friend Strom, but I do think he will live. For now, we must let him rest."

* * *

Under clear blue skies, the *Dragon's Wing* skimmed the waves, Jessub Tillerman just barely managing the role of flightmaster. Even with experience gained during the long and arduous journey back to the Firstland, the entire crew was exhausted and no one, including him, wanted to take the ship any higher than necessary. On occasion they clipped tall waves, slowing their progress, but it was still far faster than traditional sailing. Capable of maintaining flight, albeit without great confidence, Jessub had also learned to provide thrust. The only time he could practice was when they were in the water, but Gwen proved a skilled teacher. Jessub was unable to return the favor, and flying the *Dragon's Wing* unassisted remained beyond her abilities. Providing thrust came to him more easily than acting as flightmaster, but there was no one else aboard to replace him. It was a feeling that would take some getting used to.

Not long before Windhold and the natural harbor came into view, regal dragons flew out to meet them. Valterius and Gerhonda cried out to Sinjin and Kendra. It was in many ways a joyous reunion, and Kenward was not ungrateful for the escort.

No one was certain how the dragons had known they were coming. Most chalked it up to them sensing those they bonded. Their cries were both merry and mournful. Flying in close, Kenward thought they might land on the *Wing*, but perhaps they sensed the crew was already strained and chose not to distract them.

When Jessub eased the ship back into the water, he did so with growing confidence and skill.

"Well done," Fasha said. The crew hooted and hollered their agreement, though some commented on how many times it had taken him to get the hang of it.

Dragons waited on the shoreline, and Benjin dropped anchor in the shallows. With the boats lowered, weary crew and passengers climbed down the boarding nets and crossed the final barrier separating them from land. Growing winds drove white-capped waves ashore, making the final row treacherous.

Kenward joined Kendra and Sinjin in one of the boats, and despite nearly capsizing, they did eventually gain the shore. The dragons cooed and bobbed their heads up and down until Sinjin and Kendra stroked their foreheads. Valterius offered his wing to Sinjin, and Kenward's friend hadn't looked that happy in months. He smiled, albeit a bit sadly.

Tension between Kendra and Gerhonda was apparent, but Kenward chalked that up to both being female--complicated creatures, those. The embrace was longer in coming but no less enthusiastic. Soon the two ferried supplies up to Windhold, saving the need to carry everything up the steep climb.

Drakon followed suit and when the cargo had been unloaded, they carried weary travelers up to the hold. Kenward watched the first few go and turned a bit green as they slipped into the mountain. He was a brave man, but some things were beyond even his courage; putting his life in a giant flying lizard's control was among them. He'd never admit it to those around him. Climbing on foot was statement enough. He was not alone, though, and that gave him comfort.

Reaching Windhold left Kenward mentally and physically exhausted. So many questions and ideas rattled in his mind, he could make sense of none of it, which left him unsettled.

Near where a member of the Dragon Clan unsaddled Valterius, Sinjin and Kendra stood, their heads hung low. Durin's absence cast a pall over everything they did.

"Our world continues to change," Sinjin said to those gathered. A few people were still filing in at the back of the crowd. "Our stores have been taxed, and all the things we've worked so hard for are at risk. We must be vigilant. We must be strong." Windhold rang with a cheer of agreement. "We've guests to feed as well. Hunting and fishing duties are to be redoubled. I know it's a lot to ask, but I ask it nonetheless. We can no longer overlook the need for defenses and secure housing for the Drakon and Dragon Clan alike."

Even after time had passed, Kenward sensed the Dragon Clan's disappointment. They had chosen to dedicate their lives to dragons but had not been rewarded with a bonded dragon of their own. Kenward could only imagine how that must feel, and he gave those people credit for not being more bitter and for supporting their more fortunate brethren.

"It seems like long ago that we found an ancient place high atop the peaks. The time has come to focus our resources on seeing if this place can support us," Sinjin continued.

This statement was received with some enthusiasm. Life within Windhold was difficult, and any advantages they could gain would be most welcome. An outsider, Kenward wasn't a part of these efforts, and he felt selfish for having hoped Sinjin would make his requests a priority. Looking to his right, he caught Fasha's eye. She gave him a sad smile. Kenward couldn't help but feel a bit jealous of his sister in that moment, and he felt a smaller person for it, but she always managed to have a serviceable ship when he did not.

"I've already asked much of you, but there's one thing more," Sinjin said. Windhold fell silent, save the rushing wind and the occasional rattle of harness. "The Drakon and Dragon Clan do not forget those who help them." This brought a cheer. "We don't forget a friend who needs us, and despite everything else that must be done, I ask all of you to rise to this challenge and show just how we treat those we care about."

Sinjin's words evoked a rush of emotion that flooded the hall. Kenward's face flushed, and when he looked back at his sister, tears threatened to fall from her eyes. The very one he'd been jealous of a moment ago was overwhelmed with emotion. Kenward was ashamed.

"We've work to do, my friends," Sinjin said with a flourish and a grin. "We've a ship to build."

Overcome with emotion, Fasha could not hide it, and tears clouded Kenward's vision. Never before had he been honored so, and he took a ragged breath before speaking. When he did regain his composure, his words stunned everyone.

"You are gracious and kind," he said. "But if we're going to go to the trouble of building a ship, perhaps we could attempt something a bit more ambitious?"

* * *

Nora Trell preferred a sturdy deck beneath her feet and water around her, but she had to admit the landbound served a purpose or two. Though the sea provided most of what she needed, the food on land was worth a bit of risk and occasional discomfort. Fruits and other nutrient-rich foods were essential to supplement the sea's bounty. Such ingredients weren't always easy to come by, even for a trader. Buying a variety of items in small quantities was nothing like brokering large shipments. Trading was about relationships, and Nora maintained her connections carefully, knowing those who weren't vital at one time could well be in another.

Not all contacts were equal. Some were more dangerous and dealt with darker business than others. The Trells had never been ones to meddle in landbound politics. There were just too many rules and invisible lines determining what belonged to whom. No one owned the seas, not that the landbound didn't try. Where land meets water, fortunes can be made but not without risk. Aware of the danger, Nora turned onto a narrow street. This was not a well-patrolled avenue or a sanctioned trade route; this was the kind of place a person could disappear. Tiny houses stacked atop one another formed a haphazard maze of the landbound's castoffs.

Distrustful eyes watched between slats in shoddily constructed walls. Nora kept her head down but her eyes up. Avoiding eye contact with anyone, especially the hooded, black-robed figure walking toward her, she slowed. Within the narrow alley, there was not always room for two to pass. Stepping to the side as far as she could, Nora hoped she wasn't invading anyone's personal living space. This was an easy way to spring a leak.

Looming over her, it was clear the hooded man could do as he wished with her and nothing would stop him. No one would interfere or cry for help. The jagged, crumbling walls closed tighter, pressing in on her. The sky darkened. Taking a deep breath, Nora remembered why she spent her life at sea. She couldn't imagine people choosing to live like this. Most had no choice, which only made the feeling worse. If she'd been born on land and unable to sail the sea, surely she would have gone mad. This, of course, explained most of her experiences with the landbound, a dangerous and unpredictable lot.

As the robed figure passed, he bumped into her, knocking her off balance. Never had she felt so vulnerable. Part of her wanted to run, to leave this awful place and never come back, but the other part--the part that usually won--knew this was important. Her future was at stake, and she cast her fears aside. The big man's hand glided across hers, leaving a parchment scrap in her palm. After casting him a surly glance, Nora moved on. Still people watched, the danger far from averted. Some things were worth the risk.

Chapter 11

A skilled flightmaster sculpts air into art only a fortunate few can see.
--Pelivor, flightmaster

***

Windhold buzzed with activity. Never had Kenward known such joy and pressure at the same time. Always before he'd had control over his ship's construction, but he'd been limited by time, gold, and manpower. Now he lacked materials and expertise. The Drakon had proven good to their word and helped him gather the bulk of what he needed.

Benjin stood stroking a prized piece. Bearing the exact curves they needed with richly grained wood, the massive tree had been close to impossible to get into dry dock, but six dragons working together somehow made it happen. Kenward was amazed at what these people could do with flying lizards even if he really had no desire whatsoever to fly on one. Knowing he might no longer have a choice in the matter, Kenward turned his attention back to the drawings. Benjin knew his business and needed no guidance. He'd criticized the *Serpent's* masthead, and Kenward was hardly in a position to argue when the man offered to carve this new one. The likeness of Valterius was a nice touch. This time his ship wouldn't be a poor imitation; it would be the first of its kind . . . at least in this age.

Sinjin had provided the desk and dried fronds on which Kenward could draw out his designs. There were multiple gaps in his plans, but he had to push on anyway. Somehow they would find a way to fashion what they needed from what they had. Years before, Kenward would have balked at raiding the *Slippery Eel*. He'd lost the *Serpent* in the meantime, and somehow that gave him distance from the loss of the Eel. Now he tried to look at things differently. Rather than desecrating the Eel's resting place, he gave parts of the ship a new life. It still hurt but it also gave him hope. It was worth it.

Much of what he lacked now was skill, which he hoped to replace with experimentation. After all, the things he didn't know how to do were just the things he'd never had to do before. The metals and canvas from the *Slippery Eel* had been the deciding factor. The Firstland had no mining operations and thus no access to ore. The *Dragon's Wing* carried additional sails but for a reason, and Kenward couldn't ask when he had access to canvas of his own.

Overseeing the operation had been difficult, but it was something he simply could not trust to someone else. He would never have been able to forgive himself for sending someone in his stead on that particular expedition. Kenward's ships were pieces of himself, and though he inevitably risked and lost, his treatment of them mirrored how he treated himself.

Again, he poured over the drawings, trying to find some other task that needed doing, some other purpose more important than finding the lightwood he needed. In spite of describing it to Sinjin in abundant detail, no one had been able to find any of the precious wood. This frustrated Kenward more than anything else, and he did his best not to mutter under his breath. When he glanced over his shoulder, Sinjin and several of the Dragon Clan worked to saddle Valterius. The dragon seemed to miss Durin as much as anyone else and refused to cooperate. Three people went down with a single swipe of the dragon's tail, and Kenward wondered how anyone could work with a creature capable of killing them at any given moment. He thought it inevitable, but he hoped he was wrong.

When Sinjin started his way, Kenward swallowed hard. He'd found no suitable excuses. It was his fate at stake, his vision, his dream. Kenward could not expect someone else to achieve his destiny. He could ask for help and no more. He'd asked and received help in abundance, but some things remained up to him.

He'd considered combing the forest floor on foot but had enough sense to realize how much faster they could search from the air. Part of him wanted to say he might not recognize the trees from above but given the amount of time he'd spent telling Sinjin how to spot it from that exact vantage, his ruse would be thin at best.

"So?" Sinjin said. There was no need to say more.

Kenward just nodded in acceptance of his fate. He donned the heavy jacket and goggles Sinjin provided, feeling foolish. He'd always thought the goggles made people look like frogs, and now he was the frog. On trembling knees, he approached Valterius. The dragon watched with knowing eyes and remained still. Kenward had secretly been hoping the dragon would misbehave and make this trip somehow impossible. The dragon's expression was unreadable, but Kenward got the sense the dragon knew his thoughts and enjoyed a good laugh at his expense.

Leaning down and extending his wing, Valterius invited them to mount. Sinjin went first, climbing nimbly up and sliding into the saddle like greeting an old friend. Kenward grabbed Sinjin's extended hand tentatively, afraid he would somehow hurt the dragon and end up being its lunch. Valterius watched him with amusement. With a deep breath, he pulled himself up. It felt as if his boots were digging into the dragon's flesh, and Kenward tried to hurry. This unfortunately caused him to be clumsy and he nearly fell back to the stone when his boot got caught in the straps. After putting all his weight on the other foot, Valterius issued a woof.

Eventually Kenward found himself in the seat behind Sinjin. He let his friend secure the straps, afraid he would do it incorrectly and end up smeared across the rocks below the keep. His breathing was rapid when

Sinjin gave his straps one last check. His friend gave him a firm nod and a pat on the knee. It didn't help.

Kenward was about to ask for information that could mean the difference between life and death, but Valterius ran out of patience. Before Sinjin could turn back around, the dragon hit a full run.

"Valterius!" Sinjin scolded, which drove the dragon faster.

Being supported by nothing but the translucent wing membranes was a big part of what Kenward had been dreading. Little did he know that should have been the least of his fears. He had no idea what the dragon's cry meant, but the meaning became quite clear. The dragon had been waiting for this moment, and now he would have his revenge.

Valterius did not extend his wings. They dropped from Windhold and spun like a falling seed pod, the world around them alternating between stone and sky. Kenward thought he might pass out before they all died. He did not. Mere hand widths above the rocky soil, Valterius pulled up, stabilizing their flight. In case Kenward had not gotten the message, Valterius turned and met his eyes.

In that instant, Kenward vowed never again to think of dragons as flying lizards.

* * *

Sevellon made it as far as the waters off the coast of the Falcon Isles before the *Nightfist*'s crew tossed him overboard. Grateful he was not full of holes, Sevellon swam to the nearest rock he could find. Swimming was not his strongest skill, but he had survived worse. The Falcon Isles were in many ways a series of small rocky outcroppings jutting from the sea, and he would have to swim only the distances between them. Buoys tied to some of these formations gave evidence fishermen would come as well, but Sevellon did not want to rely on the generosity of others.

From the little bit the men aboard the *Nightfist* told him, few ships frequented the Falcon Isles these days. Fears of feral dragons and demons persuaded most to find trade closer to home. Those who remained on the island had little choice, and most were desperate, including the jungle savages.

Sevellon wondered just how much of the happenings in his life were the thief's luck and how much was manipulation. He began to feel the strings tug, as lights once again appeared in the water. This ship he did not recognize, which was something of a relief. There was no denying the fact that it came straight for him, though, which made no sense. Bright light shone on the rock where he huddled defenseless, cold and wet. Few times had he ever found himself in a more desperate state. Part of him wanted to slip into the water and hide, but they would find him, every advantage theirs. From the masthead looked down a mighty wolf, and it almost seemed as if it spoke.

"Are you the man they call Sevellon the Thief?"

The question came as a blow to Sevellon's confidence and ego. Most of his life had been spent avoiding that exact question, and now it had been for naught. "I am," he said.

A rope ladder fell from above, and Sevellon the thief decided to trust his luck. Grabbing the rope, he climbed aboard an unknown ship where people already knew his name and profession. Getting out of this alive might be a trick.

"Have no fear," said an older man with a hard jaw. "My name is Jharmin Kyte, and you are welcome aboard my ship. I have something for you."

Though perhaps meant to soothe Sevellon's fear, the words increased it instead. He knew who this man was, and his presence meant Catrin or someone had been manipulating him this entire time. Part of him wanted to be angry with them, and part of him was angry with himself. They had figured him out and used him as a tool. The fury began to grow. "How did you know to find me here?"

It took a moment before Jharmin Kyte replied, his expression thoughtful. "It was a rather uncomfortable experience," the man admitted. "But I do believe I was spoken to by the lady Catrin's dragon, Kyrien."

Having his suspicions confirmed reinforced Sevellon's fear. His eyes scanned his surroundings, searching for a way out, understanding the threats and looking for ways to neutralize them.

"I ask nothing from you, except that you take what Catrin has asked me to give you," Jharmin said.

"And if I choose not to take it?"

Jharmin shrugged. "You seem like a nice enough fellow, but I don't suppose we'd take it very kindly. I mean you no harm, mind you, but Catrin's family. It is my wish to carry out her desires in this instance, and I will gladly transport you back to the Godfist along with this."

Wrinkling his nose and backing away even before the blanket came into contact with him, Sevellon could not imagine a less appealing object. Smelling of wet dog, it looked like nothing more than a heavy, dirty blanket.

"I'm hoping you know what you're supposed to do with this," Jharmin said.

Sevellon was busy trying to figure out who was the greatest threat: Jharmin, Catrin, or Kyrien. In the end, he decided it was the last. With a sigh, Sevellon turned back to Jharmin Kyte and said, "I'll do as the lady requires."

* * *

Once Valterius wasn't actively trying to kill him, Kenward recognized Sinjin's wisdom. It would take months to explore on foot what they could cover in a single afternoon adragonback. Cutting through the air at high speeds was less familiar to Kenward, but he did enjoy the sensation of flying. The lack of control he didn't like, but he was in no position to complain.

Most of the foliage belonged to hardwoods, far too heavy for the main structure of Kenward's new ship. There would be elements of the ship carved from hardwood, and Kenward made note of where the oldest specimens appeared to be. Tall, straight hardwoods were essential components in some of his newest designs. The designs were not something he assumed full credit for since much of the inspiration came from books Sevellon had given him. Clearly the man had felt bad about deceiving them. Kenward understood shame and remorse. There were people he'd wanted to avoid for large chunks of his life out of embarrassment over mistakes he'd made. Kenward had told the thief he'd forgiven him, but the man didn't appear to believe. Guilt and shame were powerful emotions, indeed.

The books filled Kenward's mind with incredible visions. Described within were machines far beyond Kenward's feeble abilities to replicate, but some things aligned with what he'd learned building the *Serpent*. Ancient knowledge had led him to that construction, and this was the perfect opportunity to take things to the next level, or perhaps up a few levels. Anything worth doing was worth overdoing in his opinion. Well, almost anything.

Sweeping low into a valley clogged with jagged rock formations, Valterius flitted back and forth, sometimes with just a tilt of his wings and sometimes with rigorous flapping. Kenward did his best to anticipate the dragon's next move, but he was terrible at it, which left the straps to hold him in place. He soon learned that clinging to Sinjin and leaning whichever way his friend did made for a smoother flight.

Then Valterius pulled up sharply.

"Hold on!" Sinjin shouted.

What did he think he'd been doing, Kenward asked himself, not prepared for anything worse than what they had already been through.

Using every bit of the speed he'd been able to muster, Valterius sent them straight up a vertical face. Peaks leaned out over the cliffs like claws. The higher they flew, the less speed they carried, leaving Kenward momentarily weightless, a feeling he knew from nightmares.

At the zenith, a flash of green light amid the peaks caught Kenward's eye. It seemed likely they would slam into the same peaks at any moment. Turning until they faced downward, Valterius partially extended his wings and reached speeds that took Kenward's breath. Leaning over, he thought he might be sick, but his eyes caught sight of the very prize they sought: lightwood trees.

Distinguishable by their flaky, white bark; roughly triangular leaves; and shorter stature, the trees grew best where high winds were not prevalent. This hidden valley provided an ideal environment for them to flourish. Sucking in air and trying to speak, Kenward remained mute. As if proving he knew Kenward's mind, Valterius circled lower and landed by a rock outcropping that dominated the clearing.

Dismounting first, Sinjin said nothing about his dragon's choice of landing place. Kenward tried not to appear rushed in his escape from the saddle, but Valterius watched him intently. This was unnecessary since the dragon apparently knew his thoughts.

After stretching until his bones popped and shifted, Sinjin regarded his friend. "Sorry for the rough ride. Valterius gets a little carried away sometimes."

Kenward just grunted. Trapped in this remote place, he didn't want the dragon to hear his words. "Does he read your thoughts?"

"It seems that way sometimes, but no," Sinjin said.

"Are you sure?"

The question unnerved Sinjin. "Well, I mean, we communicate without words if that's what you're asking. But even that is mostly body language and physical contact . . . I think." Sinjin was no longer certain of his words.

"Why did we land here?"

Sinjin nodded as if understanding. "He landed here on his own. Sometimes he just needs a break. Why do you ask?"

"Because there's a grove of lightwood trees over those hills."

This took Sinjin back a step. "And you saw them . . ."

"Right before we landed."

Sinjin turned to Valterius, who gazed back at the two of them with an unflinching stare. With a shrug, he turned back toward where Kenward indicated. "Let's go have a look."

In no way clear, the walk was, in many places, more of a climb. "He could've set us down a little closer," Kenward said.

"I'm telling you. He may have excellent instincts, but I seriously doubt he can read your thoughts."

"Laugh all you want," Kenward said. "Mael has been playing with all of our heads for decades. Think about it! How many of the events that shaped your life were driven by an ancient dragon trying to get free of his prison?" He really hadn't meant to say the words, but they poured out nonetheless. "I'm sorry," he said before Sinjin could respond.

"Don't be. You're correct. I cannot change what Mael has done. But do not attribute his deeds to all dragons. They're like us, you know. There are good dragons and greedy dragons and malicious dragons. I'll admit there's an entire breed with debts to settle, but that doesn't change the good Kyrien and the Drakon have done."

"Sorry," Kenward said again, not knowing what else to say.

Ahead, flashes of white could be seen, and soon the lightwood trees became visible. Kenward counted as they walked, knowing there needed to be at least twice the number of trees he required for his ship. Only a fool would cut down all the trees to build a ship. All too soon, though, elm, oak, and pine intruded, blotting out the sun the shorter lightwood trees craved. Not seeing enough to satisfy his conscience, Kenward did the next best thing. "Help me gather the seed pods," he said.

"What for?" Sinjin asked.

"We'll need to cut down more than half of these trees to get the very minimum lightwood I'll need. I may be a man of the sea, but what kind of steward would I be if I did not replace what I take? We can pot these and water them to help them along. Then when we cut the trees, we'll do so strategically and plant new trees in place of those we take."

Sinjin nodded. "It's a good plan. I'm just trying to figure out how we get all these trees out of this valley."

"We don't," Kenward said with an evil grin. "We just need to bring the other components here."

"Oh, sure. No problem. You do remember the ride in, don't you?"

This point Kenward could not argue. It was a maddening situation. He had found all the components he needed yet couldn't quite bring the pieces together. It made him want to scream.

"I am sorry, though," Sinjin said, perhaps sensing his mood. "I would've liked it if this were easier. Unfortunately the trip out of the valley is not much better than the way in. We're sort of trapped in a little bowl, surrounded on all sides by steep peaks."

Those were the exact conditions that made it perfect for lightwood to grow. Kenward sighed. Nothing was ever easy. "Well, at least we know there's lightwood growing on the island. Perhaps we can search for some that are more accessible."

"A reasonable plan but not today."

"We still have some daylight left," Kenward argued.

"We do, indeed. Building your inventions is not my only priority."

Nodding, Kenward reminded himself just how much he asked of the Drakon and the Dragon Clan. He consumed almost all of their time, which caused their resources to dwindle. Sinjin had goals of his own, and caring for his people trumped Kenward's dreams. If not for the fact that his new ships would greatly benefit the people of the Firstland and the rest of the world, he might have felt bad about it.

"I need to make a stop on the way back to Windhold," Sinjin continued. "Getting there might be a bit of a bumpy ride. We could probably come back for you if you would rather abstain."

"Might?" Kenward asked, already knowing Sinjin and his dragon would not leave his sight until he was back within Windhold. Sinjin he trusted. He tried not to think the next thought and hoped Valterius was too far away to know. It had the potential to be a terrifying ride, and Kenward's guts churned.

Valterius watched them approach with impatience in his unflinching gaze. It made Kenward feel like prey, another thought he hoped was his alone. Sinjin mounted with practiced ease and offered his hand. To his credit, Kenward found his seat easily this time, and Valterius barely complained. He did give a huff while the two strapped themselves in. Sinjin was still double-checking straps when Valterius launched, his powerful wing strokes sending dust into the wind. Kenward pulled his goggles back on, now thankful for them.

After going almost straight up until they cleared the trees, Valterius turned on his wingtip and soared along the steep walls. The valley's end approached faster than Kenward would have thought, and he held on to Sinjin with all his might, trying unsuccessfully to determine what the dragon would do next.

Sending them straight up into the air but without enough speed to escape the valley, Valterius flipped over backward and spun. Now pointed back at the treetops, they raced on trimmed wings, gaining even more speed. Twice more Valterius picked up momentum before escaping the bowl-shaped valley. It was clear these trees were beyond their reasonable reach.

Chapter 12

Never stand in the shadow of dragons.
--Benjin Hawk, father

* * *

With Larissa watching over them, the Black Spike was not nearly as frightening. Durin sat, cross-legged, with a blanket wrapped around his shoulders. Strom and Osbourne both paced the area to which they were restricted. Larissa had not forbidden them from going anywhere else, but she had asked them not to go near the tree or the glistening pool. Whatever they needed, she brought them, and no one had any desire to venture back into the darkness, even with the amber figurines.

"You'll not have to wait here much longer," Larissa had said, but she quietly declined to elaborate.

Escape from this place was perhaps more than they could wish for. Even if they could get past the stone defenses that had closed behind them during their descent, they would have no way to tell the dragons they were ready to leave. Durin and Valterius were going to have a long talk if he managed to survive this and track down the ornery dragon.

When Larissa returned, she brought cool water; large, thick nuts Durin didn't recognize; and a bit of honey in which to dip them. It was delicious and restored his spirit. He tried not to think about his wounds. The saltbark leaf had undoubtedly saved his life, and many of his injuries were no longer visible, but he felt fragile and weak, as if he might crumple from any sudden movement.

Strom and Osbourne had explored the immediate area and reported a sizable stone landing jutting into cold seawater. From that direction came a muted roar. Rising slowly to his feet, he and the others were on full alert, though Larissa continued to wear a placid smile. It made Durin feel a little better. He was in no condition for a fight.

Walking toward the growing noise, Strom held the amber figurine high. Osbourne grabbed the other and followed. Despite Larissa's reassurance, Durin trembled and nearly passed out when a dragon's fierce visage appeared in the water, air bubbles dancing around it as it rushed toward the surface. All three took a step backward.

Kyrien emerged in his full glory to dominate the hall. On his back rested Catrin's original leather saddle.

"He's going to take us out of here," Strom said after a long stare from Kyrien. The smith appeared torn.

"We should let him take Durin first," Osbourne said. "Getting him back to the sunlight would be best."

The last of the regent dragons gazed at them, his eyes focusing on Strom.

"All three of us go at once," Strom said.

"But--" Osbourne started. A look from Kyrien silenced him.

"Climb up, Osbourne," Strom said. "I'll show you how he wants us to strap ourselves in. It's not perfect, but it should work."

Durin didn't like the sound of the word should, but he liked the thought of staying here forever even less, no matter how pleasant Larissa's company.

"Before you go," she said, "I've a gift for each of you."

The dryad presented each of them with a glistening saltbark leaf--a precious gift indeed. Strom and Osbourne pressed theirs in parchment Larissa provided. For Durin and Kyrien, however, the dryad placed the leaf on their tongues. There was magic in that placement Durin didn't understand but was somehow undeniable. Her actions also proved her bravery. Not many would have had the courage to place something on a dragon's tongue.

Kyrien, though, bowed his head in respect of Larissa and moved his forehead closer to her. She laid her hands on him, and his eyes closed. For some time they stood in silent communion, and Durin wondered what transpired between them. Strom and Osbourne stashed the amber figurines in their jackets to protect them.

Reaching down, Strom pulled Durin up and showed him where to put his legs. It didn't look as if it would work, but it was more comfortable than he had feared. Soon Strom had all three of them strapped in. They turned almost as one to say a final farewell to Larissa, who waved with tears in her eyes. She hadn't known them long, but Durin suspected she would be all alone again after they departed. He also knew the tears were more likely for the loss of Kyrien's company. Still, Durin almost felt bad for leaving--not that he had any choice.

He was still trying to figure out just how they would get out of the Black Spike without drowning when Kyrien leaped into the water. Durin's scream cut short as he was almost instantly submerged. Somehow the dragon moved fast enough and with enough force that a cavitation formed in the water behind his massive head. In his own terror, Strom raised a fist holding the spider stone, blue plasma crawling over his outstretched arm.

Lightning and sheets of plasma pressed outward on the water and added to the effect. Moving in a bubble of compressed air, Durin's ears popped just before Kyrien burst into the open sky. The sudden change in pressure made him queasy, but gulping fresh air outweighed all else in that moment.

* * *

His stomach churning, Kenward hoped Valterius wouldn't need to do any more aerial acrobatics. Things didn't go his way. Wind gusts made flying erratic, and Kenward didn't care for being pushed around in the air. Aboard the *Serpent*, he'd always compensated for wind, but he never intentionally flew so close to rocks and trees and all sorts of things waiting to impale them.

Sinjin was confident and flew without worry; it disgusted Kenward. How could anyone be so calm when hurtling toward peaks of black rock? Valterius twisted and turned, just barely clearing the peaks before crystals came into view. What Kenward saw was distressing. The place resembled the Grove of the Elders. Green crystals as big around as greatoaks but only a little taller than the average man ringed a black stone carving that must have once been beautiful. Now though, the place looked as if Vestra had struck it with a hammer.

Deep fissures divided the ancient carving into hundreds of smaller pieces. Smoking chasms glowed orange, the air shimmering above them. Of the gem plinths themselves, all appeared damaged save one. The others existed in various states of disarray. One had almost completely disintegrated into fist-sized chunks. Others remained largely whole, save for visible cracks bifurcating them.

Valterius hovered above the broken stone, the heated updraft suspending him. The air was cooler than Kenward would have expected, and he wondered if the heat were the only source of the wind. It felt as if he could step off the dragon and hang in the air, not that he would dare such a thing. Kenward Trell was loosely wrapped, but he wasn't that crazy.

"Put us down outside of the ring, please," Sinjin said.

It took a moment for Valterius to obey. Kenward got the sense the dragon was basking in the energy there. Like the other keystones, there was an immediate sense of power when one entered their sphere of influence. In spite of the damage done to the crystals and stone, the energy persisted, and somehow that gave Kenward comfort.

"I thought you wanted a whole team to come up here," Kenward said, unsure if he wanted to explore this place. Going into holes in the world was not something the sailor ever wanted to do again. Dragonhold had been enough for a lifetime, but caves were what Sinjin wanted to explore. Kenward knew he was in trouble when he saw the damage done to the ancient barriers blocking the entrances.

"It's a dangerous place to get to," Sinjin said, and Kenward knew the truth of his words all too well. "And I wanted to take a look for myself."

"Thanks for bringing me along."

"This shouldn't take much time," Sinjin said, and he pulled a herald globe from his jacket.

"You knew we were coming here and didn't mention it on purpose."

Sinjin just grinned. "Come on. It won't be so bad."

Kenward mimicked him in a most unflattering way. In truth, he owed Sinjin for what the Drakon and Dragon Clan were doing for him, but he couldn't help his sarcasm. It came naturally and unbidden.

Free of his burdens, Valterius immediately returned to the air above the broken stone and hovered, his eyes mostly lidded.

"At least he's having a good time," Kenward said.

Exploring was far less fun than it sounded. Mostly, in this case, it involved moving large pieces of rock while hoping the rest didn't suddenly fall on them. Help was a long ways off, and Kenward didn't want to find out how Valterius was at moving rocks unless he could watch from a great distance.

Due to the shift in the landscape, it wasn't all that long before Sinjin slipped into the darkness, the herald globe's light showing the way. For several long moments, Kenward tried to decide whether to follow or guard the entrance. Valterius was the only other living creature there, but the sense of ancient power and the creepiness of the broken crystals and the giant carved black stone made him not want to be left alone. Looking into the cave, he saw the ring of light moving away.

After a deep breath and a fair amount of cursing, Kenward slipped into the semidarkness. "Wait for me."

"I thought you might guard the dragon," Sinjin said with a malicious grin.

"You're just a little bit evil. Do you know that?"

"I wonder where I get it," Sinjin said, and Kenward couldn't help but laugh. "Looks like this cave goes back for quite a distance and there's plenty of room in here for more than one dragon."

"You're really thinking about moving in here?"

"We need a much more defensible position with better protection from weather and other natural threats," Sinjin said.

"And I thought being landbound was bad enough. Now you have to live in a hole in the ground. What has this world come to?"

"We'll get you back in the air soon enough, I hope," Sinjin said. "And I'm not saying the place couldn't use a little . . . freshening up."

The detritus of ages littered the cave floor, but the walls and ceiling were rounded and smooth. As they moved deeper, the entranceway opened into a much larger chamber honeycombed with what could be sleeping nooks for dragons larger than regals.

"I knew it!" Sinjin said. "I knew this had to be where the ancient dragon riders lived."

"I see evidence of dragons," Kenward said. "I see nothing to indicate riders . . ."

The silence was all that told of Sinjin's thoughts. Looking as if he would move deeper into the cave, he held the herald globe high. There were carvings in the stone above, but the lines were wide and deep, as if dragon claws had made them. Kenward had never wondered if animals and other creatures might be artistic, and the thought bothered him more than he would have expected. If dragons created art, then what separated them save their physical forms? The question rang in Kenward's consciousness, and as with all things, the more he tried not to think about it, the more it persisted.

The cavern's acoustics made even small sounds echo loudly. Kenward tried to imagine what it would be like with dragons and people living in there but failed. A chill ran down his body when a distant roar cascaded through the hall. Neither had to say a word. Both moved back toward the entrance and Valterius.

Knowing more than a few tales of Valterius's behavior, Kenward prayed the dragon was still there and wouldn't leave them stranded. Sinjin moved with renewed urgency. Kenward did his best to keep up; failure meant being left in the dark, and he wanted nothing to do with that. The place gave him the crawls.

Smaller rocks tumbled down as Sinjin climbed, and he waited impatiently for the way to be clear. Then, feeling the specter of darkness at his back, he scrambled up with exaggerated urgency.

"Are you hurt?" Sinjin asked. "Your hand is bleeding."

"I'll be fine." Kenward sucked his thumb. To his relief, Valterius waited for them, still hovering in an apparent state of bliss.

"We need to go," Sinjin said. Valterius ignored him. "Didn't you hear that? We need to go!"

As if to remind Sinjin of his place, the dragon took a few moments more before opening his hooded eyes and winging over to where they stood. Knees trembling, Kenward waited for Sinjin to mount. He dreaded the ride back but certainly didn't want to be left behind. When the dragon turned his level gaze on them, he tried to think of anything else. Never anger the dragon you are about to ride became one of Kenward's life rules.

The journey out of the valley was shockingly easy. Valterius turned a tight circle over the shattered keystone. The hot air and whatever other forces were in effect pushed them higher and higher until Valterius simply turned on a wingtip and soared back toward Windhold. Shouts and cries cut across the distance, and even Valterius showed some sense of urgency.

Triple-checking his straps, Kenward quailed, hearing another deep roar. Most times, Valterius and the other dragons approached Windhold at a moderate speed. This was not one of those times. Knuckles and knees clenched, Kenward screamed as Valterius plummeted toward Windhold's main flight deck. "You're going to get us killed!" He could almost see Sinjin's grin. The tables had turned.

One instant they raced toward the hold; the next, they were screaming through it with Kyrien roaring at them. Speeding past the last of the regent dragons was among the most terrifying things Kenward had ever experienced, with the noted exception of their high-speed landing. It left him with the taste of blood in his mouth, and he teetered in his seat.

Before Kenward could regain his senses, Sinjin dismounted and ran to Kyrien. Kenward was less enthusiastic. He did smile a moment later when Sinjin returned, Durin on his heels, scolding him about not caring for Valterius before dashing off to visit.

"It's good to have you back, my friend," Sinjin said. "Strom and Osbourne too!" The older men waved from across the wind channel.

"I bet," Durin said. His bravado was still there, Kenward noted, but the younger man kept shifting his weight as if in pain. "You probably had no one to unsaddle your ungrateful dragon. In fact, I think you might want to get Valterius out of here before Strom decides to come this way. Leaving us atop the Black Spike was a poor way to foster good relations." He said the words while staring down the dragon, who just gave a great woof and stepped on his toes. "Some things never change."

When Strom did approach, he did not appear angry. "The dragon tells me you need help building a ship," he said to Kenward. "What happened to the last one?"

Not many would dare ask the captain such a question, but Kenward just grinned. "Someone parked a ship on top of her, and then someone else used her for kindling. My ships do have a bad habit of coming in handy."

"It'll be an honor to get you back in the air, or water, or whatever it is you choose."

"You said the dragon told you?" Kenward said.

"Kyrien and I had a lot of time to talk. He said you were working on a new airship and you might need help making some pretty strange things. He even sent me pictures in my mind, but I still haven't made sense of them. What exactly are you building?"

Unsure he should answer, Kenward had to wonder if the dragons weren't manipulating all of them. How had Kyrien known his plans? Were they really his plans? After thinking about it, he realized he couldn't spend the rest of his life wondering if he was being manipulated. In this case, if the dragons wanted him to have the greatest airship ever constructed, he agreed.

"I'm building the future," Kenward said. "Thanks for being willing to help. Building the future is harder than it sounds."

* * *

Days later, Kenward Trell ducked beneath his new ship, narrowly avoiding the massive carved tree that formed both keel and masthead. It dangled beneath Kyrien and was subject to the wind. The larger dragon's aid had been critical in getting the wood they needed and moving the completed pieces from the staging area to the dry dock.

Fasha watched from nearby and shook her head. "What kind of ship are you building, my brother?"

Kenward just grinned. "You'll see."

"I've heard that before."

"And have I failed to impress?" Kenward asked.

"No, you have not. But I'd be lying if I told you I'm not a little concerned. I've seen some of the parts people are working on, and I can't make sense of it. What kind of madness is this?"

"We're at the beginning of a brave new age," Kenward said with a wink. "The ancients possessed knowledge we've long since forgotten, and I've seen some of those things. Now I'm going to build my own version of what the manuscripts describe and see if my ideas truly fly."

"And if they don't?"

Kenward shrugged. "There are risks. Look out!"

A sudden wind gust caused the masthead to swing directly toward where Fasha stood, but she hadn't lived as long as she had without being quick on her feet. Once the keel was set, Fasha inspected the rectangular framing. "It looks like a brick. Except for the carving of Valterius; that's nice."

"A flying brick," Kenward said. "It doesn't have to be pretty. It just has to fly. But I agree the masthead is a work of art. Your husband just couldn't have me sailing around with a poor imitation."

At that Fasha laughed. "I'd tell you Mother wouldn't approve, but that never stopped you from doing anything."

"Mother taught me to follow my gut," Kenward said. "Unfortunately, after that, my gut never agreed with anything else she said. A pity, really."

"Somehow you'll be the death of us all, and somehow you'll make us all laugh with our last breath. I expect nothing less, you know, so don't disappoint me."

Kenward took a bow and looked back at his ship. He used hardwood sparingly in his design, but having it would provide the stability the *Serpent* had always lacked. This ship would be heavier and more tightly built. Sinjin probably hadn't realized what he'd agree to until he saw how much canvas needed sewing. Kenward did what he could to reduce the workload, maintain efficiency in their build process, and train the people so they could work as proficiently as possible, but there was only one of him. He was grateful for his friends. If not for everyone around him, none of this would be happening.

"Now that this is in place, I need to check in with Strom and the hardwood workers."

"You've got this entire island swarming like a kicked anthill. You know that, don't you?"

"Yeah, I know," Kenward said with a grin. "But you only live once, Sis; might as well live big!"

The two climbed and continued to pick on one another, but both knew the way they really felt underneath. The jokes had always helped them cope with difficult situations and were a part of their relationship. It drove their mother to distraction, but that had never stopped either of them.

"I need more heat," Strom said when they reached the impromptu smithy. The facility was sorely lacking. "And I need ore . . . and bricks . . . and I still need to make an anvil. Have you ever made an anvil? Do you have any idea how much heat and work it takes to make an anvil? Of course not. But I'm just supposed to pull one out of my shirt pocket."

Kenward had heard the complaints before; at least the list was shorter this time. Progress had been made. "The mud bricks are almost dry," Kenward said.

Strom scoffed.

"Have you asked Benjin if there's any more metal on the *Dragon's Wing*?"

"Grubb told me anyone who comes near his stove or his last cook pot will be the next meal," Strom said.

Kenward sighed. "I guess we'll have to make the tank walls a little thinner, then."

"Easy for you to say," Strom said, his sweaty, soot-covered arms crossed over his chest. "You're not the one who'll have to hammer it all thin."

"Trust me," Kenward said. "I'd rather have the walls thick. I just don't know where to get any more metal. Do the best you can, my friend. I thank you."

The smith just grunted and returned to his work. Trying to do things on the Firstland the smith had been perfectly set up for within Dragonhold had to be frustrating. In Windhold, he had few of the tools he needed to do things right. When everything was a workaround, everything took longer and produced a lower-quality product. Kenward was just glad the man was willing to continue.

Walking toward where sails were being sewn into windsocks, Kenward was about to ask how things were going when a strong wind gust tore through the hold and sent an expansive section of sail into the air. Kenward's breath caught in his throat, but the Dragon Clan and Drakon were crafty. Within moments, they had retrieved the massive canvas and had it laid out, workers sewing once again. Entire sections of canvas had been reduced to threads just to facilitate the stitching of what might be the largest windsocks Godsland had ever known--five of them in all. Kenward couldn't wait to see the vision in his head made a reality, and it kept pushing him forward in spite of so many obstacles.

When they reached the area where the more experimental and complex parts were being assembled, Fasha raised an eyebrow in unspoken question.

"You'll see," Kenward said, unable to verbalize his full vision. The best he could do was explain each piece to the person making it. Once it was all put together, he'd let them judge for themselves. When he was honest, he wasn't certain any of it would work. He tried not to think of how all these people and dragons would react if he failed. In the end, he was trying to change the world for the better, and sometimes that meant taking risks.

His mother definitely would not approve.

Chapter 13

If you were insane, would you know?
--Ain Giest, sleepless one

* * *

Walking amid the chaos within Windhold, Brother Vaughn's trepidation grew. His life had forever changed, and he knew not exactly how to tell people what they really faced. Would it make any difference? he asked himself. Would knowing the extent of the danger change their actions? He suspected not. Nonetheless, his conscience would not allow continued silence.

Part of him wished he'd stayed behind with Catrin and Pelivor. They would understand this situation better and might actually be able to do something about it. Still, he couldn't just leave them all ignorant. Even Kenward might change his ambitions if he knew. They might not even believe him. It was a thought that had troubled him throughout his life. He'd learned important things about the return of Istra, things he now knew to be true. For exploring ideas outside the accepted doctrine, the Cathurans had shunned and ridiculed him. This was different, though. People here had seen Mael for themselves. How could they deny it?

Walking to where Sinjin, Kenward, and Strom huddled over rough drawings on coarse papyrus, Brother Vaughn sighed. Nothing in this place was quite what it should be, and he acknowledged how much of his lifestyle he'd taken for granted; many of civilization's accomplishments had seemed as if they'd always been there. Now he came to see just how magical those comforts really were. In a place such as this, without the materials or craftsmen to shape them, many things that had been a basic part of life on the Godfist were impossible to produce here.

Reading Kenward's plans gave a glimpse into the man's twisted genius. His ideas were radical, but when one looked more closely, his designs addressed real problems they all faced. Perhaps discouraging the good captain was not the best thing to do. Brother Vaughn had rarely been so torn. Honor had been the driving force for most of his life, and he wasn't about to change that now. "I need a word with you all."

His statement and tone brought those gathered to attention. "Just us?" Sinjin asked with concern on his face.

"I've a tale to tell you that you're not going to like, but it may change all of our lives."

"Durin," Sinjin said. "Please blow the gathering horn."

Durin retrieved a polished horn of wood and bone. Those around him pretended not to notice how slowly he stood from bending down. His face spoke of pain and embarrassment, which clearly shamed Sinjin. Brother Vaughn empathized with each of them.

"Could you blow this for me?" Durin asked Strom, who took it without a word. "I'm having a bit of trouble catching my breath." The words upset the young man, but life had been unkind to him. First he'd taken an assassin's bolt meant for Sinjin, and now his wounds from the breaking of the keystones were only beginning to mend.

"Healing requires more patience than most possess," Brother Vaughn said, "but your strength will return."

The younger man made no response, and Strom blew a long note on the gathering horn, sparing him the need. Doing so wasn't actually as easy as it looked, and the early part of the note came out sounding like a wounded duck. After a moment, he found the proper technique.

Strom's taking the task from Durin didn't save Durin's breath as he'd hoped since he choked from laughter. Strom gave him a disapproving look, but then even he laughed and patted the gasping Durin on the back. When the Drakon and Dragon Clan gathered along the wind channel, he was still red in the face.

"Brother Vaughn has information that is important to all of us," Sinjin said. "I gathered you all to allow him to tell his tale once. But first I want to thank you for your commitment to everything you do. The work you've all done to help our friend Kenward makes me proud. Thank you."

Those gathered returned a muted cheer, somehow knowing not all of what they heard would be praise or good news. Brother Vaughn's hands trembled. "What I'm about to tell you is a story I learned during my childhood within Ohmahold. It was not part of my formal studies but a tale told beside the evening fire. If I'm honest, I must admit I never believed . . . until recently."

His words caused many of those gathered to shift uncomfortably.

"Had any of you ever heard the name Mael prior to the discovery of his prison?"

No one answered.

"I had," Brother Vaughn continued. "The only time I ever heard the name was in an old tale that tells of three sorcerers who achieved the pinnacle of their abilities during the last Istran phase. Their names were Mael, Aggrezjhon, and Murden. Individually these people were dangerous, but when they allied themselves, they threatened the entire world."

"Why have we never heard of these men?" Kenward asked.

"I believe it is because their names were intentionally forgotten and left out of the histories as a way to punish them for the evil they conspired to do. And they were not all men. Aggrezjhon made Murden his bride before their imprisonment."

"How did the ancients imprison the most powerful sorcerers of their day?" Sinjin asked.

"In a way not so different from what Trinda Hollis did to your mother," Brother Vaughn said. "The less powerful sorcerers were no match for them individually, but they did outnumber the triumvirate, so they built traps. Obviously just any trap would not do. The ancients built the most elaborate and expensive prisons ever conceived. One you all now know well: Dragonhold."

Those gathered knew the truth of his words, and Brother Vaughn could feel the collective anxiety building.

"Another prison was constructed using the most valuable object in the entire ancient world: the Noonspire," Brother Vaughn continued, not wanting to make the people wait longer than needed. "This was said to be a noonstone crystal pulled from the depths of the Endless Sea. It towered above the people, and in the hands of a powerful sorcerer, could shatter the foundations of the world. The ancients built a fortress around the Noonspire in the middle of the Jaga under the pretense of keeping the towering crystal out of the triumvirate's hands."

Mention of the Jaga sent another ripple of discomfit through the assemblage, and Brother Vaughn swallowed. Kenward watched him intently, doing his best to select his words with care. "The less powerful sorcerers expended all their power, skill, and arcana to convert the massive energy source into a prison. The story said any who accessed the Noonspire's magic would become trapped within the black crystal for all time."

Brother Vaughn could not overlook the strangeness of reciting mythology, now believing it was real. It made him wonder how many of the other things he'd written off as fantasies were actually historical fact. As time passed, more and more of the things he thought he knew proved to be false. It was a fairly humiliating experience, but he did his best to be strong for those who needed him. Looking out across a sea of faces, he knew that to be a large number of people.

"The story ends when the triumvirate attacks the Jaga hold, defeating the substantial yet intentionally insufficient defenses erected around the Noonspire. Aggrezjhon tapped the Noonspire's power first and was hopelessly snared. Within seconds, they say Murden was also pulled bodily into the giant crystal."

"You said these were people," Jessub said. "But Mael's a dragon, right?"

"And that is the final part of the story," Brother Vaughn said. "Seeing his brethren imprisoned within the crystal and feeling its pull on his very humanity, it's said Mael changed physical form on instinct. It goes to show just how powerful these sorcerers were. At the very least, it appears Mael really did turn himself into a dragon and somehow escaped to Dragonhold."

"There's a keystone within the Jaga," Kenward said, though he looked as if he hadn't meant to say it out loud.

"What do you mean?" Brother Vaughn asked.

"How else would Mael have gotten into Dragonhold if not through the keystone," Kenward said. "We all know they also served as portals . . . before they were broken, that is."

"It's for the best," Brother Vaughn said. "I'm sure."

Kenward hesitated. His curiosity about the Black Queen had already generated a few tall tales, and Brother Vaughn couldn't blame the good captain for falling silent.

"It would stand to reason that Mael could have used the keystones to escape to Dragonhold," Brother Vaughn said, "only to have the Fifth Magic sprung on him."

"You think the Fifth Magic had been used before?" Strom asked, appearing unconvinced.

"It's purely speculation," Brother Vaughn admitted. "I know I don't have rock-solid facts for you today, but I wanted to tell you what I knew nonetheless. If nothing else, be aware the Noonspire might really exist, and it could have as much or more power to corrupt the world as Mael."

"It would explain a great many things," Kenward said.

"Does the ancient one still live?" Arakhan asked.

Brother Vaughn held out his palms. "We don't know." It was the only honest answer he could give.

"We must get word to Catrin about this," Osbourne said. "It seems like something she should know."

A prolonged silence followed this statement.

"We never did find out if messages could be reliably sent in and out of Dragonhold using the river," Strom said.

Standing near Sinjin, Kendra visibly tensed, and Brother Vaughn felt compassion. Having the death of another on your hands was not something anyone should have to experience.

No one else got the chance to speak. The light in the hold dimmed, and the air pressure shifted. Blotting out far more of the entrance than the regal dragons did when coming in for a landing, Kyrien made the opening appear far less generous in size. When he did land, his forward-facing wing flaps buffeted them.

Bringing his enormous head in close, he looked at Brother Vaughn and all who had assembled. Then he stared at Strom.

"The message will be delivered," the smith said a moment later. "Kyrien says he has done what he can to help, but now we must complete the work on our own. He says, if we need him, I can call for him." The well-muscled smith still appeared uncomfortable in his communications with the last of the regent dragons.

Kyrien was a remarkable beast, indeed, Brother Vaughn thought, wishing once again that the species had not been effectively wiped out. Kyrien's lineage would live on in the regal dragons, but Brother Vaughn doubted there would ever be another to match him.

With a parting roar, Kyrien spread his wings and let the prevailing wind carry him from the hold. Within moments, he disappeared into the clouds.

* * *

A light breeze and blue skies dotted with occasional clouds presented ideal conditions for launch. Kenward looked out over the horizon, noting the absence of whitecaps. A good sailor knew the wind might blow in one direction in one place but in a completely different direction a league away. The wind was, indeed, a fickle mistress. Kenward didn't mind. He'd danced with the air currents many times and had come to enjoy the challenge.

"Some of the things you've done in the past have been ill advised," Fasha said, "but this might just be more risk than even you can survive."

Kenward nodded. "I know."

Fasha pursed her lips and nodded in return. "You should have only those aboard who know the risks and believe in you anyway."

"I can't do it all by myself," Kenward said with a rueful grin.

Raising one eyebrow, Fasha put her hands on her hips. "I'm going with you."

Looking surprised, he said, "Thank you," his voice thicker than he'd intended.

Fasha took his hand and gave it a squeeze. "I believe in you."

"Forgive me for eavesdropping," Farsy said from not far away where he'd been coiling rope, "but you ain't leaving without me."

"I dare you to try leaving me behind," Bryn said, and Kenward grinned.

Gwen cleared her throat. "And you're going to need someone who knows how to use these thrust tubes."

Kenward braced himself.

"I want all the Drakon in the air, flying support," Fasha said, "and no funny business." The last part was said with a wag of her finger at Valterius. The dragon had the good sense to appear cowed.

"What are you going to name this brick?" Fasha asked with a gleam in her eye. "The barge of the skies?"

In truth, her jibe wasn't far from the mark. Kenward had built this ship to transport goods, among other things, between the Godfist and the Firstland. The design had weaknesses, such as being highly indefensible from dragons and other airships. Though his family was the first to create successful airships, experience taught him there would be others soon; best to prepare now. It was the kind of thinking that had kept him alive this long. Provided these test flights didn't go terribly, the reward should be worth the risk. At least he hoped so.

"Keep it low and slow until you have a feel for how that thing flies. If it flies," Fasha said. "I believe in you, but that thing scares me. And those things on your deck terrify me. Leave them strapped to the deck. How about testing one radical design at a time?"

Kenward grinned. The "things" on his deck were two roughly bird-shaped single-person aircraft, each its own distinct design. The more attractive of the two Kenward called a howler. Carved from hardwood, it bore a lustrous sheen. Seat and harness were recessed into the body along with pedals connected to wing flaps. Thrust tubes hung underneath, straddling the sleek body and a pair of waxed skis. Strom had taken pride in the springs he'd made to connect the skis, and Kenward hoped those who could fly them would have soft landings.

Only a thrustmaster could fly a howler, but he firmly believed the talent could be cultivated. Catrin and Gwen had both learned to do it and so would others. The comet storm's power grew still and would continue for many years to come. The goddess would touch people, and Kenward would find them. Never would he have dared ask Gwen, but his niece had simply insisted. If the howler fell from his deck with her on it, what was he to do? At the very least, she would test the ship moving under thrust. That alone gave Kenward a thrill.

Nothing like his other creation, though, was the one he called a bumblebee. Firmly secured, it waited for him at middeck. This aircraft Kenward would test himself. It wasn't as pretty as the howler, but the bumblebee was an entirely different creature. Made from the lightest materials possible, it resembled something one might find on a shipwreck. Canvas and line connected to a stalkweed frame with lightwood joints and sub frame. Though crude and limited, it could change the world. Having more nimble aircraft that did not require the use of Istra's powers could allow Kenward to protect his fleet, thrustmasters or not.

The thought of employing a flightmaster and thrustmaster as his sister did was not altogether unappealing. However, Kenward detested relying solely on skills he did not himself possess. It had been a source of trouble for him over the years. In the end, he had decided it wise to use Istra's power when possible and supplement with perhaps more mundane but equally advanced design and innovation.

Benjin burst from the boiler house. "That's a lot of heat, Kenward. I'm not sure the boiler walls are thick enough to handle that kind of pressure."

"I need the steam and compressed air," Kenward said with a shrug. "It should hold."

Benjin shook his head and turned to his wife. "Stay away from the boiler house." He didn't say anything about Gwen. He'd not said a word to his daughter since she insisted on going. "Perhaps you should test the big ship first," he said after a moment, "and then test the . . . other . . . things on a subsequent voyage once you've worked out any kinks."

It was sound advice he'd already been given, and Kenward acknowledged it. Benjin stepped off the deck as the main windsocks inflated. Smaller, round windsocks, tethered to each corner of the ship, filled quickly, and soon timbers creaked.

"Are you going to name this vessel before she leaves dock?" Fasha asked.

"I dub this ship the *Portly Dragon*."

His sister shook her head in disbelief. Kenward grinned, and no one suggested a more fitting name for the blocky ship. If not for the skillfully crafted masthead, one might say the *Portly Dragon* was ugly and would have no way to know which end was the bow and which the stern. Kenward had recognized this problem early on and had port and starboard painted on the decks to make sure there was never any confusion over his orders. He'd also had danger zones clearly marked, such as the area in front of the thrust tubes.

Largely unobstructed, the deck was surrounded by ropes attached to iron rings at the corners and along the edges. Boiler house and deckhouse stood opposite one another for the sake of balance, hugging the outer edges of the ship to keep the center of the deck clear from one end to the other.

Black smoke poured from the chimstack, and a loud whistling warned the pressure might, indeed, be too much. "Everyone keep clear of the boiler house!" Kenward shouted. "Don't all crowd the other side, either. Mind the distribution of weight."

"I told you," Benjin said just as the ship left the dry dock's timbers, caught the breeze, and glided out toward the sea. Dragons filled the air around them, ready to assist if needed. Kenward sincerely hoped their presence proved unnecessary; still, he was glad they were there.

The fires had been stoked and would continue to burn on their own. Kenward did not plan to add more fuel for this flight. A safe cruising altitude was his first goal, immediately followed by testing the howler and bumblebee. As excited as he was about the *Portly Dragon's* maiden flight, the other craft had filled his dreams for weeks, and he couldn't wait to see his vision made real. Not many got the chance to see their ideas through to fruition. This day would change the rest of his life, one way or another.

Sitting between the thrust tubes mounted on a rotating platform at the stern, Gwen applied her will, and the *Portly Dragon* moved faster for a brief time. To Kenward's delight, the ship possessed greater stability than the *Serpent* had ever achieved. Outfitted as she was, cargo would be limited. On the Godfist he'd have access to materials for sturdier boilers. After that, his cargo capacity would be five times that of the *Dragon's Wing*. The steam-powered propeller with its sharp whistle generated far less thrust than Gwen, but it did move the ship forward. The *Portly Dragon* could not match the *Wing's* speed or maneuverability, but it could fly under its own power, and that meant something to Kenward.

It was for that reason the bumblebee existed. The howler required someone with the skills of a thrustmaster and, to a lesser extent, a flightmaster. Kenward hoped the bumblebee would allow him the same type of freedom he expected the howler to give Gwen. The anticipation was almost too much for him, but they had agreed not to take off until shallow, rocky waters had been left behind. The *Dragon's Wing* moved under wind and sail alone, heading for the deeps.

Kenward had argued the aircraft would be easier to recover if they crashed in shallow seas, but Benjin insisted deeper water meant less chance of his daughter hitting the bottom. This logic was difficult to ignore, and Kenward paced the deck until they reached dark water.

Farsy and Jessub inspected ropes and anchors, checking for any weakness in the ship's construction. Already, Farsy had expressed concern over a number of the cleats where the ropes were secured, but he didn't seem overly alarmed. Kenward pretended not to notice.

When the *Dragon's Wing* and the *Portly Dragon* reached water deep enough to suit Benjin, Kenward grinned at Gwen and gestured toward the howler. The girl practically ran to the experimental aircraft and strapped herself in. Walking across the deck, which barely moved under his boots, Kenward felt as if he walked on solid ground. Sinjin on Valterius and Kendra on Gerhonda flying in escort, watching their every move, made this strange experience even more surreal.

After one final check, Kenward patted Gwen on the back, reminded her to secure her goggles, and wished her the luck of the gods.

The world stood still for Kenward in that moment; Gwen wore a grin to match his own. Waxed skis glided over polished hardwood. Making good on its name, the howler issued an earsplitting report. For a moment Kenward worried the small aircraft wouldn't have enough speed at runway's end, but then Gwen pushed forward the pedals controlling the wing flaps, and the spring-loaded skis left the deck. With runway to spare, the howler took flight. If the driving force hadn't made it worthy of its namesake, the sound Gwen made riding it would have.

Few things rendered Kenward Trell speechless, but seeing the howler screeching through the air did the job. He stood with his mouth hanging open as Gwen outran the regal dragons flying in support. After a graceful, easy turn, she passed the Dragon and gave Kenward an enthusiastic thumbs-up. After two more passes, Gwen sent the howler straight up--a maneuver no airship could replicate. Then the air went silent. Losing speed, the howler fell over backward and raced back toward the seas below. In a move that made Kenward more proud of Gwen than he'd ever been before, she turned up the thrust. The *Portly Dragon* and *Dragon's Wing* swayed as she cleaved the air between them. It was the most the deck had moved under Kenward's feet since they had taken off.

Even with the wind and the howler's report filling the air, Benjin's shouting could be heard coming from the *Dragon's Wing*. Gwen ignored him for two more passes before making a slower pass over the runway. This was the part Kenward feared most. Taking off from the deck of a moving airship was one thing, but landing on that same deck was something entirely different. They had planned for Gwen to make two practice approaches before deciding to attempt the landing or to ditch the howler in the water. Valterius waited, ready to pluck Gwen from the howler if she chose to bail out.

Much slower on her second approach, Kenward worried it was too slow. If she lost any more momentum, there would be no pulling up. She was already committed by the time Kenward and others tried to wave her off. Nothing anyone could have said would change the situation beyond that moment. Kenward's crazy ideas would be tested here and now. If Gwen got hurt in the process, he'd never forgive himself. He'd probably also spend the rest of his life running from his brother-in-law.

Despite having lined the howler up perfectly with the runway, Gwen did not have time to correct when a sudden gust twisted the howler sideways. The left ski hit the deck first, the angle sending the aircraft spinning back in the other direction. The second ski touched down but missed the polished hardwood runway, encountering drag instead as it slid across the much rougher lightwood.

Gwen held on as best she could but was slapped back and forth three times before the howler stabilized, still carrying too much speed. Kenward thought she might have to abandon the landing, but then she did something he'd never considered. Reversing the air flow, Gwen used the thrust tubes as brakes. Skidding to a halt mere hand widths from the edge, she raised her hands and cheered in triumph.

Benjin's cursing could be heard for some time to come.

Chapter 14

What is grotesque to one is art to another.
--Matteo Dersinger, mad prophet

* * *

Watching the ancient dragon sleep, Pelivor told himself the mighty beast was truly unconscious and not just waiting for him to make the wrong move. The giant jaws could engulf him in a single bite, and Pelivor tried his best to keep that image from his mind. Catrin needed him, and the rest of Godsland would suffer if Mael escaped. The energy stored in the massive green crystals was largely dissipated, and his form still vibrated from the release of it.

"We're going to have to do that again, aren't we?" Pelivor asked.

"In time the charge will build back up, yes," she said. "For now, we've left it far lower than it was when we arrived. Mael had not yet been able to escape even with that energy at his disposal, so I think we'll have some time."

"And if he's awake and guarding it when we return?"

"Then we knock him back out," Catrin said. "Koe is fully charged, and any energy the crystals here impart to Mael will also be available to us."

Pelivor just shook his head and hoped with all his might he didn't have to face Mael again. Something about that dragon was more terrifying than all the rest, and it wasn't just his size. Dragon fire was a part of it, but there was something else. He couldn't quite place it, but it nagged at him, making him feel foolish for not understanding.

"So we just leave him here?" Pelivor asked.

"What would you do?" Catrin asked softly. There was a dangerous note in her voice.

Pelivor could not back away from the truth. "Kill him now. Free his spirit if not his body. End it."

Looking thoughtful, Catrin was silent for some time. "I don't want to kill him."

There was no explanation and perhaps none needed. Pelivor knew Catrin well enough to know she didn't like to kill anything, let alone something completely defenseless. "We may come to regret that decision."

"Then so be it." Catrin's voice was hard and cold.

"I'm sorry," Pelivor said a moment later. "I don't like killing things either, but it is sometimes necessary. Such a powerful enemy within the hold frightens me. Already he's manipulated us. What's to stop him from doing it again?"

"Now we know what he was doing, and we'll be on the alert. We've reduced his power. Worry no more over this for today. There are things we must do."

Nodding, Pelivor climbed down and joined Catrin at the stone god's feet. The waters continued to rage through his open mouth. Fish and sometimes driftwood and other debris entered the cavern. Much of it continued away, disappearing into the closed channel carrying the river water deeper into the hold. Always when Pelivor had seen the underground oasis where the river water once again emerges, he'd thought the river entered the hold there. Never would he have guessed that it passed through here first.

Those who remained within Dragonhold had done what they could to restore order. Despite none of them knowing the name of the god depicted, the cavern was undoubtedly a holy place. This was part of what bothered Pelivor about the ancient dragon's taking up residence there. The dragon's presence desecrated the now scarred and fire-scorched landscape.

"Come," Catrin said, offering him her hand. "Let's go see the state of the shield."

Taking one last glance back, Pelivor caught a flash of color in the river water . . . then another and another. "Wait," he said. "Look."

At first he thought Catrin might be annoyed with him, but as soon as she saw the apples, she rushed to the water's edge. More and more apples flowed into the pool. Fish devoured many but others floated by, still whole. Catrin bent down, retrieved one from the water, and took a bite. An instant later, a hay bale stuffed with red leaves appeared with a grayish lump tied onto it.

Catrin drew a sharp breath. There was no time to waste. Soon the bale would flow out of the cavern and be lost. Pelivor grabbed Koe from Catrin's hands and dived into the frothing river. She drew a sharp intake of breath as the cat figurine struck the cold water. Driving a wall of air before him, Pelivor gave the predatory fish no chance to find out if he tasted good. Lightning leaped across the water, hissing and popping. The backlash stung Pelivor like a whip, but he was undeterred.

"Be careful!" Catrin shouted from shore, looking ready to blast any fish unwise enough to get close. His sudden and dramatic entrance frightened them, and most swam as far from him as they could get. Some prey just wasn't worth the trouble.

Grabbing the bale with one hand, Pelivor showed how people taught to swim in the middle of the ocean could do it. However, even with all his training, pulling the waterlogged bale out of the water was a difficult task. Catrin helped him drag it to shore.

"A man with your abilities," Catrin said, shaking her head, "and you dive into the water headfirst. What were you thinking?"

Pelivor shrugged. "I just reacted. My other . . . talents . . . take some getting used to."

Catrin nodded in understanding. She stepped closer and inspected the thing lashed to the hay bale. An inescapable smell wrinkled her nose and she laughed. "No wonder Sinjin and Kendra hated it so much."

* * *

Never before had Sevellon felt so violated and used.

"Cheer up," Jharmin said. "I'll take you anywhere you want to go."

The thief walked in silence, his thoughts whirling. Was he even now acting in his own best interest? Was he being manipulated? Not knowing drove him to distraction. Personal freedom had been among the greatest draws of a thief's life, and to lose it without even realizing it was the most frightening thing imaginable. Under normal circumstances, he would've been reluctant to board a ship with Jharmin Kyte, a man who introduced himself by speaking Sevellon's full name and profession. This alone was unforgivable, yet Sevellon found himself liking the man. It made his teeth hurt.

Jharmin's ship, the *Wolf's Head*, bore a masthead to match her name. The carving managed to appear both formidable and wise. Staying on the Godfist was not an option Sevellon wanted to consider, even if he had fulfilled his quest on Catrin's behalf; they would know he'd betrayed them. He didn't want Kendra Volker or Trinda Hollis to get their hands on him either. Jharmin's ship was the quickest and easiest way to achieve his first goal. For that reason, his boots continued to carry him closer to shore and the longboats.

"Where will you go?" Jharmin asked, not for the first time.

Still, Sevellon let the silence hang between them. He had not decided. And even if he had, he wasn't certain he wanted Jharmin to know the truth yet. Old habits died hard; those very habits had kept him alive this long.

"There's almost always work to be had in Endland Bay," Jharmin said, specifically not mentioning Sevellon's profession. "The Cathurans won't let anyone in these days, so don't bother going to any of their strongholds. The Inland Sea is also not currently safe, not that it ever was."

Sevellon suspected Jharmin was talking just to try to make the thief feel better, perhaps more accepted, but the strangeness of their relationship would not allow him to let down his guard. He kept waiting for the moment Jharmin would reveal that he would be thrown in jail and left to rot for the rest of his days. But so far, the man had just treated him with kindness and respect, although with an authoritative air with regard to carrying out Catrin's requests.

Silence persisted for the rest of the walk, until they encountered patrols. Seeing them made the thief's innards clench. Even Jharmin recoiled when the armed soldiers approached. Catrin was not well loved south of the Wall, and claiming allegiance to her could equal a death sentence rather than safe passage. Instead, Jharmin passed himself off as a trader, and given his rich attire, it was an almost believable tale. But the man's mannerisms and posture spoke of real power.

"Move along. Don't cause us any trouble, and we'll cause you none," the burliest among the guards said.

No more words were required, and the group moved through Harborton with purpose. When they reached the docks, Jharmin once again turned to Sevellon. "Where will you go?"

"As far away from dragons as possible."

"Wise choice," Jharmin Kyte said with a wry smile. "Very wise choice."

* * *

"Allette knew things that weren't revealed to me," Catrin said to Pelivor, Chase, Morif, Millie, and a few others who'd gathered to hear what she and Pelivor would do next. The assemblage included most of the people remaining within Dragonhold. Those not present were likely occupied with their tasks. After so many escaped, Dragonhold was short of hands. Pelivor assumed those who remained were loyal to Catrin, but nothing was certain.

"I thought you said she could hide nothing from you," Chase said.

"I did," Catrin responded. "That's why I don't think it was Allette who hid it from me."

"You think Mael did it?" Chase asked.

Catrin just shrugged in response.

"And now you're going to do the same thing again, not even knowing if the dragon is conscious and ready to manipulate your very thoughts?"

"Correct," Catrin said. "And I need your help."

Chase walked away, muttering to himself; sometimes waving his arms in the air and ranting.

"What's your plan?" Morif asked.

"To go to the one place it seems Mael does not want me to go. To the place he made sure Allette did not reveal to me. I will go to the heart of the Jaga. I'm missing a piece of the puzzle and will not be able to solve it until I know exactly what it is we're facing."

"It's a bad idea!" Chase insisted as he walked by, continuing to grumble under his breath afterward.

"There are things about Mael I don't understand," Catrin continued, ignoring her cousin, which clearly infuriated him, "and this is the only way I know to find out."

"We can do what you need," Morif said, "but we'll not be able to sustain it long given the limited numbers within the hold. We're already stretched thin."

"There are more than enough supplies to feed those who remain," Catrin said, accepting excuses from no one. "Prepare enough rations for twenty-one days. Then there will be plenty of people available to do as I require."

Pelivor noted that Catrin neither asked nor demanded, she simply required. It was a nice trick.

One of Miss Mariss's helpers left the hall at a run.

"Twenty-one days?" Chase asked with a raised eyebrow. "No food. No water. For twenty-one days?"

"An overestimate," Catrin said. "I expect it to take significantly less than that, but I've learned caution."

Chase crossed his arms. "That's debatable."

"There's no other way," Catrin said. Her tone made it clear the argument was over.

"I'll go with you," Pelivor said. "You and I both know the dangers. You need someone to watch your back."

Catrin gave him an exasperated look. "Last time, you nearly exploded." Pelivor flushed, remembering his headlong tumble into the heart of darkness. The end of that memory made him even more determined not to let Catrin go alone. "And both of us going will consume the limited power we have twice as fast."

"Then you need to just see whatever it is you need to see," Chase said, "and get back here without dawdling."

Everyone knew the words were out of concern for his cousin, and his point was not ill made.

"I agree," Morif said.

"As do I," Millie said, crossing her arms.

Catrin sighed. Pelivor read the thoughts on her face, and it was clear the irony of being the most powerful person on the planet and not having the ability to win a simple argument was apparent. "Fine."

"I'm sorry." Pelivor felt as if that were all he ever said to Catrin.

"There are consequences," Catrin said softly. "I told you what happened when Allette and I traveled. It was unavoidable and irreversible. Are you certain you wish me to know your every thought and memory? It's more than a little humiliating."

The thought did make Pelivor cringe, and it took him a moment to respond. It was not for his personal purposes he wished to go but to protect Catrin. That desire hadn't lessened, and the feeling in Pelivor's gut told him he wouldn't be able to stand still until she returned. His only choice was to go with her, so he nodded an affirmative.

When word came from the kitchens that rations had been prepared to Catrin's order, the reprimand from Miss Mariss was palpable. "The time has come," Catrin said. "Let us be done with this."

"May you find that which you seek," Morif intoned, and the ancient axiom had never been quite so appropriate.

Millie said a prayer behind them. A bead of sweat grew on Pelivor's forehead; he hoped Catrin didn't notice.

The main hall thrummed with discordant energy, and occasional thunder split the air, echoing loudly through the hold. They had been hearing it for some time, but so close to the source, it became overpowering. Catrin walked toward Dragonhold's main entrance, not content to take the word of others. Pelivor was glad. He also wanted to see for himself. His spirit would have to pierce that barrier, and he wanted to understand the state it was in before doing so.

"Don't go too close," Chase warned. "The lightning also strikes inside the hold. We've had two people struck already. No sense in adding two more to that list."

Pelivor sensed Catrin wanted to heed her cousin's advice, but it was difficult to see from a distance. The closer they drew, the more irritated Chase became.

"That's far enough. Don't you see the black spot right in front of where you're standing?"

This time Catrin did stop. Pelivor stood on his toes, trying to see the broken spire's base, but all he could see was that it leaned outward, disrupting the energy flow. Swirling vortices danced across the plasma barrier like tears in the fabric of the prison itself. Through these rifts clear sky was visible, Istra's energy slipping through the otherwise impermeable barrier in hints and whispers.

The ever-shifting surface captivated Pelivor. Having been locked away from the light, any chance to bask in its warmth was more than welcome. When Catrin pulled him away, he left reluctantly.

With the stone chairs in place, their polished metal–streaked surfaces standing out against the monotonous walls of Dragonhold, a different energy filled the viewing chamber. Perhaps the least comfortable seat Pelivor had ever occupied, the stone chair invoked memories of being sore for days after the last time he'd sat in it. The chairs had rested in the *Slippery Eel's* hold at the time. Pelivor wondered for a moment why they had not experienced the same melding effect that Catrin and Allette had. There must be something about the design of this specific viewing chamber, he decided.

In the next instant, no more time for contemplation remained. The chanting began softly but almost immediately grew louder. Voices became clearer as their confidence developed, and soon Pelivor floated on the vibrations they provided. When Catrin grabbed his hand, placed it on Koe's back, and kept her hand on top of his, he changed his guess: it was the common power source that bound them. There was no need to tell Catrin. He was naked before her, every thought exposed. His dreams, desires, and failings were hers to know, and he received the same from her.

Nothing could have prepared him for the knowledge that flowed between them. Knowing what Catrin knew turned out to be far more responsibility than Pelivor had anticipated. From her memories, he learned the power to enslave, coerce, and even to destroy Godsland itself. For the rest of his days, he would bear knowledge he'd never desired. Catrin had told him there would be consequences. He hadn't fully comprehended. She had known that. The knowledge shamed him.

The exchange took place in both directions, and Catrin experienced revelations of her own. The ability to communicate while experiencing each other's lives made the process even more complex.

"You were so brave," Catrin said during what was one of the most deeply buried memories in Pelivor's consciousness. Taken from the woman who'd raised him, he'd managed to leave without crying. A kind family took him in and gave him every opportunity. He would always be grateful to Nora Trell for what she'd done for him. He hadn't known it at the time, but the woman he considered his mother had been dying and had wanted to spare him the pain. The irony was not lost on him.

Pelivor suspected tears fell from his physical form, but he really had no way of knowing. Traveling in his astral form made it feel as if he had no body at all. He existed on that plane as a being of energy and light. It was glorious, save it lacked the tactile presence the real world provided. He could not handle objects and manipulate them while exploring them with his sense of touch. Instead he was left to exert what little force his energetic form could muster. The wind ignored them as well, making travel easy and fast, but he missed the feel of it on his face.

Many of the experiences that came to Pelivor were painful and frightening. Catrin's life had taken such a horrific turn. He'd never known such fear. When he experienced their kiss from Catrin's perspective, he was certain his physical face shone bright red. Catrin's own discomfort at sharing the memories flowed through the bond, and Pelivor reminded himself to take heed when Catrin warned him of consequences. This thought made Catrin laugh. Even that was invasive since he hadn't intentionally shared. It was as strange an experience as Pelivor had ever gone through.

Letting Catrin guide them, Pelivor was able to relax and process the mountain of new information entering his mind. Neither had anticipated the hidden benefit of their melding, but it soon became clear Pelivor understood things about Istra's energy Catrin had never gleaned. His was a mind of logic, math, and reason. Catrin was defined far more by her feelings, and seeing things from Pelivor's clinical view changed the way she used Istra's gifts, even as they soared over the Endless Sea.

For as much as he had to teach Catrin about using her power to fly and how to get a sizable result from a limited amount of energy, it was nothing compared to the things Catrin had to teach him. Her time within Dragonhold and the Black Spike had not been wasted, the amount of studying exhausting. So much information filled her head, he wondered if his might explode. Perhaps the use of her power had somehow enhanced her mental capabilities, he thought.

When the Jaga came into view, it approached so fast, Pelivor erected wing structures to slow their approach.

"We've no time or energy to waste," Catrin scolded across the bond. She was not angry with him; she was just worried they would be unable to accomplish what they had come for and that both would be at risk. Koe held a finite amount of energy, and neither of them knew how much remained. Perception of time and space were different on this plane.

Gliding along silently, Pelivor did his best not to be an obstruction. Neither wanted to find out what would happen if they drained the reserve Koe held. Nothing good could come of it.

Thick foliage crisscrossed with glistening black waterways raced beneath them at speeds that made the journey even more surreal. When the darkness began creeping into the greenery, turning it to ashen gray, their progress slowed. Their combined anxiety flooded the bond, and both were at their most alert.

Even in the astral plane, the air above the black swamp was foul. The energy reeked of wrongness, and nothing could escape the rotting decay. Pervasive, it crept into the pores of Pelivor's soul. Traveling here meant risking everything; he'd known that at the onset. Catrin had warned him, but he'd insisted on coming. Now she had less energy to defend herself because of his insistence. She was angry with him, and he felt guilty. Both knew instantly.

She forgave him, though he had more trouble forgiving himself. If he'd known then what he knew now, he would not have come. He would have known Catrin could take care of herself and his presence distracted her and divided her power. They were fools, all of them. Pelivor experienced Catrin's frustration, as well as her guilt for having such feelings. In a way, it made him feel better. At least he wasn't the only one to have such thoughts.

The deeper they moved into the black swamp, the more the scale of the place was apparent. It was not ubiquitous death and decay; it was filled with what might have once been a rich and beautiful landscape. To see such beauty fouled burdened Pelivor's spirit.

As they moved closer to the swamp's heart, they soared faster. Pelivor had to wonder for an instant before Catrin's panic registered. She had not increased their speed, and neither had he. Exerting their combined will to slow their progress, both despaired. Still they accelerated and soon found themselves hurtling toward a black fortress as inviting as death. Like a monument to fear, it was all sharp angles and points, as if made of dragon's teeth.

Every part of Pelivor's being wanted to flee, to get away from the madness sucking them in. Inexorably they were pulled into the black fortress and sent into a downward spiral. Everything that moved in this place was twisted and malformed--the essence of corruption. It made what Mael had done seem a petty thing.

This was the work of Aggrezjhon and Murden. The thought came neither from Catrin nor Pelivor, though he did vaguely remember the names from his studies. It was clear Catrin had never heard them before. Now they would be forever burned into her consciousness. The sense of these powerful beings was overwhelming, such skill and might undeniable. Catrin and Pelivor were but babes in the presence of masters.

Deeper their spirits soared as if spiraling into the darkest depression. Nightmares clawed at them as they passed. Feral dragons in numbers no one would have wanted to believe lived within this massive cavity. Reaching the heart of the seething wrongness brought pain and revulsion. Something endeavored to crush his spirit, and it was close to succeeding. Not even Catrin was immune, as the sorcerers trapped within a massive noonstone crystal used her every mistake against her. They showed her all those who had suffered for the sake of her cause. Images of death assaulted them over and over again, picking the memories from their worst nightmares.

Pelivor could not allow such treatment and gathered his will, which was promptly used against him. The harder he railed, the more Aggrezjhon and Murden pressed their advantage. The two spirits were nearly impossible to distinguish. They had been trapped together for millennia, and Pelivor got the sense they suffered madness similar to that of Enoch and Ain Giest. The very thought of those names sent Aggrezjhon and Murden into attack mode. The pain was unbearable.

"What do you want?" Catrin screamed the question.

Freedom.

The response was singular, as if of one mind. Pelivor tried once again to resist, but the towering crystal drew them forward, closer and closer to its glossy surface. Shadows waited within--four of them. Two he recognized and two he knew must be Aggrezjhon and Murden. This crystal was a prison just as much as the Fifth Magic, and within were Allette Kilbor and Trinda Hollis. It appeared the two had escaped Dragonhold only to end up in far worse circumstances, their spirits embattled and their physical forms suspended by the crystal's energy.

Eventually their bodies would decay and die, leaving them trapped inside the crystal spire for eternity, just like the two sorcerers. How long the energy would preserve their mortal shrouds remained unclear. Pelivor and Catrin were about to share a similar fate. Though the ancients could find no way out, they could draw others in.

A tremendous roar built in intensity, and Pelivor looked back. Racing toward them, following the threads reaching back to their physical forms, came a dragon of fire and lightning. Kyrien blazed, rivaling the sun, and he struck the crystal spire like a hammer on white-hot metal. Sparks and lightning flew, and the Noonspire shimmered on impact. The shadows within were knocked askew.

Howls of anger and regret followed them back to Dragonhold, where their pale forms waited.

Just before their consciousnesses separated, Kyrien delivered Brother Vaughn's message.

Now you tell us, Catrin thought in response.

Chapter 15

Light, unlike most things, becomes more powerful when divided.
--Gemino, sorcerer and artist

* * *

"They're calling us off, sir," Bryn said.

Indeed, those adragonback waved their arms, calling off any more maneuvers. A brisk wind had picked up, and clouds gathered along the horizon. Despite the threat of weather, Kenward walked calmly toward the bumblebee. Even Gwen I cast him sideways glance as he approached the flimsy contraption.

"I'm just going to check the lashing," Kenward said, not looking toward Benjin and pretending he couldn't hear any of the things the man said, most of which were unpleasant and somewhat uncomplimentary. The pirate captain did what he did best and chased his dream with unrelenting passion. Climbing into the bumblebee's cockpit, despite all those who now protested, Kenward released the straps and threw open one of the valves.

Hissing issued from the back of the bumblebee, and anyone caught in its wash soon fled, though the craft had yet to move. Undeterred, Kenward slid the right-hand lever forward. Increased thrust produced a rhythmic thumping, and the bumblebee started toward the *Portly Dragon's* edge. There was no more time for contemplation or design changes. This was the last chance Kenward would get before the weather came in. Patience had never been one of his strong points, nor was taking orders from others.

"At least let the dragons get below you before you fire that projectile," Gwen said.

Her words made good sense, and he held his breath a bit longer before releasing the brake. At that point, he could no longer hear Benjin, though the looks on the dragonriders' faces showed disapproval. As soon as he eased off the brake, the bumblebee leaped forward but lacked the speed Kenward needed. He'd foreseen this and reached for the pull release. Had he been wiser, he would have realized that reaching forward was more difficult when being pressed back into your seat. Crossing the last distance remaining between the bumblebee and clear skies, Kenward grasped and pulled the release. Twin water jets escaped the tanks, propelled by highly compressed air. The burst lasted a brief moment, but it launched the aircraft higher.

The bumblebee lurched sideways, leaving the deck at a bad angle. Immediately sent into a long, exaggerated spiral, there was no time for thought. Fidgeting with gadgets and valves while hurtling through the air was more difficult than expected, but he had designed this aircraft, and using that knowledge, he leveled off the flight. The thumping lowered in frequency the longer he flew, limiting the amount of time he could remain in the air. No matter the current limitations, Kenward flew on his own without Istra. It was a start--a very good start.

People could say what they would, but Kenward Trell would always be the first man to fly solo without the use of Istra's power or a dragon. Worried shouts from the *Portly Dragon* changed to shouts of encouragement as Kenward brought the bumblebee higher.

Lining up for a landing on the Dragon's deck also proved more difficult than anticipated. Windsocks and the ropes attaching them were far greater obstacles than he'd imagined. After bringing the bumblebee around and realizing just how small the target was, he reconsidered, knowing what waited if he missed his mark.

Ditching the bumblebee was far from the most attractive option; however, it might cause the least bodily harm provided one of those dragons was close enough to catch him. Casting wildly about, Kenward spotted Sinjin and Valterius, and he wondered if Al'Drak was truly on his side. It was something he had always wondered about dragons in general; riding Valterius had only reinforced those concerns. Squeezing his eyes shut, he hoped, once again, the dragon could not read his thoughts.

The thumping within his aircraft grew softer and less frequent, only a small amount of compressed air remaining. The winds around them grew still, and for a single moment in time, the bumblebee aligned with the *Portly Dragon's* deck; even his trajectory was correct. Subtle corrections were all he needed to land the bumblebee. With trembling hands, Kenward eased back on the right-hand valve, making certain not to touch the one on the left. Even with the wind in his favor, the aircraft struck the deck hard, pitching to one side, digging the wing into the deck, and spinning the aircraft sharply.

With a bleeding lip and a somewhat battered backside, Kenward climbed from the bumblebee, arms raised high in victory. While these had been only trials, they proved his creations were the most innovative and functional aircraft seen in eons. The glory of this victory was marred by those who now flew in close, demanding they return to shore.

"You're never going to hear the end of this," Gwen said.

"I know," Kenward said with a grin. "And I'll never let them forget just who was first to sail the skies."

* * *

Walking down the smooth cobbled streets along New Moon Bay, amid the shops with glass windows and ornate doors, Nora Trell was no more at home than in the slums. Here, one was less likely the get a knife in the ribs since this area was heavily patrolled by guards. The solution was, in its own way, the problem. As a trader, Nora did her best to understand the laws and customs wherever she worked. Ever present were those who wanted a share of any trade passing through their ports. Whether through tariffs, docking permits, blackmail, or downright theft, the landbound would take their cut. It had always rankled. These people got fat off her hard work, which left less to divide among the crew. This treachery had real economic impacts, and the Trells had been known for finding creative ways to circumvent such things. There were, no doubt, people looking for her, Kenward, and Fasha. She had no desire to grant them an audience.

Already she'd been seen. Though Kenward and Fasha kept low profiles, their faces known to only a certain few, Nora had been the public face of the Trell family for years. Best to do what needed doing and quickly move on. She turned a corner and walked along a twisting side street, this one clean and quiet, almost quaint. Between two shops displaying lamps and other glassware, she descended a flight of steps. At the bottom, a plain door with much of the wood visible through chips of green paint waited. Just looking at it made Nora's stomach hurt, as if she might go in and never come out. After double-checking the note from her informant, she opened the door.

A tinkling bell announced her entrance, but Nora didn't see anyone inside. Feeling self-conscious, like a stowaway on an unknown ship, she broke into a sweat. Along a collection of tables, each a different height and length than the others, rested a haphazard collection of oddities. Much of it was flawed glass art--seconds not meeting the standards of the shops above. While some of it truly was interesting, Nora had come here for one thing alone. Walking along the cloth-draped tables, she wondered if she had found the correct place; the object she sought nowhere to be seen.

"Can I help you?" an old woman's voice barked.

Nora jumped. "I . . . uh . . ."

"Most folks don't just sneak in here and poke around, you know. Most folks announce themselves."

Trying not to look at the bell on the door, Nora did her best to keep her composure. "Sorry," was all she said.

"You must've come here for something. Folks don't just wander in here for no reason."

"I have a son," Nora said, deeply hoping this woman might one day find herself on the deck of the *Trader's Wind*. They would have a very different conversation. "He likes pretty things."

The shopkeeper nodded knowingly. Nora had come up with the ruse but regretted giving the woman any more reason to look down on her. It wasn't something she was skilled at dealing with. Did the landbound have no manners at all?

"Lots of pretty things for those with the coin to pay."

This woman was determined to get under her skin, but Nora knew better than to rush. What this woman thought of her wasn't important as long as her purchase drew no unwanted attention.

"These are pretty," Nora said, pointing to glass figurines of sea creatures with metallic tips on the fins.

"And expensive."

While considering whether to have her contact burn this place down when she was done, Nora did her best not to lash out. "They look fragile. He sometimes breaks things."

With another knowing look, the shopkeeper appeared offended at the very notion of something she sold getting broken. "Perhaps wooden toys would be better. There's a shop down the street."

"No," Nora said, as nicely as she could. "Glass. Do you have any marbles?"

Now the woman's eyes narrowed. "If you came for marbles, why didn't you just say so in the first place?" In spite of her apparent suspicion, the shopkeeper pulled a cloth-covered tray from behind the tables. She twitched the cloth away, revealing marbles of varying size and quality reflecting the meager light.

"I like this one," Nora said, grabbing a large, poorly made marble. The look the shopkeeper gave her said she had known Nora would go for the cheap ones. "And this one," she said, pointing to a much nicer, clear marble with a well-crafted flower inside. Nora truly did like the marble and wondered how the glass smiths got the flowers in there.

"Expensive," the woman said.

"Even with the flaw?" Nora asked, letting a bit of her irritation show. "There's an air bubble right on that petal."

"If you want perfection, go upstairs."

"I also like this one," Nora said, trying to keep the excitement from her voice. Clearly of better quality than the others, this marble was half clear, half filled with a swirling metallic vortex and backed with colored, metallic glass in a geometric pattern that shimmered in the light.

"You have expensive taste. That one is old and rare."

"I thank you," Nora said. "Nevertheless, how much for the three?"

The woman reappraised her and, after a brief whistle, said, "Seven silvers."

"Five."

"Seven," the woman said.

"Six."

"Seven," the shopkeeper said again.

Feeling as if she'd played the game enough, Nora fingered her purse and produced seven silvers without looking. She would have paid a hundred times that without a second thought, which made her smile inside.

Again, suspicion filled the shopkeeper's eyes. "How did you know to come here?" she asked while wrapping the marbles in coarse linen, specifically not meeting Nora's gaze.

"I asked a man at the docks," Nora said, knowing the reaction she would get.

The shopkeeper made a gesture as if to ward off evil spirits. To the landbound, especially those along New Moon Bay, the docks were where the lowest among them worked and dwelt. There anyone could make a little coin without anyone asking too many questions. The woman just handed Nora the linen-wrapped marbles bound in string and made it clear it was time for her to leave.

Leaving the shop behind, Nora waited until she was well away before grinning openly, one step closer to her family's future. As ever, things still needed doing, and she walked with a determined stride.

* * *

"You do realize that if you had crashed that thing into the sea, no one would have known how to fly the *Portly Dragon* back, right?" Kendra stood on her toes, so she could stare Kenward level in the eye while berating him.

"I would not have sailed with a crew that doesn't know their business," Kenward said. "They've flown my ships plenty of times when I was otherwise occupied." A few brave enough to risk Kendra's wrath nodded at that.

"If you had listened to what every person flying air support for you was screaming, then you'd have known strong winds were coming," Kendra continued, her face flushed.

The good captain took the verbal lashing without much complaint. He must know she was right. The flight back had been harrowing, and getting the *Portly Dragon* back into dry dock had come dangerously close to crushing Sinjin and Valterius. "I kept my test flight brief," he said. Kendra leaned closer. "And the winds would've caught up with us either way."

Sinjin dropped his face into his hands.

Surely Kenward knew he should stop, but it just wasn't in his nature. "I promise I'll take you for a ride once I get a couple wrinkles worked out."

With her eyes closed and looking as if she might explode, Kendra turned and stormed away in every sense of the word.

"Why do you do these things to me?" Sinjin asked, exasperated. "You know I have to live with her, right?"

Kenward's grin never faded. "I know. Sorry. She's just too easy, and she makes it so much fun."

"Fun for you," Sinjin said. "You get to leave and fly off in . . . whatever those things are. I have to stay here and pay for your insolence."

"I'd offer you the life of a pirate, my friend, but I know it wouldn't suit you. Look at it this way: at least you have dragons."

Sinjin shook his head and smiled. "You do have a point. Though I have to ask, what's in this for you? Why are you doing this?"

"You know that little lady that I just riled up?" Kenward asked with a wry grin. "The one you will go home to? I want those who have such a thing to keep it and those who don't to find it."

Sinjin nodded, knowing Kenward wished some things to remain unspoken.

"And you should thank me for irritating your wife."

"Why would I do that?" Sinjin asked.

"Because I've given her someone else to be mad at other than you. You're welcome."

Sinjin shook his head again. Kenward had a way of disarming those who were angry with him. All perhaps save Kendra . . . and Nora . . . and Fasha. Sinjin reconsidered Kenward's abilities.

With the *Portly Dragon* secured and everything upon the flight deck lashed down, the Drakon and the crew of the *Dragon's Wing* returned to their own work. Kenward was left to grin at his crew and figure out what his next move would be. Sinjin climbed atop Valterius, strapped himself in, and returned to Windhold to face his wife's wrath. He did have to admit, though, that Kenward would take the brunt of Kendra's anger, and in some small way, that might take the pressure off him. Still, Sinjin considered the possibility there might be times his wife was happy and did not want to throttle him.

The truth was that life was hard and their circumstances more than a little grim.

"What do you think we should do?" Sinjin asked Kendra upon seeing her. The words left his lips before he fully considered them, and he almost instantly regretted the question.

Looking up from the saddlebag she was unpacking, Kendra glared. "I say we kill Kenward."

These had not been the words he expected, and he gaped in response.

"He's been trying to kill himself for years but doesn't quite seem to have the right stuff. I'm starting to think we should help him out before he gets one of us killed."

Sinjin wanted to say Valterius had had everything under control, but he knew better.

"And if he doesn't kill us, he'll just bleed us of resources making his contraptions."

"They did fly," Sinjin said before his good sense kicked in.

No words emerged from Kendra's lips; her expression said all there was to say.

"Kenward is an unsolvable puzzle," Sinjin said.

"They're all unsolvable! That's the problem. We've a dozen puzzles with half the pieces all mixed together and the other half missing. At the moment, I'm not certain we can manage not to starve."

Their reserves would last through the winter, but he understood Kendra's point nonetheless. They were powerless, and no matter what they decided, it was unlikely it would make a difference. "Some things we can do," he said, shaking off the darkness. "For one thing, we can send a small armed force back to the Godfist and see if we can establish communication through the barrier."

"I've been thinking about that," Kendra said. "I think we could establish visual contact using smoke."

"From where? In the Pinook Valley?" Sinjin asked and she nodded. "I suppose that could work. Most of the valley is within the barrier, but there were a few sizable clearings outside as well. Not sure how we could do much beyond getting their attention, though."

"Kenward and your mom know the signal language."

"Do you think my mom will remember what little she once knew?"

"Perhaps not, but Miss Mariss is from a family of pirates, don't forget."

Sinjin had not forgotten, but it also had not occurred to him that she might be fluent in the signal language. "So we have a plan and a backup plan. Good."

"Almost," Kendra said. Sinjin nearly dropped his face into his hands again, but he knew that annoyed Kendra, and now was not the time. "Kenward doesn't want to go back to the Godfist."

"Oh?"

"Kenward wants to invade the Jaga."

Unable to formulate a response to that statement, Sinjin just waited for Kendra to go on and tried not to appear as dumbfounded as he was. The mental image of Kenward flying the *Portly Dragon* into the black swamp didn't help.

"You can't have missed the connection between Kenward and Allette," Kendra said, finally getting to her point. "Kenward thinks Allette is back within the Jaga, and he's going to go there and save her from the darkness."

"He told you this?" Sinjin asked, now fully incredulous in spite of his efforts.

"Not in so many words, no, but his actions tell the tale of his heart. The *Portly Dragon* is obviously nothing but a platform for war."

"To hear him tell it, the *Portly Dragon* is the barge of the sky, an extension of his family's rich history in trade."

"And you believe that?"

"Yes," Sinjin said. "He's my friend and I believe him when he tells me why he's building the craziest aircraft the world might ever know." Doubt crept in.

"See?" Kendra said, reading his face. "We can't let him go alone."

"Wait. What?" Sinjin shook his head as if making sure his brain hadn't developed a rattle.

Kendra sighed. "Clearly," she began, looking at Sinjin as if he were daft, "Kenward built the howler and the bumblebee to protect the slower and less nimble *Portly Dragon*. And those craft are not suited for carrying weapons into combat."

Despite his training in military matters, Sinjin could never manage to think like someone with a soldiering background. Though Kendra had never officially served on a fighting force, her mother had taught her well, for good or ill. Some of those lessons had taught her what to do; others taught her what not to do. The latter were far more powerful lessons, reinforced with pain.

"And you think the Drakon are better suited?" Sinjin asked, not wanting the answer.

"Vastly," she said. "The glass lances are proof of weapons used against dragons while adragonback."

"No one knows how to make those, and they would be of limited use against just about any other foe."

Kendra nodded, silent. Sinjin didn't know what to think. Such things rarely happened. "I don't know what to do," she finally admitted.

It was tempting to make a sarcastic remark, but Sinjin could not blame his wife in the least. He also had absolutely no idea of how best to proceed.

* * *

Within the makeshift forge, sweat ran into Osbourne's eyes and burned. Both his hands were occupied, helping his friend work hot metal, at least to the best of his ability. Osbourne was accustomed to the heat, though he preferred working hot glass, but their current forge lacked the shielding that had always insulated him from the fire's raw power. Working hand-built bellows while holding a pair of crude tongs, Osbourne wished for better gloves. His hands were desensitized to heat after years of working with glass, but even he could feel when he was being burned. While there were others, perhaps more capable and better suited physically to this job, Strom needed all the experience he could get. The working conditions compromised everything he did, and both knew the stakes.

"You really think we should be doing this?" Osbourne asked again.

Strom responded by repeatedly hammering red-hot metal. White hot was what they really wanted, but sometimes bright orange was the best they could accomplish. Working metal at lower temperatures was more difficult and compromised the product's integrity, but it was at times the best they could do. Osbourne worried most about the pressure tanks and the valves associated with them--or the lack thereof. When working with steam, it didn't take long for one to realize the need for pressure release, but Kenward insisted they had neither the time nor the resources. He was right. But in truth they had neither the time nor the resources to build experimental airships.

"Some of the things we've done in the past have been ill advised," Osbourne continued, "but this pushes the limits."

Strom stopped hammering for a moment, put down his tool, placed his hand on his hips, and stared at Osbourne. Still working the bellows, Osbourne went silent. Strom took the opportunity to stare at him a little bit longer just to make certain he'd made his point before he once again picked up his hammer. Using the extra energy from not talking, Osbourne concentrated on getting the metal white hot.

* * *

Despite the freedom and power of flight, it was sometimes nice to get where you were going on your own two feet. This was the case for Sinjin, who had left Valterius in Durin's care. He felt bad about asking his friend to work while he was still healing, but having something useful to do might reinforce his sense of purpose.

He could not change the harm that came to his friends and those he loved, and Sinjin let the physical exertion exorcise some of his worries. Not far away, the *Portly Dragon* waited in dry dock. The ship had grown since Sinjin had last seen it. Tar bladders the size of the deckhouse had been wrapped in sailcloth. Nearby, Kenward's crew worked to remove the inner sections from lengths of stalk weed, providing slender, unobstructed cylinders.

"What's all this?" Sinjin asked when he reached the place where Kenward worked, huddled over plans scribbled in charcoal on fresh-cut planks. When the pirate wiped away his most recent drawing upon hearing Sinjin's voice, it was no coincidence.

"Making a few adjustments," Kenward said, not looking up.

Taking it all in, Sinjin decided his wife was either a complete genius or entirely delusional. The same could be said for Kenward Trell, and he wondered, not for the first time, about the company he kept.

"We're not far from finished," Kenward continued. "I am sorry about using so many of your resources, but I vow to come back laden with tools and implements of all varieties. I may even find a way to get your smith an anvil, heavy as the devils are."

"Where will you go first?" Sinjin asked, trying his best to be subtle. If

Kendra had been there, she'd have rolled her eyes at his lack of tact.

"Wherever the wind takes me is probably the only honest answer I can give. Unless you've a spare thrustmaster or three."

"Not today," Sinjin said.

Kenward sighed. "I didn't think so. I'm going to have to figure that part out eventually. At sea, one can drop anchor and ride out a contrary wind. It's not so easy from the air. We've rope and sail and we know how to use them, but I must confess they can't do what a single thrustmaster can. But no worries! We're a crafty lot. I've more ideas to test, and you never know what we'll come up with."

Increasingly grateful for Valterius, even if dragon flight had its own drawbacks, Sinjin tried not to think about the complexities of flying airships.

"Still, it may take me a while to return," Kenward said.

The words were said without emotion, and Sinjin wasn't certain what to read into them. His wife's suspicions had him looking for alternate meaning in everything. It was maddening. "Are you going to invade the Jaga and try to save Allette?" Sinjin finally asked, unable to keep up the subtle game.

It took Kenward a moment to respond. "I suppose . . . if that's where the wind takes me."

"We'll go with you," Sinjin said before Kenward could utter another word.

"No. They'll not harm me. I've been invited."

Invited. The word rarely carried such sinister connotation, and Sinjin was afraid to ask by whom.

Kenward considered his offer for a moment. "You would do that for me?"

Sinjin nodded.

"It would likely be a one-way trip for some of us," Kenward said. "Though I'm sure the crew would return to you should anything ever happen to me."

"Was it Allette who invited you?" Sinjin asked, primarily because his wife would ask him that question, and for once he wanted to have the answer.

Unfortunately Kenward shrugged in response.

Sinjin tried to think of something else to say when his eyes landed on a growing pile of coconuts. "What are all those for?"

"Water storage," Kenward said, and it was clear to Sinjin he would get no more information that day. Once the man started giving one- and two-word answers, the dismissal was obvious.

"Is there anything else you need?" Sinjin asked, despite the fact that he'd probably already given too much.

"A couple flightmasters and a handful of thrustmasters if you can scare them up."

Chapter 16
Some ships are propelled solely by their crew's will.
--Fasha Hawk, sailor

* * *

Pelivor would not approve, but what he really needed were a few more days to rest. Catrin had a great deal more experience with astral travel, and even she felt the weariness, as if her soul were in tatters. Walking through darkened halls, like a thief skulking in the night, she couldn't help but feel bad for leaving him behind. Some things needed doing no matter what anyone else thought. She knew Pelivor's feelings. Now she knew almost everything he did. Their lives and memories diverged once their energies had been torn apart, but the cores of their beings were known to one another.

The deeper Catrin moved into the hold, the more Mael's presence could be sensed. Not knowing if he was conscious or not, she moved in silent trepidation. Though glossy and slick in her hand, Koe was streaked with white. The meager energy stream penetrating the barrier had not been enough to fully recharge the dragon ore carving. There was a chance she could draw energy from the giant green crystals, but they should also be mostly depleted. This would be a dangerous encounter. She had wisdom enough to recognize those with greater knowledge and skill than she. The most powerful individuals of the last Istran phase might also prove to be the most dangerous of this age. Like a child alone in a thunderstorm, Catrin felt small, powerless, and afraid. Mael was awake.

Even knowing this, Catrin remained undeterred. Her life had ceased to be the important factor long ago; most of what she did was for the benefit of others. Sinjin and his wife were chief among those, and even that made Catrin feel selfish. The entire world relied on what she did to save them, and all she could think about was her own debts. It proved just how small and self-centered she really was. Knowing Mael played with her feelings and tampered with her thoughts did not prevent them from stinging and hitting home.

It came as no surprise to see Mael wrapped around the ancient god's head, back in the place worn smooth over time. He watched her enter with distrust glittering in his eyes, and she couldn't help but notice the way he reacted when she pointed Koe in his direction. No matter how powerful he may be, he knew the sting of the carving and wisely backed away.

You're a fool for coming here.

Catrin made no statement in response but merely nodded her head, Koe never leaving her hand.

Why did you not kill me? His eyes glittered with rage, but a semblance of humanity remained even after all these years.

"Because, in you, I see myself," Catrin said. These words hung in the air for a long time before anyone moved or spoke. Catrin could feel him tinkering with her memories, playing with her motivations, and trying to get her to fall back under his influence, but the knowing prevented any of it from being subtle enough for the skillful sorcerer to apply.

I need pity from no one.

"It is not pity. I feel for you, ancient one. It is empathy. You, Aggrezjhon, and Murden were the most powerful people of your time. You were feared and misunderstood. No matter what your motivations were. This I understand better than anyone else alive."

The ancient dragon shifted.

"I've been to the Noonspire."

You think I'm unaware of this? There's nothing you can hide from me.

Perhaps most would have taken the dragon's word, but Catrin had seen the surprise when she mentioned the Noonspire, no matter how much the old sorcerer had endeavored to hide his reaction. The sheer size of his visage made even the slightest emotion visible.

Your friends will die. My colleagues will make sure their souls never escape the prison that has held them for so long.

The dragon's harsh words echoed painfully. Catrin knew he referred to Allette and Trinda, and while she would not consider them friends, they were better allies than this dragon was proving to be. Catrin had come here seeking help and knowledge in the hopes she and Mael would find common ground, but now she felt like the very fool he said her to be.

As if reading her thoughts, Mael chose that instant to launch his attack. What had seemed a leisurely posture soon proved to be an aggressive position of power. Lightning and fire rained down from on high, and the true glory of Mael's might was apparent. He must have known this time would come, a time when Catrin would be unprotected, when Pelivor would be left behind. Patience this sorcerer had in abundance. Thousands of years he'd waited to exact his revenge, his perspective far longer reaching than hers might ever be. In spite of the defensive structures she erected, Catrin was not immune to his attacks. Reaching deep into Koe for what reserves he held, she endured the pain, despite knowing her wounds were not purely physical. Using emotional anguish, the dragon mage carved deep rifts into Catrin's psyche.

The Herald of Istra knew power as well, though, and had not come unprepared. Ignoring the sting of Mael's attack and the smoke rising from her clothing, Catrin launched a potent attack of her own. Leveling Koe at the fearsome dragon, she used the carving's strength to exploit what she hoped was a weakness. Inanimate, Koe had no thoughts or feelings to manipulate. Born from Catrin's imagination, he could not easily be corrupted and used against her. Only if Mael could possess the carving itself could he claim its power, much as Thorakis had done years before.

"I do not wish to destroy you."

Then you truly are a fool. I'd very much like to rid the world of you. Especially now that you've damaged the shield without having the decency to destroy the blasted thing. The vibration makes my teeth hurt, and I blame you.

When the echoes of his anger had settled, Catrin let the silence hang between them, sensing a deeper undercurrent. Mael needed her, no matter what he said, and for more than just destroying the shield. This was not something the dragon wished to be true or wanted to admit, but Catrin would use it to her advantage. "What if I were to help you escape?"

Dark, menacing laughter occasionally reverberated within the cavern. Catrin doubted anyone in the hold still slept. Pelivor would be on his way, and Catrin would soon have to explain herself. Coming here had been a mistake. The ancient sorcerer lacked much of the humanity he'd once born and did not even respond to simple empathy. Catrin had underestimated what three thousand years in a prison could do to a soul.

"I've brought you a gift," Catrin said, ignoring the hatred being projected at her, understanding, at least to some extent, that the people of the last age had created this monster. If not for her friends and family and those who cared for her, Catrin might have suffered a similar fate. For those reasons she refused to give up on Mael, insisting some vestiges of humanity must remain. Otherwise, her own future looked grim, indeed.

Mael appeared dubious Catrin would have any gift worthy of his attention. The Herald of Istra knew something of what sorcerers found valuable. Moldy old tomes were unappreciated by some, but the right books in the right hands--or perhaps claws--were magic. When Catrin placed the tomes on the grassy landscape, not far from where black scars still tore through the soil, it was clear they piqued Mael's interest. A normal dragon may not have seen the books' value, but Catrin knew he could read without ever turning a page. She and Pelivor had left little power within the green stones, but there was enough to afford him that.

Your kindness may one day be your downfall, but I must nonetheless thank you.

"We need not be enemies," Catrin said. "Perhaps there are ways we can help one another."

These words clearly made Mael uncomfortable, and he shifted in the lap of the mighty stone god, his tail sending spray from the waterfall onto the plain below.

I've known allies before. They betrayed me.

It was some time before the dragon spoke again, but then the expression on his visage softened.

You've shown me kindness, Catrin Volker. I'll not forget this. Do not think this makes us friends. If you wish to save the child queen and the Black Queen, you must move quickly. This information I impart to you in return for the gift you brought me. Those trapped within the Noonspire seek new bodies since their old mortal trappings have long since turned to dust. Those new vessels must be prepared in order to receive such vast knowledge and powerful souls, so you do have some time, but not much.

"Sadly I'm as much trapped here as you are." Catrin's words were sincere, but they brought a strange smile to the dragon's eyes. She waited, silent, hoping to understand the nature of this smirk.

There is another way.

Catrin wasn't certain if she detected humor, kindness, or lies. Her life would likely depend on which it actually was. As if to show his power, Mael placed the idea deep within Catrin's mind without ever uttering the words. It was unsettling at best, but at least Catrin Volker had the information she'd come for.

May the gods forgive what she did next.

* * *

When Pelivor awoke, his head ached. With parched lips, he looked for something to drink and found a pitcher of cool water waiting on the nightstand next to him. Not far away, on the bed where he had expected to see Catrin resting, were clean, smooth sheets. Almost immediately, he began to curse. He loved Catrin and knew her now better than anyone else in the world, save perhaps Allette Kilbor. She must be doing something of which he would not approve.

"You'll want to sip this," Miss Mariss said. "The hunger may be overwhelming, but drinking this too fast is sure to give you a headache. Do yourself a favor and learn from Catrin's mistakes."

These words did little to still Pelivor's anxiety. "Where has she gone?"

Miss Mariss simply shook her head and walked from the room, leaving Pelivor alone with his melancholy thoughts. Then the thunder started. He'd guessed Catrin had gone to see the dragon, but now no doubt remained. Few others within the hold could create such thunder, and this was not the result of a natural or even supernatural storm. This was the result of his friend going off on her own, unprotected, into the realm of an ancient dragon sorcerer with unknown powers. The words that left his lips were not fit for ears. He got out of bed too quickly and stumbled against the nightstand, knocking the pitcher over with a clatter of metal against wood.

Miss Mariss came rushing back into the room at the sound. "Oh, no," she said. "I won't have you running off and risking yourself just because

Catrin does foolish things. We need you, something I think the two of you often forget."

"I cannot let her face the dragon alone," Pelivor said. "I'm sorry."

When deep laughter reverberated through the hold, making it clear Mael was awake and still had access to power, Pelivor could no longer be restrained. Miss Mariss shook her head in disappointment but did not bar his path. The laughter unnerved her as well, and even if she were angry with Catrin, they were friends. No one wished ill on those they cared for.

With his head aching and his body failing to react with the alacrity he would have desired, Pelivor did his best to make his way back to the dragon's chamber with as much speed as possible. There was no way to cover such distances quickly, at least no natural way. Pelivor realized this in an instant and used his flightmaster experience to full advantage. Applying his will, he sent himself hurtling through the halls at breakneck speed. If he misjudged, the results could be fatal since hard stone flew past in a blur. Practically flying down the main hall, he soon saw Catrin walking toward him, solemn but determined. No words were needed to tell him what she'd done, no explanation required. Instead, Pelivor simply slowed and allowed his feet to once again touch cold stone. His knees trembling from the exertion, he faced his friend with fear in his heart.

"There's another way out," Catrin said. "We must go."

"Wait. He told you this?"

Nodding, she tried to pull Pelivor back toward the main keep. It was an extremely difficult thing, knowing her mind up until a certain point then having no way to know what Catrin thought going forward. He could guess, based on the sum of her experiences, but had no way to predict what she would do next. She always had his best interests at heart; that he knew. For this reason alone he allowed her to pull him back the way he had come.

"What else did he tell you?" Pelivor asked.

For a while longer, Catrin walked in silence. Pelivor knew she was choosing her words. "He said Aggrezjhon and Murden wanted to use Allette and Trinda's bodies since they lost their physical forms long ago."

These words darkened Pelivor's soul, and he began to see why Catrin would want to go to save them. The things she didn't say terrified him.

"We must first scout the way," Catrin said. "We take no one else. No one is to know where we've gone. The way is not safe, and I don't want their blood on my hands as well."

"So you're just going to leave Miss Mariss and all the others without any information and let them wonder what happened to us?"

"I don't like it any better than you, but I've no better ideas."

"I really don't like it," he said.

Nodding, Catrin accepted it. "I need my pack. I have one prepared for you as well."

Pelivor raised an eyebrow.

"I had a feeling and stashed them not far away."

Much of the way they walked was a common thoroughfare, a major hall leading back to areas of the keep that had been inhabited for much longer. The stump of an old torch still resting in the sconce was just what he'd been searching for. "A moment," he said.

Catrin stopped, turned, and waited without much patience. Pelivor leaped up to the sconce and grabbed the butt of the old torch. Using the blackened charcoal, he scratched a crude message onto the floor. He didn't get much more than their initials and the words will return written on the stones of the roadway before the rest of the torch completely disintegrated. It would have to be enough.

Soon Catrin turned from the main thoroughfare, going out of her way to avoid contact with anyone else. Most of the tunnels they now strode were seldom used. It was a good thing; Catrin's pack reeked of that dreadful blanket.

When they arrived in a circular chamber, its floor divided into symmetrical tiles, each bearing a pictograph, Pelivor's stomach grew cold. This chamber had been used successfully to turn on the water within the hold and also to travel to the mountaintop, a trip that would currently be suicidal by Pelivor's estimation. Though each time had recovered utility from the long past, both had come with a price, and Pelivor wondered what this would cost them.

Catrin gave Pelivor no chance to second-guess; grabbing his hand, she pulled him onto a tile bearing a series of rectangles, each surrounded by four circles. Not quite ready and pulled off balance, he took a hesitant step and stumbled into her, forcing her back as his foot hit the tile she occupied. A low grinding noise followed after she inadvertently depressed the wrong tile, this one having three thick vertical bars intersected by a wavy horizontal line.

Having no idea what this represented, Pelivor closed his eyes and held his breath. Nothing else happened. "Sorry," he said.

"It wasn't your fault. I shouldn't have pulled you like that. I don't know what I was thinking."

Both silently acknowledged their luck. Catrin joined him then smiled, shrugged, and exerted greater force on the stone tile upon which they stood. At first it only wiggled, but then Pelivor took her hand and synchronized their movements. Without warning, the tile dropped, leaving both waving their arms, trying to keep their balance. The movement started slowly, almost imperceptibly, but increased until soon they were falling at a rate that had Pelivor's insides tingling. Catrin's grip on his hand tightened.

After plunging into unknown depths, the circular stone floor slowed, pressing up into their boots. From her pocket Catrin pulled a herald globe and used Koe to give it an extra charge. It revealed a foreign landscape unlike anything else within Dragonhold. Above were sweeping lines, right angles, and stonework straight from the hands of masters. Below, the stone resembled the work of giants armed with enormous hammers. Even the smallest facet in the stone face was taller than Catrin and Pelivor standing on top of one another.

A strange sound filled the hall. Not hesitating, Catrin stepped onto roughhewn black stone.

Pelivor followed with trepidation. "What is this place?"

Four cylindrical rails lined the halls. Two were suspended from either wall, one dominated the center of the floor and another hung from the ceiling. Whistling and a rush of air were all the warning they received before a projectile of metal, wood, leather, and glass soared through the room.

"What was that?" Pelivor asked.

Catrin walked to a series of black metal levers set into the wall. "That was our ride."

"You're not planning to get into one of those things, are you?" Pelivor asked.

"There's no other way," Catrin said. "I've no idea exactly how far we need to travel or if we'll use up the precious little energy Koe has stored. So far beneath the land, the air is completely devoid of Istra's power; I know you can feel it. We must conserve. And as you can also see, the mine cars travel in ways we would never be able to accomplish."

Pelivor sighed and watched Catrin. The way she operated this foreign device's controls, as if she knew them, made him suspect Mael had imparted this information--and more, which worried him. Despite his concerns, the mine car slowed and stopped right in front of them. Catrin immediately climbed aboard, but Pelivor took a few more moments to inspect the car to make sure there was nothing that had rotted over the ages. It was a testament to the ancients' construction skills that any of this worked at all. Albeit under a patina of age, the mine car was in near pristine condition, making Pelivor wonder what other marvels the ancients had accomplished.

The mine car itself was remarkable. Pelivor would have expected something suitable for carrying ore, but this car was designed to transport people rather than cargo. Two seats, side by side, filled the bottom of the car. A series of controls near the front bore indecipherable labels, and a glowing amber lamp shed light on what lay ahead. Pelivor cleared dust and grime from the lens, allowing them to see more.

"Let's go," Catrin said.

Having inspected the car to the best of his ability and really having no way to address any of the things he found questionable, Pelivor resigned himself and climbed aboard.

"If I'm right," Catrin said, "we're just taking a short service loop to pick up speed."

"And if you're wrong?"

Catrin shrugged. "Hold on."

There was no more time for misgivings. Sliding the controls forward, Catrin sent the car gliding along the rails. The metal structures supporting them bore a glossy sheen. Pelivor did not know how long the cars had been running. It was possible they had operated continuously over the eons, but it seemed far more likely that recent events within Dragonhold had reactivated them.

No matter how long it had been, using the cars was far from safe. The speed alone was dizzying. Halls barely wide enough to allow for the car and rails led to a steep downward slope. Soon they dived through an expansive cavern with many rails suspended from cables. The cylindrical shafts, supported by metal structures, rarely intersected. Where they did, the rails appeared designed to allow the car to switch tracks. Rather than coming together at right angles, the tracks merged smoothly then separated with equal grace.

Dust and detritus of ages coated some rails. Upon seeing those, Pelivor made the mistake of looking down. There, at the bottom of a deep pit, Catrin's overbright herald globe shone on dented and destroyed cars launched from no-longer-complete spans. Certain his screams could be heard all the way back in the main hold, Pelivor watched in despair as they crossed over broken tracks and launched into an upward arc. When the tracks continued, he tried to catch his breath.

Shiny rails indicated the track was whole the entire way around, but Pelivor could not be certain. When the controls and the circular shaft reappeared, he knew Catrin had been right. Still, that did nothing to ease his anxiety since he'd seen no place appropriate for them to disembark. The pitch of his screams rose even higher when Catrin threw one of the levers forward. A loud clang reverberated through the halls, setting Pelivor's teeth on edge. A junction raced toward them, smooth and clean on one side, dusty and unused on the other. The smooth side would get them nowhere. Despite the graceful appearance of the transition, the car slammed left and vibrated over disused rails.

Still whisking along the track, the mine car sent dust, grime, and refuse of ages flying. Bits of wood that may have once supported the tunnels and rusted metal hung in the shaft before them. It was everything Catrin and Pelivor could do to keep their heads down and avoid decapitation.

"Get ready to jump!" Catrin shouted.

Had she given Pelivor the opportunity to protest, he would have, but life was moving at high speed, and there would be consequences. He was certain. There was no way to know just how much longer there ride would last until Catrin drew a sharp breath. She stood and leaped, grabbing his shirt collar as she went. Unable to stand in time, Pelivor was yanked bodily from the car by Catrin's grip alone, and he thought she might have broken his collarbone. Screaming, the two landed on a pile of unforgiving rock. This was, however, far preferable to the fate of their mine car. Pelivor now had a full view, and he was thankful for Catrin's quick reflexes. If only she hadn't gotten them into this in the first place.

A short distance ahead of the doomed mine car, the tracks ended in a pile of rocks where the tunnel had long ago collapsed. Whistling and screaming, the car collided with the rocks at near full speed, sending sparks and a thunderous boom into the air. Pelivor would have despaired if not for delicate beams of sunlight piercing the darkness.

Chapter 17

Beware the dreamers, for they know not their own weakness and are therefore not limited by it.

--Osbourne Macano, glassblower

* * *

"He's going to need a thrustmaster, sir."

Benjin Hawk smiled at the young man who had grown up before his eyes. Jessub Tillerman was a man of his word, and Benjin truly had no hold over him. Nonetheless, Jessub asked permission to join Kenward Trell's crew. Doing so would endanger the young man's life, but who was he to say no? "Are you sure that's what you want?"

"I always said I was going to be an adventurer," Jessub said, his grin contagious.

"Indeed you did, my boy. Indeed you did. I must admit, you've perhaps not chosen the safest career path," Benjin said, getting a chuckle from Jessub. "But I'll support you in whatever you decide."

"Thank you, sir."

"But don't think I'm going to tell my wife on your behalf. Or that I'm going to tell her this was my idea. That, my friend, is on you."

The young man blanched, proving he had good sense, in spite of his choice of ship. "Yes, sir."

Benjin chuckled and patted the boy on the shoulder. Something seemed to be irritating his eyes; he kept rubbing at them but would admit nothing. Jessub cast him a sideways glance but also remained silent. Gwen and Fasha stood nearby, talking, which would make the conversation even more difficult for Jessub, but that was not his problem. If this boy thought he could survive the *Portly Dragon*, then he would have to brave Benjin's wife and daughter first.

Of course, it could be said that taking advice on women from Benjin Hawk was a bad idea. And once again the two people he thought he knew best surprised him. There were no stern words or reprimands; instead tears of joy and sorrow mixed on his shoulders. Jessub Tillerman was a brave man. It went neither unnoticed nor unrewarded.

"Come on, young man," Benjin said after the girls had finished falling all over Jessub. "Grab your things and let's go talk to your new captain."

The *Portly Dragon* sat in dry dock, looking much like the barge she was designed after. Kenward Trell watched them approach with a crooked smirk.

"Permission to come aboard, sir?" Jessub asked.

Kenward grinned like a fool at the sight of the bag slung across the young man's shoulder. "I would never have asked you to come."

Benjin nodded in acknowledgment of his statement, knowing it was partly intended for him. Out of respect, Kenward Trell had not sought anyone from the *Dragon's Wing*.

The good captain could scarcely contain his enthusiasm. "Having a thrustmaster aboard, even a novice, will greatly increase our chances of success."

Benjin wore a sad smile. "Take good care of him. The boy's been getting under my feet for so long, he's like family." Jessub flushed and could not meet his eyes.

"He is just as fine and strong a young man as I've ever seen," Kenward said, coming to the aid of the boy's ego. "I'm certain will get along very well."

"I'll say one last thing, Kenward. I don't expect Martik would take kindly to you putting his only born son in the drink."

And with those words, Benjin released responsibility for one he considered his own. It was a difficult parting, and he worried about Jessub's future and safety, but he'd done everything in his power to train the boy, as had Martik, Fasha, Gwen and others. There was nothing more they could do.

Before Benjin left the *Portly Dragon's* deck, he couldn't help but notice tanks attached to the sides of the howler and bumblebee. Not to mention the long stalk weed sections he'd seen them hollowing out, which were now connected to those very tanks. Shaking his head, Benjin Hawk stepped back onto dry land, silently wishing those aboard luck.

A crowd gathered to see the *Portly Dragon* off on its true maiden voyage. With air and sea trials behind, leaks had been fixed, adjustments made, and provisions loaded. The strange ship left the ground slowly. Daylight streamed between the ship and the dry-dock footings for a mere instant before it came slamming back down. Twice more they bounced, black smoke and steam billowing from the boiler house. Gusting winds pulled at the windsocks. Even when the airship cleared the dry dock, one corner dragged along the sand, sending the ship twisting onto the wind.

But then the *Portly Dragon* found its wings and flew. Valterius and Gerhonda soared in close, their riders latching on to ropes attached to the ship's corners to lend stability.

"Thrust, Jessub!" Kenward shouted as the rocks drifted closer. "We need more thrust!"

Jessub straightened his back and applied the full force of his will. A charge built up until lightning pulsed within the thrust tubes. Despite the disconcerting sight, the *Portly Dragon* moved through the air, howling as she went. An escort of regal dragons stayed nearby--just in case.

* * *

Replacing Pelivor hadn't been easy. His departure had truly left a hole in Nora Trell's crew--not that she would ever admit it to him. In every way she wished him well, and a sad part of her admitted she'd never found his match. Emmon was a capable boy; he just lacked spark. It was a pity. He'd come from a trusted family who'd long sought a share in the *Trader's Wind.* The boy did everything asked of him without complaint, but he had not the will to learn on his own. It had been the primary thing that had set Pelivor apart; the spark burned brightly in that one.

Emmon would serve as first mate in Pelivor's lingering shadow. It would suffice. There were other purposes, however, for which her needs were very different. The young man was far more at home on land, and Nora was getting a better sense of him as a result. Part of her wanted to keep him ignorant in the event he jumped ship. Another part knew no one would ever believe him. In the end, she decided to see how he handled a small amount of knowledge. The first insight was that Nora feared stairs. More than two or three steps seemed like asking for trouble. Going up was perhaps not as bad, under the right conditions, but coming down would allow the boy to see. Letting others see her weaknesses wasn't something Nora was accustomed to doing, but she thought there might be a thing or two she could learn from that fool son of hers--not that she would ever admit it to him. The boy convinced his crew to take the most incredible risks, and they obeyed not out of fear or even simple respect. His crew believed in him. It was a remarkable feat considering what he asked of them.

When they reached the stair, Emmon looked confused, clearly sensing Nora's unease. The boy certainly could read her.

"Go up a couple steps and wait."

Showing his better sense, Emmon nodded and did as he was told. Reaching out with his hand, he put his arm where she could grab it if needed. What the boy lacked in spark, he made up for in the oddest ways. Perhaps, over time, others would fight to get out of his shadow. Pelivor had been young and ignorant once too, and no doubt innocent. Nora reminded herself to judge the boy fairly. It just wasn't always easy.

An orange glow emanated from heavily occluded glass windows. A fire burned within. Struggling with the old, stubborn lock, Emmon quickly became frustrated. He must have wanted to be inside as much on her behalf as his since the stairs seemed to bother him not at all. Nora remained calm and closed her eyes, waiting for the sound of the door opening.

"I thought I heard someone out here scrabbling," Gregorric of Dorn said. "Come in. Come in."

Hearing the man's voice instantly put Nora at ease, though she most certainly did not look down. The line of Dorn had long been a vital trade partner for the Trells, and once inside, his house was no longer terrifying-- at least on the first floor. Winding stairs led to upper chambers Nora remembered as a child but no longer cared to see.

"How's Fasha?" Gregorric asked, as he always did. Nora smiled. "How's Kenward?" he asked with a wry grin, as he always did. Nora shook her head. "What are you going to do with that boy?"

She shrugged. Emmon watched the exchange with a mixture of awe and confusion.

"What are you up to?"

She grinned. "You don't really think I'm going to tell you, now do you?"

"It would be nice. I have to tell their families something."

"I've told you," Nora said. "I'm interviewing potential candidates to be my new first mate."

After choking, Emmon tried to be very small if not invisible.

"So you did," Gregorric said. "And yet, you had some pretty specific criteria that raise reasonable questions."

"Does it raise the question of the first mate's potential share?"

"It does," the man conceded.

Nora nodded as if this were enough explanation.

"Come in here, girl," Gregorric said. "I know you're listening."

When a girl of perhaps nineteen summers emerged from the next room, dressed in sturdy traveling pants and a snug wool top, Nora thought she might lose Emmon. Smacking him on the back of the head, she said, "Stop gaping. You look like a fish."

"This is Gret. Gret, this is Nora and that's Emmon, but then you already knew that, didn't you?"

The girl flushed and averted her eyes. Emmon looked as if he might defend her. "Sit still," Nora whispered in his ear. Turning deep red, his ears looked as if they were on fire. "Hello, Gret. I'm Captain Trell. You may call me Captain Trell."

"Yes, ma'am," the girl said.

Nora gave her a look she saved for the truly daft.

"I mean, yes, Captain Trell."

"You sure about this one?" Nora asked Gregorric. Now the girl flushed as deeply as Emmon, just as she'd intended. "Emmon, take Gret outside. We'll meet you in the street."

He held out his arm and escorted Gret outside.

"You're a devious, evil woman, manipulating them already."

"I have to start at some point," Nora said with a grin. "The boy hasn't a chance, but I gave him an edge. Maybe it'll make him feel like he's got a shot. Sometimes that's all it takes."

Gregorric just shook his head. "Shall I help you down the stairs, m'lady?"

Nora accepted with a nod. Asking for help was difficult. Gregorric of Dorn was an old friend, and that made it perhaps a little easier. He was wise enough never to use it against her; except perhaps by living in a place surrounded by lethal staircases. By the time they reached the streets, it was clear Emmon and Gret were uncomfortable.

"Come on, you two," Nora said. "We need to go find some place out in the open."

"What kind of place?" Gregorric asked.

"Someplace where there's nothing anyone might miss if it falls down."

Her old friend shook his head and laughed. "Go that way," he said, pointing toward the bay.

Emmon and Gret exchanged a glance. She quickly looked away as if annoyed.

"Let's go," Nora said. "Now you two hold hands." All three looked at her as if she were perhaps the cruelest person of all, and Nora Trell laughed. "Just kidding."

"And people wonder where your son gets it," Gregorric said.

Nora just made a gesture some might consider rude and headed inland, ignoring his advice and her yearning for the sea.

* * *

With Istra's energy caressing his skin, Pelivor reveled in the feeling, the pain of his bruised collar bone the only distraction. "How'd you know?"

"Mael did not tell me; he showed me," Catrin said.

The thought of the old sorcerer in Catrin's mind gave Pelivor the crawls, and he dared not think what else the dragon had showed his friend. He knew why she held her silence. He wanted answers nonetheless. The forsaken blanket smelled even worse when exposed to sunlight, which didn't help. Catrin wore it over her shoulders, letting it block out most but not all of Istra's light.

When a dragon appeared on the horizon and steadily grew larger, Pelivor was not surprised. Catrin's calm demeanor confirmed his suspicion Kyrien would come for them. Riding a regent dragon with the Herald of Istra was not something many people got to do in their lives, and Pelivor couldn't help but take note of the interesting and challenging times in which he lived.

Dropping from the sky and slamming into the ground with thunderous force, his hide crisscrossed with scars, Kyrien presented an imposing figure. Clear eyes spoke of intelligence, and they focused on Catrin and Pelivor. It was the kind of thing one might never get used to. After a trumpeting call,

Kyrien extended his wing and allowed them to climb aboard his back, where a leather saddle awaited.

"Double-check your straps," Catrin said.

Pelivor had done little else since getting strapped in. Despite knowing he could easily float to the ground using Istra's power, he had no interest in flying loose in the middle of a dragon fight. Given where they were going, a warm welcome was unlikely.

"You don't have to go, you know."

"I know," Pelivor said. "You'll just have to forgive me for coming anyway."

Catrin smiled. It was such a wonderful thing, Pelivor lamented its rarity.

Kyrien launched himself into the air without warning, and Pelivor held on with white knuckles. In spite of all the time he had spent on airships and his skills as a flightmaster, there was nothing that compared to the powerful thrusts of a *Dragon's Wing*s. Leaving the Godfist was bittersweet, knowing those who stayed within Dragonhold to serve them were now left behind. It was not without purpose, but he felt empty, hollow, and sad. Catrin felt much the same. Both were driven to save them all, even though both knew it was beyond them. The way was rarely clear nor the path easy.

Using their combined knowledge and skills, Catrin, Pelivor, and Kyrien raced through the skies at speeds never before seen. Roiling mists erupted behind as the dragon showed off, dragging his claws along the water and leaving rainbows in the air. Once again, they were free.

* * *

What Emmon lacked in spark, Gret made up for in fire and spark. It was plain to see. Even Emmon seemed to sense it. He gave the girl as wide a berth as Nora would allow. Neither of these two was accustomed to life on a ship, and they would be made uncomfortable many times to come.

"Build a fire, Emmon," Nora said. The boy looked at her as if he would ask an inane question but then thought better of it. She supposed he thought it was a test, which was good since it was. Gret risked making eye contact and shook her head. "He's a good kid," Nora said when Emmon was out of earshot gathering wood.

Gret just grunted in response. "Didn't you say we needed a clear area?"

"I did."

After looking around, Gret glanced back to Nora with a somewhat sarcastic question in her eyes.

"Yes. This spot will do nicely . . . but not yet. We've other business to attend to first. Chances are we'll want to leave in a hurry when we're done."

Gret rolled her eyes, which pleased Nora; she needed to test the girl's temper in a controlled environment. Selecting someone with the wrong temperament could be disastrous.

When Emmon returned, he carried a few pieces of dead wood, some dried leaves and couple of rocks. It really didn't look all that promising, but Nora wasn't giving up on him yet. To his credit, the boy started with some dry wood fiber he'd pulled from somewhere, and he placed small sticks and leaves around it, leaving the larger pieces of wood off to one side. Given the dampness in the air, he had a difficult road ahead, but he seemed determined, which was a good sign. In many ways, this was more a test of character than fire-making skills. Nora fingered the tinderbox in her pocket while Emmon smacked two rocks together, trying to generate enough spark to ignite the fibers.

Gret rolled her eyes. Still, Emmon tried. Harder and harder, he smacked the stones together, occasionally sending small sparks where he needed them but not enough to catch. His face reddening from the effort and the embarrassment, he smacked harder and pinched his thumb. Clearly in pain, the boy did not stop, now determined not to let his ego be so crushed, in spite of the tears that ran down his cheeks. Even Gret seemed to take pity on the boy. Staring at the shavings, she looked as if her thoughts were far away. Nora watched closely, her test working even more brilliantly than even she'd intended. A spark flew, landing on the fibers and glowing orange for an instant. Looking as if it would wink out, just as the others did, it nonetheless held on, Gret's eyes never leaving it. Smoke, first just a trickle then more, leaked from around the now growing glow. Emmon blew softly, and the orange glow winked out for a moment before coming back even brighter. Soon he was adding larger and larger pieces to the fire.

"Well done," Nora said. Gret nodded just the slightest bit. Emmon went into the woods, presumably to gather more wood and perhaps to compose himself. There would come a time for kindness between them, but she also needed to harden him some. He was too fragile. Experiences such as these would give him practice and pride. No matter what folks said about her offspring, Nora Trell had not raised soft children. Yet somehow, fostering other people's soft children was her lot in life. At least she'd had practice, she thought with a sigh.

"Are we waiting for something?" Gret asked. Her voice was respectful, which was the only reason Nora answered.

"Yes."

No more words were said, which was just how Nora wanted it. Soon these two would know their places and would be better prepared to fit in on her ship. What might seem callous or cruel was for a reason and toward their ultimate benefit as well as her own.

Frequently looking over his shoulder, Emmon returned with a small armload of twigs. From within the forest came a deep melody, almost indistinguishable at first but growing clearer and louder over time. Nora smiled. She hadn't been certain her friend would come, and hearing his voice did her good.

"Greetings, landfriend," said a deep voice. Emmon looked ready to flee, while Gret took on a defensive posture. The girl had potential.

"Greetings, friend Veterbas."

"Always you must come back to land," the burly man said. He was tall and round, but none of his girth was fat. There were few men Nora would wager could defeat the druid in a fair fight, if there even was such a thing. She doubted it. "You claim to be a creature of the sea, and yet here you are again."

Knowing he enjoyed this part very much, she let the man have his fun. What he said contained a grain of truth; never could she completely sever her ties with land.

"But it's the trees you need, I suspect, and not dear old Veterbas. Do I see it true?"

"You do," Nora said, knowing argument would only prolong the process. Better to let the man think himself correct and get on with it.

"I fail to understand how you can need more wood for ships, Nora Trell. How many ships does one person need?"

"It doesn't help that my fool son keeps sinking them or leaving them on top of mountains."

The druid whistled at this. "To sink a ship seems an easy thing. To leave one on a mountain is a special kind of lunacy."

"Thank the gods I have but one son."

"So I have," Veterbas said. "So I have."

"I need to know where I can find certain kinds of trees but all in the same place."

Veterbas looked thoughtful as she listed a half dozen species. "You are not one to ask easy questions, Nora Trell. Why do you want to know this?"

"I have need of the wood."

"To quote my old friend Barabas, 'Trees are the noblest of creatures, for they provide us so much without complaint. But while the trees might not complain, I will. If you take too much, the land and animals suffer."

"We'll replant whatever we take."

The druid grunted, as if he'd heard it all before.

"The land will suffer more if we do not face the storm."

At this, Veterbas nodded. "So it is. I do not take this lightly, Nora Trell. You must do as you say and care for the land. Do not simply plant again what you've taken, nourish the land with your very being. Commune with it and thank it for the gifts you so desire."

"It will be so."

Even with that said, the druid hesitated, but then he seemed to see the truth. Darkness was coming, one way or another, and perhaps the land could be spared; perhaps this offering would appease the gods. Though his thoughts appeared to be written on his face, his words surprised her. "Perhaps Kenward could be encouraged to take up some profession that requires less wood."

"Perhaps he and Emmon could build fires together," Gret said with a wicked grin.

Though the notion seemed to disturb Veterbas deeply, Nora Trell laughed. This girl had fire and spark to spare.

Chapter 18

Sacrifice is the highest form of honor.
--The Pauper King

* * *

The sea called to Nora Trell, but landbound work remained. Her last stop, at least, was back along the shoreline. Consoled by the sea's scent on the air, she grinned, thinking about the night before. Gregorric had chosen well. Gret did, indeed, have talent to spare. Having had some of the ancient stories verified, Nora could move with greater confidence. It was one thing to read about power in an ancient text and quite another to see someone with a healthy dose of spark produce a breathtaking result. Neither Gret nor Emmon had spoken since. Nora understood. Gret was confused and worried but did not want it to show. Emmon most likely feared for his life. Nora couldn't blame him either. She could have warned him, but where would have been the fun in that?

The sunset reflected from the windows of a shop, making it harder to see the man inside. He worked with a small, round-tipped hammer. Nora waved as they approached. His straggly beard moved as he smiled, and his eyes behind metal-rimmed goggles twinkled. He always saw her coming.

"I didn't know it was my lucky day!" Ebrem said. "My favorite customer just shows up like the wind. I suspect you'll float out just the same."

"Hello, Ebrem, I am once again in need of your services."

"Did your boy put another one on the bottom?"

"No. And to be fair, he left the last one on a mountaintop."

"I can't help with that, unless said mountain is under water."

"Sadly not."

"That boy of yours is a piece of work, he is."

"You can say that," Nora said. Ebrem nodded. "I did, however, lose something dear to me." He looked as if he wanted to ask what but showed restraint. This was why Nora trusted him; that and he was the cleverest man she knew. He also happened to know a lot about diving. "I roped it at three hundred knots."

"Three hundred!" Ebrem's eyes bulged. "Outrageous."

"What's the deepest you can go now?"

"One seventy-five."

"What's limiting you?"

Now, it seemed, she had his attention. Nora knew the man well enough. Once he saw where she was going, his mind took over. He could see the possibilities. Even the most brilliant people sometimes need a little inspiration and motivation.

"Air is the problem," he said, his eyes going distant. "We need a more powerful pump."

"And what's it going to take to build said pump?"

"Time. Gold."

"I'll give you one of the two," Nora said, laying gold on the counter. He seemed to be doing the math in his head. "I need it now," she said, doubling the gold. This made the math much easier.

"It's going to be big," he said, scratching down notes.

"I can do big. How long? Realistically."

"Sixty days if I put off everything else."

"Too long," Nora said. "I need it in fourteen days."

Ebrem's eyes bulged again. "Can't be done."

"Why not?"

Ebrem looked at her as if she were daft; it was not something most people dared to do. "Just getting that much metal hot and then cooled down again takes time."

"Then don't make it out of metal."

That statement confounded the man, but then his mind was fully engaged. He began sketching a spoked wheel. "We can make much of the structure from wood, but it won't last."

"If we paint the wood, it'll last a year," Nora said.

Ebrem nodded. "Yes . . . with proper maintenance."

"And that will give you a year to build one out of metal."

Blinking twice, Ebrem stopped. "That could work but it's going to be expensive. I'm going to need help from people with real talent. These things aren't easy, you know. People don't just dive to the bottom of the sea to recover . . ." He raised his eyebrows and waited.

"Something precious to me." Nora added another stack of gold coins.

"In fourteen days," he said, grinning, "we go diving, eh?"

"Fourteen days." Soon she would be ready to sail. When they left the shop behind, Nora turned to Emmon and Gret. "He's a genius but sometimes you have to do the thinking for him."

* * *

While not a swift ship, the *Portly Dragon* could sail without wind. Given time and practice, Jessub Tillerman might one day be just as effective a thrustmaster as Gwen. Though he possessed some ability as flightmaster, it was tenuous at best and he was glad this ship did not require it. Thunderheads, dark green and occasionally lit from within, were still reason for concern. The ship had not been designed to fly through storms.

Kenward stood at the clearly labeled stern. Some had laughed but he knew better. His ship had no broad side. With the exception of the masthead, there was really no such thing as a bow or stern. He continued to use them because that was what his crew understood. Such terms no longer fully applied to the ships in his mind, his imagination capable of so much more than the technology at his disposal. Construction techniques had already improved, and he himself learned from knowledge the ancients left behind, but there was much still to learn. Lessons at sea rarely came without pain.

"Some of the cleats are coming loose, sir," Bryn said. Having already fetched the tool they made for that task alone, Farsy made it clear he agreed. Bryn stomped on the deck, allowing Farsy to find the place where he stood from belowdecks. There the exposed bolt and nut would be located. Driving bolts through the massive timbers that made up the *Portly Dragon's* deck had been a tremendous amount of work at the time, but the strength of these attachment points was paramount. Not long after, Farsy could be heard from below, albeit muffled and faint.

"Excellent work," Kenward said. "Call for me if you find any other trouble."

Walking toward the thrust tubes, Kenward avoided the parts of the deck painted with warnings, keeping to the space between the tubes, where the air was calm and smooth. "How are you feeling, my boy?"

"I'm fine, sir," Jessub said. "I'm just feeling a little hungry. Maybe if Grubb could bring me something to eat . . ."

"No. The *Portly Dragon* does not require thrust to stay in the air. When you're tired, when you are hungry, when you thirst, you may stop and satisfy your needs unless I tell you otherwise. There will be times I'll asked you to provide thrust until such a time as we no longer need it. There will come a time I'll ask from you more than you have to give. Be ready. We'll face the winds soon enough, and I'll want a refreshed thrustmaster when that time arrives. All I ask is that you use great care when you cease. When Catrin did it best, she reduced the thrust over time."

"Yes, sir," Jessub said, easing out of the thrust, allowing the *Portly Dragon* to slow gradually.

"Well done," Kenward said, and the rest of the crew hooted their approval. Jessub walked to the deckhouse with a lopsided smile on his face. Kenward Trell was determined to make the boy the adventurer he'd always wanted to be. He was well on his way. "How are those cleats coming?"

"We've still got a few more to cinch up, sir," Bryn said. "But Farsy says some of the bolts are cracking."

"Move those lines to spare cleats," Kenward said. "Then bring the cracked bolts to the forge. We'll see about reinforcing them." One advantage of steam-based travel was always having fires burning. Kenward had planned for this eventuality. All he had to do was reinforce the undersized bolts, one at a time, before any snapped. It was risky but no one complained. Those aboard knew what they had taken on, and they trusted him; the last bit was the hardest to believe. "And while he's down there, tell him to make sure there aren't any gaping holes in the hull." Putting the ship to sea for repairs wasn't Kenward's first choice but it never hurt to be safe. His mother would laugh.

After scouting the seas and weather conditions, Sinjin and Kendra returned with concern on their faces. "Permission to board?"

Despite the fact that Kenward had already told Sinjin and Kendra they could land on his deck whenever they wanted, he shouted in return, "Permission granted."

Having landed the bumblebee on the decks of the *Portly Dragon*, Kenward marveled at the ease with which Valterius and Gerhonda gained the decks. No sooner did they land than did Sinjin and Kendra remove their straps and march toward him, their faces sour. Dragons flanked the boiler house, lying down to rest. Kenward wasn't sure if this was to shield their riders in the event the boilers failed or if the dragons just liked keeping warm. Either way, Kenward particularly liked the look of dragons on deck, rather than just as the masthead. Still, they could be unreliable creatures, and he hoped they behaved. It seemed unlikely.

"Bad weather coming," Sinjin said. "How's the ship holding up?"

"We haven't found any gaping holes in the hull, sir," Bryn said from nearby with a grin.

"She's doing just fine…just fine," Kenward said. "How many people did you say those dragons can carry?"

* * *

The *Trader's Wind* was a purpose-built ship rarely called to do anything but what she was specifically designed to do. On this day, though, the crew would witness a spectacle. While the Wind was far from the ideal exploration ship, she did have a few advantages. Her cranes and pulleys were built to lift massive cargo, and her decks, large enough to hold both an enormous pump and the barge that would soon support it. Getting the barge into the water was an impressive but simple enough affair. Getting the pump oriented properly, lowered onto the barge, and secured proved a more difficult and dangerous endeavor.

Nora held her breath as the diver struggled against the waves while trying to tighten the straps. Two men used long poles to push the barge away from the ship since it was naturally drawn toward the *Trader's Wind*. Once the top and bottom straps had been secured, the crew took their places on the barge. On deck waited a suit of metal and oiled leather with a helmet that looked a lot like a cookpot with a hose coming out of it.

Carefully the suit was secured to the hoist and readied for lowering to the barge.

"Are you going to tell us what we're looking for yet? Is it a shipwreck? Lost treasure? What is it?" Ebrem asked. He had insisted on coming to fix any problems that might occur with his experimental pump. It was a beauty, painted black and gold, looking like a machine of the new age.

Nora grinned. "You are sworn to secrecy." Ebrem nodded in acceptance as the loading crane lifted his pressurized dive suit from the deck. Nora reached in her pocket and pulled out a black crystal. "This is what we're after."

Ebrem reached out his hand and grabbed the stone. Nora reluctantly let go. It was among her most precious possessions. "I don't get it. I've seen prettier crystals than that . . . and darned easier to get."

Nora said nothing. She hated watching from above rather than from the barge itself. She felt disconnected from the operation but had learned to get used to such things. The climb was simply more than she could handle. She could have ridden the crane down, but as she was always so quick to point out to Kenward, that would create a risk not worth taking. If the crane malfunctioned, she would be in serious trouble. No, the deck was better-- just frustrating and nerve wracking. She wanted to yell to them to triple-check the air supply before the suit dipped beneath water. Weighted down as it was, the suit sank like a stone, leaving a trail of air bubbles behind it.

From her vantage, the suit disappeared almost immediately. All she could do was wait while those aboard the barge took turns using their full body weight to turn the massive wooden wheel that drove the oversized air pump. It was a graceful and stressful ballet the crew performed, lining up to jump onto the spokes at just the right time then riding the spoke down. Before it reached the bottom, the crewmen needed to jump off or be pulled through the framework that held the wheel and pump assembly in place. Nora was proud of their brave efforts, but she worried for them. This would all have been difficult enough on dry land, but compensating for the motion of the barge and pushing off the hull of the *Trader's Wind* made for an unsettling spectacle. Always when she needed them, her crew was there, and she prayed for their continued safety.

"I just don't get it," Ebrem said, scratching his head.

"Show him," Nora said to Gret, knowing he would never let it go. Again with reluctance she handed the noonstone crystal to the young woman. Nora could not blame Ebrem; she, too, had been unconvinced until Gret managed to test the ancient technique. Now she understood and soon so would he.

"Come with me," Gret said. "This is most safely done inside. Captain Trell would not be happy if I lost her crystal."

Thoroughly intrigued, Ebrem followed the young woman to the forward deckhouse. He watched in silent fascination as Gret produced a wooden cylinder and some string. When Gret suspended the crystal within the wooden tube and ran her hand over it, the man's eyes went wide. Soon he, too, came to see the truth.

"They're coming back up," someone shouted.

Nora beat the rest to the door, but they quickly matched her pace. None was rude enough to leave her behind, and they instead walked at an awkwardly slow pace. Air bubbles erupted from the sea nearby; watching that spot, they waited. Silence hung heavily while they waited to see movement, to know the larger pump had truly provided enough air even at such depths. When the diver brought his hands up, the people cheered. They cheered even louder when the sizable crystal he carried was pulled onto the barge.

Nora Trell smiled. Gret, Emmon, and Ebrem all seemed to realize what this larger crystal might be capable of.

"Now I get it," Ebrem said.

* * *

Wind tickled Onin's beard. He was free but he was not. "We're going to have to fly around it!"

Jehregard ignored him, flying ever closer to the darkness and fog that shrouded the land Onin called his home. Only when he turned to look out to sea did he once again see nature as it should be. Darkness had consumed the great swamp. For as long as he had known this place, the Jaga had been dangerous and, in places, dark and twisted, but this was different. Now the darkness was pervasive, it leeched into the land and permeated everything. Once pristine shorelines now dripped with ooze that stained the sands.

The tierre within which Onin sat tilted backward as Jehregard put them into an upward spiral, sending them higher and higher, using the unnatural thermals emanating from the fetid land below. The hot air stank, and Onin wished they had flown around the Jaga, just as he had asked the dragon to do. Never had Jehregard been a particularly obedient dragon, but in this instance, it could be deadly. When they reached the altitude where the smell finally dissipated, Onin found himself short of breath. Cursing age and a stubborn dragon, Onin looked down. "By the gods!" he said without meaning to.

His stubborn dragon had brought them high over the Jaga, high enough to see the central feature, a place that had clearly been hidden for centuries if not thousands of years. It was an impossible place. Onin knew that it had always been; he remembered it from his flights over the Jaga and how it had made him feel. That feeling still existed, only now it was magnified many times over. No longer did marsh water and soil obstruct his view to the source of that feeling. From deep within the land rose and unholy spire. Inky black, yet filled with murky shadow that moved and writhed along its glossy surface, the mighty monolith dominated the land. Through some unknown force, it repelled the water in the mud and the black slog and held it at a distance.

Onin of the Old Guard had dug holes within the Jaga and seen them fill with water immediately. And here rose what looked like an entire city ringing the ancient crystal. It emerged from the mire, sprung from some nightmare eons old. He could feel the evil of it, the wrongness, the corruption. It nearly made him wretch. And yet there was beauty to it. The architecture, though dark and foreboding, contained amazing symmetry and precision. How could anyone construct such a place? Power was the answer, Onin knew. Lightning danced along the walls of the cavern from the crystalline megalith to the suspended water, soil, and roots of the Jaga. It was like seeing a cross-section of the greatest known wilderness on Godsland at full scale. Architecture and twisted swamp life were almost indistinguishable. The mighty cylindrical fortress surrounding the Noonspire seethed with life, as if the fortress breathed.

Continuing to take them closer, albeit going no lower, Jehregard kept ignoring Onin's input. "One of these days, I'm going to find a big enough hammer to knock some sense into this dragon."

If Jehregard heard him, he gave no indication. When finally they were directly above the giant crystal, Onin looked down into his worst nightmare. What he had thought was simply architecture was something entirely different. Feral dragons of all sizes lined the gaping chasm surrounding the Noonspire. The entire structure and complex writhed. Through the gaps, the true architecture was visible, and symmetry did exist, but much of the darkness came from its inhabitants.

Never had Onin seen so many dragons. Warnings he'd given those within the Heights rang in his mind. There was no joy in being right; he deeply wished he'd been wrong. No matter what he wished, the danger he'd warned of was before his eyes and even greater than he'd imagined. Lightning flashed along the top of the spire, and Onin looked into the uppermost facets. Within, he saw the dark forms of two women, a man, and a small child. Feeling his heart tighten, the old warrior knew remorse and despair. Somehow he could feel how desperately they wanted to be free from that prison--those who had been there since the last age of power and those who had just arrived.

Lightning leaped upward then, racing toward them, striking Jehregard's legs and underbelly. Finally the stubborn verdant dragon realized it was time to go. Turning on a wingtip and using their altitude to gain speed, the verdant dragon took advantage of the nimbleness so many of his kind lacked. Thankful that everything in his tierre was secured, or at least most everything, Onin did his best to dodge the rest. Wind tore at them as Jehregard continued to gain speed. The farther away from the spire they got, the lower they went. Onin watched the black swamp attentively. If there were enough feral dragons to fill that chasm, then there would be more.

Dense fog obscured his view of the Midlands, and when the Heights appeared, this sight was similarly obfuscated. It was not unusual or unheard of for the Heights to be surrounded in clouds, but this time those clouds were filled with smoke and fire.

* * *

Deep within Dragonhold, within the lap of a forgotten god, a dragon came as close to a smile as its physiology would allow. Mael was most pleased.

THE SEVENTH MAGIC

Chapter 1

Writing can influence the world long after we've departed.
--Enoch Giest, the First One

* * *

Deep within Dragonhold, signs of recent battle marred a once-beautiful cavern. The dragon sorcerer Mael rested on the lap of a god whose name even he did not know. The Herald of Istra had done him real harm, and part of him wanted to rest. While basking in the meager energy algamyte crystals gathered and soaking in amber sunlight tempted him, it would not move him toward his goal. The time had come for Mael to act. Not all things had gone as he'd planned, but in the end, everything went his way. No sorcerer controlled every outcome. Knowing how to use uncontrollable events to your fullest advantage was the trick.

Even the slightest movements brought echoes of pain. He had something extra special planned for the Herald, no matter how useful she'd proven. Few who had ever hurt him lived. Catrin Volker was historically insignificant and deserved no more of his thoughts. His plans overshadowed all other motives. Even that infernal damaged shield making his head and teeth ache could not keep Mael still.

One last time, he looked around the cavern. Fractured but not destroyed, the keystone lay broken. It was for the best, he knew, but after thousands of years, the ancient sorcerer found the strangeness unnerving. With a single reckless action, the Black Queen had damaged two of the great magics of the last age, thus weakening all the rest. He'd been a part of creating the keystones and other magics. All of them were inherently connected, even those developed in isolation. Ain's machine was built under the Black Spike surrounded by deep water, a work of genius tainted by madness. They had called it the Sixth Magic. No matter its power; it was flawed and unclean from the beginning. Mael's last accomplishment was supposed to elevate the magics above the stain of Ain's madness. It was not to be. With ferocity he banished the memory.

The change he'd wished for had come, invigorating but terrifying. Each of his favorite sleeping spots called to him. The herds he'd tended for so long, and even the fish he'd cultivated into fat, juicy morsels all enticed him to stay. Here nothing threatened; he was comfortable.

Outside, he would be exposed. This thought reinforced his plans. Vulnerability outside the hold meant not truly being safe within. In spite of his previous thought, he had to admit even novices such as Catrin Volker posed a threat. With education and experience, she might best them all. Without it, she might destroy the world. Though Mael would never reveal the extent and nature of the barrier between himself and Istra's energy to anyone, it existed. The thought of Catrin Volker in but a few years' time, constantly awash in energy, made even him shiver. Had not the need been great, she would already be dead. No matter how dangerous, she'd served him well. With nothing more than a nudge and a missed step, she'd made this moment far easier. He hadn't been looking forward to gnawing his way through the underwater stone grate blocking his escape. With his enemy's help, he was another step closer to achieving his goals.

Before slipping into the roiling waters at the waterfall's base, Mael ate a final meal of his favorites. The remaining fish did their best to escape and hide. Away from the fall, the subterranean river grew still; only a pair of draconian eyes remained visible. With what might have been a tearful blink, the sorcerer Mael closed his eyes and submerged.

* * *

Had Martik Tillerman ever seen the mighty wheel within Dragonhold from this angle, he would never have started the machine. Mael had always known this. He'd shown Trinda and the others just enough to get them to do as he needed. Von of the Elsics and the rest had been fools to think they could contain him in this prison, especially since no one stood guard. None had been a match for him, and neither was their construction. His former allies remained trapped within the Noonspire, which gave evidence of how close they had come to succeeding. Mael grinned at the memory. He had at least escaped that fate.

Here, too, stood a noonstone crystal of respectable size. Though no match for the Noonspire, it was more than adequate. Rushing water and a giant flywheel drove a massive stone cylinder and gears nearly as tall as the mountain. Though few had ever seen such mastery, Mael laughed. They had been such children. Within the gears moved algamyte crystals similar to those the stone god held. A pang of loss surprised him. He suppressed it.

This entire mechanism formed interplay, moving algamyte crystals through intersecting orbits around the noonstone core. Should those orbits ever falter . . .

Again, Mael laughed. Had this machine not existed, he would have struggled to absorb enough energy to escape cold stone. This deep within the land, energy was scarce even during the Istran Noon. In their attempts to make sure he never escaped, the fools had given him the exact thing he needed. They probably should have warned their descendants.

After relishing his victory a moment longer, the mighty dragon turned, sending his tail crashing into the stone cylinder. The first strike sent vibrations through the hold; the second, deeper in pitch. The third hit brought about all Catrin, Martik, and Trinda's fears. By the time they realized the danger, it was already too late.

They had also not known the mighty cylinder and flywheel served multiple purposes. While initially used to start the Fifth Magic moving, their secondary purpose was equally important. Once the crystals obtained orbital velocity, the reaction would drive the crystals faster. A spinning granite shaft, reinforced with metal, connected the orbital mechanism to the giant stone wheel. The massive weight regulated speed and prevented the reaction from escalating beyond control. With a final strike of his tail, Mael smashed the link into catastrophic failure. Even the mighty dragon's thick hide felt the sting of stone and metal fragments erupting from the mechanism.

Bone-chattering vibrations followed, and the huge stone cylinder bucked a single time before digging in. A mighty chasm grew with deafening resonance. It felt as if the Godfist had been torn in two. A rain of rock sent Mael looking for cover. More rock fell as he retreated, shielding his eyes with his tail. Blinding light and heat raged from the accelerating reaction, intensifying with every passing instant.

The fools.

Mael dived back into the river. Rocks rained into the water as well, but at least it dampened the reverberations. The damaged shield's constant buzzing grew in volume and pitch. Even beneath the water, his head felt as if it might explode. Perhaps a few more days to recuperate might not have been so bad, the ancient sorcerer thought.

An impossible note cut even into the water just before and everything stopped and went dark. For an instant Dragonhold fell silent.

* * *

Not for the first time, Miss Mariss asked herself what she was doing. All the changes in her world and life had come with far greater responsibility than a simple innkeeper, and rarely was there time to take stock--literally or figuratively. Many a sleepless night had been spent inventorying supplies, but now the need was less. Fewer people remained within the hold, and no one to suddenly demand two weeks' rations prepared on an instant's notice. Or to leave her behind, locked within a prison set to explode in the future with nothing more than "We'll be back" to go by. She chuckled at that. Catrin was her friend and coconspirator and, in many ways, her leader, but she was infuriating at times. Still, Miss Mariss would do it all again.

None of that eased the impending sense of doom. No matter how well concealed her worry, Martik must have sensed it. Getting all the rest worked up would do her no good at all.

"I have no idea what to do now," Martik said. "I probably should have gone to the Firstland. Clearly Catrin and Pelivor didn't need my help."

"Probably doesn't change now a hair. Not one hair."

Martik just grunted.

"Don't come around here talking to me about 'probably' this or 'should have' that," Miss Mariss continued. "What are you going to do now? That's what I want to know."

Again, Martik grunted his response.

"You sound just like my grandfather. He was a grumpy old codger," she said, and Martik laughed.

"What will you do?" he asked a moment later.

It took even longer for her to respond. "Maintain order. When they return, Dragonhold will be ready and operational. That's what I aim to do."

Deep, foreboding laughter traveled through the hold, sounding far closer and louder than it had in the past. No less terrified now, Miss Mariss reconsidered her words. Martik was dumbstruck. Then the thumping started, each jolt more frightening than the last. Dragonhold trembled and shook, and it sounded as if the hold were being torn to pieces. Stone rained around them, knocking Miss Mariss down. She came to her senses while being dragged from the kitchens.

"I can walk," she gasped, hoping he would stop dragging her. Already her shoulder and hips ached.

The keep settled but Martik pulled her up and toward the great hall. "Thank the gods. I thought we might lose you."

"I'll survive." After a few steps, she added, "I think."

Mael's laughter rang through the hold once again, and both moved with increased urgency. Others flooded into the halls as well, looking for guidance or information. No one said a word but moved to assist Miss Mariss and Martik toward the great hall. She hadn't even noticed his limp until after Bradley helped him.

Heat on her back warned of more trouble. Even the great hearth did not radiate with such intensity. Ever-increasing brightness urged them on. Others gathered near the main entrance, and it was there the group ran. Visible beyond the shattered gates, the plasma barrier brightened and flared. Now constant, relentless lightning left the smell of burned stone in the air. Cowering in pools of overlapping light, Miss Mariss and the others shielded their eyes and waited. With a suddenness that stole her breath, everything stopped. Darkness was immediate, the last echoes of thunder dwindling. The keep was still, and no one dared breathe. The barrier was gone. No one knew for how long, but already people struggled with the life-or-death decision: stay or go.

"Go!" Miss Mariss screamed. "Escape the hold!" For an instant, everyone turned and looked at her instead, effectively locking her in. "The evil one is loose. Move!"

No one asked any more. An orderly but high-speed evacuation made

Miss Mariss proud. Chase arrived during the commotion and directed those around him. She told herself they were prepared, that they had trained and lived through worse. She was wrong.

Dragonhold erupted like a volcano of light and smoke. The initial blast left no one standing. Ash and dust spouted from every orifice in the hold, blinding them even more effectively than the light or darkness had before.

"Crawl to the entrance," Chase commanded through his coughing fit. "Hold cloth over your mouth and eyes."

Unable to hold a cloth over her mouth and crawl at the same time, Miss Mariss held her breath and moved what she thought was toward the gates. Strong hands grabbed her. On the remains of the stair, the air was clear enough to see Chase, breathing hard. Already Martik searched for a safe way down. Miss Mariss just stood, coughed, and rubbed her eyes. More people trickled out, for which she was grateful, but a towering cloud filled with lightning reached into the sky like the finger of doom. Fire and ash rained on those below, slowly crushing all hope. Then Miss Mariss saw something that would haunt her dreams. Amid soot and ash, gleaming gold undulated. In the light of a hundred comets, lightning encased glistening scales, pulsing with rhythmic movement.

When Mael burst from the cloud, released from a prison that had held him for ages, he shone like a second sun. For the first time since he'd become a dragon, his scales bathed in comet light, shining gold and revealing his true nature. Here was a dragon like no other. Nothing stood in his way. In his triumph, Mael swooped over them, his deep baritone laughter echoing within the Pinook Valley.

They were free of the Fifth Magic but at what cost?

* * *

It had been a long time since Nat Dersinger had stood in the sacred chamber. The journeys alone took a toll on his body, but the visions he feared. Each took something from him until he'd begun to feel hollow.

"Shh." Neenya's sharp hiss brought him out of his ruminations and back to their journey. Concern softened the disapproval. Grabbing his hand, she guided him away from a paper hornet nest.

She felt guilty and when Nat was selfish about it, he allowed her partial blame. They had come on her instincts. He would just as soon have stayed within the village and lived the rest of his life without another vision. He'd done his part. Now he just wanted the world to leave him alone. Few people on Godsland could understand how he felt, Catrin Volker among them. When he was feeling cranky, he lumped a hefty portion of blame on her shoulders, even knowing she'd wanted no more to do with it than he had. Being pulled through the jungle reinforced the feeling they were but pawns in a game they scarcely understood.

Through the canopy the viewing spire appeared. They were close. The jungle did not allow the spire to be seen from many places. Even after all these years, Nat couldn't find the place on his own. This didn't worry him much since he really didn't want to go there.

While he dragged his feet in the jungle, he did not do the same once they had started climbing. The stair provided no cover. Wind and sand scoured the skin from their bones, and he climbed with all the speed he could muster. It mattered little. Such a long climb, like penance, required he put in the time.

Reaching the top brought little joy save respite from the wind. Rubbing his hands against the persistent stinging sand, Nat waited for the familiar feelings to engulf him, to remove him from this reality and show him a twisted future. Always his visions had proven true yet distorted or misunderstood. That was part of what made him hate the premonitions so much. What good were they if he couldn't even fully understand them until after the events they portended took place? It was either a curse or a completely useless gift.

Distant thunder interrupted his mental tirade. Neenya gasped, and Nat turned. In the early evening sky appeared a cloudlike column, glowing from within. Based on the direction, it came from the Godfist. None of the usual feelings accompanied this vision, though he did feel himself drawn and held, staring toward a bright light emerging from the cloud. Faster it came and brighter it grew. Nat's sense of time left him. A gleaming dragon bore down on the spire, holding his attention. Neenya screamed and Mael laughed; his name and identity suddenly known to Nat. Information flooded his mind, showing him the future through the dragon mage's eyes. Previous visions had never been so terrifying.

As Nat Dersinger collapsed into Neenya's arms, Mael breathed a fountain of fire.

Chapter 2

Those in pain are most vulnerable to the darkness.
--Thundegar Rheams

* * *

Fires dotted the landscape. Though the cloud forest was too wet to burn, the trees below had no such advantage. Smoke and ash choked those high above. A hazy pall hung over everything. The Heights were under siege, something he'd never imagined possible. Still, an army of men painted black with mud camped in the foothills. They did not scale the mountains or brave the cloud forest to batter themselves upon painted cliffs. Clever and devious, they used fire at the base of the mountain to fight those above.

Despite verdant dragons and their crews, fires continued to grow, setting fires being far easier than putting them out. Still, verdant dragons dumped huge mouthfuls of seawater on the fires, which made for an even greater spectacle. Smoke and embers posed a problem, but greater dangers ascended on the thermals. Balloons of woven reeds carried vials of flaming pitch and floated up in waves, threatening even well-secured areas. The cloud forest, too, slowly fell victim to pitch-fueled fires.

More recently, the balloons contained unpredictable explosive devices. Some detonated with spectacular effect long before reaching the Heights, others sprinkled the cloud forest with glowing embers, but some reached their intended destination. Not far from Onin, a flaming balloon and its cargo landed, smoldering. Nearby dragon grooms worked to calm their frightened charge. Onin moved. The weapon now sparkled and hissed, but he was too slow. Jehregard swung his giant head in front of Onin. Before he could shout a warning, Jehregard used his mouth to fling the weapon from the hold. It didn't get far before it exploded, and Jehregard shied away, crying out in shock and pain.

A flash of heat and the shock wave were all Onin felt, for which he was grateful. Jehregard nudged him and Onin patted the great oaf's head. He appeared uninjured, though darkness marred one side of his face. The dragon alongside them finally stopped prancing, but the whites of his eyes still showed. Onin empathized with his grooms. It would be a dangerous day. Frightened animals can be deadly--dragons even more so.

As he walked toward the inner chambers and the hall of the council, Onin knew it would be a dangerous day for them all. Most of the guard already waited within, and the expressions greeting Onin crossed a wide spectrum. Some afforded him the respect earned through a life of service, but many viewed him as an unwanted relic from a past best not discussed. He reminded them their society was not as honorable as they liked to believe. Here existed greed and pride like anywhere else, and that stung their egos.

This Onin found ironic. "I've been an ugly old man most of my life," he said in way of greeting. "I doubt I'll get any prettier."

Chuckles faded to silence. Some had the courage to glare at him. He did not care.

"Rise and greet your lord chancellor," Sensi said with an unenthusiastic flourish. His expression shared a joke with those in the room while his voice remained serious. Onin still chuckled when the lord chancellor entered. Their eyes met, getting them off to a bad start, and he shook his head. When would he learn?

"This is a military meeting," the lord chancellor began without preface. "Those not part of the current guard are dismissed."

Knowing his rights, Onin remained. An uncomfortable silence held.

"Must I have you removed?" the lord chancellor said.

"You may try," Onin said.

"Is that a threat?"

Onin shrugged. "Anyone who violates my rights will encounter resistance."

"So it is a threat!" the lord chancellor said, his voice higher in pitch.

"Only if you plan to violate my rights."

Cold silence followed. The lord chancellor seemed to be gauging his own standing in the room. Powerful he may be, but the guard was sworn to protect the people and their rights. If the lord chancellor issued orders contradicting that oath, loyalty would be tested. Revolutions had started over less, of which Onin was acutely aware.

"Fine. Stay," the lord chancellor said, red in the face. "But do not cross me."

Onin nodded, knowing he walked a fine line. Experience had made this abundantly clear, but his sense of self-preservation wasn't what it used to be. "We need to stop hiding up here and get into the fight." These words stirred the guard, as Onin had known they would. With a single statement, he'd shifted opinion in his favor. Much of what he knew he kept hidden, sure they would not believe. Someone else must also see what he'd seen.

"The dragons and the new guard are our most precious resources," the lord chancellor said. "We cannot risk them."

Pandering to the guard and insulting Onin in a single statement showed the lord chancellor did not come to this battle unarmed. Onin considered his options and decided to keep his mouth shut. Awkward and overlong, the silence unnerved all those present.

"The ferals are concentrated at the center of the Jaga," Jordic of Kern said. He was a good man, Onin knew. "If we stay along the coastline, we should be able to avoid the ferals and the weather."

The stormy season would be as much a danger as the ferals.

"I've sent word to the Midlands, apprising them of our needs," the lord chancellor said. "If they wish continued trade and prosperity, they will comply."

Onin shook his head, the disappointment in the room obvious. The lord chancellor did not deal with the Midlands on a regular basis. To him, they were but a faraway land to be called on when in need and good for little else. The guard knew otherwise, one and all, old and new. The Midlands fed the Heights in exchange for precious metal. In times of war, the cost of food increased. The cost of some metals increased dramatically and others decreased. Iron was more valuable than gold for the making of weapons, and platinum fed no starving children. In this instance, the people of the Heights were in no place to ask favors. Among their few applicable assets, dragons might be their only hope.

"I wish to fly a scouting mission along the coast," Jordic said. It was a risky move. "I can take iron and copper and trade for grain."

"Even a single dragon is too much to risk," the lord chancellor said.

"Then I'll go," Onin said. Jordic glared at him. Onin almost felt bad.

"That's a risk I can accept," the lord chancellor said with a smile. "Any chance you could scout the center of the swamp while you're at it?"

"Already have." This statement brought silence. "Not on purpose, mind you. My dragon just doesn't steer all that well." This brought laughter from almost the entire guard--even Jordic. "It would probably be best if you sent Jordic of Kern with me to make sure I don't get lost. After all, my little dragon can't carry much."

"Useless," the lord chancellor said. "Fine! Go."

Onin turned to Jordic and winked. The younger man shook his head and smiled.

* * *

Following a path Emmon widened before her, Nora Trell walked and grumbled. It wasn't the boy who raised her ire; he was doing quite nicely. Holding a branch aside, he let her pass and raced around to get back ahead of her and clear the trail as best he could. Why would anyone choose to live this far out in the wilderness? She knew the answer was partly to keep people like her from asking favors. It didn't make the walk pass any more quickly.

When at last they reached a well-made fence with rolling green pasture beyond, they had found Madra's farm. Emmon ducked down to climb through the fence.

"Wait," Nora said, backing up. The boy looked confused but did as he was told and took a step back. For another moment they stood in silence.

331

Then came a loud snort from not far away. Trees and brush blocked the view, but something was coming. Emmon back away farther when a bull charged, its sharp horns long enough to reach through the fence and kill.

"How'd you know?" Emmon asked.

"Never go into a field without checking, boy. And I've been here before. Madra's known for saying, 'Who needs guard dogs when you've got bulls?' Madra's known for saying a lot of things."

"Now what do we do?"

"Yell 'Madra' as loud as you can."

The boy shrugged and managed an impressive effort. Moments later, dressed in chaps and cursing, came Madra. "What kind of idiot just goes around shouting in the woods? Do they even consider that I might have a horse standing over me?"

"It's Nora Trell," Emmon shouted after a nod from Nora.

"Oh. That kind of idiot. I should've known."

"Could you corral your dog, please?" Nora asked.

Madra made a rude gesture but grabbed a metal bucket from nearby. A good shake and the bucket made a rattling sound. The bull turned immediately and ran toward the fence where Madra stood, looking as if it might impale her, but instead it slowed and gently grabbed the ear of corn Madra held. With her other hand, she yanked on a rope that pulled the gate shut, corralling the bull off from the rest of the field.

"How'd she do that?" Emmon asked, not moving toward the fence, his skin pale.

"If you always feed them in the corral and rarely close the gate, you don't even have to work at it. And now we can safely cross the field."

"Are you sure?"

"Well, you did make Madra angry with all that yelling you did."

The boy gave her a wry but unappreciative look.

"What do you want?" Madra asked when they reached the barn. She had her knees bent and a colt's hind leg resting between hers, and she finished crimping the nails of a loose shoe. Nora just waited for her to give them her attention. "That'll have to do until the farrier comes back. Turn him back out on the hill, Chelby."

After pulling up a wooden chair with a leather seat and wheels, Madra looked them over and chuckled. "You must want something, Nora Trell. Otherwise you wouldn't have gotten off your pretty ship and trudged through all those trees and bugs and snakes. You did tell the boy about the snakes, didn't you? Boiling things look just like branches, but one bite and it's all over."

The size of Emmon's eyes nearly made Nora laugh, but why spoil the joke? "I need your help."

Madra snorted.

"I need food."

"You walked all the way here for some food?"

"Rather a lot of it, actually."

Madra's eyes narrowed. "You have an army to feed?" The silence hung. "I had an army once, dreadful things. Noisy and they smell terrible. They're like children. Speaking of children, Chelby!"

"Yes?"

"Nora here needs rather a lot of food. You know what that means, don't you?"

"No."

"It means I'm going to need a drink. Fetch my metal flask, will you?" Chelby did as she asked.

"Don't ask about his brother while he's standing here," Madra said when her son walked away. "Those two have been fighting again. Idiots. At least I did not raise boring children."

"I'll drink to that," Nora said. "Twice."

Emmon pretended not to hear.

"So where exactly do you need all this food?"

"West of here," Nora replied.

When Chelby returned, Madra took a deep pull before handing the flask to Nora. "West of here, you say? Well, there's not a whole lot west of here, now is there? Won't be sending wagons that way, that's for certain. How much can the boy carry?"

With a laugh, Nora pushed Emmon toward the door. "Why don't you go play with the bull?"

"Watch the pointy bits," Madra said as he rushed out. After he was gone, she asked, "You think that one's going to make it? He's a little doe eyed, don't you think?"

"He'll live," Nora said. "Not sure how much of that living he'll do on my ship, but I doubt I'll have to throw him overboard."

"So you want supplies by barge, I assume?"

"That would be best. I'll need multiple shipments over time." Nora did not shrink under Madra's glare. There was a reason she'd trudged through the forsaken wilderness to seek out Madra. Others could get what she needed but not and maintain secrecy. Few people had the courage to ask Madra many questions.

"You never ask for anything easy."

"What fun would that be?"

* * *

Leaving the Heights involved far less activity for Onin and Jehregard than Jordic and his dragon, Tanaketh. Among the largest verdant dragons,

Tanaketh was young and proud. Most verdants were supported by a guard and ten grooms. Jordic commanded a full thirteen grooms to deal with the dragon. Tanaketh's size and disposition made him both a greater asset to the Heights and a greater threat to those in power.

Getting them away from the Heights was the first priority, and they left with as much haste as possible before anyone changed their minds. While he would have liked some time to confer with Jordic, there were ears everywhere. Even once they were in the air, shouting sensitive information between them would be unwise.

Jordic's request for a wing transfer still came as something of a surprise. The practice had been frowned upon in Onin's day and was all but outlawed. Still, Onin had done it himself in the past, and he believed the talent should be maintained even if not often used. In battle, such skills could mean the difference between life and death. Patting his dragon on the neck, he said, "All right, old boy, behave yourself for once." Jehregard grunted in response. "Just keep straight and level."

Tanaketh flew in close, overlapping Jehregard's wing with his own. Though crowded by the larger *Dragon's Wing*tip, Onin dared not insult the giant oaf. Jordic walked Tanaketh's wing with confidence but stepped down onto Jehregard's hesitantly. Tanaketh wheeled away almost immediately. The change in air pressure pulled Jehregard's wing upward, causing Jordic to stumble.

When Jordic wormed his way into the small tierre, Onin smiled. He liked this young man more and more. Wing walking took guts.

"Why'd you do it?" Jordic asked almost immediately.

"Do what?" Onin asked just to be contrary.

"You know. Offer to go with me--or in my stead--depending on how you look at it."

Onin shrugged. "Our lord chancellor may have some strong points, but dealing with the Midlands is not among them. Diplomacy in general seems to be a problem."

Jordic smiled at this statement. Such conversations were unusual. They had been trained to take orders not ask questions. Onin had always had difficulty with that. In Jordic, he saw himself.

"We can't just ask them to send us all their resources when they are surely also preparing for war," Jordic said.

Onin nodded. "That is the reason."

"Is it the only reason?"

"I don't like smoke."

That made Jordic laugh. "I think we need to reinforce relations with the Midlands," he said after a moment, his voice once again serious. "They have things we need, and we have things they need. When we work together, like during the Jaga War, we are all stronger."

"I agree," Onin said. "The problem is that the lord chancellor understands neither our strengths nor our weaknesses. He views the Midlands as a threat to his absolute power."

"But you know that's not the case," Jordic said with passion.

"I do. But I'm probably not the person you want to quote to get his chancellorship's approval."

"Not even Sensi can convince him of this," Jordic said.

Onin had his own issues with Sensi, but at least the man had tried.

"So how do you plan to fix this?" Jordic asked.

Again, Onin shrugged. "At least we're not breathing in smoke." Jehregard trumpeted his agreement.

"They say you're crazy."

Onin nodded.

"I say it's hard to tell the difference between bravery and lunacy," Jordic continued. "You're a good man, Onin of the Old Guard, even if you don't want to admit it."

"You, too, are a good man, Jordic of Kern. Though, I must admit, I've been trying to think of what I'll say to your parents if you don't survive the wing walk back."

Jordic took the hint and summoned Tanaketh. The big dragon moved in fast, once again crowding Onin with his wingtip, flaunting his size. Jehregard must not have taken kindly to this. As soon as Jordic grabbed Tanaketh's wing, Jehregard dived, leaving Jordic hanging.

"He was a brave kid," Onin ruminated out loud, Jordic's cursing in the background as he pulled himself up. "A little slow . . . but a good kid."

* * *

Allette Kilbor knew nothing. She shared memories with the most powerful person on the planet, along with her own life experience, but nothing prepared her for this. Slipping through the keystones had been risky once she'd cracked them but had seemed safer than remaining in the cavern with Mael. Knowing she had destroyed his way out, she doubted he would have shown her any mercy. Seeing the Jaga through the fractured keystone, she'd thought fate smiled upon her; in actuality it was about to stand on her neck.

She had walked into a trap not knowing the danger she faced. And Trinda Hollis, thinking to capitalize on Allette's good fortune, rushed headlong into the very same trap. The Black Queen almost felt bad about that. The child queen had been manipulated along with the rest, and Allette's animosity toward her waned. Even without the knowledge of Mael's influence, Allette and Trinda faced a common foe. Both were trapped and working together might be their only chance of escape.

Both had been separated from their physical forms, which rested not far away within an altar presumably constructed for that purpose. Energy flowed to those bodies, sustaining them in their suspended state. Within the Noonspire, Allette and Trinda were mere shades of their physical forms, their spirits reflecting how they perceived themselves. Wearing a perpetual frown, Trinda clearly felt guilty for what she had done.

Allette's spirit looked much as she had aboard her father's ship. It was there her identity had formed and that self she clung to. Their captors seemed not to care. Both Allette and Trinda had learned not to attract Aggrezjhon and Murden's attention. Almost indistinguishable, they often resembled a single spirit, but sometimes they disagreed and the two grew more recognizable and distinct. Allette could only imagine what ages in a prison such as this would do to a person. She tried not to wonder. Thinking too much might raise their ire.

When their captors did pay attention, it was to dominate them and crush their spirits. The ancient magic users were extremely skilled, and Allette hoped never to experience it again. Too many times, she knew, and she would cease to exist. This was their true goal. Once their spirits had been subdued, Aggrezjhon and Murden could inhabit Allette's and Trinda's physical forms and finally escape their prison. That would, of course, leave Allette's and Trinda's spirits in their place. That thought alone kept Allette fighting to maintain her identity.

Even when the sorcerer and sorceress ignored them, their thoughts radiated through the crystal. They had seen Mael through the keystone and blamed him for their imprisonment. He had betrayed them. He had helped build this forsaken prison and lured them into it. He would have gotten away with it if not for their quick thinking and teamwork. These thoughts ran in circles, reinforcing each other and creating a predictable pattern.

During a rare moment when Aggrezjhon and Murden were transfixed on something in the outside world, something flying high above them, Allette reached out to Trinda and held her hand. Even if only in spirit, the contact was reassuring. Though they had never been friends, Allette was glad Trinda was there. She understood much of what Allette had been through, and at least she wasn't alone. Whenever she came close to losing herself, she leaned on the child queen, and Trinda leaned on her. It was a small thing, but in circumstances such as these, small things could make all the difference.

Across their bond, Trinda sent a mere whisper of thought. "Together, we will survive."

It was enough for Allette to know she had at least one ally in this world.

* * *

Sleeping upon a broken spire, mostly submerged in cool water, Mael enjoyed his freedom. After so long, he'd forgotten the sheer variety of things to see, smell, eat, and drink. Never would anyone take it from him again. That thought niggled at him, preventing him from enjoying his newfound freedom. It wouldn't last. They were still out there. They did not want him to be free. Waiting for eons could have made him act in overenthusiastic haste, but he had learned true patience. Thus far, he'd used little more than gentle nudges to move the puzzle pieces into place.

A smile crept over him as he remembered when the humans rediscovered the keystones. After so much silence, their inane conversations had been the most interesting thing in the world. Of course the humans had no way to know how susceptible they were to persuasion when using the keystones. Just a little nudge in the right direction, here and there, was all it had taken. It was a good thing since power had been available in such minute quantities. He'd been agonizing over pulling every last bit of energy from the air beneath a mountain, and now he soaked in sun and comet light. The potent combination left him giddy.

Saltbark trees provided an excellent restorative. He'd eaten three trees whole before the effects kicked in. Now he floated above a natural energy flow. Though cracked, the keystones remained powerful. It was a reminder. Eventually Aggrezjhon and Murden would have access to enough power to escape their prison. He'd done his best to keep them occupied, but their interference had already cost him. If he'd not had secondary, tertiary, and quaternary plans, he might have remained trapped. Surely his former colleagues had plans of their own.

Now he had an advantage, just as he always had. He'd always been just a little bit better than the other two. That was why she had married Aggrezjhon and not him. No one had ever said it but he knew; he'd always known. No matter how close they had been at times, he could not forgive betrayal. Memories of their last days had played in his mind ever since. The others had remained true until the very last moment, when the Noonspire trap was sprung. Weaker and slower, Aggrezjhon and Murden had fallen almost instantly. There had been no time to save them. He'd barely saved himself. Had they not turned on him then, he would have broken free. Trapped and realizing they had lost everything, they became jealous and made certain he did not get away.

Without them to offset his power, he would have been unstoppable. He would have been . . . That thought had run through his mind so many times, it ignited familiar fury. His colleagues--his friends--had latched on to his very humanity and would not let go. Jealous, they had exacted one last vile act of revenge against him. Even then they had been lesser beings, their combined effort not enough to ensnare his spirit. Still, they took something from him. Fully assuming dragon form cost him his humanity. He'd long since forgotten what that meant or why it was important; he was, after all, a dragon.

Without another thought he flew toward the Noonspire.

Chapter 3

To put the well-being of another above your own is the highest form of existence.
--Mother Gwendolin, Cathuran monk

* * *

Kenward Trell paced the deck. "Wherever bolts aren't holding, I want the joints wound in rope and torqued. Is that clear?"

"Yes, sir," his crew responded.

With such a large ship and so many bolts to reinforce, the work took time.

Eventually Farsy emerged from belowdecks. "Good thinking, sir. The ropes are doing a better job than the bolts were."

Kenward wasn't certain he liked the word were. "You fixed the bolts, right?"

Grinning, Farsy held up a leather bucket filled with cracked and bent metal. Kenward swallowed. He'd intended the ropes to be a temporary fix to reinforce the bolts. Now he flew a ship held together with string. His mother and sister would be so proud.

"The thing is, sir, the ropes provide a sturdy connection but also allow for some flex. The bolts would just break again and damage the beams. This is better."

It had been Kenward's idea, but he still wasn't so sure. "Repair the bolts anyway," Kenward said. Farsy never stopped grinning, which unnerved the good captain as few things did. "How much rope do we have left?" he asked as an afterthought.

"Enough to build another ship," Farsy said. "I'll get you a damage and status report, sir."

Kenward nodded. Farsy frequently managed to stay one step ahead.

When the Jaga coast came into view, Kenward had second thoughts about everything. This place no longer followed the natural order. For miles, the waters along the coast were fouled. What should be white sands and blue water were covered in noxious brown and black ooze. A child of both land and sea, Kenward was repulsed. Beyond that waited a pervasive sense of doom. Allette was trapped within a pit of pure evil. He spared a thought for Trinda as well; whatever he did for Allette he also did for the child queen. It was enough.

Sinjin and Kendra guided their dragons back toward deck. They had been flying ahead but no longer. Scouting inland would have been pointless since the Jaga threatened from the very start.

"You are a good man, Kenward Trell," Kendra said, coming to his side. "You've a noble heart, and she knows how you feel. Dying is a poor way to prove your love." Reasoned, convincing words delivered in a measured tone.

Kenward listened without looking at her, his tears falling to the deck. "I can do nothing to save her. I am weak, helpless, and impotent at the very moment I so wish to be strong. I can fix so many things . . . but I can't fix this."

"There is no dishonor in turning back," Kendra said.

Kenward nodded and turned to his skeleton crew. Those he trusted most and who trusted him stood at the rails, watching madness approach. "If you plan to see the morning, get off the *Portly Dragon* now. The last favor I will ask of my dragon-riding friends is that they fly you all to safety."

Dragons stood ready to transport the crew, but no one stepped forward. Kenward swallowed hard. It was one thing to sacrifice himself, entirely another to take his crew and friends--his family--down with him. Kenward Trell faced an impossible decision, feeling as if he were being physically torn apart. Jessub Tillerman moved to his place between the thrust tubes. The rest returned to their work. They knew what they faced, and they stood ready to do their jobs. Proud of his crew, he would not dishonor their bravery.

"Sinjin, Kendra," Kenward said, "you may take your leave. The *Portly Dragon* sets sail for the Noonspire with all haste."

"You're just going to fly in there and save her?" Kendra asked.

"The Dragon will get me close, and I'll take the bumblebee in the rest of the way. If all goes well, we leave with one more than we came in with."

Kendra shook her head. The time for persuasion had passed. "Travel well, my friend. May we meet again on the other side."

Sinjin and Kendra said their final good-byes and climbed back atop their dragons. Running to the part of the deck marked stern, he looked out to see two verdant dragons coming fast, one significantly smaller than the other. Kenward felt relief on recognizing Jehregard. Still, the larger dragon approaching at such high speed intimidated. Roaring as it passed, the mighty beast left the air roiling, which shook the *Portly Dragon*, her rope-bound joints screaming in protest.

The two regal dragons took flight. Kenward watched the large verdant dragon as it executed a wide turn, hoping to be recognized as friends. Onin's voice could soon be heard bellowing the words, "Turn back! If you wish to live, turn back now!"

Kenward really didn't need another reminder, but he appreciated the effort nonetheless. He couldn't say he hadn't been warned.

"The heart of the Jaga is lousy with ferals," Onin said as Jehregard flew circles around the *Portly Dragon*. "And the Noonspire presents a far greater danger. We must join together if we're to defeat this darkness."

Kenward knew the wisdom of his words.

"Leave them!" came shouting from a tierre atop the second verdant dragon. The sheer size of the beast made it terrifying, its bellowed displeasure no more reassuring. "You've warned them; now let's move on. You've seen. There's no more time."

"Evil threatens us all," Onin said after a brief pause. "I must go. I must do my duty."

"Be well, Onin of the Old Guard!" Kenward yelled with a wave. "Jessub, take us into the darkness."

* * *

The problem with living remote enough to keep away the fools is that you occasionally have to come out. Even knowing the shortest route to a serviceable wagon and team of horses, Madra of Far Rossing was already tired.

"We're not hauling all this stuff ourselves, right?" Chelby asked while hooking up both horses.

"Of course not. But if you happen to be negotiating for large quantities of food, you might as well fill your own wagon on the cheap."

Chelby laughed. "Knowing you, they'll pay us to fill the wagon." He turned serious then. "Do you remember the last time we filled the wagon?"

"Oh, I remember."

"Do you think we could negotiate for some help unloading?" Chelby asked, looking hopeful.

"And by unloading, I assume you mean carrying it all the way to the root cellar?"

Chelby nodded.

"We'll see," Madra said as only a mother could.

"It's not like Medrin will be there to help!"

Both quieted as they turned along the wagon trail leading to Mackey's place.

"Oh, look! Madra has come. And she's brought her wagon!" Mackey shouted from the barn doorway. Young Jarn peeked from the hayloft.

"And two horses, pa!" Jarn added.

"You are a little predictable," Chelby said with a laugh.

"A wise boy is a quiet boy," Madra said. Chelby laughed again. He was most certainly her son.

"What do you need a wagonload of today?" Mackey asked, grinning.

"She probably needs it real bad, pa! Real bad."

"Not a wise boy to be seen," Chelby muttered.

Madra ignored them and walked into the barn. Mackey followed. Chelby stayed outside to play ball with Jarn.

"What have you got that's for sale?" Madra asked.

"All of it is for sale. Or at least enough to fill that wagon of yours."

"What if I needed to fill that wagon many times over?" Madra asked while thumbing through bushel baskets of dried corn. "Many many times. How much for all of it? Including what comes out of the smokehouse. All of it."

"Well . . . I . . . uh . . . What are you feeding? An army?"

"Yes. That's it. I'm building another army of the infirm to save us all. Do you want to join?"

Mackey just shook his head and scribbled a number on vellum with charcoal. Madra grabbed them and wrote some figures of her own. Mackey's eyes bulged. "I can't do that! It's just too much."

"With enough gold," Madra said, "you can do just about anything. I need you to do this for me."

"I'd have to buy from others in the surrounding areas," Mackey said. "And that would create a shortage, which would make the price . . . Yes. I'll do it. What do I tell people?"

Madra shrugged and added an additional stack of coins to her deposit. "Tell them whatever you want. Tell them your crop failed or your cows are extra hungry this year. I don't care. Just don't tell them it's for me."

Mackey nodded slowly, looking half lost in thought. Chelby came through the door, smiling.

"Oh, that reminds me," Madra said. "I'm going to need some things loaded onto my wagon."

It wasn't until they were loaded and halfway down the rutted drive before Chelby said, "I notice you left some room in the wagon. Are we going to see our young baker friend?"

"We are."

Dancing in his seat while he drove, Chelby urged the horses just a little faster.

"Don't beat me to death on the way there, boy."

The dilapidated condition of the trails out this way gave evidence to how seldom they were used. Even these made Madra feel exposed, and she was glad when the aroma of baking bread was all she could smell. Another small farm, this one far more accessible than the last, came into view. A mud brick farmhouse backed up to grain bins, chicken coops, pasture, and fields beyond. Two other wagons, each single horse, were tied beneath the trees. Madra waited.

"You're killing me," Chelby said. "Can you not smell that? How can you just sit here and wait patiently? We could go in and have a pastry while we wait for every other person with a nose gets theirs."

Madra grinned and waited. It didn't take all that long before the two local farmers headed back toward civilized lands, as they called them.

"They're gone," Chelby said. "Come on."

Waiting a little longer just for spite, Madra then urged the horses out of the trees and along the smoother trail leading up to Timit's place. Smoke poured from all three chimneys. She would always think of old man Timit, though his son had been the heart of the farm for many years. A small bell announced their entrance, the tinkling sound not quite sweet.

"Greetings, Miss Madra!"

"Greetings to you, Timit son of Timit."

"I see you've brought your wagon," Timit said while peering out the window. Chelby chuckled.

"Feed my boy before he starves," Madra said.

"I want one of those and two of those," Chelby said before Timit could respond. The baker put the pastries on a wooden paddle and slid them into the closest brick oven.

"How is business?" Madra asked.

"Slow," Timit said. "Rumors of war in the east. Talk of dragons attacking villages. People don't want to leave their homes."

"Well, that's good," Madra said, and Timit looked confused. "I'm going to need everything you can sell me."

"What? Are you building another army?"

"I've decided to remarry," Madra said. "I can't have all my suitors starving while they wait their turn."

Timit was flummoxed.

"Here's what I need," Madra said, handing him a strip of parchment.

Timit's eyes went even wider. "I can't do that. I'd have to turn away all my other customers."

"Are your other customers here?" Madra asked, the coins in her hand making a clinking sound. "Did your other customers pull you from your momma and smack your bottom?"

"But--"

"Do you want me to put you back where I found you?"

"No, ma'am," Timit said. Madra put coins in the young man's hand. "Do you want anything else?" he asked Chelby, who nodded and pointed, his mouth still full.

"About my wagon," Madra said.

* * *

The *Portly Dragon* flew without joy. Beneath them passed a landscape reeking of death and wrongness. Soon the entire Jaga would be a rotting quagmire. Along the edges of the corruption, where lush greenery could still be seen, gathered the animals. Trees bent low, laden with creatures never meant to live so close together. The lack of feral dragons brought no comfort. Kenward suspected a multitude gathered around the heart of this madness. There, too, he would find the most complex and fascinating creature he'd ever known.

Allette Kilbor was the one thing Kenward Trell wanted most but could not have. He knew unrequited love. He'd known the sting of rejection, but this was different. She felt the same for him. He was certain. He'd seen it in her eyes. Someone or something else had stood in their way and kept them apart. It infuriated him and gnawed at his soul. When the Noonspire appeared on the horizon, Kenward quailed. Nothing he'd imagined prepared him for the scale of what had been buried under the swamp. The Noonspire sank beneath ground level to dizzying depths. The land around it had been thrust away, a wall of plasma and fire holding the soil, rock, water, and everything else out.

Rock formations with symmetry and order formed an intricate architecture protruding through the plasma barrier. A ripple passed through the column, making it breathe. Feral dragons clinging to the structure moved like a single organism. In the spire's light, they basked.

How could she survive here amid such evil? Kenward asked himself. He'd come here to save her from whatever influence this place had, but it was not simply the place. He could feel it now. There would be no negotiations; they were already at war. "Stoke the fires!" he shouted. "Full thrust!"

The massive Noonspire facets reached out to them, pulling them closer. Within the crystal, shadowy occupants could be seen. Madness, hatred, and impatience waited there. Kenward saw fear and worry and guilt but also love. Which feelings came from which figures, Kenward could not know for certain, but he could guess.

Go away! a voice boomed in Kenward's mind, knocking him from his feet. Farsy ran toward him, but Kenward could not hear his friend's words.

Come closer, another said in a calm but commanding voice.

Farsy pulled Kenward back to his feet, his mouth moving but no intelligible words coming out.

Go, now, Kenward! Or surely you will lose me.

This thought came with a vision of Allette. He smelled her hair and felt her gentle touch. He had to go. They had to get away that instant. Her voice pounding within his mind made everything clear. Holding up two fingers, he called for thrust. The *Portly Dragon* lumbered through turbulence, lightning clawing the air beneath them. Pumping his fist, Kenward called for more fuel on the fire. Farsy and Bryn appeared worried. Jessub Tillerman looked panic stricken. The young man held out his hands to his sides to indicate his efforts weren't working. Kenward already knew. Too slowly did they drift, some force pulling them back despite the thrust.

Kenward held on as the *Portly Dragon* listed heavily, "Prep the howler and bumblebee!"

"Fire!" Farsy yelled.

"Abandon ship!" Kenward shouted. "The *Portly Dragon* is going in!"

Lightning reach the ship then crackled along the lowest corner, the ropes now smoking. Orange flames gushed from the boiler house, and steam rushed out with a deafening squeal. Coconuts rolled into the heat. Kenward had almost forgotten about them amid the chaos but now could think of little else. Running toward the smoldering coconut that was filled with something an ancient book claimed more powerful than the fire snakes Brothers Gustad and Milo had rediscovered, Kenward hoped to buy his crew time.

Before he reached it, sparks flew from the mud-sealed opening. Spinning and leaping, it rolled from the deck and fell, moments later exploding with a thunderous boom. Sparks and smoke blasted the ship from below.

Like a single, massive creature, feral dragons attacked.

"Go now!" Kenward cried.

The deck's pitch increased, making the bumblebee difficult to reach. Farsy had orders to meet him there. Bryn and Jessub would take the howler. Though he'd never flown the experimental aircraft, Kenward was confident Jessub would figure it out. He was a thrustmaster, the most important skill required. Gwen had taken to it almost instinctively.

No one had expected to come out of this alive, and the odds hadn't improved. Feral dragons filled the skies around them but did not attack. Dangerously close to the megalithic crystal, the *Portly Dragon* was free of ferals. As if protecting against something, they blotted out the night sky, making escape on the smaller aircraft unlikely.

When Kenward reached the bumblebee, Farsy was already there. Jessub crossed the pitching deck between him and the howler. Bryn still shoveled coal onto the fires.

"Bryn!" Kenward shouted. The young man ignored him. "Bryn!" he screamed, knowing it would soon be too late.

Finally Bryn acknowledged him, tossed down his shovel, and ran toward the howler. Jessub strapped himself in. Kenward watched with detached horror. This couldn't be happening. Surely he would wake soon and it would all be over. No such luck.

With jarring impact, the *Portly Dragon* struck the Noonspire. Squealing in protest, the ship ponderously spun, the gaping chasm ready to consume them. Lightning assaulted the rigging, and Kenward knew time had run out. Farsy patted him on the shoulder, signaling he was ready, and Kenward slammed the pressure release forward. Nothing happened. A brief inspection revealed part of the controls had come loose. Blasted connecting rods!

The howler preparing to take off made him turn his head. Bryn wasn't on board, and the howler was still secured. Sprawled on the deck, Bryn moved but not fast enough. With the deck pitched, Jessub had been unable to release the straps.

"Hurry, Bryn!" Jessub shouted. "Hurry!"

Time ran out. Jamming the connecting rod back onto the shaft, Kenward hoped it would hold. Gradually he opened the air tank. After three forceful thumps, the bumblebee came up to song and launched across the deck at an upward angle. Looking left one last time before leaving the deck, he saw Bryn release the howler. It immediately got away from him and slid into the abyss. Staring up from the doomed *Portly Dragon*, Bryn saluted.

Kenward Trell's heart broke.

* * *

Onin of the Old Guard was a practical man, not prone to flights of fancy. Emotional acts were a good way to end up dead. Still, he couldn't help but wonder his friends' fates. He'd warned the fools to leave, and they ignored him. All the worry was their fault, and he cursed them for it.

Soon he, too, was driven to reckless action. Flying Jehregard closer, Onin stepped out onto the wing, an especially daring move considering what he'd done to Jordic the last time. Tanaketh behaved and let Onin pull himself up. Events such as this emphasized how different Jehregard was. Full-sized verdant dragons possessed undeniable majesty, but Jehregard had proven far more versatile and self-sufficient than his lumbering brethren.

It wasn't the length of the walk that made Onin think these beasts had grown too large, though it didn't help matters. The wind threatened to throw him into open air, and he had no desire to test Tanaketh's loyalty. Jehregard stayed nearby.

Onin had long thought the verdants would be bred into extinction. For many lifetimes, dragons had been mated to produce ever larger offspring, but there was a practical limit. The current generation was dangerously close by his estimation. He would have continued his mental rant but was glad, instead, to enter Jordic's tierre.

The younger man grinned at him. "Not as much fun as you'd think, is it?"

Onin grunted in response.

"You must want something," Jordic said, his eyes twinkling with mirth. "Surely you didn't come over here just to grunt at me."

Again, Onin grunted.

"Okay. Maybe you did."

"We need to talk," Onin finally said.

Jordic had the good sense to keep his mouth shut.

Chapter 4

The world moves forward. If you resist change, you fall behind.
--Brother Vaughn, Cathuran monk

* * *

Chaos reigned, ground and sky looking much alike. Disoriented, Kenward struggled to control the bumblebee. Even with the improvements made to the design, this aircraft's primary flaw was the ability to fly for only a short time. He wasn't even certain how long. It would become apparent soon enough.

Jessub passed them on the howler, looking absolutely terrified. His speed remarkable, even ferals left him room to pass. Kenward and Bryn approached much more slowly, and the mystical portal through which Jessub had gone just as suddenly closed. Between them and freedom flew a wall of teeth and claws.

In that moment, though, the *Portly Dragon* broke over the Noonspire. Sharp cracks reverberated and echoed. A small blast ignited the explosives-filled coconuts and started a chain reaction. The resulting blast sent sparks, steam, and chunks of metal into the air, overwhelming the bumblebee and the dragons above. Kenward was grateful for the straps holding him in. Farsy screamed.

Struggling with the controls, Kenward righted the aircraft just as they burst from the smoke and ash. Blackened with soot, coughing and smoking, they escaped the Jaga's heart. Feral dragons would not be so easily evaded; three barred their path. The howler's call was all the warning they got before Jessub burst through the dragons, sending them in all directions. It wouldn't be enough, but Kenward appreciated the effort. Jessub Tillerman was an adventurer, indeed. Tales would be told and songs sung, provided someone survived.

Breaking free, Kenward knew the victory would be short lived. The bumblebee lacked the howler's speed. The longer they flew, the less frequently the thumps came. Soon he might regret being strapped in. Without thrust to provide lift, it would fly like a rock.

"We're going to have to bail out!" Kenward shouted to Farsy, who already loosened his straps. Kenward might have said more, but a shimmering orb racing toward them blinded him with its brilliance. What had at first seemed a deadly weapon ready to incinerate them was actually a regent dragon bearing two riders. Catrin rode at the front, Koe held before her, both shining like fire. That same power washed over Pelivor and Kyrien, as if they were made of lightning.

Focused on the ferals, Catrin paid them no mind, but Pelivor met

Kenward's eyes. The skilled flightmaster then did something Kenward would never quite understand. Somehow, across the distance between them, Pelivor forced air back into the bumblebee's holding tanks, and the thumping grew faster than ever. With Farsy holding on, Kenward aimed for the coast. A quick getaway and a safe landing were the best he could hope for. For those lost or still in the fight, he shed a tear.

Even with the extra compressed air Pelivor provided, the bumblebee would not get them all the way to the coast. Knowing they would likely nose-dive into the vile, twisted marsh if he let the compressed air completely run out, Kenward searched for a place to land. Nothing looked safe. They could either touch down in black water crawling with snakes and other predators or make an abrupt stop amid the trees and vines.

They hadn't seen or heard from Jessub, which worried Kenward as much as anything--that and Bryn's fate. Few things had ever pained him as much as leaving the young man behind. Bryn's death would forever be on Kenward's conscience, and that made it heavy, indeed. No amount of tears would change reality, and Kenward concentrated on saving Farsy. That, at least, he might actually achieve.

A trumpeting bellow announced company. Kenward sighed in relief on seeing Onin and Jehregard approaching with Jordic and Tanaketh not far behind. The larger dragon's size alone would ward off all but the most determined foes, but they were still a ways off. He hoped the compressed air would last. Changing tactics, he climbed ever higher, aiming for the dragon. The vital thumping inexorably slowed.

Eventually, the small craft would go no higher. Kenward used the altitude to gain speed and raced toward Onin and Jehregard.

Onin yelled. "We'll circle back and get underneath you."

While Kenward would have complied, fate removed the choice from his hands when the bumblebee quite suddenly went silent. Their trajectory would have taken them well over Onin's head, but the sudden loss of thrust caused them to drop.

Onin screamed as the bumblebee nosed into his flight path. Jehregard's last-second evasive maneuver kept the bumblebee from crashing into the front of the tierre. Instead, the out-of-control projectile wedged itself into the tierre's side, the bumblebee almost touching Onin's backside. He looked back and shook his head. "You people really do know how to make an entrance. Whoa!" he shouted as soon as he turned to watch where they were going.

Kenward turned as well. The skies above the Noonspire blazed with reflected light and sheets of what might be heat lightning. The air writhed with dragons, most dark and shadowy, but one shone like the brightest comet, glittering light surrounding him. Those aboard Kyrien cast out chains of fire, but the feral dragons came in overwhelming numbers. Seeing just how many dragons followed them, Kenward's courage fled.

Though far from secure where he was, Kenward remained frozen in place, unable to climb into the damaged tierre in mid flight. Jehregard's sudden movements threatened to dislodge the aircraft and send it tumbling to the swamp below. As the bumblebee came loose, Onin grabbed the aircraft with a gnarled hand, grunting from the effort.

The rest of the ride would haunt Kenward's nightmares. Feral dragons flew in close, but did not attack; instead they herded Jehregard back toward the Noonspire. Onin did what he could to fight it, but too many ferals surrounded them. Tanaketh cried out but was soon cut off from Jehregard. Once Catrin saw them driven back in that direction, her attacks intensified in pitch and scale; over and over she struck down feral dragons, only to have more take their place. Nearly overwhelmed, Pelivor guarded her back, wielding light like a whip.

In near silence, ferals harrying them, Jehregard glided back to the Noonspire. Kenward didn't know what they wanted with him, Farsy, Onin, and Jehregard, but his imagination created horrific visions of mad sorcerers trapping them all within the towering crystal prison. More likely, they were meant as a distraction or a price to be paid.

When Kyrien dived straight toward the spire, feral dragons blocking his path, Catrin stole Kenward's breath. Lighting up from within, she released the straps and dived from atop Kyrien.

The dragon pulled up, Pelivor still fighting from his back, but then a blinding flash emanated from the spire. The blast wave nearly knocked the bumblebee loose. Onin's grip kept them in place, but his white knuckles made no promises.

* * *

Seeing Jessub and the howler fall from the *Portly Dragon* put Bryn's heart in his throat. He'd sacrificed his life to see the young man saved, and it looked as if he'd failed. Screaming and the howl of thrust proved him wrong a moment later as Jessub sailed past, moving up and out of the chasm. Part of him wanted Jessub to come back for him, but it would do no good. The *Portly Dragon* imploded upon the Noonspire. Pulling himself along the coarse deck, trying to get as far from the boiler house as possible, Bryn feared he simply delayed the inevitable. It might be far less painful and agonizing to jump into the gap and fall to his death, but life had a tenacious grip, and he wasn't ready to give up.

When the boiler house blew, he feared he'd made a mistake. Getting behind a collapsing wind sock, Bryn avoided the fiery blast. The next detonation split the ship into pieces and rattled the world. His ears ringing and his eyes watering, Bryn fell. His descent ended as abruptly as it began.

When his senses returned, he found himself resting on a mostly deflated wind sock stretched between two wooden planks. One end rested on the architecture of the outer column; the other end hissed and popped from contact with the Noonspire itself. Even with his thoughts clouded, Bryn knew his situation was deadly.

Whispers emerged, growing louder and more insistent.

Come closer.

Yes . . . closer.

Bryn closed his eyes, hoping they would go away. They did not. He could feel the energy emanating from the crystal and reaching out toward him. It pulled at his spirit, tugging his soul.

"A mere morsel, this one," the first voice said. It was impossible for Bryn to tell male from female. He didn't suppose it mattered.

"A tasty morsel."

Bryn didn't care for being described as tasty. His head pounded as the energy continued to assault him, steadily leeching the life from him. He hadn't realized how much closer he'd gotten to the Noonspire, and Bryn pulled himself away with great effort.

"A will, this one has."

"A tasty will."

"I am not tasty!" Bryn shouted, holding his hands over his ears. The voices laughed loudly in his mind, proving he was helpless before them and could do nothing to keep them out. He should just give up and let them take control. It would be so much easier. No more decisions. No more heartbreak. His reflection gleamed in the Noonspire, and Bryn realized he'd moved closer without intending to. Pushing himself backward, he tried to get away, but the energy clung more tightly now, as if tiny hooks dug more and more deeply into his very spirit.

"The struggle makes it more painful."

"The struggle makes it tastier!"

Screaming, Bryn pulled himself forcefully away. It felt as if his body moved but his soul remained, snared by Aggrezjhon and Murden, their names seared into his memory. His insignificance amusing, they dominated him. Claimed by numbness, Bryn was lost.

A terrible roar split the air. He barely noticed. Wind buffeted him, almost throwing him from the canvas. The ends contacting the Noonspire glowed orange, and flames licked the edges. Soon Bryn's perch would fail, and he likely wouldn't know the difference. The fight seemed far away now. It was none of his concern. He'd done his part and made a noble sacrifice. He was satisfied and could now let go.

Sensation returned in an overwhelming rush. Aggrezjhon and Murden released their draining grip as a new threat arrived. Not quite understanding, Bryn saw Catrin Volker descending, glowing like a goddess, her translucent hair flowing around her and taking on the color of the surrounding light. She did not come to him, as he expected. Instead, she slammed into the Noonspire with percussive force. Blinding light and another blast dulled his senses, and it barely registered when Kyrien reached in and grabbed him with mighty claws.

Atop Kyrien's back, Pelivor fought as if the world's fate rested on his shoulders. As Bryn's senses returned, he supposed it did.

From within the crystal came a command so forceful, every living creature not already trapped complied.

"Go!"

* * *

In the moment the howler slipped from the *Portly Dragon's* deck, Jessub Tillerman realized the value of a quiet life on the farm, of playing in the fields and racing back to a simple cabin when the rains came. Always when he'd had it, he had wanted more. Seldom had he simply enjoyed what he had. Now all of it was lost. The adventure he'd always craved was now likely to end his life. Suddenly it didn't seem worth it. The thoughts flashed across his consciousness even as his limbs moved. Though trembling from fear and adrenaline, he gripped the controls and exerted his will, thrust tubes howling. After tumbling, the aircraft pointed straight into a sky filled with dragons. Jessub could no longer see how close the ground was, but much of the Noonspire towered over him.

Gradually the howler slowed before changing direction, the force of his will finding purchase. Bryn cried out from where he clung to remains of the *Portly Dragon*. If Jessub could have, he would have landed and brought Bryn aboard, but it was impossible. The best he might be able to do is distract the ferals and buy him some time. It didn't feel like it would be enough, but it was better than doing nothing. To do it, though, he needed speed. Still climbing, he presented an easy, slow-moving target. When dragons closed in, there was no more time to consider.

He turned the howler on its wingtip and dived toward wild madness and flames reaching out from the Dragon's remains. Without warning, explosions rocked the stonework surrounding the giant crystal. Sparks and debris pelted, stinging and burning as the howler picked up speed and raced by. When next he climbed, he did so with speed no dragon could match and a report that made the air tremble. Ferals blocked his escape, gathering tightly together before him. Below there was not enough room to maneuver, and he might soon find himself overwhelmed. He just needed a bit of clear sky to make a good run at them.

Claws, teeth, scales, and wings were all he could see, and he issued his best battle cry. Applying all his strength, he sent the howler hurtling toward the ferals with even greater speed. Perhaps the dragons had thought he would flinch, but instead they cleared a path for him at the last instant. Jessub Tillerman hooted and hollered after breaking free, allowing himself an instant of jubilation before executing a wide turn. Sweat soaked his clothes, and his goggles pressed back into the flesh around his eyes, his cheeks rippling from the wind resistance.

His escape had taught him something important: ferals have a healthy sense of self-preservation. Either they were in control or whoever controlled them did not do so with absolute authority. Jessub had seen what that looked like. His survival would depend on proving this hypothesis. It was foolish and risky and exactly what Kenward Trell would do. The last part worried him most.

With his turn complete, the chaos around the Noonspire was fully apparent. What he saw couldn't be real, yet it did not dissolve away like the remnants of dreams. It persisted. Second and third thoughts would not be put aside as he approached. Part of his plan depended on the ferals seeing him coming and moving out of his way. The skies ahead were filled with dragons, but all were now facing the other direction, intent on something he could not see.

Now his battle cry sounded weak and shrill. The dragons ahead did not react, as if completely oblivious to his existence. In the next instant, the skies were afire. Lightning spiderwebbed, reaching out and promising a deadly embrace. The air stank of fear and smoke.

Through gaps in the ferals, Jessub saw beings of light astride a pulsating dragon. Those gaps just as suddenly closed, and though Jessub pulled up, it was too late. Ferals did not hear him until the last instant, and those that fled obstructed his flight path. His battle cry now a scream, Jessub flew into the malevolence. Dodging from side to side as best he could, Jessub could not avoid them all. In an instant, the howler's wingtip struck a feral in the abdomen, sending him spinning out of control. Not knowing if his aircraft was whole and near to passing out from the forces applied, Jessub did his best to maintain control. If he lost consciousness, he lost everything. Then came an undeniable command, one so powerful, it pulled him from the edge and urged him away. With the fog cleared from his mind, he flew.

* * *

Sinjin Volker had never felt so useless. He'd had almost no impact on events at the Noonspire. He and Kendra hadn't even gotten close to the giant crystal, and he'd had no chance at all of saving his mother. He saw what she did. It had been her choice. It was very like his mother to sacrifice herself to save the people who would miss her most. He cursed her at that moment but only because it hurt. Life had done everything it could to come between them, and he might never see her again. The Noonspire had imprisoned the powerful for thousands of years, and he had no reason to believe his mother would be any different.

Beside him, Kendra brooded. She hadn't said a word in hours. It was her way, and he gave her the time and space to think. When she needed him, she'd tell him; of that he had no doubt. Valterius flew without input. As long as they moved away from the Jaga and toward open sea, Sinjin would not protest. He'd lost sight of the others and hoped to be reunited with them soon. They needed a plan, some way to save his mother. He spared a thought for Allette and Trinda, but it was his mother who really mattered. It was a selfish thought, but he did not feel guilty for having it.

Not far from the shoreline, they saw a familiar silhouette. Kyrien flew to greet them, Pelivor on his back and something, or rather someone, clutched in his claws.

"I didn't know," Pelivor said when they got closer. "That wasn't at all what we had planned."

"It's her way," Sinjin said. Those simple words seemed to impale Pelivor. He said nothing in response. "Do not blame yourself. It's not what she wants. It's not what I want."

"It hurts." Pelivor had tears in his eyes.

"I know," Sinjin said. "I know.

A long silence hung in the air.

"Who?" Kendra asked, pointing at Kyrien's claws.

"Bryn," Pelivor said. The fact that he said no more spoke volumes.

"Have you seen anyone else?"

"They went east," Pelivor said.

"Thank you," Sinjin said. "We'll go meet up with them."

Kyrien interrupted him then, roaring at Valterius and Gerhonda. Both roared back in unison. Before Sinjin could say another word, Valterius turned back toward the Firstland. Gerhonda did the same, and little could be heard over his wife's cursing. The only thing soothing Sinjin's guilt over leaving the others behind was that Kyrien flew in the direction Pelivor said they had gone. All he could do was hope they survived.

* * *

Along a rocky shoreline east of the Midlands plateau, Jehregard landed. Jordic circled above, his dragon, Tanaketh, unable to land in such a place. For Onin, this confirmed his feelings about the verdants, and his thoughts wandered. What kind of dragon could not land anywhere it liked? He cursed fools who thought of nothing but the gold lining their coffers. Kenward cleared his throat, and Onin remembered his guests. Destroying a man's tierre while he's trying to help you is not the best way to engender good relations. Onin released his grip on the bumblebee. Loud creaking preceded several thuds. Onin assumed his passengers had disembarked.

Jehregard seemed to find this all quite amusing. He'd caught Kenward and Farsy on his wing and stared at Onin as if to rub in spoiling the old man's fun.

"I guess you'd better get up here and help me fix this," Onin said.

Kenward stood on the sands, rubbing his hind side. "Maybe I should walk from here."

"Wouldn't recommend it. Mids don't like climbers."

"If we help you fix it to the best of our abilities, will you leave us here with no hard feelings?" Kenward asked.

After thinking awhile, Onin nodded.

"Should we look for stalk weed and rope weed before climbing back up?"

"That's the smartest thing I've heard you say," Onin said, and he tossed down a long knife.

Moments later, Kenward perked up. The howler was coming, growing louder over time. Soon Jessub Tillerman appeared along the horizon. It didn't take him long to spot them. Not far from shore, he slowed, apparently trying to find shallow water to land in. A moment later, Kenward ran for the waves. He wasn't sure if Jessub had misjudged his speed or was hit by a downdraft, but the result was an unpleasant spectacle. The howler struck the water and dug in, slowing dramatically. The tail pitched forward, snapping the howler in half. Thrown clear, Jessub continued for a short distance before hitting the water face first.

Waves crashed over his stunned form, and Kenward pulled him to shore. After a coughing fit, Jessub said, "I'm so sorry."

"Don't worry about it, kid. You did your best."

"Bryn," Jessub said, looking haunted.

"I know. I know. Sometimes all you can do is live harder to honor those who never got the chance."

Another trumpeting call split the air, and Kyrien appeared, Pelivor on his back. Coming in fast, he sent sand into the air as he flapped his wings hard. Rather than landing, he hovered mere inches above the sand and released his claws. Bryn's still form rolled out. Flying backward a short distance, Kyrien landed. Jehregard and Tanaketh roared in greeting.

Kenward left Jessub's side to check on Bryn. Though his clothes were burned and torn and his skin was soot covered, he did at least appear to be moving. "Say nothing," he said when Kenward reached his side. "I've got the goddess of all headaches."

They were the sweetest words Kenward had ever heard.

Jessub should have stayed where he was but could not. "I'm so sorry," he whispered to Bryn.

"You did exactly what you should have done. Otherwise Kyrien would've had to save us both."

Kenward wasn't certain how much Kyrien understood, but he roared in response. Given Kenward's recent experiences with dragons, he had to rethink his preconceptions. It seemed certain they would soon prove him wrong once again. They were good at that.

"We need to get back," Jordic called from above.

"Go!" Onin said. It wasn't the first time.

"You started this," Jordic said. "If you're not there when I return, the council won't hear my report. Don't let them destroy our homeland because you gave them an out."

Onin finally nodded. "I'll take you all where you want to go after we've met with the Midlands and reported back to the council. It will take time. I am sorry."

The tierre was far from repaired, but Onin had cleared most of the pointy bits. Kenward and Farsy helped Bryn and Jessub aboard before climbing up themselves. Soon they flew alongside Tanaketh. Kyrien joined them in the air, and Pelivor waved farewell. The last of the regent dragons, though, had other plans. Flying up next to Jehregard, Kyrien synchronized their flight. A distant look came over his eyes, and Kenward wondered at the ways of dragons. Moments later, he trumpeted and winged away.

Jehregard turned out to sea, far off course from heading to the Midlands. Tanaketh roared in displeasure. Kyrien went to him next. The massive verdant dragon dwarfed Kyrien, yet he calmed under the regent dragon's influence. When the two parted, the verdant dragon continued toward the Midlands. With Pelivor on his back, Kyrien turned and headed, presumably, wherever it was he wanted to go. Kenward wished his old friend luck.

Chapter 5

The secret to hope is that it can exist without reason.
--Mother Gwendolin, Cathuran monk

* * *

Seeing Windhold was bittersweet. While Sinjin longed to live a peaceful life with his family and people, he could do nothing but worry about his mother. Kyrien had sent him home. The thought nagged at him. Kendra remained silent, as she had for much of the journey. Even the dragons were subdued. Upon their entrance, Windhold fell silent. "Things have not gone well," Sinjin said, not wanting to keep the people in suspense. "Keep doing what you've been doing, and you will help us all greatly. I thank you."

No one pressed for more information, though questions waited in Durin's eyes. His friend moved a bit more fluidly than when he'd left, and that gave him some small measure of peace. When the dragons had been cared for, Kendra joined Sinjin and Durin. Strom marched across the wind channel, a pillar of strength amid a perpetual storm. His hair flew out sideways and his clothes flapped in the wind, but his gait was unerring. Osbourne and Brother Vaughn followed, looking concerned.

"I need a word with you," Strom said by way of greeting.

Sinjin just nodded and waited.

"Is it true?" he asked softly. "Is your mother trapped within the Noonspire?"

Sadly Sinjin nodded again.

Strom couldn't control his reaction, though he did somehow refrain from cursing. "I saw it all. I mean . . . I dreamed it all. Give that dragon a hand, and he'll take your arm."

One's dreams were very personal things, much like one's thoughts. Having either encroached on seemed a deep violation of privacy. Sinjin could understand why Strom was so unnerved. Kyrien had invaded his unconscious thoughts in addition to his conscious thoughts. What frightened Sinjin most was that other dragons and sorcerers possessed similar abilities. No one could know how many Mael had influenced and manipulated over the years. Archmaster Belegra's machinations had been clumsy, brute-force enslavement in comparison. With real power and knowledge, coercion is a subtle art far more difficult to detect.

"I don't like it," Strom said, "but I have a message for you. Tomorrow we leave for the Godfist."

Sinjin shook his head in surprise. "Wait. What? Who?"

"Why?" Kendra interjected.

Holding up a hand, Strom sighed and took a deep breath. "Kyrien--at least I hope it was Kyrien--says we need to go to the Godfist and retrieve the sword he demanded I make for your mother. The one she lost."

A note of bitterness accompanied that statement. Still, Sinjin knew Strom was just upset and not really angry over a weapon lost in battle. Catrin had always said the sword served its purpose well. Now he had to wonder. "Kyrien sent us back here," Sinjin said. "He spoke to our dragons. It seems likely he also communicated with you."

Strom appeared unconvinced.

"Can't you just make another?" Kendra asked.

Strom looked as if he might throw her from Windhold for asking such a question. "Do you have any idea what it took to make that sword?" he asked, his voice several octaves higher than usual. "It took every tool and technology available. Trying to make another here would take me years; if I could do it at all."

"I was just asking," Kendra said, her face as close to pouty as her pride would allow. It was enough.

"I'm sorry," Strom said. "It's just . . ."

No one had to ask. All of them had plenty to be upset about. Being angry with each other would help none of them.

"So you're saying you know where the sword is?"

"I was hoping you would know," Strom said. "All I have to go on is a vision of the oasis in the Arghast desert where Catrin struck the well."

Sinjin had been there once. The notion his mother had created such a place from only dry sand was unfathomable. So much of what his family did seemed impossible, but he'd somehow grown accustomed to it. "Do you think the tribes have it?"

Strom shrugged. "Seems as good a place to start as any. If not, perhaps they could help us search for it. Right before the vision of the oasis, I saw Catrin strike a feral with the glass lance. The sword formed the handle and was jerked from her hand. That's all I know, except that Osbourne and I are going with you."

"Why?" Kendra asked, knowing more passengers would add time to the trip.

"We were there," Strom said, his face cold and hard. "We witnessed the striking of the oasis. This will not have been forgotten. Sinjin visited the place as a boy, for certain, but you have never been there, correct?"

Kendra nodded, though it was clear she did not wish to do so. Strom spoke no more.

"Gather the people," Sinjin said. "Everyone deserves to know why we must once again leave them."

* * *

Soaring above snowcapped peaks, Kenward looked at Bryn and Farsy before shaking his head and turning to Onin. "Are you sure your dragon heard Kyrien correctly?"

Onin grunted.

"I could see New Moon Bay or maybe Drascha Stone, but we're headed the wrong way. There are ports along the Inland Sea but few friendly to people like us."

Shrugging, Onin otherwise ignored him, just as he'd done for most of the trip.

"We're heading in the general direction of Madra's place and even Wolfhold," Farsy added.

Kenward had no desire to go to either place. He was a child of both land and sea, but he preferred his visits to land be as brief as possible. And he could think of no reason Kyrien would send him there. Jharmin Kyte was a capable sailor in his own right, and Madra was an old lady. He had a twinge of guilt at that thought, but it was true nonetheless.

Jehregard had stayed at high altitudes to avoid the mountain peaks, but as they soared over the forests of Astor, he sped lower. These lands were mostly uninhabited, but woodsmen cried out as they passed overhead.

Try as he might, Onin could get the dragon to go no higher. Well within bow and ballista range, they moved over farmsteads reaching outward from central towns like spokes. Now many saw them coming, and chaos played out below. Most had never seen a dragon of such girth, and fewer still had encountered dragons that meant them no harm.

"Now you'll have the whole place in a panic," Onin scolded Jehregard, but the dragon continued to ignore him.

"The more I fly with dragons," Kenward said, "the more I like airships."

"Maybe you should stop crashing them into things."

That silenced Kenward for a time.

Inland from the farmsteads were areas more densely populated. Cities and towns dominated the landscape, and here defenses would be more prevalent. Only surprise allowed them safe passage over heavily armed battlements and ramparts. Before anyone thought to attack, they were beyond weapon range. It was a slim defense, and Kenward continued to wish the verdant dragon would take them higher. At times he dipped below the rooflines and soared between buildings. Architecture rushed by in a dizzying blur that left Kenward queasy. A single miscalculation or lapse in judgment would send them all crashing to the cobblestones below.

Alarms rang and signal fires ignited. Jehregard bellowed a challenge to all who would listen. In the distance a shoreline loomed. A wraith in the mists, Adderhold appeared from the fog, already intimidating. From what Kenward had heard, a mercenary held the place and had declared himself king. So far, no one had seen fit to argue the point. Kenward deeply hoped the dragons hadn't plotted to drop him there. This troubled him most. For the bulk of his life, he'd worried about what other people plotted. Now he worried what the dragons were up to, so much of what they did made no sense at all.

"The Inland Sea," Farsy whispered. He did not say Adderhold, but Kenward knew he was thinking it.

Arrows and ballista bolts flew as Jehregard approached, making no effort to hide. From the snakelike structure came thunder and fire, but the dragon was ready. Using his agility and uncanny judgment, he dodged the projectiles. Dark ships leaked from beneath the serpent fortress, filling the waters around the keep. The place was well defended, by Kenward's estimation; all the more reason to avoid the Inland Sea.

Winds buffeted them over the most unpredictable waters known, the air no more stable. Turbulence shook the compromised tierre terribly at times, their makeshift repairs insufficient for such punishment. Whenever the damage and shoddy fixes caused problems, Onin grumbled about where idiots landed their insane creations. Kenward made sure the older man never saw him grin. He had no desire to swim the Inland Sea.

"Where are you taking us?" Kenward shouted when land was lost from view on all sides. Few ships dared these waters, and he doubted anyone heard. He hadn't expected an answer, but the mighty verdant dragon issued a reverberating roar. Kenward decided it might be best if he kept his mouth shut.

Reds and purples shaded the skies by the time the Inland Sea's western shores came into view. Here existed wild lands, uncivilized since the Zjhon wars. Beyond that, the Westland, a place fouled by ancient weapons. Few ventured there after the detonation if the Statue of Terhilian; tales of a devastated and corrupted land kept most fools away. Beyond the Westland waited unfriendly seas. Besides a few patches of uninhabited islands, little was to be found there. Still, the thought of being dropped off along the western coastline, especially the southwestern coast, was not all that unappealing. This would have reassured had not Jehregard begun to slow, a thin column of smoke from a narrow clearing the only sign of habitation for miles. Towering ridgelines blocked the view beyond as they moved lower.

When Jehregard landed in the clearing, a bad feeling churned in Kenward's gut. No water visible for miles, this kind of place terrified him. What had this dragon done? Walking toward the lone cabin as if in a dream, his thoughts whirled. The door opened before he reached the threshold, and there stood his mother, Nora Trell, captain of the *Trader's Wind*; the most profitable trade ship ever to sail.

"Mother!" he shouted, running forward.

"Get inside, fool boy."

Kenward found the inside far better appointed than the exterior. Then his eyes landed on his sister, Fasha. "What the--?" he began involuntarily.

Hard, stoic faces surrounded the table. Grubb cooked over a black metal stove. Emmon, the one Kenward called "the new kid," stood in a corner looking uncomfortable.

"Sit," his mother said.

Kenward immediately slid a roughhewn wooden chair from the table and sat, staring.

"Your sister keeps me informed of your antics." This conversation was not going to go well. So much for reunions. "Your actions reflect on the rest of the family, my son. We make our living from our name. This is not to be taken lightly."

Though he'd heard the words before, Kenward had to contain his frustration. If circumstances had been different, his flying ships could have been a huge success. Instead, he was being lectured about the family name. The looks Fasha gave him didn't help. After staring her down for an appropriate interval, he stuck his tongue out. His mother saw it.

"Pay attention to me for once, fool boy!"

"Sorry, Mom. I know what a disappointment I must be."

His mother had healed well and was a good bit quicker than when he'd seen her last. Before the words had left his mouth, she stepped up and smacked him on the back of the head. "You'll be the death of me yet."

Fasha stuck her tongue out. Nora massaged her temples. "This is why I cannot leave the *Trader's Wind* to either of you."

And there was the heart of the matter. For years Kenward and Fasha competed for the right to inherit the greatest trading ship the world had ever known. The thought had always made him a little sick. Where was the adventure in buying and selling? If he were truly honest with himself, he'd done much to make sure his mother would never leave him the ship, though some of the things he'd done for fun probably had the same effect. The look on Fasha's face was worth the trip.

"Don't gape, girl," Nora said. "You look like a fish."

Kenward had never really expected to inherit; he'd just enjoyed making his sister work for it. She was the far more practical of the two and a darn fine sailor, not that he'd admit it out loud.

"Since there is no one to inherit, I've decided not to retire. I'd rather die on my ship, knowing she's well cared for." Kenward smiled in spite of himself. She'd probably outlive them all. "If I left the ship to you," she continued, turning to Fasha, "you'd rather be off flying that giant canoe your husband carved out of a tree, and just think how jealous your brother would be."

Kenward laughed.

Nora glared at him. "And if I left the mightiest trade ship in the world to you, my dear son, you'd probably dock her on top of a mountain, and then your sister would kill you. Can't have that."

Fasha nodded, glaring at Kenward.

"So now what?" Kenward asked when no one else would speak. "You go die on your deck, Fasha gets to play house in her big canoe, and I get left to rot in the woods?"

"Something like that," Nora said.

Grubb winked at him, and Kenward found himself confused.

"This is the way I see it, Kenward. If I leave you alone, you'll build terrible airships that fly just long enough to crash into something."

Onin, who had been otherwise silent, could not contain his laughter.

Nora stared him back into silence. "If I put you on the *Trader's Wind*, you'll find a way to sink us. If I put you on the *Dragon's Wing*, your sister will kill you. You leave me little choice, my son."

It was all true, but Kenward couldn't help it. He was who he was, and nothing could change that.

"If the Trells build airships," Nora continued, "then we're going to build the best airships the world has ever seen. Is that clear?" The smile finally came to his mother's eyes, and his sister threw salted fish at him--just like old times. "I can't have just one of the greatest airships. I'll need at least two. And I'll need a captain for each. Think I'll have trouble finding any?"

"No, ma'am," Kenward said, tears in his eyes. Never before had his family so deeply believed in his vision. He had no illusions that building airships in partnership with his mother and sister would be a drama-free experience, but he also knew their tenacity, attention to detail, and just pure desire to make him do things better would improve the end result.

"So why have you brought me out here to the middle of a tainted land?" Kenward asked. "There are no sailable waters within many miles from here."

"Fool boy. If you're building airships, what do you need water for?"

"Drinking mostly," Fasha said. "And washing."

Kenward made a face at her.

"What do you need to build airships?" Nora asked as if speaking to a slow child.

"Lightwood."

"For certain applications, yes, but not and entire ship unless you're desperate."

Kenward took offense on behalf of the *Serpent*. The fact that the ship no longer existed kept his mouth shut. No sense providing an easy target. It was among the first things one learned as a part of this family.

"Balsa, spruce, cedar, lightwood, and shakewood combined with a ready supply of rope weed," Nora said. "Now that would be how you build airships. A correct tool exists for every job and a correct material for every purpose. Remember, sailing is the fun part. Building the ships that make sailing fun is the hard part."

Kenward knew the truth of her words. He'd yet to build a proper airship, but he'd not yet had the materials needed. "Good luck finding all those things in one place."

Nora Trell smiled.

* * *

Behind the small cabin, across a narrow ravine with a moss- and mushroom-covered bridge of hewn logs, Fasha led Kenward toward the place his mother said had everything he needed. Occasional echoes filled the valley, much of it obscured by a noisy creek filled with a series of waterfalls. The smell of fires came to his nostrils as the wind blew toward the cabin where his mother and the others waited. While she could have made the climb with them, her time was far better spent caring for Farsy and Bryn; at least that was what she said.

Scrabbling up a ravine to the ridgetop, Fasha stood triumphant. Barely a step behind her, Kenward stumbled when he saw what lay beyond. A vast lowland plain made the perfect staging area and dry dock, already partially constructed. Shipbuilders, carpenters, smiths, and foresters numbering in the hundreds made the landscape move. These people knew what they were doing.

"You've seen the future, my brother," Fasha said. "We've seen what you can do on your own. Now let's see what you can do with the full force of the Trell family behind you."

Few times in his life had his sister rendered him speechless, but this time she utterly succeeded. The *Dragon's Wing* resting in a dry dock that took up just a fraction of the size of the entire operation helped Kenward understand the scale at which his mother and sister were thinking. Surely they were just as crazy as he. They had simply hidden it better. "They're going to be huge!" he said.

Fasha grinned.

"How long have you known?"

"Mom and I have been working on this for a while," Fasha admitted. "We didn't always know it would be airships we'd be building, but it did seem likely since the Eel and the *Dragon's Wing* had both flown when they had not been designed to do so. Purpose-built flying ships were the likely evolution, which you've proven in your own spectacular fashion."

"Thanks, Sis."

"Don't thank me. I'm just going to use this opportunity to kick your tail with all things equal. No excuses. Fair's fair. Deal?"

"You're on," Kenward said, grinning back. "What're the stakes?"

"Knowing you? Our lives."

Kenward barked a laugh.

"First, though, I think you'd be wise to fix Onin's tierre."

His sister made good sense, but while he had her alone, he had to ask one more question. "Have you seen any walnuts?"

Suspicious, she replied, "No. Why? What do you needs walnuts for?"

"Nothing," Kenward said. "I just like walnuts."

"Uh-huh," Fasha said, walking back toward the cabin.

"Have you seen any bats?"

Fasha turned and regarded him with one of those looks. "What are you up to?"

"Oh, nothing."

Chapter 6

To see the power and majesty of creation, look to the skies. To experience that same power and majesty, look inside.
--Catrin Volker, Herald of Istra

* * *

Many gathered to see Sinjin, Kendra, Strom, and Osbourne off. Most did not want them to leave but understood nonetheless. Durin's hands trembled when loading extra water skins and rations into the saddlebags, but already he'd grown stronger. Still, Sinjin hated leaving him behind, especially when so much work needed to be done. Matters of survival had fallen by the wayside. There would come a point he'd have to make extremely difficult decisions.

Arakhan and Mikala approached. They would be in charge of the Drakon in his and Kendra's absence, the strength he could not be for his people. Both deserved to be Al'Drakon more than he, but that choice had been left to Valterius. Sinjin often wondered if the dragon had made a mistake. Sometimes he thought Al'Drak might wonder as well. Arakhan checked Strom's straps, where he was secured behind Kendra, and Mikala checked Osbourne's. Arakhan leaped down from Gerhonda and slapped her on the hindquarters. The regal dragon swatted at him before leaping into the wind.

Just before Mikala jumped down, she whispered in Sinjin's ear. "Don't go. They'll kill you." He barely heard the rest of her words as Valterius chose to follow Gerhonda before Mikala was on the ground. She held on long enough to deliver her cryptic message--"It's not you they want"--before leaping to safety. An instant later, the dragons and their riders hurtled through open air. Valterius trimmed his wings and dived, gaining tremendous speed before chasing after Gerhonda. The people within Windhold watched, knowing the dragonriders' to go to the Godfist. But both dragons turned sharply, heading back inland.

"Where are we going?" Kendra screamed as they flew through all-too-familiar valleys.

"I wish I kn--" Within the otherwise pristine forest, something dark and twisted moved, cutting his words short. Silently Sinjin directed Kendra's attention until she, too, saw it. Ash-painted warriors and demons approached land they had so easily taken years before. Windhold was defenseless against them, as it had always been. So much time lost, and now it had run out.

Osbourne's grip on Sinjin's shoulders tightened, physically turning him to see giants emerge from an adjoining valley. They were easy to spot as the lumbering brutes howled their displeasure. Reaching down, the twisted, oversized creatures grabbed massive river stones and hurled them at the approaching dragons. Osbourne screamed as one of the mighty stones whizzed past with a rush of stinging wind and sand.

Dipping low, Valterius slipped between two giants. Each swung at them as they passed, both just a little too late. Carried by their momentum, they struck each other instead and bellowed in rage. More corrupt forces poured from ships moored along the northwestern coast. Sails crowded the horizon, all coming from a direction not easily visible from within Windhold. The valley ahead appeared pristine. These armies were just arriving, not yet ready for full-scale attack.

"What are we going to do?" Kendra shouted.

"I don't know," Sinjin yelled in response.

A sheer face loomed ahead. Tenacious bushes and trees reached out, ready to claw anything that came too close. Saddles creaked from downward force. Looking over his shoulder, Sinjin could see one of the giants coming after them, a river stone in each gnarled, twisted hand. The higher they flew, the slower their ascent. Proving giants weren't stupid, the massive beast waited. Carefully timing the attack, its aim was true.

Valterius's last-second evasive moves were all that saved them from certain annihilation, turning a direct hit into a glancing blow, though enough to shake them nonetheless.

"Are you hurt?" Sinjin shouted back to Osbourne.

No response came. At their peak, Valterius turned, providing a clear view of the keystone and the green crystals surrounding it. All the entryways were clear. No rock littered the area around the keystone, and rubble previously blocking the entrances was gone. Soon they raced back down the rock face toward the enraged giant. Beyond, archers formed ranks. They were in trouble. When red lightning erupted from huddled figures in dark robes, the world exploded. Turning, they avoided direct hits, but Sinjin felt the sting of even a graze. Valterius roared from pain of his own.

The valiant regal dragon soared upward, aiming his claws for the giant's eyes. The mighty beast raked the air, massive, filthy hands more like claws swatting at them. With a roar, the giant bent down and grabbed an angular chunk of granite from the valley floor. Clumps of grass and a tree still clung to it.

Diving and gaining speed, Valterius raced toward the dark-robed figures. Twice their attacks scraped the regals, but for the most part, the dragons avoided the streams of noxious energy. Their passengers flailed, jerked back and forth with dizzying suddenness.

While giants had proven they weren't stupid, neither were they brilliant. Hurling the massive granite boulder with all its might, the giant launched a devastating projectile . . . just where Valterius wanted. Anticipating the attack, the dragons dodged. The mass of granite raced beneath, plowing into the valley floor with land-ripping force. The dark-robed sorcerers were no more. Arrows and rocks filled the air in volleys, threatening to take them down, but the dragons knew this land better than anyone else alive. Circling back, they raced toward Windhold. Sinjin expected them to land, expected to orchestrate the evacuation. The speed at which they approached, though, made it clear there would be no stopping.

"We're under attack!" he screamed as they passed stunned faces. Dragons roared and shouts filled the hold. "Make for the keystone in the peaks! Something's opened them up!"

In the next instant, they soared through open air, racing toward an approaching fleet.

* * *

Having skilled artisans at his disposal made almost everything easier for Kenward Trell. Not since the *Slippery Eel* had he played the role of wealthy shipbuilder. His past two ships had been built from sweat and tears. These new ships would be built from that rare combination of the best materials and pride. A well-made, well-maintained, skillfully sailed ship could span generations. The *Trader's Wind* was such an example. Recent discoveries rendered the ship largely obsolete but not entirely. Kenward tried not to get ahead of himself. His ships would have their time.

For the moment, he was content to scale the ridgeline separating his mother's cabin from the main worksite. Onin had been more patient than Kenward would have expected. In some ways the man had been downright pleasant. Even skilled artisans needed time to produce quality work, and Onin had said there was no sense repairing his tierre if not to fix it correctly. This meant disassembling undamaged parts to be replicated for the side someone had flown the bumblebee into. Kenward had been thinking hard on how to improve the design.

The parts were heavy, but Bryn, Farsy, and Fasha helped. Onin was content to let them do all the work, which Kenward grudgingly supposed was only right. He'd expected the older man to come see the work site, but Onin had said he'd see plenty when he flew over. The walk got easier as they went, though the carved parts seemed to get heavier over time. Wood smoke from the cabin mixed with spices and cook smoke, and the smell kept them moving. After staging the new and old parts for reassembly, Kenward was the first to the door.

He was about to ask what smelled so good, but no one noticed him enter. Onin and Nora laughed so hard, they had tears in their eyes. Grubb fidgeted.

"And then she poured the potatoes on his lap!" Nora said after a few deep breaths.

Reddened and breathing hard, Onin held his ribs. "Enough," he gasped. "No more. You're killing me."

"Are you two all right?" Kenward finally asked.

"Shut up and eat," his mother said, which set them both to laughing again.

Shrugging, Kenward moved to where Grubb cooked. "What smells so good?"

His old friend shoved a plate full of all Kenward's favorites into his hands. "Shut up and eat."

You didn't have to tell Kenward twice, but it didn't hurt. Onin giggled like a little boy, and Nora wiped her eyes. Fasha and the others were no fools. They grabbed plates for themselves and did as Kenward had been told.

"Are you going to let us in on the joke?" Fasha asked when her plate was clean.

"No," Nora and Onin said at the same time, and this set them giggling again.

"That tierre isn't going to reassemble itself, you know," Farsy said when done eating. When walking past the stove, he added, "I thank you as always, friend Grubb."

Kenward took the hint, finished the last of his food and followed Farsy to the door. Bryn came with them. Fasha stayed behind.

"What do you suppose was going on in there?" Kenward asked when they were well clear of the cabin. Farsy looked at him as if he were daft. "Well, I know the whole men and women thing and the flirting, but really? Do you think? Onin . . . and my mom?"

Bryn remained silent.

"Don't look at me," Farsy said. "I just see what I see and know what I know."

"And what do you know?" Kenward asked, already knowing the punch line.

"I know how to tie knots."

"That you do. That you do."

The joke was Farsy's way of telling Kenward to shut his mouth and do what needed doing. Onin's tierre was a remarkable bit of construction, and Kenward had never intended to crash into it. It just worked out that way. Seeing it restored was satisfying. Jehregard watched from nearby, his look disapproving. Kenward wasn't looking forward to getting the heavy structure back on the towering dragon.

"We're going to need a hoist," Farsy said, as if reading Kenward's thoughts--something that appeared far too easy for the good captain's comfort. "That's what the dragon is accustomed to, and that's the safest way I know."

"I'll get the forestry crew to come set us up one," Kenward said, ready to walk away from the final reconstruction.

"Really? You're not even going to help us finish this thing?"

"Time's a wasting my friend," Kenward said as he walked away. "Things need doing."

* * *

Mikala had warned Sinjin not to come. Though he didn't fully comprehend Arghast legends and beliefs, he knew they expected the Herald to come for the sword. He could hardly believe ancient prophecies had predicted she would lose her sword over the desert. Prophecies were funny creatures, though. Mikala had described the sword as the Dragon's Tooth, a mighty weapon that would come to the Arghast from the sky. Sinjin hadn't heard anything about a sword in that, but Mikala had seemed convinced. He could do little more than pray she and the others escaped to the keystone caverns. There, at least, they had a chance to defend themselves.

Now he wished he had listened to her words. His homeland covered in dark, gritty ash looked foreign, and the Arghast were hardly welcoming. Valterius and Gerhonda had thick hides, but even they were vulnerable to the rows of spears surrounding them.

"Leave the dragons, and you walk away," said a man in full headgear.

"No," Sinjin said before anyone else could act or speak. His wife shot him a heated glare but remained silent. "Surrender the Dragon's Tooth, and you walk away."

"What are you doing?" Osbourne asked from behind him.

Sinjin made no response. He knew what he was doing. He was Al' Drakon. These people knew it. If he came from a stance of weakness, he and his friends would be dead. Instead, he played his role as tribal leader.

"I was here," Strom said, and Sinjin bit his tongue. He had hoped everyone would be smart and remain silent. He'd been wrong. "You pledged loyalty to the Herald of Istra. This is her son."

"We swore no oath of fealty to the Herald of Istra's son," the tribesman said. "Any who take what is hers are thieves and will be treated as such. We've seen the golden dragon. The master of lies has escaped."

Those words sent a chill through Sinjin. Evidence of a dark future was mounting and he liked it not one bit. He needed the sword and knew only one way to get it. "I am Al'Drakon," he said, "and I claim the right of challenge."

These words sent a ripple through the spears. Sinjin hoped the words invoked a less prevalent prophecy as Mikala believed. She'd said it was dangerous but hadn't been able to tell him how or why. He wished Valterius had given her more time to speak.

The tribesman who had spoken for the Arghast flexed his tanned, oiled muscles. "I accept your challenge."

Sinjin swallowed, wondering what he had just done.

* * *

A scouting patrol returned, telling Durin and the others what they already knew. They were under attack. Black sails crowded the horizon, and dark storm clouds roiled overhead, filled with unnatural lightning that never stopped. The darkness had come for them. He hoped Valterius and Gerhonda would bring back Sinjin, Kendra, and the others. They were far better suited to lead. What did he know about battle?

"If they're right, we can fall back to the keystone caverns," Brother Vaughn said as he approached. Durin continued helping Mikala and Arakhan saddle Grekka and Atherian. "Do you think we can get everyone out of here in time?"

"No," Durin said. "Pray I'm wrong."

Brother Vaughn did just that.

"I need to know what the situation is up there," Durin continued, leading in spite of himself. "Mount up."

Brother Vaughn looked up in surprise.

"Mount up," Durin said again. "And bring your herald globe."

Tapping his pocket, Brother Vaughn accepted Arakhan's hand, and the powerful man practically pulled him into the saddle. With straps barely secured, Atherian leaped into the air, Grekka right behind. There was no time to waste, and the dragons also knew it. The stubborn beasts sometimes appeared to communicate quite well. It was a puzzle that had kept Durin up more than a few nights. If he lived through this, the memories of their flight would also haunt his dreams. The approaching armies no longer made any attempt at surprise, spreading across the land, making them more difficult to attack from the air. It was among the few advantages they had. Given enough time, the keystone caverns might provide even greater advantage. Based on the numbers pouring from ships and marring the landscape, they would need all they could get.

Giants waited in the valley, howling in rage on seeing the dragons. Durin hadn't expected to engage the enemy directly at all, let alone so soon. He'd gone from the normalcy of his daily business to a life-or-death battle in far too short a time. Reconciling what he saw proved difficult. Boulders--each one the size of a house--hurled at them hardly looked real. A rain of arrows pushed them higher, and a boulder slammed into the cliff face. Rock fragments pelted them, sparks thick in the air.

Atherian flew to the other side of the valley, giving Grekka room to maneuver. Both dragons used every trick to gain speed, racing up and down valley walls, elusive and unpredictable while at the same time gaining momentum. The sheer face loomed ahead far too soon, and it didn't feel like they were moving fast enough to gain the peaks. Massive stones whizzed past far too close to hitting their marks. Every evasive action slowed them, and the high valley remained out of reach. At the top of their arc, the dragons folded their wings and dropped. A barrage of stones hit the spot where they had been a moment before, showering them in fragments.

Frustrated by so many missed attacks, the giant rose to its full height. The massive beast effectively blocked the valley floor. Speed was not on the giant's side, and he moved too soon, giving the dragons time to avoid him by racing up opposite valley walls. One more turn and they would have the speed they so desperately needed. The giant, quicker than he'd made himself appear, waited for them when they turned.

The sudden appearance of other dragonriders distracted the mighty giant. Spears and rocks hurled from adragonback caused the monster to swat and duck away. The Drakon had disobeyed his orders and likely saved his life. This time they approached the cliff wall with more speed. Hurtling skyward, Durin couldn't help but cry out. Only Brother Vaughn's screams beside him made him feel any better.

They cleared the peaks and swiftly descended upon the thermals. The valley nestled among the peaks appeared in far better order than when Durin had seen it last. Crystals knocked askew during the breaking of the keystones stood almost straight, and all the debris had been cleared from the entranceways, leaving them as they must have been so long ago.

"What in the world happened here?" Brother Vaughn asked.

Durin shrugged.

Chapter 7

If others define your self-worth, they'll always be better than you.
--Sinjin Volker, Al'Drakon

* * *

You've served me well, Nat Dersinger, Mael's voice purred in Nat's mind. Do not fear me. I am most pleased.

Neenya's nails dug into Nat's flesh, and he knew this was as much reality as vision. Never before had his second sight overlaid the real world; always it had supplanted it. Now, though, Mael was at his full power, basking in Istra's light and able to apply his art with subtle mastery. Not since the last age had such sorcery been known to Godsland. The Herald of Istra was a child playing with toys compared to Mael and Nat quailed. For all her faults and flaws, Catrin was his friend.

Those thoughts angered Mael. Nat's vision turned red. Through this bond, bits of the sorcerer were revealed. He did not hate Catrin but was jealous. Such steadfast loyalty she commanded despite being so much less powerful.

Nat pretended not to notice these things. Through mortal eyes, he gazed on a figure part man, part dragon--at this point mostly dragon, but man he'd once been. Never could all traces of humanity be cast aside. This, too, was instinctively understood.

You must come willingly if you are to be useful. Trust me and history will be thick with your name.

Having a choice in this matter was incomprehensible. How could his desires matter to one so magnificent? No longer did he wonder if the dragon heard his thoughts.

This form has advantages. But it also has . . . limitations. Together we are more powerful. I have prepared you for this task. I raised you to be strong.

Raised him. The words struck a nerve. Matteo Dersinger had raised him--in his own way. Truly Nat had resented his father and the madness most perceived him to have. How much had Mael been responsible for? How many tragedies in his life could be traced back to a meddling dragon trapped within Dragonhold? Thinking of the glass viper that took his beloved Julet from him, Nat's spirit broke. Nothing had ever hurt him more, and he'd been searching for someone to blame ever since. He'd vented anger at those partially responsible but mostly at himself. Now he knew the true source of that most vile evil.

I've asked a great deal from you and will now ask even more. You must forgive me for introducing challenges into your life.

"Challenges!" Nat screamed. Neenya trembled behind him, her tears soaking his back. "You killed my true love and drove my father mad, what could you be but a monster?" He expected anger, resentment, rage but none came. Instead, he received understanding.

I've asked much.

Memories returned to Nat, filled with revelations. Now he saw lines of manipulation, gentle nudges influencing his decisions. It had been Mael, too, who'd led him to Neenya, who had proven his father's words, who had provided absolution when everything else was lost. Nat sobbed.

You must come willingly if you are to fulfill your destiny, Nat Dersinger. What will you do?

"I don't know."

Neenya wrapped her arms around him, squeezing him hard, as if she knew he must choose between her and the dragon. And the dragon was winning.

What will you do?

When no answer came, Mael released the towering spire and soared away, disappearing over the sea.

* * *

Using the light of his herald globe, Brother Vaughn led the way. Durin followed. Arakhan and Mikala flanked them, ready to defend if needed. Wind howled, trespassing on the silence but not touching the eerily still valley. Deep fissures bifurcated the keystone, making it look like glass beneath a hammer blow, but no longer did the fissures issue smoke and fire. Like scar tissue from an old wound, smooth stone filled the cracks. It was not the same, but it was whole, much like Durin.

"We already explored that one," Brother Vaughn said, pointing. Arakhan scouted the area, searching the land for clues as to what had happened and whether or not it was safe for the Drakon to bring the Dragon Clan here. They had no time to waste, and Brother Vaughn wanted to do as little exploring as possible. While strange, the place appeared safe to him--far safer than anyone would be within Windhold. In spite of his impatience, he knew Arakhan and Mikala did not want to make the situation even worse. Skilled trackers, they understood things he did not. He let them do as they felt necessary. Someone had done them a tremendous service by clearing out the obstructions. The caverns themselves were defensible from within, apparently designed with that in mind.

The entranceways were not much larger than regal dragons needed. As long as no one waited within the caverns, Brother Vaughn was confident they would be better off here, though nowhere was truly safe.

"Look at this," Arakhan said a moment later, waving for the others to join him. He pointed to a wide trail in the moss leading to one of the caverns.

Brother Vaughn wondered how he had missed it. "What would make a mark like that?" he asked.

It looked like a trail made by a giant snake or perhaps a dragon's tail, but he hoped someone would prove him wrong. They could be walking into a trap.

A sharp intake of breath caused him to look toward Mikala, who'd worked her way in front of the rest. Glittering in the light of his herald globe waited sights that simultaneously invoked primal fear and a glimmer of hope.

The trail continued across the dusty cavern floor, snaking its way toward a central pedestal, which sat empty. The trail went no farther, and it did not turn or double back; it simply ended before the empty pedestal. The rest of the cavern was an altogether different story. Rows upon rows of weapons and armor stood meticulous and orderly. Glittering staves waited in purpose-built racks, and colorful glass spheres filled with magnificent designs rested on slender stands. Edging forward like a thief, Brother Vaughn pulled one from its resting place. Like a comet trapped in glass, it swirled in an endless vortex, somehow looking impossibly deep.

"Go," Durin said, his tone firm. "Bring our people here."

Mikala hefted a staff that gleamed even in meager light. Texture and contrast illuminated masterful construction, like silver and copper intricately melded together. Atop the staff rested a glass sphere not unlike the one Brother Vaughn held but with a ghostly design he couldn't quite make out. Arakhan went straight to the most plentiful weapon, something akin to a crossbow with an icy blue crystal embedded in the stock.

"We'll be back," Mikala said.

Brother Vaughn watched them go with hope and trepidation. Could they possibly get the Dragon Clan evacuated in time? Would these weapons even work? Were they even weapons? Did they require the hands of the gifted? So many questions ran through Brother Vaughn's mind. Durin took a more direct approach and took one of the crossbowlike weapons. If these proved potent, they could better arm the Drakon. Mikala's choice of staff might reveal what other, perhaps more powerful, weapons they possessed.

Durin pointed the crossbow at the nearby rock and pulled the trigger.

"Be careful with that!" Brother Vaughn said, but nothing happened. It wasn't a good sign.

"I think the trigger's broken on this one," Durin said. "It's like it didn't even try to fire." Reaching down, he picked up another, inadvertently pointing it at Brother Vaughn.

"Watch where you aim that thing."

Turning back toward stone, Durin tried a second weapon to no effect. No bolts or other projectiles were present, and Brother Vaughn's guts tightened. Walking back to sunlight, Durin brushed the dust from the bluish-white crystal, which made a slight click. A faint glow grew stronger, and the crystal pulsed with life. Short bursts of thunder echoed through the valley, and Durin ran to a nearby rock formation. The young man tried to climb up and was visibly deflated when he failed. It was something he could have done easily before his injuries.

Brother Vaughn rushed to his side and gave him a boost.

"By the gods!"

If not for his own physical limitations, Brother Vaughn would have climbed up to join the young man. "Tell me what you see!"

"Arakhan and Mikala are trying to clear a path for the Drakon. They're bringing the Dragon Clan, or at least a bunch of people. Oh, wow!"

"What?" Brother Vaughn asked, frustrated and tempted to make the climb himself in spite of the risks. He had to know what was going on.

"Wait."

A click was followed by a high-pitched thump. Durin stumbled backward, almost falling on top of Brother Vaughn.

Stepping back, the monk looked into the sphere he held. Terrified, he decided it would be better if someone with more power and experience tested it. With great care, he moved back into the cavern and returned it to the cradle that had held it for so long. It glowed brighter than all the rest. In his attempt at being careful, he slipped and nearly knocked the too-tall stand over. Who would place dangerous objects in such unstable places? The ancients continued to mystify him. They possessed such mastery yet did things that made absolutely no sense.

After seeing what the bow's kick did to Durin, Brother Vaughn searched for another option. The young man had been right about one thing: they could provide effective cover from this vantage.

"Giants!" Durin shouted, his weapon firing over and over with mere breaths in between. It seemed an impossible thing, but he was thankful for it nonetheless. No time to think about the empty pedestal; that mystery would have to wait. The monk continued his scan, searching for a weapon more suitable to a man his size and age. In a corner behind the full-sized bows rested a few smaller ones.

Grabbing the closest, Brother Vaughn hefted the weapon. It felt good in his hand. As a man who had taken vows of peace and honor, it frightened him when a tool of death brought joy and comfort, but this one did. Running back to the sunlight, he searched for a place from which he could gain a better view. Finally Durin put down his weapon long enough to pull Brother Vaughn up. A moment later, he stood, staring down at chaos. His bow clicked, trigger extended and ready.

Before he fired at approaching giants, Durin stayed his hand. Try as he might, Brother Vaughn could not locate the Drakon until they suddenly filled the air around him. Some just barely cleared the stones.

"Get out of the way!" Mikala shouted.

Durin went to his knees and lay flat, as did Brother Vaughn. Wings and claws pelted them, scrabbling at the stones around them, but then it was over. The Dragon Clan dismounted with trembling knees. Some went straight to the ground and kissed the soil. Others ran immediately into the cavern on Arakhan's command. Considering the chaos they had flown through, it was an impressive feat. As soon as passengers dismounted, Drakon leaped back into the air. Brother Vaughn flattened himself against the stone, but it was unnecessary. In tight spirals, Drakon rode the air above the keystone. Whether an effect of the geography or some trick of the ancients, some magic remained.

"Don't shoot the Drakon," Durin said.

The urge to fire on the enemy was difficult to resist, which worried Brother Vaughn. Knowing he fought for the light had to be enough. When the Drakon reached the bottom of their arc and began racing along the valley floor, Brother Vaughn aimed at anything behind them. Such an amazing vantage the ancients had capitalized on. He could fire into the enemy with almost complete impunity.

From below, a dark figure cast red lightning, but it fizzled before reaching the mountaintops. The smell of ozone was heavy in the air until gusting wind threatened to toss Brother Vaughn from the dizzying height. Another blast hit, and the world went three shades darker. It was then he knew he was in real trouble. Shouts rose up around him as others found themselves under similar assault. Rolling onto his back, a feral dragon's fierce visage bearing down on him, he pulled the trigger.

The initial blast cast the dragon backward, but it shook off the pain and regarded Brother Vaughn as one might a troublesome bug. Under the dragon's gaze, the weapon took far too long to recharge. He was powerless, insignificant, and about to die. A slight click momentarily banished dragon fear. With a simple squeeze, he fired. Knocked backward by the close-range attack that struck above the dragon's eyes, the giant beast tumbled head over tail.

Shaking off the deadly lethargy, Brother Vaughn moved. More dragons would come. Approaching footsteps brought a glimmer of hope. Somehow amid the dragon wind and the armies below, he heard many soft clicks. The Drakon opened fire. He and Durin found themselves in a bad place, and they stood back-to-back, weapons at the ready. Standing together and remaining still meant the Drakon could fire with greater confidence. This Brother Vaughn told himself repeatedly as the dragon he'd shot in the head turned to regard him. It wore something akin to a smile.

Durin fired first, his aim true. Brother Vaughn tried to still trembling hands. Squinting, he held his breath and didn't have to search long to find a target. Still he hesitated. Missing when firing at an enemy within their defenses could mean killing their own. Drakon fired into the air, stemming the incoming flow of feral dragons. As if realizing they would soon lose Durin and Brother Vaughn, they turned their fire on those who'd landed. The world lit up, leaving them shading their eyes. Leaping into the air, the dragon lashed out with its tail, sending both tumbling.

Though a single shot may have only stunned the dragon, repeated hits proved lethal. Drakon continued concentrating fire on the large dragon, and he fell into the valley below, taking out troops gathering at the cliff's base.

It took Brother Vaughn a moment to regain his feet, but then he half ran to where Durin lay. It was all the speed he could muster. Durin pushed himself up, and Brother Vaughn hoisted him to his feet. Putting the young man's arm over his shoulder, the monk did his best to take advantage of the brief lull to get them behind the Drakon line. Focused and organized, they stood as if they had been trained for this very task. Brother Vaughn was glad they were on his side.

"I just need to know one thing," Durin said as they gained the cavern.

"What's that?"

"How did we not see that coming?"

The monk gave no answer.

Armed with weapons from a forgotten age, Drakon were a deadly wind. None could withstand their speed and agility. Fire rained from the skies. As Brother Vaughn had suspected, more potent and powerful weapons existed in smaller numbers. No one had yet dared to test the glass spheres. If anything like herald globes, they could perhaps be used as thrown weapons, but Brother Vaughn expected their use was something completely different, the designs far too artful to be thrown at an enemy.

Staves proved an early favorite but functioned in the hands of only some. A young man tried three different rods before one responded to his mental commands; others found none. Durin did his best to coordinate the chaos. The Dragon Clan worked to arm and train new arrivals. The keystone caverns soon bristled with deadly weapons in the hands of willing if inexperienced wielders.

"How many more trips will it take?" Durin asked Arakhan before they took off once again.

His muscles gleamed with sweat and his breathing was rapid, but the Drakon shrugged. "There's fighting in the hold. I do not know how many will remain." With those words, they leaped back onto the thermals.

Reality poignantly clear, Brother Vaughn felt useless. Others were far more capable of handling the bows, and he handed his to a young woman desperate to defend her people. Walking back to the mystical comet orb, he grasped it firmly and removed it from its stand. After walking outside, he studied it in the light, trying to unlock its secrets. Information existed in the design; if only he understood it. The swirling vortex within reminded him of comets and Istra's power. The metallic pattern on the back looked mechanical yet smooth and sleek. Some mixture of art and machine was all he could gather.

With light streaming through his fingers and growing brighter, Brother Vaughn held it high and hoped he proved brave rather than foolish. Feral dragons fell upon them like a rain of death. The Drakon were unable to land with so many ferals attacking. And the regals were at their most vulnerable while they carried loads of passengers, giving them less opportunity to make evasive maneuvers.

Brother Vaughn stood, exposed at the keystone's center, his hand held high. Members of the Dragon Clan watched from the cavern entrances, each group covering part of the sky. For this purpose the entrances were ideal. They seemed to recognize what he did and gave him an unspoken acknowledgment. His eyes squeezed closed, Brother Vaughn engaged his will, knowing feral dragons descended. With all his might, he thrust upward, focusing his energy on the task. A ferocious roar resulted. Opening his eyes, he looked up to a wavering column of air that erupted from his outstretched fist. Feral dragons were cast away, folding like moths in a thunderstorm. A cheer rang out from the Dragon Clan, and Drakon arrived moments later, able to unload another precious load of passengers.

"One more trip," Arakhan said between gulping breaths.

Brother Vaughn worried the warrior and dragon alike might die from the effort. Flying in battle, especially when evading attacks, was far from a passive operation. Synchronizing movements with their mounts and dodging attacks used every muscle in their bodies. Firing his weapon occupied his hands, leaving him to grip the saddle with his thighs. The remaining Drak and Drakon pushed beyond their physical limits. Others had lacked the strength. Fewer dragons returned from each trip.

"I hope some remain," Arakhan said as the Drakon took flight, making a final desperate attempt to help their clanmates.

Proud to be among them, Brother Vaughn considered the source of his newfound strength and once again marveled at the ancients' skills.

Chapter 8

Fires of war forge our greatest achievements.
--Kendra Ironfist, Drakon

* * *

Larissarelatarenfall.

The name sounded unfamiliar in spite of being a shortened version of her own. The dryad had longed for companionship but not like this. "You have me at a disadvantage," she said, despite seeing the shadows the creature cast across the seaport.

You know who I am, and you know why I'm here. But you are correct about the disadvantage. That I'll grant you.

"There is nothing for you here. Go in peace."

Shall it be in peace or in pieces?

The dryad gulped, wanting to slide back into her tree and wait for the ancient dragon to leave. Though far younger than he, Catrin had given her the dryad's gift. Her brethren's combined knowledge provided history and perspective, things she would have otherwise lacked in her solitary existence. Catrin had been good to her, even if unable to be the person Larissarelatarenfall truly needed. She'd done her best. The dryad owed her very existence to Catrin, who had carried her spirit in seed form to the Black Spike and planting he tree beside the Well of Sight so she might watch over the world. In the long years Catrin hid within the tower, she and Kyrien had been the dryad's only other contact with the world.

She left something in your care, I believe. If you wish me to leave in peace, give me what I've come for.

"It's not here," the dryad said, her hands never leaving tree bark.

The ancient sorcerer crept closer and eyed her from around the corner.

What a pretty tree.

The words sent a chill through Larissarelatarenfall, and she caressed the bark, unsure what she would do if anything happened to any of it. The thought made her want to cry, but Catrin had told her to be strong. It was an impossible thing to ask of someone, to be strong when one is all alone. She was always alone. No one loved her. The thoughts hammered her consciousness, and she barely found the strength to dip her fingers into the viewing well. Wind rushed into the Black Spike through every orifice, threatening to implode the towering architecture. Sand and debris pummeled Mael as wind rushed into the small space, creating immense pressure.

"Do you want to die under a pile of rock?" the dryad asked, her voice betraying no fear. She had prepared for this. She'd known the ancient sorcerer might be more than she could handle, and she had but a single failsafe.

"You're not the first to try," Mael sneered. "But there is no need. I can smell the truth. Who has taken that which is mine?"

Larissarelatarenfall tried not to think of Kyrien and Pelivor, but the image leaped into her mind unbidden--at least unbidden by her will.

Thank you.

Exaggerated sweetness made the dryad's skin crawl.

Tell me one more thing, and I'll truly leave you in peace. Somehow covering the space between them in less time than she would have thought possible, Mael reared back and towered above her. Do you think I don't remember?

Larissarelatarenfall tried not to faint.

I helped make the great magics of the last age, you fool. And they will likely be the greatest magics of this age as well. Who is there to match my skill? No one not currently trapped within one of those magics.

"I don't want any trouble."

That made the dragon laugh, and Larissarelatarenfall thrust her fist into the viewing well. The waters at the seaport rushed higher, forcing Mael physically away from the well.

You think to use my creation against me? The dragon chuckled, a deep drumming sound, but then his eyes narrowed. Enough of this!

Fire seared the air and left the dryad smoking. Sap bubbled and hissed, leaves smoldered. Again he attacked, and leaves caught fire. Screaming, Larissarelatarenfall plunged both hands into the well and used the device itself as a weapon, contrary to its design and nature. It was like grabbing a red hot log from the center of a campfire, as likely to injure the wielder as the target.

"No!" Mael shrieked but it was too late. Charged liquid rushed out and pinned the ancient dragon. Struggling against its caustic grip, Mael screamed his anger and sent bluish orange flames from his nostrils. Again Larissarelatarenfall and her tree were seared, her defenses useless. Debilitating pain ended her attack. Involuntarily she relented.

Mael sank down against the far cavern wall. "You've made this far more difficult and painful than needed, but I don't suppose I blame you." The dragon moved to the well, looking into metallic waters that so clearly showed the world outside. "I just need to see a couple things."

Behind her tree, the dryad cowered, letting the dragon do as he would. She had failed Catrin. She had failed herself. Surely the world would pay for her mistakes.

Dipping his claw into the metallic water, Mael controlled the well with familiar skill, but the dryad felt he desecrated the place before her eyes. Still, she watched to see what was so important. When the Jaga came into view, she recoiled from such perversion of nature.

They thought it necessary. They said this was a small price to contain those who could rend the world.

She knew what was there. Catrin had watched the place, forcing the dryad to see things she wished she'd never seen. That would not make them exist any less. The well showed the skies above the Noonspire, a thick knot of comets coming in for a close pass. Someday those comets would come too close, but this was not the day. They would come just close enough. If he knew his colleagues, they would take advantage of the first opportunity. His thoughts rang through the cavern as if he shouted, but his jaws never moved. The true scale and majesty of the Noonspire and the massive construction surrounding it were soon apparent. Isn't she beautiful?

Larissarelatarenfall could not have disagreed more. It was cold and foul and ugly in most every way in spite of symmetry and impeccable craftsmanship. Fewer dragons clung to it now, revealing more ancient stonework. Nothing to rival it had been built since.

They called her the Seventh Magic.

Beneath the light of comets shining brightly in the midday sun, the Noonspire rotated. Every dragon within took flight, scattering across the winds. A cloud of dust and spray followed. Terrific noise projected from the viewing well, which swelled the sorcerer with pride. Then the architecture began to shift; what had looked like mere building blocks showed their true nature: cogs within a massive machine. Water and vegetation spewed from the chasm, which pulsed and glowed, still preventing the land from collapsing inward.

Colossal weights on massive cables dropped into the abyss. The land bucked twice before the Noonspire began to rise. Like a harbinger of the end of days, the monolithic crystal thrust into the full light. Stone frameworks continued to churn and settle into place, just as the ancients had set them three thousand years before. No one then would believe the audacity of sacrificing the world's most powerful artifact to imprison the mighty.

It had fooled them all back then but would not do so now. Mael knew exactly what he faced, and seeing the Noonspire rise from the depths, exposed to the full light, he'd been right to prepare for war. It was a matter of time. Still, it would keep Catrin occupied. That alone made all he'd done worthwhile. The dryad trembled but could not look away. The world was changing, and she was witness. Mael cast her a sideways glance before shifting the view. The cloud forests burned, immersing the Heights in cinders and soot, while armies camped where food was plentiful, especially since the fires forced game downward.

In the Midlands towering war machines rolled toward cliffs previously thought impossible to scale. No one from this age would have dared imagine siege engines large enough to take the Midlands cliffs, but Mael had seen it all before. He knew this strategy as well as they did. The world relied on alliances. Attack any one nation, and allies rush in. This approach required a great deal of setup and timing. One had to build up massive forces and materials without tipping off enemies then attack all one's enemies at once. Concentrate your might on the weakest enemy, and your empire will soon grow.

Aggrezjhon and Murden had been busy, but so had Mael. When he shifted his view to include the Firstland, he laughed out loud. Larissarelatarenfall huddled behind her tree, praying he would go away.

* * *

"Thief," they called him. Sinjin hated the name but accepted the insult. Now was not the time. Better he prepare to fight for his life. Following the Arghast riders, they flew.

"There must be another way," Osbourne said from behind.

"No. I have to do this."

"What would you have me do?"

"Stay with Valterius and Gerhonda," Sinjin said. "I don't know where we're going, but we may need to make a quick escape." Leaving the dragons seemed like foolishness, but he'd given his word, and he knew what that meant--especially to the Arghast.

"And you think leaving me with them will make some sort of difference?"

"Well," Sinjin said. "At least you can warn anyone foolish enough to try and take them. I'm sure having Strom there will also be a deterrent."

"So you're just going to let that guy beat the tar out of you in front of your wife?" Osbourne asked.

Caught off guard, Sinjin almost laughed. What else was he supposed to do?

The trail of horses stopped near a dark patch in the sand. Valterius landed fast and hard, as if to show the Arghast just how tough he really was. Gerhonda followed suit. It made for a bone-jarring landing, but Sinjin couldn't blame them. A great many Arghast spears pointed in their direction.

A single escort waited. Sinjin had rights as the challenger, and the Arghast were a strict people, even when it worked to their disadvantage. Some sort of mystical portal waited beyond. "Stay here with the dragons. Kendra and I will go in and get the sword."

"Are you kidding?" Strom said. "No way."

"None of you have to go," Sinjin said, not even looking at his wife. There was no need to ask. He already knew where she stood on the matter.

"Try to keep me away." The smith crossed his arms.

"You're not leaving me here alone," Osbourne said and went to stand by Strom. So Sinjin, his wife beside him and his mother's good friends following in their wake, walked away from Valterius, hoping the dragons could take care of themselves. It did not escape him that he was likely in far greater danger. Perhaps he should worry about his own survival.

Square corners and runic inscriptions marked the entranceway; sand covered the rest. Sinjin could not imagine how such a structure could exist amid massive dunes and not be entirely filled with sand, but here, at the threshold, they were asked to remove their shoes. He expected them to ask for his weapons as well, but they did not. The Arghast were a strange people, he thought; swords were just fine, but where do you think you're going with those shoes . . . in the middle of the desert? Madness.

Within awaited an even more unlikely place. Lush carpets colorfully depicting Arghast history decorated walls and floors. Deeper within, paintings adorned the stones themselves, faded and chipped but still beautiful. The air itself spoke of age, mysticism, and power, making Sinjin's arm hair stand on end. Ahead awaited a chamber one could only describe as an arena. Here, under the sands, hid a small field. Though Sinjin had no idea what games were usually played there, the sight of the tribal leader waiting for him made it clear what would happen today. The man's size was perhaps the only thing Sinjin could hope to exploit. Smaller and quicker, he could perhaps outlast a larger man.

Kendra grunted behind him. Sinjin looked back and noticed she and the others were kept from staying with him. No one else was allowed to follow, and his friends had little choice but to sit on stone benches with the crowd. A small bubble surrounded them as none chose to sit close to them. They were on shaky ground. This had the potential to be a very bad day. Duty to his mother was all that kept him from running away. Everything Uncle Chase had taught him became jumbled in his mind; he hoped for muscle memory from all his sparring time. It was a thin hope.

An older man waited along with Sinjin's opponent. He raised his hand and asked, "Will you fight?"

The question surprised Sinjin since he had issued the challenge. Still, he answered to satisfy protocol. "Yes. I will fight."

The crowd erupted. The older man raised his hand again and turned to the tribal leader, whose muscles flexed. "Will you fight?"

"No," the big man said. An even louder roar filled the arena, the acoustics somehow amplifying the sound, making it seem as if thousands were present. "I use my right to a champion."

The hooting and celebration in the crowd indicated they all knew something he did not.

"Sarjak of the Scorpion Clan, will you fight?"

The arena exploded with activity. Skirmishes broke out in the crowd, bets were made, and more than one person fainted. Sinjin had a very bad feeling.

Cheers followed a young man emerging from the crowd. Shoulder-length black braids and coarse facial hair were signs of manhood, but he was smaller in stature than most Arghast. Sinjin wondered if it was a joke, but his spear and graceful gait said otherwise. His weapon was scaled down from what most Arghast warriors used, but the way Sarjak of the Scorpion Clan carried it made it appear just as deadly.

Standing beside the older man, Sarjak waited, grinning. It was a tactic Sinjin's uncle had taught him: intimidate the enemy by showing no fear. He'd always had a hard time pulling it off. This occasion was no exception. The tribal leader tossed a rigid wooden spear at his feet and left the field, sitting not far from Kendra. She slid closer, obviously making him uncomfortable.

The older man looked both men in the eye. Then, throwing his hands in the air and walking away, he said, "Kill each other."

The arena fell silent, and Sarjak continued to grin. Sinjin held his ground, pivoting to follow the smaller man's movements. Intimidation was an effective tactic, and Sarjak was well trained. His movements catlike, he stalked Sinjin. Leaping high, his legs carved precise lines. Kicking the air didn't impress Sinjin but did show how nimble and skilled his opponent was. Still, the man had already expended a great deal of energy without landing a blow.

Though armed with an inferior spear, Sinjin was not untrained and had advantages of his own, though he suspected the use of Istra's power during such a fight would incite greater violence. Still, he wasn't against using his gifts to save his own life. Pivoting again, he watched the diminutive warrior prepare to do another of his flips. Sinjin was trying to decide if this was his opportunity to strike when Sarjak of the Scorpion Clan launched a surprise attack. What had seemed the setup to a harmless move was actually a devastating strike. As he thrust his spear into Sinjin's side, bringing pain and warmth, Sarjak grinned.

This was when most fighters made mistakes. He could almost hear his uncle coaching from the past. "Don't rush in to soothe your pride. Wait 'til you've got the advantage; then strike. Pride is a dead man's weapon."

He hadn't always understood or appreciated the words, but they saved him from a quick death. Though small, Sarjak was a potent enemy.

Pivot and feint. Sinjin tried to elicit some response. He hadn't wanted to hurt this man, but blood soaked his pant leg. He wouldn't last much longer. Sarjak could let him bleed to death. Again, Sinjin made a sloppy attempt at provoking an ill-timed attack out of Sarjak, and again the man held back. Each pivot and turn, Sinjin's movements got a little sloppier, dizziness driving him to one knee. As he picked himself up, the crowd booed. "Thief," they chanted, which raised his ire, but he didn't let it get to him. He just needed Sarjak to move a little closer. Louder the crowd grew, and Sarjak turned his attention away for just an instant.

Sinjin was already moving when Strom opened his shirt, revealing the amber figurine. Without a word, the smith caused the statuette to shine brightly, further distracting Sarjak. It was all the break he needed to land a blow across the Arghast warrior's knees. Exerting his will, the mundane spear struck with more force than the swing alone would have imparted, which sent the small man tumbling over backward, clutching his knee in pain.

Circling, Sinjin looked for an opening, knowing the show of weakness could be false, but Sarjak struggled to stand. Still Sinjin suspected a farce. When he stepped in for a feint, Sarjak sent the presumably injured leg soaring toward Sinjin's unprotected face. Perhaps it was all the years of living with Kendra, but Sinjin knew how to dodge. He managed to get his face clear and take a swing at the exposed knee. Sarjak's scream gave evidence the knee truly was injured.

With no more tricks and dizziness starting to set in, Sinjin pushed harder than he should have. Suddenly seeing a keystone previously blocked from view distracted him. Sarjak's bare foot landed on his jaw.

The crowd launched to their feet and shook the foundation with their shouts. Strom and Kendra tried to reach him. Trying to sneak around where no one was looking, Osbourne also came. They would not be fast enough. Though no taller than Gwen Hawk, Sarjak of the Scorpion clan held his spear poised for a deadly strike.

* * *

The forests of Astor might be the worst place on Godsland as far as Nat Dersinger was concerned. It would all likely be over soon, his fate already determined. A waxing gibbous moon hid among the comets. Not so long ago, the dead god's periodic light had set the meter for life. Now, though, every night was brighter than the closest fullest moon he'd ever known. They said the dead god had been closer once, looming larger in the skies and pulling the tides to extremes. Now, though, one had to search for the moon amid Istra's brilliance. Could he even be certain the moon was not yet full? The light played tricks with his eyes. He could not afford to be fooled this time.

Snow capped the mountains in the distance, and the peaks shone like burnished copper. Within those peaks rested Ohmahold, perhaps the oldest fortification on the Greatland. Using the contours of converging mountain ranges, the ancients had constructed a safe haven within the most formidable natural defenses possible. Nature had assisted greatly, but it did not come without a price. Weaknesses of which few were aware and fewer still were mindful of had existed since before the rise of civilization. Again, Nat shivered at the thought.

Any time he followed in Catrin's footsteps, even in reverse, Nat worried. She was a bright flame. Getting too close meant risking the burn. Even she and Brother Vaughn had not known about the items Nat had been sent to retrieve. No one born in the past thousand years knew--until now. Excitement vied with worry. The dragon had treated him kindly as well as unkindly, but there was something more in this for Nat, who'd been ostracized for warning of these very events. Now he had the opportunity to be a part of those events as they unfolded and to uncover knowledge once lost.

Common thought was that the ancients had left them gifts to help them along when Istra finally returned. In actuality, the ancients had left gifts for themselves and hidden them well. Growing familiarity provided glimpses into Mael's feelings and motivations. It was both terrifying and oddly comforting. He made himself think of other things, knowing the dragon was likely nearby, watching him and reading his thoughts.

When a steaming pool backed up to a rock face appeared ahead, he knew a long night waited. The druids watched these forests closely, and a fire was a sure way to draw their attention. Nat had no problem with druids; they were generally kind folks so long as you didn't abuse the land. But in these parts, druids and the Cathurans were tightly aligned. Nat also had no problems with Cathurans, except that he was about to rob them, he hoped without their ever knowing.

Nat backed off from the pool, looking for a sheltered place to spend a night. Not much presented itself. This was not the kind of place anyone would want to stay for long. Sun-bleached bones lined the shores of the pool, a clear warning that obviously some ignored at their own peril. Knowing he was one, Nat quailed. Though still safe on land, the thought of soon entering the water and possibly being eaten by daggerfish prevented him from getting any restful sleep. His dreams were of teeth and red water.

When a full day passed, clouds blew in with the sunset. No matter how bright or full, the moon could not be seen. As a fisherman, he'd used the cycles of the moon his entire life, but this one time he worried he was wrong, that he had somehow miscalculated. Never before had his knowledge of the dead god's cycles been an actual matter of life and death. The clouds also prevented him from keeping accurate time, and he thumbed his sand clock, trying to decide what to do.

If he entered the water too soon, before the moon was high, he would be almost certainly eaten going in. If he waited too long, he would either become trapped inside Ohmahold or be eaten on his way out. He suppressed thoughts of surrendering to the Cathurans. Visions of Mael clawing his way into the hold made him quail.

A rabbit skin was his only assurance. His legs shaking, Nat wrapped the skin around a rock and tossed it into the mist-covered water. Though it bobbed and floated, the skin remained otherwise unmolested. Nat said a prayer that the fish weren't just good at recognizing living prey. Stripping down to naught but a loincloth, he stood by the pool and shivered from more than just the cold. He picked up a small waxed bundle and an amber figurine. Not understanding how the figurine worked, he hoped the light would last long enough. If everything went as planned, he would be in and out in a single night. But it was an audacious plan.

Unable to stand the thought of waiting too long, Nat slowly walked into the water, risking only toes at first. With every step, he was more vulnerable and would have a more difficult time escaping. When he ducked his head under the water, he was beyond hope if daggerfish attacked. Small forms brushed up against him in groups, feeling like loose stones that danced through the water. If not for holding his breath, he would have cried out. What had he done to offend fate, he asked himself while swimming through the blackness and still feeling stone overhead. It was then he questioned if he'd found the right pool or even the right tunnel leading from the pool. Panicking, he scrabbled harder, knowing it was too late to go back the way he'd come. When at last he broke the surface, he coughed and sputtered, trying to regain his breath. The sounds echoed through the ancient mines beneath Ohmahold.

Quickly Nat emerged, dried himself as best he could, and donned the leather slippers he'd wrapped in a waxed pack. Feeling cold and vulnerable, he trembled on his legs. In no way was Nat Dersinger made for stealth. Running through darkened halls, racing against the sand clock and wearing nothing but a loincloth and slippers, he could not have felt more like a fool. The dragon had better be right.

Chapter 9

The creative mind accelerates over time.
-- Osbourne Macano, glassblower

* * *

"Stop!"

The booming voice echoed from nowhere. Sarjak of the Scorpion Clan hesitated. His posture resembled his clan's namesake, his spear like the arachnid's tail, its tip ready to lash out with speed and force. Strom wanted to go to Sinjin, to stop the fight before Catrin's son was dead, but tribesmen stood ready to prevent just that. His figurine would no longer be much use. Fingering the spider stone, Strom knew another way, one which terrified him.

Catrin's voice, though twisted and distorted, drew Strom's gaze toward a stone grove at the back of the arena and away from Sarjak's spear. Previously obscured from view, the stone grove cleared as the Arghast moved away from the keystone with haste. Looking again, Strom cursed himself for being unobservant. Signs of recent damage marred the area. Flickering amber light danced around the keystone. Pain filled Catrin Volker's visage when she appeared above the circular artifact, as if she, too, were fractured and torn.

"Give my son the sword," Catrin's shade said. Dark shadows danced around her, laughing and encroaching on her spirit. Lightning split the air above the keystone and Catrin recoiled.

"Mom!" Sinjin yelled, no longer under threat from Sarjak's spear.

The Arghast warrior who'd been so close to ending Sinjin's life now rushed toward the keystone. Catrin, still trapped within the Noonspire and under attack, lashed out with ropes of fire before her image flickered and faded away.

"For the Herald!" Sarjak of the Scorpion Clan yelled as he leaped into the shattered portal. His high-pitched scream ended abruptly as the keystone fell dark and silent.

Sarjak was gone.

The men blocking Strom moved. The mood shifted. It had been clear all along this was a sacred, holy place. Catrin's appearance was a significant event, and it seemed to have triggered some knew belief. While Strom detested prophecies, they did on occasion come in handy. Reaching Sinjin's side, he was grateful for this instance. He examined the wound, which was still bleeding rapidly. The young man was already weakened. Kendra reached him a moment later, tearing strips from her garments and applying pressure to stem the blood flow. "Get the sword," she said to Strom in a low growl, "and then get us out of here."

The smith just nodded and searched for the man who'd challenged Sinjin in the first place. It was an impossible task. The man had been wearing headgear, and only minor variations in his garb gave any indication of his identity. Strom remembered his physical form well, but these were a lean, muscular people, so he didn't stand out. It didn't help that no one wanted to face them. Most formed an orderly line, leaving the building in subdued silence. Strom was not far from losing his temper and demanding they all stop what they were doing and take the desert apart if that was what it took to get Catrin's boiling sword. An older man approached. Strom recognized him as the man who'd given the order to start the fight.

"Please accept our humble apologies," the man began.

Strom grunted.

"I've sent for water, clean bandages, and herbs for the Herald's son."

"Where's the sword?" Strom asked with a command in his tone. The Arghast respected strength, and he knew that, but he'd also had about all he could stand of the tribesmen. Perhaps the Drakon and Dragon Clan were more flexible in their beliefs due to the changes they had seen in their own lives, but for whatever reason, the Arghast on the Godfist were more steadfast. When honest, Strom had to admit the fact that their prophecies kept coming true probably had something to do with it. Still, a big part of him believed prophecies fulfilled themselves. Would Catrin have had to come through the keystone if the Arghast had not believed she needed to in order to fulfill their role? It wasn't a question that would be answered any time soon.

"I have sent for the sword."

"Where is it?" Strom repeated.

The older man hesitated, and Strom leaned closer. "A sacred place," he said.

"Take us there. Now."

"I cannot," the man said. "I have sent the fastest horses."

"We have dragons."

"About that . . ."

Not waiting to hear what the man said, Strom marched toward the entrance. Though the Arghast had been true to their word and white-robed figures worked to clean and dress Sinjin's wound, anger continued to build within the smith. Burning like a forge under full bellows, his rage grew. "Out of my way!" he barked at the last of those seeking to make an orderly exit. The line parted before him, and he knew he must resemble a charging bull. It was something he'd worked on over the years, which sometimes proved useful.

When he reached the sands above, he wondered again how they managed to keep sand from filling the entire place and hiding it beneath the dunes forever, but the question was soon driven from his mind. The dragons truly were gone. Cursing, Strom turned back toward the arena like a gathering thunderhead. The older man met him at the entranceway.

"What's your name?" Strom asked, no warmth in his voice.

"Thane."

"What happened to our dragons, Thane?"

"I don't know," the man said.

Strom growled.

"I am told they simply flew away."

The big smith wanted to be angry with Thane, to blame all this on him, but he could not. For all he knew, the dragons had abandoned them of their own volition. It wouldn't be the first time.

"We're sorry for how you've been treated," Thane apologized again.

"This is twice," Strom said, looking Thane directly in the eye. "If I ever come back here again, you all had better be nice. Is that clear?"

Thane nodded.

Moving back inside, Strom pushed through the crowd, which again parted before him.

Sinjin was on his feet, his abdomen wrapped in clean dressing.

"How are you feeling?" Strom asked, sounding like a completely different person.

"I've been better . . . but I'm not dead. Thanks."

Strom grinned at him. Thane said nothing but nodded in understanding and silent apology.

Kendra was about to say something sarcastic when a shout from the entranceway drew everyone's attention.

"Dragons!" someone shouted.

"Out of our way!" Strom barked as they practically carried Sinjin from the arena.

When they reached open air, Strom almost turned around and rushed back in. Feral dragons approached, though were still some distance away. Even closer, though, were Valterius and Gerhonda, each bearing a heavy load. Both worked hard to maintain their altitude. Beneath them, their loads flailed and writhed, making the task more difficult. When Strom realized the dragons carried horses, each with a rider still in the saddle, he prepared himself for more trouble. This was not the kind of thing the Arghast took lightly.

The horses did arrive with far greater speed than they would have achieved without "help," and with ferals on the way, every instant mattered. Valterius bugled in triumph when he set the horse and rider gently before Sinjin, like a hunting dog delivering a fat duck. The rider teetered in his saddle, his horse sidestepping and wheeling, the whites of his eyes visible in his panic. Bearing a bundle wrapped in blankets, he presented it on trembling knees.

Taking his arm from around Kendra's shoulders, Sinjin accepted the cloth-wrapped sword with a wince. Pulling back the oiled cloth revealed Strom's masterpiece. Though he'd never wanted to create death machines, the smith had to admit this sword was beautiful and unique. Unlike single-bladed swords that were the pinnacle of technology developed over hundreds of years, everything about this sword was superior and advanced. Strong but brittle metals mixed with softer, malleable metals were apparent in acid-etched lines along the blade. Wisplike joins fused hardened metal that formed the cutting edges. Even while he'd been forging the sword, Strom had not understood. Now, looking at it with fresh eyes, he still did not completely understand all the reasons for the things he'd done. It had all come from Kyrien, the knowledge a specter he'd chase for all his days.

Gerhonda placed the other horse and rider as gently as she could on the ground then whined at Kendra, looking back toward the ferals. There was no time for words. Strom helped Sinjin and Osbourne mount Valterius and get strapped in. Sinjin looked better already. Pain was clear on the younger man's face, but it was accompanied by unquestionable determination that made Strom proud.

Kendra reached down a hand, and Strom used the leverage to gain the saddle. Gerhonda decided he could finish strapping in from mid air. It was not a decision he appreciated until he looked back to see just how close the ferals had gotten--far too close, indeed. Reaching deep into his pocket, he fingered the spider stone, praying he would not need to use it.

* * *

Making their way back to the dry docks and staging fields, Kenward Trell had to admire his mother's foresight and wisdom. Everywhere he looked in these hills, he found raw materials. Though primarily made of wood, and specific types of wood for different purposes, metal was a critical component in shipbuilding. The craftsmen his mother had assembled needed ore, and finding it locally would be far cheaper than shipping it in. His family earned their living through trade and needed to continue doing so if they wanted to finance such an elaborate construction operation. His mother had never been one for half measures. She hid things from him still; just as he withheld information from her; most of the time the arrangement suited them.

Jessub Tillerman walked alongside Kenward in silence. It was good to see the boy getting his strength back. Three plates a day wasn't hurting matters. His mother had planned ahead, and they were perhaps too well stocked. Kenward had stolen a peek at the latest inventories, and there was far more than needed. Perishable items troubled him most. His mother was not one to waste food. Such things gnawed at his curiosity.

"How are you feeling?" he asked Jessub.

"Better. I appreciate everyone who has cared for me and fed me. But I don't want to be a burden. I can go back to work whenever you have need."

"Funny you should say that," Kenward said. Jessub showed surprise, as if he'd expected Kenward to say no, to tell him it was still too soon. "I know you've still got healing ahead, but maybe a brief thrust test on the stinger would help loosen you up."

Jessub grinned back. "It couldn't hurt."

"Well, not as long as my mother and sister don't find out."

It was a long walk back to where the new aircraft prototype was still being sanded to remove rough edges. What Kenward had learned from the howler and the bumblebee, he had applied to the stinger. It was not a perfect aircraft, but it was a step closer to realizing his vision. Walking past the massive construction that was the *Kraken's Ghost*, Kenward felt familiar chills. This experience was without a doubt the best thing his mother had ever done for him. Though he drove her to distraction at times, he knew she did what she thought was best for them all. Knowing she thought chasing his crazy visions and dreams was best for the entire family brought a heavy mist to his eyes.

"Do you really think she'll fly, sir?" Jessub asked before realizing just what he'd said. "I mean . . . it's just . . . she's so big. It's difficult to imagine."

With a knot in his gut, Kenward knew this worry well. It was one thing to fly the *Serpent*, completely another to fly a ship many times larger. Lessons recently learned should make a ship like the *Kraken's Ghost* possible. No matter what doubts remained, it also felt good to pay tribute to his very first ship--one he'd sunk long ago. Finally he was ready to redeem himself.

Not far away rested the foundation of a similar yet very different ship. Sleek and smooth, the *Vengeful Shark* resembled its namesake in many ways, all the pointy bits hidden away until needed. The *Kraken's Ghost*, a sprawling, multilimbed ship promising death from every angle, also resembled its namesake. The lines of the *Kraken's Ghost* were shorter but no less graceful. Craftsmen, drafters, and architects struggled to enact his vision of incorporating the kraken form into the ship's functionality rather than as mere decoration. He'd built ships hastily in the past, but this one he intended to hand down someday. This was a generational ship, like the *Trader's Wind*, and Kenward understood the significance. This was his family's future, a thought that never drifted far from his mind or his sister's.

Having airships to guard and supplement the traditional fleet made perfect sense, which was most likely why his mother was so driven to see it happen. Still, these ships might never actually fly. It was an epic gamble. They could have built one ship at a time and tested before launching into full-scale construction of two massive ships, but his mother had some other agenda. Though she would not say why, she levied more gold toward this project than Kenward knew the family possessed. It was a sickening amount and it tested his courage.

When the stinger came into view, Jessub whistled. He hadn't been near an aircraft since his crash, and Kenward wasn't certain how the young man would react. He turned to Jessub and said, "Well, it's like my mother always told me, 'If you fall off the horse, what the heck were you doing on land?'"

With a laugh that ended in a cough, Jessub closed the remaining distance between him and the stinger. While similar to the howler, the proportions were different. No air tanks or firing tubes were visible. These elements had been cleverly incorporated into the main body along with munitions storage. The stinger was ready to earn its name. This craft had more in common with the *Vengeful Shark* than the *Kraken's Ghost*. Long, sleek lines contoured smooth surfaces.

The men working on the stinger stopped when Kenward and Jessub approached. "We're almost done, sir. We just need to fine-tune the thrust tubes."

"And that's why we're here," Kenward said.

"Let us get her strapped down tight, sir, and then we can safely test."

These men had been talking to his mother and his sister. "No need," Kenward said. "Jessub has excellent control, not to mention he's still a little weak. No need to waste time."

The craftsmen looked as if they might protest, but Kenward just gave Jessub a boost into the pilot's seat. Then he climbed up behind the younger man. The seat fit him well and had far fewer straps to worry over. With a couple of buckles cinched tight, he was ready to fly.

"How's it feel?" he asked Jessub, who just kept running his hands over the wood.

"Fine, sir. Just fine."

"Do you think you can give the thrust tubes a little test? Not too much now, mind you."

The workmen backed away from the aircraft when Jessub nodded, even if without much enthusiasm. Nothing happened at first, and Kenward feared the boy might have lost his nerve or perhaps even his access to Istra's powers. He was just wondering if that were even possible when a low-pitched growl emerged from the thrust tubes. Tuned to specific harmonics, these thrust tubes represented the height of engineering and design. Ancient knowledge combined with tenacity and ingenuity made the impossible possible once again.

"How's it feel?" Kenward asked again, a wide grin on his face.

Jessub turned back with a twinkle in his eye. "It feels real good, sir. Do you want me to give it a little more?"

"No," the lead engineer shouted. Jessub pretended not to hear. Kenward shrugged. Eventually this series of events would have to be explained, and he didn't want it said it was his decision. He liked Jessub but didn't feel the slightest bit bad putting this one on the young man. Those women find enough reasons to irritate me, he thought. Besides, it was good training for the boy.

Sawdust and wood chips filled the air behind them along with shouts from those caught in the wash. Jessub gave people time to move out from in front and behind before he truly applied himself. With trembling knees, Kenward hoped this didn't end like Jessub's last flight. Part of his reason for coming along was to show the boy he believed in him, but he had other reasons as well. Seeing the *Kraken's Ghost* and the *Vengeful Shark* from above would give him additional perspective he needed; it would also help settle some things he'd been trying to reason out.

Once every had given them a wide berth, Jessub fully applied his will. The stinger's report, deeper than the howler's, bore a resonant note like the striking of a harmonious chord. The engineers' shouts were drowned out. Vibrations in the wood structure ceased as Jessub found a sweet spot. Gliding forward along the dry dock's rails, the stinger moved faster. Jessub pulled back on the flaps and shouted for joy when they gained the air.

"You've got no skids!" someone shouted. He'd overlooked the missing landing gear. Normally he would have searched for a soft place to land, but that hadn't worked out well last time. Jessub looked back. Based on his grin, it was unlikely he'd heard the warning. No sense telling him now. Better to have a look around first. Kenward pointed up.

The higher they flew, the clearer the picture became. Workers below were like insects crawling over giant turtles, and the true scale became apparent. Looking at these enormous ships knotted his guts. Who could think such machines would fly? It would take all the canvas in the Greatland and a mountain of coal to generate enough lift. Even with the best and lightest woods, these ships would weigh more than the *Trader's Wind* and would be just as easy to get into the sky.

A wiser man might have called it a day and signaled for Jessub to land, but Kenward might not get another opportunity any time soon, especially once his mother and sister found out about this test flight. Pointing up, he urged Jessub to take them even higher. The aircraft flew with such fluid grace, Kenward could hardly believe it. Relaxed at the controls, Jessub could presumably fly like this for hours--at least once he'd gotten his strength back.

Altitude didn't do much to change Kenward's thinking on the two airships, but it did give him a better bearing on their location. In the distance, he could see waves, and that alone gave him comfort. Beyond a tall ridge waited something that made him question his mother's sanity. Construction dwarfing Kenward's and Fasha's airships combined lay below.

It was audacious and ludicrous. It was also now clear on which side of the family the insanity ran. "I need to talk with my mother! Take us down."

Nodding, Jessub began looking for a suitable landing site. Kenward could feel the young man's anxiety growing. This was the part that would make them or quite physically break them. When the young man appeared torn, Kenward sighted a spot back across the second ridgeline between them and his mother's cabin. There, by coincidence or design, waited a long strip of cleared ground that appeared smooth from above. Kenward tapped on Jessub's shoulder and pointed.

Having no better options, or perhaps because he wanted to be able to blame Kenward, Jessub circled back and tried to line the stinger up with the narrow strip of land. Had he stopped to think about it, it would have bothered the good captain that the young man might have used his own techniques against him. At that moment, though, he was more concerned with the landing. "Easy! Easy!"

Carrying too much speed, Jessub struggled against buffeting crosswinds. This operation would have been tricky enough in still air, but the skies above so many mountain peaks and ridgelines were as turbulent as the varied landscape below. When they reached the treetops, Kenward braced himself, feeling as if they would be dashed amid the branches at any moment. It was everything Jessub could do to avoid this fate.

The young man showed his worth, though, and guided them toward the center of the clearing. Still whizzing through the air at incredible speed, Jessub slowed them abruptly. The stinger dropped from the skies, and Jessub tried to abort the landing. His reaction just a little too late, the aircraft's tail struck grassy soil. Trying to pull them back into the air, Jessub did manage to right the aircraft . . . just in time to crash into Nora's cabin.

Once certain no one had been killed, Kenward grinned. This could only go well.

Chapter 10

Pride is best placed in one's work.
--Martik Tillerman, architect

* * *

Jordic of Kern returned to the Heights to find the situation worse than when he'd left. Ferals maintained a perimeter around the hollow mountains. Facing them alone was futile. Tanaketh cried out to his brethren before the ferals saw them coming. The mighty bellow sent a ripple through the darkness, and moments later, great behemoths burst through the ferals in every direction. The move was not without consequences, and Jordic trembled under the weight of those who died to save his life. They may not yet know it, but the cargo Jehregard carried was far more valuable, not to mention lethal. Grain dust in confined spaces could become explosive, but it was the rest of his cargo that concerned him. Though securely stored and kept isolated, the materials of war could just as easily incinerate them as the enemy.

Three verdants crowded in close, seeing how heavily loaded Tanaketh was, and escorting him in. Others dropped lower, raining stone and boiling water on the armies below. The ferals' numbers thinned, as many swooped lower in defense. Jehregard came in dangerously low. Within the upper range of enemy weapons, they were vulnerable. As if they knew the nature of his cargo, the forces of darkness launched fiery projectiles that splattered when they struck, spreading the flames.

Only with the help of verdant dragons flying alongside did they reach a safe altitude. Those within the Heights watched and prepared for a crash landing. All three dragons entered the hollow mountain together, just barely squeezing close enough to fit. Left with nowhere to hide, many dropped to stone for safety.

"Brace yourselves!" Jordic yelled to his passengers just before Tanaketh struck stone. The impact knocked the wind from him, and their inertia carried them forward, skidding and smoking across the wind channel. "Put out the fires quickly!"

As soon as they were stopped, people rushed in and did as he commanded. Soon only smoke and steam remained. After helping his passengers disembark, Jordic climbed down. Taking back to the skies one at a time, their escort rejoined the fray. Provided the room they needed, dragon grooms attended Tanaketh and unloaded his potentially deadly cargo. Jordic spoke with the load supervisor before seeking the council. Most of the verdants had now returned to their wind channels, and the guard congregated. Jordic walked to join them.

"Well met, brothers," he said. "We wouldn't have made it without you."

"Onin?" one asked.

"Alive," Jordic said. This brought a mixture of reactions, as he had expected. Onin had sponsored the mission; in their minds he should either be here or be dead. Sweating and still smelling of battle, the guard converged on the council chamber. None were happy.

Sensi and the others were present. Only the lord chancellor remained absent, and Jordic suspected it was on purpose, as it usually was. Those among the guard bristled at the all-too-common insult. Many tolerated it in times of peace, but when they were at war, the guard expected alacrity. Intentional delays for the sake of nothing more than pompous arrogance was an outrage.

When the lord chancellor did finally enter the council chamber, he was met by steely, smoldering gazes, which he completely ignored. "Onin of the Old Guard sponsored this mission and is charged with reporting."

Jordic stood tall, his head high. Others rolled their eyes.

"Onin?" the lord chancellor asked as if not already fully aware of the man's absence.

"He's not here," Jordic finally said.

"Is he dead, then?"

"No, sir." Saying the words made Jordic feel sick.

"Wounded?"

"No."

"Incapacitated?"

"No."

"Then he is a traitor," the lord chancellor said, almost gleeful.

The delegation from the Midlands had watched in silence, but one of the older men bristled. "Onin of Sparrowport is a good man. You're lucky to have him."

It was a dangerous statement. Had the lord chancellor chosen to challenge the man, things might have gotten worse, but he ignored the Midlander instead. "We will deal with the matter of treason momentarily. Must I remind you that we are at war?"

Jordic clenched his teeth in hopes of restraining his tongue.

"Since Onin of the Old Guard has failed to perform his sworn duty, it falls to you, Jordic of Kern, to report."

Not looking at the lord chancellor, Jordic spoke to the council as a whole. "The danger we face is greater than any we've ever known."

The lord chancellor rolled his eyes. "Why do those with no one to corroborate their stories tell the tallest tales?"

An angry murmur ran through the guard, but no one spoke up. Those who'd come from the Midlands continued to look uneasy, but not as much as Jordic of Kern. Sweat ran into his eye, but he let it burn rather than show weakness. "The reality of my words will be inescapable soon enough.

Already the one the Greatlanders call the Herald of Istra has fallen to the Noonspire." These statements created a great commotion in what was a normally solemn chamber.

"And the tales grow taller," the lord chancellor said. "If this ancient myth truly exists, then why has no one ever seen it?"

"I have."

The lord chancellor laughed. "Why has no one else?"

"Because we've acted like cowards," Jordic of Kern said, knowing his life was at stake. The lord chancellor almost smiled but maintained his act of being furious. "Because we've become overly cautious and weaker because of it. When was the last time any of you flew low over the very heart of the Jaga?"

No one made a sound.

"Of course they haven't. That would be foolish," the lord chancellor said.

"And now we know why it would be foolish," Jordic said. "Though it may have been buried beneath the black swamp for who knows how long, the Noonspire does exist, and Istra's return appears to have brought it back to life. Onin and I saw it, surrounded by the biggest hole in the ground you've ever seen and crawling with ferals." Perhaps the mention of Onin was ill advised, but Jordic bore no guilt. He'd done what was right and was not sorry for his actions.

"So you're saying there is a giant noonstone crystal in a hole at the center of the swamp--a hole that's not full of water, you say?" The lord chancellor smiled. "Truly, Jordic, you stretch your credibility thin. You've spent too much time with Onin."

"The Noonspire was in a giant hole in the ground, yes. Now it is not. Now it towers above the swamp, by what magic I do not know. I suspect whoever is in control there has been quietly building their strength. Once discovered, there was no more reason to hide, and they fully exposed themselves. With the Noonspire soaking in comet light, they'll be even more powerful. There's no time left. We must attack with all our strength."

Again the chamber erupted in arguments and exclamations.

Emel, captain of the guard cleared his throat and stood. "You say the Noonspire was beneath the ground on your way to the Mids and above when you returned?"

The lord chancellor cast him an annoyed glance but did not chastise him for speaking out of turn.

"Yes, sir."

"Was the Noonspire already under attack when you first saw it?"

"No, sir," Jordic said. He would not lie. "We passed the Noonspire, and it was mostly dormant, though it pulsed with life and was surrounded by ferals."

Emel frowned. The lord chancellor's smile widened.

"We encountered an airship that was heading straight for the Noonspire," Jordic continued, knowing only in the truth might he exonerate himself and Onin but, more important, convey the danger to his countrymen. "We warned them and then I urged Onin to continue on to the Midlands. He knew the Greatlanders, and he was worried about them."

"I'm certain he worried more about them than doing his duty," the lord chancellor said.

"He wanted to do both, sir. I was there with him, and I also did not want to see those people die. Onin asked that we turn back and do what we could to save them. I eventually agreed."

"Traitors!" the lord chancellor shouted, now standing and shaking his fist at Jordic.

Emel ignored this. "Tell us the rest."

"We could not save them, sir. The airship crashed into the Noonspire and only Onin's bravery saved two of the Greatlanders. The Herald of Istra fought and saved others, but she, too, was lost. It looked as if the crystal itself consumed her." Outrage, disbelief, and harrumphs interrupted him. He raised his voice to be heard above them. "Afterward the Greatlanders wanted Onin to take them somewhere, but he refused, saying he had to do his duty first."

Again, the lord chancellor made a rude noise but quieted under Emel's level glaze.

Jordic continued. "Kyrien, the last of the regent dragons, came to us, ridden only by the Herald's companion. Kyrien communicated with Jehregard and Tanaketh directly. It was the dragons who decided where Onin and I went."

No longer was any sense of order maintained. Sensi and the lord chancellor backed slowly toward a concealed exit. They did not flee, but they stood ready. Jordic had known this would not go well, but he hadn't been prepared for this. "Jehregard took me to the Midlands where I negotiated a trade for valuable goods and skills. With me are five of the Midlands' finest weaponsmiths, and we brought most of the materials needed to defend the Heights and the Midlands. We need them to help us make the weapons, and they need us to defend their homeland. I did my duty, and Onin did his. We must accept and acknowledge the fact that the dragons have agendas of their own, including verdants. We are not always in control."

"Lies!" someone shouted, and a scuffle broke out. Jordic wondered if he'd gone too far, but he knew what was right and would defend it to his grave.

Only when dragonriders fresh from the fight entered the chamber did order return.

The lord chancellor grew bold once again. "We can believe nothing this man says. It is my judgment Jordic of Kern and Onin of the Old Guard are traitors."

"What madness is this?" yelled one. His leathers and furs still smoked from battle, and the smell alone reminded of stark realities. When no one spoke, he made his report. "Scouting patrol just returned and reported some kind of giant plinth rising from the Jaga."

"It's the Noonspire!" one of the Midlanders shouted before clamping his hands over his mouth.

Sensi and the lord chancellor moved to escape the chamber.

"Onin of Sparrowport is no traitor," shouted a gnarled man missing two fingers and a thumb on his right hand. "We came here to help you and to help our homeland, but you betray your own. We accompanied Jordic of Kern. We saw what he described, and yet you do not even think to ask us, as if we could not be trusted to verify his words. You disgust me."

"I agree," Emel said, and the room went silent. "I challenge the lord chancellor's judgment."

Men blocked the lord chancellor's escape, knowing full well where the exits were. On trembling knees, Jordic of Kern waited, his life hanging in the balance. Never before had the captain exercised his right of challenge, mostly because it required a unanimous vote among the council and the guard. Such a thing he'd never witnessed. It took only a moment for the guard to form a unified front, standing in support of their captain, Jordic, and Onin. Two council members rose almost immediately to join them, but most remained where they sat. The lord chancellor looked smug. Sensi, at least, had the good sense to be afraid. Sweat poured from his pale flesh.

Emel stared down at two of those councilors who remained seated, saying nothing, his expression never changing. After only a moment, they joined him. Three council members remained, but when Emel turned on them, they no longer hesitated. Only Sensi and the lord chancellor remained in opposition. Only then did Jordic join the others in staring Sensi down. The big man quivered and shook, and after issuing a terrible wail, he ran to Jordic's side.

"The lord chancellor's judgment has been challenged and unanimously rejected. Jordic of Kern will receive a commendation for flying what may be the most dangerous flight of this war. Onin of the Old Guard is now an honorary member of the New Guard and due all the rights as such. Upon his return, he will be treated with respect."

"Fools!" the lord chancellor shouted before being allowed to finally flee the room.

* * *

"Kenward, you fool! Are you trying to kill someone?" Nora Trell screamed at her grinning son.

Stepping from the stinger and taking a bow, Kenward promptly slipped on a loose shingle. "Could someone just lean the ladder against this wall, please?"

Shaking his head and despite Nora's glare, Farsy brought the ladder and held the bottom. Jessub said nothing and tried to turn invisible. So far, it wasn't working. Fasha didn't take her eyes off him; the boy was in serious trouble. It almost made Kenward giggle. Seeing the look on his mother's face made the problem worse. The good captain did his best to appear cowed, but his mother and sister were having none of it. Workers dodged in and out, and the women barked orders before turning back to glare at him.

"Now look at what you've done," Nora said.

"It's not so bad," Kenward said. "The stinger took barely a scratch. Nothing a good bit of polish won't fix, I imagine."

Nora put a hand on her hip and raised an eyebrow. "And what about my roof?"

"I am sorry about that. A slight miscalculation, I'm sure. The winds are tricky around here, you know."

"I'm aware of this fact," Nora said, her face reddening. "One of the reasons I liked this place was that you'd have to be a fool to try to fly into it. Which I think was proven true today. I like having a mountain between my house and experimental aircraft."

"Or two," Kenward said. Nora silenced him with a glare. He chose a different tack. "I'll have some of the people working on the *Kraken's Ghost* come up and remove the stinger. I'm sure one of them will know how to fix a roof. Looks like tricky business to me."

"Fool boy."

"What?" Kenward asked, trying to appear innocent.

"I'm paying those people, and you waste their time."

"Not a waste, Mother. In the air I gained perspective, not to mention an otherwise successful test flight of the stinger . . . if you overlook the landing. Plus I got to see . . . other things." With the last part, he raised his eyebrows at his mother.

Fasha stopped glaring at Kenward and turned to in disbelief. "What are you hiding, old woman?"

Jessub laughed uncontrollably but then bit his lip and tried to make himself invisible. He failed.

A moment later, there came a rushing sound outside. Bits of the roof fell in as a massive downdraft struck. Kenward looked up in shock to see the stinger lift off. It couldn't be. Running to the door, he opened it to see the stinger resting on the grass nearby, undamaged. Six people saluted, all in uniforms both familiar yet new. Kenward was speechless. Fasha stared, open mouthed. Now both knew why their mother had been unconcerned about finding enough thrustmasters and flightmasters to get the massive ships off the ground.

"I knew you were up to something big," Fasha said with an accusing glare at Nora.

"You didn't think I was going to let you have all the fun, did you?"

Four men and two women entered the cabin with military precision and formality. Kenward giggled and Nora glared at him. "Ever since Catrin Volker flew the *Slippery Eel*, I knew this day would come. Once I'd seen it done, it became obvious; my own eyes allowed me to believe my wildest dreams might really come true. How many times have I paced the decks, waiting for wind to push me along? How many times have I wished to fly like a bird and leave cold waves behind? I love the sea, truly I do, but this is business."

"Speed is speed," Kenward said, and this time Nora smiled at his words. "And size is size."

These words made Nora purse her lips. Fasha's eyes smoldered. Kenward stayed silent but it wasn't easy.

"These fine people: Vik, Raja, Devin, Wenli, and Gret are our new shipmasters. Two will be assigned to each ship."

Kenward seemed to be taking in the term shipmaster, but Fasha did the math. "There's a third ship?"

Nora didn't answer; instead she just looked at Kenward, closed her eyes, and inclined her head. He needed no more permission. Leaping up from his chair, he said, "It's huge, Sis! You've got to see this thing. It's way bigger and crazier than what we're building. We're rational and staid compared to that madwoman." More than a few of those gathered looked uncomfortable. "I've never seen anything like it. What are you going to name that thing, the Flying Island?"

"The *Trader's Skies*."

For all his joking, that name struck Kenward's heart. This was the opportunity of several lifetimes, and his mother was going big. With that statement, she had explained everything. Kenward was about to ask what the heck a shipmaster did when Nora got up and signaled for everyone to go outside.

Kenward walked out beside Fasha, who muttered in disbelief. Ahead walked the one he thought was named Vik or Vix or something like that.

"I think the old bag might have finally lost it, Sis."

Fasha rolled her eyes.

Vik or whatever his name was stiffened and walked faster. Kenward reminded himself not to select old Vik when the time came--too stuffy.

"Show them," Nora said, and she nodded at Vik.

The man stepped forward, straightened his arms, and flexed his muscles. Kenward wasn't impressed until the rush of air burst from his hands, lifting him from the ground and spraying everyone else with leaves and other debris. Kenward wondered if he'd judged too soon.

Then Nora pointed at Gret; the smallest person in the group by a noticeable margin. Then she pointed at the towering, ancient trees across from the cabin, away from just about everything else. "Show him."

Bending her knees and establishing a firm stance, Gret leveled her fist at the trees. She and Vik both held something in their hands, but Kenward couldn't make out what they were. When the woman applied her will, Kenward took two steps back. Without so much as flinching, she cast a column of rotating air across the distance with such violence, trees ripped from the ground were sent spinning into anything still standing. Within seconds, the land was cleared. Now Kenward understood how they had cleared the valleys in such a short time and how so many trees had been brought down and stacked in staging areas.

"How are you not crushed by such force?" Kenward asked. "Or thrown backward?" He had seen the challenges flightmasters and thrustmasters faced. This brought entirely new possibilities."

"The ancients knew things we still don't understand," Nora said. "These devices are among them. Clearly the vortex orbs allow tremendous thrust but also counteract it. Somehow the user is not subject to those forces unless desired."

"May I?" Fasha asked Gret, holding out her open palm.

Looking to Nora first, Gret received a nod in answer. With a sheepish look, she handed the glassy orb to Fasha. She'd seen such things before but never quite like this one. Part of the spherical object was perfectly clear; within, a glittering maelstrom swirled, impossibly deep and complex. The back was covered in metallic green and orange creating an intricate pattern. Form, function, and design created breathtaking art.

"For all the money I've spent building these ships," Nora said. "These cost me twice that; not to mention years of research. We need more, but it is a start."

"You got me, Mom," Kenward said. "I'm impressed."

"You haven't seen anything yet, fool boy." Nora wore an impish grin. "The next part is just for you." Rarely had she ever commanded Kenward's attention more completely. "Show him, Raja."

The man stepped forward with no expression on his face. He was good, Kenward thought. From his pockets, Raja produced four rocks, a couple of pieces of string, and a tiny thrust tube with hooks around the outside and a black crystal mounted at its center. Kenward recognized noonstone. He'd seen the largest piece in the world, and this was surely the same material. With those thoughts came pain, and he tried to push it away. What Raja did next partially succeeded. First he tied the thrust tube to the rocks and placed it at the center.

"Start the reaction," Nora said. Placing his hand over the crystal, a tiny blue spark and a pop were followed by rushing air. A pleasant breeze resulted. "Now provide no more energy."

Kenward gaped. Floating above the table, the miniature thrust tube continued to pump air, presumably with no input from the shipmaster. Such a thing could allow the ungifted to fly continuously on their own, Kenward realized with a jolt.

"Now we just need a whole lot of noonstone." Fasha said.

Nora grinned. "Funny you should mention that."

"Mother," Kenward said. "You are an evil genius."

"It's about time you all figured that out. Now somebody fix my roof!"

Chapter 11

A passionate life inspires.
--unknown bard

* * *

"I'd wager you never thought this would be your day," Nat Dersinger said to the man in Kyte livery, who leaped in surprise. "Left here practically alone to guard empty chambers. It must have seemed the most boring assignment possible."

Reaching for his sword, the young man turned to see Nat, backlit by the comets beyond the open balcony.

"Now before you do anything foolish, ask yourself this: Do you really want to cross a man capable of sneaking into the most secure part of Wolfhold?" Feeling bad for the young man, Nat could hardly believe he was there. No previous experience had prepared him for this. Mael's thoughts tickled his mind. "I don't want to kill you. This should be evident based on the fact that I could easily have killed you already."

Watching the young man's every move, Nat sensed his belief. Victory must have shown on his face. The young man looked as if he might try to make a run for it, presumably to seek help, but then thought better of it after Nat spoke. "Lord Kyte will not even miss what I am here to retrieve. It was left here long before the Kyte family occupied this structure. I will, in fact, be giving you and your lord a magnificent gift at a small price." The young man didn't look at all convinced but did not flee. "What is your name?"

"Jenneth," he said, his eyes downcast.

"I'll make you a deal, Jenneth. If you trust me and do as I say, I will leave you alive and more popular than you've ever been before." The young man's expression told Nat he just needed to set the hook. "Imagine telling Lord Kyte about how you found the ancient stash of art and artifacts that had been hidden within Wolfhold for ages."

Emotions played across Jenneth's face.

Hero.

Nat felt the nudge, recognizing it for what it really was; always before he had called it intuition then visions. Now he understood the true source and marveled at Mael's skillful manipulation. A single thought at the right moment was all it took to change the course of human history--or at the very least Nat's life and now Jenneth's.

"I'll do it," Jenneth said, "but do not think to cross me. One does not get to guard the lord's chambers, empty or not, without reason."

Nat did his best not to undo what Mael had helped him accomplish. He could have pointed out how much good that had done Jenneth, but he knew better. Instead he closed his eyes and inclined his head. It was enough.

"You've been taught to defend this place," Nat said. "You know how to trigger the cave-in mechanisms to isolate this part of the hold." The young man appeared to have second thoughts. "I need the key."

Looking over Nat's shoulder, Jenneth blanched. Knowing what the young man saw, Nat did not blame him for his fear; the dragon mage frightened him as well. No matter what he sensed beneath a seemingly endless well of resentment, Mael was no gentle flower. Jenneth said nothing but glanced at the fireplace. Stifling a laugh, Nat walked to the ornate hearth and inspected the tools hanging alongside. Amid the tongs and pokers rested a different kind of implement. Covered in soot, it fit with the rest, save the more skillfully crafted handle. Nat grabbed the key and walked toward the inner halls, indicating Jenneth should lead the way.

"How did . . . ?"

"Never take up gambling, kid. They'll just take all your money."

Hanging his head, Jenneth nodded. "I already learned that lesson."

Again came a twinge of guilt, but he just had to take solace in the fact that the young man would see another day. Beyond that was not his responsibility.

"Where are we going?" Jenneth asked, his voice trembling.

"To the secondary juncture," Nat said. Jenneth was again appalled by how much information Nat possessed. Mael had told him this would be the case. This was the final fallback position in the keep's defense. The Kyte family's early discovery and use of the keystones had made them extremely easy to manipulate. And they had brought other places within the sorcerer's reach. Ohmahold, Drascha Stone, even parts of the Godfist outside Dragonhold. Now Nat recognized the brilliance, amazed at what Mael had accomplished with so little access to Istra's light.

I saved the last bit of energy from when Istra last departed this world. Such a sad parting. I longed to use that power every day for three thousand years. I had to be patient.

Such resolve would have been unimaginable to Nat before Mael, but having been touched by this ancient mind and shown a glimpse, he was in awe.

Jenneth led the way reluctantly. He did not deviate from what Nat knew was the shortest path to the juncture. At least he was no fool. After two turns, Jenneth stopped. His eyes went to the ceiling, and he looked back as if he might be sick.

Nat joined him and looked up to see a beautiful mural of a wolf pack caring for pups. As much as he hated to do it, Nat hoisted the key.

"Do you have to?" Jenneth asked before Nat made another move. "Are you sure?"

"You know this is the location of the cave-in release, correct?"

Thoroughly defeated, Jenneth nodded.

"Then they would not place anything truly priceless here, knowing it would be destroyed."

Appearing unconvinced and worried, Jenneth wrung his hands and paced. Nat could not waste time. More guards would be stationed within the hold, though fewer than usual given Jharmin's current absence. Ramming the pointed key through a wolf pup, plaster and other bits falling away, Nat found what he was looking for. Jenneth went pale. Using the key to clear away the decorative covering, Nat revealed a small orifice, just large enough to admit the key. He had to move the handle to different angles to get more intricate parts of the design within. With a final twist, the key caught on something. Pushing Jenneth back toward Lord Kyte's chambers, Nat gave a good yank. At first the painting cracked and chipped, the cave-in not as instantaneous as one might expect. Already Nat was aware no shower of rock would follow, but Jenneth knew no such thing.

With a few more yanks, a much larger opening appeared. Starting just above where the ceiling had been, a series of indentations were carved into the stone: a ladder leading into darkness. Pulling a herald globe from his robes, Nat once again brought shock and marvel to Jenneth's eyes. Everyone knew what herald globes were and what they looked like, but few had ever actually held one.

"Don't drop it," Nat cautioned. "Now up you go." Bending his knees and knitting his fingers, Nat prepared to give the young man a boost. It was a good thing Jenneth had not done anything stupid, or it would have been a difficult climb.

Accepting the herald globe with fear and awe, Jenneth pulled a cloth from his uniform and wrapped the globe as if it were the most fragile object in the world before putting it in an inside pocket. He checked three times before he was satisfied the globe was secure, and he put a hand on Nat's shoulder. For the first time, the young man's fear was gone, excitement and the thrill of discovery in its place.

With a grunt, Nat lifted with all his strength.

"A little higher," Jenneth said.

"Stretch," Nat said through clenched teeth. Far too old for feats of strength, a cry escaped his lips as Jenneth did as he was told, which put more pressure on Nat's aging joints. Soon it was over and Nat struggled to stand straight. He was not weak, but no longer was he young and spry.

"By the gods! You spoke truly. Look at it all!"

"You will bring me three specific items that belong to . . . my companion. The rest you may keep or turn over to Lord Kyte. I make no judgments or suggestions. Get me the items I require, and I will be gone."

* * *

Dragons.

All Sevellon the thief wanted was freedom from dragons, yet no matter what he did, they found him. Whether painted on signs or engraved in furniture, they were inescapable. No matter how far he fled, they chased him down and pinned him beneath hungry gazes. His dreams were thick with them, but a single serpent dominated them all. This dragon was different. It wanted something and would not leave him alone.

Asking Jharmin Kyte to take him back to the Godfist had been among the most difficult things Sevellon had ever done, and it was, in almost every way, against his will. The only part of him that agreed with going back was the part that wanted to remain sane. Every day the dreams had worsened, the urge to throw himself into black water almost too much to resist. Compulsion to get back to the Godfist had overwhelmed all else, including self-preservation. He'd begun to fear sleep. Some people walked while dreaming, and he was afraid he'd wake up cold, wet, and drowning. Leaving Jharmin Kyte's ship, the *Wolf's Head*, was in many ways sweet parting; in other ways it was terrifying.

Back in Harborton, he was no more welcome than he'd been the last time. Somehow he'd have to get into the Masterhouse, but he had no information, no plans for the construction, no maps, nothing. All he could do was watch the entrances and make notes. Matters of defense often followed schedules and patterns. These fostered vigilance but were also tools the thief could exploit.

Pictures in his mind surfaced, but he forced them back down. If the dragons needed his expertise, then they could very well stop tinkering with his thoughts. Feeling a strong sense of aloneness afterward, he wanted very badly not to admit he missed the presence once it was gone. No matter how much he valued his freedom, having pertinent information pop into your consciousness provided reassurance. In matters of life and death, Sevellon tried not to be picky.

What the dragons wanted with an ugly stone, Sevellon did not know. He'd heard of the sky stone and how the gods had sent it so the Zjhon might defeat the Herald, but it hadn't actually worked out that way. He tried not to put much stock in the words of prophets and minstrels, especially since people still clung to legends already proven false.

Moving from shadow to shadow, Sevellon searched for a place from which he could monitor the Masterhouse. No one was going to bring the sky stone out to him, which meant going in. He'd have to access the most sacred inner chambers and carry a heavy, ugly, and presumably valuable stone away from those who cherished it. This was not a job he'd ever have taken, but choice was no longer his.

"... need skilled hands," a man said.

Peeking around the corner, Sevellon spotted a tall guard lingering near the blacksmith shop.

"What for?"

"The masters want the same kind of comforts within the Masterhouse as are available within Dragonhold."

"Look what it got them," the smith said.

The guard shrugged and moved on.

Rubbing his hands together, Sevellon moved away, knowing it would be best to let at least a little time pass before approaching the blacksmith. Sometimes a thief had to be subtle, a master thief even more so.

Chapter 12

Be the inspiration for a young person that you needed at their age, and you can travel in time.

--Master Jarvis, teacher

* * *

Pulling the spider stone from his sturdy inside pocket, Strom knew outrunning the ferals was unlikely. Clear skies left nowhere to hide. Valterius and Gerhonda had expended large amounts of energy getting the horses and riders back to Sinjin and the others. Now they faced jagged peaks, seaside cliffs, and the Arghast desert. Valterius chose the open sea beyond the cliffs. Gerhonda flew below and behind. Ferals appeared from the peaks around Catrin's Oasis, and Strom growled at the thought of them fouling the place.

More dragons, previously clinging to the cliffs, had been lying in wait. With the extra weight, the regal dragons gained altitude more slowly and were less nimble in their movements. The feral dragons took full advantage and did their best to surround the regals. They were succeeding. If only the Drak had less weight to bear, Strom thought, and he reached for the straps holding him in. He wouldn't survive the fall, but his sacrifice might give Sinjin a chance to grow old. It was not an easy choice or one made lightly, but air pressure changes pulsating with mighty wing flaps told him it might already be too late.

With the spider stone in hand, he tried to find the feral dragon he knew was so close. Through some trick the predators possessed, the huge creature hid from the smith until claws raked the air near his face, and that was when Strom unleashed his fury on the dragon above. Like a fiery snake, lightning pulsed and writhed. A thunderclap split the air, and the dragon above crumpled, quite suddenly bearing down on them, forcing them closer to rock-strewn waters.

Gerhonda whined as Valterius struggled to get away from the dead feral. Dropping below the cliffs they just so recently cleared, they plunged into the shadows. Here the land also shaped the air, and Valterius employed the turbulence to his advantage. Using a rolling updraft formed by the prevailing wind as it encountered the cliffs and mountains, Valterius rolled out from under the feral dragon and spread his wings. The sudden change in direction took Strom's breath and Sinjin screamed. Strom did his best to support his injured friend.

A cloud of ferals harried Gerhonda, and the smith despaired. Osbourne had no way to defend himself. They were helpless. Valterius worked to gain altitude, but it was clear it would not be enough. Trying to predict the dragon's movements, Strom took aim at the ferals but would just as likely hit Gerhonda.

"Give me a straight shot," Strom shouted, not knowing if the dragon would listen or understand. He never found out.

Rolling thunder tipped with screams and high-pitched thumps made it sound as if some leviathan had risen from the deep and joined the battle. To Strom's utter amazement, it appeared this new monster was on their side. Beams of fire and blue light raced into gathered ferals, scattering them. Gerhonda dipped lower, trying to get closer to Valterius. Her flight wobbled but she appeared mostly whole, those riding her injured but not dead.

Seeing the true nature of their salvation, Strom hollered with joy. The Drakon had arrived, and they flew as never before. Like Valterius and Gerhonda, they each carried an extra passenger, but the Dragon Clan rode facing backward, something Strom would never have considered. It was not the seating arrangement that was so remarkable, rather the speed at which they flew. As if propelled forward by the Dragon Clan, the Drakon split the air with speed no feral could match. They carried weapons like nothing Strom had ever known. Catrin and others had wielded the Staff of Life, but never had he seen gleaming metal staves glow with intricate fury.

Arakhan stood out amid the rest, his staff emitting structured light, forming geometric patterns and symbols. Around his arm, shields of blue light connected to rods and gears of pure plasma, man and staff together forming a larger machine. Strom watched in utter amazement as Arakhan pulled his arm back, engaging the mechanism, before releasing a blade of energy that sliced the air and anything it touched.

"Al'Drakon!" came their battle cry, sounding strange as they whizzed past.

Aerial chaos took on a more orderly form as the ferals began their retreat. Arakhan, Mikala, and the others soared after the fleeing dragons, while Valterius and Gerhonda made for the coastal cliffs. Not wasting any time after the valiant beast touched the rocky sands, Strom unstrapped himself and checked on Sinjin. The fighting had loosened his bandages and reopened the wound. The young man was far from defeated and worked to secure his own dressing. Strom handed him a water skin.

"By the gods!" Osbourne exclaimed, looking out over the water. In the distance, the Drakon fought. Ferals made a stand above black-sailed ships approaching the coastline. Red lightning leaped from the assembled ships, dark art once again threatening. Drakon faced danger from above and below; it was a lot to ask of anyone. The resultant light show caused the thin clouds, now gathering above the ships and growing darker, to glow from within.

"Be watchful," Kendra said. "They might not have all flown away."

She was right. Still, the horrific spectacle drew the eye. Somehow a second passenger and some sort of magical weapons had turned regal dragons into a lethal force. Never had Strom seen anything fight with such tenacity, accuracy, and deadly impact. But even with that, numbers were not on their side.

It was to the protection of their fleet the ferals had run. Seeing the Drakon make one last attack on the ferals while doing their best to avoid those on the ships below, Strom could not believe the raw power of their combined might. Peeling away, the Drakon took casualties in their retreat but still faired far better than the other side. The thought made Strom sick. Those were his friends and countrymen, and he vowed not to let their deaths go unavenged. Part of him wanted to take the fight to the ships and unleash the spider stone upon them, but protecting Sinjin and Kendra was more important. He had decided to trust Kyrien after their long flight back from the Black Spike, and he had to continue to believe, or all this might prove to be for naught.

The surviving Drakon returned with amazing speed, though they slowed upon approach. Regal dragons gathered along the same cliffs from which Nat Dersinger had once pushed Catrin.

Breathless, Brother Vaughn managed to say, "We found a cache of ancient artifacts."

Strom could see in the man's face he didn't tell them everything, but he didn't press the issue.

"How badly are you hurt?" Brother Vaughn asked Sinjin.

"I've lost some blood. We've got the bleeding stopped again. Given time, I'll heal."

The monk pulled a wooden box from the leather satchel he carried and mixed three powders together on a dried leaf. "Here. When the pain is high, take a pinch with water."

Sinjin took the leaf, looked at it for a moment, then poured the contents into his mouth. Brother Vaughn produced a water flask. The young man grimaced and drank more water than advisable but to his credit did not spit it out. He handed the leaf back to the monk, who waved it off. "Chew on it," he said. Again, he did as he was told and popped the leaf into his mouth. He made another face but kept chewing. That was when Strom knew it really hurt.

"I have my mother's sword," Sinjin said, the leaf tucked in his left cheek. "But I have no idea what I'm supposed to do with it. With no additional information, I can only assume I'm to take it back to the crystal. If my mother objects, she is clearly capable of telling us to leave." No one could argue his point. Sinjin watched the horizon, ever vigilant in spite of his pain, and Strom was embarrassed when the wounded man proved more observant than he. "Fires." Multiple smoke columns rose from behind not-so-distant mountains. "That looks like Harborton and the Lower Pinook."

"They've not even recovered," Kendra said, shaking her head in dismay.

Sinjin limped toward Valterius.

"You must go to your mother," Arakhan said, stepping between Al'Drakon and Al'Drak.

"This is my homeland," Sinjin said.

"And ours as well." As if to bolster his words, formations of Arghast riders appeared, heading toward the Pinook Valley. It was an awe-inspiring sight. "We will protect our homeland. You must go."

With a sad nod, Sinjin extended his hand to Arakhan. "Take good care of them."

"You must take weapons and thrust spheres," Arakhan said. Sinjin considered protesting, but Arakhan gave him a look that told him just how foolish it would be.

Strom looked at the delicate glass sphere someone handed to him.

Brother Vaughn approached Strom. "Just point that away from everyone and think about a strong wind."

Strom somewhat reluctantly did as he was told, and the roar was immediate. He sighed. Osbourne extended his trembling hand. Strom gave him an unreadable look as he handed the orb to his friend. Closing his eyes and squinting, Osbourne held the thrust sphere out toward the desert and concentrated. Nothing happened. His face was a mixture of disappointment and relief.

"Try the staff," Brother Vaughn said.

Strom almost punched him. When the monk handed him the work of metal art, the smith was enamored. Such craftsmanship he'd never seen, and just a quick glance taught him things. This was a treasure beyond measure. Grasping it lightly, he pointed it toward the sands as Brother Vaughn instructed and applied his will but was surprised and a little disappointed when it didn't work.

"Not every staff works for every person," Brother Vaughn said. "We're still figuring this stuff out. For now, though, looks like it's a light bow for you."

Strom accepted the weapon with no small amount of trepidation. If what they said was true, and he had no reason not to believe them, this weapon was from the last Istran phase. Most things he'd encountered from the last age had tried to kill him. Pulling the trigger seemed dangerous folly. Still, he lived in dangerous times. With a deep breath, he turned the weapon toward the sands and fired. The high-pitched thump sounded even different from that vantage point, and Strom could see the utility of such a weapon. With that said, wielding it terrified him, knowing he might accidentally incinerate his friends.

"Most importantly," Brother Vaughn said, "don't shoot the dragon."

Valterius trumpeted his agreement.

"Without the ability to provide thrust, I'll be of little use," Osbourne said.

The comment was aimed at Brother Vaughn, who'd already proven his use of the thrust sphere. Strom hated to see his friend left behind, but perhaps it was for the best. Maybe one would survive. A thrust sphere had been recovered from a fallen friend, and Strom accepted it with reluctance. He strapped the light bow over his shoulder, and Sinjin had his at the ready. It felt strange facing backward, but Brother Vaughn climbed up behind Kendra and looked much the same as he did. Testing the straps one more time, he hoped he was truly secure.

"Let's get in the air before you use those things. And remember, don't shoot the dragons."

"Got it," Strom said.

More fires sent smoke into the air over the Upper Pinook Valley. From between the columns came a flight of dragons--each bearing a rider. Strom cursed. Drakon took flight.

In tight formation, the ferals flew low over the desert, creating a dust plume. Red lightning painted the clouds. The ferals moved faster than they could achieve on their own. Great, Strom thought. What had seemed a huge advantage might just level the field.

"Go!" Arakhan shouted.

It should have been Al'Drakon giving the orders, but all that would matter little if none survived. Arakhan was right and Sinjin obeyed. He was Al'Drakon, but he was no fool. Valterius pointed them out to sea, and Strom tested the thrust sphere with more intent than before. Holding out his hand, he concentrated and applied his focus to moving the air behind him. At first it felt as if nothing happened, but he could see the turbulent wash he'd created from mists roiling above the water. Trying again, he concentrated on thrust, applied to him and ultimately Valterius. The result was immediate, and Strom thought they might spin out of control. Valterius trimmed his wings and kept them upright in the turbulent air, his roar lost to the wind.

The speed was too much, but Strom lacked control. With deep breaths, he lowered his heart rate, slowed his breathing, and eased off the thrust. When they reached a speed less likely to tear them all to pieces, Valterius turned and gave him an unyielding stare.

"Sorry," Strom said.

Sinjin grunted. "Might need to go easy on that."

Looking back, Strom saw just how far behind Gerhonda had fallen. Ferals gained on her, in spite of Brother Vaughn's efforts. If not for Arakhan, the rest of the Drakon and the Dragon Clan, they would have been overwhelmed. The Drakon were now battle tested, and it began to show.

Arcane power flooded from those aboard feral dragons, but much of their energy went into speed. Strom watched them come, seeing the energy they radiated. Rather than using thrust as the Dragon Clan did, these sorcerers pulled at the air, tearing it apart, somehow forcing a bubble of relatively still air through the cavitation. The effect propelled them forward with a strange tearing sound, those aboard looking as if they felt nothing but a soft breeze, dark robes barely stirring.

Projectiles of electric blue light raced toward the dragons as the Drakon coordinated their efforts, careful not to fire into their own ranks. Following Arakhan, they let him select the targets, and they attacked each before moving on to the next. The ruthless tactic maximized the weapons' effects. Had they been spread out, striking various targets without eliminating them, they would still face most of the ferals. Using this technique allowed them to reduce the enemy's numbers more quickly. But the dark-robed figures aboard the ferals were no fools, nor were the dragons they rode. Soon they shifted their efforts from speed to defense.

"Go!" Arakhan yelled again.

Gerhonda picked up speed, and when she caught up with Valterius, Brother Vaughn looked exhausted. Hoping he would hold up, Strom waved in encouragement; the monk gestured weakly. Sitting as he was, Strom could do little but look back at the still-raging battle and feel guilty for leaving those he cared about. Osbourne should be by his side at a time like this. He wished his old friend well.

* * *

The only advantage ash fall provided was that camouflage was inherent and inescapable. Everything blended together, stained by pumice. Sevellon the thief carried a rock through the wilderness. This was the last thing he would do in service to dragons, he told himself. He had trained to facilitate the flow of valuable objects between wealthy families and organizations. This was generally best done in cities. Surviving alone on the Godfist tested the limits of his survival skills. While he knew how to create fires that emitted very little smoke, he would need something to cook.

Turning over rocks, looking for bait, and putting them back as they were, he left as little evidence of his passing as possible. His senses heightened, every noise was suspect. Fishing would put him out in the open, which meant night fishing. Unless thick clouds blew in, there would be plenty of comet light, more than he actually needed or wanted. He would be exposed. Dragons and other enemies aside, the Godfist was already a dangerous place. Plenty of hungry predators were about, and snakes provided yet another threat. Shivering, he tried to think about something else, something nice. Somewhere waiting for him was a city where no one knew his name, a place where the things lurking in the darkness were other people. He could handle people.

With every step north, the land grew wilder. Less evidence of humans coincided with more signs of . . . other activity. Dragon bones became more prevalent along with gouges in the land. Warnings such as these would normally have sent him back in the direction he'd come, but he stayed his course, knowing he'd never be rid of dragons if he did not complete this task. The creatures were terrifying to fight but perhaps even more frightening because of their ability to manipulate people's thoughts without their ever knowing. Looking back on his life, there were times when the urges of supposed instincts had been overwhelming. He would be a pawn no more. After this, he had a very simple plan: stay alive and avoid dragons. Perhaps living underground was not such a terrible idea after all.

Memories of his time within Dragonhold and aboard the *Slippery Eel* brought with them regret. No matter how he tried to push them away, Sevellon felt them acutely. He was getting old and losing his edge. Though now almost certain he'd been manipulated by dragons, likely more than one, he took responsibility for his actions. Unsure how this would change his life, he moved deeper into forested foothills.

A sound like thunder came from nearby. Sevellon froze. There was not a cloud in the sky. Deep, guttural woofs and grunts sounded, disturbing the relative stillness. Covered in sooty ash, Sevellon did his best to be invisible. By the size of the nose that came into view a moment later, he also hoped the pumice masked his smell.

Snuffling a wuffing, the giant crawled along the forest floor, grunting and whining as it went. The thief watched in fascinated horror. Fingers as large as he was gently swept much of the ash fall aside, allowing the beast to sniff out toadstools. Whining and grunting with each one found, the giant was in every way unlike what Sevellon had expected. Its masters had fled the Godfist, and this creature at least appeared to have returned to its natural state. This was only a small consolation since that state was huge and ravenous.

At times, the thief's luck seemed to wander off, and the giant found a particularly bountiful toadstool patch nearby. Excited by its find, it squealed with delight and shook the trees. A fallen branch struck Sevellon, but he remained quiet and still. Long moments passed while the giant ate, its knees coming dangerously close to where the thief hid. Not long after, though, the creature yawned and rolled onto its side. By the time the sun dipped below the ridgeline, the beast snored and twitched in its sleep. Crying out and thrashing as if having a nightmare, the giant was perhaps as dangerous asleep as awake. Nonetheless, Sevellon knew this might be his only chance to escape. No matter how docile the giant may seem, he didn't want to find out what would happen if it realized he was there.

Moving toward a nearby clearing, Sevellon cursed branches and leaves that made stealth slow and arduous. Still the giant snored, shaking the foliage. During a brief pause between snores, the thief slipped, his boot landing on a dead branch that snapped on impact. Movement made Sevellon freeze, the trees around him stirring. The last of the regent dragons reared and towered above, gazing down on him.

Eyes closed, Sevellon did the only thing he could think of and held the sky stone over his head, hoping the creature didn't take his arms off with it. Instead, the stone was lifted away without tooth or claw touching him as he'd feared. Wind buffeted and shook the forest. When Sevellon opened his eyes, he saw Kyrien's silhouette against the backdrop of comets, both beautiful and terrifying. At his feet, the thief found a pack filled with tools and provisions that would have been an enormous help in getting him there. At least he would have them for the way out. The dragon's voice in his mind reminded him of what he needed to do.

Go. Run.

It was then Sevellon realized he no longer heard the giant's snore. Turning back, he found the creature watching him with far too much interest. Though its visage was more inquisitive than vengeful, Sevellon had no desire to satisfy its curiosity. Slinging the pack over his shoulder, he ran.

* * *

Miss Mariss tried not to despair, but it was difficult. She'd rebuilt her life and those around her before; she could do it again. Helplessness drove her to distraction. The events shaping her world were far beyond her control. Much of what she had done might not even have been of her own volition. Mael's influence tainted everything they had accomplished, much of which he'd already managed to destroy.

While she and the others hadn't built Dragonhold, it was in many ways her home, and she took pride in the work done to restore the keep. So suddenly that had been taken away--and with so much damage--and what remained was covered in ankle-deep soot. If Durin were there, she'd have told him to start shoveling. That thought didn't help. So many of those she cared about were gone; even if some had driven her to distraction, she missed them.

Most were busy salvaging what supplies they could when the shouts came. Nearly screaming in frustration, Miss Mariss couldn't imagine what else could go wrong.

"We're under attack!"

Those words seemed impossible to her. What was there to take? A filthy hold with a giant hole in it and a few tenacious people? It made no sense.

"Started seeing fires to the south," Bradley said, out of breath and holding his shirt over his face to keep out the black dust hanging in the air, "but more come from the north."

It still made no sense, but that changed the realities of the situation very little. They could not surrender; that would be suicide. The best she could think of was to hole up in the kitchens and defend the halls as best they could. The cave-in mechanisms had all been triggered in previous battles, and none had been re-created. It was obvious now they should have put those defenses back into place, but there had been so little time and so many things needing doing. It was a wonder they had kept everyone fed. No matter the excuses, the result was the same.

Chase approached, cursing as he came.

"My feelings exactly," Miss Mariss said.

"We need to fall back and just let them have the place," Chase said.

"We don't even know what, if anything, survived Mael's escape."

Nodding, Chase considered their situation. It was one of the reasons she trusted him. The man had the good sense to think instead of just telling her why she was wrong. Distant screams and explosions rang within the hold followed by shouting.

"We'll do as you say," Miss Mariss said, knowing they had no more time to consider.

"Fighting in the valley!" someone shouted from the great hall.

In the background ululating calls were punctuated by the words, "Al'Drakon!" Blue light filled the outer hall, and Miss Mariss could not help but run with Chase and the others to see what was happening. None foolish enough to charge into an ongoing battle, they armed themselves as best they could. Knowing the Drakon had come to fight for them, though, gave them ample reason to help in any way possible. A tear came to her eye as she ran, and she wiped it away. They had not been abandoned. Despair lost a bit more of its grip.

Regal dragons whizzed past the main entrance in a blur, rolling thunder behind them. Flickering blue light illuminated the littered hall in a way that chilled Miss Mariss's blood. Then it was time to go. At the lip of the broken stair leading into Dragonhold came an enormous hand then another. With a terrible roar, the giant pulled itself upward.

"To the kitchens!" Chase commanded. "Evacuate to the kitchens!"

More figures emerged from below, a towering giant guarding them. Miss Mariss stumbled when strange, high-pitched sounds echoed within the hold. Blue-white light was brighter now, and the giant's roar changed to a scream. Regal dragons entered the hold with deadly speed. Any mistake would surely be fatal, but any slower and they would have been easy targets. Each dragon carried two riders armed with weapons like nothing she'd ever seen.

The rush of wind came with the Drakon, and they sent the dust swirling around the great hall. No one had ignored Chase's orders, and most jammed the hall leading to the kitchens when Miss Mariss reached it. She turned once again to see the Drakon landing around her, all facing her. She wasn't certain she understood until the rush of air grew. Seated backward, each passenger held some sort of glowing object in his or her hands, and the wind rushed from them like an unnatural hurricane. Under ordinary circumstances, this would have been difficult for anyone in the main hall to withstand for long, but the thick layer of pulverized rock made for a powerful scouring agent. Had they been in the Pinook Valley, they would have seen a roiling black cloud billow from the mountainside and blot out the light.

Chapter 13

Gullibility invites harm.
--Allette Kilbor, the Black Queen

* * *

Providing thrust did not come without effort; one could do so for only so long. Both Strom and Brother Vaughn had done what they could, but even the dragons tired from flying at such high speeds. For every advantage, a price was paid. Sinjin loosened straps. Hopping down to the sandy atoll proved difficult. Whether from the wound itself or as a result of his favoring the injury, his stiff back ached. Though uninhabited, this nearly complete ring of rock and sand provided an excellent place to rest. A few trees grew along the thicker sections of the island, and food was plentiful. Fresh water was not. They would need to conserve until opportunity to replenish their supplies presented itself.

"I just don't understand," Kendra said, breaking the silence. It had been difficult to talk while flying. "What are you supposed to do now?"

"All I can do is hope Kyrien knows what he's doing."

Strom grunted. "Seems we've little choice in the matter."

"I just don't see how sacrificing yourself will help your mother."

Sinjin nodded silently. He didn't know either.

"We don't even know why she sacrificed herself in the first place."

"I'm sure she had reasons," Strom said.

"Pelivor said he thought she had planned it all along and just didn't want him to know until it was too late. He knows my mother better than just about anyone else in the world, and he said it was just the kind of thing she would do. I tend to agree."

Strom nodded.

"We know she's alive, or at least she was yesterday," Sinjin continued. "She knows I've retrieved the sword, and she didn't tell me not to come. It's all I have to go on."

"I just think we'd all like a little more than that," Brother Vaughn said.

Sinjin shrugged.

"We come in at night," Strom said after a long silence. "There should be plenty of light to see by close up but not enough for them to see us coming from afar. I can use the figurine to blind them."

"And the rest of us," Brother Vaughn added.

"Good point," Strom admitted. "When I yell 'darkness,' cover your eyes."

It seemed an awfully thin plan to Sinjin, but he was thankful to the smith. He'd thought he might have to drag them there against a mountain of protest. At least Strom understood the necessity. He suspected Kendra and Brother Vaughn did as well, but that didn't mean they had to like it.

"When we reach land," Strom continued, "I suggest we stop using the thrust spheres. We can come in quieter that way, and we'll be fresher when speed is needed."

Valterius grunted. Sinjin reminded himself none of this was easy on the dragons either. Without them, they'd surely be lost. Valterius sighed, as if reading his thoughts.

"She showed me how to get in," Sinjin finally added. "From the top."

"You're not really planning to jump in there too, are you?" Kendra asked, having a way of making the question a threat.

"I don't know what else to do. We could just fly over and drop the sword, but something tells me that's not going to work. We could take on every feral dragon, giant, demon, and soldier and see how we make out, but I suspect it won't end well. Or I can follow my mother, bring her what she needs, and hope to survive." Even Kendra remained silent after those words, no doubt feeling the sting of his sarcasm. "Sorry."

"If you die, I'm going to kill you," Kendra said, and Sinjin couldn't help but laugh. After hugging his wife a little harder than advisable, he winced from the pain. It was worth it.

When they took off again, the air was uneasily still, the need for stealth greater than speed. Sinjin and the others had grown accustomed to propelled flight. Now flying at normal speeds felt strange and dreadfully slow. Perhaps taking offense from this very notion, Valterius put them into a dive. Dragons were plenty fast on their own. Sometimes Sinjin envied his mother's ability to communicate directly with Kyrien, but he'd come to have his own bond with Valterius. They may not speak in each other's minds, but they shared a deep, somehow inherent understanding of body language, posture, muscle movements, and other outward expressions of the inner self. And even with all those things, Sinjin had absolutely no idea what his dragon thought about their destination.

Gerhonda, too, had been subdued and just a little too predictable. Sinjin had come to believe they behaved themselves only when humans did what they wanted. His life's path had largely been dictated by dragons, and he had to rethink just where he fit into the equation. Knowing what he did of Mael's influence on world events, he couldn't help but feel violated. In his desire to escape from Dragonhold, Mael had subverted the lives of Sinjin, his family, and everyone else on the planet. It seemed too much to believe but evidence mounted. Once aware of the ancient sorcerer's machinations, proof and instances to support it sprang to mind until it was obvious. He was not alone in feeling like a fool.

Strom had been right about the light. Istra sent three large comets scudding across the sky, bits breaking off and streaking across the horizon.

"Are you sure about this?" Kendra asked, her voice sounding too loud in the stillness.

Sinjin wasn't certain at all, but he would not let his mother down. She had helped him get the sword, and he would take it to her one way or another. "I think Valterius, Strom, and I should go on alone from here. But what I think about that doesn't matter."

"You're darned right it doesn't," Kendra said.

Nodding in acceptance, Sinjin let the silence hang again. His gut churned. He'd expected Kyrien to meet them. His mother's boiling dragon sent them on this quest and had not yet seen fit to tell him why or what he was supposed to do. Kyrien made a good target for his anger. The dragon had endangered everything Sinjin loved with mysteries and riddles. He suspected Kyrien had reasons for what he did, but at that moment, it didn't matter. He was frightened. His wife wanted answers, and he didn't have any. He wanted her to live a long and happy life, but it was not his to decide. He wanted to live that life with her but might not get the chance. For his mother, he would throw himself into the depths, and for her love of him, his wife would follow. The pain was deep and physical.

Strom, Brother Vaughn, and the dragons were just in the wrong place at the wrong time. It was unlikely to end well. The thrust might give them some chance, but Sinjin lacked optimism. Gathering the Drakon and joining forces with their allies would take time, and he somehow knew it would be too late. Cursing dragons that played with his thoughts, he watched the horizon.

Bits of light streamed across the skies far faster than anything else. Comets farther away moved more slowly. It created a sky filled with dancing light beams, some streaking from horizon to horizon in a single breath. Not even a wisp of cloud obscured the view. Reflecting the light, the landscape looked more like a glittering jewel than a black swamp. Birds flew beneath them in the preternatural light, painted orange and purple, beacons of life and hope. It was a strange but welcome omen.

Still distant, the Noonspire created a similar display. In the daylight it had looked like a smoky black crystal engulfed within the land itself. Now it towered above the Jaga, gleaming in comet light. The glossy surface reflected the skies, shifting like a rainbow of fire. Oranges, reds, and yellows made it appear as if it were engulfed in a massive conflagration. Even from a distance, the power was unmistakable. He'd been warned Aggrezjhon and Murden would soon have the power to free themselves, but seeing the Noonspire somehow risen from the depths, he had to wonder if they weren't already powerful enough. Mael had escaped his prison, or at least Sinjin presumed. The height of power was coming, and the future of all the people on Godsland were at stake.

The Cathuran maps indicated thousands of comets would crowd the skies during the Istran Noon. Large comets would sometimes come very close. At these times, it was said Istra sent great bursts of energy. Sinjin just hoped they didn't burn up in her bounty. Already the air was thick with energy. What it would be like in fifty years was unimaginable.

Riding what warm air he could find, Valterius took them higher. Despite ample light, the landscape lacked contrast. Rather than rich color and texture, it was shades of blackness, making individual shapes difficult to distinguish. Higher they went and Sinjin began to notice a pattern below. The closer they got to the spire, the darker the land grew. It was as if the center of the swamp had dried up and did not reflect the light in the way the moisture-laden vegetation did, or Sinjin realized, something waited there, covering up the swamp, ready to ambush anyone foolish enough to come close. The truth came far too late.

Like any other illusion, it burst when recognized. The land crawled with life, large and small; at least some of it looked small from above. Masterfully carved stone blocks that hadn't been there before now radiated from the Noonspire's base. Much of the surface was glossy and slick, but some areas revealed lighter-colored stone with irregular texture, like an enormous sculpture. Reaching toward the clouds, the Noonspire dominated the landscape.

Thinner and colder, the air became more difficult to breathe as Valterius took them higher, putting space between them and the prison. Near the megalithic crystal's tip, a facet reflected orange light tinged with greens and blues, setting it off from the world around it. Inside, Sinjin saw a raging battle. His mother's spirit tugged at him, pulling him closer. Then it was as if something else grabbed a hold of him. Downward they spiraled, Kendra's shouts unintelligible. No words survived the cacophony.

Dragged lower against his will, a primal insult to any flying creature, Valterius bellowed in rage. From the ground came a great barrage of projectiles, many leaving a trail of fire behind and casting even brighter light on the horrific scene. What must have been thousands of feral dragons leaped into the sky at once, many with hooded riders on their backs. Sinjin's blood went cold. Valterius avoided attacks as best he could, but their flight path was no longer fully under his control. Stronger the attraction grew until it became apparent they were being pulled to the ground and not into the top of the crystal as Sinjin had thought. Howling madness waited to consume them. "Just get us pointed at the sky!" he shouted to Valterius. The dragon did not immediately respond. "Give us all the thrust you've got, Strom!"

It was soon apparent Kendra had given a similar command because she and Brother Vaughn flashed past. Kendra got three shots off with a light bow before she and Gerhonda were lost from view. Sinjin cursed, wishing his wife were someplace safe. Then the thrust pushed him back into his seat, the leather saddle creaking under the strain and the straps tightening around his body. He sucked in shallow breaths, unable to bear the pain of breathing deeper. The distance it put between them and the spire was worth it. Though he was moving away from his intended destination, Sinjin was pleased. When they dropped past the peak of the spire, he knew in his heart something was wrong, that he needed to go into the top, just as his mother had.

It was almost as if she said the words to him, and he took comfort from being close to her, even if they might as well be in two different worlds. It didn't matter. She needed him and he was there. She, too, was there for him. He was both in need and needed at the same time. This was the true nature of his life. Weakness revealed strength. The feeling of connection with his mother was cut off then, the fires within glowing anew. A great battle raged, and he hoped she fared well.

Ferals crowded the skies above, and projectiles ranging from arrows to entire tree trunks filled the air below. The gap was closing, no matter their speed, and Valterius was once again forced lower.

"We've got a problem!" Strom shouted. "Give me the bow."

Sinjin turned to see a feral flying in their wake and gaining on them, three hooded, dark-robed figures on its back. Before he could hand the bow back to Strom, a spiral web of red lightning struck with ferocious intent. Valterius reeled and Sinjin lost his grip on the precious weapon. In his effort to save the bow, Strom diverted all his attention. Though he did manage to grab it, it left him in an awkward position, and all thrust had ceased. This, the feral had not expected. The gigantic dragon sailed forward, carried by momentum and the propulsion hooded riders continued to produce. The delay cost them.

Ducking its head, the feral narrowly avoided being struck in the eye by Valterius, but those atop his back were not so fortunate. Two were knocked free, sent spinning into the air. The third clung to the feral's tail. The impact sent a shock of pain along Sinjin's side. He was relieved to see no dragon behind them, but when he turned to look ahead, he nearly fainted from fright. Before them reared a massive feral dragon, claws extended and bearing a rider of equal proportion.

This alone would have been a startling sight, but hooded figures held in the giant's grotesquely oversized claws terrified Sinjin. One launched a column of spiraling air that tore at his *Dragon's Wing*s. The other sent red and orange fire, searing Sinjin's very soul. Strom recovered and applied the thrust, putting some distance between them and the feral-mounted giant. Howling in anger, the giant shifted his grip to the hooded form's lower body, twirled the figure three times overhead, then threw the dark sorcerer with all his might.

The hooded figure flew with single-minded intent, not crying out or flailing in the air, but instead preparing a single, lethal attack. Focused solely on Sinjin, the figure held clawed fingers out before it, and a ball of darkness rimmed with fire formed. With a single shot, while still providing thrust, Strom sent a knife of fire into the dark hood. Sinjin tried to determine what kind of creature the dark sorcerer was, but it fell away soundlessly, revealing no more.

Pounding on his dragon in frustration, the giant forced more speed from his mount. The feral cried out and thrust forward, ready to take out its pain on them. This time the giant threw the remaining hooded figure like a spear. Claws outstretched and forming a sharp point, Sinjin thought it might simply impale them, but instead a blinding white pulse no larger than a firefly raced toward them. It pierced Valterius's wing membrane, and Sinjin experienced physical pain at his mount's cry. Favoring his right wing, Valterius sent them into a spiral. The hooded figure flew past, and Sinjin did not see where he went, though he did see another flash of light strike Valterius in the tail.

"He's been hit!" Sinjin yelled through gritted teeth. Strom made no response, the continued thrust the only evidence he still lived. More feral dragons took off from around the Noonspire, almost all bearing giants. Unerringly they flew toward Valterius. They had been marked. It also occurred to him they might sense the sword or recognize him. That thought alone made him quail. Soon after he was busy ducking river stones and whole trees.

Raked by roots still wet from the swamp, Sinjin reeled. Leaning hard to one side, the straps all that held him in, Sinjin saw the dragon-riding giant snatch a ballista from the ground. The soldier who'd been loading the weapon hung on for his life. When the giant held the ballista high, the mud man reached up, grabbed the trigger string, and yanked. A mighty thump announced the sharpened tree truck now sailing over their heads. Had it not been for something slamming into the giant and exploding, the bolt would surely have landed on its mark. As Valterius continued to spiral, Sinjin tried to locate the source of the attack. A familiar, albeit deeper and louder, thumping accompanied a scaled-up version of the bumblebee that streamed black smoke and fire out the back. At the controls, grinning like a fool, was Kenward Trell.

Chapter 14
The key to flying is avoiding going entirely too fast in entirely the wrong direction.
--Kenward Trell, inventor and airship captain

* * *

Rhythmic thumps from the stinger's exhaust were drowned out by the strange sound Kenward's air pressure–powered repeating weapon made when fired. His vessel might be a dangerous mixture of compressed air, flammable liquids, and powdered explosives, but on a good day, those things should remain isolated from each other. Opening the valve forced air into the stalk weed shafts, which ejected explosives-filled walnut shells at high velocity. The effect was a devastating weapon that looked as if it might self-destruct at any given moment. Looks did not determine how well something flew, Kenward told himself. Sometimes it was better to appear weak. A ship that appears invincible might inspire an enemy to throw everything they have at it.

Many of his walnut shells missed their intended target, and some exploded in midair. Kenward just hoped they all made it away from the stinger before they detonated. Those that did strike worked exactly as intended, creating fear and chaos in dragons and giants alike. He had to remind himself to watch the skies around him since there were so many other aircraft and dragons to avoid. Jessub Tillerman sliced between Kenward and the dragon harrying Valterius. A brief hesitation was all that prevented Kenward from shooting Jessub's growler. A feral soared close behind, and Kenward reacted, pulling his weapon release wide open. The air rang with a foreign phong, phong, phong followed by random detonations.

Some walnuts did little more than annoy those they struck, but the others made up for it. Time slowed while he passed through the madness surrounding the Noonspire. Bringing the stinger back around, Kenward had a full view of aerial chaos. Wings, explosions, and lightning surrounded stingers and growlers. The *Kraken's Ghost* loomed in the distance, Fasha's ship well hidden elsewhere.

After pulling his straps tight, Kenward Trell opened the fuel-air mixture valve full stop. The thumps grew in frequency and amplitude, the speed giving the good captain a thrill like nothing else he'd ever known. He'd flown at speed atop a dragon, but he'd had no control. This was in every way a superior experience, save one. Tapping on the glass face of the fuel gauge, Kenward hoped it malfunctioned. He'd used most of his air firing the weapons, which meant he would have little pressure remaining should the main engine run short on naphtha. Learning from the ancients changed things so quickly, they hadn't quite perfected everything yet.

Jessub and Gret flew alongside, each able to fly for long periods of time without any need for fuel or compressed air. The growlers did have air tanks, but those capable of flying them without could refill them in flight. As much as Kenward hated relying on the gifted, they had their advantages. Feral dragons and those riding them did not take kindly to the flyby and were in pursuit. Kenward just needed to get back within what he called the Ring of Fire.

Tapping the glass once again, he shrugged. It would either be enough or it wouldn't. The ferals gained, and already Gret was under fire. "Don't wait on me," Kenward said. "I'm taking a shortcut!" Reaching down with his left hand, Kenward pulled a lever he hadn't been certain he'd ever have the guts to use. If he did nothing, the dragons would catch them; it was either fly or bail out. Given that choice, Kenward decided to fly. With a yank, he pumped the rest of his compressed air through the pitch-fired thumper engine. The result sent him hurtling through the air at uncontrollable speed, his flight path leaving a squiggly line of black and white smoke.

Left behind, Jessub and Gret had plenty of speed to outrun the dragons, or at least he hoped they did. The growlers depended on thrust from Istra's power, which was not granted in equal measure. Gret was a good bit faster than Jessub, though he had greater control over his landings. Kenward was still working on those. Soon landing became his highest priority since the *Kraken's Ghost* moved toward him at an unbelievable rate. Reaching down, Kenward was about to ease the compressed-air valve closed when the pulse engine winked out, going dark and silent. No thump came from the compressed-air backup since Kenward had used it to get his burst of speed. He came in fast and low.

Pulling back on the flaps, Kenward stood the stinger on its tail, using the wings themselves as brakes. The deck of the *Kraken's Ghost* came up fast but provided plenty of room for error, which turned out to be a good thing. Not reacting quickly enough, Kenward let the stinger's tail strike the deck before he had leveled out, which sent the nose crashing downward. Thankful they had taken the time and materials to spring load the skids, Kenward still bit his tongue during the rough landing.

Jessub, Gret, and the rest of their flight, or at least those who'd returned, must have made it within the Ring of Fire because the *Kraken's Ghost* showed her teeth. With scaled-up versions of what the stinger and growlers carried, the *Ghost* fired melon-sized shot with a terrific report. The sound alone was a weapon that struck fear in approaching ferals. Ballistae fire sent flaming bolts through the air, marking the *Ghost*'s air space.

Farsy ran to Kenward's side. "Are you hurt?"

"No, but it's pretty ugly out there. Fuel me up, load me heavy, and pack the air tanks full. I almost didn't make it back." Farsy looked at him as if he were daft. Then his old friend shook his head. "And load the bay with some of the big shot this time."

"You've bent up the landing gear," Farsy said.

"Hit it with a hammer a couple of times if that's what you have to do, but get me back in the air!"

Frowning, Farsy did as Kenward asked but clearly didn't like it.

* * *

Watching Kenward and the others go, Sinjin hoped they had the sense to stay away. No matter how much he appreciated their help, the darkness was too powerful here. Valterius was out of the fight. Wounded, the valiant beast carried on as best he could. Strom kept the thrust low to prevent the air from thrashing the regal dragon too much. The sky above them thick with ferals, it was as if Kenward and the others hadn't been there at all; like a keel moving through water, the darkness simply rushed back in.

Gerhonda took the fight to the ferals against all probability. Sinjin's wife carried one of the larger light bows, and Brother Vaughn wielded a glowing orb. How the monk snatched dragons from the sky and dashed them on the armies below was a mystery until smoke and debris made the spiraling vortex obvious.

"Look," Sinjin shouted, pointing. He didn't know if Strom heard until dragons descending on them folded like moths in a hurricane. The ancients' orbs were truly mysterious, complex, and dangerous objects. For now they worked in their favor, but such tools might later haunt them. The herald globes were perfect examples of useful implements turned powerful weapons.

A deep growling filled the air a moment later, and three more aircraft like the one Jessub had been flying soared past. Sinjin watched as Gwen opened fire on nearby ferals, continuing to force them lower. Rings of mist rolled through the air after each projectile left the stalk weed shafts, only to be ripped apart by the wind. Some walnuts had little apparent effect, while others exploded with concussive force. Throwing his arm against shards of walnut shell knifing through the air, Sinjin watched the aircraft roar past, staying in tight formation. Ferals reached for them--not quickly enough.

Gerhonda soared in close, given breathing room by Gwen and the others. "We've got to get him out of here," Kendra said.

"Might be too late," Sinjin said. His wife glared at him. "Maybe with help . . ." If aircraft kept ferals off their tail, they might have a chance. No matter how fast, nimble, and well armed, it was unlikely. Gerhonda used her wing to lend Valterius support. He whined. Gwen and her companions made pass after pass, turning back when their fuel, air, or munitions were exhausted.

As soon as they departed, Kenward returned, his aircraft still belching fire. Flying in low, he yanked on a lever beside his seat. Nothing happened. Kenward shook the aircraft back and forth--still nothing. Executing a tight turn revealed explosives-filled melons stuck together and jamming the bomb bay. Still Valterius spiraled downward as if in a trance, only at a slower rate because of Gerhonda's aid. Twice Sinjin lost sight of Kenward but then saw the flying machine far too close to the ground and taking heavy fire from below. Approaching an armed fortification, Kenward pulled up sharply, arrows sticking out of his aircraft. The force dislodged the two explosive melons, whose irregular size made them perhaps less than perfect for the task. When they struck the ballista, though, they worked just fine.

The blast sent a wave of destruction across the plain, leaving a circle of devastated landscape. If not for cover fire from the other two aircraft, Kenward Trell would never have made it away from the fight, yet he flew on. Sinjin wished him well and tried to figure out what to do next. So far he'd had little choice in the matter and even less understanding of what was expected of him. Gripping the sword, he clenched his teeth. Perhaps landing in the area Kenward bombed would buy them a few brief moments, but it seemed suicide.

"I need to get back to the top of the Noonspire," he said. "Valterius is wounded. I need Gerhonda to take me." It was a painful admission, and Valterius whined, looking back at Sinjin.

"We can't land," Kendra said. "They'll overrun us in an instant. And Kenward might drop the next bombs on us."

Sinjin would have laughed under other circumstances. "We need to wing walk."

Kendra gave him a look that said she thought he was insane but offered no alternative. "Are you sure you want to do this?" she asked, her voice betraying fear.

He couldn't blame her; the thought was more terrifying than anything he'd ever done. But to land was to die. His mother's influence on his mind was subtle, but he recognized it.

You can do it.

Without responding, Sinjin unstrapped and pushed up onto his knees. "Take him out of here," he said to Strom. "Use all the speed he can handle."

Kendra had moved onto the wing.

"Are you crazy?" came Gwen's voice, clearly incredulous, as she flashed past, firing on ferals in her path all the while.

Sinjin knew the answer but stepped out onto Valterius's injured wing, careful to stay clear of the hole burned in the membrane. Gerhonda's wing supported the weight from below, but he wasted no time. Passing Kendra was the most difficult part, and it occurred to Sinjin that this would have been far safer had he let her cross first, but there simply was no time. He just hoped it didn't get them killed. Lightning split the skies, leaving hazy ghosts in his vision.

Claws raked the air nearby. Last-second bursts of thrust kept them alive, which caused the dragons to shift underfoot. When he made it to Gerhonda's saddle, the sword over his shoulder, Sinjin reached for the straps.

The ferals had been waiting.

Kenward was gone. Gwen and those in the other aircraft were distant. Three feral dragons collided with Gerhonda in a coordinated attack, nearly knocking Sinjin from the saddle. Holding on took most of his concentration. Kendra soared in front, pulling on a single strap before Valterius was overwhelmed.

What Sinjin saw next made him question his own eyes. Gleaming like a comet embodied, Kyrien bore down on them. In his mother's dragon ore saddle, Pelivor rode in a suit of intricate metallic armor. In one hand, he held a metal staff; in the other, a thrust sphere. Lightning seared the air. Giant claws ripped Sinjin from the sky and bore him away. It took him a moment to realize Kyrien had grabbed him. Pelivor applied thrust, his lightning assaulting nearby ferals.

The giants made one last push to keep Sinjin away from the Noonspire. Sacrificing themselves and their dragons, they flew in close and launched whatever they had. Kyrien and Pelivor defended as well as they could, but ferals and giants attacked from all directions. Sinjin screamed when a whole tree struck him, knocking his breath away and possibly breaking ribs. He would have grabbed his side if not for a hooded figure being thrown at him. Reaching out with clawed hands, the assailant grabbed on to Sinjin, making the pain worse. In their struggle, the figure's hood fell open, revealing a form more dragon than human, and Sinjin felt sick. A perverse combination of two creatures, forced on nature, shrieked at him. An instant later, it fell away, its eyes going distant. Kendra stared up at him before turning her light bow on the ferals surrounding her and Valterius.

Despair washed over Sinjin in massive waves threatening to crush his spirit. They were lost. Images of the accomplishments humankind had achieved since Istra's return flashed through his mind. All the things his mother had done, and even he and the Dragon Clan--it was all for naught. How could he possibly win where the most powerful people in the world had failed? It was folly.

His fearful tirade was interrupted as a barrage of information flooded his mind. Now he understood Strom's reaction to thoughts invading without warning or request.

You could not know.

Kyrien's voice in Sinjin's mind was overwhelming and absolute. It allowed no other thought, even as they moved closer to the top of the Noonspire, even with Pelivor waging a battle like nothing seen in a hundred lifetimes.

If you had known, they would have stolen the knowledge and used it against us all.

Stunned, Sinjin tried to make sense of new realization and understanding. Visions showed him the choices Kyrien had made. Tears welled and flowed freely as he saw his father, Prios, stealing an egg from the regent queen. When a single egg glowed brighter, Prios selected it. It had started then, for Kyrien, but everything he'd done since was toward this purpose--this singular moment in time when all would be decided. There had been no other way.

When I saved the sky stone from being destroyed, and in doing so saved Master Edling from your mother's wrath, I did so for a reason.

With that thought came images. Kyrien plucked Sinjin's grandfather from before the headsmen's axe and later rescued his mother just before she would have killed Master Edling. Then there came a gift from above. A melon-sized rock descended, its surface pocked and pitted yet worn smooth. How Pelivor managed to lower it and still fight was beyond his knowing, but Sinjin latched on to it. There was no question as to what the stone was, but he would have to sheath his sword to carry it securely.

More images rushed in. High above the Inland Sea, Kyrien and Catrin soared toward the Westland coast, taking down Seethe and Thorakis the Builder. He'd seen this event from much farther away, from a balcony within Ravenhold. Now he saw what he had always suspected. The dragons twined around each other, locked in a mating dance. They had plummeted like stones, his mother still strapped to Kyrien's back. The pain returned full force, even knowing his mother had survived. For years, he'd believed that to be the moment of his mother's passing. The pain was no less real.

I did not tell Strom why such a sword was needed. Nor did I tell your mother. I did not tell you why you must retrieve the sword, even if at great cost. You could not have known. Now you must know everything. You must understand and do what is required, no matter what.

Visions of the regent queen's death and the loss of all the rest of Kyrien's kind made Sinjin understand. No greater purpose existed. Only then did he see Kyrien's brilliance, somehow knowing what he would do and become before his birth. Such a burden unimaginable, Sinjin's own responsibilities pressed down on him. Determining humanity's fate had been difficult for his mother, and now he understood why.

You have the knowledge, the character, and the spirit to do what must be done. Fail not.

Those were the last words before Kyrien released his grip. Tumbling toward the top of the Noonspire, Sinjin Volker wondered what he'd gotten himself into.

Chapter 15

The human mind is weak and easily tricked.
--Mael, sorcerer

* * *

Falling toward the Noonspire, Sinjin could not imagine a more perilous perch. The height and wind would make most people quail, but the battle in the air surrounding the spire made it downright terrifying. He could not let fear rule and clenched his jaws, ready to do what had been asked of him. Those within saw him coming, despite a pitched battle taking place within the spire itself. Aggrezjhon and Murden knew he approached, and they probed his thoughts. The reaction was almost immediate. Tinged with fear and apprehension, a crown of lightning erupted from the Noonspire, reaching out with deadly intent, only to arc and bend toward the sky stone Sinjin clutched with one hand. In his other, he held the sword, ready to do what was needed.

Streaks of fire leaped forth, and feral claws swiped at him. The sky stone absorbed the fire as if it had never been, but the claws got far too close. Only the efforts of Kyrien and Pelivor along with Kenward and Gwen kept Sinjin unharmed.

Fires erupted atop the spire, searing air belching upward. Covering his face against the heat, Sinjin was suspended by the forceful updraft, ancient sorcerers probing his thoughts. They knew what he planned. They knew all Kyrien's secrets. No hope remained. Nothing would stop the greatest powers ever to walk Godsland.

Helpless, Sinjin floated and endured the mental assault. Doubt undermined his confidence, making him question Kyrien's intentions and reconsider his commitment. No more time remained, though, as claws forced Sinjin downward. Flames reached higher. Sinjin screamed but knew what he had to do. Lightning and fire poured into the sky stone, which grew hotter and hotter. His sword ready, he aimed downward and thrust.

The flames wavered as he approached and everything changed.

Those within had been trying to repel him but seemed to have given up and suddenly began drawing him closer, trying desperately to pull him within the smoky black crystal. Images flooded his mind then, visions of his mother and father and the life they had shared. Scenes of his younger self playing pranks with Durin would have brought a smile to his face were he not in such a perilous position. Sinjin held on tightly, but the sky stone was torn from his grip. It plummeted to the charred, smoking swamp below. Sinjin wrapped both hands around the sword hilt, driving it into the mighty facet waiting to devour him. This was how his mother had entered the crystal structure, and this was how Aggrezjhon and Murden meant to pull him in as well. Flames still licked the top of the spire, but the portal opened to receive him, pushing the fire away. Moving unerringly toward that spot, Sinjin was drawn with terrific force. Nothing he could do would change his trajectory. Fire leaped out to his now unprotected hands grasping the sword hilt, but Sinjin would not release, could not relent. The consequences would not allow it. Screaming, he held on with a viselike grip.

A single breath later, his sword struck the Noonspire a mighty blow. Right behind it, he encountered hard, slick crystal. The flames exacted a price before winking out. The air went silent, except the sword. Vibrating at a specific frequency, it sang a powerful note. Resonating, the crystal trembled, unable to resist. Getting to his feet, Sinjin Volker straddled the peak. Like a gearsmith's clock, he repeatedly struck the spire at a precise and measured pace.

The fight for the skies continued, looking surreal. Seeing the Drakon engaged gave Sinjin heart. No longer could the din be heard, and the light took on a different hue. Within the crystal, battle raged. Shades vied for control. Kyrien had known the sword's solitary note would temporarily alter the Noonspire's structure. He'd known each strike would stun those within, and they would likely need all the time between blows to regain their composure. Still, Sinjin did not know what would happen next. His strikes might render Aggrezjhon and Murden helpless for brief moments in time, but it would do the same to all those within.

Not knowing any other way to help his mother, Sinjin committed himself to doing as Kyrien asked. Over and over he rang the crystal like a giant bell until his arms felt as if they might fall off. Nonetheless, bright flashes within gave evidence the fight continued.

* * *

Within the Noonspire the light was distorted and weak. Still, it fed Catrin's soul and sustained her despite being tainted with the hatred of eons. Others might have struggled to wield Istra's powers within the crystal, which was among the reasons it had been used as a prison, but Catrin absorbed all the energy around her. Unless trapped under stone or that foul-smelling blanket of Jharmin Kyte's, it was unavoidable.

Even with greater access to power, Catrin could achieve little. With the exception of projecting herself through the fractured keystone, reaching anything outside the crystal had proven impossible. The designers would likely have left the keystone out, given the choice, but it was the entire reason the Noonspire had been located there in the first place. Its existence had also made the disguise more effective since who would build a prison for sorcerers upon a sacred place of power. In spite of all that, this very prison had functioned for thousands of years.

Perhaps the ancients planned on finding some other solution but never had. Catrin couldn't help but think they left the problem for her generation to deal with. Those who made this place were long since dead, along with their great-great-great-grandchildren. Now power had returned to the world and was ever growing. A prison this would be no more. If not for Catrin and the others, the tipping point would already have been reached, unleashing Aggrezjhon and Murden on the world in their new bodies.

The battle taking place outside was distorted and strange. Though close in proximity, it was a world away. Bright flashes brought no thunder, and the silence belied the true nature of what transpired. Trinda Hollis stood nearby, wringing her hands, her white dress stained and fouled. Allette Kilbor crouched, a cornered animal ready to lash out, her allegiance highly questionable. She'd no doubt been under these sorcerers' influence for years, and trust would be difficult to grant. It did not escape Catrin that she herself might have been under Mael's influence for an even greater time, but that made trusting Allette no easier. All had been played for fools and pawns, dangerous pawns--and prickly.

Being trapped within a place inhabited by angry, vengeful spirits dampened the soul. Hopelessness and oppression coated everything and left even those whose inner fires burned brightly in a deep malaise. Insanity would come for them all, sooner than later, and it might be best to just let the sorcerers win. Then they could all escape and bask in untainted comet light once again. Outside they could breathe deeply the smell of renewed life. Outside they would be powerful once again, ready to face any foe. It was a lie, and Catrin knew it. She could only hope the others possessed the fortitude to resist coercion. Doing so was becoming increasingly difficult.

Those with living bodies remained huddled together for whatever strength it afforded them. Sarjak of the Scorpion Clan alone was not touched by Istra's powers. Part of his robes were missing, and his spear was a good bit shorter than when he'd leaped through the damaged keystone, but he had some magic of his own. Catrin didn't know by what luck he survived; the damage to his garment and spear spoke of other, more gruesome, possibilities. She doubted the man could do anything to protect against their hosts, but having a trained fighter at her side somehow gave her strength. Memories of Benjin, Chase, Pelivor, and others filling a similar place in her life almost brought a smile.

Aggrezjhon and Murden lost their physical forms so long ago, even they had trouble remembering how they once looked. Seldom did they fully manifest, always blurry and out of focus. It would not take long for the others to join them in formlessness. All the old sorcerers had to do was wait. Catrin's physical body would be absorbed into the crystal, gradually leeched away, just as theirs had so long ago.

The sorcerers did not want to wait. They wanted out. At first Catrin had thought Allette and Trinda had been taken for just that purpose. She'd been wrong. The two women were bait. Catrin was the vessel Aggrezjhon and Murden desired, her body already acclimated to massive power, her barriers obliterated. Even in the previous age, that had been a rare thing. Either would be invincible given her form. That fact was perhaps Catrin's salvation; they could not both have her.

Evening skewed the outside light, it did not bring about darkness but instead accentuated the comet light no longer drowned out by Vestra's rays. The light shifted in hue and angle but did not diminish; however, it did make those within the crystal look like the specters they would soon become. The world reeked of power, and Catrin knew this prison, no matter how massive and effective it had been for eons, was about the fail. When it did, those within would either escape or perish.

Having bided their time, the sorcerers came without warning, neither willing to allow the other an edge. The ferocious assault knocked Catrin from her feet, her head smacking against the rune-engraved stones encircling the fractured keystone. Buckled and cracked, sharp stone bit into flesh. The warm sensation of blood brought instincts to the fore.

Aggrezjhon and Murden assaulted her psyche with unmitigated ferocity, each trying to wipe out any trace of identity in a single massive blow. The simultaneous attacks were more than any person should ever endure, but they worked against each other, lessening the efficacy. Had the two cooperated, Catrin would have been lost. It was a realization she wished she could take back since the shades read her thoughts. After the briefest lull, they combined their respective energies into a single overwhelming attack.

Feeling herself slip away, Catrin reached out to those around her, desperately seeking help. What assistance Allette and Trinda provided was weak and unfocused. It did little to stem the tide wrought by Aggrezjhon and Murden. Grasping on to memories, Catrin clung to that which meant the most to her: Sinjin.

As if that single thought summoned what she needed most, Catrin looked up. Her son dangled from Kyrien's claws. Seeing them bolstered her strength in a way nothing else could. It also distracted the sorcerers, who repelled Sinjin and lashed out with malicious intent. Their attacks found no purchase.

How her son defended himself so completely remained a mystery until she recognized the pocked stone he carried. Master Edling had used that very artifact against her and Prios; it had nearly been her downfall. Now, though, it provided protection to the one she cherished most. He'd come for her, and seeing the pocked stone ripped away and sent tumbling to the swamp below inspired reckless action. Screaming, she rushed Aggrezjhon and Murden. Sarjak of the Scorpion Clan ran at her side, issuing a ululating battle cry. He should have stayed behind.

No training or physical skill could prepare one for fighting wraiths. Noble and gallant, the Arghast tribesman crouched low and arched the remainder of his spear to resemble a scorpion's tail. Rushing forward and getting ahead of Catrin, Sarjak fell. There was no flash, no lightning or thunder. Aggrezjhon's shade simply pointed a finger at the nimble fighter and drew the life from him.

"No!" Catrin cried out, seeing yet another soul sacrificed for her. Weight enough rested on her shoulders, and this threatened to crush her. But Sinjin gave her strength.

Knowing she would attack, Aggrezjhon and Murden reversed whatever tactics they had been using and now tried to draw Sinjin into the Noonspire. That she could not allow. With all her might, she did as she'd done long ago, before breaking down the barrier between her and Istra's light. Rather than simply channel the flood of power washing over her, Catrin gathered energy from around, squeezing it from the crystal and focusing it. A being of light, she attacked the darkness.

She was a fool, a babe in the presence of masters. For lifetimes these sorcerers had lain in wait, and it was too late when the traps were sprung. Like tentacles of fire, ropes of energy lashed out at Catrin's spirit, grabbing on to her and embedding themselves deep within her psyche. Rather than recoiling, as her instincts demanded, she charged forward, intent on triggering every defensive mechanism the sorcerers had managed to create. It was unclear how much power the two saved throughout the ages, but they had somehow remade the prison's interior to suit their purposes.

Through sheer determination and strength of will, Catrin Volker charged forward, intent on scattering one of the shadows to the winds. That same finger that took Sarjak's life pointed at her chest. In that very instant, her son landed atop the Noonspire. The world trembled. Losing her step, she stumbled forward, no longer under control. No one could manipulate her then. She was fully committed, and nothing stood between her and Aggrezjhon, his finger still extended. The ringing, though, interrupted the power flowing within the crystal. Each time Sinjin struck, it was as if Istra's powers ceased to exist. Though jarring, she was alive in spite of the finger still aimed at her heart.

Colliding with Aggrezjhon was a mistake. Though she did achieve her goal of scattering his spirit, he seeped into her, the traps holding her fast. Sucking a deep breath, she expelled him with all the self-determination and identity she could muster. He'd goaded her and she'd fallen for it. Now he had an edge over Murden, though being a woman was an advantage she pressed. The ringing of Sinjin's sword interrupted the energy, preventing any of them from gathering more than a pittance of power. Having it ripped away with every other heartbeat made it feel as if she were being torn apart. The shades struggled as well. Lacking physical forms, their very existence was tied to the energy stored within the Noonspire.

Two against one, it was but a matter of time. Flashing lights from the outside world made the crystal prison's walls dance as Catrin fought. It was all she could do.

Never had she known such gratitude as what she felt for Trinda and Allette. They could have let her be destroyed; both had vowed to see her dead at one point or another. But instead they came to her aid, using scraps of power coerced from the air. It wasn't much but it shifted the balance. Even with the assistance, Catrin reeled from the attacks. Already astral travels with Allette and Pelivor had damaged her identity and sense of self. The knowledge of multiple lives bottled up in her memory made her question her sanity.

And then there was Mael.

Mael.

The name thundered like coming doom. Laughter rang in the Noonspire, and Catrin looked up to see the dragon mage with Nat Dersinger on his back; it could be no other. Secured by a dragon ore saddle and carrying a glowing metal staff, he rode in a coat of shining mail. His long hair flew free, his eyes as wild as a bobcat's.

Allette and Trinda continued their slow advance, the shades not launching any counter attacks. Only when Trinda met Catrin's eyes and gave her a sad, knowing smile did she understand. With an extended arm, Murden's shade leveled a single finger at Trinda Hollis, releasing energy stored up over time. The child queen and daughter to Baker Hollis dropped to cold stone, her burdens and responsibilities forever removed. Catrin silently wished her spirit a swift journey.

* * *

Sinjin Volker watched in horror as Trinda Hollis fell. Even from his unusual vantage point, he knew what he saw. His resolve faltered. She'd been an irritant and an enigma, but in some ways, she'd been his friend. His sword strokes lost their cadence, and he struggled in his mourning to achieve his former rhythm. In spite of the defenses in the air above him from Drakon and aircraft alike, ferals crept closer and closer to where Sinjin stood, exposed.

An especially large male got close enough to latch on to the giant crystal, his legs finding meager purchase on the glossy surfaces. As the feral dragon reared its head, Sinjin readied himself for death with a glance down at his mother. By some strange trick of the light, or from the power she held within, Catrin looked otherworldly, illuminated from behind. Lighting reflected off the feral dragon's scales as it readied to strike, but its visage shifted from victorious apex predator to that of hunted prey.

It was then Mael came into view, on his back, a rider glittering with power, wild hair flying in every direction: Nat Dersinger. An instant later, Kyrien and Pelivor flashed by. Jessub Tillerman circled overhead in his aircraft, not leaving the fight as others had. Still Sinjin swung his mother's sword, ringing its one repeating note. Hands numb and shoulders aching, he was afraid he would falter. Part of him expected Mael to attack, but Kyrien and the golden dragon circled lower and lower before landing amid charred ruins at the spire's base. Pelivor dismounted and stood, facing east. Nat Dersinger climbed down and faced west, his back to Pelivor. The two dragons, each unique, regarded one another. What transpired between them, no one else could know.

Again, Sinjin nearly faltered from the desire to see what transpired below. With a grunt of effort, he resumed his rhythmic strikes. Tension filled the air. Facing each other, the dragons looked as if they might tear each other apart. After long moments, the two seem to reach some sort of agreement. Together, they turned toward the Noonspire.

Newcomers, like wisps of smoke, materialized into slender forms emerging from the dark swamps. Barely recognizable as such, dryads marched on the Noonspire. Unnoticed, they had gathered around the last of the regent dragons and the man-become-dragon. Dingy and mud stained, the dryads surrounded the spire and raised their hands in a silent gesture perhaps they alone understood. They parted long enough to let the dragons pass.

Climbing opposite sides of the spire, Kyrien and Mael ascended, wrapping themselves around the giant crystal until they became intertwined. Sinjin stood to deliver his next blow, struggling more with every strike and not knowing how much longer he could go on. In a semiconscious stupor, he concentrated on the next swing.

Eyes closed, Kyrien and Pelivor looked as if they were both in a trance. With little more than a look, Mael sent feral dragons to the winds. None dared defy him as he stood guard over Sinjin and Kyrien. Even in his trancelike state, Sinjin had to wonder why. His eyes made contact with Nat Dersinger. The man had been friends with his mother but still looked like a madman. In his eyes, though, Sinjin found peace and understanding. It was impossible to say why anyone would align themselves with Mael, but it was clear Nat believed he was in the right. Weariness overcame him then. The last thing he heard was the dragon mage humming that sounded like a lullaby.

Chapter 16

Judge not by the loudest among them but by those who remain calm.
--Catrin Volker, Herald of Istra

* * *

The coming dawn brought with it a unification of the heavens. Vestra cast his warmth across the land, bathing it in color and texture, making even the black swamp appear vibrant. Most comets faded in the sun god's light, only to reappear with the coming night, but not all. Large comets, close to Godsland, radiated sufficient light to remain visible for most of the day. For those who'd been born under Vestra's light alone, it was a difficult thing to get used to. For those born under Istra's light, this was all they knew. The idea of pinpricks of light at fixed locations in the skies was entirely foreign to them, and would be for more than a hundred years to come. With the moon passing close to Godsland, it dominated one side of the horizon so even the Dead God was represented.

It was an omen, an ending and a beginning.

Sinjin Volker did not know how long he'd managed to keep striking the Noonspire with his mother's sword, but his shoulders and arms ached in remembrance. He didn't remember stopping. To sleep in such a place was unthinkable. Wind gusts and smooth facets could easily have sent him to his death, not even taking feral dragons into consideration. With the sudden recollection of a haunting melody, Sinjin realized Mael was gone. Forcing visions of the dragon mage from his mind, he pushed himself to his feet, straddling the peak, his boots slipping on the smooth surface. Everything within many miles was visible from this vantage point through clear skies.

Above, Jessub Tillerman still circled, apparently watching over him. "He's up!"

A cheer arose from those gathered below. The *Dragon's Wing* rested in nearby shallows, nowhere near enough water to actually float her, but better than landing on rock, Sinjin supposed. Vestra rose higher, revealing more details and shifting the hues toward what most would consider true, natural light. The ferals were gone. Regal dragons patrolled the skies along with verdants. The marshes surrounding the Noonspire crawled with life, like ringlets of water radiating out from a cast stone. Demons, mud men, and even a few giants fled. Part of Sinjin wanted to attack them now, to eradicate them before they reorganized and threatened peace once again.

Something new filled the air, though. As if a dark veil had been removed, the world around him grew brighter and more colorful. The surrounding swamp was still twisted and covered in foul ooze, but the change was there; he could feel it. In years past, he'd written such feelings off as superstition or unrealistic dreams of power. Now he knew better. He, too, had changed. He'd lived in his parents' shadows most of his life. Even as Al'Drakon, he'd never fully left their overpowering influence behind. He loved them and would never forget the lessons they'd taught him and the love they'd showed him, but they no longer defined him. Subtle changes resulted in a monumental shift.

When he looked down, though, he recognized the biggest change around him. Shining like polished gemstone, Kyrien twined around the mighty spire, his eyes lidded, his visage peaceful. The Noonspire itself had changed. No longer dark and smoky, the largest noonstone crystal ever found had been transformed into dragon ore--the rarest and most potent material on all Godsland--as only regent dragons could achieve. It seemed impossible and yet he stood atop it, basking in its warm glow. While Sinjin wondered how he would get down from such a perilous height, the pressure around him changed. Valterius landed beside him.

The valiant beast held his head low, as if expecting reprimand, but Sinjin just wrapped his arms around the dragon and shed joyful tears. His companion and friend was alive and could still fly. Extending his uninjured wing to Sinjin, Valterius helped his exhausted rider gain the saddle. With hands that refused to cooperate, it took time to work straps and buckles, several of which he didn't fish through the keeper, which normally held the ends of the straps in place. It was the kind of laziness he chastised in others. Expecting a brief flight, he allowed himself this weakness.

Showing his concern, Valterius spread his wings and took flight far smoother than any time they left Windhold. As he turned on a wingtip to soar lower in a graceful spiral, Valterius gave Sinjin an even better view. Enormous airships hovered along the coastlines, which alone was difficult to believe. The air around them held a myriad of flying machines along with the Drakon.

Dryads now radiated away from the spire. Though they remained gaunt, wispy figures, their gait and bearing conveyed a very different message. They had arrived looking defeated but dispersed with renewed life. It was a feeling mirrored in his own spirit. He'd begun to fear hope, thinking it too much to ask and worried embracing optimism would allow harsh realities to crush his spirit. Now he knew it had been among the few things keeping him alive. Without hope, he would have given up a thousand times. It was impossible to imagine what the world would look like had he done so.

He'd seen nothing within the spire, no sign of his mother, Allette, or the others. The memory of Trinda Hollis falling haunted him, tarnishing his salvation with bitter regret. He should have been so much kinder to the girl. She'd been a victim of manipulation as much as or more so than anyone, and Sinjin had mistreated her. She'd tried to explain it to him, but he'd been unable to hear her words. Only now that she was gone did he come to see

Trinda Hollis's true nature. He mourned her death while trying to keep from speculating on his mother's fate. That knowledge would have to wait. Valterius did not rush their descent, giving Sinjin time to sort his thoughts, or to at least make the attempt. Feelings washed over him, from joy to anger to remorse. All were real. All were valid and he embraced each one, allowing himself to feel the full force of those emotions and know from whence they came. It was something his mother had taught him; something Benjin Hawk had taught her; and if his memory served, something Mother Gwendolin had taught him. He was grateful.

Moments later, Valterius landed in a small clearing surrounded by Sinjin's friends and loved ones. Seeing them brought fresh tears to his eyes.

Not waiting for Al'Drak to set foot on land, Kendra rushed forward and embraced him before he got the first strap loose. Climbing up the rest of the way, she helped, clearly aware of his physical state. "I don't know how you managed to persevere. Most would have fallen long before you quit."

"I don't remember."

Nodding, Kendra pursed her lips. "You were brave and strong," she said, unable to keep her voice from cracking. "I was afraid I was going to lose you, but you proved yourself more powerful than anyone would have given you credit for."

"I'm just glad I didn't fall off."

Chuckling, Kendra helped him get his sore leg over the saddle. He grunted with effort, but no one laughed at that. He was lucky, though. His wounds would heal. Sore muscles would mend. Even his wife walked with a limp, favoring her right side. Others had not been so lucky; the knowledge weighed heavily. It had not been the kind of night to leave one without scars.

From below, the Noonspire appeared even taller than it had from above. Facing east, Sinjin watched Vestra illuminate the megalithic dragon ore crystal from within, setting it ablaze. At that moment, a seam appeared at the crystal's base. Previously invisible doors swung open without a sound, as if moved by the hand of an unseen god. Dwarfed by the massive portal, two figures leaned on one another. In spite of sore legs, Sinjin moved toward his mother with all the speed his body could gather, stumbling and nearly falling as he went. The two figures waited for him. Others followed in silence. Kenward Trell matched his pace.

Kyrien uncoiled with the most graceful movements and lowered himself to the ground. Not stopping, Sinjin reached out to his mother until her glowing spirit raised a single hand, bidding him to hold.

"We are not yet done," Catrin said, her words loud enough for people miles away to hear. "Come."

The command was not meant for Sinjin or anyone outside the spire; that was clear without additional instruction. The Herald of Istra communicated with more than simple words and inflection. Every syllable conveyed feeling. This higher form of communication used words more like vessels than the content themselves. It made his tongue feel clumsy and inadequate, no matter how eloquently he might speak.

Gradually, imperceptibly at first, two forms began to materialize before Catrin and Allette. No longer did they manifest as dark, twisted shades, but instead resembled what their physical forms must have been so very long ago. Though the crystalline prison had long since absorbed them, somehow memory survived. Aggrezjhon and Murden stood in the light for the first time in many centuries, the world outside visible to them once again without the Noonspire to shade it. The wonder was visible on their ever more distinct facial features, their bodies gone but not entirely forgotten.

"You are free," Catrin said.

The words echoed and resonated within the prison. Seeing confusion on the sorcerers' faces, Sinjin swallowed hard. What was she doing? It occurred to him then that Aggrezjhon and Murden both needed physical forms to leave the prison, and only two remained within. "No!" he shouted, but his mother held up a hand to silence him. Even her gestures conveyed greater meaning.

"Allette Kilbor and I will leave this place; whole--or at least as whole as when we entered. But Aggrezjhon and Murden, you have been punished enough. No soul should be imprisoned for eternity, no matter their crimes, and certainly not for being who and what they are. My powers are no more my fault than those your brethren feared in you."

Her voice washed over Sinjin, bringing absolution, humanity audible in her words, conveying regret and remorse. She had not asked to be the most powerful person on the planet, and perhaps she no longer was, but she knew the burdens such power imposed. She understood what it was like to be feared and hated because she possessed abilities others did not.

"I accept you for who and what you are," Catrin said. "You must accept me for who and what I am. My form is my own and will remain so. My spirit is my own and will remain so. I am connected to all of you, but you may not inhabit this mortal shell. That is for me alone."

Understanding washed over Aggrezjhon and Murden, though their faces still showed disbelief. Sinjin could only imagine how they must feel. They had been imprisoned for thousands of years and had been free for a mere fraction of that time prior to their imprisonment. It must be strange and exhilarating as well as frightening.

"For a brief time, the way will be clear," Catrin said. "I grant you leave of this place."

"But where?" Murden's voice whispered yet boomed. "How?"

Behind the two sorcerers, light bloomed and swelled as Vestra showed his full glory above the horizon. From that light stepped a diminutive form in a pristine white dress. Smiling like Sinjin had never seen her do before, with light and warmth finally reaching her eyes, came Trinda Hollis. She walked with deliberate slowness, beaming with newfound bliss. Standing between Aggrezjhon and Murden, the girl known as the child queen reached up and took their hands. With an almost shy smile, she said, "Come on, sillies. It's this way."

No more words were required. Sinjin stared into the blinding light until they were gone, and even then he had trouble pulling his gaze away. Towering ghosts clouded his vision long after he turned back to his mother and Allette. Six long steps it took them to reach the natural light, and they transformed as they crossed the threshold, as if they had not truly been physical beings while trapped within the Noonspire. Lines gathered around his mother's eyes. What might be an unwanted sign of aging to some showed his mother's humanity and were beyond value.

His legs feeling leaden, Sinjin stepped forward. Pelivor passed him, the smell from the blanket he carried preceding him. Kenward Trell also walked past but not without patting him on the shoulder on his way by; even that light touch brought pain. It was going to be a long recovery.

"No," Catrin said when Pelivor attempted to wrap her in the blanket. "For what time I have left, I will stand in the light. I can hide from it no longer."

Those words knotted Sinjin's gut. He'd wanted to believe this was the end of his troubles and hers, but perhaps a peaceful, trouble-free existence was too much to ask. His mother and many of his friends had survived, and from that he took solace. For the moment, it was enough. There would be time to worry over the future, and likely a number of people were already doing that worrying for him. No sense in spoiling the moment.

The sentiment was reinforced when Kenward Trell approached Allette Kilbor. The woman had said nothing. She'd been imprisoned within the Noonspire for longer than Catrin, and Sinjin worried over the damage done. Kenward's posture showed he had similar concerns. He opened his arms and stood with palms out. The woman who'd been known as the Black Queen stepped forward with tears in her eyes. Saying nothing, she walked into Kenward's arms and wrapped him in a tight embrace, looking as if she might never let go.

It was a good day, Sinjin Volker thought, a good day, indeed.

"Oh, dear," came Nora Trell's voice from behind him. "What's that fool boy gotten himself into this time?"

Seeing a form reemerge from the light startled Sinjin even as he laughed, but Murden's spirit held a finger to her lips. Unable to breathe, he waited.

"Before we go," Murden said loud enough for all to hear, "there is one last thing I can do to repay you. The Seventh Magic was once beautiful. So it should be again."

Reaching out, she stroked the crystalline walls. While it had no outward effect at first, it soon became clear there would be widespread consequences. Like the workings of a woodsmith's toy, the interlocking blocks supporting the Noonspire and those forming the smooth stone ring around it began to shift and move. Some lifted upward and rotated; others dropped down, leaving cavernous openings. Those who stood surrounding the spire remained rooted in place, the stones on which they stood the only ones not moving.

Murden once again melted into the light, which dimmed behind her as the sun reached its zenith. Whatever doorway or portal they had passed through was now gone, and Sinjin suspected it would not return for thousands of years. Outside the spire, the transformation continued. What had been smooth and flat was no more. An entire city, as if premade, arose from the heart of the Jaga, hidden for millennia. Here was the fabled city written of long ago--not lost but transformed. Seeing the city in its original state was awe inspiring, even if its true nature was now known. Perhaps this place could evolve into something greater than a prison, Sinjin thought. Another hand on his shoulder made him wince.

Benjin Hawk gave him a knowing smile. "There'll be a lot of work to get done."

Good old Benjin, always reliable and ready to remind him of his duties. Sinjin grinned back. "I'm sure we'll find someone to do it."

Laughing, Benjin squeezed Sinjin's shoulder a little too hard. It was all he could do to remain standing. When his mother came to him, her eyes filled with knowing sadness, his resolve failed and his lip quivered.

"It is to you, my son, I owe the greatest apology," Catrin said, her voice calm and smooth despite the pain in her eyes. "I was stolen from you, over and over again, and there are years I can never give you back. It matters not what authority or responsibilities I had; it only matters that I was not there when you needed me most. I can promise no better in the future, my Sinjin. For that I am most truly and humbly sorry."

"You don't have to be sorry," Sinjin said through barely contained emotion. "You just have to be my mom."

Chapter 17
The spirit's true might is not known until duly tested.
--Ain Giest, sleepless one

* * *

The return to Dragonhold was like a dream. So much had changed in Sinjin Volker's life since he called this place home, and indeed even the face of the Godfist had changed. From above, the gaping chasm created during Mael's escape stood as a colossal reminder of dangers they yet faced. It was otherwise easy to forget. The sun shone brightly once again, and peace had come to most of the world. It would not always be so. Best to enjoy good times while they lasted.

Beside him, Kendra whistled. "I never believed Trinda when she said the Fifth Magic might break the Godfist, but it looks like she wasn't far from the mark."

"She said a lot of things I didn't believe," Sinjin agreed, Valterius taking him closer to Kendra and Gerhonda so he did not have to shout to be heard.

"You can't blame yourself," Kendra said--not for the first time.

"I know. But I must learn from my mistakes and, at the very least, not make them again."

"You will be a good leader, my son." The words came from above as Kyrien descended from the clouds. No matter how much he'd been through, Sinjin still had trouble believing it. "It's true no matter what you believe. This was a lesson I learned and a mistake I'll not make again."

Riding behind her, resplendent in his fine blue silks, Pelivor nodded in agreement. Part of Sinjin lamented his father's absence; it was he who should ride with his mother, but the thought was fleeting. Prios was gone and nothing could change that. Pelivor and his mother deserved happiness no matter how Sinjin wished the past to change. "How far out is the fleet?" he asked, knowing his mother and Kyrien flew in escort.

"Close. We flew ahead to make sure there were no surprises."

It was a wise move. Though Aggrezjhon and Murden no longer presented a threat, there were no guarantees regarding the rest of the world. This was an age of power, and change was inevitable. No matter how much Sinjin wanted to let down his guard and live a carefree life, he knew better. Moments later, he spotted the *Dragon's Wing* moving at high speed off the Godfist's west coast. Benjin and Gwen were visible, even from afar, and Sinjin smiled. The ship's masthead, carved in Kyrien's likeness, now boasted much larger wings that extended over starboard and port sides. At mid deck stood a device resembling a giant ballista, only in place of a bolt, it was loaded with an aircraft. Sinjin shook his head; the girl was as bad as her uncle.

The three dragons circled above the Chinawpa and Pinook valleys, looking down on a scarred land only beginning to heal. When the *Dragon's Wing* drew close, an old sailors' tune became audible. "Give me a fair wind and gentle seas, and no one will be happier than me. Give me waves capped in white, I'll find me an inn and bid you good night."

Sinjin added his own verse to the tune, "Give me a dragon who obeys my commands, I'll have no need of inns or lands. Give me a dragon with a will his own, perhaps I'd best just stay at home." His words brought laughter, and the healing continued. There had been times it felt as if brevity would never again exist, but somehow they had overcome. It was among the most magical parts of his life. Some he'd thought lost had been returned to him, which made it a little easier to bear the thought of those who had not.

Soon the main body of the trade fleet materialized on the horizon. No more would Kenward Trell be forced to carry a pittance of freight between continents. Now he and his family dominated the air aboard the *Vengeful Shark*, the *Kraken's Ghost* and the *Trader's Skies*. Regal dragons patrolled the area, accompanied by aircraft of ever-evolving design. So much had changed, yet so much stayed the same.

Seeing the fleet, Benjin eased the *Dragon's Wing* back out to deeper waters and lowered her into the sea. Within moments, Gwen was strapped in to the stinger perched atop the giant ballista. Sinjin could almost hear Benjin grumbling and admonishing his daughter to be careful. He did hear her command, "Release!"

Like an arrow shot from the mightiest bow, Gwen and her aircraft launched into the air. Had it not been for the thrust she applied, they would have plunged directly back into dark water, but she knew her business. Growing in volume and pitch, the sound that had given the original howler its name filled the air and echoed through the valleys below. Fingering the thrust sphere in his pocket, Sinjin considered his friend's unspoken challenge, but one glance at his wife made him think better of it. There would be time for that to come.

No one knew what they would find within Dragonhold save devastation, which was obvious from above. They'd had no word of survivors and so far had seen no signs of life from below. Sinjin's guts twisted, knowing so many people he cared about had been left here to fend for themselves. It wasn't something he or any of them were proud of, but it was another thing he'd been told he could not blame himself for. Sadly he'd been told that about a great many things of late, but still he felt responsible. So many seek influence and power, but no one ever mentioned the cost: innocence and peace of mind.

After passing them at high speed, Gwen raced through the Pinook Valley, apparently trying to get a better understanding of what they faced. Sinjin turned to Kendra, and she nodded; the two soon cut the air in Gwen's wake, seeing what she saw and finally having some sense everything would be as it should. Here and there, people worked in the Pinook Valley, planting crops and cleaning up the debris left after so much destruction. Shy and fearful at first, the people looked up in surprise, never having seen the likes of Gwen and her stinger before. When the dragons came behind, however, a cheer rose up from the valley below, and when at last Kyrien showed himself, with Catrin and Pelivor on his back, great jubilance erupted from those who must have thought themselves lost and abandoned.

A single pass showed Gwen what she needed, and she sailed upward, across the peaks and back over the Arghast Desert. Even there, cheers rose from tribesmen racing toward Dragonhold, their horses' manes flowing in dark, glossy waves.

"Send someone to the top of the peak!" Sinjin yelled as he and Kendra made another pass through the valley. More people heard his command and moved back toward Dragonhold. Even seeing a dozen survivors eased anxiety and allowed him once again to hope. When he saw Miss Mariss and Martik Tillerman standing within Dragonhold's main entrance and waving to them, Sinjin could not keep the tears from his eyes. So much guilt and worry washed away then, and when he looked over to his wife, she dabbed at her eyes.

It took time for people to make their way through the hold, and only a few were privy to Dragonhold's inner workings, but before too long, Miss Mariss and Martik stood atop the tallest spire within the Pinook Mountains. Valterius soared in close and landed gracefully beside them.

"You're a sight to see," Miss Mariss said, her voice cracking with emotion. "We thought you all lost."

"And figured we weren't far behind you," Martik said. "Dragonhold is an indefensible mess."

Having seen the gaping crater near what Sinjin thought was the center of the mountain fortress, he understood where Martik was coming from, but it was the dark gray grit coating everything that made it obvious.

"Whatever that dragon did," Miss Mariss said, looking as if she might spit, "he ground half the keep to dust and spread it thick throughout the entire hold."

"It might be a complete loss," Martik said, earning a glare from Miss Mariss.

"Nonsense. It might take a few years to clean it up and mend what we can, but it'll still be livable. You young people just have no patience or the stomach for hard work."

It was clear Martik had heard this before and already knew there was no sense arguing. "What on all of Godsland is that?" he asked instead, pointing out over the Arghast Desert.

Grinning, Sinjin said, "The Trell family has been hard at work."

"May the gods help us all," Miss Mariss said. "My nephew is fool enough for all of us, but this is beyond even his audacity. This has my sister written all over it."

Sinjin would have laughed, but something else lay beneath the humor: Admiration? Respect?

"That can't be real," Martik whispered, watching the mighty airships approach, smaller craft and dragons of varied sizes surrounding them.

"Onin," Miss Mariss whispered, allowing the true nature of her heart to be seen. It was a rare occasion for one who prided herself on keeping her own counsel, and it only made Sinjin think more highly of her. She'd been a difficult taskmaster in his youth, and he'd sometimes wanted to avoid her, but she'd always been fair and mostly kind. Durin might have argued otherwise, but even he had come to see the value of lessons she'd taught them. Faced with feeding and entire hold, Miss Mariss had never shied from duties she'd essentially volunteered for. She'd been in no way responsible for Dragonhold or its occupants, but it was simply her nature to take charge of a situation and make sure what needed doing got done.

Now though, she faced an even more daunting task. Gerhonda landed beside Valterius a moment later, and Miss Mariss rushed to embrace Sinjin's wife before she could even release her straps and climb down. "It is so good to see you! I can't tell you how happy I am that your husband and mother-in-law did not manage to get you killed."

This brought a grin to Sinjin's face, and Kyrien flew in close. The circular pedestal upon which they stood wasn't large enough to hold them all at once, and the larger regent dragon was forced to cling to the mountainside, just as Seethe had once done. No feral dragons had been seen since Aggrezjhon and Murden departed this world, but no one forgot.

"It is good to see you as well, Catrin, Pelivor, and Kyrien!" Miss Mariss shouted, blowing them kisses.

No words were said as the *Trader's Skies* approached. The airship dwarfed any ship ever built on Godsland, even the *Trader's Wind*, which had made the Trell family their fortunes. The *Trader's Skies* represented a bright future if one cared to see it, and it left those gathered with a collective sense of awe. Thrustmasters and flightmasters stood at attention near the giant thrust tubes resting upon articulating mounts that allowed a wide range of mobility. The massive airship moved with quiet grace, unlike the stingers and growlers patrolling the skies around them.

Jehregard left the formation and soared closer, allowing Onin the opportunity to speak without shouting. "Nora's going to bring the ship in and dock," he said with a nod to Miss Mariss. "It might be best if you all give her some room to maneuver." Without another word, Jehregard tilted to one side and soared away.

Reaching out, Sinjin offered Martik his hand to pull the man up behind him on the saddle. The man who'd accomplished so much already in his life paled and did not extend his grip. Kendra made the same offer to Miss Mariss, who giggled and moved without hesitation. Perhaps shamed by his fear and her bravery, Martik took Sinjin's hand. Kyrien pushed himself away from the peak and soared lower, still circling the spire. After helping Martik strap himself in, Sinjin prepared to make his intentions known to Valterius. The dragon turned his head, looked Martik in the eye, and came as close to grinning as his visage would allow.

"Maybe I should--" Martik managed to say before Valterius leaped from the heights, trimmed his wings, and dropped toward the valley floor. His screams could be heard for miles.

Edging ever closer, the *Trader's Skies* backed up her growing reputation. With graceful ease, she hovered close enough to the flat-topped spire to extend a loading ramp. The air beneath the ship sent loose rock and scree into the wind, but otherwise did no harm. Using a polished wooden cane with a kraken's likeness wrapped around it, Nora Trell walked down the ramp. "You all didn't have to run and hide," she said. "You'd think I didn't know how to dock my own ship!"

After Kendra returned Miss Mariss to the platform, she crossed the distance and embraced her sister. "Then perhaps you should not have sent Onin of the Old Guard to shoo us away."

"Men," was all Nora said, and the two sisters shared a hearty laugh along with more than a few knowing looks.

"You know I'm grateful for all you've brought," Miss Mariss said softly, the humor gone from her voice. "But I don't know what to do with it. The hold is a disaster. If we take stores in, they'll only end up fouled with this forsaken dust." She reached down and grabbed a handful of the coarse grit still covering much of the circular stone platform.

"Sinjin warned us," Nora said. "And I think we may be able to help. First, though, we've got to preserve what supplies remain within."

It took three days to seal off the kitchens and smithies, along with the entrance to the God's Eye and a few other places where Dragonhold's survivors had already made progress clearing away the dust and debris. Even after those people had spent weeks cleaning, it would have taken them years at the pace they moved. Miss Mariss had been right about Sinjin and his generation lacking the patience for such work, though he didn't necessarily see this as a bad thing. Impatience was sometimes the force that drove innovation, and this case was no different.

"We've sealed the halls," Martik reported to those gathered in the main hall. "I'm not certain there's much else we can do in the short term."

Sinjin questioned his mother's plan, but ankle-deep rock dust convinced him things couldn't get much worse. The hold itself was eerily quiet, having been evacuated of all but those critical to this operation and those with dragons. Catrin, Pelivor, Gwen, and the gathered thrustmasters and flightmasters mentally prepared themselves for something the likes of which no one had ever before attempted. Even the dust clouds their steps sent into the air made breathing difficult, and things were about to get much worse.

Once freshly planted crops were covered with cloth and the valleys evacuated, Catrin made her orders clear, and those remaining moved to their assigned positions. They would start with the great hall and apply whatever lessons they learned to the rest of the hold, assuming they survived this unprecedented attempt. Valterius ferried people to Upperton, well away from the anticipated dust cloud, and Kendra gave a final wave before departing. Sinjin remained beside his mother, determined and unafraid. Whatever happened would happen, and fear would change it not one bit.

Martik Tillerman was the last to leave the hold, having triple-checked the barriers they built to protect what meager supplies remained. After watching Valterius take Martik away, Sinjin turned to his mother.

"It's been too long since we've done something together," she said and he smiled. This was not the average mother-son effort. Both pulled wet scarves over their noses and mouths. "Be ready! On my command . . . now!"

The air pressure within Dragonhold changed as a dozen thrust spheres were activated. A twisting wind howled toward the main entrance. Carrying coarse sand and grit, it wore away at the rock itself. Clouds of black dust roiled and billowed, blotting out the light and leaving them in near darkness, but still they continued, knowing they were not to stop before the Herald's command. It was a testament to the bravery of those who served that day when the air within the hold began to clear, showing the stone columns gleaming in the meager sunlight. Though the skies high above were clear, thick gray dust clogged the air in the Pinook Valley.

Aiming his thrust to one side, scouring away the filth from every crevice in the main hall, Sinjin saw ancient carvings in the walls now revealed from beneath millennia of lichen and calcified mold. Overzealous effort sent tiny stones flying across the floors, damaging parts of the ancient artwork, and Sinjin did his best to clean the hold without destroying it.

"Concentrate on the main entrance," Catrin shouted above the roar of artificial wind, and the air within the great hall cleared even further as the group cooperated, forming a mighty vortex of air that sucked the remaining dust from the great hall. When the air was clear, the Herald held her fist in the air. "Cease!"

It took only a moment for those gathered to obey, and Sinjin smiled at his mother. "That wasn't so bad."

She grinned in return. "For the people of Dragonhold, it was the very least we could do."

With that sentiment, Sinjin wholeheartedly agreed. The keep had been theirs for years before it fell to Trinda Hollis upon his mother's departure, and perhaps it had truly belonged to Mael all along, but now he, too, was gone--or at least Sinjin presumed. The mysteries of Dragonhold were far from solved, and no one could guess what they might yet discover.

For the next week, Catrin and those temporarily under her command did everything within their abilities to restore the hold to its former glory. Deep within, where the Fifth Magic had detonated, there was little to do but remove the remaining dust. Stone floors that had perhaps never before seen the open sky now bathed in sunlight. After sealing many damaged halls, their exploration a task for some later date, Martik declared the keep once again defensible, if barely.

"There's a great deal more work to be done," he said. "Perhaps more than any of us might achieve in a lifetime. But no matter what some may say"--he looked crossways at Miss Mariss--"my generation knows the value of what will remain when we're gone and of tasks not to be achieved in our lifetimes. That which is not begun now will only be delayed, and I very much wish to leave this place better than when I first arrived here, better than when the Herald herself discovered it."

Sinjin half expected his mother to voice her disagreement, knowing it was her father and Benjin who had truly rediscovered the place and the ancients who had made it what it was. In days past, his mother would have made certain everyone knew to whom the true credit belonged, but she had changed. All of them had changed. The validity of what one believed was sometimes secondary to what those beliefs drove one to achieve. Sometimes it was better to leave those to believe what they will so long as it serves the rest. Truth was a rare thing and did not always lead to salvation.

When Miss Mariss and the others returned to the great hall, their expressions spoke volumes. "You mean to tell me we spent weeks shoveling that forsaken dust and all we had to do was wait for you all to arrive? The gods have a twisted sense of humor."

Few had the courage to laugh in the face of her anger, but Onin of the Old Guard proved himself either brave or foolish. Sinjin suspected both. Ruddy from barely suppressed chortles, Onin found himself confronted by a red-faced and puffing Miss Mariss. What would have cowed most men sent the old warrior into a hysterical fit threatening to consume him.

"Men!" was all Miss Mariss said before walking away in a huff.

"You're going to pay for that later," Martik said in a low voice.

Onin barked a laugh. "That I will, m'boy. That I will. But I like a woman with fire, and sometimes you just have to fan the flames."

It took time to gather all those who chose to continue residing within Dragonhold. Their numbers had dwindled from war and from peace. Many the invasions had forced underground sought new lives outside the hold. Those who remained were committed, out of love for either the hold itself or others who remained. Still, Sinjin was grateful for those hearty folk, ready to take on the task of several lifetimes.

"You've done well," Catrin said when everyone had gathered. "You've served me well. You've served the people of the Godfist well, and you should be proud of yourselves."

"We knew you would return to us," someone said from the back of the crowd, and Sinjin wished he knew who had spoken. In the end it did not matter since the same sentiment was echoed by many of those gathered. It was then he sensed his mother's will faltering.

"I'd stay with you if I could . . . but I cannot." Her voice trembled.

Dismay rolled through the hall. Sinjin had heard the talk; many believed her the rightful ruler of this place. These people had endured Trinda Hollis's rule on the hope Catrin would come back. Some of those had blamed Catrin for failing to adequately protect them long ago. Emotion thickened the air making Sinjin queasy.

"I've done what I can do here, and now I must move on. Great things remain to be done. You all are the heart of this hold. Without you, none of this would have been possible. I am forever in your debt, and I leave this place to you. It's yours."

The silence that followed was like a living thing devouring them all.

Morif finally spoke. "It is the greatest gift I've ever known." All eyes turned to him. "I don't deserve this honor, but I pledge myself to all those here. I will do everything within my power and until my very last breath to see Dragonhold restored and inhabited by the people of the Godfist."

Millie stepped forward and echoed his vow. One by one, people joined them. Bradley, Simms, and others made their solemn vows before the Herald, though she'd asked for none. When all who wished to do so had offered themselves to this task, silence reclaimed the hall.

"It is truly the greatest gift," Bradley said. "But who will lead us? Who will guide us so that we share common purpose and goals?"

"I do not know," Catrin admitted, "except that it cannot be me. I'm sorry."

"A vote," Morif said at last.

Others within the hall murmured in agreement. Not all of those gathered could read or write and a silent ballot was abandoned. "I say it should be Martik," someone shouted from within the crowd. Again, Sinjin did not know who it was who had spoken but he agreed.

"The choice is yours," Catrin said, unwilling to cast her own vote.

"Martik," came another cry, and Bradley stepped forward to add his agreement. No other names were offered, and soon the name Martik was repeated everywhere.

The man who'd come to them as a conscripted soldier in the Zjhon army stood stunned and speechless. "Why me?" he asked in a voice barely above a whisper. "Surely I cannot."

"Ah, but you must, Martik Tillerman," Catrin said. "As my last act within this hold, I declare you steward. In accordance with the vote just passed, this place is granted to you and your line for all the days to come. Consider well your actions from here on out, my friend, for many will count on you." She leaned toward him and whispered in his ear, "You can do this, Martik. You were born for this."

Chapter 18
Those with a hero's soul are often unaware until need arises.
--Morif, soldier

* * *

Nothing moved within the black spike, and a foul smell clung to the air. Kyrien snorted in distaste. Patting him on the neck, Catrin dismounted. Pelivor followed; he'd refused to do anything else. This pain was personal, and he knew that; he knew far too many things, as did she. Accepting it, she walked slowly, as if rushing would change what she would find. Wilted, twisted, and blackened, a saltbark tree reached out of blasted and scorched soil. Now covered in soot, the walls had lost their sheen.

"Larissarelatarenfall."

Dying leaves shifted at the sound of that name, some dropping to the ruined ground below. When at last a hand appeared on the tree trunk, sliding around the tree from behind, it moved with painful care and slowness, trembling all the while. The dryad looked every bit as bad as the rest of the place and Catrin sobbed. "I'm so sorry."

The wounded dryad responded with nothing more than a trembling wave. Catrin understood. She'd been given the dryad's gift long ago; she knew their secrets and weaknesses. Mael did as well, and Catrin's fury raged. Dryads, even those of saltbark trees, whose leaves bring tremendous healing to all the world's creatures, could not heal themselves. An undamaged tree would eventually heal the dryad's form, given sufficient time, but a dying tree and a wounded dryad meant a long and unenviable end.

Walking forward, Catrin knew what she had to do. Just as Brother Vaughn had taught her years before, she embraced the tree and pressed her forehead against the bark. A price would be paid for taking on the tree's pain, but she didn't hesitate. This she could do. The tree did not yield, and bark painfully pressed into her face. The tree did not want to hurt her; the sense of it was overwhelming. They both knew what would come. Catrin had brought this tree here, planted it herself. What had once been a striped seed that fit in her palm was now a beautiful saltbark tree, so full of vigor and life. These thoughts she projected with gentle might.

At a gradual but consistent rate, her head moved forward, into the dying tree. When she'd been given the dryad's gift, she hadn't understood. Only later, when another dryad woke the gift within her, had Catrin begun to understand. Planting the seed the dryad in the shallows had given her, she'd gained better understanding. Over time, her relationship with the remarkable tree blossomed, just as the tree so swiftly grew in that magical place.

With growing empathy came greater anguish, and she could not contain her screams. Through fire and pain, Catrin felt cleansed, her sacrifice enough to counter damage done. When misery reached its height, at a point she could no longer withstand, a familiar calm came over her. Kyrien wrapped himself around her, perhaps in physical form, outside the tree, but also within. She'd never considered the possibility of dragons communicating directly with trees, but now it seemed so obvious. Pelivor lent them his energy like so many times in the past. Together they bore the brunt of Larissarelatarenfall's pain. Images of what had taken place between the dryad and Mael flashed over Catrin's consciousness.

The end came. Pain relented, ebbing as they reached a vision of Catrin, Kyrien and Pelivor, come to save them, tree and dryad alike. Scars there would be, but that which had been broken was mended. The connection ended without warning. Perhaps that was why she felt so dizzy afterward, or maybe it was the other way around. Falling to the ground, her hands came up covered in blackened moss.

From behind the tree, the dryad moved more steadily, though still with a pronounced tremble. "Rest." The word came as barely a whisper, as if from parched lips long unused. Catrin did as she said, her hand resting on Kyrien, who slept. The tree's appearance hadn't improved, nor had the dryad's, and Catrin despaired; she'd wanted so badly to heal them. Perhaps they were just too far gone; perhaps Mael had made certain she would fail. The last thought struck a sour note; he'd saved her. How could she loathe one she owed her life, to whom they all owed their lives. It was irreconcilable.

Larissarelatarenfall reached out her hand, though always remaining in contact with the tree. "Look," she said. Turning tear-filled eyes up, Catrin saw the dryad lift away a dead leaf, its crystals falling away and crumbling to dust. It was painful to watch, but the revelations touched deeply. A single, emerald green leaf coated in gleaming crystals protruded from where the dead leaf had fallen. From old life came new. "Thank you," the dryad said.

Catrin cried.

* * *

Watching the trade fleet approach Windhold was difficult to believe, and Durin had to wonder if his eyes were working properly. Having the *Trader's Wind* come to the Firstland would have been cause for celebration; such a sizable ship could carry enough goods to modernize the Firstland and feed the people for a year. Smaller trade vessels and swift defensive ships accompanied her, bringing goods and skilled workers. Airships hovering above dwarfed them. Surrounded by scouting ships, including the *Dragon's Wing* and a growing myriad of aircraft, the trade fleet was unlike anything else in the world.

The *Kraken's Ghost*, though smaller than the *Trader's Skies*, stood out from the rest, perhaps because of its unpredictable movements, but more so because it so closely resembled its namesake. Where the *Vengeful Shark* was sleek and smooth, the Kraken was ready to envelope anything that came too close within barbed tentacles and devour it. Lightning pulsed over the engines, and the cacophonous roar grew as they approached.

Jessub Tillerman was the first to reach land, and he soared past the wind channel where Durin stood, waving on his way by. Others gathered around to watch the spectacle, and in some cases awaiting someone in particular. Casting a sideways glance at Onin of the Old Guard, he noted a twinkle in the soldier's eyes he'd never seen before. It was a good day.

Sinjin and most of the Drakon had flown out to welcome the fleet, and they added to the aerial chaos. Shouts of greeting and warning mingled in the air, as those airborne did their best not to collide with each other.

Brother Vaughn walked up alongside him. "Never thought I'd see the day."

"Hard to believe, isn't it?" Durin asked.

Nodding, the monk said, "For most of my life, I dreamed of soaring the skies. Now I can do just that, and it terrifies me."

Durin laughed. "Thank the gods for those with less sense than us. I'd just as soon watch from here."

"A sound plan if you ask me," Brother Vaughn said. "There'll be plenty of work to be done on firm ground."

The truth of his words struck Durin. Cut off from so many things he'd taken for granted, they had struggled. The Godfist was a difficult place to live, requiring the people to be clever and hearty, but they had nails and leather and anvils and books, none of which existed here. The Firstland was the kind of place where everything was improvised and nothing done as his grandfather would have seen fit. It had bothered Durin all along. He'd been raised to meet a certain standard with his work, even if he'd failed to appreciate it in his younger years. Here that level of competence was simply impossible. Anything they achieved was a lot of hard work combined with a healthy dose of luck.

When the *Trader's Skies* blocked out the horizon, everything changed. Extending from her deck was a loading ramp wide enough for a verdant dragon. Steam rising in gouts and a roaring howl accompanied the lowering of the bridge but was silenced once the mighty structure rested on stone. Durin didn't know if such a ship ever visited Windhold in the past, but he doubted anything had ever matched this.

From within the holds, walking up long ramps with a gentle slope, came pack animals loaded with goods. Watching the animals go by was like being in a dream. Tools, metal goods, rope, and canvas passed. So many things that had been impossible to create on the Firstland were now carried past him as if it were the simplest thing in the world. Truly, everything had changed.

When Miss Mariss appeared, a cloud cat running alongside her, attacking invisible things along the way, Durin smiled. Again he cast a glance at Onin, who'd flown in a month before with a long list of preparations to be made. Never would he mention the tears running down the man's face.

* * *

"This thing itches," Onin said, fussing with the frilly shirt the girls had picked out. Sinjin stifled a laugh.

"The last thing I saw dressed up like this was a turkey," Kenward added. "It was delicious."

Shaking his head, Sinjin could no longer hide his mirth.

"What are you grinning at?" Onin asked.

Shrugging, Sinjin remained silent, knowing what side he was on. His entire reason for being there was making sure neither groom ran off under pain of his wife's wrath--and that of Miss Mariss and Allette Kilbor. No, he would say nothing. They knew.

"I've married people on my ship a number of times," Kenward said. "It's a half-a-day affair at the very most. A few words, a little food, and the rest takes care of itself."

At that even Onin laughed. Planning for this affair had been going on for weeks. Sinjin suspected half what the trade fleet brought had been solely for this wedding.

"Stand still," Nora said a moment later. Sinjin hadn't even seen her approach, or he might have remembered having something else to do at that moment. "I've got two weddings to plan and you two look like a couple sheep headed to slaughter. Sloppy sheep at that. Stand still!"

By the time Nora was done fidgeting with his beard, Onin's patience was at its end. Sinjin had to side with him on this point since he'd never seen either man look sharper. Onin had combed his beard for what felt like hours and had redone all his braids, using his finest beads and circlets. Polished boots wore a reflective sheen, his leathers showing no signs of wear or holes. Kenward's clothes were a slightly different style but were in no worse condition. His shirt was similar to Onin's, but his pants and boots were lighter in color and with a textured surface as opposed to Onin's gloss.

"I've a swift ship in dry dock," Kenward said when Nora walked away.

"And I've a dragon waiting with his tierre on," Onin added.

"Neither of you are going anywhere," Sinjin said. Both men turned on him, making it clear he was as likely to stop an avalanche, "without leaving me with at least a couple black eyes. A fat lip wouldn't hurt."

Barking a laugh, Onin slapped him on the shoulder. "It would either be us or them, m'boy. Either way, your luck's run out."

"I'm not sure they'll know when to stop," Sinjin said, leaning to one side to staunch the pain.

"If you all don't hush, you're going to ruin everything," Kendra said, Sinjin's ear in her viselike grip. "Be quiet and do as you're told."

"And now you know what awaits you both," Sinjin muttered after she walked away. The look she sent him made it clear he'd spoken too loudly.

"They're ready," Millie said from within Catrin's Vale.

Walking behind the two grooms, Sinjin caught a glimpse of his mother. In a dress of light blue sparkling with finely cut gemstones and Pelivor by her side, Catrin's presence was like a warm, comforting embrace. "The time has come, my friends," she said with a wide smile. Musicians played softly in the background, and Allette Kilbor walked from behind a folding curtain of pale blue silk.

Sinjin almost whistled involuntarily at the sight of her in her dress of cream and white with highlights of blue, her jet black hair bound with a golden clasp. Kenward drew a sharp breath, and someone in the crowd giggled. Allette smiled then, looking more beautiful than ever before. A moment later, Miss Mariss stepped from behind a similar curtain on the opposite side of the clearing. The *Slippery Eel*, somehow made even more beautiful over time, completed the backdrop. The wood retained its luster, except where moss and lichen had encased it. The detailed workmanship appeared to grow out of the mountain rather than being inexorably consumed. Even that was rendered mundane by the sight of Miss Mariss. Sinjin had known her his entire life, and never had he seen her look so beautiful. Though given to plain, sturdy work garments, the woman who had kept them fed for much of their lives was resplendent in a dress similar to what Allette wore but essentially in reverse. What was cream on Allette's dress was pale blue on Miss Mariss's and vice versa.

It was her expression that made the biggest difference in Sinjin's mind. Never had he seen her so relaxed and happy. That alone brought peace to his heart. Many had speculated Catrin and Pelivor would also marry this day, but Sinjin's mother had confessed to having other plans. That was all she'd told him, so he had little more to go on than anyone else. Kendra caught his eye and wiped away a tear. His wife was not one to admit such emotion, thinking it a sign of weakness, and she averted her eyes before he could smirk at her.

The sun moved behind Catrin as it set, streaming between two peaks and illuminating her from behind.

"Who would take these women as their wives?"

Only then did Onin and Kenward look their parts. Gone were the complaints and jokes, and in their place pride and expectation. Stepping forward and into view of those gathered, both brought comments of their own. Sinjin had to agree; the men did clean up nicely.

Presiding over the wedding suited his mother perhaps better than any other role, and Sinjin was proud. Kendra looked at him just as he wiped a tear and smirked before turning away.

"You may seal the vows with a kiss," Catrin said at last. Kenward and Onin raced to claim the prize first. Both Allette and Miss Mariss beamed as their new husbands wrapped them in their arms, kissing them soundly. If it had been a competition, it would have been a draw, and all those assembled cheered. Jessub Tillerman flew above them then, releasing flower petals to rain down on them. It was a nice touch, Sinjin had to admit, knowing it had been his wife's idea.

With the music playing louder, the dancing began. Nearby foods of all varieties waited on wide, glossy fronds.

"Never thought I'd see the day," Benjin said after moving to Sinjin's side, which happened to be right near where the brisket and smoked vegetables had been laid out.

"Which day is that?" Sinjin asked. "The day Kenward is dressed better than his sister, or the day Onin smiled at someone other than his dragon?"

"Both," Benjin said, not looking up from his food.

"Look at them," Fasha said as she and Kendra approached. "They haven't even danced with their wives yet and already they're making a mess of themselves."

Sinjin held up clean, empty hands in his own defense, but it did not matter. Kendra smacked him on the rear and dragged him into the clearing where the newlyweds still danced. Never would he have guessed Onin would be the best dancer among them, with Miss Mariss quite neatly keeping up with him. Kenward and Allette didn't care. They moved much more slowly, turning in lazy circles, their eyes locked in a longing gaze. Sinjin did his best not to step on Kendra's toes.

As the sun set, leaving them under the comet and moon light, the celebration began in earnest. Songs were sung, tales told, and the finest ale shared among friends. It was as good a time as Sinjin could remember, and he vowed never to forget how this day felt. Hard times would come, but these moments would sustain them when darkness encroached. For a time, he simply allowed himself to be happy and enjoy being in the presence of those he loved.

With bellies full and a cool breeze blowing, most gathered on blankets laid about the vale and watched the skies. The last thing Sinjin remembered before falling asleep was his mother's voice lifted in song. He recalled no words, and the melody fled like a scent on the wind, but the feeling crept into his soul, where it would forever remain. His mother had promised him nothing, and said she had plans of her own. He fell asleep knowing it was enough.

Chapter 19

Sometimes things are as they should be. Cherish it.
--Catrin Volker, Herald of Istra

* * *

Morning arrived with the promise of new life. Sleep slow to clear from his mind, Sinjin looked around without fully understanding at first. Others had gone to their ships and homes for the night, but he and Kendra and a few others had stayed until no more of the magical day remained. Had he known the cost, Sinjin would have stayed awake all night, taking every moment with his mother. She was gone. It was first among a number of realizations to bring clarity.

Beside him, Kendra stirred and stretched with a yawn. Silent, Sinjin allowed her to reach conclusions in her own time. "What?" she asked over a barely stifled yawn.

At first, Sinjin maintained his silence, not wanting to say the words. Eventually though, he had to face reality, had to face the new day with all the strength his parents had fostered in him. "They're gone," he said. "She told me she could promise no more, and now I understand what she meant."

"But why?" Kendra asked, a catch in her voice.

"I don't know for certain. I suspect it's because there is simply too much power in the world now. I can't blame her for not wanting to spend the rest of her days wrapped in a foul-smelling blanket or trapped in a prison of rock. At least she's not alone."

Standing, Kendra helped Sinjin to his feet and they both walked toward the newest occupants of Catrin's Vale. No longer flesh and blood, three granite stones now stood, one far larger than the others. The two smaller stones leaned against one another as if in an eternal embrace. The third monolithic stone encircled the two smaller ones in what could only be described as its tail. When Sinjin squinted just right, he could almost see his mother, Pelivor, and Kyrien huddled together and taking strength from one another.

There Catrin had first encountered regent dragons and heard Kyrien's wails. The dragons told his mother this place belonged to her, and they had asked her to save him. Perhaps ask wasn't the right word, but they had left her a choice, and she had taken on the task, not because the dragons demanded it, but because she could not abide any creature being in such agony. The dragons had only reinforced her own desire to save Kyrien from the fate Archmaster Belegra had planned. It had been that same day his mother and father met for the first time, at least on the physical plane. So much history, so much pain, and yet salvation had come in the end. It was fitting, too, the *Slippery Eel* would not waste away alone after having saved them all at the cost of her own seaworthiness.

No matter how fitting or well reasoned, Sinjin wept. He'd already dealt with losing his mother in the past, yet he found the pain cut just as deeply. Memories of his father threatened to crush what little resolve remained, but Kendra's soft touch pulled him back from the edge of despair.

His mother had as much as told him this was coming. Part of him was angry she hadn't said more, but it wouldn't have made things better. He would have tried to convince her to stay, tried to find some way to fix that which was broken, and failure may have made it hurt even worse.

Life had taught him many things, not the least of which was that each person should choose his or her own destiny. It was not always so, but knowing his mother had chosen her own fate helped. Though she was not in the form he was used to, he could at least visit her here. Their presence palpable, Sinjin laid his hand on what looked like roughhewn granite to find the surface smoother and warmer than expected. Peacefulness washed over him, and he was thankful she was not completely lost, as she had seemed the first time.

Though others had been in the vale when Sinjin awoke, no one remained. Perhaps, upon waking, the others had reached the same realization as he, and they had chosen to give him this time with his mother, Pelivor, and Kyrien--a final chance to say good-bye. For this, he was grateful. Only Kendra was there to see him finally release all the emotions stored up within him, pushed down until such a time as he could deal with them. Peace had come to Godsland, at least for a time, and Sinjin allowed himself to grieve those they'd lost. So many had sacrificed themselves to make this day possible, not knowing if they would truly succeed. To those people, Sinjin felt the greatest gratitude and enormous debt. They had given their lives, and he had an obligation to make the very best of it. Others would rely on him moving forward. His leadership would be required to make things as his mother and the others had always dreamed they could be.

Taking Kendra's hand, Sinjin kissed her softly and thanked her for being there with him. She did not speak, her gentle caress saying more than words ever could. It was a new day, a new life, and the future would wait for no one. So much still needed doing, and he cast a final glance at the standing stones. Vowing to make them proud, he took Kendra's hand and led her away. Perhaps a trick of the wind, Sinjin thought he heard the words, I love you, my son, carried on the breeze. He smiled.

"I noticed something, you know," Kendra said. "Your mother has that dreadful blanket."

Sinjin specifically hadn't mentioned it and maintained his silence.

"If the thief lives and let me think him dead all this time, I'm going to kill him."

* * *

Jharmin Kyte returned to Wolfhold knowing difficult times were ahead, but it felt good to be home.

"The lady Lissa is on her way from Ravenhold," the first of many messengers relayed. Others brought tidings and requests for help from every direction. Before he'd even gained his ancestral home, a line of people had formed, awaiting his attention.

"We have a problem," said Grethen, captain of the Wolfhold guard. Jharmin gave him a withering look. "And a surprise. And another problem."

"I just want to go to my apartments and refresh myself after a long journey," Jharmin said. "You all managed to live without me for this long; pretend I am still at sea. That is, after you bring me food and a hot bath."

Grethen laughed. "Well, sir, we'll walk right past the first problem, then. Can't miss it."

"Great. Just great." Jharmin had known Grethen for a very long time. He would say no more about the matter. Walking through familiar halls, the ground so very still beneath his feet felt alien. Those bonded with the sea are more connected to the world through the water's movements, whereas the land was rigid and unforgiving. Still, a warm bath in a proper-sized tub and a full belly awaited, at least once this "problem" was resolved.

Shock stopped him immediately upon turning a corner. Never would he have expected to see Jenneth in restraints and standing beneath the ruination of one of his favorite murals, which he also knew has a trigger point for the cave-in mechanism. "What happened here?"

"Wait until you hear this story," Grethen said.

"Has Jenneth killed anyone?" Jharmin asked.

"No, sir."

"Then remove his restraints."

"Yes, sir." Grethen did as Jharmin asked, as he always did, even if he almost as often had something to say about it.

Jenneth rubbed his wrists and bowed deeply to Jharmin. "Lord Kyte, forgive me."

"I'm confused. Forgive you for what, exactly?"

"There was a man, sir, and a dragon," Jenneth stammered. "They came silently from the balcony. I was at my post, sir, but I did not see or hear them come. Suddenly the man was just there. He said he would let me live if I let him take something left here long ago." The young man's face went so red, he looked as if he might pass out. "He also said he would reveal gifts for you. I'm sorry, sir. I did not fight him. Had it been just a man, I would have taken him down, but . . . the dragon . . ."

"Describe this man to me, and why isn't there a big pile of rock blocking this hall? That's it?" Jharmin asked, pointing to a small pile of plaster and debris, pieces still showing wolf pups at play.

"He was tall, and his hair stuck out in all directions--"

"And the look of a madman in the corners of his eyes?"

"Yes, sir? Do you know this man?"

"Perhaps," Jharmin said then pointed at the debris. "What of this?"

"We left it just the way we found it," Grethen said.

"That was nice of you. Jenneth?"

"He was right, sir. This was a false cave-in release. Above is a hidden cache of ancient artifacts."

It took a moment for Jharmin to absorb the information. At first he was taken aback by the fact that any of the cave-in releases could be false, along with his sense of security. Second was the notion that Wolfhold still held secrets. Grethen brought a ladder and lamp from nearby.

Jharmin said nothing, climbing the ladder in silence.

"We left everything just as we found it. Not so sure about Jenneth, though. Some items have quite obviously been removed."

Jharmin ascended into darkness, and Grethen followed and handed up the lamp. Seeing treasures that had hidden above his head for all his life, all Jharmin Kyte could do was whistle.

"What do you want us to do about this?" Grethen asked.

"Clean up this mess, and place a guard. And send birds to Nora Trell. Tell her I have what she's looking for."

"Consider it done, sir. What about him?"

"Jenneth and I are going to talk this over. I'll handle this from here."

Grethen might have wanted to say more, but he kept his mouth shut for once.

"What did the man want?" Jharmin asked.

"A suit of armor, a metal staff, and a ball of glass with a design in it."

"Is that it?"

"Yes, sir."

"And did you take anything for yourself?"

"No, sir." Jenneth met Jharmin's eyes.

"Help Grethen clean this up, and then return to duty. I'm going to take a bath and eat fruit and figure out how to repay Nat Dersinger for making me wreak havoc on Wolfhold."

"You don't mean?"

"Of course we're going to have to release them all now!" Jharmin ranted. "How else will we know which are actually protecting us and which are hiding the gods know what?"

"When do you want us to do that?" Jenneth asked, going pale.

"We'll have to begin immediately, of course."

"Lady Lissa will be here in a matter of days, sir."

Massaging his forehead, Jharmin said, "I guess you'd better get started, then, hadn't you?"

"Yes, sir. Anything else, sir?"

"If I'm not sitting in hot water, eating cherries, soon, you get to tell Lady Lissa why we destroyed all the paintings, and the carpets and the moldings she loves so much."

Jenneth took off at a run.

* * *

Atop the needle spire, Nat Dersinger waited. As far as he could see, the forests crawled with activity. This was a new kind of settlement; a new way of living with nature instead of against it. Neenya and the Gunata worked tirelessly with the druids and the Cathurans to show newcomers the way and to make certain the laws of preservation were obeyed. The Falcon Isles accepted all those who came, no matter how strange or unusual they may be. As long as those people obeyed the laws and honored the land and their neighbors, they would be left unmolested. This was how Nat had always wanted it, and finally he had the resources and the power to effect the change he desired.

Some had resisted, even Neenya, but they'd come to see his way of thinking. Few things in this world were as difficult as convincing others of new ideas. So many clung to the old ways because they were safe and comforting, and Nat knew the value of old knowledge, but sometimes they had no choice but to face the new. Istra's return made it unavoidable, pushing even naysayers into supporting him. No one questioned the source of Nat's wealth, as long as he was willing to share. It was a convenient arrangement.

You've done well.

Going immediately to his knees, Nat said, "Yes, lord."

Soon I will regain my strength and your services will no longer be required. Not yet, though. Get up. Look at me.

Returning to his feet, Nat Dersinger shaded his eyes. Mael shone as bright as a comet, his scales like hammered gold. On his neck, a package was secured, and Nat could only stare.

Take it!

Mael's impatience urged him forward, and Nat reached out to the ropes securing the package, ignoring the towering height over which he stretched. The dragon shifted. Nat feared he would tumble to the treetops far below but kept his grip. The dragon stared at him now, projecting his authority. Nat loosened the ropes, clutched the package in one arm, and thrust himself back into the chamber atop the needle spire.

Enormous eyes watched with a sort of glee as Nat opened the bundle. Seeing his reaction, the dragon laughed.

"You are kind, lord," Nat said, believing the words he spoke.

Perhaps. When it suits me.

"You underestimate your own generosity, lord. You saved her."

Indeed. I did. It was the expedient thing to do. Had Aggrezjhon or Murden seized Catrin Volker's form, they would have been formidable enemies. Now they are gone, along with that wretched child. It doesn't matter how you win, as long as you get what you want.

Flying away from the needle spire, Mael fully spread his wings, basking in the light. Seeing Nat Dersinger's efforts had brought him cheer. Had he still a human face, he would have smiled.

Debts have been paid. Vengeance is mine. So long as man and dragon do as I require, there is no need for conflict. Give them peace, and soon they will forget.

* * *

Kenward Trell walked the sturdy, well-joined, and finished wood decks of the *Trader's Skies* hovering above one of the highest peaks on the Firstland. Below, a broken keystone was surrounded by green algamyte crystals. Regal dragons flitted like birds in and out of recesses in the land, most bearing riders. Others patrolled the skies.

Shipmaster Gret orchestrated flightmaster and thrustmaster, contributing to their stable flight. To a great extent, towering balloons supported the ship. Rising from a central peak along a deckhouse large enough to support an army and from each of the ship's corners, wind socks almost looked like cloud formations. Significantly larger than the *Ghost* or *Shark*, the *Trader's Skies* provided far more runway space than needed.

"Are you ready to lose some coin?" Fasha asked.

Kenward just grinned. With Gwen and Jessub on his crew, he was confident of victory. He wasn't certain which one had suggested it first, but neither could resist a race. With the *Shark* and the *Ghost* offshore in opposite directions, the three ships formed the racecourse.

"You did somehow end up with my flightmaster," Fasha pointed out.

"I did you a favor, and you know it. That boy's thrust all the way. You'll see."

"Are you two fighting already?" Nora asked from not far away. "Just get you rear ends over here and let's do this."

Neither could argue and they raced there. Kenward nearly knocked Nora down when he lost his balance, be he hurled himself to one side to make sure she was safe.

"Fool boy."

Rubbing his shoulder, Kenward joined his mother and sister. Signal fires on the *Kraken's Ghost* and the *Vengeful Shark* had been lit, and everyone not engaged in essential duties gathered to watch. Two growlers waited almost on the edge of the nearest runway. Gwen, Jessub, Gret, and Vik were at the ready. The rivalry already obvious, the pairs ignored each other. One flightmaster and one thrustmaster per aircraft. A single thrust sphere was allowed for each team.

"Keep it clean and fair," Fasha said. "As long as my crew wins."

"Cheat if you can, but win either way," Kenward said, echoing his sister's sentiment.

"I taught my children well."

Gleaming in the light, the polished hardwood growlers were sleek works of art, appearing to be in flight even while firmly strapped to the deck. Vik walked with a limp and added a small pillow to his seat before climbing in. Torches were brought out, and there would be no more waiting once the smokers were lit. Gwen and Jessub both held up their hands, indicating they were ready. Vik fidgeted before joining Gret in doing the same.

"Light them up!" Fasha shouted with a grin. Gwen and Jessub's smoker ignited immediately and filled the air with red smoke. It took an instant longer for Gret and Vik's white smoker to ignite. "On the count of three. One. Two. Th--"

Gret's growler roared to life perhaps an instant early and gained an advantage. Both aircraft launched immediately, leaving the deck well before reaching the edge. Squeezing in close to Gwen, Gret managed to gain the lead. White smoke engulfed Gwen and Jessub, and both aircraft dropped from sight.

Running toward the edge of the ship, Kenward wondered if this had been a bad idea.

* * *

Choking, Gwen did what she could to avoid Gret's smoke stream and not fall from the sky. It was a delicate balance. Dipping down into the valley to separate themselves, she gained clear air but put them in far greater danger. Seconds later she burst back out from behind a looming ridgeline to fall in behind Gret again--now even farther behind.

"More!" Gwen shouted, barely audible above the roar. Rolling thunder growing louder was only the indication Jessub heard her. Every bit of extra speed came from guts and determination, and Jessub did her proud. Closing the gap, Gwen swung to one side, ready to make a pass. The *Vengeful Shark* was not that far off shore, and she wanted to position herself on the outside of the turn, hoping to hold their speed. Still Gret maneuvered to engulf them in smoke, which was suddenly filled with something. White feathers pelted Gwen and choked them both. When she caught a glimpse of Vik, he grinned, aiming thrust at them and letting air suck the feathers from his pillow. When an egg struck her, Gwen was no longer amused.

There was no need to shout a battle cry or yell to Jessub; he was already giving his best, and she wasn't certain how long it would last. Cheers erupted from the *Shark* as they approached. Gret mirrored Gwen's plan, leaving her little choice but to cut the corner tighter and faster. Banking hard, she strained the growler to its limits. While she was perfectly capable of flying the aircraft alone, having Jessub and a thrust sphere aboard made entirely new things possible. Even facing backward, Jessub reasoned out the situation and executed a move that made Gwen's guts jump toward her chin. Rather than aiming thrust straight back to propel them, Jessub held the orb high, forcing the aircraft's tail to rip through the air and cutting almost too tight a turn given their original flight path.

Jessub had turned them around, but they maintained very little speed, and the *Vengeful Shark* was straight ahead. If she crashed into the only thing in the skies for a mile, she'd never hear the end of it. Jessub wasted no time and exerted thrust laterally once again. Gwen applied all her strength to the thrust tubes beneath the growler's wings. As they skimmed past the *Shark*, people ran in all directions. Gwen smiled. Never before had such a maneuver been conceivable.

When once again synchronized with Gret and Vik, the two growlers flew side by side. Using Jessub's technique, they should be able to get ahead in the next turn. Then all they had to do was land, get unstrapped, and have both team members standing on deck. It all seemed simple enough, but execution was everything. Each having an assigned landing strip meant there should be less trouble with interference, but experience dictated caution.

Ahead, a decision waited. Windhold rose up before them. Avoiding it would require flying around or over several more mountains; the valley beyond cut straight through. "Don't flinch. Give me all you've got!"

Waiting until the chance was nearly past, Gwen made a sharp course correction. "Turn!" she shouted. Jessub whipped them through the air. Windhold was far from abandoned, and people cleared the wind channels on seeing their abrupt turn.

Howling loudly enough to be heard above the growler and Jessub's thrust, they soared through Windhold at incredible speed. It took only an instant before they emerged into the narrow valley beyond. Almost immediately the choice seemed unwise. Gwen had told Jessub not to flinch and he hadn't. Now she couldn't get the words out to tell him to let up. Feverishly working the controls, she watched as trees reached out to claim them. In a moment of epiphany, Gwen abandoned the thrust tubes and exerted her will downward. Sensing the change, Jessub angled his thrust upward. Looking straight up at the skies, Gwen returned to the thrust tubes and Jessub blasted the peaks until they soared higher.

Gret and Vik flew off shore, roiling mists behind them. Now with a relatively clear path, Gwen concentrated on speed, disappointed to learn their dangerous risk had actually cost them time.

"We're going to turn even tighter," she yelled. "I'll plan ahead so we aren't dodging the ship this time!"

Jessub barked a laugh in response.

Approaching the *Kraken's Ghost*, Gret cut a tight line, looking as if they, too, would attempt to shorten the turn. Gwen cursed. It didn't take long for them to copy the move. Experience had already taught her things, and she began controlling the thrust tubes individually. The results were dramatic, and flying sideways cost them speed. No time remained for experimentation. "Get ready!"

Jessub snarled with effort. Maintaining peak output was exponentially more difficult than normal flight. Vik showed no signs of slowing, and the distance between them grew. Speed carried Gret and Vik forward faster than the tight turn radius would allow, and the aircraft wobbled as they executed the turn. Overshooting, they soared out over the waves. It was then Gwen realized they were throwing away the *Ghost* turn to get a better angle of approach on the *Trader's Skies*. Growling, Gwen wished she'd thought of it. Already committed, she yelled, "Now!"

Jessub had learned as well. Flexing and creaking, the growler approached its limits as they rapidly slowed, turned, and reversed direction in a very tight arc. No dragon could do that. Gret and Vik soared wide, lining themselves up for a quick approach and landing. Approaching the *Trader's Wind* from the side, Gwen and Jessub would have to execute a sharp turn. Under normal circumstances, she would have swung out wide, but there was no time. Already, Gret was lined up and inward bound.

"Hold on," Gwen shouted.

"I've been holding on! Don't do anything cra--"

Not waiting for him to finish, Gwen made up her mind. No one had said which direction she had to come in, just that she had to land. "If you trust me, unbuckle yourself. We can win this."

"I trust you!" he said. The following scream did not fully support the statement.

Shouts from aboard the *Trader's Skies* made it clear they didn't think she was going to make it. Many pointed and shouted. Too late, Gwen looked over to check on Gret and Vik's progress; they were on a collision course. Gwen and Jessub would cross over Gret and Vik's assigned landing strip before reaching their own designated strip, just on the other side of the deckhouse. With all her might, she reversed the airflow on one side, yanking the growler sideways and slowing it, which allowed Gret and Vik to whisk past. Having lost altitude along with speed, Gwen didn't have time to warn Jessub before they clipped the deckhouse. Only through brute force did she keep them from nose-diving into the deck. People ran from the thrust wash. With a single bounce and quick turn, the growler came to rest mostly on the assigned runway.

Climbing out, Gwen grabbed Jessub by the collar. He looked as if he might be sick. Dragging him out, she helped him down and propped him up. For a moment, she stood there, breathing hard and laughing between the tears, not knowing who had won. It didn't matter. The experience was amazing and worth every risk. The fact that Jessub chuckled and cried along with her made her feel a little better.

"Are you insane?" Nora asked when she reached them.

"Did we win?"

"That answers that question," Kenward said. "That's my niece."

"I don't know which of you will be the death of me first. It's not a competition, you know."

"But there are some really great prizes," Gwen said, surprising everyone. Even Kenward's eyes went wide. Nora laughed the hardest.

"Pay up, Sis," Kenward said.

"You're calling that a landing? I call that a crash site."

"Pay up."

* * *

Walking along New Harborton's streets, Sinjin Volker smiled. In a few short years, east Firstland had been transformed from a vast wilderness into a thriving metropolis. While the west remained untamed, filled with creatures of all descriptions, east Firstland recaptured the glory of ages past and perhaps even exceeded it; Sinjin wasn't sure. Much of the knowledge and technology they used came from ancient texts found in the past twenty years, but even that knowledge had been built on and improved.

Crews worked to lay new wooden piping along the cobbled streets. Side by side in the trenches they dug were tightly sealed ducts for fresh water and air. Sewer lines had been built in the previous year, solving one of the largest problems they had faced considering such rapid population growth. The Firstland had become known as a land of limitless opportunity where freedom was treasured as much as gold. The trade fleet making New Harborton its home port had a great deal to do with their success. Sinjin was grateful. The Trells were more to him than just friends; they were family.

Fresh water would soon flow to all the businesses and homes that crowded the newly cobbled streets along with ancient roads uncovered by work crews. Compressed-air technology fueled innovation and growth. Kenward Trell had been at the forefront of this research, expanding on ancient knowledge, and he rarely let anyone forget it. Sinjin didn't mind. His friend deserved all the credit; after all, he risked his own life when testing each new development. Word came from Martik Tillerman along with each return of the trade fleet and sometimes via dragon or bird. Knowledge now flowed around the world, and each innovation benefitted them all.

People waved and saluted as he passed, something Sinjin would never grow accustomed to. He'd once known every face and name of the people who lived here, but those days were gone. New people arrived every day: craftsmen, scholars, and others seeking a better life. Here those willing to work for their share were afforded land and opportunity. Some earned their keep with their backs; others, through art and culture. No matter what they brought, the result was the same. The Firstland had grown to have a life of its own, far from Sinjin Volker's control. Forming the Council of Thirteen had been perhaps his greatest accomplishment. The truth was that he'd done it to relieve himself of responsibility for so many lives; better the people govern themselves. Decisions reached together were more popular than a single ruler's mandate, their own goals and dreams providing far greater motivation.

Though it had removed some pressure, Sinjin was still Al'Drakon. Valterius waited not far away, watching over the other dragons within the lower stables. He and the other dragonriders could stay high above, within the keystone caverns, but such divisions served no one. The Drakon were no better than anyone else on Godsland, something Sinjin did his best to remind those who might forget. They had a responsibility to protect these people from whatever threats they faced. The world might have become more peaceful, but danger still lurked. True peace required vigilance.

The craftsmen's quarter, filled with water-powered hammer mills, smithies, and shops, assailed his ears with the sound of industry. Hissing air drove pumps and bellows and even provided the force needed to deliver fresh water from the reservoirs through the aqueducts and into the homes and shops of all those who lived and worked there. The Council of Thirteen had deemed these things every citizen's right, and budgets set aside were more than adequate to pay the workers needed to build the required infrastructure. Many came to the Firstland because they heard about a place where more coin was available than workers to earn it. At some point the scales would tip, Sinjin knew, but for now he smiled. His mother would have liked this very much.

When he reached the vendors' district and the open-air market, Sinjin was reminded of the Godfist. Things they had missed so dearly were now available to all. Hard-won progress was worthwhile in the end. The trade fleet meant they no longer had to make everything they needed, yet progress allowed them to do just that. Self-sufficiency had been among his mother's greatest goals, and Sinjin took pride in making her visions reality.

Anonymity was not something he'd ever possessed, yet the greetings called out wherever he went made him a bit uncomfortable. He carried no coin because no one would accept it from him. He asked for nothing because the mere sight of him brought merchants and vendors into the streets, each wanting no more than to please him. Trying to remember their names was among his greatest challenges, but some were familiar nonetheless.

"Took you long enough," Onin of the Old Guard said, his wry smile betraying his words. "You know how much she likes to serve cold food."

"I know," Sinjin said with a grin.

"And it won't be you she blisters with her words," Onin continued, all the while holding open the door of the Last Inn. Having rebuilt the Watering Hole multiple times, Miss Mariss said it was time for a new tradition. Nonetheless, this place held all the comforts of the previous inns and perhaps a few more. Four mighty hearths graced the common rooms that extended from a central bar and the kitchens. A joyful noise greeted them.

Having beaten him there, Kendra waved and pulled out the stool next to her. Doing so revealed the extra girth she carried along with the glow radiating from her like light from a comet, and perhaps just as magical. Sipping her tea, his wife beamed, and for Sinjin Volker, that was enough.

"To Al'Drakon!" someone in the crowded common room shouted, and the rest echoed the cheer.

Flushing, Sinjin Volker raised the mug Miss Mariss slid to him in silent salute. He might never get used to such treatment, but his wife's gentle touch assured him everything was as it should be. "To the future," he said loudly enough to be heard over the din.

"To the future!"

* * *

Like humans, dragons are creatures of habit, and patterns formed over thousands of years were hardest to break. Though free, Mael had not slept properly in years. Coming back to the prison that had held him for so long seemed the greatest foolishness, but prison it was no more. It was a strange confliction that drove him. Like a prisoner who falls in love with his captor, he longed for his home. It would be a simple enough thing to drive everyone else from Dragonhold, but that would make the rest of his plans more difficult to achieve. Better to leave them alone and let them build it all for him--far better, indeed.

Even seeing him would raise their suspicions and consciousness of him too much. He needed to fade from the collective memory like so much dust. Only then would he truly be free to encourage development along a specific path.

Long years without proper sleep left him feeling worn thin and snappish. When rain finally came, providing darkness and cover, Mael slipped into the Pinook River. A glistening serpent, he moved through the water with terrific speed, even against the current.

While he could have gone all the way to his former home before surfacing, the dragon mage hesitated when dim amber light shone on the water, stored up during daylight and diffused through massive crystals above. Even before breaking the surface, change was evident. The scale of time had changed for him, and it seemed as if the humans rushed headlong into everything, not stopping to consider the more distant future. A series of waterwheels lined the shore, driving shafts protruding from wooden structures. Wood deteriorated, and to Mael's eye, it already looked weak. Copper tanks stood taller than the mills, looking no more permanent.

"Mark the line," a voice said from nearby. Mael remained mostly submerged, only breaking the surface enough to see and hear. "Twenty-five paces and mark it. Walk it twice."

A young woman staked the white string line and walked back to where the older man stood. Then she paced off the distance, marked it, and verified it. The two repeated this process until a rectangle had been delineated. At least the impatient creatures had the sense to keep things straight and plumb. Whatever humanity remained in the mage had long since been overwhelmed by his time in dragon form. While he knew he'd once been one of them, he took no pride in that heritage, realizing he'd chosen a far superior species. He was not jealous of natural-born dragons, for few had access to real power and none had the benefit of truly understanding humans. It was this connection that allowed him to control them so easily. There was perhaps one dragon in existence with power to challenge Mael, but he was a pitiful creature--far better to be the first of your kind than the last.

"Why do we need another mill, Papa? It was prettier here without them."

"Perhaps. The hold must support itself. If we're to reopen the mines, then we need a hammer mill to break down ore-bearing rock. Perhaps the Arghast can just dig up salt in blocks, and on the Firstland they pull gemstones from pockets in the ground, but here we have to do things the hard way. Sacrifices must sometimes be made."

"Can't we use the other mill?"

"The grist mill doesn't work the same way and is used for food. The air mill provides compressed air for half the hold. The hammer mill will break down nonfood items."

"If you say so," the girl said, kicking at the grass. When her gaze turned toward Mael, he froze, suddenly uncomfortable and afraid a little girl might see him. Cursing himself and his pounding heart, the dragon mage nonetheless remained perfectly still. Human frailty simultaneously played to his advantage and disadvantage. Bored, the girl expected to see nothing, and that's what she saw.

"We need to mark out a roadway."

Sighing, the girl turned back to her work.

No matter what he told himself, seeing the young woman stirred something within him, something long since lost. Her scent triggered deeply repressed memories. With them came shame and rage. Mael suppressed the feelings, dipped beneath the water and glided silently from the cavern. When light poured through the water next, change was once again evident. This, however, was his own doing. The destruction of the Fifth Magic left part of the river exposed to open air and passing through what was now a park and marketplace. Though it appeared all had gone to their beds, parting clouds allowed enough light to illuminate vendor carts shuttered for the night. An alluring smell emanated from one, and for an instant, he considered taking the cart with him, but that would surely spoil all his efforts at stealth.

When at last amber-hued light colored the water, Mael felt himself relax for the first time in years. It wasn't that he was afraid when outside since there was no one in the world as powerful as he, yet he did not feel comfortable or at home in any of the places he'd dwelt since leaving. No matter how perfect the locations might have seemed, each lacked something.

Now he was home--such a bizarre feeling. His heart rate slowed and eyelids drooped before he'd even fully pulled himself from the water. It was as if he'd been off on a grand adventure and finally made it back to safety and warmth. Too many fish crowded the waters. With two bites, Mael reduced their number. For so long, he'd maintained the balance in this place, caring for the fish and deer and other creatures, most of which he'd rescued from the rushing water. All were there for a reason and were part of the ecosystem. In an environment this small, any shift in the balance could be catastrophic. With any piece of the puzzle missing, the rest would slowly fall apart; it offended the dragon's sensibilities.

Snapping up three deer in a single strike, Mael took them with him to the nameless god who'd kept him company across the ages. Seeing the massive visage spewing water into the cavern soothed Mael like nothing else. Change had come to his cavern as well. Humans had cleaned up much of the damage, but his presence could not be erased. Still, they had done their best to cover it up. What remained must be a stark reminder of dangers they yet faced. They knew he existed and that he had escaped. They must wonder what had become of him, which made the dragon chuckle. He understood why they might avoid this place, given the insecurity it would foster. Better to clean it up, seal it off, and ignore it. Mael was just fine with that. Curling into his familiar place in the stone god's lap, he savored the meal. Everything tasted different outside. Knowing what he now knew, it might be difficult to leave. With the crook of his jaw resting in a familiar groove, Mael closed his eyes and slept better than he had in years.

Epilogue

Never trust old people. They have all the power.
--Kira Longbow, adventurer

* * *

Commemorating what would have been Catrin Volker's ninetieth birthday, this Herald's Day was to be the largest pilgrimage in history. Such an opportunity would not come again for another decade. Never before had the trade fleet left the Godsland carrying more people than goods. With so many gone to the Firstland, the Pinook Valley felt desolate and abandoned, no longer resembling the wilderness it had once been or more recently a thriving town. Lowerton's streets, narrow, twisted, and usually packed, were eerily vacant, save a few souls carrying gifts and steaming trays to neighbors.

The place's construction was congested and appeared haphazard at first glance, though some said it was beautiful. Kira Longbow disagreed. What might have once been a natural treasure was now cobbled, paved, and overbuilt. Compressed-air lines and transport tubes crowded already narrow roadways. Cylindrical packages whisked through the communications tubes at incredible speed, issuing a high-pitched squeal as they went. It grated on worn nerves.

What galled most was still wanting things only civilization could provide. In the wild, she could find or hunt for everything needed to survive, but never could she make some of the things she craved. No one could. Only because of the trade fleet did all the ingredients from across the world come together in one place. Only then and given skillful hands and the right tools could a delicate Midlands pasty dusted with saffron and smothered in whipped truffle butter become possible. The thought made her mouth water.

Walking cobbled streets in spike-heeled boots was not a task for those with weak ankles. Kira almost managed to walk with confidence. A voice in the back of her mind told her she would be successful and she believed. Such a quest required belief, and her faith in herself was unwavering.

"Never thought I'd see the day," Bent said from a darkened alley.

Unflinching, Kira turned and glared at him. "What are you doing out here?"

"I had to see how you were dressed."

She raised her eyebrows and gave him a steely look.

"The corset is a nice touch."

"Just go do what you're supposed to do," Kira said, now self-conscious. Most days, she could come to Lowerton in leathers and muddy boots, and most would leave her be. On this night, though, she needed to look like anyone else.

"Even with so many people gone, there are still a lot of first-lighters in Dragonhold."

This was not news. Large portions of the population traveled to the Firstland on pilgrimage. Those with good sense stayed behind, but they were far fewer. Celebrations outside the hold were small and mostly family affairs. Within Dragonhold was a completely different matter. For one night, the hold was open to all, only the most dangerous places cordoned off and guarded. Fortunately for Kira, not all those on guard this night were happy about it.

First-lighters were those born before Istra graced the skies. In these people her power ran most deeply, sustaining them, keeping them vital and vibrant. For those like Kira, power was like smoke on the wind. While she might know it's there and even sense it, she could never pull the smoke from the air and hold it in her hand. Still, among her generation, talents manifested, and some had more than their fair share. "I'll take my chances."

"The hair beats all," Bent said. "Are you a rainbow?"

Again Kira flushed. Every part of her outfit served a purpose, and her hair was no exception. She used lemon to bleach it until it was almost white, left the roots undyed, and applied purple along its length, red at the tips, and capped them in black. Using slick gel, she'd formed her long hair into dual spirals that jutted straight backward, as if she stood in a strong wind. "Don't touch it," she said. "And stop gawking."

"I'll be ready and waiting," he said, drifting back into the shadows. "Be prepared for the ride of your life. No saying I didn't warn you."

Kira stuck her tongue out and walked on. His whistle at her back made her blush one last time. The winding roadway leading to Dragonhold was among Martik Tillerman's most significant achievements. Some said he remained within the hold; others reported he'd made a final pilgrimage to see his old friends. Kira hoped it was the latter. The fewer authority figures within, the better.

Passing the statue of Catrin, Kira reached up and rubbed her Herald's charm for luck. Bent claimed to be a nonbeliever, but she'd seen his Kyrien pendant enough times to know better. Some would say what she did was against the Herald's principles, but Kira knew better. Catrin would want her to find that which was hidden, especially when the very tool she needed was not even in use and collecting dust.

Sweeping turns and switchbacks made for a long walk, but were traversable by horse-drawn wagons and pop cars alike. Fortunately neither could be seen anywhere. Guards in ceremonial garb and holding metal staves flanked the grand entranceway that was adorned with buntings and fine draperies. From within the hold came a muted din that chilled Kira's blood. People--and a lot of them--all within a confined space. At that moment her courage nearly fled, the feeling of constriction shortening her breaths. But this day would not come again, and her chance would be gone. All her work, and Bent's and others', would have been for naught.

Taking a deep breath, she walked between the guards and returned polite nods. The custom of wearing thick make-up or a ceramic mask to honor the Herald also worked to Kira's advantage. Though she was not entirely well known, she had drawn the attention of the guard perhaps a few too many times. None who knew her would expect her to look as she did. The skirts she wore barely covered her knees, leaving a tantalizing bit of leg visible above her bootlaces.

Though her hair drew a few glances, others within the hold were similarly dressed. Kira had watched the entertainers practice for weeks, and her dress was near enough to their costumes to be mistaken for one of them, yet different enough to avoid suspicion--she hoped. The growling of her stomach announced her coming as she approached a table laden with pastries, and the man ahead of her, his face painted white, smiled. "Swallow a dragon?"

"Two," Kira said.

"After you, then."

Others turned to see what the fuss was about. Having so much attention focused on her was unnerving. "Thank you," was all Kira said. Eventually people turned back to the business of selecting the perfect pastry. Kira already knew what she wanted, though she chided herself that her grand plan just had to include pastries. Bent would never let her hear the end of it, which was why she was never going to tell him.

Still warm, the morsel was everything she had dreamed of while scrounging for food in the wilderness. Though she knew she shouldn't, she grabbed another, hoping no one was looking. Then, after a moment, she grabbed a third.

"Perhaps you swallowed three dragons," the man said, clearly thinking himself clever.

"The night is young," Kira said in spite of the need for anonymity.

The man hadn't been expecting such a response and choked on a pastry of his own. While he recovered, Kira moved to where a pair of young men in Dragonhold livery dispensed hot cider. Accepting a steaming wooden cup from one of them, she had everything she needed.

"May I offer you some company?" the man who'd been choking asked, hurrying to catch up with her.

Kira stepped faster, moving awkwardly in spiked heels. "I'm meeting friends."

"I'll gladly escort you to them," he said, his eyes wandering up and down. "I see you have both hands full. Please, allow me to hold your cup so you may enjoy your pastry."

At least he was wise enough not to mention that it was her third. "Of course," she said, knowing refusal would only make her look even more suspicious. "But I have only a brief moment."

Taking her by the arm, he guided her to a nearby column, away from the crowd. Only when he had her alone did he take the cup from her hand. "Please, eat your pastry."

"This one is for a friend," she said. Had he moved his hand to her back, surely he would have felt the slender copper canisters concealed there.

"Well, that explains it. Your secret is safe with me, little lady."

Trying to decide what to do next, Kira fingered a folded paper in her sleeve. "Is that Lord Martik?" The man could not resist looking, and Kira poured the white powder from the folder paper into the cider and onto the pastry.

"I don't see him. Where did you say he was?"

"I can't see him now either. I'm sorry. I must have been mistaken." The man continued to look for the master of Dragonhold, presumably ready to impose himself upon the man.

Kira took the cup from his hand and said, "I must be going. Thank you for your kindness."

Perhaps it was her ruse, or maybe he'd finally lost interest in her, but he let her go. Thankful she hadn't had to make him drink or force feed him the pastry, she moved on. Keeping her eyes down, she did her best to slip away and not draw anyone else's attention. Her outfit made it even more difficult. Many of the ladies wore their best gowns on this day, and a few might wear a corset underneath to enhance their figures, but none would go quite as far as Kira. Bent said she took unnecessary risks, but who would expect someone in a corset and high-heeled boots would make a run for it?

When she neared the area cordoned off as a stage, she did her best to appear as one of the guests and not an entertainer. Here gathered too many of those her hair and dress emulated. Keeping people between her and the performers and hoping no one noticed, she turned toward the God's Eye. It was her first time in years, and an old sense of anxiety crept up on her. Childhood fears wet her brow. No one guarded the side halls, and when she turned, she knew she approached areas where she had no business. It would be difficult to pretend she'd gotten there by accident, but that was exactly what she did.

Torchlight illuminated a junction ahead, and a single guard stood, bored and resentful. Kira knew him. He'd been complaining ever since the assignment to work this night came down. Everyone still in town knew guardsman Erril was unhappy.

"You can't come this way," he said. "You'll have to go back."

"I'm sorry," Kira said, doing her best to sound innocent and vapid. "I think I had a little too much cider, and now I'm lost. I was looking for a place to eat my pastry, but now I don't feel so good."

Looking torn, Erril finally said, "You can rest here a moment. Here, sit." He took the cup and eased her to the cold stone floor. When she handed him the pastry, he looked as if he were being tested.

"I'm not hungry anymore. You can have it."

"Are you sure?" he asked, but the pastry was already halfway to his lips before she nodded. The cider had cooled to a reasonable drinking temperature, and Kira nodded again when he asked with his eyes. Within a few moments, he joined her on the floor, certain to sleep for at least two days. It was almost too easy, but she credited all her planning and hard work. Now it was all paying off. Her time was limited, though; she had no way to know if anyone would come to check on Erril or when. It was among the flaws in her plan that Bent had been so eager to point out.

Grabbing the torch from the sconce, she moved into the chamber she knew waited. If this information was wrong, it would be on Bent. It had been one of his girlfriends who had revealed the location of the amberlite statuette. Few had seen the famous wonder but everyone knew the stories. It was not for its historical value but for practical reasons Kira needed the statuette, and she would gladly find a way to return it when she was done. She was convinced the Herald would want her to use the tool rather than let it be used as a mere reading light. It seemed a crime. When a yellowish glow became visible ahead and to her left, Kira's heart beat faster.

There it was, everything the stories said it was: a skillfully carved female form that glows from within for no one knew exactly how long before needing to be exposed once again to Istra's light. Bent had said that was why it was here. A Cathuran studying amberlite wanted to find out how long it would continue to shine in the darkness. As her hand wrapped around it, the monk's experiment was over. After wrapping it in cloth and concealing it in her pocket, she moved swiftly away, feeling bad about ruining the Cathuran's research.

Her knees trembled and never before had she felt so alive. When she turned back onto the main thoroughfare, she felt exposed, as if anyone who saw her would immediately know what she'd done. When a pair of guards entered the hall, walking toward her, she was certain her nerves would give her away. Perhaps it was the festivities or the heavy makeup she wore, but they paid her no mind. She was nearly to the great hall when she heard one cry out. "Stop that woman!"

Time seemed to slow as she kicked the stone walls with the heels of her boots, knocking away the thick soles and spiked heels. Softened leather soles and uppers that conformed to her feet were revealed. The bottoms had been rubbed with pitch then pressed in gravel, which provided excellent grip. At a fast walk, she moved through the crowds and back toward the main entrance. When the guard burst into the main hall, she ran.

The pounding in her ears blocked out all other sound, though the shock on people's faces and in their reactions was clear.

The man she'd encountered earlier blocked her path, a knowing grin painting his face. Without an instant's hesitation, Kira leveled her arm at him and snapped her closed fist upward. The movement activated a hidden release in her sleeve. Super-compressed gas in the copper cylinders escaped through jointed metal tubes that provided a long, straight, cylindrical flight path for the projectiles waiting to be sucked into the barrel by the forceful expulsion. The sound was unlike anything else, making a fump, fump, fump sound. Tiny, thick-walled, glass vials filled with greenish liquid flew toward the overbearing man. The first struck him in the chest, and his eyes flew wide. The second hit him in the neck, the liquid within forcefully injected into his system. He took one step and dropped. Knowing he would have a week-long headache when he awoke did not dampen Kira's humor. The guards flanking the exit did.

Crossing their staves in a practiced maneuver, the men sufficiently blocked her path. Raising her arms and cocking both fists, she sent glass vials spraying in their direction. One man managed to deflect her attacks with his shield, but the second was struck in a narrow strip of exposed flesh on his leg. Going to one knee, he looked as if he might stand. Kira leveled her arms at both men again, knowing she might already have used all her ammunition. Two more vials flew from her left arm, causing the first guard to flinch. The second collapsed to the floor, leaving her an opening. Running as fast as she could, Kira's hearing suddenly returned. Shouts behind her drove her forward. The remaining guard stood ready to sweep her legs from beneath her. Instead, she applied her skills and training. Leaping into the air, she tucked and made herself very small. Spinning just over the swinging staff, she extended into a pike position before letting bent knees absorb the landing. Without missing a step, she ran across the roadway, ignoring the long series of switchbacks.

The direct route, though obstructed by statuary, ornamental trees, and other artistic landscaping elements, presented a steep slope. Most would have been sent tumbling by the unsure footing, which was entirely intentional on the designers' parts, but Kira had trained for this exact route. Every turn had been memorized, every side step and jump practiced. Whistles blew long notes, bringing what guards remaining in Lowerton to full alert. She had hoped for a little more time. Bent had better be ready.

No matter how much conditioning and training she'd endured to prepare for this night, Kira breathed hard and sweat ran into her eyes, making it difficult to see even in the preternatural comet light. Rock and moss had looked solid from the roadway on her many trips up and down, studying the landscape. Now, though, the land twisted and shifted under her feet. The first two bad steps she recovered from, but already off balance, she turned her ankle in the loose soil. Carrying so much speed, the fall could easily have been deadly, but she had trained for this as well, knowing it was a possibility.

Even as she tumbled, she heard the sound of pop cars thumping to life. Those coming from above did not worry her as much since they would need to snake down the mountainside. The ones below, however, posed a real threat. Surely someone would have stayed at the airing station, and that meant a fully operational defense turret between her and Bent. Not good.

Rather than fighting the fall, Kira did her best to use it to her advantage. The result left the taste of blood in her mouth but also brought her closer to the bottom with great speed. When at last she did regain her stride, a pair of retrofitted wagons blocked the lower roadway. Most pop cars were little more than horse-drawn wagons redesigned to run on compressed air. Spoke wheels and rigid axels limited their speed, which Bent said was their primary weakness. She could only hope her old friend was right. Given his building and engineering skills, she'd always chosen to believe in him. Now that her freedom and perhaps her life were at stake, she wondered if that had been wise. She'd never even seen this invention of his and prayed it was as good as he claimed.

So much of what they had done required stealth. Certain risks were unavoidable, but that did little to settle her raging nerves. What the pop cars lacked in speed, they made up for in firepower. Kira's plan was falling apart before her eyes as multiple air cannons pointed in her direction. Oversized air tanks at the vehicles' rears and self-feeding ammunition in vats could provide continuous fire. Accuracy was no longer needed, which sickened Kira as a trained hunter. A single well-placed shot was far better than a dozen poorly aimed. But in this instance, she knew they would do the job nicely.

Passing the statue of Catrin at a stumbling run, she gained flat ground and subsequently her stride. Pumping her arms and kicking as hard and as fast as she could, there was no escaping the guard. They, too, had trained, and she'd underestimated them. When the repeated thumping sound started and was joined by more, she readied herself for the pain or possibly worse. The corncob rounds they were usually loaded with would sting, but rock or metal load could be lethal. A wooden round exploded on cobblestones just before another struck her in the calf. At least her countrymen showed some kindness and aimed low. The result knocked her from her feet, and she hit the stones hard, lying very still except for breathing rapidly. It was over. She had miscalculated and would pay the price for having gambled and lost. Screeching and a low rumble issued from a side street, the intersection where Kira pushed herself to one knee was dark until gas-fired lights focused on her.

Like the sound of several pop cars somehow meshed together into a single vehicle, Bent's air car sang a beautiful song. A symphony of science, mechanics, and audacity raced toward her. Twice more she was struck in the legs with wooden rounds, and she went back down before Bent reached her. Putting the air car between her and the guards tested the vehicle's mettle immediately. Bent hadn't said what it was made of, but wood shot bounced off the bodywork, leaving only small dents.

"Get in!"

Kira tried but Bent pulled her in before she could coerce her body to move. A moment later, she strapped in and held on. Thrown back in her seat as Bent opened the accelerator full stop, Kira couldn't believe the force with which the car moved forward. Like a leaping deer, it sped along the streets. The pop cars followed, their turrets still functional, though the accuracy became deplorable as the cars bounced over the cobblestones. Looking at the leather bags flanking her seat, Kira realized the wheels were not directly connected to the frame. Instead, reinforced air bags absorbed the vibrations, giving them a much more controllable ride. Bent used that to his advantage.

Her friend claimed to be the best driver on the Godfist, but she'd always had her doubts. On this night he proved himself as he never could before. "There's an air gun back there," he shouted as they sped along a short stretch of straight road. "Aim for their lights! Use the mirrors. You'll figure it out."

Even in the rush of wind, her hair stayed slicked back and out of her eyes. Finding the control handle, Kira looked into the mirror before her, now realizing it would allow her to aim and fire the weapon without turning around. Having to do everything in reverse was the only disadvantage. Handling the weapon as she would a crossbow, she fired and missed, taking out a flowerpot in a shop window. That bit Kira truly felt badly about, but the time for personal preference had passed. Squeezing the controls, she let the wood shot fly. Neither she nor Bent wanted to hurt anyone, but they also knew the risks. This had all better be worth it.

In a single sweep, the flurry of fire blasted out lights on the two closest pop cars. Each one exploded with the sound of shattering glass. It sickened her a bit that spraying felt as good as true marksmanship. Losing their lights didn't present much of an issue on well-lit streets, but they approached the countryside. Once over Martik's bridge, tall trees would obscure even bright comet light. No clouds graced the sky, which worked to their disadvantage, but the guards apparently agreed with her assessment.

At an intersection, the two lead pop cars split, turning left and right. Three more with working lights continued pursuit, now firing more frequently as buildings became fewer and wider spaced. Ahead, the bridge waited. There was no one posted there this night; at least there wasn't supposed to be anyone posted there. A solitary figure blocked the entrance to the massive, rope-suspended bridge. Though the bridge was weight limited, their little pop car was barely enough to make it move. Had the guards in pursuit been closer, it might have made for a much more interesting crossing. The bridge guard got off three shots before leaping to safety. Kira heard a pop and breaking glass, the light ahead no longer as bright as it had been.

Three times more, shot struck the car, but they quickly moved out of range. Sewn leather tires filled with air absorbed much of the shock and provided traction. The smell of pitch grew stronger as the tires heated. The land beyond the bridge dropped away, and anyone with good sense took the exit nice and slowly. Bent hit the lip wide open. As they soared through the air, Kira realized each tire had its own air tank, whereas most pop cars had a single tank to drive the rear wheels.

Landing along the slope kept impact from being fatal, but it did knock the wind out of Kira. This part of the escape route would be the most dangerous. Smooth dirt tracks allowed pop cars to move with far greater speed, and Bent showed what his car could do given the chance to pick up momentum. While she'd seen two-speed impeller transmissions before, Kira had never seen one on each wheel. It made sense given the individual air tanks but required far greater technical sophistication and controls. She was still trying to puzzle out the advantages of such a system when Bent yanked hard on a lever beside him, sending the car into a hard left turn, the tires on the left side no longer turning as fast as those on the right.

Using the accelerator along with differential drive, he sent the car skidding through the turns, the rear end sliding out to the side, making it feel as if they would crash into the thick foliage lining the roadway.

After a series of sweeping turns, the lights behind them were no longer visible. Bent had been counting on it. Throwing the car completely sideways, he skidded off the main trail toward a cluster of farmsteads. Bent hadn't accounted for the dark marks his turn left behind. It was unlikely the guards would miss them, but time was short.

Extending from a nearby hayloft was a ramp. Bent aimed for it and drove up into the loft and through a narrow channel between stacks of hay, and he didn't stop until midway through the loft. From beside the door, Chaffy and Galen pulled the ramp in and closed the doors. Bent had mentioned needing to air up before the last leg of their journey, but Kira doubted they could fill the tanks fast enough. Again Bent surprised her, revealing quick-release couplings on each tank. Rather than fill them, he swapped them out for prefilled tanks waiting amid hay bales. Not only did they swap the tanks in less time than it would have taken to fill a single one, but they also swapped out the tires for new ones of similar design but with metal spikes along with tar and gravel for traction.

Before Kira would have thought possible, Bent opened the accelerator.

Clumps of hay flew, assaulting Chaffy and Galen. Traction was limited even with the spikes, and Kira couldn't see what was beyond the barn's back door. Inside, though, was a small ramp. Given the height of the ramp they'd used to come in, it seemed ludicrous and their speed too slow. Bent never flinched. When they struck the ramp, it was all Kira could do to keep from screaming.

What hadn't been obvious was that the barn had been built into the side of a hill, part of it exposed and part carved into the mountainside. After only a short drop, the ground sloped downward and provided a smooth landing. A cart path led into the woods, getting rougher and muddier as they went. Bent's choice in tires now seemed wise. Only a little farther, and they could escape into the wilderness, back into the places where she was powerful and skilled. Towns had a way of making her feel weak. The aches in her calf and ribs didn't help.

When lanterns appeared in the forest ahead, Kira cursed.

"Plan B!" Bent said, turning his head so as not to shout. The guards ahead were on horseback, far faster on a woodland trail than any ordinary pop car. The sound of the car announced their approach, and stealth was no longer possible. "Hang on!"

Already the trees whisked by, and Kira's hands ached from holding on so tightly, but she did her best to prepare herself for something worse. Horses jammed the trail ahead. Bent pulled a handle that caused an earsplitting whistle to cut the air. Even the well-trained horses were unprepared for it and cleared out of his way, where the sound was most intense. After racing past, he closed the whistle and yanked on another lever. Nothing seemed to happen. After a moment, though, a rumbling roar grew and became a continuous series of booms. With the sound came increased speed.

Bent worked the controls with frenzied movements, the car gaining momentum. Using the compressed-air drive, he did his best to control the constant thrust provided by what could only be a pitch-fired pulse jet. Soon Kira's seat became almost too hot to sit on, and she knew it was true. They were rocketing through the woods, spitting fire like runaway bits of an airship. Though it was clear Bent had no control over the volume of thrust once the pulse jet was lit, he must have had foresight enough to limit the supply of fuel.

"I've one more tank of pitch," he said when the jet blew out, "but I don't want to use it."

"I don't want you to use it either," Kira said.

Ahead, a stone bridge crossed one of many creeks. It formed a short, steep arc, forcing them the slow. "I should have enough air to get us to Harborton. If I have to light the jet again, we're likely going in the water. Be ready."

Kira had no chance to reply before he sent them hurtling across the countryside, only one headlamp to show the way. The closer they drew to Harborton, the better maintained the cart trail. Carrying speed, they passed an airing station, its turret unmanned. At least one thing had gone their way. As the car chattered down the main cobbled thoroughfare, Bent looked to his mirrors, checking for pursuit. Seeing none, Kira was ready when Bent locked up the rear wheels and sent them skidding and smoking to a halt, sparks flying from spiked tires. Squarely facing a cellar door, they waited only an instant before Chaffy's little brother Hamm opened it. "Hurry," he said, fear in his eyes.

Easing on the air, Bent drove down the ramp laid over the steps. Hamm waved and made a run for it, leaving the cellar door open. A bucket of cold water waited, and Kira wasted no time in climbing from the car, no matter how much her body complained. Putting weight on her leg was the worst but she endured. Dunking her head in the water, she worked to remove the water-based dyes. She would have used soap to scrub away the remaining color, but there was no time. Wrapping herself in a plain, brown cloak, she limped toward the open door, looking back to Bent with worry.

"Go," he said. "I'll slip out the back and make a swim for it. This had better all be worth it. If you've put us through all this for nothing, well . . ." He just shrugged and slipped into the darkness.

Pain made the climb difficult, and she struggled to close the door. Hearing horses coming, she left it slightly ajar. Immediately crossing the street, she endured the pain, walking with a forced gait, not letting her limp show. Her hair still wet, she pulled it back, just before horses turned the corner. Amber light shone from within her cloak, and she quickly concealed it.

With her head down, the guard passed her by. Stepping faster, she turned toward the waterline. From a doorway across the street, a man in a fine-quality black suit watched. The fit spoke of tailoring, something most in these parts could scarcely afford. Kira pretended not to see but could not resist a glance as she passed. His eyes met hers, and she quickly looked away but not before noticing the glint of golden cufflinks.

Walking faster, she hoped this would all be worth it. Still feeling the man's gaze on her back, she hastened toward the next intersection. Had she looked back, she would have seen him smile. Instead she followed that little voice in the back of her mind, the one that told her everything would be fine; all she had to do was believe.

BrianRathbone.com